Overwhelming praise
for these *New York Times* bestselling authors

NORA ROBERTS

"There's no mystery about why Roberts is a
bestselling author of romance and mainstream novels:
she delivers the goods with panache and wit."
—*Publishers Weekly*

"Her stories have fueled the dreams of
twenty-five million readers."
—*Entertainment Weekly*

ELIZABETH LOWELL

"There is no finer guarantee of outstanding romance
than the name of Elizabeth Lowell."
—*Romantic Times Magazine*

"For smoldering sensuality and exceptional
storytelling Elizabeth Lowell is incomparable."
—Kathe Robin, *Romantic Times Magazine*

HEATHER GRAHAM POZZESSERE

"Award-winning Pozzessere combines mystery
with sizzling romance."
—*Publishers Weekly*

"An incredible story-teller!"
—*Los Angeles Daily News*

With over 40 million copies of her books in print worldwide and six titles on the *New York Times* bestseller list in one year, **Nora Roberts** is truly a publishing phenomenon. She has published over a hundred novels and her work has been translated in over twenty-five different countries to high acclaim. According to the *Los Angeles Daily News*, she is "a word artist, painting her story and characters with vitality and verve."

In addition to her amazing success in mainstream fiction, Nora remains committed to writing for the category romance audience, which took her to their hearts in 1981 with her very first book, a Silhouette Romance novel.

Elizabeth Lowell is one of romance's most versatile and successful authors. The author of over thirty contemporary and historical romances, she's also known as Ann Maxwell for science fiction and romantic suspense and, with her husband, Evan Maxwell, as A.E. Maxwell. There are over 13 million copies of her stories in print throughout the world. She is also a recipient of the Romance Writers of America's Lifetime Achievement award, as well as a *New York Times* bestseller.

A master storyteller with over 10 million copies of her books in print around the world, **Heather Graham Pozzessere** describes her life as "busy, wild and fun." Surprisingly, with all her success, Heather's first career choice was not writing but acting on the Shakespearean stage. Happily for her fans, fate intervened and now she is a *New York Times* bestselling author! Married to her high school sweetheart, this mother of five spends her days picking up the kids from school, attending Little League games and taking care of two cats. Although Heather and her family enjoy traveling, southern Florida—where she loves the sun and water—is home.

NORA ROBERTS

ELIZABETH LOWELL

HEATHER GRAHAM POZZESSERE

FOREVER MINE

Silhouette Books

Published by Silhouette Books

America's Publisher of Contemporary Romance

SILHOUETTE BOOKS

ISBN 0-373-83400-4

FOREVER MINE

Copyright © 1998 by Harlequin Books S.A.

The publisher acknowledges the copyright holders of the individual works as follows:

REBELLION
Copyright © 1988 by Nora Roberts

RECKLESS LOVE
Copyright © 1990 by Two Of A Kind, Inc.

DARK STRANGER
Copyright © 1988 by Heather Graham Pozzessere

Printed in U.S.A.

CONTENTS

REBELLION   9
Nora Roberts

RECKLESS LOVE   175
Elizabeth Lowell

DARK STRANGER   407
Heather Graham Pozzessere

Rebellion

NORA ROBERTS

This story is told for the MacGregors,
all who came before, all who come after.

Prologue

❦

Glenroe Forest, Scotland, 1735

They came at dusk, when the villagers were at their evening meal, and the peat fires sent smoke curling from the chimneys into the chill November air. There had been snow the week before, and the sun had beaten down and then retreated until the frost had set hard as rock under the bare trees. The sound of approaching horses rang like thunder through the forest, sending small animals racing and scrambling for cover.

Serena MacGregor shifted her baby brother on her hip and went to the window. Her father and the men were returning early from their hunting trip, she thought, but there were no shouts of greeting from the outlying cottages, no bursts of laughter.

She waited, her nose all but pressed against the window glazing, straining for the first signs of their return and fighting back her resentment that she, a girl, was not permitted to join hunting parties.

Coll had gone, though he was barely fourteen and not as skilled with a bow as she herself. And Coll had been allowed to go since he was seven. Serena's mouth became a pout as she gazed out through the lowering light. Her older brother would talk of nothing but the hunt for days, while she would have to be content to sit and spin.

Little Malcolm began to fuss and she jiggled him automatically as she stared down the rough path between the crofts and cottages. "Hush now, Papa doesn't want to hear you squalling the minute he walks in the door." But something made her hold him closer and look nervously over her shoulder for her mother.

The lamps were lighted and there was the scent of good, rich stew simmering over the kitchen fire. The house was neat as a pin. She and her mother and her little sister Gwen had worked all day to make it so. The floors were scrubbed, the tables polished. There wasn't a cobweb to be found in any corner. Serena's arms ached just thinking of it. The wash had been done and the little lavender sachets her mother loved so much were tucked in the chests.

Because her father was laird, they had the best house for miles around, built of fine blue slate. Her mother wasn't one to let dust settle on it.

Everything looked normal, but something had set her heart to racing. Grabbing a shawl, Serena wrapped it around Malcolm and opened the door to look for her father.

There was no wind, no sound but the horses' hooves beating against the hard frost on the path. They would ride over the rise any moment, she thought, and for a reason she couldn't name, she shuddered. When she heard the first scream, she stumbled backward. She had already righted herself and started forward when her mother called out to her.

"Serena, come back in. Hurry."

Fiona MacGregor, her usually lovely face pinched and pale, rushed down the stairs. Her hair, the same red-gold shade as Serena's, was pinned back and caught in a snood. She didn't pat it into place, as was her habit before welcoming her husband home.

"But, Mama—"

"Hurry, girl, for God's sake." Fiona grabbed her daughter's arm and dragged her inside. "Take the bairn upstairs to your sister. Stay there."

"But Papa—"

"It's not your father."

Serena saw then, as the horses crested the hill, not the hunting plaid of the MacGregor but the red coats of English dragoons. She was only eight, but she had heard the tales of pillage and oppression. Eight was old enough to be outraged.

"What do they want? We've done nothing."

"It's not necessary to do, only to be." Fiona closed the door, then bolted it, more out of defiance than of any hope it would keep out intruders. "Serena—"

A small, slender woman, she gripped her daughter's shoulders. She had been the favored daughter of an indulgent father, then the adored wife of a loving husband, but Fiona was no weakling. Perhaps that was why the men in her life had given her their respect, as well as their affection.

"Go upstairs into the nursery. Keep Malcolm and Gwen with you. Don't come out until I tell you."

The valley echoed with another scream, and with wild weeping. Through the window they saw the thatched roof of a cottage rise in flames. Fiona could only thank God her husband and son hadn't returned.

"I want to stay with you." Serena's wide green eyes overwhelmed her face, damp now with the beginnings of tears. But her mouth, the one her father called stubborn, firmed. "Papa wouldn't want me to leave you alone."

"He would want you to do as you're told." Fiona heard the horses stop at the door. There was a jingle of spurs and the sound of men shouting. "Go now." She turned her daughter and pushed her toward the stairs. "Keep the babies safe."

As Malcolm began to wail, Serena fled up the steps. She was on the landing when she heard the door burst in. She stopped and turned to see her mother face a half-dozen dragoons. One stepped forward and bowed. Even from a distance, Serena could see that the gesture was an insult.

"Serena?" little Gwen called from the stairs above.

"Take the baby." Serena pushed Malcolm into Gwen's pudgy five-year-old arms. "Go into the nursery and shut the door." She lowered her voice to a whisper. "Hurry—keep him quiet if you can." From her apron pocket she dug a sugarplum she'd been saving. "Take this and go before they see us." Crouching at the top of the stairs, she watched.

"Fiona MacGregor?" said the dragoon with the fancy stripes.

"I am Lady MacGregor." Fiona kept her shoulders back and her eyes level. Her only thought now was to protect her children and her home. Since fighting was impossible, she used the only weapon at hand—her dignity. "By what right do you break into my home?"

"By the right of an officer of the king."

"And your name?"

"Captain Standish, at your service." He drew off his gloves, waiting, hoping, to see fear. "Where is your husband...Lady MacGregor?"

"The laird and his men are hunting."

Standish signaled, sending three of his men on a search of the house. One overturned a table as he passed. Though her mouth was dry as dust, Fiona held her ground. She knew he could order her home torched, as easily as he had her tenants' cottages. There was little hope that her rank, or her husband's, would protect them. Her only choice was to meet insult with insult, and calmly.

"As you've seen, we are mostly women and children here. Your...visit is ill-timed if you wish to have words with the MacGregor or his men. Or perhaps that is why you and your soldiers come so bravely into Glenroe."

He slapped her then, sending her staggering backward from the force of the blow.

"My father will kill you for that." Serena flew down the stairs like a bullet and launched herself at the officer. He swore as she dug her teeth into his hand, then swept her aside.

"Damn devil's brat drew blood." He lifted his fist, but Fiona flung herself between him and her daughter.

"Do King George's men beat small children? Is that how the English rule?"

Standish was breathing fast. It was a matter of pride now. He could hardly let his men see him bested by a woman and child, especially when they were Scottish scum. His orders were only to search and question. It was a pity the sniveling Argyll had convinced the queen, in her role as regent, not to enforce the Bill of Pains and Penalties. Scotland would indeed have been a hunting ground if she had. Still, Queen Caroline was furious with her Scottish subjects, and in any case she was hardly likely to hear of an isolated incident in the Highlands.

He signaled to one of the dragoons. "Take that brat upstairs and lock her up."

Without a word the soldier scooped Serena up, doing his best to avoid her feet and teeth and pummeling fists. As she fought, she screamed for her mother and cursed the soldiers.

"You raise wildcats in the Highlands, milady." The officer wrapped a fresh handkerchief around his hand.

"She is unused to seeing her mother, or any woman, struck by a man."

His hand was throbbing. He would not regain his men's esteem by thrashing a puny child. But the mother... He smiled as he let his gaze wander over her. The mother was a different matter.

"Your husband is suspected of involvement with the murder of Captain Porteous."

"The Captain Porteous who was sentenced to death by the courts for firing into a crowd?"

"He was reprieved, madam." Standish laid a hand lightly on the hilt of his sword. Even among his own kind he was considered cruel. Fear and intimidation kept his men in line; the same would work with one Scottish whore. "Captain Porteous fired on a group of rioters at a public execution. Then he was taken from prison and hanged by persons unknown."

"I find it difficult to sympathize with his fate, but neither I nor anyone in my family know of such matters."

"If it's found differently, your husband would be a murderer and a traitor. And you, Lady MacGregor, would have no protection."

"I have nothing to tell you."

"A pity." He smiled and moved a step closer. "Shall I show you what happens to unprotected women?"

Upstairs, Serena beat on the door until her hands were raw. Behind her, Gwen huddled with Malcolm and wept. There was no light in the nursery but for the moon and the flames from the fired cottages. Outside she could hear people shouting, women wailing, but her thoughts were all for her mother—left below, alone and unprotected, with the English.

When the door opened, Serena stumbled back. She saw the red coat, heard the jangle of spurs. Then she saw her mother, naked, bruised, her beautiful hair a wild mass around her face and shoulders. Fiona fell to her knees at Serena's feet.

"Mama." Serena knelt beside her, touched a tentative hand to her shoulder. She'd seen her mother weep before, but not like this, not these silent, hopeless tears. Because Fiona's skin was cold to the touch, Serena dragged a blanket from the chest and wrapped it around her.

While she listened to the dragoons ride off, Serena held her mother with one arm and cuddled Gwen and Malcolm with the other. She had only the vaguest understanding of what had happened, but it was enough to make her hate, and to make her vow revenge.

Chapter One

London, 1745

Brigham Langston, the fourth earl of Ashburn, sat at breakfast in his elegant town house and frowned over the letter. It was certainly one he'd been expecting, one he'd been waiting and watching for. Now that it was here, he read each word carefully, his gray eyes serious and his full mouth firm. It wasn't often a man received a letter that could change his life.

"Damn it, Brig, how long are you going to keep me waiting?" Coll MacGregor, the quick-tempered, redheaded Scot who had been Brigham's companion on certain journeys through Italy and France, seemed unable to sit quietly while Brigham read.

In answer, Brigham merely lifted one narrow hand, white-skinned and foaming with lace at the wrist. He was accustomed to Coll's outbursts, and for the most part enjoyed them. But this time, this very important time, he would hold his friend off until he'd read the letter through again.

"It's from him, is it not? Damn you to hell and back, it is from him. From the Prince." Coll pushed away from the table to pace. Only the manners hammered into him by his mother kept him from tearing the letter from Brigham's hand. Although the knowledge that, despite the difference in size and girth, Brigham could hold his own in a fight might also have played a certain role in his decision. "I've as much right as you."

Brigham looked up at that, letting his gaze pass over the man who was now striding around the small salon with enough force to make the china rattle. Though his muscles were tense and his mind was shooting off in a dozen directions, Brigham's voice was mild.

"Of course you do, but the letter is, nonetheless, addressed to me."

"Only because it's easier to smuggle a letter to the high-and-mighty English earl of Ashburn than it is to a MacGregor. We're all under suspicion of being rebels in Scotland." Coll's sharp green eyes were alight with challenge. When Brigham merely returned to the letter, Coll swore again and dropped into his chair. "You're enough to try a man's soul."

"Thank you." Setting the letter beside his plate, Brigham poured more coffee. His hand was as steady as it was when he gripped the hilt of a sword or the butt of a pistol. And, indeed, this letter was a weapon of war. "You

are quite right on all counts, my dear. The letter is from Prince Charles.''
Brigham sipped his coffee.

"Well, what does he say?"

When Brigham indicated the letter with a wave of his hand, Coll pounced
on it. The missive was written in French, and though his command of the
language was not as good as Brigham's, he struggled through it.

As he did, Brigham studied the room around him. The wallpaper had been
chosen by his grandmother, a woman he remembered as much for her soft
Scottish burr as for her stubbornness. It was a deep, glassy blue that she'd
said reminded her of the lochs of her homeland. The furnishings were elegant,
almost delicate, with their sweeping curves and gilt edges. The graceful Meis-
sen porcelain figurines she had prized still stood on the little round table by
the window.

As a boy he'd been allowed to look but not to touch, and his fingers had
always itched to hold the statue of the shepherdess with the long porcelain
hair and the fragile face.

There was a portrait of Mary MacDonald, the strong-willed woman who
had become Lady Ashburn. It stood over the crackling fire and showed her
at an age very close to what her grandson claimed now. She'd been tall for
a woman and reed-slim, with a glorious mane of ebony hair around a narrow,
fine-boned face. There was a look in the way she tilted her head that said
she could be persuaded but not forced, asked but not commanded.

The same features, the same coloring, had been passed down to her grandson. They were no less elegant in their masculine form—the high forehead,
the hollowed cheeks and full mouth. But Brigham had inherited more than
his height and his gray eyes from Mary. He'd also inherited her passions and
her sense of justice.

He thought of the letter, of the decisions to be made, and toasted the
portrait.

You'd have me go, he thought. All the stories you told me, that belief in
the rightness of the Stuart cause you planted in my head during the years
you raised and cared for me. If you were still alive, you'd go yourself. So
how can I not?

"So it's time." Coll folded the letter. In his voice, in his eyes, were both
excitement and tension. He was twenty-four, only six months younger than
Brigham, but this was a moment he had been awaiting for most of his life.

"You have to learn to read between the lines, Coll." This time Brigham
rose. "Charles is still holding out hope of support from the French, though
he's beginning to realize King Louis would rather talk than act." Frowning,
he twitched back the curtain and looked out at his dormant gardens. They
would explode with color and scent in the spring. But it was unlikely he
would be there to see them in the spring.

"When we were at court, Louis was more than interested in our cause. He
has no more liking for the Hanoverian puppet on the throne than we," Coll
said.

"No, but that doesn't mean he'll open his coffers to the Bonnie Prince
and the Stuart cause. Charles's notion of fitting out a frigate and sailing for
Scotland seems more realistic. But these things take time."

"Which is where we come in."

Brigham let the drapes fall back into place. "You know the mood of Scotland better than I. How much support will he get?"

"Enough." With the confidence of pride and youth, Coll grinned. "The clans will rise for the true king and fight to the man behind him." He rose then, knowing what his friend was asking. Brigham would be risking more than his life in Scotland. His title, his home and his reputation could be lost. "Brig, I could take the letter, go to my family and from there spread word throughout the Highland clans. It isn't necessary for you to go, as well."

One black brow rose, and Brigham nearly smiled. "I'm of so little use?"

"To hell with that." Coll's voice was bluff, his gestures wide. Both were as much a part of him as the rumbling cadences of his homeland and his fierce pride in it. "A man like you, one who knows how to talk, how to fight, an English aristocrat willing to join the rebellion? No one knows better than I just what you can do. After all, you saved my life more than once in Italy and, aye, in France, as well."

"Don't be boring, Coll." Brigham flicked at the lace at his wrist. "It's unlike you."

Coll's wide face folded into a grin. "Aye, and there's something to be said for the way you can turn into the earl of Ashburn in the blink of an eye."

"My dear, I *am* the earl of Ashburn."

Humor kindled in Coll's eyes. When they stood together like this, the contrasts between the men were marked. Brigham with his trim build, Coll with his brawny one. Brigham with his elegant, even languid manners, Coll rough-and-ready. But no one knew better than the Scot just what lay beneath the well-cut coats and the lace.

"It wasn't the earl of Ashburn who fought back-to-back with me when our coach was attacked outside of Calais. It wasn't the earl of Ashburn who damned near drank me, a MacGregor, under the table in that grimy little gaming hell in Rome."

"I assure you it was, as I remember both incidents very well."

Coll knew better than to banter words with Brigham. "Brigham, be serious. As the earl of Ashburn you deserve to stay in England, go to your balls and card parties. You could still do the cause good here, with your ear to the ground."

"But?"

"If I'm going to fight, I'd like to have you beside me. Will you come?"

Brigham studied his friend, then shifted his gaze up and beyond, to the portrait of his grandmother. "Of course."

The weather in London was cold and dank. It remained so three days later, when the two men began their journey north. They would travel to the border in the relative comfort of Brigham's coach, then take the rest on horseback.

For anyone who remained in London during the miserable January weather and chose to inquire, Lord Ashburn was making a casual journey to Scotland to visit the family of his friend.

There were a few who knew better, a handful of staunch Tories and English Jacobites whom Brigham trusted. To them he left in trust his family home, Ashburn Manor, as well as his house in London and the disposition of his servants. What could be taken without undo notice, he took. What could not, he left behind with the full knowledge that it probably would be months, perhaps even years, before he could return to claim them. The portrait of his grandmother still stood above the mantel, but on a sentimental whim he'd had the statue of the shepherdess wrapped for the journey.

There was gold, a good deal more than was needed for a visit to the family of a friend, in a locked chest beneath the floor of the coach.

They were forced to move slowly, more slowly than Brigham cared for, but the roads were slick, and occasional flurries of snow had the driver walking the team. Brigham would have preferred a good horse beneath him and the freedom of a gallop.

A look out the window showed him that the weather to the north could only be worse. With what patience he'd learned to cultivate, Brigham sat back, rested his booted feet on the opposite seat, where Coll sat dozing, and let his thoughts drift back to Paris, where he had spent a few glittering months the year before. That was the France of Louis XV, opulent, glamorous, all light and music. There had been lovely women there, with their powdered hair and scandalous gowns. It had been easy to flirt, and more. A young English lord with a fat purse and a talent for raillery had little trouble making a place in society.

He had enjoyed it, the lushness and laziness of it. But it was also true that he'd begun to feel restless, fretting for action and purpose. The Langstons had always enjoyed the intrigue of politics as much as the sparkle of balls and routs. Just as, for three generations, they had silently sworn their loyalty to the Stuarts—the rightful kings of England.

So when Prince Charles Edward had come to France, a magnetic man of courage and energy, Brigham had offered his aid and his oath. Many would have called him traitor. No doubt the fusty Whigs who supported the German who now sat upon the English throne would have wished Brigham hanged as one if they had known. But Brigham's loyalty was to the Stuart cause, to which his family had always held true, not to the fat German usurper George. He'd not forgotten the stories his grandmother had told him of the disastrous rebellion of '15, and of the proscriptions and executions before and after it.

As the landscape grew wilder and the city of London seemed so far away he thought once again that the House of Hanover had done little—had not even tried—to endear itself to Scotland. There had always been the threat of war, from the north or from across the Channel. If England was to be made strong, it would need its rightful king.

It had been more than the Prince's clear eyes and fair looks that had decided Brigham to stand with him. It had been his drive and ambition, and perhaps his youthful confidence that he could, and would, claim what was his.

They stopped for the night at a small inn where the Lowland plains started to rise into the true Highlands. Brigham's gold, and his title, earned them dry sheets and a private parlor. Fed, warmed by the leaping fire, they diced and drank too much ale while the wind swept down from the mountains and hammered at the walls. For a few hours they were simply two well-to-do young men who shared a friendship and an adventure.

"Damn your bones, Brig, you're a lucky bastard tonight."

"So it would seem." Brigham scooped up the dice and the coins. His eyes, bright with humor, met Coll's. "Shall we find a new game?"

"Roll." Coll grinned and shoved more coins to the center of the table. "Your luck's bound to change." When the dice fell, he snickered. "If I can't beat that..." When his roll fell short, he shook his head. "Seems you can't lose. Like the night in Paris you played the duke for the affections of that sweet mademoiselle."

Brigham poured more ale. "With or without the dice, I'd already won the mademoiselle's affections."

Laughing thunderously, Coll slapped more coins on the table. "Your luck can't hang sunny all the time. Though I for one hope it holds for the months to come."

Brigham swept his gaze upward and assured himself that the door to the parlor was closed. "It's more a matter of Charles's luck than mine."

"Aye, he's what we've needed. His father has always been lacking in ambition and too sure of his own defeat." He lifted his tankard of ale. "To the Bonnie Prince."

"He'll need more than his looks and a clever tongue."

Coll's red brows rose. "Do you doubt the MacGregors?"

"You're the only MacGregor I know." Before Coll could begin an oration on his clan, Brigham asked quickly, "What of your family, Coll? You'll be pleased to see them again."

"It's been a long year. Not that I haven't enjoyed the sights of Rome and Paris, but when a man's born in the Highlands, he prefers to die there." Coll drank deeply, thinking of purple moors and deep blue lochs. "I know the family is well from the last letter my mother sent me, but I'll feel better seeing for myself. Malcolm will be nigh on ten now, and a hellion, I'm told." He grinned, full of pride. "Then so are we all."

"You told me your sister was an angel."

"Gwen." The tenderness invaded his voice. "Little Gwen. So she is, sweet-tempered, patient, pretty as new cream."

"I'm looking forward to meeting her."

"And still in the schoolroom," Coll told him. "I'll be around to see you don't forget it."

A little hazy with ale, Brigham tilted back in his chair. "You've another sister."

"Serena." Coll jiggled the dice box in his palm. "God knows the lass was misnamed. A wildcat she is, and I've the scars to prove it. Serena MacGregor has the devil's own temper and a quick fist."

"But is she pretty?"

"She's not hard to look at," said her brother. "My mother tells me the boys have started courting this past year, and Serena sends them off with boxed ears, scrambling for cover."

"Perhaps they have yet to find the, ah, proper way to court her."

"Hah! I crossed her once, and she grabbed my grandfather's claymore from the wall and chased me into the forest." The pride came through, if not the tenderness. "I pity the man who sets his sights on her."

"An amazon." Brigham pictured a strapping, ruddy-cheeked girl with Coll's broad features and wild red hair. Healthy as a milkmaid, he imagined, and just as sassy. "I prefer the milder sort."

"Isn't a mild bone in her body, but she's true." The ale was swimming in Coll's head, but that didn't stop him from lifting the tankard again. "I told you about the night the dragoons came to Glenroe."

"Yes."

Coll's eyes darkened with the memory. "After they'd finished shaming my mother and firing roofs, Serena nursed her. She was hardly more than a bairn herself, but she got my mother into bed and tended her and the children until we returned. There was a bruise on her face where that black bastard had knocked her aside, but she didn't cry. She sat, dry-eyed, and told us the whole."

Brigham laid a hand over his friend's. "The time's past for revenge, Coll, but not for justice."

"I'll take both," Coll murmured, and tossed the dice again.

They started out early the next morning. Brigham's head ached, but the cold, blustery air soon cleared it. They went on horseback, allowing the coach to follow at a sedate pace.

Now they were truly in the land he'd been told of as a child. It was wild and rough, with crags rising high and moors spread out and desolate. Prominent peaks pierced the milky gray of the sky, sometimes cut through with tumbling waterfalls and icy rivers thick with fish. In other places rocks were tumbled as though they had been dice rolled by a careless hand. It seemed an ancient place, one for gods and fairies, yet he saw an occasional cottage, smoke belching from the central opening in the thatch.

The ground was heaped with snow, and the wind blew it in sheets across the road. At times they were nearly blinded by it as Coll led the way up the rising, rut-filled hills. Caves opened out of rock. Here and there were signs that shelter had been taken in them. Lakes, their waters a dark, dangerous blue, were crusted at the edges with ice. The effects of the ale were whisked away by a damp cold that stung the air and penetrated even the layers of a greatcoat.

They rode hard when the land permitted, then picked their way through snowdrifts as high as a man's waist. Cautious, they bypassed the forts the English had built and avoided the hospitality that would have been given unhesitatingly at any cottage. Hospitality, Coll had warned Brigham, would include questions about every aspect of their journey, their families and their destination. Strangers were rare in the Highlands, and prized for their news as much as their company.

Rather than risk the details of their journey being passed from village to village, they kept to the rougher roads and hills before stopping at a tavern to rest the horses and take their midday meal. The floors were dirt, the chimney no more than a hole in the roof that kept as much smoke in as it let out. The single cramped room smelled of its occupants and of yesterday's fish. It was hardly a spot the fourth earl of Ashburn would be likely to frequent, but the fire was hot and the meat almost fresh.

Beneath the greatcoat, which now hung drying in front of the fire, Brigham wore dun-colored riding breeches and a shirt of fine lawn with his plainest riding coat. But though it might be plain, it fit without a wrinkle over his broad shoulders, and its buttons were silver. His boots had been dulled a bit by the weather but were unmistakably of good leather. His thick mane of hair was tied back with a riband, and on his narrow hands he wore his family seal and an emerald. He was hardly dressed in his best court attire, but nonetheless he drew stares and curious whispers.

"They don't see the likes of you in this hole," Coll said. Comfortable in his kilt and bonnet, with the pine sprig of his clan tucked into the band, he dug hungrily into his meat pie.

"Apparently." Brigham ate lazily, but his eyes, behind half-closed lids, remained alert. "Such admiration would delight my tailor."

"Oh, it's only partly the clothes." Coll raised his bicker of ale to drain it, and thought pleasantly of the whiskey he would share with his father that night. "You would look like an earl if you wore rags." Anxious to be off, he tossed coins on the table. "The horses should be rested; let's be off. We're skirting Campbell country." Coll's manners were too polished to allow him to spit, but he would have liked to. "I'd prefer not to dally."

Three men left the tavern before them, letting in a blast of cold and beautifully fresh air.

It had become difficult for Coll to contain his impatience. Now that he was back in the Highlands, he wanted nothing so much as to see his own home, his own family. The road twisted and climbed, occasionally winding by a huddle of cottages and cattle grazing on the rough, uneven ground. Men living here would have to keep an eye out for wildcat and badgers.

Though they had hours to ride, he could almost scent home—the forest, with its red deer and tawny owls. There would be a feast that night, and cups raised in toasts. London, with its crowded streets and fussy manners, was behind him.

Trees were scarce, only the little junipers pushing through on the leeside of boulders. In Scotland, even the brush had a difficult time surviving. Now and then they rode by a rumbling river or stream, to be challenged by the eerie, consuming silence that followed. The skies had cleared to a hard, brilliant blue. Above, majestic and glorious, a golden eagle circled.

"Brig—"

Beside Coll, Brigham had suddenly gone rigid. Coll's horse reared as Brigham pulled out his sword. "Guard your flank," he shouted, then wheeled to face two riders who had burst out from behind a tumble of rock.

They rode sturdy garrons, shaggy Scottish ponies, and though their tartans were dulled with age and dirt, the blades of their fighting swords shone in the midafternoon sun. Brigham had only time enough to note that the men who charged had been in the tavern before there was the crash of steel against steel.

Beside him, Coll wielded his sword against two more. The high hills rang with the sounds of battle, the thunder of hooves against hard-packed ground. Gliding overhead, the eagle circled and waited.

The attackers had misjudged their quarry in Brigham. His hands were narrow, his body slender as a dancer's, but his wrists were both wiry and supple. Using his knees to guide his mount, he fought with a sword in one hand and a dagger in the other. There might have been jewels on the hilts, but the blades were fashioned to kill.

He heard Coll shout and swear. For himself, he fought in deadly silence. Steel scraped as he defended himself, crashed when he took the offensive, driving at one foe and outmaneuvering the other. His eyes, usually a calm, clear gray, had darkened and narrowed like those of a wolf that scents blood. He gave his opponent's sword one final, vicious parry and ran his own blade home.

The Scot screamed, but the sound lasted no more than a heartbeat. Blood splattered the snow as the man fell. His pony, frightened by the smell of death, ran clattering up the rocks. The other man, wild-eyed, renewed his attack with more ferocity and fear than finesse. The violence of the advance nearly cut through Brigham's guard, and he felt the sting of the sword on his shoulder and the warm flow of blood where the point had ripped layers of clothing and found flesh. Brigham countered with swift, steady strokes, driving his quarry back and back, toward the rocks. His eyes stayed on his opponent's face, never flickering, never wavering. With cool-headed precision, he parried and thrust and pierced the heart. Before the man had hit the ground, he was swinging back toward Coll.

It was one on one now, for another of the attackers lay dead behind Coll, and Brigham took time to draw a deep breath. Then he saw Coll's horse slip, nearly stumble. He saw the blade flash and was racing toward his friend. The last man of the band of attackers looked up to see the horse and rider bearing down on him. With his three comrades dead, he wheeled his pony and scrambled up the rocks.

"Coll! Are you hurt?"

"Aye, by God. Bloody Campbell." He struggled not to slump in the saddle. His side, where the sword had pierced it, was on fire.

Brigham sheathed his sword. "Let me see to it."

"No time. That jackal may come back with more." Coll took out a handkerchief and pressed it to the wound, then brought his gloved hand back. It was sticky but steady. "I'm not done yet." His eyes, still bright from battle, met Brigham's. "We'll be home by dusk." With that, he sent his horse into a gallop.

They rode hard, with Brigham keeping one eye out for another ambush and the other on Coll. The big Scot was pale, but his pace never faltered. Only once, at Brigham's insistence, did they stop so that the wound could be bound more satisfactorily.

Brigham didn't like what he saw. The wound was deep, and Coll had lost far too much blood. Still, his friend was in a fever to reach Glenroe and his family, and Brigham would not have known where else to find help. Coll accepted the flask Brigham put to his lips and drank deeply. When the color seeped back into his face, Brigham helped him into the saddle.

They dropped down out of the hills into the forest at dusk, when the shadows were long and wavering. It smelled of pine and snow, with a faint wisp of smoke from a cottage farther on. A hare dashed across the path, then crashed through the brush. Behind it, like a flash, came a merlin. Winter berries, as big as thumbs, clung to thorny limbs.

Brigham knew Coll's strength was flagging, and he paused long enough to make him drink again.

"I ran through this forest as a child," Coll rasped. His breathing came quickly, but the brandy eased the pain. He'd be damned if he would die before the true fighting began. "Hunted in it, stole my first kiss in it. For the life of me, I can't think why I ever left it."

"To come back a hero," Brigham said as he corked the flask.

Coll gave a laugh that turned into a cough. "Aye. There's been a MacGregor in the Highlands since God put us here, and here we stay." He turned to Brigham with a hint of the old arrogance. "You may be an earl, but my race is royal."

"And you're shedding your royal blood all over the forest. To home, Coll."

They rode at an easy canter. When they passed the first cottages, cries went out. Out of houses, some fashioned from wood and stone, others built out of no more than mud and grass, people came. Though the pain was streaking up his side, Coll saluted. They crested a hill, and both men saw MacGregor House.

There was smoke winding out of the chimneys. Behind the glazed windows lamps, just lighted, were glowing. The sky to the west was ablaze with the last lights of the sun, and the blue slate glowed and seemed to turn to silver. It rose four stories, graced with turrets and towers, a house fashioned as much for war as for comfort. The roofs were of varying height, strung together in a confused yet somehow charming style.

There was a barn in the clearing, along with other outbuildings and grazing cattle. From somewhere came the hollow barking of a dog.

Behind them more people had come out of their homes. Out of one ran a woman, her basket empty. Brigham heard her shout and turned. And stared.

She was wrapped in a plaid like a mantle. In one hand she held a basket that swung wildly as she ran; the other hand held the hem of her skirt, and he could see the flash of petticoats and long legs. She was laughing as she ran, and her scarf fell down around her shoulders, leaving hair the color of the sunset flying behind her.

Her skin was like alabaster, though flushed now from delight and cold. Her features had been carved with a delicate hand, but the mouth was full and rich. Brigham could only stare and think of the shepherdess he had loved and admired as a child.

"Coll!" Her voice was low, filled with the music of laughter, rich with the burr of Scotland. Ignoring the horse's dancing impatience, she gripped the bridle and turned up a face that made Brigham's mouth turn dry. "I've had the fidgets all day and should have known you were the cause. We had no word you were coming. Did you forget how to write or were you too lazy?"

"A fine way to greet your brother." Coll would have bent down to kiss her, but her face was swimming in front of his eyes. "The least you can do is show some manners to my friend. Brigham Langston, Lord Ashburn, my sister, Serena."

Not hard to look at? For once, Brigham thought, Coll hadn't exaggerated. Far from it. "Miss MacGregor."

But Serena didn't spare him a glance. "Coll, what is it? You're hurt." Even as she reached for him, he slid from the saddle to her feet. "Oh, God, what's this?" She pushed aside his coat and found the hastily bound wound.

"It's opened again." Brigham knelt beside her. "We should get him inside."

Serena's head shot up as she raked Brigham with rapier-sharp green eyes. It wasn't fear in them, but fury. "Take your hands off him, English swine."

She shoved him aside and cradled her brother against her breast. With her own plaid she pressed against the wound to slow the bleeding. "How is it my brother comes home near death and you ride in with your fine sword sheathed and nary a scratch?"

Coll might have underplayed her beauty, Brigham decided as his mouth set, but not her temperament. "I think that's best explained after Coll's seen to."

"Take your explanations back to London." When he gathered Coll up to carry him, she all but pounced on him. "Leave him be, damn you. I won't have you touching what's mine."

He let his gaze run up and down her until her cheeks glowed. "Believe me, madam," he said, stiffly polite, "I've no desire to. If you'll see to the horses, Miss MacGregor, I'll take your brother in."

She started to speak again, but one look at Coll's white face had her biting back the words. With his greatcoat flapping around him and Coll in his arms, Brigham started toward the house.

Serena remembered the last time an Englishman had walked into her home. Snatching the reins of both horses, she hurried after Brigham, cursing him.

Chapter Two

There was little time for introductions. Brigham was greeted at the door by a gangly black-haired serving girl who ran off wringing her hands and shouting for Lady MacGregor. Fiona came in, her cheeks flushed from the kitchen fire. At the sight of her son unconscious in the arms of a stranger, she went pale.

"Coll. Is he—"

"No, my lady, but the wound's severe."

With one very slender hand, she touched her son's face. "Please, if you'd bring him upstairs." She went ahead, calling out orders for water and bandages. "In here." After pushing open a door, she looked over Brigham's shoulder. "Gwen, thank God. Coll's been wounded."

Gwen, smaller and more delicately built than her mother and sister, hurried into the room. "Light the lamps, Molly," she told the serving girl. "I'll need plenty of light." She was already pressing a hand to her brother's brow. "He's feverish." His blood stained his plaid and ran red on the linen. "Can you help me off with his clothes?"

With a nod, Brigham began to work with her. She coolly sent for medicines and bowls of water, stacks of linen were rushed in. The young girl didn't swoon at the sword wound as Brigham had feared, but competently began to clean and treat it. Even under her gentle hands, Coll began to mutter and thrash.

"Hold this, if you please." Gwen gestured for Brigham to hold the pad she'd made against the wound while she poured syrup of poppies into a wooden cup. Fiona supported her son's head while Gwen eased the potion past his lips. She murmured to him as she sat again and stitched up the wound without flinching.

"He's lost a lot of blood," she told her mother as she worked. "We'll have to mind the fever." Already Fiona was bathing her son's head with a cool cloth.

"He's strong. We won't lose him now." Fiona straightened and brushed at the hair that had fallen around her face. "I'm grateful to you for bringing him," she told Brigham. "Will you tell me what happened?"

"We were attacked a few miles south of here. Coll believes it was Campbells."

"I see." Her lips tightened, but her voice remained calm. "I must apologize for not even offering you a chair or a hot drink. I'm Coll's mother, Fiona MacGregor.''

"I'm Coll's friend, Brigham Langston."

Fiona managed a smile but kept her son's limp hand in hers. "The earl of Ashburn, of course. Coll wrote of you. Please, let me have Molly take your coat and fetch you some refreshment.''

"He's English.'' Serena stood in the doorway. She'd taken off her plaid. All she wore now was a simple homespun dress of dark blue wool.

"I'm aware of that, Serena.'' Fiona turned her strained smile back to Brigham. "Your coat, Lord Ashburn. You've had a long journey. I'm sure you'll want a hot meal and some rest.'' When he drew off his coat, Fiona's gaze went to his shoulder. "Oh, you're wounded.''

"Not badly.''

"A scratch,'' Serena said as she flicked her gaze over it. She would have moved past him to her brother, but a look from Fiona stopped her.

"Take our guest down to the kitchen and tend to his hurts.''

"I'd sooner bandage a rat.''

"You'll do as I say, and you'll show the proper courtesy to a guest in our home.'' The steel came into her voice. "Once his wounds are tended, see that he has a proper meal.''

"Lady MacGregor, it isn't necessary.''

"Forgive me, my lord, it's quite necessary. You'll forgive me for not tending to you myself.'' She picked up the cloth for Coll's head again. "Serena?''

"Very well, Mother, for you.'' Serena turned, giving a very small and deliberately insulting curtsy. "If you please, Lord Ashburn.''

He followed her down through a house far smaller than Ashburn Manor, and neat as a pin. They wound around a hallway and down two narrow flights because she chose to take him down the back stairs. Still, he paid little notice as he watched Serena's stiff back. There were rich smells in the kitchen, spices, meat, from the kettle hung by a chain over the fire, the aroma of pies just baked. Serena indicated a small, spindle-legged chair.

"Please be seated, my lord.''

He did, and only by the slightest flicker of his eyes did he express his feelings when she ripped the sleeve from his shirt. "I hope you don't faint at the sight of blood, Miss MacGregor.''

"It's more likely you will at the sight of your mutilated shirt, Lord Ashburn.'' She tossed the ruined sleeve aside and brought back a bowl of hot water and some clean cloths.

It was more than a scratch. English though he might be, she felt a bit ashamed of herself. He'd obviously opened the wound when he'd carried Coll inside. As she stanched the blood that had begun to run freely, she saw that the cut measured six inches or more along a well-muscled forearm.

His flesh was warm and smooth in her hands. He smelled not of perfumes and powders, as she imagined all Englishmen did, but of horses and sweat and blood. Oddly enough, it stirred something in her and made her fingers gentler than she'd intended.

She had the face of an angel, he thought as she bent over him. And the soul of a witch. An interesting combination, Brigham decided as he caught a whiff of lavender. The kind of mouth made for kissing, paired with hostile eyes designed to tear holes in a man. How would her hair feel, bunched in a man's hands? He had an urge to stroke it, just to see her reaction. But one wound, he told himself, was enough for one day.

She worked competently and in silence, cleaning the wound and dabbing on one of Gwen's herbal mixtures. The scent was pleasant, and made her think of the forest and flowers. Serena hardly noticed that his English blood was on her fingers.

She reached for the bandages. He shifted. All at once they were face-to-face, as close as a man and woman can come without embracing. She felt his breath feather across her lips and was surprised by the quick flutter of her heart. She noticed his eyes were gray, darker than they had been when he'd coolly assessed her on the road. His mouth was beautiful, curved now with the beginnings of a smile that changed his sharp-featured aristocratic face into something approachable.

She thought she felt his fingers on her hair but was certain she was mistaken. For a moment, perhaps two, her mind went blank and she could only look at him and wonder.

"Will I live?" he murmured.

There it was, that English voice, mocking, smug. She needed nothing else to drag her out of whatever spell his eyes had cast. She smiled at him and yanked the bandage tight enough to make him jerk.

"Oh, pardon, my lord," she said with a flutter of lashes. "Have I hurt you?"

He gave her a mild look and thought it would be satisfying to throttle her. "Pray don't regard it."

"I will not." She rose to remove the bowl of bloodstained water. "Odd, isn't it, that English blood runs so thin?"

"I hadn't noticed. The Scottish blood I shed today looked pale to me."

She whirled back. "If it was Campbell blood, you rid the world of another badger, but I won't be grateful to you for that, or anything."

"You cut me to the quick, my lady, when your gratitude is what I live for."

She snatched up a wooden bowl—though her mother would have meant for her to use the delft or the china—and scooped out stew and slapped it down so that more than a little slopped over the sides. She poured him ale and tossed a couple of oatcakes on a platter. A pity they weren't stale.

"Your supper, my lord. Have a care not to choke on it."

He rose then, and for the first time she noticed that he was nearly as tall as her brother, though he carried less muscle and brawn. "Your brother warned me you were ill-tempered."

She set her fist on her hip, eyeing him from under lashes shades darker than her tumbled hair. "That's fortunate for you, my lord, so you'll know better than to cross me."

He stepped toward her. It couldn't be helped, given his temper and his penchant for fighting face-to-face. She tilted her chin as if braced, even anxious, for the bout. "If you've a mind to chase me into the wood with your grandsire's claymore, think again."

Her lips twitched even as she fought back the smile. Humor made her eyes almost as appealing as anger. "Why? Are you fast on your feet, *Sassenach*?" she asked, using the Gaelic term for the hated English invader.

"Fast enough to knock you off yours if you were fortunate enough to catch me." He took her hand, effectively wiping the smile from her eyes. Though her hand curled into a fist, he brought it to his lips. "My thanks, Miss MacGregor, for your so gentle touch and hospitality."

While he stood where he was, she stormed out, furiously wiping her knuckles against her skirts.

It was full dark when Ian MacGregor returned with his youngest son. After his quick meal, Brigham kept to the room he'd been given, leaving the family to themselves and giving himself time to think. Coll had described the MacGregors well enough. Fiona was lovely, with enough strength in her face and bearing to add grit to beauty. Young Gwen was sweet and quiet with shy eyes—and a steady hand when she sewed rent flesh together.

As to Serena...Coll hadn't mentioned that his sister was a she-wolf with a face to rival Helen's, but Brigham was content to make his own judgments there. It might be true that she had no cause to love the English, but for himself, Brigham preferred to weigh a man as a man, not by his nationality.

He would do as well to judge a woman as a woman and not by her looks, he thought. When she had come racing down the road toward her brother, her face alive with pleasure, her hair flying, he'd felt as though he had been struck by lightning. Fortunately, he wasn't a man who tarried long under the spell of a beautiful pair of eyes and a pretty ankle. He had come to Scotland to fight for a cause he believed in, not to worry because some slip of a girl detested him.

Because of his birth, he thought as he paced to the window and back. He'd never had any cause to be other than proud of his lineage. His grandfather had been a man respected and feared—as his father had been before death had taken him so early. From the time he was old enough to understand, Brigham had been taught that being a Langston was both a privilege and a responsibility. He took neither lightly. If he had, he would have stayed in Paris, enjoying the whims and caprices of elegant society rather than traveling to the mountains of Scotland to risk all for the young Prince.

Damn the woman for looking at him as though he were scum to be scrubbed from the bottom of a pot.

At a knock on the door he turned, scowling, from the window. "Yes?"

The serving girl opened the door with her heart already in her throat. One peep at Brigham's black looks had her lowering her eyes and bobbing nervous curtsies. "Begging your pardon, Lord Ashburn." And that was all she could manage.

He waited, then sighed. "Might I know what you beg it for?"

She darted him a quick look, then stared at the floor again. "My lord, the MacGregor wishes to see you downstairs if it's convenient."

"Certainly, I'll come right away."

But the girl had already dashed off. She would have a story to tell her mother that night, about how Serena MacGregor had insulted the English lord to his face—a face, she'd add, that was handsome as the devil's.

Brigham fluffed out the lace at his wrists. He had traveled with only one change of clothes, and he hoped the coach with the rest of his belongings would find its ponderous way to Glenroe the next day.

He descended the stairs, slender and elegant in black and silver. Lace foamed subtly at his throat, and his rings gleamed in the lamplight. In Paris and London he'd followed fashion and powdered his hair. Here he was glad to dispense with the bother, so it was brushed, raven black, away from his high forehead.

The MacGregor waited in the dining hall, drinking port, a fire roaring at his back. His hair was a dark red and fell to his shoulders. A beard of the same color and luster covered his face. He had dressed as was proper when receiving company of rank. In truth, the great kilt suited him, for he was as tall and broad as his son. With it he wore a doublet of calfskin and a jeweled clasp at his shoulder on which was carved the head of a lion.

"Lord Ashburn. You are welcome to Glenroe and the house of Ian MacGregor."

"Thank you." Brigham accepted the offered port and chair. "I'd like to inquire about Coll."

"He's resting easier, though my daughter Gwen tells me it will be a long night." Ian paused a moment, looking down at the pewter cup held in his wide, thick-fingered hand. "Coll has written of you as a friend. If he had not, you would now be one for bringing him back to us."

"He is my friend, and has been."

This was accepted with a nod. "Then I drink to your health, my lord." He did, with gusto. "I'm told your grandmother was a MacDonald."

"She was. From the Isle of Skye."

Ian's face, well lined and reddened by wind and weather, relaxed into a smile. "Then welcome twice." Ian lifted his cup and kept his eye keen on his guest. "To the true king?"

Brigham lifted his port in turn. "To the king across the water," he said, meeting Ian's fierce blue gaze. "And the rebellion to come."

"Aye, that I'll drink to." And he did, downing the port in one giant gulp. "Now tell me how it happened that my boy was hurt."

Brigham described the ambush, detailing the men who'd attacked them, and their dress. As he spoke, Ian listened, leaning forward on the big table as though afraid he might miss a word.

"Bloody murdering Campbells!" he exploded, pounding a fist on the table so that cups and crockery jumped.

"So Coll thought himself," Brigham said equably. "I know a bit about the clans and the feud between yours and the Campbells, Lord MacGregor. It could have been a simple matter of robbery, or it could be that word is out that the Jacobites are stirring."

"And so they are." Ian thought a moment, drumming his fingers. "Well, four on two, was it? Not such bad odds when it comes to Campbells. You were wounded, as well?"

"A trifle." Brigham shrugged. It was a gesture he'd acquired in France. "If Coll's mount hadn't slipped, he would never have dropped his guard. He's a devil of a swordsman."

"So he says of you." Ian's teeth flashed. There was nothing he admired so much as a good fighter. "Something about a skirmish on the road to Calais?"

Brigham grinned at that. "A diversion."

"I'd like to hear more about it, but first, tell me what you can about the Bonnie Prince and his plans."

They talked for hours, draining the bottle of port dry and cracking another while the candles guttered. Formalities faded and disappeared until they were only two men, one past his prime, the other only approaching it. They were both warriors by birth and by temperament. They might fight for different reasons, one in a desperate attempt to preserve a way of life and land, the other for simple justice. But they would fight. When they parted, Ian to look in on his son, Brigham to take the air and check the horses, they knew each other as well as they needed.

It was late when he returned. The house was quiet, fires were banked. Outside the wind whistled, bringing home to him the isolation, the distance from London and all he held familiar.

Near the door, a candle had been lighted to show him the way. He took it and started up the stairs, though he knew he was still far too restless for sleep. The MacGregors interested him—they had since the first time he and Coll had shared a bottle and their life stories. He knew they were bound together, not just through family obligation but through affection and a common love of their land. Tonight he had seen them pull together with unquestioning faith and loyalty. There had been no hysterics when he had carried Coll inside, no weeping and fainting women. Instead, each had done what had needed to be done.

It was that kind of strength and commitment Charles would need over the next months.

With the candlelight sending shadows leaping, Brigham walked past his room to push open the door to Coll's. The bedcurtains were pushed back, and he could see his friend sleeping yet, covered with blankets. And he saw Serena sitting in a chair beside the bed, reading a book by the light of another taper.

It was the first time he'd seen her look as her name described. Her face was calm and extraordinarily lovely in the soft light. Her hair glowed as it fell down her back. She had changed her dress for a night robe of deep green that rose high at the throat to frame her face. As Brigham watched, she looked up at her brother's murmur and placed a hand on the pulse at his wrist.

"How is he?"

She started at the sound of Brigham's voice but collected herself quickly. Her face expressionless, she sat back again to close the book she had in her lap. "His fever's still up. Gwen thinks it should break by morning."

Brigham moved to the foot of the bed. Behind him, the fire burned high. The scent of medicine, mixed with poppies, vied with the smoke. "Coll told me she could do magic with herbs. I've seen doctors with less of a sure hand sewing up a wound."

Torn between annoyance and pride in her sister, Serena smoothed down the skirts of her robe. "She has a gift, and a good heart. She would have stayed with him all night if I hadn't bullied her off to bed."

"So you bully everyone, not just strangers?" He smiled and held up a hand before she could speak. "You can hardly tear into me now, my dear, or you will wake up your brother and the rest of your family."

"I'm not your dear."

"For which I shall go to my grave thankful. Merely a form of address."

Coll stirred, and Brigham moved to the side of the bed to place a cool hand on his brow. "Has he waked at all?"

"A time or two, but not in his right head." Because her conscience demanded it, she relented. "He asked for you." She rose and wrung out a cloth to bathe her brother's face with. "You should retire, and see him in the morning."

"And what of you?"

Her hands were gentle on her brother, soothing, cooling. Despite himself, Brigham imagined how they might feel stroking his brow. "What of me?"

"Have you no one to bully you to bed?"

She glanced up, fully aware of his meaning. "I go when and where I choose." Taking her seat again, she folded her hands. "You're wasting your candle, Lord Ashburn."

Without a word, he snuffed it out. The light of the single taper by the bed plunged them into intimacy. "Quite right," he murmured. "One candle is sufficient."

"I hope you can find your way to your room in the dark."

"I have excellent night vision, as it happens. But I don't retire yet." Idly he plucked the book from her lap. "*Macbeth*?"

"Don't the fine ladies of your acquaintance read?"

His lips twitched. "A few." He opened the book and scanned the pages. "A grisly little tale."

"Murder and power?" She made a little gesture with her hands. "Life, my lord, can be grisly, as the English so often prove."

"Macbeth was a Scot," he reminded her. "'A tale told by an idiot, full of sound and fury, signifying nothing.' Is that how you see life?"

"I see it as what can be made of it."

Brigham leaned against a table, holding the book loosely. He believed she meant just what she said, and that interested him. Most of the women he knew could philosophize about no more than fashion.

"You don't see Macbeth as a villain?"

"Why?" She hadn't meant to speak to him, much less hold a conversation, but she couldn't resist. "He took what he felt was his."

"And his methods?"

"Ruthless. Perhaps kings need be. Charles won't claim his throne by asking for it."

"No." With a frown, Brigham closed the book. "But treachery differs from warfare."

"A sword is a sword, thrust in the back or in the heart." She looked at him, her green eyes glowing in the light. "If I were a man I would fight to win, and the devil take the method."

"And honor?"

"There is much honor in victory." She soaked the cloth and wrung it out again. For all her talk, she had a woman's way with illness, gentle, patient, thorough. "There was a time when the MacGregors were hunted like vermin, with the Campbells paid in good British gold for each death. If you are hunted like something wild, you learn to fight like something wild. Women were raped and murdered, bairns not yet weaned slaughtered. We don't forget, Lord Ashburn, nor forgive."

"This is a new time, Serena."

"Still, my brother's blood was shed today."

On impulse he placed a hand over hers. "In a few months more will be shed, but for justice, not revenge."

"You can afford justice, my lord, not I."

Coll moaned and began to thrash. Serena turned her full attention to him again. Automatically Brigham held him down. "He'll break open his wound again."

"Keep him still." Serena poured more medicine into a wooden cup and held it to Coll's lips. "Drink now, darling." She poured what she could down his throat, murmuring, threatening, coaxing all the while. He was shivering, though his skin was like fire to the touch.

She no longer questioned Brigham's presence, and she said nothing when he stripped off his coat and tucked back the lace at his wrists. Together they bathed Coll with cool water, forced more of Gwen's mixture past his dry lips and kept watch.

During Coll's delirium Serena spoke to him mainly in Gaelic, as calm and steady as a seasoned soldier. Brigham found it strange to see her so unruffled when from almost the first moment of their acquaintance she had been animated by excitement or fury. Now, in the deepest part of the night, her hands were gentle, her voice quiet, her movements competent. They worked together as though they'd spent their lives doing so.

She no longer resented his assistance. English or not, he obviously cared for her brother. Without his aid she would have been forced to summon her sister or her mother. For a few hours, Serena forced herself to forget that Lord Ashburn represented all she despised.

Now and then, over the cloth or the cup, their hands brushed. Both of them strove to ignore even this minor intimacy. He might have been concerned for Coll, but he was still an English nobleman. She might have had more spine than any other women he'd known, but she was still a Scots terror.

The truce lasted while Coll's fever raged. By the time the light turned gray with approaching dawn, the crisis had passed.

"He's cool." Serena blinked back tears as she stroked her brother's brow. Silly to weep now, she thought, when the worst was over. "I think he'll do, but Gwen will have a look at him."

"He should sleep well enough." Brigham pressed a hand to the small of his back, where a dull ache lodged. The fire they had taken turns feeding during the night still roared at his back, shooting light and heat. He had loosened his shirt for comfort and a smoothly muscled chest could be seen in the deep V. Serena wiped her own brow and tried not to notice.

"It's almost morning." She felt weak and weepy and tired to the bone.

"Yes." Brigham's mind had shifted suddenly, completely, from the man in the bed to the woman by the window. The first hints of dawn were behind her, and she stood in shadow and in light. Her night robe cloaked her as if she were royalty. Her face, pale with fatigue, was dominated by eyes that seemed only larger, darker, more mysterious, for the faint bruises beneath.

Her blood began to tingle below her skin as he continued to stare at her. She wished he would stop. It made her feel...powerless somehow. Suddenly afraid, she tore her gaze from his and looked at her brother.

"There's no need for you to stay now."

"No."

She turned her back. Brigham took it as a dismissal. He gave her an ironic bow she couldn't see, but stopped when he heard the sniffle. He paused at the door. Then, dragging a hand through his hair and swearing, he moved toward her.

"No need for tears now, Serena."

Hurriedly she wiped at her cheek with her knuckles. "I thought he would die. I didn't realize how afraid I was of it until it was past." She swiped a hand over her face again. "I've lost my handkerchief," she said miserably.

Brigham pressed his own into her hand.

"Thank you."

"You're welcome," he managed when she handed it back to him crumpled and damp. "Better now?"

"Aye." She let out a long, steadying breath. "I wish you would go."

"Where?" Though he knew it was unwise, he turned her to face him. He only wanted to see her eyes again. "To my bed or to the devil?"

Her lips curved, surprising them both. "As you choose, my lord."

He wanted those lips. The knowledge stunned him as much as her smile did. He wanted them warm and open and completely willing under his own. Light broke through the sky and tumbled like gold dust through the window. Before either of them were prepared, he reached out so that his fingers dug through her hair and cupped her neck.

"No," she managed, amazed that the denial was unsteady. When she lifted a hand in protest, he met it, palm to palm. So they stood as the new day began.

"You tremble," he murmured. Lightly he ran his fingers up her neck, kindling small fires. "I wondered if you would."

"I've not given you leave to touch me."

"I've not asked for leave." He drew her closer. "Nor will I." He brought their joined hands to his lips, dropping a soft kiss on her fingers. "Nor need I."

She felt the room tilt and her will drain as he lowered his head toward her. She saw only his face, then only his eyes. As if in a dream, she let her own eyes close and her lips part.

"Serena?"

She jerked back, color flaming into her face at the sound of her sister's voice. Shaken, Serena gripped her hands together as Gwen stepped into the room. "You should be resting yet. You've only slept a few hours."

"It was enough. Coll?" she asked, staring toward the bed.

"His fever's broken."

"Ah, thank God." Her hair more gold than red, curtained her face as she bent over him. In her pale blue night robe she looked very much like the angel Coll had described. "He sleeps well, and should for a few hours yet." She glanced up to smile at her sister and saw Brigham by the window. "Lord Ashburn! Have you not slept?"

"He was about to retire." Serena moved briskly to her sister's side.

"You need rest." Gwen's face puckered into a frown as she thought of his shoulder. "You'll do your wound no good else."

"He does well enough," Serena said impatiently.

"For your concern, I thank you." Brigham bowed pointedly to Gwen. "As it appears I can be of no further use, I will seek my bed." His gaze swept down Serena and up again. Beside her sister she, too, looked like an angel. An avenging one. "Your servant, madam."

Gwen smiled after him as he strode out, her young heart fluttering a bit at the sight of his bare chest and arms. "So handsome," she sighed.

With a sniff, Serena brushed at the bodice of her robe. "For an Englishman."

"It was kind of him to stay with Coll."

Serena could still feel the determined press of his fingers on the back of her neck. "He's not kind," she murmured. "I don't believe he's kind at all."

Chapter Three

Brigham slept until the sun was high. His shoulder was stiff, but there was no pain. He supposed he owed Serena for that. His lips curved into a grim smile as he dressed. He intended to pay her back.

After he had pulled on his breeches, he glanced at his torn riding coat. It would have to do, as he could hardly wear evening dress. Until his trunks arrived he would be roughing it. He ran a hand over his chin after shrugging into the coat. His stubble was rough and his lace far from fresh. How his valet would have cringed.

Dear, dour Parkins had been furious at being left in London while his lord traveled to the barbarous Scottish Highlands. Parkins knew, as few did, the true purpose of the trip, but that had only made him more insistent about accompanying his master.

Brigham tilted the shaving mirror. Parkins was loyal, he thought, but hardly competent to do battle. There was no finer—or more proper—gentleman's gentleman in London, but Brigham hardly needed, or wanted, a valet during his stay in Glenroe.

With a sigh, he began to strop his razor. He might not be able to do anything about the torn jacket or the drooping lace, but he could manage to shave himself.

Once he was presentable, he made his way downstairs. Fiona was there to greet him, an apron over her simple wool gown. "Lord Ashburn, I trust you rested well."

"Very well, Lady MacGregor."

"If you're a man such as I know, you'll be wanting to break your fast." With a smile, she laid a hand on his arm and began to walk. "Would you care to sit in the parlor? It's warmer than the dining hall, and when I have a solitary meal I find it less lonely."

"Thank you."

"Molly, tell the cook that Lord Ashburn is awake and hungry." She led him into a parlor where a table had already been set for him. "Shall I leave you now, or would you prefer company?"

"I always prefer the company of a beautiful woman, my lady."

With a smile, she accepted the chair he held out for her. "Coll said you were a charmer." Apron or not, she sat as gracefully as any drawing room miss Brigham had known. "I wasn't able to thank you properly last night.

I'd like to make up for that now and give you all my gratitude for delivering Coll home.''

"Would that I had delivered him under better circumstances."

"You brought him." She offered her hand. "I owe you a great deal."

"He's my friend."

"Aye." She squeezed his hand briefly. "So he's told me. That doesn't lessen the debt, but I won't embarrass you." Molly brought in coffee and Fiona poured, pleased by the opportunity to make use of her china. "Coll asked for you this morning. Perhaps after you've eaten you would go up and speak with him."

"Of course. How does he?"

"Well enough to complain." Fiona's smile was maternal. "He's like his father, impatient, impulsive and very, very dear."

They spoke idly while his breakfast was served. There was porridge and thick slabs of ham, portions of fresh fish with eggs and oatcakes and numerous jams and jellies. Though he chose coffee over the breakfast whiskey, it occurred to him that, while remote, this Highland table could easily rival one in London. The lady sipped her coffee and encouraged Brigham to eat his fill.

He found her burr charming and her conversation direct. While he ate, he waited for her to ask him what he and her husband had discussed the night before. But the questions didn't come.

"If you'll give me your jacket this evening, my lord, I would mend it for you."

He glanced at the ruined sleeve. "I fear it will never be the same."

Her eyes were sober when they met his. "We do what we can with what we have." She rose, bringing Brigham to his feet. Her skirts swished quietly into place. "If you'll excuse me, Lord Ashburn, I have much to see to before my husband returns."

"The MacGregor has gone?"

"He should be home by evening. We all have much to do before Prince Charles makes his move."

Brigham's brow lifted as she left. He'd never known a woman to take the threat of war quite so complacently.

When he returned upstairs, he found Coll a bit pale and shadowed around the eyes but sitting up and arguing.

"I won't touch that slop."

"You will eat every drop," Serena said threateningly. "Gwen made it especially for you."

"I don't care if the Blessed Virgin dipped her finger in it, I won't have it."

"Blaspheme again and you'll wear it."

"Good morning, children." Brigham strolled into the room.

"Brig, thank God," Coll said feelingly. "Send this wench on her way and get me some meat. Meat," he repeated. "And whiskey."

After crossing to the bed, Brigham raised a brow at the thin gruel Serena held in a bowl. "It certainly looks revolting."

"Aye, that's just what I said myself." Coll fell back against the pillows, relieved to have a man on his side. "No one but a thick-skulled woman would expect anyone to eat it."

"Had a rather nice slab of ham myself."

"Ham?"

"Done to a turn. My compliments to your cook, Miss MacGregor."

"Gruel's what he needs," she said between her teeth, "and gruel's what he'll have."

After a shrug, Brigham sat on the edge of the bed. "I've done my bit, Coll. It's up to you."

"Toss her out."

Brigham fluffed his lace. "I hate to disoblige you, my dear, but the woman terrifies me."

"Hah!" Coll set his chin and eyed his sister. "Go to the devil, Serena, and take that slop with you."

"Fine, then, if you want to hurt little Gwen's feelings after she nursed you and took the time and trouble to make you something fit to eat. I'll just take it down and tell her you said it was slop and you'd rather have nothing than touch it."

She turned, bowl in hand. Before she'd taken two steps, Coll relented. "Hell and damnation, give it to me, then."

Brigham caught her smirk as she swept aside her skirts and sat. "Well done," he murmured.

Ignoring him, she dipped the spoon in the bowl. "Open your big mouth, Coll."

"I won't be fed," he said just before she shoved in the first bite of gruel. "Curse it, Serena, I said I'll feed myself."

"And spill gruel all over your clean nightshirt. I'll not be changing you again today, my lad, so open your mouth and be quiet."

He would have sworn at her again, but he was too busy swallowing gruel.

"I'll leave you to your breakfast, Coll."

"For mercy's sake." He grabbed Brigham's wrist. "Don't desert me now. She'll yap at me, nag and bluster and set me mad. I—" He glared as Serena pushed more gruel into his mouth. "She's the devil of a female, Brig. A man's not safe with her."

"Is that so?" Smiling, Brigham studied Serena's face and was rewarded by the faintest rising of color.

"I haven't thanked you for getting me home. I'm told you were wounded," Coll said.

"A scratch. Your sister tended it."

"Gwen's an angel."

"Young Gwen had her hands full with you. Serena bound me up."

Coll looked at his sister and grinned. "Ham-fisted."

"You'll be swallowing the spoon in a moment, Coll MacGregor."

"It takes more than a hole in my side to devil me, lassie. I can still put you over my knee."

She wiped his mouth delicately with a napkin. "The last time you tried you walked with a limp for a week."

He grinned at the memory. "Aye, right you are. Brig, the lass is a Trojan. Kicked me square in the—" he caught Serena's furious look "—pride, so to speak."

"I'll remember that if I ever have occasion to wrestle with Miss Mac-Gregor."

"Beaned me with a pot once, too," Coll said reminiscently. "Damn me if I didn't see stars." He was drowsy again, and his eyelids drooped. "Fire-eater," he muttered. "You'll never catch a husband that way."

"If it was a husband I wanted to catch, so I would."

"The prettiest girl in Glenroe." Coll's voice wavered as his eyes shut. "But the temper's foul, Brig. Not like that pretty Frenchie with the gold hair."

What pretty Frenchie? Serena wondered, sending Brigham a sidelong look. But he was only grinning and fiddling with the button of his jacket.

"I've had the pleasure of discovering that for myself," Brigham murmured. "Rest now. I'll be back."

"Forced that gruel on me. Nasty stuff."

"Aye, and there's more where that came from. Ungrateful oaf."

"I love you, Rena."

She brushed the hair from his brow. "I know. Hush now, and sleep." Serena tucked him up while Brigham stood back. "He'll be quiet for a few hours now. Mother will feed him next, and he won't argue with her."

"I'd say the arguing did him as much good as the gruel."

"That was the idea." She lifted the tray with the empty bowl and started past him. Brigham had only to shift to block her way.

"Did you rest?"

"Well enough. Pardon me, Lord Ashburn, I have things to do."

Instead of moving aside, he smiled at her. "When I spend the night with a woman, she usually calls me by my name."

The lights of war came into her eyes, just as he'd hoped. "I'm not some golden-haired Frenchie or one of your loose London women, so keep your name, *Lord* Ashburn. I've no use for it."

"I believe I have use for yours...Serena." She delighted him by snarling. "You have the most beautiful eyes I've ever seen."

That flustered her. She knew how to handle flattery, how to accept it, evade it, discount it. Somehow it wasn't as easy with him. "Let me pass," she muttered.

"Would you have kissed me?" He put two fingers under her chin as he asked. Serena held the tray like a shield. "Would you have, this morning, when the need for sleep was all over your face and the light just going gold?"

"Move aside." Because her voice was husky, she shoved the tray at him. Brigham caught it instinctively to keep it from falling. Unencumbered, Serena headed for the door with him two steps behind. The sound of running feet stopped them both.

"Malcolm, must you sound like a great elephant? Coll's sleeping."

"Oh." A boy of about ten skidded to a halt. His hair was a deep red that would probably darken to mahogany with age. Unlike the other men in his family, he had fine, almost delicate features. He had, Brigham noticed immediately, the deep green eyes of his sister. "I wanted to see him."

"You can watch him, if you're quiet." With a sigh, Serena shook his shoulder. "Wash first. You look like a stableboy."

He grinned, showing a missing tooth. "I've been with the mare. She'll foal in a day or two."

"You smell like her." She noticed from the mud in the hall that he hadn't done a thorough job of cleaning his boots. She would sweep it up before their mother saw it. She started to speak to him about it, then noticed he was no longer attending.

Brigham found himself being studied and assessed, quite man-to-man. The boy was lean as a whippet and smudged with dirt, and there was sharp curiosity in his eyes.

"Are you the English pig?"

"Malcolm!"

Both ignored her as Brigham stepped forward. Calmly he handed the tray back to Serena. "I'm English, at any rate, though my grandmother was a MacDonald."

Mortified, Serena stared straight ahead. "I will apologize for my brother, my lord."

He shot her a look ripe with irony. Both of them knew where Malcolm had come by the description. "No need. You would perhaps introduce us."

Serena's fingers dug into the tray. "Lord Ashburn, my brother Malcolm."

"Your servant, Master MacGregor."

Malcolm grinned at that, and at Brigham's formal bow. "My father likes you," he confided. "So does my mother, and Gwen, I think, but she's too shy to say."

Brigham's lips twitched. "I'm honored."

"Coll wrote that you had the best stables in London, so I'll like you, too."

Because it was irresistible, Brigham ruffled the boy's hair—and grinned wickedly at Serena. "Another conquest."

She lifted her chin. "Go wash, Malcolm," she ordered before she flounced away.

"They always want you to wash," Malcolm said with a sigh. "I'm glad there'll be more men in the house."

Nearly two hours later, Brigham's coach arrived, causing no little stir in the village. Lord Ashburn believed in owning the best, and his traveling equipment was no exception. The coach was well sprung, a regal black picked out with silver. The driver wore black, as well. The groom, who rode on the box with him, was enjoying the fact that people were peeking out their doors and windows at the arrival. Though he'd complained for the last day and a half about the miserable weather, the miserable roads and the miserable pace, he felt better knowing that the journey was at an end and that he'd be left to tend to his horses.

"Here, boy." The driver pulled up the steaming horses and gestured to a boy who stood beside the road, ogling the coach and sucking his finger. "Where will I find MacGregor House?"

"Straight down this road and over the rise. You be looking for the English lord? That be his carriage?"

"You got that right."

Pleased with himself, the boy gestured. "He's there."

The driver sent the horses into a trot.

Brigham was there to meet them himself. Braced against the cold, he stepped out as the coach pulled up. "You took your sweet time."

"Beg pardon, my lord. Weather held us up."

Brigham waved a hand at the trunks. "Bring those in. The stables are around the back, Jem. Settle the horses. Have you eaten?"

Jem, whose family had been with the Langstons for three generations, jumped down nimbly. "Hardly a bite, milord. Wiggins here sets a mad pace."

Appreciating the truth of it, Brigham grinned up at the driver. "I'm sure there will be something hot in the kitchen. If you would—" He stopped as the coach door swung open and a personage more dignified than any duke stepped out.

"Parkins."

Parkins bowed. "My lord." Then he studied Brigham's attire, and his dour face changed. His voice, filled with mortification, quivered. "Oh, my lord."

Brigham cast a rueful glance at his torn sleeve. Undoubtedly Parkins would be more concerned with the material than with the wound beneath. "As you see, I have need of my trunks. Now, what in blazes are you doing here?"

"You have a need for me, as well, my lord." Parkins drew himself up. "I knew I was right to come, and there can be no doubt of it. See that the trunks are put in Lord Ashburn's room immediately."

Though the cold was seeping through his riding coat, Brigham planted himself. "How did you come?"

"I met the coach yesterday, sir, after you and Mr. MacGregor had taken to horse." A foot shorter than Brigham, and woefully thin, Parkins pushed his shoulders back. "I will not be sent back to London, my lord, when my duty is here."

"I don't need a valet, man. I'm not attending any balls."

"I served my lord's father for fifteen years, and my lord for five. I will not be sent back."

Brigham opened his mouth, then shut it. Loyalty was impossible to argue with. "Oh, come in, damn you. It's freezing."

Cloaked in dignity, Parkins ascended the stairs. "I will see to my lord's unpacking immediately." He gave a shudder as he studied his master's attire once more. "*Immediately.* If I could persuade my lord to accompany me, I could have you suitably clad in a trice."

"Later." Brigham swung on his greatcoat. "I want to check on the horses." He strode down the steps, checked, then turned. "Parkins, welcome to Scotland."

The faintest ghost of a smile touched the thin lips. "Thank you, my lord."

Jem the groom seemed well on the way to making himself and the horses at home. Brigham heard his cackling laughter as he pushed aside the wooden door.

"You're a right one, ain't you, Master MacGregor? Sure and Lord Ashburn has the best stable in London—England itself, for that matter—and it's me who's in charge of them."

"Then I'll have you look at my mare, Jem, who'll be foaling soon."

"Pleased to have a look at her I'll be—after I've seen to my loves here."

"Jem."

"Eh—" He turned and saw Brigham standing in a beam of thin winter light. "Yes, sir, Lord Ashburn. I'll have everything set to rights in a twinkle."

Brigham knew that Jem couldn't be faulted with horses, but he also had a free hand with the bottle and language the MacGregors might not deem proper for their youngest. So he lingered, supervising the settling of his team.

"Fine horses they are, Lord Ashburn." Malcolm had taken a hand in the grooming. "I can drive very well, you know."

"I wouldn't doubt it." Brigham had stripped off his greatcoat, and since his jacket was ruined in any case, he added his weight to the work. "Perhaps we'll find an afternoon so you can show me?"

"Truly?" There was no quicker way to the boy's heart. "I don't think I could handle your coach, but we have a curricle." He gave a manly sneer. "Though my mother won't let me drive anything but the pony cart by myself."

"You'll be with me, won't you?" Brigham swatted one of the horses' flanks. "They seem to be in good shape, Jem. Go have a look at Master MacGregor's mare."

"Please, sir, would you look in on her, too? She's a beauty."

Brigham laid a hand on Malcolm's shoulder. "I'd be delighted to meet her."

Satisfied he'd found a kindred spirit, Malcolm took Brigham's hand and led him through the stables. "She's Betsy." At the sound of her name, the mare poked her head over the stall door and waited to be rubbed.

"A lovely lady." She was a roan, not beautifully distinguished, but dignified and trim enough. As Brigham lifted a hand to stroke her head, she pricked up her ears and fixed him with a calm, questioning eye.

"She likes you." The fact pleased Malcolm, as if he often trusted the opinions of animals over those of people.

Inside the stall, Jem went about his business in a calm, capable way that impressed the young Malcolm. Betsy stood tolerantly, sighing occasionally so that her heavy belly shook, and switching her tail.

"She'll be foaling soon," Jem pronounced. "Another day or two by my guess."

"I want to sleep in the stables, but Serena always comes and drags me back."

"Don't fret about it, Jem's here now." With that, Jem stepped out of the stall.

"But you will send word when it's time?"

Jem looked at Brigham for affirmation, got it and grinned. "I'll send up a shout for you, never fear."

"Could I impose on you to show Jem to the kitchen?" Brigham asked. "He hasn't eaten."

"I beg your pardon." Abruptly proper, Malcolm straightened his shoulders. "I'll see that the cook fixes you something right away. Good afternoon, my lord."

"Brig."

Malcolm grinned at the man, and at the hand he was offered. He shook it formally, then skipped out, calling for Jem to follow.

"A taking little scamp. If I may say so, milord?"

"You may. Jem, try to remember he's young and impressionable." At Jem's blank expression, Brigham sighed. "If he begins to swear like my English groom, the ax will fall on me. He has a sister who would love to wield it."

"Yes, milord. I'll be the soul of propriety, I will." Breaking into a grin, Jem followed Malcolm out.

Brigham didn't know why he lingered. Perhaps it was because it was quiet, and the horses good company. It was true that he'd spent a good part of his youth in the same way as Malcolm, in the stables. He'd learned more than a few interesting phrases. He could, if necessary, have harnessed a team himself in only half again as much time as his groom. He could drive to an inch or doctor a strained tendon, and he had overseen his share of foalings.

Once it had been his dream to breed horses. That had changed when the responsibilities of his title had come to him at an early age.

But it wasn't horses or lost dreams he thought of now. It was Serena. Perhaps because his thoughts were on her, he wasn't surprised to see her enter the stables.

She'd been thinking of him, as well, though not entirely kindly. Throughout the day she hadn't been able to concentrate on ordinary things. Instead she concentrated, unwillingly, on that moment she had stood with him by her brother's window.

She'd been tired, Serena assured herself as she wrapped the plaid securely around her. Almost asleep on her feet, if it came to that. Why else would she have only stood there while he touched her in that way…looked at her in that way?

And how he'd looked. Even now, something stirred in her at the memory. His eyes had gotten so dark; they'd been so close. She knew what it was to have a man look at her with interest, even to have one try to steer her into the shadows to steal a kiss. With one or two, she'd permitted it. Just to see if she might care for it. In truth, she found kissing pleasant enough, if unexciting. But nothing before had come close to this.

Her legs had gone weak, as if someone had taken out the blood and replaced it with water. Her head had spun the way it had when she'd been twelve and sampled her father's port. And it had felt, Lord, as though her skin were on fire where his fingers had touched it. Like a sickness, she thought.

What else could it be? She shook the feeling off and straightened her shoulders. It had been fatigue, plain and simple. That, and concern for her brother, and a lack of food. She was feeling a great deal better now, and if she chanced to come across the high-and-mighty earl of Ashburn she would handle him well enough.

She shook off her thoughts and peered around the dim stable. "Malcolm, you little heathen," she called, "I'll have you out of those stables and into the house. It's your job to fill the woodbox, hang you, and I've done it myself for the last time."

"I regret you'll have to hang Malcolm later." Brigham stepped out of the shadows and was pleased to startle her. "He isn't here. I've just sent him along to the kitchen with my groom."

She tossed up her chin. "Sent him along? He's no servant of yours."

"My dear Miss MacGregor." Brigham stepped closer, deciding that the dull colors in the plaid were the perfect foil for the richness of her hair. "Malcolm has formed an attachment for Jem, who is, like your brother, a great horse lover."

Because her heart was softest when it came to Malcolm, she subsided.

"He's forever in here. Twice this week I've had to bundle him up and drag him into the house past his bedtime." She caught herself and frowned again. "If he pesters you, I'd appreciate it if you'd let me know. I'll see that he doesn't intrude."

"No need. We deal together easily enough." She was frowning over that as he stepped closer. She smelled of the lavender that always seemed to waft around her. "You need more rest, Serena. Your eyes are shadowed."

She had nearly stepped back before she was able to resist the unusual urge to retreat. "I'm as strong as one of your horses, thank you. And you're very free with my name."

"I've taken a liking to it. What was it Coll called you before he fell asleep? Rena? It has a pretty sound."

It sounded different when he said it. She turned to study his horses. "You've impressed Malcolm with these, I'm sure."

"He's more easily impressed than his sister."

She glanced over her shoulder. "You have nothing that could impress me, my lord."

"Don't you find it wearing to despise all things English?"

"No, I find it fulfilling." Because she was feeling weak-kneed again, and needful, she turned on him, letting anger replace longings she did not yet understand. "What are you to me but one more English nobleman who wants things his way? Do you care for the land? For the people? For the name? You know nothing of what we are," she spat out. "Nothing of the persecutions, the miseries, the degradations."

"More than you think," he said softly, guarding his own temper.

"You sit in your fine house in London or your manor in the country and dream by the fire of values and great social change. We live the fight every day, just to hold on to our own. What do you know of the terror of waiting in the dark for your men to return, or the frustration of not being able to do more than wait?"

"Do you blame me, too, for your being born a female?" He caught her arm before she could spin away. Her shawl fell away from her hair and onto her shoulders so that the evening light struggling through the doorway and the chinks in the wood glowed over it. "I might curse myself for preferring you that way." He resented bitterly his automatic response to her. "Tell me the truth, Serena, do you despise me?"

"Aye." She said it with passion, wanting it to be true.

"Because I'm English?"

"It's reason enough to hate."

"It's not, but I think I'll give you one."

To please himself, he thought as he dragged her against him. To undo the knots in his stomach, calm the thunder in his loins. She jerked back and might have landed a blow, but he was prepared for her, and very quick.

The moment his mouth came down on hers, she went still. He heard her breath suck in, then only the buzzing in his own head. She had a mouth like rose petals, soft, fragrant, crushable. With an oath, he wrapped an arm around her waist and locked her to him. He could feel her breasts yield and her body tremble. His own was rigid with the shock of the sensation that poured through him.

Behind them the horses blew and shifted weight. Dust motes danced in an errant sunbeam.

She couldn't move. She thought she might never move again, because all the bones in her body had dissolved. Behind her eyes was a rush of colors, so vivid, so brilliant, that they would certainly blind her. If this was a kiss, then she had never experienced one before, for this was all heat, all light, all movement, in one meeting of lips.

She heard a moan, such a soft, such a sweet moan, and never recognized it as her own. Her hand was on his arm, fingers tangled in the tear of his sleeve. She might have swayed, but he held her so close.

Was she breathing?

She had to be, for she lived still. She could smell him, and the scent was much the same as it had been on their first meeting. Sweat, horses, man. And he tasted... Her lips parted, she thirsted for more. He tasted like honey warmed in whiskey. Wasn't she already drunk from him?

Her heart began to thunder, drumming in pulses she hadn't known existed. If there was more, she wanted to find it. If this was all, it was enough for a lifetime. Slowly she slid her hands up his arms, over his shoulders and into his hair. Her kiss changed from one of shock and surrender to one of demand.

He felt her teeth nip at his lip and a fire centered in his loins. Suddenly desperate, he pressed her back against a post and savaged her mouth even as it opened and invited him in. In that instant he was more her prisoner than she his.

He surfaced like a man drowning, gulping in air and shaking his head to clear it. "Good God, where did you learn to do that?"

Right here, right now. But shame and confusion stained her cheeks. However it had happened, she had let him kiss her and, Lord help her, she had enjoyed it. "Let me go."

"I don't know if I can." He lifted a hand to her cheek, but she jerked her head away. Struggling for patience, Brigham stood where he was and tried to catch his breath. A moment ago she had kissed him in a manner to rival the finest French courtesans. But now, right now, it was painfully clear she was innocent.

He could kill himself—if Coll didn't beat him to it. Brigham set his jaw. Seducing the sister of his friend—the daughter of his host—in the stable, as though she were a tavern wench. He cleared his throat and stepped back. When he spoke, his voice was stiff.

"I offer my deepest apologies, Miss MacGregor. That was unforgivable."

Her lashes swept up. Beneath them her eyes were not sheened with tears but bright with anger. "If I were a man, I'd kill you."

"If you were a man," he said, just as rigidly, "my apologies would hardly be necessary." He bowed and went out, hoping the cold air would clear his head.

Chapter Four

She would have enjoyed killing him, Serena thought. With a sword. No, a sword was much too clean, much too civilized, for English vermin. Unless, of course, she used it to sever small pieces from him one at a time rather than end his worthless life with one thrust through the heart. She smiled to herself as she imagined it. A quick hack there, a slow, torturous slice here.

Her thoughts might have been gruesome, but no one would have guessed by looking at her. She was the picture of quiet feminine occupation as she sat in the warm kitchen and churned butter. It was true that when her thoughts darkened she brought the plunger down with unwarranted force, but the energy, whatever its source, only made the job go faster.

He'd had no right to kiss her that way, to force himself on her. And less right than that to make her like it. With her hands wrapped around the wooden staff, Serena sent the plunger dancing. Miserable English cur. And she had patched up his hurts with her own hands, served him a meal in her own house. Not willingly, perhaps not graciously, but she had done it nonetheless.

If she told her father what Brigham had dared to do… She paused for a moment as she dreamed of that possibility. Her father would rage and bellow and very likely whip the English dog within an inch of his miserable life. That made her smile again, the picture of the high-and-mighty earl of Ashburn groveling in the dirt, his arrogant gray eyes clouded with terror.

She began to churn faster as her smile turned into a snarl. The picture was right enough, but she'd prefer to hold the whip herself. She would make him whimper as he sprawled at her feet.

It was true, and perhaps sad, Serena thought, that she had such a love of violence. It concerned her mother. No doubt it was a pity she hadn't inherited her mother's temperament rather than her father's, but there it was. It was rare for a day to go by when Serena didn't lose her MacGregor temper and then suffer pangs of guilt and remorse because of it.

She wanted to be more like her mother—calm, steady, patient. The good Lord knew she tried, but it just wasn't in her. At times she thought God had made the tiniest mistake with her, forgetting the sugar and adding just a dab too much vinegar. But if God was entitled to a mistake, wasn't she then entitled to her temper?

With a sigh, she continued the monotonous chore of working the plunger up and down.

It was true enough that her mother would have known exactly the proper way to handle Lord Ashburn and his unwanted advances. She would have become frigidly polite when he'd gotten that look in his eyes. That look, Serena thought, that told a woman instinctively that he meant mischief. By the time Fiona MacGregor had been done with him, Lord Ashburn would have been putty in her hands.

For herself, she had no way with men. When they annoyed her, she let them know it—with a box on the ear or a sharp-tongued diatribe. And why not? she thought, scowling. Why the devil not? Just because she was a woman, did she have to act coy and pretend to be flattered when a man tried to slobber all over her?

"You'll be turning that butter rancid with those looks, lassie."

With a sniff, Serena began to work in earnest. "I was thinking of men, Mrs. Drummond."

The cook, a formidably built woman with graying black hair and sparkling blue eyes, cackled. She had been a widow these past ten years and had the hands of a farmer, thick fingered, wide palmed and rough as tree bark. Still, no one in the district had a better way with a joint of meat or a dainty fruit tart.

"A woman should have a smile on her face when she thinks of men. Scowls send them off, but a smile brings them around quick enough."

"I don't want them around." Serena bared her teeth and ignored her aching shoulders. "I hate them."

Mrs. Drummond stirred the batter for her apple cake. "Has that young Rob MacGregor come sniffing around again?"

"Not if he values his life." Now she did smile as she remembered how she had dispatched the amorous Rob.

"A likely enough lad," Mrs. Drummond mused. "But not good enough for one of my lassies. When I see you courted, wedded and bedded, it'll be to quality."

Serena began to tap her foot in time with her churning. "I don't think I want to be courted, wedded or bedded."

"Whist now, of course you do. In time." She gave a quick grin as her spoon beat a steady tattoo against the bowl. The muscles in her arms were as solid as mountain rock. "It has its merits. Especially the last."

"I don't want to find myself bound to a man just because of what happens in a marriage bed."

Mrs. Drummond shot a quick look at the doorway to be certain Fiona wasn't nearby. The mistress was kindness itself, but she would get that pinched look on her face if she heard her cook and her daughter discussing delicate matters over the butter churn.

"A better reason is hard to find—with the right man. My Duncan, now there was a man who knew how to do his duty, and there were nights I went to sleep grateful for it. Rest his soul."

"Did he ever make you feel—" Serena paused a moment, groping for the right words "—well, like you'd been riding fast over the rocks and couldn't get your breath?"

Mrs. Drummond narrowed her eyes. "Are you sure that Rob hasn't been around?"

Serena shook her head. "Being with Rob's like riding a lame pony uphill.

You think it'll never be done with." Her own eyes were bright with laughter as she looked up at the cook.

That was the way Brigham saw her when he walked in. Her long fingers were wrapped around the plunger, her skirts were kilted up and her face was alive with laughter.

Damn the woman! He couldn't keep himself from staring at her. Damn her for making him want just by looking!

He made little sound, but Serena turned her head. Their eyes locked, briefly, almost violently, before Serena lifted her chin away and went back to her churning.

The look had lasted only an instant, but that had been long enough to show Mrs. Drummond what had put Serena into a temper. Or rather who.

So that's the way of it? she mused, and couldn't prevent a small smile. Locked horns, without a doubt. It was as good a way to begin courting as she knew. She'd have to think on it, she decided. But the earl of Ashburn was certainly quality, as well as having a face and form that made even a widow's heart flutter.

"Can I serve you, my lord?"

"What?" Brigham turned to stare through Mrs. Drummond before his eyes slowly focused. "I beg your pardon. I've just come from Coll's room. He's complaining for food. Miss Gwen says a bit of your broth would do him."

Mrs. Drummond cackled and went to the pot by the fire. "I have my doubts he'd think so, but I'll spoon it up and have it sent. Would you mind me asking, my lord, how the lad does?"

He had made the mistake of looking at Serena again as she lazily stroked with the plunger. If anyone had told him that watching a woman churn butter could dry a man's mouth to dust, he would have laughed. Now he couldn't see the humor in it. He tore his eyes away, cursing himself. It would pay to remember that he had already spent one sleepless night because of her, two if he counted the one they had spent together nursing Coll.

"He seems to fare better today. Miss Gwen claims his color's good enough, though she'll have him stay in bed a while yet."

"She could do it. The good Lord knows no one else could deal as well with the lad." Mrs. Drummond tutted over the man she considered the oldest of her charges. She slanted a look at Serena and saw that she was watching Brigham from under her lashes. "Would you care for some broth yourself, my lord? Or a bit of meat pie?"

"No, thank you. I was on my way to the stables."

That had the color lifting into Serena's cheeks as she banged wood against wood. He lifted a brow. Though she set her chin and moved her bottom lip into a pout that had his stomach muscles clenching, she didn't speak. Nor did he as he gave a brisk nod and strode out.

"Now that's a man!" Mrs. Drummond exclaimed.

"He's English," Serena countered, as if that explained everything.

"Well, that's true, but a man's a man, kilt or breeches. And his fit him mighty true."

Despite herself, Serena giggled. "A woman's not supposed to notice."

"A blind woman's not supposed to notice." Mrs. Drummond set the bowl of broth on a tray and then, because her heart was soft, added a gooseberry tart. "Molly! Molly, you lazy wench, come fetch this tray to the young master." She set the tray aside and went back to her stirring. "The man Lord Ashburn brought with him from London, lassie, the proper-looking gentleman?"

"Parkins." Serena flexed her cramped hands and sneered. She found it odd that her heart rate had leveled almost to normal as soon as Brigham had swept out. "His English valet. Imagine, bringing a valet here to fuss with the cut of his coat and the shine on his boots."

"Quality's used to having things done a certain way," Mrs. Drummond said wisely. "I hear Mr. Parkins is an unmarried gentlemen."

Serena moved her shoulders. "Probably too busy starching Lord Ashburn's lace to have his own life."

Or he hasn't met a woman with life enough for two, Mrs. Drummond mused. "Seems to me, Mr. Parkins could use a bit of fattening up." She grinned, then set the bowl aside to shout for Molly again.

Quality, Serena thought with a sniff a few hours later. Just because a man had a trace of blue blood in his veins didn't mean he was quality. It didn't make him a gentleman, either. All it made him was an aristocrat.

In any case, she wasn't going to waste her time thinking about the earl of Ashburn. For nearly two days she had been tied to the house, to the day-to-day chores, which were increased by Coll's needs. Now she had some time free. Perhaps she was stealing it, but she could make it all up later. The truth was, if she didn't get out and off by herself for just a little while she might burst.

Her mother probably wouldn't approve of her taking a ride in the forest so close to mealtime. Serena shrugged that off as she saddled her mare. Her mother would approve even less of the old work breeches she wore. Hanged if she had the patience to ride sidesaddle, she thought as she led the mare out of the stables. She would take care that her mother wouldn't see her so that her mother wouldn't have to be disappointed in her behavior. With luck, no one would see her.

Swinging astride, she led her mount to the rear of the stables, then over a low hill dotted with spindly briers and lichen. Surefooted, the mare picked her way over the uneven ground until they were almost out of sight of the house. Serena veered south, sending up a brief prayer that no one in her family be looking out the window. The moment the forest swallowed her, she kicked the mare into a gallop.

Oh, God, she had needed this more than food, more than drink. One wild ride through the naked trees with the wind on her face and a horse straining for speed beneath her. It might not be the proper thing, but she knew as well as she knew her name that it was the right thing for her. She didn't have to be a lady here, a daughter here, a sister here. She had only to be Serena. With a laugh, she spurred the horse on.

She startled small game and sent birds whirring upward. Her breath puffed out white, then vanished. The plaid she had wrapped around her shoulders held off the bite of the wind, and the exercise, the freedom, were enough to warm her. In fact, she welcomed the tingle on her skin from the cold winter air, and the sharp clean taste of it.

She had a fleeting wish, almost instantly blotted out by guilt, that she might continue to ride and ride and ride with never another cow to be milked, never another shirt to be washed, never another pot to be scrubbed.

It was probably an evil thought, she decided. There were those in the village who worked from dawn to dusk, who never had an hour they could set aside for dreaming. She, as daughter to the MacGregor, had a fine house to live in, a good table to eat from, a feather bed to sleep on. She was ungrateful, and would no doubt have to confess to the priest—as she had when she had secretly, then not so secretly, hated the convent school in Inverness.

Six months out of her life, Serena remembered. Six months wasted before her father had seen that her mind was made up and she would have none of it. Six months away from the home she loved to live with those simpering, giggling girls whose families had wanted them to learn about being ladies.

Bah.

She could learn everything there was about running a household from her own mother. As to being a lady, there wasn't a finer one than Fiona MacGregor. She was a laird's daughter herself, after all, and had spent time in Paris and, yes, even in England, long ago.

There were still times, when the chores were done and the fires burning low when Fiona played the spinet. Hadn't she taught Gwen, whose fingers were more clever and whose mind was more patient that her sister's, how to ply a fancy needle? Fiona could speak French and engage any visitor in polite conversation.

To Serena's mind, if she needed to be polished, she would be polished in her own home, where the talk was of more than hooped skirts and the latest coiffures.

Those giggling whey-faced girls were the kind of ladies Lord Ashburn preferred, she imagined. The kind who covered their faces with fans and fluttered their lashes over them. They drank fruit punch and carried vials of smelling salts and lace handkerchiefs in their reticules. Empty-headed twits. Those were the kind of women whose hands Brigham would kiss at fancy London balls.

As she neared the river, she slowed the horse to a walk. It would be pleasant to sit by the water for a little while. If she had had time, she would have ridden all the way to the loch. That was her special place when she was troubled or needed time by herself.

Today she wasn't troubled, Serena reminded herself as she slid from the saddle. She had only wanted to take a breath of air that was hers alone. She laid the reins loosely over a branch, then rested her cheek against the mare's.

Fancy London balls, she thought again, and sighed without any idea that the sound was wistful. Her mother had told her and Gwen what they were like. The mirrors, the polished floors, the hundreds and hundreds of candles. Beautiful gowns sparkling. Men in curling white wigs. And music.

She closed her eyes and tried to see it. She'd always had a weakness for music. Over the sounds of the rushing river she imagined the strains of a minuet. There would be reels later, Serena thought. But to start, it would be a slow, lovely minuet.

She began to move to the music in her head, her eyes still closed, her hand held out to an invisible partner.

Lord Ashburn would give balls, she thought. All the beautiful women would come, hoping for just one dance with him. Smiling a little, Serena executed a neat turn and imagined she heard the sound of petticoats rustling. If she were there, she would wear a dress of rich green satin, with her hair piled high and powdered white so that the diamonds in it glittered like ice on snow. All the men with their foaming lace and buckled shoes would be dazzled. She would dance with them, one by one. As long as the music played she would dance, twirling, stepping, dipping into low, graceful curtsies.

Then he would be there. He would be dressed in black. It suited him. Aye, he would wear black, black and silver, just what he had worn that night he'd come into Coll's room, when there had been only candle and firelight. It had made him look so tall and trim. Now the light would be blinding, flashing in the mirrors, shimmering on silver buttons and braid. As the music swelled they would look at each other. He would smile, in the way he did that softened his eyes and made her heart melt just a little.

He would hold out his hand. She would lay hers on it, palm to palm. A bow from him, then her curtsy. Then… Giddy, Serena opened her eyes.

Her hand was caught in an easy grip. Her eyes were still clouded with the dream as she looked up at Brigham. The light was behind him, and as she stared up, dazed, it seemed to form a halo around his face. He was wearing black as she had imagined, but it was a simple riding coat, without the fancy silver work or the sparkle of jewels.

Slowly he raised her to her feet. Because she would have sworn she still heard music, she shook her head.

"Madam." Smiling, he lifted her hand to his lips before she could recover. "You seem to be without a partner."

"I was…." Dumbly she stared at their joined hands. Light glittered on his signet ring and reminded her of time and place and differences. Serena snatched her hand away and clasped it with the other behind her back.

"What are you doing here?"

"I was fishing." He turned and pointed to the pole he'd propped against a tree. Beyond it, his horse grazed lazily on the turf of the bank. "With Malcolm until a short time ago. He wanted to get back and look at Betsy."

She could already feel the color sting her cheeks as she thought how ridiculous she must have looked in her partnerless minuet. "He should have been about his lessons."

"I'm assured he did his duty by them this morning." Because he couldn't resist, Brigham stepped back to take a long, thorough study. "May I ask if you always dance alone in the wood—in breeches?"

Her eyes kindled as she chose anger over embarrassment. "You had no right spying on me."

"You quite took me by surprise, I promise you." He sat on a rock, crossed his ankles and smiled at her. "Here I was, contemplating how many more trout I might catch, when a rider comes barreling through the forest with enough noise to frighten every fish for miles." He didn't add that her wild approach had had him drawing his sword. Instead, he buffed his nails on his coat.

"If I had known you would be here," she said stiffly, "I would have ridden another way."

"No doubt. Then I would have missed the delightful sight of you in breeches."

With a sound of disgust, she whirled toward her horse.

"Such a fast retreat, Serena. One might think you were…afraid."

She spun toward him again, eyes flashing, and planted her feet. "I'm not afraid of you."

Magnificent. There was no other way to describe her as she stood, her body braced as though she held a sword in her hand, her eyes molten, her hair tumbling like firelight down her back. She had ridden through the forest with a speed too great for safety and with a skill few men could have matched. However much she aggravated him, Brigham could not deny her courage or her style.

Neither could he deny that the way she looked in breeches made him uncomfortable. However ill-fitting, they showed the enticing length of slim legs and the slender curve of waist and hip. With the homespun shirt tucked and cinched, he could see the gentle sweep of breasts that even now rose and fell in agitation.

"Perhaps you should be afraid," he murmured, as much to himself as to her. "As I find myself plagued with all manner of dishonorable intentions."

Her stomach quivered at that, but she held her ground. "You don't worry me, Lord Ashburn. I've dispatched better men than you."

"So I imagine." He rose and saw what he had wanted to see—the quick, and just as quickly controlled, flash of unease in her eyes. "However, you have yet to deal with me, Serena. I doubt you'll manage to box my ears."

She would have backed up a step if pride hadn't rooted her where she stood. "I'll do worse if you touch me again."

"Will you?" Why was it that the more the woman spit at him, the more he wanted her? "I've already apologized for what happened in the stables."

"The stables?" She lifted a brow, determined not to give an inch. "I fear whatever that might have been, my lord, was so unimportant as to be already forgotten."

"Cat," he said mildly, though not without admiration. "If you continue to sharpen your claws on me, you're bound to break them."

"I'll risk it."

"Then let me refresh your memory." He stepped closer. "You were as hot as I, as pleasured as I. It wasn't a swooning girl I held in my arms but a woman, ripe for loving, damned anxious for it."

"How dare you?" The words came out in a sputter. "No gentleman would speak to me so."

"Perhaps not. But no lady wears breeches."

That stung. It was true, she was not a lady, would never be one, though she wished constantly to find the way within her, to please her mother. "Whatever I choose to wear, I won't have you insult me."

"Won't you? By God, that's rich. You've done nothing but insult me since you first clapped eyes on me." Goaded past caution, he grabbed her arm. "Do you think because you're female I should tolerate your sneering comments about myself, my lineage, my nationality? Damn me if you can have it both ways, Serena. You dress like a man, talk like a man, then choose to hide behind your petticoats when it suits you."

"I hide behind nothing." She tossed back her head and glared at him. Through the bare branches of the ash trees the sunlight poured, turning her hair to molten gold. "If I insult you, it's no more than you deserve. You may have charmed my family, but not me."

"Charming you," he said between his teeth, "is the least of my concerns."

"Aye, your concern lies with the fall of your lace and the shine of your boots. You ride into my home with your talk of war and justice, but you do nothing."

"What I do, what I mean to do, is no business of yours."

"You sleep under my roof, eat at my table. Where were you when the English came to build their forts, to take our men off to their prisons and their gallows?"

"I can't change history, Serena."

"You can change nothing, nothing that has gone before, nothing that is yet to come."

His fingers tightened on her arm. "I won't discuss my plans with you, but I will tell you this—when the time comes, a change will be made."

"To benefit whom?"

He yanked her toward him. "Which means?"

"What does the fate of Scotland mean to you or any English nobleman? You came from England on a whim and can return as easily, depending on the way the wind blows."

His face paled with rage. "This time, my dear, you go too far."

"I'll say what I choose." She tried to wrench away but found her arm caught in viselike fingers. "You give me no reason why you align yourself with our cause, why you choose to raise your sword. Therefore I am free to think what I like."

"You may think as you choose, but words require payment."

She hadn't seen him truly angry before. She hadn't known his eyes could blaze or that his mouth could harden until it seemed as though his face were carved from granite. She nearly yelped when his fingers dug still more deeply into the tender flesh of her arm.

"What will you do," she managed, coolly enough, "run me through?"

"As you're unarmed, that pleasure is denied me. But I have a mind to throttle you." Whether the gesture was made in earnest or merely to frighten, Serena couldn't be sure. He lifted his free hand and circled her throat. His fingers pressed, not gently but not quite hard enough to cut off her air, and his eyes stayed on hers, dark and hard. "You have a very slender neck, Serena," he said silkily. "Very white, very easily snapped."

For a moment she froze, as a hare does when a hawk makes its killing dive. Her hand fluttered helplessly at her side, and her eyes widened. Her breath, when she managed to draw it in, was shallow.

Because her reaction was no more or less than what he had looked for, Brigham smiled. The wench needed to be taught her manners, and it pleased him very much to be her instructor. Then it was he who sucked in his breath as her boot caught him hard on the shin.

His grip relaxed as he stumbled back, swearing. Deciding against assessing the damage, Serena spun on her heels and dashed for her horse. Still swearing, he caught her in three strides.

He lifted her off the ground, his arms locked firmly around her waist, while she kicked and cursed. She didn't fight like a woman, with shrieks and scratches, but with hands knotted into fists and muttered oaths. He discovered she weighed next to nothing and could wriggle like a snake.

"Hold still, damn you. You'll pay for that."

"Let go of me!" She struggled and tossed her weight backward, hoping to unbalance him. "I'll kill you if I get the chance."

"Well I believe it," he said bitterly. Her struggles broke his grip, and his hand moved up and over her breast. The contact shocked both of them, and the combat took on a new desperation. "Be still, damn it." Out of breath and patience, he tried to find a purchase that was less arousing. Seeing her chance, Serena sank her teeth into the back of his hand. "Bloody viper," he managed before her heel connected with his still-tender shin and sent them both tumbling to the ground.

He told himself it was instinct, certainly not any concern for her welfare, that had him cushioning her fall. The impact knocked the breath from both of them and left them tangled together like lovers. The moment she had recovered, Serena brought her knee up, barely missing her mark.

They rolled over a bed of pine needles and dried leaves while she fought like a wildcat, pounding him with fists and spitting Gaelic curses. Blinded by her hair, he made a grab for her and found himself gripping her bare flesh where her shirt had loosened.

"Name of God," he muttered as the blood stirred in his loins. She twisted, and her breast filled his hand. It was soft as water, hot as fire. "Bloody hell." Though it cost him, he drew his hand back and made a frantic grab for her arms.

Her breathing was shallow. A pulse had begun to thud in her throat when he had touched her. Her breast still tingled from his fingers. More than his threats, more than his anger, the unfamiliar reaction of her body frightened her. She was furious, she hated him. But oh, if he touched her like that again, she would melt like butter in high summer.

He scissored his legs until hers were trapped between them. Intimately, without the cushion of petticoats, they pressed center to center so that she felt for the first time the shock of a man's desire against her vulnerable womanhood. Heat flickered, then spread, in her stomach. The muscles of her thighs went lax. For an instant her vision blurred, giving him the advantage.

He braceleted her wrists in one hand and held them over her head. It was a movement meant as much to give him a moment for clear thinking as to allow him to protect himself. Her skin was glowing as the blood pounded hot beneath it. Tangled with leaves, her hair spread out like tongues of flame and melted gold.

His mouth dry, Brigham swallowed and tried to speak, but she was arching beneath him. Her continued struggles for freedom kindled fires in both of them that threatened to rage out of control.

"Rena, for God's sake, I'm only flesh and blood. Be still."

Her own movements were making her ears buzz and her limbs weak. There was an excitement that had somehow become tangled with panic, making her all the more desperate to get away. In defense she twisted from side to side and pulled a moan from Brigham.

"You don't know what you're doing," he managed, "but if you continue, you'll find out soon enough."

"Let me go." Her voice was steady, and arousingly husky. As she watched him, her breasts rose and fell with each agitated movement.

"Not quite yet, I think. You'll still rip into me."

"If I had had a dirk—"

"Spare me the details. I can imagine." He had nearly caught his breath, and he let it out now, slowly, cautiously. "My God, you're beautiful. It tempts me to keep you on the edge of fury." With his free hand he traced a fingertip over her lips. "It simply tempts me."

When he started to lower his head, her lips warmed and parted. Stunned by her own reaction, she turned her head quickly to avoid the kiss. Brigham contented himself with the tender flesh just below her ear, and the slender line of her throat.

This was different from a kiss, she thought hazily as a moan escaped her. Less and more. It felt as though her skin were alive and yearning for him as he nuzzled and dampened and nibbled. Instinctively she lifted her hips and sent shock waves of pleasure and frustration through him. He felt her hands stiffen beneath his grip, then go limp with her shudder.

Her hair smelled of the forest, he discovered when he buried his face in it. Earthy, seductive. Her body was as taut as a bowstring one moment, pliant as warm tallow the next. Hungry, he bit lightly at her ear, along her jaw, then slowly, almost triumphantly, at her waiting lips.

He tasted the breath that shuddered through them as he teased the tip of her tongue into movement with his own. There was so much he could teach her. Already he knew she would be a student eager for knowledge, and skillful at applying it once she learned. Her lips softened when they merged with his, then parted with the gentlest of pressures. In the age-old rhythm, her body moved shamelessly beneath his.

She hadn't known there was so much to feel, not just wind and cold and heat, not simply hunger for food and fatigue. There were hundreds, thousands of sensations to be discovered by the merging of lips, the locking of bodies.

There was the scent of a man's skin and, she discovered as she traced her tongue along the column of his throat, the taste of it. There was the sound of her own name being murmured thickly against her own mouth. There was the feel of strong fingers on her face, tensing, stroking, the frantic beat of heart against heart. Then the feel of those same fingers caressing her breast, covering that heart and turning her muscles to jelly.

"Brigham." She thought she might float away, weightlessly, painlessly, if only he would continue to touch her.

Her breast swelled in his hand. Unable to resist, he brushed his thumb over the nipple and felt it go taut. He yearned to draw the peak into his mouth, to experience the heat and the flavor. Instead he crushed his mouth to hers, desperately, almost brutally, as for the moment, just a moment, he let the wildness take him.

Sharp points of passion replaced the languor, and she ached with it, all but wept with it. Her hands were still trapped by his. Though she pressed for freedom, she was unsure whether, if she gained it, she would use her hands to drag him closer or to thrust him aside.

It hurt. This grinding, overwhelming need clawed through her, pounding in her center, raging through her head until she feared she would be burned alive.

It pleasured. The sensations he brought to her, the promises he gave her glimpses of. If there was a border between heaven and hell, he had led her to it, and now he had her teetering on the edge.

When the trembling began she fought against it, against him, against herself.

At her muffled whimper, he lifted his head. It was there in her eyes, the fear, the confusion and the desire. The combination nearly undid him. He saw that his hand still locked her wrists where, undoubtedly, bruises would form. Cursing himself, he dragged himself from her and turned away until he could find some measure of control.

"I have no excuses," he managed after a moment. "Except that I want you." He turned back to see her scramble to her feet. "God knows why."

She wanted to weep. Suddenly, desperately, she wanted to weep, wanted him to hold her again, to kiss her as he had at first in that gentle, that patient way. She dragged a leaf from her hair and, after crumbling it in her fingers, tossed it aside. She might not have had any dignity left, but she had pride.

"Cows and goats mate, my lord." Her voice was cold, as were her eyes, as she was determined to make her heart. "They do not have to like each other."

"Well said," he murmured, knowing precisely how she felt about him. He only wished he could be as certain at that moment of how he felt about her. "Let us hope we are a bit above the cattle. There's something about you, Serena, that tugs on my more primitive emotions, but I assure you I can restrain them under most circumstances."

His stiff manner only made her want to fly at him again. With what she felt was admirable control, she inclined her head. "I've yet to see it." Turning, she strode toward her horse. As she took the reins, she stiffened at the touch of Brigham's hand in her hair.

"You have leaves in your hair," he murmured, and fought back an urge to gather her close again, to just hold her in his arms.

"They'll comb out." When he put a hand on her arm, she braced herself to face him.

"Did I hurt you?"

That was almost her undoing, the regret in his eyes, the kindness in his voice. She was forced to swallow so that her answer could be steady and flat.

"I'm not easily broken, my lord." She shook off his offer of help and launched herself into the saddle. He stood back while she wheeled the horse and set off at a gallop.

Chapter Five

"If you think I'm keeping to my bed like an old man while you and my father ride out to do the Prince's work, you're a madman."

As Brigham watched, Coll pushed himself out of bed and uncertainly gained his feet. His head swam more than a little, but he braced himself against one of the bedposts and tugged off his nightshirt.

"Where in hell's name are my clothes?"

"My dear Coll," Brigham said dryly, "how should I know?"

"You must have seen what was done with them."

"I regret I can't help you there." Brigham flicked a speck of lint from his sleeve and continued in the mildest of tones, "Nor will I carry you back to your bed after you faint and fall from your horse."

"The day a MacGregor falls from his horse—"

"I hasten to remind you you've already done so once." When Coll merely swore and staggered to a chest to look for his clothing, Brigham clasped his hands behind his back. "Coll," he began, picking his way over tender ground, "I sympathize, believe me. I'm sure it's miserable to be tied to a sickbed day and night, but the simple fact is you're not well enough for the journey."

"I say I am."

"Gwen says not."

Frustrated at finding no more than linen and blankets, Coll slammed the chest shut again. "Since when does that slip of a girl run my life?"

"Since saving it."

That silenced Coll, who stood naked as a newborn in the early-morning sunlight. He had allowed his beard to grow since leaving London, and the roughness it gave his face suited him.

"I have no doubt she did," Brigham added. "And I wouldn't care to see all of her hard work go for nothing because you were too proud to rest until you were able to be of use."

"It's a black day when a Campbell stops me from riding with my father to gather the support of the clans for the Stuarts."

"Oh, there will be time yet. It's just beginning." Brigham smiled then, knowing that Coll's temper was easing, allowing him to see sense. He was much like his sister in the way that temper kindled as fast as dry wood. The pity was, Serena's didn't cool as quickly. "And I'll have you remember, we're riding out today for nothing more than an innocent hunting party. It wouldn't do for it to be rumored otherwise."

"I trust I can speak my mind in my own house," Coll muttered, but subsided. It was a bitter pill, but he knew he was far from ready for the journey west. Worse, if he insisted on going, he would slow the rest of the party down. "You'll meet with the MacDonalds and the Camerons?"

"So I'm led to believe. The Drummonds and Fergusons should be represented."

"You'll need to speak with the Cameron of Lochiel. He's always been a strong supporter of the Stuarts, and his voice is listened to." Coll dragged a hand through his mane of red hair. "Hell and damnation. I should be there, standing with my father, showing I stand for the Prince."

"No one will doubt it," Brigham began, then stopped when Gwen entered with a breakfast tray. She took one look at her brother, standing naked and furious, and clucked her tongue.

"I hope you haven't pulled any stitches out."

"Damn it, Gwen." Coll grabbed up a blanket and covered himself. "Have some respect."

With a gentle smile she set down the tray and curtsied to Brigham. "Good morning, Brig."

He touched a handkerchief to his lips in a futile effort to hide a grin. "Good morning."

"Brig, is it?" Coll sputtered. He knew that if he tried to stand five minutes more he'd embarrass himself. "You've become damn familiar with my sister, Ashburn."

Brigham nearly winced, thinking just how familiar he'd become with Coll's other sister. "We dispensed with formality shortly after we mopped up your blood." He picked up his greatcoat. "I fear you'll have trouble with your patient today, Gwen. He's in a foul temper."

Gwen smiled again and moved over to tidy Coll's bed linen. "Coll never gives me any trouble." She fluffed his pillows. "You may feel better after your breakfast, Coll. If you're up to taking a short walk, I'll go along with you. But I think you might dress first."

Stifling a chuckle, Brigham sketched a bow. She might not have the bite of her sister, but Coll's little angel knew how to get her way. "Now that I see you're in good hands, I'll take my leave."

"Brig—"

Brigham merely laid a hand on Coll's shoulder. "We'll be back within a week."

Too weak to argue, Coll let himself be led back to bed. "God go with you."

Brigham left them with Gwen tugging a fresh nightshirt over Coll's shoulders. He started for the staircase, then stopped short when he saw Parkins waiting for him, stiff backed, thin lipped and carrying a valise.

"Decided to return to England, Parkins?"

"On the contrary, my lord, I mean to accompany you on your hunting trip."

Brigham gave him one brief, incredulous look. "I'm damned if you do."

Parkins's pointed chin came up, the only sign of his agitation. "I will accompany your lordship."

"Don't be daft, man. If I wanted to take someone along, I'd take Jem. At least he'd be of some use with the horses."

Though he gave an inward shudder at being compared to a lowly groom, Parkins remained resolute. "I'm convinced Lord Ashburn will have need of me."

"I'm convinced I won't," Brigham responded, and started past.

"Nonetheless, I will accompany you, my lord."

Slowly, almost certain he had misunderstood, Brigham turned to see Parkins standing, a figure of righteousness, at the top of the stairs. "You are ordered to remain," he said in a very quiet, very dangerous voice. Parkins's stomach lining turned to ice, but he remained unbroken.

"I regret that your orders fail to persuade me that my duties are not best carried out in your company, my lord. I will accompany you."

With his eyes narrowed, Brigham ascended a step. "I'm of a mind to dismiss you, Parkins."

The pointed chin quivered. "That is your lordship's prerogative. That being the case, I will accompany you still."

"Damn your eyes, Parkins." Exasperated, Brigham stormed down the steps. "Have it your own way then, but you won't care for the pace or the accommodations."

"Yes, my lord." Fully satisfied, Parkins smiled at Brigham's back.

Surly, Brigham strode out of the house and toward the stables to have a word with his groom. Barely dawn, he thought, and already he'd been engaged in two arguments. He flung on his greatcoat as he went, his long, purposeful strides eating up the frosty ground. God, it would be good to get in the saddle and ride. Away from here, he thought, glancing back and homing in unerringly on Serena's window. Away from her, he corrected, almost savagely.

She had managed to avoid him all through the evening. Or when she could not, Brigham remembered with some fury, she had spoken to him in a voice as frigid as the ground he was treading on.

He could hardly blame her, after his treatment of her.

He did blame her, completely.

It was she who had raged and ranted at him until his temper had snapped. It was she who had fought him like some kind of hellcat until his passions had torn loose. Never, never in his life had he treated a woman with any form of physical violence. In lovemaking he was known to be passionate but never harsh, thorough but never forceful.

With Serena he had barely restrained himself from ripping the clothes from her back and plunging into her like a man gone mad.

She was the cause. If he had managed to make it to midway through his third decade without ill-treating any woman save one, surely that woman was at fault. She goaded him, he thought viciously. She taunted him.

She fascinated him.

Damn her. He kicked a pebble out of his way—the mark on his lordship's gleaming boot would distress Parkins severely—and wished Serena could be dispatched as easily as the stone.

He would have the better part of a week away from her. When he returned, this madness that had taken hold of him would have passed. He would then treat her with cordial respect and disinterest, as befitted the sister of his closest friend.

He would not, under any circumstances, think of the way her body had felt, melting beneath his.

He would certainly not pause to reflect on the way her lips had tasted, warmed and swollen with his kisses.

And he would be damned if he would allow himself to remember the way his name had sounded when she had spoken it, just once, in the depths of passion.

No, he would do none of those things, but he might murder her if she got in his way again.

His mood filthy, his temper uncertain, he came to the stables. Before he could pull open the door it was pushed outward. Serena, all but swaying on her feet, stepped out. Her face was pale, her eyes were exhausted, and the bodice of her dress was smeared with blood.

"Rena, my God." He gripped her by the shoulders hard enough to make her cry out. Then he was gathering her tight against him. "What happened? Where are you hurt? Who did this to you?"

"What? What?" She found her face pressed into the folds of his greatcoat, and the hand that stroked her hair was trembling. "Brig—Lord Ashburn..." But it was difficult to think when she was being held as though he would never let her go. When she was being held, Serena realized dimly, as though she was someone to be protected and cherished. She fought back an urge to snuggle into him. "My lord—"

"Where is he?" he demanded, dragging her away again, one hand supporting her waist as he drew out his sword. "By God, he won't live longer than it takes me to kill him. How badly are you hurt, my love?"

Her mouth simply hung open. He was holding her gently, as though she might break, even as murder kindled in his eyes. "Are you mad?" she managed. "Who do you want to kill? Why?"

"Why? Why? You're covered with blood and you ask me why?"

Confused, Serena looked down at her dress. "Of course there's blood. There's always blood at a foaling. Jem and I have been working half the night with Betsy. She had twins, and the second didn't come as easily as the first. Malcolm is nearly beside himself with delight."

"Foaling," he said blankly while she stared at him.

Serena moistened her lips and wondered if he needed one of Gwen's potions. "Are you feverish?"

"I'm quite well." His voice was stiff as he stepped back and sheathed his sword. "I beg your pardon. I mistook the blood for your own."

"Oh." She looked foolishly down at her dress again, both warmed and confused by his explanation. So far as she knew, no one had ever raised a sword in her name before. She could think of nothing to say. He had leaped to her defense as though he would have fought an army for her. And he had called her his love. Serena pressed her lips together to moisten them. Perhaps he was feverish. "I should wash."

He cleared his throat and felt ten times the fool. "Do the mare and the foals do well?"

"Very well, though everyone but Malcolm is exhausted." She tucked her hands into the folds of her skirts, not knowing what to do next. Oddly enough, she wanted to laugh. It was laughable, after all—Brigham drawing his sword like an avenging angel. Or devil. And herself smeared with dirt and sweat and birthing blood. "I beg your pardon, my lord," she managed as a giggle escaped her. She might enjoy fighting him, but not for the world would she embarrass him deliberately.

"This amuses you, madam?" His voice was cold, cracking like ice on a pond.

"No. Yes." With a sigh, she wiped at her eyes. "I'm terribly sorry for laughing. I'm tired."

"Then I will leave you to find your bed."

She couldn't let him go that way, she thought as he put his hand on the door. If their parting words had been a shout, it would have contented her. But to have made him cringe when he had tried to protect her would keep her awake at night.

"My lord."

He turned back. His eyes were calm again and very cool. "Yes?"

Her tongue tied itself into knots. This wasn't the kind of man you could thank with a smile and a quick word. The other man would have understood—the one who had held her so gently. But not this one. "You, ah, ride with my father and his men today."

"Yes." The reply was curt as he drummed his fingers on the hilt of his sword.

"I will wish you luck...with your hunting."

He lifted a brow. So she knew, he thought. Then, that she would of course know, and being a MacGregor, would go to the grave with the knowledge if need be. "Thank you, madam. I shan't keep you longer."

She started to leave, then turned, the passion in her eyes again. "I would give so much to go with you today." Gathering up her skirts, she raced toward the house.

Brigham stood where he was, in the chill air of early morning, the light breeze ruffling his hair. It had to be madness. It had to be the gravest error of judgment, the sharpest of ironies.

He was in love with her.

Letting out a long breath, he watched her until she had scrambled over the rise. He was in love with her, he thought again, and she would sooner plunge a dagger into his heart than give hers to him.

It was a long, rough ride over land wilder than that he and Coll had traveled through on their way north. There were echoing hills and naked rock thrust like deeply gouged teeth from the bare ground. Gray peaks and crags glittered with snow and ice. For miles they would see hardly a hovel. Then they would come across a village where peat smoke rose thick and people clamored out for greetings and news.

It was very much the Scotland his grandmother had spoken of, hard, often barren, but always fanatically hospitable. They stopped at midday and were pressed into a meal by a shepherd and his family. There was soup, the makings of which Brigham didn't care to know, and bannock and black pudding. He might have preferred the supplies they had brought with them, but he ate what was offered, knowing it was as gracious a feast as could be afforded in the lonely hills. It was washed down with Ian's own ale.

There were a half-dozen children, all but naked, though happy enough, and the shepherd's wife, who sat near the fire working a spindle. The turf house smelled of the compost heap that lay just outside the door and of the cattle that were housed in the room beyond.

If the family considered their fate bitter, they didn't show it. The shepherd drank with gusto and pledged his loyalty to the Stuart king.

All the men were welcomed, and food was pressed on each, though the portions were meager. Brigham couldn't resist a grin at the sight of the proper Parkins struggling to swallow the mysterious soup while removing a pair of small, grimy hands from his spotless sleeve.

Dozens of excuses had to be made before the travelers could convince their hosts that business prevented them from remaining overnight. When they set out again the wind was rising, bringing with it the taste and the scent of snow.

"I feel as though we've caused them to starve for the next week," Brigham commented as they continued west.

"They'll do well enough. Their laird will see them provided for. That's the way of the clans." Ian rode like a man half his age, straight in the saddle, light wristed, tireless. "It's men like him darlin' Charlie will need to make Scotland thrive."

"And the Camerons?"

"Good fighters and true men." Ian settled into an easy, ground eating lope. "When we meet at Glenfinnan you'll judge for yourself."

"The Jacobites will need good fighters, and good generals, as well. The rebellion will only be as successful as the Prince's advisers."

Ian shot him a glittering look. "So you've thought of that."

"Yes." Brigham looked around him as they rode. The rocky, tumbled ground was a perfect field of war for the Highlanders. The men who rode behind them, the men who lived in it, would know its advantages and hardships well. "If we bring the battle here, we'll win. Britain will be united."

"It's my wish to see a Stuart on the throne," Ian mused. "But I'll tell you I've seen wars before. In '15, in '19. I've seen hopes raised and hopes dashed. I'm not so old that my blood doesn't warm at the thought of battle, at the hope of putting old wrongs right. But this will be the last."

"You'll live to see others, Ian."

"This will be the last," he said again. "Not just for me, lad, for all of us."

Brigham thought of those words as they neared Glenfinnan.

The waters of Loch nan Uamh were a dark, violent blue. As they arrived at the great stone fortress, the snow was just beginning. Overhead the sky had turned to a thick steel gray, and the wind whipped the waters of the lake into fury.

Their coming had been heralded by the playing of pipes, and the high, eerie music lifted into the thin air. Such music was used to celebrate, to mourn and to lead soldiers to battle. As he stood with the snow swirling about his feet, Brigham understood how a man could weep, or fight, to the sound of such notes.

Inside, servants were dispatched with what luggage had been carried on the journey west, fires blazed high and whiskey was pressed into every waiting hand.

"Welcome to Glenfinnan." Donald MacDonald held up his cup of whiskey. "Your health, Ian MacGregor."

Ian drank, and his eyes approved the caliber of MacDonald's whiskey. "And to yours."

"Lord Ashburn." MacDonald signaled for more whiskey to be poured. "I trust my old friend has made you comfortable?"

"Very. Thank you."

"To your successful stay at Glenfinnan." MacDonald toasted and drank again. Not for the first time, Brigham was grateful for his head for whiskey. When he noted how easily it was downed by his companions, he decided that he had inherited it from his grandmother. "So you're kin to Mary MacDonald of Sleat in Skye."

"Her grandson."

MacDonald was then compelled to offer a toast to her. "I remember her. She was a bonny lass, though I was hardly whelped when I visited her family. She reared you?"

"From the time my parents died. I would have been nearly ten."

"Since you're here, I can't doubt but she did a good job of it. You'll be wanting food, gentlemen. We have a late supper for you."

"And the others?" Ian asked.

"Expected tomorrow." MacDonald glanced at the doorway, and his rather doughy face creased into a smile. "Ah, my daughter. Ian, you remember my Margaret."

Brigham turned and saw a small, dark-haired woman of about eighteen. She was dressed in a wide hooped gown of midnight blue that matched her eyes. She dropped into a curtsy, then came forward, hands extended to Ian, with a smile that brought out dimples in her cheeks.

"Why, here's a lass." With a great laugh, he kissed both of her cheeks. "You've grown up, Maggie."

"It has been two years." Her voice was soft, with a lilt.

"She's the image of her mother, Donald. Thank the Lord she didn't take her looks from you."

"Have a care when you insult me in my own home." But there was a ring of pride in MacDonald's warning. "Lord Ashburn, may I present my daughter Margaret."

Maggie dropped another curtsy and extended her fingertips to Brigham. "My lord."

"Miss MacDonald. It's a pleasure to see a flower on such a bitter night."

She giggled, spoiling the elegant curtsy. "Thank you, my lord. It's not often I hear flattery. You are a great friend of Coll's, are you not?"

"Yes, I am."

"I had thought..." She glanced from Brigham to Ian. "He did not accompany you, Lord MacGregor?"

"Not for lack of wanting, Maggie. And not so many years ago it was Uncle Ian."

She dimpled and kissed his bearded cheek. "It's still Uncle Ian."

He patted her hand as he turned to MacDonald. "Coll and Brigham ran into a bit of trouble on the road from London. Campbells."

"Coll?" Maggie spoke quickly, revealing more than she had intended. "Was he hurt?"

Ian's brows rose as her fingers curled into his. "He's on the mend now, lassie, but Gwen put her foot down and said he wasn't to travel."

"Please, tell me what happened. How badly was he wounded? Was he—"

"Maggie." With a little laugh, MacDonald cut off his daughter's rapid questions. "I'm sure Ian and Lord Ashburn will tell us the whole of it. Now I imagine they'd like to refresh themselves before dinner."

Though obviously impatient, she pulled herself back. "Of course. Forgive me. I ll show you to your rooms."

Gracefully she swept her skirts aside and led her father's guests out of the drawing room and up the staircase. "You've only to ask if there's anything you need. We dine in an hour, if it suits you."

"Nothing would suit me better," Ian told her, and pinched her cheek. "You've grown up nicely, Maggie. Your mother would be proud of you."

"Uncle Ian...was Coll badly hurt?"

"He's mending well, lass, I promise you."

Forced to be content with that, she left the men alone.

They dined leisurely and with elegance in the great dining hall. There were oysters bigger than any Brigham could recall seeing anywhere before, and salmon in a delicate sauce, removed with roast duck. There were wild fowls and gooseberry sauce and joints of roast mutton. The claret was fine and plentiful. Their host pressed sweets upon them. Mince pie, tarts, stewed pears and sweetmeats.

Throughout, Maggie handled her duties as hostess with an ease and liveliness that became her well. By the time she had risen to leave the men to their port, she had charmed the entire table, from Ian down to his humblest retainer.

The talk turned to politics. Louis's intentions toward England and his support of Charles and the Jacobites were discussed, debated and argued over while servants brought fresh candles and stoked the roaring fire.

Here, in this dining hall in the wild western Highlands, there was unanimous support for the fair-faced Prince. Brigham saw that these men would not only fight behind him but had come to love him for the symbol of hope he had been almost from his birth.

He went late to bed but found sleep difficult. The fire burned red, and the plaid bedcurtains kept out any drafts, though he could hear the wind whistling against the window glazing. His thoughts, no matter how he struggled to discipline them, returned again and again to Serena.

Would she be in bed now, fast asleep, her mind at rest, her body relaxed? Or would she, like him, lie awake and restless, mind in turmoil, body tensed with needs that had been stoked like the flames of the night fire?

What kind of madness drew a man to a woman who detested him and everything he was? There had been prettier women in his life, and certainly there had been sweeter. There had been women who would laugh and frolic, in bed or out, without a care as to whether he was an English lord or a French peasant. There had been women, dignified and elegant, who had been delighted to receive him for tea or to accompany him on a leisurely ride through the park.

Why had none of them caused him to lie in bed and sweat with visions of slender white hands and tumbled red-gold hair? None of them had ever made him burn with just the thought of a name, a face, a pair of eyes. They had nothing in common but an allegiance to a deposed royal house. He could find no logic here, no reason for a man to lose his heart to a woman who would have delighted in crushing it beneath her heel.

But he did love her. It occurred to Brigham that he might pay more dearly for those feelings than he ever would for following his conscience and the Jacobite cause.

When he slept he slept poorly, and he was awakened shortly after dawn by the arrival of the Camerons.

By midday, the house was swarming with men. MacDonalds from the western isles, Camerons, Drummonds, more MacGregors from the outlying districts. It became a celebration with pipes playing and whiskey to be drunk. Rough manners were overlooked and laughter rang off stone.

Gifts had been brought—deer, rabbits and whatever game had been killed on the journey. They were served at dinner, and this time the great dining hall was packed with men. The company at this meal was varied, from the chiefs and lairds to their eldest sons and men of rank to the retainers. They were all served at the same table and served well, but with subtle distinctions.

At the head of the table was venison done to a turn and fine claret. At the middle there was ale and port with substantial dishes of mutton and rabbit. At the bottom, below the salt, beef and cabbage and table beer were offered. But at all levels the food was plentiful. No man seemed insulted by the arrangements, and all ate ferociously. Servants stood behind the chairs, many of them local villagers pressed into duty for the event.

Toasts were drunk, to the true king, to the Bonnie Prince, to each clan, to the wives and daughters of the chiefs, one after another, until bottles were drained and more opened. As a man, they lifted cups to the king across the water. There was no doubt that hearts were with him. But Brigham found as talk turned to the Stuarts and the possibility of war that the table was not of one mind.

There were some whose blood ran hot enough to make them yearn to make the march on Edinburgh immediately, swords raised and pipes playing. Old grudges festered, and like reopened wounds their poison poured out. Proscriptions, executions, homes burned, kin sent to plantations and indentured, estates forfeited.

As Serena had once told him, it was not to be forgiven, it was not to be forgotten.

But others were less inclined to put their lives and their lands into the hands of the untried Prince. They had gone to war before and had seen their men and their dreams cut down.

Cameron of Lochiel, his clan's acting chief while his father remained in exile, pledged the Prince his heart, but with reservations. "If we fight without the support of French troops, the English will swarm over our land and drive us to the hills and the caves. Clan Cameron is loyal to the true king, but can the clans alone stand against the trained might of England? And a loss now will break the back of Scotland."

"So we do what?" James MacGregor, heir of Rob Roy, slapped his palm on the table. "Do we sit with our swords sheathed? Do we sit by our fires, growing old, waiting for retribution? I, for one, am sick of the elector and his German queen."

"If a sword is sheathed, it can't be broken," Lochiel returned quietly.

"Aye." A MacLeod chieftain nodded as he hunched over his port. "Though it goes against the grain to do nothing, it's madness to fight if there will be no victory. We have lost before, and paid a bitter price for it."

"The MacGregors stand behind the Prince to the man," James said with a dangerous light of battle in his eyes. "As we'll stand behind him when he takes his throne."

"Aye, lad." Keeping his voice soothing, Ian broke in. He knew James had inherited his father's loyalty, and a good deal of his guile and love of intrigue, but not his control. "We stand behind the Bonnie Prince, but there is more to be thought of than thrones and injustices. Lochiel is right. This is not a war to be waged rashly."

"Do we fight as women then?" James demanded. "With talk only?"

There had been whiskey enough drunk to bring tempers boiling. James's words had already stirred angry mutters. Before more could be said, Ian spoke again, drawing the men's attention to him.

"We fight as clansmen, as our fathers and their fathers. I fought beside your sire, James," he said quietly. "And at your side when we were both young," he added to Lochiel. "I am proud to pledge my sword and my son's to the Stuarts. When we fight, we should fight with cool heads and shrewdness, as well as sword and ax."

"But do we know the Prince means to fight?" someone at the table demanded. "We've gathered before, behind his father, and it came to nothing."

Ian signaled for his cup to be filled again. "Brigham, you spent time with the Prince in France. Tell us his mind."

The table quieted, so Brigham kept his voice moderate. "He means to fight for his rights and those of his house. Of that there can be little doubt." He paused to take stock of the faces around him. All listened, but not all seemed cheered by his words. "He looks to the Jacobites here and in England to fight with him, and hopes to convince King Louis to support his cause. With the French behind him, I think there is no doubt he could divide his enemies and cut through." He lifted his cup, taking his time. "Without them, it will take bold action and a united front."

"The Lowlanders will fight with the government army," Lochiel mused. He thought sadly of the death and destruction that would surely follow in their wake. "And the Prince is young, untried in battle."

"Yes," Brigham agreed. "He will need experienced men, advisers as well as fighting men. Don't doubt his ambition, or his resolve. He shall come to Scotland and raise his standard. He will need the clans behind him, heart and sword."

"He has both of mine," James stated, lifting his cup like a challenge.

"If the Prince's mind cannot be swayed," Lochiel said slowly, "the Camerons will fight behind him."

The talk continued into the night, and over the next day and the next. Some were convinced, their swords and their men at the ready. Others were far from encouraging.

When they took their leave of the MacDonalds, the sky was as gloomy as Brigham's thoughts. Charles's glittering ambition could all too easily be dulled.

Chapter Six

Serena sat before the crackling bedroom fire, wrapped in her night robe, while her mother brushed and dried her hair. For Fiona it brought back memories, both sweet and sad, of her eldest daughter's childhood. So many times she had stood like this, with her daughter bundled before the fire, her skin glowing from her bath. It had been simple then to ease a hurt or solve a problem.

Now the child was a woman, with, Fiona thought, a woman's needs and a woman's fears. There would come a time when her little girl would sit in front of a fire of her own.

Usually when they had this time together Serena was full of talk, questions, stories, laughter. Now she was strangely subdued, her eyes on the fire, her hands quiet in her lap. Through the open door they could hear Gwen and Malcolm entertaining Coll with some game. The laughter and crows of triumph came, muffled, into the room.

Of all her children, it was Serena who concerned Fiona most. Coll was headstrong, certainly, but enough like his father to content Fiona that he would find his way well enough. Gwen was mild and sweet-natured. Fiona had no doubt that her giving heart and fragile looks would bring her a kind man And Malcolm... She smiled as she drew the brush through Serena's long damp hair. He was full of charm and mischief, bright as a button, according to the good Father.

But it was Serena who had inherited the uncertain MacGregor temper along with a heart easily bruised. It was Serena who hated as passionately as she loved, who asked questions that couldn't be answered, who remembered too well what should be forgotten.

It was that that concerned Fiona most of all. That one hideous incident had scarred her daughter as much as it had scarred her. Fiona still bore the marks of the English officer's use of her. Not on her body, but on her heart. And she was afraid that the marks would never fade from Serena's heart, any more than they would fade from her own. But while Fiona carried her shame secretly, Serena's hate too often burned from her eyes and fell unheedingly off her tongue.

Fiona would never forget the way her young daughter had washed her, comforted her, eased both her body and heart through the misery of that night. Nor could she forget that a wildness had been born in Serena as a result of it, a recklessness that caused her to ride off unattended into the forest, to flare up at any real or imagined slight to the family. As a mother, she worried at Serena's obvious disdain of the men who came courting.

Now it was Serena's uncharacteristic silence that troubled her. Fiona wondered, not for the first time, how to mother a grown child.

"You're so quiet, my love. Do you see dreams in the fire?"

Serena smiled a little. "You always said we could, if we looked hard enough." But she had looked tonight and had seen only flaming wood.

"You've kept to yourself so much the last few days. Are you feeling poorly?"

"No, I'm just..." She let her words trail off, not certain she could explain to herself, much less her mother. "Restless, I suppose. Wanting spring." She fell silent again, staring into the fire. "When do you think Papa will be back?"

"Tomorrow. Perhaps the day after." Fiona stroked the brush tirelessly through Serena's hair. Her daughter's pensive mood had come on the day the hunting party had left. "Do you worry about him?"

"No." She sighed, and her hands moved nervously in her lap. "Sometimes I worry where it will all end, but I don't worry for Papa." Abruptly she linked her fingers together to still them. "I wish I were a man."

The statement brought Fiona some measure of relief, as it was typical. With a little laugh, she kissed the top of Serena's head. "What foolishness is this?"

"I do. If I were a man I wouldn't forever be forced to sit and wait." And want, she thought, want something so nebulous she could never describe it.

"If you were a man you would rob me of one of the greatest pleasures of my life."

With another sigh, Serena quieted. "I wish I were more like you—more like Gwen."

"You are what you were born to be, love, and nothing pleases me more."

"I wish I did please you. I wish I could."

"What, more nonsense?"

"There are times I know you are disappointed with me."

"No, not disappointed, never that." For a moment, Fiona wrapped her arms around Serena and pressed cheek to cheek. "When you were born, I thanked God for giving you to me whole and safe. My heart was nearly broken from losing the two bairns between Coll and you. I feared I'd have no more children, then there you were, small as a minute, strong as a horse. What a time you gave me with the birthing. The midwife said you clawed your way into the world. Women don't go to war, Serena, but I tell you this, there would be no children in the world if men had to bring them into it."

That made Serena laugh. She tucked her legs up and settled more comfortably. "I remember when Malcolm came. Papa went to the stables and got drunk."

"So it was with all of you," Fiona said, smiling. "He's a man who would sooner face a hundred dragoons with only a dirk than set foot in a birthing room."

"How did you know— When you met him, how did you know you loved him?"

"I'm not sure I did." Dreaming herself, Fiona studied the fire. "The first time was at a ball. Alice MacDonald, Mary MacLeod and I were the best of friends. Alice MacDonald's parents were having a ball for her birthday. The MacDonalds of Glenfinnan. Your father's good friend Donald, as you know, is Alice's brother. Alice wore green, Mary blue, and I wore white with my grandmother's pearls. We had our hair powdered and thought we were very fashionable and beautiful.''

"I know you were.''

With a little sigh, Fiona stopped brushing to rest her hands on her daughter's shoulders. "The music was very gay, and the men so handsome. Your father had Donald introduce him, and he asked me to dance. I did, of course, but I was thinking—what do I want with this great beast of a man? He'll probably tread on my toes and ruin my new slippers.''

"Oh, Mama, never say you thought Papa couldn't dance.''

"I did, and was shown contrary, as you've witnessed time and time again. No one danced with more grace and lightness of foot than Ian MacGregor.''

It pleased Serena, the mental picture she conjured up of her parents young and sharing their first dance. "So you fell in love with him for the way he danced.''

"No, indeed. I flirted with him, I confess. Alice and Mary and myself had made a pact to flirt with all the men at the ball until we had a score of suitors. We had decided we would choose only the most handsome, the most elegant and the wealthiest for husbands.''

With some astonishment, Serena looked over her shoulder. "You, Mama?''

"Aye, I was quite vain and full of myself.'' Fiona laughed and patted hair that was just beginning to show the first signs of graying. "My father had spoiled me miserably, you see. The next day, your father called on the MacDonalds, where I was staying. To ride out with Donald, he said, but he made certain I saw him striding around the house as if he owned it. Over the next weeks he put himself in my way more times than I could count. He wasn't the most handsome, the most elegant or the wealthiest of the men who called on me, but in the end, it was he I wanted.''

"But how did you know?'' Serena insisted. "How could you be sure?''

"When my heart spoke louder than my head,'' Fiona murmured, studying her daughter. So this was the problem, she realized, and wondered how she could have missed the signs. Her little one was falling in love. Rapidly Fiona ran through the names and faces of the young men who had come calling. She could not recall Serena sparing even one of them a second glance. In fact, Fiona thought with a frown, Serena had sent most of them off with their tails between their legs.

"There has to be more than that.'' As confused as she was unsatisfied, Serena plucked at the folds of her skirts. "There has to be a rightness to it, a sense to it. If Papa had been different, if you hadn't had the same beliefs, the same backgrounds, your heart would never have spoken at all.''

"Love doesn't account for differences, Rena,'' Fiona said slowly. A sudden thought had intruded, one that made her uncertain whether to laugh or weep. Had her daughter, her fiery, headstrong daughter, fallen in love with the English lord?

"My sweet.'' Fiona touched a hand to Serena's cheek. "When love nappens it's most often right, but it rarely makes sense.''

"I'd rather be alone,'' Serena said passionately. Her eyes glowed in the firelight, showing as much confusion as determination. "I'd rather play aunt to Coll's and Gwen's and Malcolm's children than find myself pining after a man I know would make me unhappy."

"That's your head talking, and your temper." Fiona's hand was as gentle as her voice. "Falling in love is frightening, especially for a woman who tries to fight it."

"I don't know." She turned her cheek into her mother's hand. "Oh, Mama, why don't I know what I want?"

"When the time's right, you will. And you, the most courageous of my children, will take it."

Her fingers tightened suddenly on Serena's cheek. They both heard the rumble of horses approaching. For a moment, in the light of the fire, both remembered another time, another night.

"Papa's back early." Serena rose to take her mother's hand.

"Aye." Degree by degree, Fiona forced herself to relax. "He'll be wanting something hot."

The men had ridden hard in their desire to sleep in their own beds. They had indeed hunted, and came home laden with fresh-killed deer and rabbit and wild duck. The house, which had been so quiet, erupted with Ian's shouts and commands. Clad in her night robe, Serena had decided to remain upstairs until she heard her father bellowing for her.

She began smoothing her hair and skirts, then stopped herself in disgust. It hardly mattered what she looked like. She came down to see her father, his face still reddened by the bite of wind, giving Gwen a hearty kiss. Coll sat near the fire, a lap robe covering his knees and Malcolm perched laughing on the arm of his chair.

With a full cup already in his hand, his other dug into his breeches pocket, Brigham stood in front of the hearth. His hair was ruffled by the ride, his boots splashed with mud. Despite her resolve not to, she found her eyes drawn to his. For the space of three heartbeats, there was nothing and no one else.

Nor was there for him. He watched her enter, her dark green robe flowing down her, her hair glowing like firelight. Brigham's fingers tightened so quickly, so violently, on the pewter cup that he thought they might leave dents. Deliberately relaxing them, he sketched her a bow. Her chin shot up, making him want more than anything else to stride across the room and crush her against him.

"There she is, my little Highland wildcat." Ian threw open his arms. "Have you got a kiss for your Papa?"

She gave him a saucy smile. "I might." Crossing to him, she gave him a very demure peck on the cheek. Then, with a laugh, she threw her arms around his neck and gave him a loud, smacking one. He responded by lifting her off her feet and twirling her twice.

"Now here's a likely lass," he told the room in general. "If a man can survive the claws, he'll have a prize worth keeping."

"I'll not be a prize for any man." She gave his beard a hard, disrespectful tug that earned her a slap on the bottom and a grin.

"You see I speak the truth, Brig. She's a lively one. I've a good mind to give you to Duncan MacKinnon, as he asks me nigh on every week."

"And so you may, Father," she said mildly. "He'll be less of a nuisance once I slice him in two."

He laughed again. Though all his children delighted him, Serena held the tightest grip on his heart. "Fill my cup, brat, and the rest besides. Young Duncan's not the match for you."

She did as he bade, passing the cup to him before walking over to add to Brigham's. It was impossible to resist raising her gaze to his, or allowing the challenge to glow in her eyes. "Nor, perhaps, is any man," she responded.

When a gauntlet was thrown down, Brigham was honor bound to pick it up. "It may be, my lady, that none has yet taught you to sheathe your claws."

"In truth, my lord, none who tried have survived."

"It would seem you're in need of a man made of tougher stuff."

She lifted a brow as if assessing him. "Believe me, I'm not in need of a man at all."

His eyes warned her he could prove her wrong, but he only smiled. "Forgive me, madam, but a high-strung mare rarely understands the need for a rider."

"Oh, please." Coll choked on his own laughter and held up a hand. "Don't encourage him, Rena. The man can go on like that for hours, and you'll never win. Have pity and bring that jug here. My cup's empty."

"As your head is," she muttered, and poured whiskey into the cup her brother held out.

"Easy, lass, don't flay me. I'm still a sick man."

"Are you now?" With a smile, she snatched the cup from him. "Then you'll be wanting one of Gwen's brews and not whiskey." She tossed it off herself before he could grab it.

"Wench." Grinning, he pulled her down in his lap. "Pour me some more and I'll keep your secrets."

"Hah! What secrets?"

He put his mouth to her ear and whispered only one word. "Breeches."

Serena swore under her breath and filled the cup again. "So you haven't been so sick you couldn't spy out your window," she muttered to him.

"A man takes what weapons he can."

"If you children would stop your bickering..." Ian waited until all eyes were on him. "We found the MacDonalds well. Donald's brother Daniel is a grandfather again. His third, which shames me." He sent a look at his two oldest children, who forgot their annoyance with each other long enough to give their father identical smiles. "Well you should grin like a couple of simpletons while neglecting your duties to the clan. A better father would have had you both married off and breeding, willing or not."

"There is no better father than our own," Serena said, and watched him soften.

"We'll pass over that. I've invited Maggie MacDonald to visit."

"Oh, good Lord," Coll moaned. "Talk of nuisances."

The comment earned him a cuff on the ear from his sister. "She's a great friend of mine, I'll remind you. When does she come?"

"Next week." Ian sent Coll a stern look. "And I'll remind you, my lad, that no guest in my home is a nuisance."

"They are when they're forever underfoot so that you can't walk but trip over them." Then he relented, knowing that hospitality was a matter of honor and tradition. "No doubt she'll have outgrown that by now and be happy in Rena's and Gwen's company."

The next days passed in a flurry of activity in preparation for the expected company. As was Fiona's wont, wood and silver were polished, foods prepared, floors scrubbed. Serena welcomed the diversion and was too used to work to resent the extra labor. She looked forward to the company of a girl her own age who had been her friend since childhood.

Now that Coll had mended, he and Brigham rode out often, sometimes in the company of Ian and other men, sometimes alone. There were discussions nightly debating the Jacobite cause and the Prince's next move. Rumors flew from hill to glen, from burn to forest. The Prince was on his way. The Prince was in Paris. The Prince was never coming at all.

Once, a messenger had been hustled into the drawing room with a dispatch for Brigham. The doors had remained shut on the men for hours, and the rider had left again after dark. Whatever news he had brought had not been passed on to the women, a fact Serena bitterly resented.

In the kitchen, with the fire blazing, Serena dealt with the washing, her share and Gwen's. She had exchanged her polishing duties for Gwen's help with the laundry. It suited her. She preferred stamping on linen in the big tub to cramping her hands with beeswax.

With her skirts kilted up, she waded in water up to her calves. She enjoyed the energy it took, just as now she enjoyed the solitude of the kitchen. Mrs. Drummond was visiting a neighbor for an exchange of recipes and gossip. Malcolm was about his lessons, and their mother was supervising the preparation of a guest room.

Serena high-stepped like a pony in the cooling water, humming to herself to make the chore less monotonous and to keep the rhythm steady.

She wondered if Brigham had found Maggie MacDonald pretty and if he had kissed her hand the way he had once kissed her own.

Why should it matter? she asked herself, and began to stamp on the wash with more vigor. The man had barely spared her a glance since he had returned, and that was precisely the way she preferred it. He meant nothing to her, at least no more than any prickly thorn in her side.

She wished he would go away. Serena began to stamp harder, until water rose to the lip of the tub. She wished he would take his cool voice and hot eyes back to London—or to hell, for that matter. She wished he would fall in the river and catch a chill, then waste slowly, painfully, away. Better yet, she wished he would come in, fall on his knees and beg her for one smile.

Of course, she would sneer.

She wished—

She stopped wishing, stopped washing, stopped thinking, when he strode into the room. Brigham was brought up short, just as she was. He had thought she was busy upstairs with her mother, or in the dining hall with her sister. For days he had made a science out of avoiding her and the discomfort and pleasure being in her company brought him.

Now she was here, alone in the overheated kitchen, her face flushed with exercise, her hair escaping from its pins, and her skirts— Dear God.

Her legs were pale and wet and as shapely as any man could dream of. Before he controlled himself, he watched a drop of water slide down from her knee, along one smooth calf and into the tub. His breath hissed out softly between his teeth.

"Well, this is an unexpected and charming domestic scene."

"You've no business in the kitchen, Lord Ashburn."

"Your father persuaded me to make myself at home. As everyone is occupied, I thought it would be less trouble for me to come in and charm Mrs. Drummond out of some soup."

"It's there in the pot." She indicated the steaming kettle. "Help yourself to it and take it away. I've got too much to do to wait on you."

"So I see." He recovered enough to walk closer. She smelled of soap and made his stomach quiver. "Madam, I assure you, I will never sleep quite the same again knowing how my bed linen was washed."

She swallowed a chuckle and began to stamp in the water again. "It does the job, *Sassenach*, and does it well. Now, if you'll be about your business, I'll be about mine before the water goes cold." Inspired perhaps by the devil, she brought her foot down hard and sent water splashing over his breeches. "Oh, I beg your pardon, my lord." Unable to prevent it, she snickered.

Brigham looked down at his breeches and gave a wry shake of his head. "Perhaps you think these need washing, as well."

"Toss them in," she invited recklessly. "I've had a mind to plant my foot on your breeches before."

"Have you?" He reached down toward the fastening and had the satisfaction of watching her eyes widen. Flushing to the roots of her hair, she stepped back and nearly tumbled down in the water.

"Brigham—"

He caught her before she could send herself and the washwater all over the kitchen. "There, I knew I would have it out of you again."

He had an arm around her waist, another on her hair. The remaining pins plopped into the water and sunk. Serena stood, flustered, with her arms trapped between their bodies. "What?"

"My name," he murmured. "Say it again."

"I've no need to." She moistened her lips, unwittingly stirring his blood all the more. "And you've no need to hold me. I have my balance now."

"But I do have a need, Rena. I've told myself three days running that I cannot, I should not, I shall not touch you." As he spoke he ran his hand up her back, down her hair, as if he could take as he chose. "But I have a need. The same one I see now in your eyes."

She hated herself for lowering them. "You see nothing."

"Everything," he corrected, pressing a kiss to her hair. "Oh, God, I haven't been able to get the scent of you out of my mind, the taste of you off my palate."

"Stop." If she could have freed her hands, she would have covered her ears with them. "I won't listen."

"Why?" The hand on her hair tightened so that she was forced to lift her head. "Because I'm English?"

"No. Yes. I don't know." Her voice rose, roughened by the beat of her pulse. "I only know I don't want this. I don't want to feel the way you make me feel."

He felt a moment of triumph as he dragged her closer. "How do I make you feel, Rena?"

"Weak, afraid, angry. No, don't," she whispered as his lips hovered above hers. "Don't kiss me."

"Then kiss me." He brushed his lips lightly over hers.

"I won't."

His lips curved as hers met them. "You already are."

With a shuddering moan, she clutched at him, taking what her heart wanted and blocking out the warning in her head. He wasn't for her, could never be for her, and yet when he held her it seemed as though he had always been for her.

His lips teased and retreated, seduced and tormented, until she was driven to take possession. Had she told him he made her feel weak? That was a lie, she thought dimly. She felt strong, incredibly strong, with energy coursing through her and pumping through her blood until it ran hot. A woman could fear weakness, but not power.

She wrapped her arms around him, let her head fall back and her lips part as she all but dared him to try to sap her strength.

It was like holding a lightning bolt, he thought. Full of fire and flash and dangerous power. One moment he was coaxing, the next he was bombarded with the heat that seemed to radiate from her. Murmuring her name, he lifted her from the water. He held her aloft for a moment, then slowly let her slide down his body until her feet hit the floor.

Then her lips were racing over his face. She slipped her hands beneath his coat to run them impatiently over the linen of his shirt. Her body was arched against his, begging to be touched. Her breasts yielded temptingly against his chest.

Knowing his only choices were to pull her to the floor and pleasure them both or stop, Brigham dragged himself away.

"Serena." He took both of her hands and brought them to his lips. "We must talk."

"Talk?" Thoughts couldn't surface in a head that swam so thickly.

"Yes, and soon, before I abuse the trust of your father and my friend more than I already have."

She stared at him a moment, and then her mind began to clear. Pulling her hands away, she pressed them to her cheeks. How could she have thrown herself at him in that way? "I don't want to talk, I want you to go away."

"Want or not, we will talk." He grabbed her hands again before she could turn away. "Serena, we can't pretend that something doesn't happen between us every time we're together. I may not want this any more than you, but I'm not fool enough to say it doesn't exist."

"It will pass," she said, desperate to believe it. "Desires come, and they go."

He lifted a brow. "Such cool and worldly talk from a woman in bare feet."

"Oh, leave me be, will you?" She shoved at him. "I was fine and happy before you came here. I'll be fine and happy when you leave."

"The hell you will." He pulled her against him again. "If I were to leave now, you'd weep."

Pride stiffened her spine. "I'll never shed a tear over you. Why should I? You're not the first man I've kissed, and you won't be the last."

His eyes narrowed to slits, darkened like onyx. "You live dangerously, Serena."

"I live as I please. Now let me go."

"So I'm not the first you've kissed," he murmured. He had a desperate and vivid desire to know the names and faces of each one so he could murder them. "Tell me, did the others make you tremble?" He kissed her again, hard enough to make her gasp. "Did they make your skin go hot and soft?" His mouth came to hers again, and this time she could do nothing but sigh against his lips and let him have his way. "Did you look at them the way you look at me now?" he demanded. "With your eyes dark and clouded?"

She clutched at his shoulders, almost afraid she would dissolve and slide through his hands. "Brigham—"

"Did you?" he demanded, his eyes dark and bright.

Her head was reeling, and she shook it. "No."

"Serena, I've finished in—" Gwen pushed open the door, then stood, her mouth forming a surprised O as she stared at her sister caught in a close embrace with their guest. Serena stood on the toes of her bare feet, gripping Brigham's beautiful coat. And he—Gwen's young imagination caused her blush to deepen.

"I beg your pardon," she managed, and continued to stand, looking from one to the other without the least idea what to do.

"Gwen." With more force than dignity, Serena pulled out of Brigham's arms. "Lord Ashburn was just—"

"Kissing your sister," he finished coolly.

"Oh." Gwen watched Serena send Brigham a furious glance. "I do beg your pardon," she repeated, wondering if it would be best to go or stay.

Amused, Brigham watched Gwen wrestle with propriety while Serena whirled to the cupboard and rattled crockery. "There's no need to beg anyone's pardon," she said testily. "Lord Ashburn wanted soup."

"So I did, but as it happens I've had all my appetite can handle at the moment. If you ladies will excuse me..." He strolled out, wincing only slightly as a bowl hit the floor.

Chapter Seven

"**K**ing Louis will not intervene." Brigham stood in front of the fire, his hands clasped behind his back. Though his eyes were calm and his stance relaxed, his voice was grim. "It becomes less and less likely as time passes that he will support the Prince with gold or with men."

Coll tossed the letter that had come earlier by messenger onto a table and rose to pace. Unlike Brigham's, his impatience needed room and movement. "A year ago, Louis was more than ready to lend support. Ready? Damn, he was eager to lend it."

"A year ago," Brigham pointed out, "Louis thought Charles might be of use to him. Since the French invasion was abandoned last March, the Prince is largely ignored by the French court."

"Then we'll do without the French." Coll turned to glare first at Brigham, then at his father. "The Highlanders will fight for the Stuarts."

"Aye," Ian agreed. "But how many?" He held up a hand to prevent his son from launching into a passionate speech. "My mind and my heart remain unchanged. When the time comes, the MacGregors fight for the rightful king. But it's unity we need, as well as numbers. To win, the clans must fight as one."

"As we have fought before," Coll said with a slap of his fist. "And will again."

"Would that were true." Ian's voice was quiet, one of reason and regret. And of age, he thought with an inward sigh. Growing old was the damnedest thing. "We can't pretend that every chief in Scotland stands behind the true king or will rally his clan for the Prince. How many, Brig, will stand against us in the government army?"

Brigham picked up the letter from the table and, after glancing at it once more, tossed it into the fire. "I expect word from my contacts in London any day."

"How much longer do we wait?" Coll took his seat again to stare into the fire. "How many more months, how many more years do we only sit and talk while the elector grows fat on the throne?"

"I think the time of rebellion comes sooner than you might think," Brigham murmured. "Sooner than we might be prepared for. The Prince is impatient."

"The Highland chiefs will meet again." Ian drummed his fingers on the arm of his chair. Like any wise general, he preferred to plan his war before raising his sword. "Care must be taken to keep such meetings from raising the suspicions of the Black Watch."

Coll swore roundly at the mention of the Highlanders recruited by the English to maintain order in Scotland.

"Another hunting party?" Brigham asked.

"I had in mind something a bit different." At the sound of approaching carriage wheels, Ian smiled and tapped out his pipe. "A ball, my lads. It's time we did a spot of entertaining. And the lass who comes visiting is, I believe, a very pretty reason for dusting away cobwebs."

Brigham twitched the curtains aside in time to see Serena dash down the steps toward the waiting carriage. A dark-haired girl descended and launched herself into Serena's arms. "Maggie MacDonald."

"Aye. She's of marriageable age, as is my own first daughter." He set his gaze on Brigham's back a moment. A man would have to be blind, he thought, not to see that there was a tune playing between his young guest and his daughter. "Nothing more reasonable than to hold a ball to introduce them to a few suitable young bucks."

Fighting back annoyance, Brigham let the curtain fall into place. He didn't want to look at Serena now, with the sun falling on her face and her eyes dark with laughter. "It will do well enough, I suppose."

Coll only scowled at the toe of his boot. "I don't care for it. Bringing another giggling female into the house now. Damned if I'm going to find myself cornered into taking her for sedate rides and listening to talk of the latest bonnets when we should be polishing our swords."

Ian merely rose to open the salon doors. "I've no doubt that Rena and Gwen will entertain her well enough without you." The moment the doors were opened, women's voices and laughter poured through. Coll grumbled and stayed stubbornly in his seat. "There's the lass." Ian's voice rumbled to the ceiling. "Come here and give your Uncle Ian a kiss."

Smiling, Maggie danced across the hall. She laughed when he lifted her off her feet, but Fiona scolded him. "The girl's already been bumped enough on the journey. Go in and warm yourself by the fire, Maggie."

With her arm still tucked in Ian's, Maggie stepped into the room.

Manners prevented Coll from scowling, and he began to rise reluctantly. Then, manners or not, his mouth fell open. She still looked hardly bigger than a doll beside his broad-shouldered father, but the skinny, smudge-faced pest he remembered had miraculously been replaced by a slender vision in dark blue velvet. Her hair, dark as midnight, fell in curls beneath a hat that framed her face. Had her eyes always been that beautiful, like the loch at twilight? he wondered as he managed to close his mouth. Had her skin always looked like fresh cream?

Maggie smiled at him. Then, because she had planned her moves carefully during the journey, she turned to curtsy to Brigham. "Lord Ashburn."

"It's a pleasure to see you again, Miss MacDonald." He took her offered hand and brushed his lips over her fingers. Behind Ian, Serena's breath came out in a quiet hiss. "I trust your journey wasn't too taxing."

"Not at all."

Because Maggie's hand was still in Brigham's, Serena couldn't prevent herself from stepping forward. "You remember Coll, don't you, Maggie?"

With a little more force than was necessary, she pulled Maggie away from Brigham and toward her brother.

"Of course I do." Maggie had practiced a friendly, almost impersonal smile in front of her mirror night after night in preparation for this first meeting. Though her heart was pounding, she put her practiced smile to use now. He was even more handsome than she remembered, taller, broader, even more exciting. Growing up had taken so long, but now, at this moment, it seemed worth it. "I'm happy to see you again, Coll. I hope your wound is healed."

"Wound?" He took her hand, feeling unbearably clumsy.

"Your father explained that you were wounded on the way from London." Her voice was mild as a spring morning. She wondered he couldn't hear the furious thundering of her heart. "I trust you've recovered?"

"It was nothing."

"I'm persuaded it was a great deal more than nothing, but it's good to see you up and about again." Because she was afraid that if her hand stayed in his another moment she would faint with delight, Maggie drew herself away and twirled around. There was a blush in her cheeks now that she prayed everyone would take for excitement from the journey. "It's wonderful to be here again. I can't thank you enough, Uncle Ian, Aunt Fiona, for asking me to come."

Refreshments were brought in, seats were taken. Rather than making the excuses he had prepared, Coll found himself jockeying for the chair nearest Maggie. Brigham took advantage of the situation and leaned close to Serena as he passed a plate of cakes.

"Will you try one of these, Miss MacGregor?" he asked. Then, in a quiet voice that was covered by the conversation: "You've been avoiding me, Rena."

"That's ridiculous." She took a cake and wondered how she had been maneuvered to the fringes of the party with him.

"I agree completely. Avoiding me is ridiculous."

Her cup rattled in its saucer. "You flatter yourself, *Sassenach.*"

"It's gratifying to see I make you nervous," he said quietly, then turned and continued in a normal tone, "Gwen, I must tell you how charming you look in pink."

He never tells me I look charming, Serena thought as she bit, almost viciously, into her cake. He never gives me gallant bows and pretty compliments as he did with Maggie. With me it's barbs and snarls. And kisses, she remembered with an inward shiver. Deep, dark kisses.

She wouldn't think of it—or of him. When a man treated a woman that boldly, he wanted only one thing. She might have been raised in the Highlands, but she was no fool when it came to the ways of the English aristocracy.

She would be no man's mistress. Certainly she would be no Englishman's mistress. No matter what magic he could make her feel, no matter what wonders he could make her dream of, she would never shame herself or her family. If she avoided him, it wasn't that she was afraid, it was that she was being sensible.

"Daydreams, my love," Brigham murmured, making her jump. "I hope they are of me."

"They are of cows to be milked," she said between her teeth. When he chuckled, she put up her chin and prepared to speak to Maggie. Her friend, at that moment, was bubbling with laughter and smiling beautifully at Coll. Her brother, Serena noted, was flushed and glassy-eyed.

"Apparently Coll doesn't find Miss MacDonald a nuisance after all," Brigham commented.

"He looks as though he's been hit on the head with a rock."

"Or struck through the heart with Cupid's arrow."

Her eyes widened at that, then narrowed consideringly. In a moment she had to smother a chuckle of her own. "Who would have thought it?" Too amused to do otherwise, she leaned closer to Brigham. "Do you suppose he'll start spouting poetry?"

He caught a whiff of her hair and imagined burying his face in it. The woman was made to drive him mad, snapping one moment, smiling the next. "Men have been known to do worse when so afflicted."

"But Coll? Coll and Maggie! A few years ago he couldn't wait to dust Maggie off his boots."

"And now she is a beautiful woman."

A little pang of jealousy warred with friendship. "Aye," Serena murmured, and wondered fleetingly what it would be like to be tiny and fragile. "You certainly seem to think so."

His brow lifted at that, and then a smile ghosted around his lips. "For myself, I've come to prefer green eyes and a sharp tongue."

She looked at him then and blushed despite herself. "I have no way, my lord, with drawing room flirtations."

"Then that is perhaps one more thing I shall teach you."

Choosing to retreat rather than fight with a dull sword, Serena rose. "Let me take you up, Maggie, and show you your room."

Maggie's company was precisely the distraction Serena needed. It had been nearly two years since they had been together, but time and distance were swept away. They talked late into the night, rode out together into the forest, walked for miles in the hills. As always, Maggie spoke whatever was in her heart, while Serena kept her innermost thoughts close. The fact that her friend was still in love with Coll didn't surprise her. The fact that Coll seemed equally besotted with Maggie did.

It pleased her. Though Serena had never believed, as Maggie always had, that Coll would fall in love with her friend, she couldn't deny what was happening in front of her eyes. He made dozens of excuses to be in their company, when just two years before he had made twice as many to be out of it. He listened to Maggie's cheerful ramblings as though she were the most fascinating person on earth. And with the sharp and always critical eye of a sister, Serena noted that Coll was taking great pains with his appearance.

She even had it from Mrs. Drummond that Coll was asking Parkins's advice on his wardrobe.

She would have laughed about it if she had not felt constant prickings of jealousy. More than once she had caught herself sulking when she thought of how rosy and dreamy being in love had made her friend. And how nervous and unhappy falling in love was making her. The weakness infuriated her, and made her only more determined to see that Coll and Maggie had their hearts' desire.

Coll accompanied them on some of their rides, which meant they more often than not rode as a foursome, including Brigham. The new situation gave Serena as much pleasure as it did discomfort.

The weather was brisk, but the bite of winter was easing. In another month, Serena thought, the trees would be greening and the first hardy wildflowers would brave their way out to the sun. For now, there was the slap of a March wind on her face as she rode. The spring thaws had not yet come, and the ground still rang hard under the horses' hooves, but there were birdcalls and occasional bright flashes of wings as the horses disturbed the midmorning quiet. Ice and frost had melted from the trees, leaving them wet and glistening.

They kept to a sedate canter that caused Serena to rein in her impatience, as well as her horse. She knew Maggie could ride as well as anyone, but her friend seemed to prefer picking her way daintily along the path.

"You would prefer a run?" Brigham asked as he came up beside her.

"I would," she said feelingly.

He shot a look over his shoulder while his own mount danced beneath him. "Let them catch up."

Though she was tempted, she shook her head. Her mother would never approve of their going in pairs rather than in a group. "It wouldn't be right."

"Afraid you can't keep up with me?" He was rewarded by a flash in her eyes.

"There isn't an Englishman alive a MacGregor can't beat on horseback."

"Easy talk, Rena," he said mildly. "The lake's less than a mile."

She hesitated, knowing proper manners dictated she remain with her guest. But a challenge was a challenge. Before she could stop herself, she pressed in her heels and sent her mount leaping forward.

She knew the way as well as she knew the corridors of her own home. With a light hand, she guided the horse through the curves and twists, whipping under low-hanging branches, leaping over or skirting fallen limbs. The path was barely wide enough for two, but neither gave way, so they rode all but shoulder-to-shoulder. She glanced over to see Brigham's face alive with laughter as he spurred his mount forward. The forest rang with her own as she leaned forward to coax more speed out of her mare.

There was a pleasure here that came as much from the company as the race. There was a freedom she experienced only with him, but one that, for now, she didn't question Brigham's part in. She only wished that the lake were ten miles away rather than one, so that they could continue to ride fast and reckless, with the sun shooting beams through bare trees.

She rode like a goddess, he thought. Brilliantly, with a careless disregard for life and limb. With another woman he would have held back, slowed the pace out of concern for her safety, and perhaps her pride. With Serena he only pushed harder, out of the sheer pleasure of seeing her fly along the path, her plaid streaming over her dove-gray riding habit. With a grin he watched her gallop half a length ahead, regretting only that she had chosen the habit over breeches.

Not so easy, he murmured to himself as he spotted the sun striking the lake's surface in the distance. With a kick of his heels they were neck and neck again, thundering down the rise toward the water.

They reached the bank together, and his heart stopped as Serena waited until the last possible instant to rein in. With a ringing whinny, her mare reared. She was laughing in the moment she hung suspended between sky and earth, her eyes dark and reckless, her body fluid. If Brigham hadn't already been in love, he would have fallen then, as quickly and as dangerously as a man hurled from a cliff.

"I won, *Sassenach*."

"The devil you did." Breathless, he patted his horse's neck and grinned at her. "I had you by a head."

"Head be damned," she said, forgetting herself. "I won, and you're not man enough to admit it." She took a deep, greedy breath of air that tasted of pine and water. "If I hadn't been hampered by riding sidesaddle, I'd have left you in my dust." Then she was laughing at him, her eyes greener than any of the lush lawns he knew in England, her flirty little hat tilted askew from the race. "You've nothing to be ashamed of," she said with her tongue in her cheek. "You're as good a horseman as any Englishman might be, and nearly as good as a lame Scot with a blind eye."

"Your compliments put me to the blush, my lady. Regardless, the race was mine, but you're too vain—or too mulish—to concede."

She tossed her head so that the hat fell off to hang by its ribbons. The hair that Maggie had labored over that morning tumbled down in a mass of sunset curls. "I won. A gentleman would have the grace to admit it."

"I won." Reaching over, he loosened her ribbons and snatched the hat away. "A lady would never have raced in the first place."

"Oh." If it had been possible, she would have stamped her foot. Instead, she swung her horse around until they were face-to-face. She didn't mind being called vain and mulish, but to have her lack of ladylike graces tossed in her face was too much. "Isn't that just like a man! The race was your idea. If I had refused, I would have been a coward. But I accept, and win, so I'm not a lady."

"Accepted, and lost," Brigham corrected, enjoying the way temper flushed her cheeks. "You've no need to be a lady for me, Rena. I prefer you as you are."

Her eyes kindled. "Which is?"

"A delightful wildcat who wears breeches and fights like a man."

She hissed at him and, on impulse, gave his mount a slap that had it leaping forward. If Brigham hadn't reacted quickly enough, or had his skill been less sharp, he would have landed headfirst in the icy waters of the lake.

"Vixen," he murmured, half in amazement, half in admiration. "Have you a mind to drown me now?"

"It would hardly be my fault if you sank to the bottom. You have a head like a stone." But she was biting her lip to keep from laughing. Tossing her head again, she looked up at the sky. It was a glorious day, perhaps the most beautiful she would ever see. Annoyance with him faded easily when she remembered that he had given her the chance for a run.

"I'll call a truce," she decided. "Coll and Maggie will be here soon. If I'm angry with you, I'll have no one to talk to while they make moon eyes at each other."

"So, I have my uses." Brigham slipped from his horse. "You warm my heart, madam."

"The race, and winning it, put me in a pleasant mood." She unhooked her knee from the saddle and laid her hands on his shoulders as he stood to assist her to the ground.

"I'm delighted to hear it." Before she had an inkling of his purpose, he had tossed her over his shoulder. "But I'll remind you, I won."

"Are you mad?" She thudded a fist against his back, not certain if she wanted to laugh or swear. "Set me down, you oaf."

"I've a mind to do just that." He took a few easy strides to the verge of the lake. Serena's eyes widened. Rather than beat against him, she dug her fingers into his jacket.

"You wouldn't dare."

"My dear, have I told you that a Langston never, absolutely never, refuses a dare?" She kicked and gave a passing thought to biting as his hand slid up her calf. "Can you swim?"

"Better than you, *Sassenach*, I'll swear. If you don't let me—" Her threat was cut off by her squeal as he feinted a toss. "Brigham, don't! It's freezing!" She began to laugh, even as she kicked and struggled. "I swear I'll murder you the moment I'm free."

"That's hardly incentive for me to release you. Now if you'll concede that I won the race…"

"I will not."

"Well, then." He had started to step closer to the water when Serena landed a blow with the toe of her boot close enough to a sensitive area to make him wince. In defense, Brigham stepped back and tripped over a root. They went down in a flurry of petticoats and curses. For propriety's sake, and his own sake of mind, he removed his hand from the taut curve of her bottom.

"We've been here before, I believe," he managed as they both struggled to catch their breath.

Serena shoved herself off him and remembered, belatedly, to cover her legs. "Damn you. You've stained my skirts."

"My lady, you came a great deal too close to ummanning me."

She grinned and pushed the hair out of her eyes. It was a glorious day, and she felt too alive to remember to be a lady. "Did I? I'll do better at the next opportunity." After a glance at the dirt on his breeches, she snickered. "Parkins will undoubtedly scold you for ruining those."

"My valet does not scold." But Brigham rubbed at the streak of dirt. "He simply looks mortally offended, which causes me to feel as though I were a schoolboy again."

Serena plucked at the turf. "What is he like, your Parkins?"

"Steady as a rock, infuriatingly proper. Stubborn. Why?"

"Mrs. Drummond has decided he would make a likely husband."

"Mrs. Drummond?" Brigham turned his head to stare. "*Your* Mrs. Drummond, and Parkins?"

Family honor brought the light of battle to Serena's eyes. "And why not? Mrs. Drummond is a fine woman."

"You'll get no argument from me. But Parkins?" Brigham leaned back on his elbows and laughed. He could do nothing else when he thought of the scarecrow-framed Parkins and the prodigiously built cook. "Does he know?"

"She'll get around to letting him." Because she had found the pairing funny herself, Serena lay back on the grassy bank and smiled at the sky. "She'll charm him with her tarts and sauces, just as Maggie is charming Coll with her pretty eyes and shy smiles."

"Does that bother you?"

"Maggie and Coll?" Serena cushioned her head with her arm and thought it through. "No. She's been in love with him for as long as I can remember. I'd be more than happy for them if they make a match, and since she's already my friend I wouldn't have to worry about hating the woman Coll chose for a wife. But—"

"But?"

"Seeing them together has made me think. Things are changing, and there's nothing to be done to stop it." She closed her eyes, content to have the chilly breeze dance over her face. "When spring comes, love comes. So they say." If her voice was wistful, she blamed it on the air. "When this spring comes, war comes. There will be nothing to stop that, either."

"No." He reached over to toy with the ends of her hair. "Would you have it stopped, Serena?"

She sighed, opening her eyes to watch the wispy clouds chased by the wind. "Part of me hates not being able to take a sword and fight myself. Yet another part, a part that seems to have just begun, wishes there was no need to fight at all. That part of me wishes we could go on living as we have been, watching the flowers come up in the spring."

He took her hand. It was too fragile to hold a sword, he thought, however strong her heart. "There will still be flowers. And there will be other springs."

She turned her head to look at him. It hadn't occurred to her that she was relaxed with him, content, even happy to be alone with him on the banks of the lake. It was her favorite place, one she came to when she was deeply troubled or very happy. Now she was there with him, and it seemed so right, somehow—the gentle call of birds, the smell of the water and damp earth, the almost harsh light of the sun.

Her fingers curled into his in a move so instinctive that she didn't know she had done it until it was too late, until the change had come into his eyes, the subtle darkening, the sharpening of intensity. It was as if in one instant the rest of the world had slipped out of its orbit and only they were left, hands linked, eyes only for each other.

"No." Quickly she pushed herself up so that she was sitting rather than lying on the bank. It had seemed a move of self-preservation, but it was a poor one, as it only put them closer together. Brigham reached out to trace the line of her jaw.

"I could let you go, Rena. It wouldn't change what's between us."

"There can be nothing between us."

"Stubborn." He nipped her lower lip. "Willful." Then he traced the ache with his tongue. "Beautiful."

"I'm none of those things." She lifted a hand, thinking to push him away, but somehow she was clutching his jacket.

"You're all of them." He bit gently at her jaw, making her eyes widen in confused desire. His lips curved at her reaction. She would be a joy in bed. Slowly, almost leisurely, he shifted to nibble her earlobe.

"Don't."

"I've waited for days to have five minutes alone with you and do just this." He dipped his tongue into her ear so that both pleasure and heat rippled through her. "There is nothing more I want than to make love with you, Serena. Every inch of you."

"I can't. You can't."

"You can," he murmured. "We will." He teased her lips apart with his.

For a moment she luxuriated in it, the feel of his lips on hers. The rightness of it. But it couldn't be right. It would never be right. "Please, stop. It's wrong for you to speak that way to me. It's wrong to— I can't think."

"Don't think." Suddenly he gripped her by the shoulders so that they were again face-to-face. "Feel. Just feel. And show me."

Her head was spinning, with longings, with warnings. With a moan, she dragged his mouth to hers. It was wrong. It was madness. But she couldn't resist. When he touched her, she wanted only for him to go on touching her. When he kissed her, she felt she might die from the pleasure of it. To be wanted like this was its own kind of torment. She could feel his desire for her in the way his fingers gripped, in the way his mouth devoured. With each passing second she could feel her will drain until she knew there would come a time when she would give everything to him.

He covered her heart with his hand, aroused to desperation by its pounding. For him. Unable to resist, he traced his fingers over her curves, trailing his lips down her throat, then up again, to find her lips warmed and waiting for his.

"My God, Serena, how I want you." His breath ragged, he pushed her away to stare at her flushed face. "Can you understand?"

"Aye." Her hand was shaking as she lifted it to her throat. "I need time to think."

"We need time to talk." Very carefully he released her, only just realizing how hard his fingers had dug into her arms. He heard the sound of approaching horses and swore. "Every time I'm alone with you I end up kissing you. We won't get any talking done this way. I need you to understand how I feel, and what I want for us."

She thought she did. And to her shame, and her excitement, she knew she was close to agreeing. He wanted her, and she would be his lover. It would be the most precious moment of her life. And then he would offer to make an arrangement. As his mistress, she would be well provided for, well housed, well clothed, well attended. And miserable. If she found the strength to refuse him, she would retain her pride, and she would be even more miserable.

"There's no need to talk. I understand." She rose to brush off her skirts. "I simply need time to think about it."

He took her hand, knowing they had only moments to be alone. "Do you love me?"

She closed her eyes, wishing she could hate him for asking what he must already know. "That isn't the only question to be answered, Brigham."

He dropped her hand and stepped back, his eyes cold again. "We're back to that, are we? I'm English, and no matter what you may feel for me, no matter what we can bring to each other, you won't forget it."

"Can't," she corrected, and wanted to weep. "No, I can't forget who you are, what you are, any more than I can forget who and what I am. I need time to see if I can live with what you want from me."

"Very well." He inclined his head. "You'll have time. But remember this, Serena. I won't beg you."

Chapter Eight

"It's going to be a beautiful ball." Maggie balanced on the rung of a ladder and polished the topmost corner of a mirror. The servants, under Fiona's eagle eye, were turning the house inside out. Family was expected to do no less. "Everything will be perfect, Rena. You'll see. The music, the lights—"

"And Coll," Serena added, rubbing her cloth over the arm of a chair.

"Especially Coll." Smiling, Maggie looked down over her shoulder. "He's already asked me for the first dance."

"That comes as no surprise."

"He was so sweet when he asked," Maggie murmured, peering closer to the mirror to give her face a careful study. She was terrified that the long, sunny rides she had indulged in would bring out freckles that Coll would despise. "I wanted to tell him there was no one else I wanted to dance with at all, but I knew that would make him go red and stutter."

"I don't remember ever hearing Coll stutter until you came to visit."

"I know." Maggie bit her lip in delight. "Isn't it wonderful?"

A sarcastic response faded from her mind when Serena looked up at Maggie's beaming face. "Aye. He's fallen in love with you, and I've no doubt it's the finest thing that has ever happened to him."

"Not just because you're my friend?" Maggie asked anxiously.

"No, because he looks happier whenever you're in the room."

Maggie felt tears sting her eyes, then blinked them away. She didn't want them red and puffy if Coll happened in. She was still floating in the fantasy that her love should see her as nothing less than perfect.

"Remember years ago when we promised each other we'd be sisters one day?"

"Of course. You would marry Coll and I would marry whichever of your cousins I—" With the cloth dangling from her fingers, Serena looked up. "Oh, Maggie, never say Coll has made an offer?"

"Not yet." Maggie tucked a loose curl back in her cap. For a moment she got the stubborn line between her brows her father would have recognized very well. "But he will. Rena, it can't just be wishful thinking. I love him so much."

"Are you certain?" Rising, Serena crossed over to lay a hand on Maggie's skirt. "We were only children when we talked that way. I know you had your heart set on him, but you're not a child anymore, and Coll's a man."

"It *is* different." With a sigh, Maggie rubbed at a spot on the mirror. "When we were children I would think of him as a prince."

"Coll?" Serena couldn't prevent a sisterly snort.

"He was so tall and bonny. I imagined him fighting duels over me, sweeping me up on his horse and carrying me off." Laughing a little, she stepped down a rung. "But now, these past few weeks, being around him has made me see him in a whole new way. He's a steady man, dependable, gentle, even shy in his way. Oh, I know he has a temper and can be reckless, but that's the part that makes him exciting, as well as steady. He's not a prince, Rena, and I love him more than I ever knew I could."

"Has he kissed you?" Serena asked, thinking that Brigham was more like Maggie's childhood vision of Coll. The earl of Ashburn was a man for duels and carrying off.

"No." Maggie pouted for a moment over it, knowing it was wrong to wish he had just once taken command of her. "I think he was about to once, but Malcolm came in." Maggie fluttered her hands. "Do you think it's wrong for me to want him to?"

"No." Serena's answer was flat and honest, but Maggie was dreaming and didn't notice the tone.

"I miss my mother more now than when she died," Maggie mused. "Not being able to talk to her about all of this. To ask her if being with my father ever made her feel as though her heart had turned upside down. Tell me the truth, Serena, do you really think he loves me?"

"I've never seen him act so stupid around anyone else. Stammering, going around dreamy eyed and slack mouthed. Whenever he looks at you he either goes pale or colors up."

"Truly?" Maggie clapped her hands in delight. "Oh, but the man's slow. I'll go mad soon if he doesn't stop looking and take."

"Maggie!" Though her laughter was scandalized, Serena gave her friend a careful study. "You wouldn't, well, agree to more than a kiss?"

"I don't know." Her color was high as she stepped down another rung. "The only thing I'm sure of is, if he doesn't declare himself soon, I'll take matters into my own hands."

Fascinated, Serena tilted her head. "How?"

"I—" Maggie stopped at the sound of approaching footsteps. Her heart fluttered once, making her certain it was Coll even before he swung into the room. On impulse, she let her foot slip off the rung and gasped in alarm as she tumbled the last few feet toward the polished floor.

Serena reached out, but Coll took the distance in a leap and caught Maggie around the waist. He had only a fleeting sensation of how tiny she was before he was swamped with concern.

"There now, lassie, have you hurt yourself?"

"How clumsy of me," she managed over the lump in her throat as she stared up into his wide, rugged face. If Serena had asked her now if she would agree to more than a kiss, her answer would have been yes, a hundred times yes.

"Nonsense." Overwhelmed by tenderness, he held her gently. "A little slip of a girl like you shouldn't be climbing ladders."

Suddenly afraid he might bruise her with his big, clumsy hands, he started to set her down. Drastic desires called for drastic measures, Maggie thought, and she let out a muffled cry as her foot touched the ground. Instantly she was gathered in Coll's arms again. She nearly swooned in earnest when she felt the rapid beat of his heart against hers.

"You have hurt yourself? Shall I call Gwen?"

"Oh, no! If I could just sit for a moment..." She fluttered her lashes and was rewarded when Coll swept her up and carried her to a chair. It took him only six steps, but he had never felt more of a man.

"You're a bit pale, Maggie. A little water should help." He was up and striding out before she could think of an excuse to keep him.

"How badly does it hurt?" Serena had already knelt by her feet. "Oh, Maggie, it would be so unfair if you couldn't dance tomorrow."

"I'll dance. And I'll dance with Coll."

"But if you've sprained your ankle—"

"There's not a thing wrong with my ankle. Don't be silly." To prove it, she sprang up and did a quick, laughing dance step.

"Why, Margaret MacDonald. You lied to him."

"No such thing." She sat again, careful to arrange her skirts in their most flattering folds. "He assumed I'd hurt myself, I never said so. Oh, Rena, how is my hair? It must be a mess."

"You fell on purpose."

"Aye." Maggie's face glowed with triumph. "And it worked."

Disgusted, Serena sat back on her heels. "That's nothing but a trick, and a demeaning one at that."

"It's not a trick, or only a small one, and there's nothing demeaning about it." She touched a hand to her cheek where Coll's beard had tickled her. "It was simply a way to make him feel as though I needed tending. A man doesn't fall in love with a woman who's a packhorse, you know. If it makes him feel good to think of me as a bit helpless and fragile, what's the harm?"

Serena chewed over that one, remembering the time Brigham had raised his sword for her when he'd thought she had been attacked. If she had acted a little more...fragile... With a shake of her head, she told herself that was for Maggie, not for her.

"None, I suppose."

"When a man's shy, he needs a bit of a push. There, he's coming back." She gripped Serena's hands and squeezed. "If you could leave us alone for just a little while."

"I will, but... It almost seems as though he hasn't a chance."

Her smile spread. "I hope not."

"Here now." Coll knelt beside her and offered a cup. "Drink a little."

"Perhaps I'll go fetch Gwen," Serena said as she rose. Neither Maggie nor Coll spared her a glance. "And perhaps I won't," she murmured, and left them alone.

Coll took Maggie's hand in his. It seemed so soft, so tiny. He felt like a bear hulking over a dove. "Are you in much pain, Maggie?"

"No, it's nothing." She looked at him from under her lashes, amazed to find herself as stricken with shyness as he. "You don't need to fuss, Coll."

Looking at her, he was reminded of one of the beautiful porcelain dolls he had seen in Italy. His need to touch her was as great as his fear that he would bruise her. "I was afraid I wouldn't be quick enough to catch you."

"So was I." Daringly, she laid her hand on his. "Do you remember, years ago, I fell in the forest and tore my dress?"

"Aye." He had to swallow. "I laughed at you. You must have hated me."

"No, I could never hate you." Her fingers curled into his. "I must have been a dreadful nuisance." She drew together her courage and looked up. "Am I still?"

"No." His throat was dry as dust. "You're the most beautiful woman in Scotland, and I—" Now his throat was not only dry but seemed to have swollen to twice its size, and his collar threatened to strangle him.

"And you?" Maggie prompted.

"I should find Gwen."

She nearly screamed with frustration. "I don't need Gwen, Coll. Can't you—don't you see?"

He did, the moment he braced himself to look into those dark blue eyes. He was thunderstruck for a moment, then terrified, and then he was lifting her out of the chair and into his arms. "You'll marry me, Maggie?"

"I've waited all my life for you to ask." She tilted her face up for his kiss.

"Coll!" Fiona stepped into the room. Her voice was ripe with warning and disapproval. "Is this how you treat a young female guest in our home?"

"Aye." He laughed and carried Maggie forward. "When she's agreed to be my wife."

"I see." She looked from one to the other. "I won't pretend I'm surprised, but—I think you'd best refrain from carrying Maggie around until after the wedding."

"Mother—"

"Set the lass down."

Stiff with annoyance, he complied. Maggie gripped her hands together, then relaxed when Fiona opened her arms. "Welcome to the family, Maggie. I can only be grateful my son is finally showing good sense."

She still couldn't believe it. As she finished up the morning milking, Serena thought over Maggie's breathless announcement. Coll was getting married.

"What do you think of that?" she asked the placid cow as milk squirted into the pail.

No one was supposed to know yet, of course. Fiona had insisted that Coll approach MacDonald with an offer first, as was proper, but Maggie hadn't been able to hold the news inside. In fact, Serena's eyes were gritty this morning because Maggie hadn't let her sleep until it had been nearly time to rise again.

There was little doubt that when MacDonald arrived later that day with many of the other guests he would agree to the betrothal. Maggie was nearly delirious at the thought of announcing the engagement at the ball that night.

Ready to dance out of her shoes, Serena thought as she squeezed and pulled the last of the milk from the bored cow. Then there was Coll, strutting around like a rooster with two tails. With a shake of her head, Serena set the milking stool aside and lifted her two pails.

Of course she was happy for them. As long as she could remember, Maggie had dreamed of marrying Coll. She would be a good and loving wife to him, calming his more radical impulses, indulging the harmless ones. She would be content to spin, ply her needle and raise a brood of raucous children. And Coll, like their father, would be devoted to his family.

For herself, she had reaffirmed her decision never to marry. She would make a poor wife. It wasn't that she minded the work, or that she wouldn't dearly love to have children of her own, but she hadn't the patience or the biddable nature to sit and wait, to nod and obey.

In any case, how often did anyone find a mate to both love and respect? She supposed she'd been spoiled by being a part of her parents' marriage. Settling for less would make her feel like a failure.

How could she marry anyone, she asked herself as she came out of the cow shed, when she had fallen in love with Brigham? How could she give herself to a man when she would always wonder what it would have been like with another? Knowing she could never be a part of Brigham's life, or he a part of hers, didn't change what was in her heart. Until she could convince herself that the love she had for him was dead, she would remain alone.

It would be harder now, watching Coll and Maggie. Serena balanced herself with the pails as she started down the rise. The sun was struggling to brighten the sky and melt the last of the winter's snow. The path was slick, but manageable for one who had made the trip day after day all her life. She moved without hurry, not for caution's sake but because her mind was elsewhere.

No, she wouldn't begrudge them their happiness because she could never have the same. That would be mean-hearted, and she loved them both too much for that. But she had to wonder at the way Maggie had claimed her heart's desire simply by tumbling off a ladder.

The way Coll had looked at Maggie! As if she were a piece of precious glass that might shatter at a touch, Serena remembered with a quick shake of her head. How would it be to have a man look at you that way? Of course, it wasn't what she wanted, Serena reminded herself. Still, just once it might be nice.

She heard the sound of boots ringing on rock and glanced up to see Brigham striding toward the stables. Without giving herself time to think, she changed directions so that they would pass each other. Offering a silent apology for the spilled milk, Serena let out what she hoped was a convincing gasp of alarm and slid to the ground.

Brigham was beside her instantly, his hands on his hips, his face already darkened by his black mood.

"Have you hurt yourself?"

It was more an accusation than a question. Serena bristled, then forced herself to play the part. She wasn't precisely sure how it was done, but Maggie had used her lashes. "I'm not sure. I may have twisted my ankle."

"What the devil are you doing hauling milk?" Disgusted, he bent down to examine her ankle. The communication that had been brought to him late the previous night was weighing on his mind. But for that, he might have seen the thunder come into her eyes. "Where's Malcolm or that scatter-brained Molly or one of the others?"

"The milking's not Malcolm's job, and Molly and everyone else are busy preparing for the guests." All thoughts of being fragile and feminine were whisked away. "There's no shame in hauling milk, *Lord* Ashburn. Perhaps your dainty English ladies wouldn't know a cow's teat from a bull's—"

"This has nothing to do with my English ladies, as you call them. The paths are slippery and the pails are heavy. So it has to do with you doing more than you're able."

"More than I'm able?" She knocked his hand away from her ankle. "I'm strong enough to do as much as you and more. And I've never in my life slipped on this path."

He sat back on his heels and let his gaze sweep over her. "Sturdy as a mule, aren't you, Rena?"

That was it. A woman could take only so much. Serena sprang up and emptied the contents of one bucket over his head. It was done before either of them could prevent it. She stood, swinging an empty bucket, while he swallowed a mouthful of very fresh milk.

"There's a warm milk bath for your soft English skin, *my lord.*"

She grabbed the other bucket, but before she could toss it in his face, his hands closed over hers on the handles. His grip was very firm, very steady, but there was smoke from a volatile fire in his eyes.

"I should thrash you for that."

She tossed her head back and watched with growing satisfaction as milk dripped down his cheeks. "You can try, *Sassenach.*"

"Serena!"

The challenging gleam in her eyes turned to one of distress when she heard her father call her name. She braced herself as she waited for him to rush the last few feet toward her.

"Father." There was nothing to do but hang her head before his glowering eyes and wait for the worst.

"Have you lost your mind?"

She sighed. Because she was looking at the ground, she didn't notice that Brigham shifted just enough to put himself between Serena and her father's wrath. "My temper, Father."

"There was a slight accident, Ian," Brigham began. Taking out his handkerchief, he wiped milk from his face. "Serena lost her footing while she was carrying the milk."

"It wasn't an accident." It would not have occurred to Serena to claim it as one and save herself. "I poured the pail of milk on Lord Ashburn deliberately."

"I had eyes to see that for myself." Ian planted his feet. At that moment, with the sun rising behind his back, his plaid tossed over one shoulder and his face hard as granite, he looked fierce and invincible. "I'll apologize for the miserable behavior of this brat, Brigham, and promise you she'll be dealt with. Into the house, girl."

"Yes, Father."

"Please." Brigham put a hand on her shoulder before Serena could make her humiliated retreat. "I can't in good conscience allow Serena to take the full blame. I provoked her, also deliberately. I called you a mule, I believe, did I not, Serena?"

Her eyes kindled as she lifted her head. She was careful to lower it again quickly lest her father see she was unrepentant. "Aye."

"I thought that was it." Brigham wrung out his sodden handkerchief. What

Parkins would say to this, Brigham couldn't even surmise. "The incident was as unfortunate as the insult, and as regrettable. Ian, I would take it as a favor if you would let the matter drop."

Ian said nothing for a moment, then made an impatient gesture toward Serena. "Take what's left of that milk into the house and be quick about it."

"Yes, Father." She sent a quick look at Brigham that was a mixture of gratitude and frustration, then ran, milk slopping at the lip of the pail.

"She deserved a whipping for that," Ian commented, though he knew he would laugh later at the memory of his little girl dumping milk all over the young English buck.

"That was my first thought." Brigham glanced idly at the ruined sleeve of his coat. "Unfortunately, on further consideration, I'm forced to admit I quite deserved it. Your daughter and I seem unable to maintain a polite demeanor with each other."

"So I see."

"She is stubborn, sharp-tongued, and has a temper that flares faster than a torch."

Ian rubbed a hand over his beard to hide a smile. "She's a curse to me, Brigham."

"To any man," Brigham murmured. "She makes me wonder if she was put here to complicate my life, or to brighten it."

"What do you intend to do about it?"

It was only then Brigham realized he had spoken his last thoughts aloud. He glanced back to see Serena disappear into the kitchen. "I intend to marry her, with your permission."

Ian let out a long breath. "And without it?"

Brigham gave him a level look. "I shall marry her anyway."

It was the answer Ian wanted, but still he hedged. He would know his daughter's mind first. "I'll think on it, Brigham. When do you leave for London?"

"The end of the week." His mind returned to the letter and his duty. "Lord George Murray believes my presence will help gain more support from the English Jacobites."

"You'll have my answer when you return. I won't deny that you're a man I would be content to give my daughter to, but she must be willing. And that, lad, I can't promise you."

A shadow came over Brigham's eyes as he dug his hands into his pockets. "Because I'm English."

Ian saw that this ground had been crossed before. "Aye. Some wounds run deep." Because he had a generous heart, he clapped a hand on Brigham's damp shoulder. "Called her a mule, did you?"

"I did." Brigham flicked his sodden lace. "And should have moved more quickly."

With a rumbling laugh, Ian gave Brigham's shoulder another slap. "If you've a mind to marry her, you'd best be a fast learner."

She wished she were dead. She wished Brigham were dead. She wished fervently that he had never been born. Setting her teeth, Serena scowled at her reflection as Maggie fussed with the curling irons.

"Your hair is so thick and soft. You'll never have to sleep in. papers all night."

"As if I would," Serena mumbled. "I don't see why any woman goes to so much fuss and bother just for a man."

Maggie smiled the wise smile of a woman in love and engaged. "What other reason is there?"

"I wish I could wear mine up." Gwen scooted around to the mirror to study her own hair. "You did make it look so pretty, Maggie," she said, afraid of seeming ungrateful. "But Mother said I couldn't pin it up until next year."

"It looks like sunbeams," Serena told her, then went immediately back to frowning.

"Yours looks more like candlelight." Gwen sighed and tried a few dance steps. This would be her first ball, and her first gown. She could hardly wait to put it on and feel grown-up. "Do you think anyone will ask me to dance?"

"Everyone will." Maggie tested the iron.

"Perhaps someone will try to kiss me."

"If they do," Serena said grimly, "you're to tell me. I'll deal with them."

"You sound like Mother." With a light laugh, Gwen twirled in her petticoats. "It's not as though I would let anyone kiss me, but it would be so nice to have someone try."

"Keep talking like that, my lass, and Father will lock you up for another year."

"She's just excited." Expertly Maggie threaded a green riband edged in gold through Serena's hair. "So am I. It feels like my very first ball. There." She patted Serena's hair before she stepped back to study her handiwork. "You look beautiful. Or would, if you'd smile."

In answer, Serena bared her teeth in a grimace.

"That should send the men scurrying to the hills," Maggie commented.

"Let them run." Serena almost smiled at the thought. "I'd as soon see the back of them."

"Brigham won't run away," Gwen said wisely, earning a glare from her sister.

"It's of no concern to me what Lord Ashburn does." Serena flounced away to snatch her gown from the bed. Behind her back, Gwen and Maggie exchanged delighted grins.

"Well, he is rather stuffy, isn't he?" Maggie put her tongue in her cheek, then moved over to check her own gown for creases. "Handsome, certainly, if one likes dark, brooding looks and cool eyes."

"He isn't stuffy at all." Serena turned on her. "He's—" She caught herself, warned by Gwen's giggle. "Rude is what he is. Rude and annoying, and English."

Dutifully Gwen began hooking Maggie's gown. "He was kissing Rena in the kitchen."

Maggie's eyes went as round as saucers. *"What?"*

"Gwen!"

"Oh, it's just Maggie," Gwen said with a move of her bare shoulder. "We always tell her everything. He was kissing her right in the kitchen," Gwen continued, turning dreamy circles as she remembered it. "It was so romantic. He looked as though he might swallow her right up, like a sugarplum.''

"That's enough." Hot and flushed, Serena struggled to step into her gown. "It wasn't romantic at all, it was infuriating and, and—'' She wanted to say unpleasant, but couldn't get her tongue around the lie. "I wish he would go to the devil.''

Maggie lifted a brow. "If you wished him to the devil, why didn't you tell me he had kissed you?''

"Because I'd forgotten all about it.''

Gwen started to speak, but was hushed by a quick gesture from Maggie. "Well, I daresay there wasn't anything special about it, then.'' Calmly she began to hook Serena's gown. "My cousin Jamie is coming tonight, Rena. Perhaps you'll find him more to your taste.''

Serena only groaned.

By the time Brigham escaped from Parkins's perfecting hands, he was frazzled and impatient. With the rumors and the unrest in both Scotland and England he felt little like partnering a bunch of simpering girls and plump matrons at a country ball. His summons back to London weighed on him. The support the Prince expected from his English followers wasn't as immediately forthcoming as he had hoped. There was a chance that adding his own voice would sway those who were straddling the political fence, but it would be a dangerous mission.

He had no way of knowing how long he would be gone, how successful he might be or, if he were found out, what would be the fate of his lands and title.

There would be dozens of Highland chiefs under the same roof that night. Loyalties would be tested, oaths would be sworn. What he learned here he would take with him to London in hopes of stirring fighting blood among those English loyal to the Stuarts. It was a war that still dealt more in talk than in the sword. Like Coll, he was growing weary of it.

As he descended the steps toward the ballroom, he was the picture of the fashionable aristocrat. His lace was snowy, foaming from his throat, falling over his wrists. His buckles gleamed, as did the emerald on his finger. A matching one winked out of the lace at his throat. His black waistcoat was threaded with silver, topped by a silver-buttoned coat that fitted without a wrinkle over his shoulders.

At a glance, it would have appeared that he was a young, wealthy man, used to the finer things and unhampered by any care. But his thoughts were as bright and as dangerous as his dress sword.

"Lord Ashburn." Fiona curtsied as he entered. Since that morning she had been fretting over what her husband had told her of Brigham's feelings for her oldest daughter. More than Ian could, she understood the warring emotions Serena must be experiencing.

"Lady MacGregor. You look stunning.''

She smiled, noting that his gaze was already sweeping the room. And she thought as she softened that the love in it was unmistakable. "Thank you, my lord. I hope you will enjoy the evening.''

"I shall, if you promise me a dance.''

"It would be a pleasure. But all the young ladies will be angry if I monopolize your time. Please, let me introduce you."

She laid her hand on his arm and led him into the room. It was already scattered with people, dressed in their best. Satin gowns glimmered and silk shimmered in the light of the hundreds of candles that floated in the chandeliers overhead or rose from high stands. Jewels gleamed and winked. Men were wrapped in dress kilts, plaids of bright reds and greens and blues contrasting with doublets of calfskin. Buckled brogues and silver buttons caught the light, vying for brilliance with the shine of women's jewels.

For the ladies' part, it was apparent that in the Highlands French fashions were watched closely. The more opulent styles were preferred, with an abundance of tinsel and silver lace in evidence. Hoops swished and swayed like bells. Heavy brocades in vivid shades were worn by both men and women, with thick gold ornamentation worked into dress coats and huge cuffs that covered the elbows. Stockings were white or clocked and worn with dressy garters.

Glenroe might have been remote, with the nearest shop half a day's ride away, but the Scot's love of fashion was no less than that of the Frenchman or the Englishman.

Brigham was introduced to the pretty and the plain by his hostess. When the music began, he would do his duty. For now, he curbed his impatience as he continued to scan the room for the one face he wanted to see. Willing or not, he was determined to lead her out in the first dance, and for as many others as he could manage.

"The little MacIntosh lass has the grace of a bullock," Coll confided in his ear. "If you find yourself shackled with her, best to offer to fetch her a drink and sit out the dance."

"I appreciate the warning." Brigham turned to examine his friend. "You look quite self-satisfied. Shall I take it that your interview with MacDonald went as you wished?"

Coll's chest puffed out. "You may take it that Maggie and I will be wed by May Day."

"My felicitations," Brigham said with a bow. Then he grinned. "I shall have to find someone else to drink under the table."

Coll snorted and fought off a blush. "Not likely. I wish I could ride with you to London."

"Your place is here now. I'll be back in a matter of weeks."

"With cheering news. We'll continue to work here, but not tonight. Tonight's for celebrating." He clapped a hand on Brigham's shoulder. "There's my Maggie now. If you want a turn with someone light on her feet, ask Serena to stand up with you. A foul temper she might have, but the lass can dance."

Brigham could only nod as Coll strode away to claim his betrothed. Beside the demure Maggie MacDonald, Serena stood like a flame, her hair dressed high, the rich green silk of the dress trimmed in gold and cut square at the neck to reveal the smooth swell of her breasts. There were pearls around her throat, gleaming dully, no whiter, no creamier, than her skin. Her skirts flared out, making her slender waist seem impossibly small.

Other women were dressed more opulently, some with their hair powdered, others with jewels glistening. They might have been hags dressed in burlap.

Serena looked up at Coll and laughed. Brigham felt as though he'd taken a stroke of the broadsword across his knees.

As the strains of the first dance began, several young ladies cast a hopeful look in his direction. Brigham found his feet and moved across the room to Serena.

"Miss MacGregor." He made her an elegant bow. "Might I have the honor of this dance?"

She had made up her mind to refuse him, should he ask. Now she found herself wordlessly offering her hand. The strains of a minuet floated through the room. Skirts rustled as ladies were led to their places by their partners. Suddenly she was certain she would never remember even the most basic steps. Then he smiled at her and bowed again.

It seemed her feet never touched the floor, and her eyes refused to leave his. She had dreamed of this once, standing in the chill air of the forest. There had been lights there, too, and music. But it hadn't been like this. This was like floating, like feeling beautiful, like believing in dreams.

His hand held hers lightly, fingertips to fingertips. It made her feel weak, as though she were caught up in his arms. They stepped together sedately, moved apart. Her heart thundered as though they were wrapped together, tumbling into an intimate embrace. His lips curved as she sank into her final curtsy. Hers warmed as if they had been kissed.

"Thank you." He didn't release her hand, as they both knew was proper, but brought her fingers to his lips. "I've wanted that dance since I found you alone by the river. Now, when I think of it, the only difficulty will be deciding whether you look more lovely in your green gown or in your breeches."

"It's Mother's. The gown—" she said quickly, and cursed herself for stammering. When he led her off the floor, she felt like a queen. "I want to apologize for this morning."

"No, you don't." Boldly he kissed her hand again. More than one murmur arose because of it. "You only think you should."

"Aye." She shot him a quick, amused look. "It's the least I can do after you saved me from the threat of a beating."

"Only the threat?"

"Father only has the heart to threaten. He's never taken a strap to me in my life, which is probably why I'm unmanageable."

"Tonight, my dear, you're only beautiful."

She flushed and lowered her eyes. "I don't know what to say when you speak like that."

"Good, Rena—"

"Miss MacGregor." Both Brigham and Serena looked impatiently at the intruder, a young son of one of the neighboring Highland lairds. "Would you honor me with this dance?"

She would have preferred honoring him with a kick in the shins, but she knew her duty too well. She laid a hand on his arm, wondering how soon it would be proper to dance with Brigham again.

The music played on—reels, country dances, elegant minuets. Serena danced with elderly gentlemen, sons, cousins, the portly and the dashing. Her love of dancing and her skill kept her in constant demand. She had one other set with Brigham, then was forced to watch him lead out one after another of the pretty guests.

He couldn't keep his eyes off her. Damn it, it wasn't like him to resent watching a woman dance with another man. Did she have to smile at them? No, by God, she didn't. And she had no business flirting with that skinny young Scot in the ugly coat. He fingered the hilt of his dress sword and fought back temptation.

What had her mother been thinking of to allow her to wear a dress that made her look so...delectable? Couldn't her father see that that young rake was all but drooling on his daughter's neck? Her bare neck. Her soft, white, naked skin, just at the point where the fragile line of her collarbone swelled into her breast.

He swore under his breath and earned a wide-eyed stare from Gwen. "I beg your pardon, Brig?"

"What?" He dragged his eyes away from Serena long enough to focus on her sister. He had no notion that his stormy looks had prevented half a dozen young swains from approaching Gwen for a dance. "Nothing, Gwen. It was nothing." He drew a deep breath and struggled for a casual tone. "Are you enjoying yourself?"

"Very much." She smiled up at him and secretly wished he would ask her to dance again. "I suppose you go to many balls and parties."

"In London, in the season, you can barely turn around without one."

"I would love to see London and Paris."

She looked very young at that moment, and he was reminded of how devotedly she had nursed her brother back to health. Some man, one day, he thought, and delighted her by kissing her fingers. "You, my dear, would be all the rage."

She was young enough to giggle without simpering. "Do you think so, really?"

"Without a doubt." Offering his arm, he led her onto the floor again and told her as many stories as he could recall about balls and assemblies and routs. Even as he spoke, his eyes were locked on Serena as she danced with her skinny partner. When the dance was over, Gwen had enough to dream on for years. Brigham had worked himself into a fine, shining, jealous rage.

He led her off the floor, watching as Serena was led in a different direction by her partner. One who was wearing, in Brigham's opinion, a particularly hideous yellow brocade. While the coat might have offended him, the possessive manner in which the man clutched Serena's hand did a great deal more.

"Who is that Serena's talking with?"

Gwen followed the direction Brigham was scowling into. "Oh, that's only Rob, one of Serena's suitors."

"Suitors?" He said between his teeth. "Suitors, is it?" Before Gwen could elaborate, he was striding across the room. "Miss MacGregor, a word with you?"

Her brow lifted at his tone. "Lord Ashburn, may I present Rob MacGregor, my kinsman."

"Your servant," he said stiffly. Then, taking Serena's elbow, he dragged her off toward the first convenient alcove.

"What do you think you're doing? Have you lost your senses? You'll have everyone staring."

"To hell with them." He stared down at her mutinous face. "Why was that popinjay holding your hand?"

Though she privately agreed that Rob MacGregor was a popinjay at his best, she refused to accept any slur on a kinsman. "Rob MacGregor happens to be a fine man of good family."

"The devil take his family." He had barely enough control left to keep his voice low. "Why was he holding your hand?"

"Because he wanted to."

"Give it to me."

"I will not."

"I said give it to me." He snatched it up. "He's no right to it, do you understand?"

"No. I understand that I'm free to give my hand to whomever I choose."

The cool light of battle came into his eyes. He preferred it, much preferred it, to the grinding heat of jealousy. "If you want your fine young man of good family to live, I wouldn't choose him again."

"Is that so?" She tugged at her hand and got nowhere. "Let me go this instant."

"So you can return to him?"

She wondered for a moment if Brigham was drunk, but decided against it. His eyes were too sharp and clear. "If I choose."

"If you choose, I promise you you will regret it. This dance is mine."

Moments before, she had longed to dance with him. Now she held her ground, equally determined not to. "I don't want to dance with you."

"What you want and what you'll do may be different matters, my dear."

"I will remind you, Lord Ashburn, only my father can command me."

"That will change." His fingers tightened on hers. "When I return from London—"

"You're going to London?" Her anger was immediately eclipsed by distress. "When? Why?"

"In two days. I have business there."

"I see." Her hand went limp in his. "Perhaps you had planned to tell me when you saddled your horse."

"I only just received word that I was needed." His eyes lost their fire, his voice its roughness. "Would you care that I go?"

"No." She turned her head away, to stare toward the music. "Why should I?"

"But you do." With his free hand he touched her cheek.

"Go or stay," she said in a desperate whisper. "It matters nothing to me."

"I go on behalf of the Prince."

"Then Godspeed," she managed.

"Rena, I will come back."

"Will you, my lord?" She pulled her hand away from his. "I wonder." Before he could stop her, she rushed back into the ballroom and threw herself into the dancing.

Chapter Nine

Perhaps she had been more unhappy in her life. But she couldn't remember when tears had seemed so miserably and inescapably close. Perhaps she had been angrier. But she could think of no time in her life when fury had raged quite so high or burned so hot.

And the fury and misery were all with herself, Serena thought as she kicked the mare into a gallop. With herself, for dreaming, even for a moment, that there could be something real, something lovely, between herself and Brigham.

He was going back to London. Aye, and London was where he belonged. In London he was a man of wealth and means and lineage. He was a man with parties to attend, ladies to call on. A line to continue. Swearing, she pushed the horse harder.

He might stand behind the Prince. She was coming to believe he was dedicated to the cause and would fight for it. But he would fight in England, for England. Why should he not? Why should a man like the earl of Ashburn waste a thought on her once he was back in his own world?

Just as she would waste no thought on him, she promised herself, once he was gone.

She knew he had met with her father and many of the other chiefs early that morning. Oh, women weren't supposed to know or bother themselves with plans of war and rebellions, but they knew. France would move on England, and when she did, Charles hoped to sway the French king to his cause.

The previous winter, Louis had planned to invade England with Charles in attendance as his father's representative. If the fleet had not been wrecked in a storm and the invasion abandoned... Well, that was another matter. It was clear that Louis had supported Charles because he wanted a monarch on the English throne who would be dependent on France. Just as it was clear Charles would use France or any means to gain his rightful place. But the invasion had been abandoned, and the French king was now biding his time.

Just because a body had to busy herself with sewing and cleaning didn't mean she had no head for politics.

So Brigham would go to London and beat the drum for the young Prince. It had become more important than ever to rally the Jacobites for the Stuarts, English and Scottish. The time for rebellion was ripe. Charles was not his father, and would not be content, as James had been, to while away his youth in foreign courts.

When the time came, Brigham would fight. But come back to the Highlands? Come back to her? No, she couldn't see it. A man didn't leave his home and country for a mistress. Desire her he might, but she already knew a man's desire was easily fanned, and easily cooled.

For her it was love. Her first. Her only. Without ever having taken her innocence, he had ruined her. There would never be another man for her. The only one she wanted was preparing even now to ride out of her life.

If he stayed, what difference would it make? she asked herself. There would always be too much between them. Had he loved her... No, even that would have changed nothing. Her beloved books had shown her time and time again that love did not necessarily conquer all. Romeo and Juliet. Tristan and Isolde, Lancelot and Guinevere. Serena MacGregor was no weak-moraled Guinevere, nor was she a starry-eyed Juliet. She was a Scot, hot-blooded perhaps, but tough-minded. She knew the difference between fantasy and fact. There was one fact that could not be ignored, now or ever.

Brigham would always be tied to England, and she to Scotland.

So it was best that he was going. She wished him well. She wished him to the devil.

"Serena?"

She whipped her head around to see Brigham racing up behind her. It was then she realized there were tears in her eyes. The shame of them, the need to keep them hers alone, had her wheeling back to drive her mount yet faster. Cursing the cumbersome sidesaddle, she made for the lake in a mad dash she hoped would leave Brigham behind. She planned to pass the water and ride up into the hills, into the rougher land where he would never be able to track her. Then she was swearing at him as he thundered to her side and snatched the reins from her hands.

"Hold up, woman. What devil's in you?"

"Leave me be." She kicked her horse, nearly unseating Brigham as he struggled to hold both mounts. "Oh, damn you to hell. I hate you."

"Well you may after I take a whip to you," he said grimly. "Are you trying to kill both of us?"

"Just you." She sniffled, and despised herself for it.

"Why are you crying?" He drew her mount in closer to his as he studied her face. "Has someone hurt you?"

"No." Her hysterical laugh shocked her enough to make her swallow another. "No," she repeated. "I'm not crying. It's the wind in my eyes. Go away. I rode here to be alone."

"Then you'll have to be disappointed." She was crying, however much she denied it. He wanted to gather her close and comfort her, but he knew her well enough by now to know her response would be to sink her teeth into his hand. Instead, realizing it might be just as foolish, he tried reason. "I leave at first light tomorrow, Serena. There are things I wish to say to you first."

"Say them, then." She began searching her pockets for a handkerchief. "And go away to London, or to hell for all I care."

After casting his eyes to the heavens, Brigham offered her his handkerchief. "I would prefer dismounting."

She snatched the cloth to dry the hated tears. "Do what you want. It doesn't matter to me." She blew her nose heartily.

He did, taking care to keep her reins in his hand. After he had secured the horses, he reached up to help her down.

After a last defiant sniff, she stuffed the handkerchief into her pocket. "I don't want your help."

"You'll have more than that before I'm done with you." So saying, he plucked her with more speed than style from the saddle. He'd finished with reason. "Sit."

"I will not."

"Sit," he repeated, in a tone dangerous enough to have her chin jerking up. "Or, before God, you will wish you had."

"Very well." Because his eyes warned her it was no idle threat, she chose a rock, deliberately taking her time, smoothing her skirts, folding her hands primly in her lap. Perversely, now that he was growling she was determined to be proper. "You wished to converse with me, my lord?"

"I wish to throttle you, my lady, but I trust I have enough control left to resist."

She gave a mock shudder. "How terrifying. May I say, Lord Ashburn, that your visit to my home has broadened my perception of English manners."

"I've had enough of that." He moved so quickly she had only time to stare. Grasping the front of her riding jacket, he dragged her to her feet. "I am English, and not ashamed of it. The Langstons are an old and respected family." The way he held her, she was forced to stand on tiptoe, eye-to-eye with him. And his eyes were dark as onyx, with a heated fury in them only a few had seen and lived. "There is nothing in my lineage to make me blush, and much to make me proud to bear the name. I've had my fill of your slurs and insults, do you understand?"

"Aye." She thought she had understood what it was to be truly frightened. Until this moment, she hadn't known at all. Still, frightened didn't mean cowed. "It's not your family I mean to insult, my lord."

"Only me, then? Or perhaps the whole of England? Damn it, Rena, I know what your clan has suffered. I know that even now your name is so proscribed that many of you are forced to take others. It's a cruelty that's already gone on too long. But it wasn't I who brought the persecution, nor was it all of England. Insult me if you will, scratch or bite, but I'm damned if I'll take either for something that wasn't of my doing."

"Please," she said very quietly. "You're hurting me."

He let her go and curled his hands into fists at his sides. It was rare, very rare, for him to come that close to losing control of both thoughts and actions. As a result, his voice was ice.

"My apologies."

"No." She reached out tentatively, to touch his arm. "I apologize. You're right, it is wrong of me to lash out at you for many things that were done before either of us were born." She was no longer afraid, she realized, but shamed, deeply shamed. She would have done more than shout if anyone had slashed so at her family. "It's wrong to blame you because English dragoons raped my mother. Or because they put my father in prison for over a year so that even that dishonor went unavenged. And it's wrong," she continued after a long, cleansing breath, "to want to blame you because I'm afraid not to."

"Why, Rena? Why are you afraid?"

She started to shake her head and turn away, but he took her arms to hold her still. His grip wasn't fierce this time, but it was just as unbreakable.

"I hope you will forgive me, my lord. And now I would prefer to be alone."

"I shall have your answer, Serena." His voice was nearly calm again, but there was a thread of hot steel through it. "Why are you afraid?"

Raising her head, she sent him a damp, desperate look. "Because if I don't blame you I might forget who you are, what you are."

"Does it have to matter?" he demanded, shaking her a little.

"Aye." She discovered she was frightened again, but in a wholly different way. Something in his eyes told her that no matter what she said, no matter what she did, her fate was already sealed. "Aye, it has to. For both of us."

"Does it matter?" He dragged her against him. "Does it matter when we're like this?" Before she could answer, he closed his mouth over hers.

She didn't fight him. The moment his lips covered hers she knew she was through fighting him, and herself. If he was to be her first, her only, she needed to take whatever could be given. Now his mouth was hot and desperate on hers, his body taut as wire and straining against hers. Part was still temper, yes, she knew it. But there was more. It was the more she was ready to answer. If she had ever had a choice, she made it now, and caution flew to the winds.

"Does it matter?" he said again as he rained kisses over her face.

"No, no, it doesn't matter now, not today." She threw her arms around him and clung. "Oh, Brig, I don't want you to go. I don't want you to leave me."

With his face buried in her hair, he memorized her scent. "I'll come back. Three weeks, four at the most, I'll come back." When he received no response, he drew her away. Her eyes were dry now but solemn. "I will be back, Serena. Can't you trust even that?"

"I trust you more than I thought I would ever trust any man." She smiled a little and lifted a hand to his face. Oh, God, if this was love, why should it hurt so? Why couldn't it bring her the joy she saw in Maggie's eyes? "No, I don't trust you'll come back to me. But we'll not speak of that." She moved her hand to cover his lips when he would have spoken. "We'll not think of it. Only of today."

"Then we'll talk of other things."

"No." She kissed both of his hands, then stepped back. "We won't talk at all." Slowly she began to unfasten the buttons of her riding habit.

"What are you doing?"

He reached out to stop her, but she slipped the snug jacket from her shoulders, revealing a simple chemise and small, high breasts. "Taking what both of us want."

"Rena." He managed her name, though the pulse beating at his throat made the word low and rough. "Not like this. This isn't right for you."

"How could it be more right?" But her fingers trembled slightly as she unhooked her skirt. "Here, with you."

"There are things that need to be said," he began.

"I want you," she murmured, halting his words and his thoughts. "I want you to touch me the way you touched me before. I want—I want you to touch me the way you've made me dream of." She stepped closer. "Do you not want me any longer?"

"Not want you?" He closed his eyes and dragged an unsteady hand through his hair. "There is no one and nothing I've ever wanted more than I want you at this moment. God help me, there may never be again."

"Then take me here." She reached for her laces, watching in a kind of dazed wonder as his gaze dipped down. "And give me something of yourself before you leave me." Taking his hand, she pressed her lips to his palm. "Show me what it is to be loved, Brigham."

"Rena—"

"You're leaving tomorrow," she said, suddenly desperate. "Will you leave me with nothing, then?"

He let his fingers trail along her cheek. "I would not leave at all if the choice were mine."

"But you will go. I want to belong to you before you do."

Her shoulders were cool to his touch. "Are you certain?"

"Aye." With a smile, she laid his hand on her heart. "Feel how fast it beats? Always when I'm close to you."

"You're cold," he said unsteadily, and pulled her closer.

"There's a plaid on the mare." With her eyes closed, she drew in his scent. As he had with her hair, she committed it to memory. "If we spread it in the sun we'll be warm enough."

"I won't hurt you." He lifted her face, and she saw that the intensity was back in his eyes. "I swear it."

She trusted him for that, trusted him to be gentle. It was in his eyes as they spread the plaid on the bank of the lake and knelt upon it. It was in his lips as he lowered them to her bare white shoulder. It was in his hands as they clasped hers, communicating care as much as need.

She knew what she was about to do, what she was about to give him— the innocence a woman could give to only one man, and only once in her life. As they knelt face-to-face with the sun warm overhead and the waters cool beside them, she knew she hadn't offered the gift on impulse or in the madness of passion, but almost quietly, with a confidence that it would be accepted with tenderness. And remembered.

She had never looked more beautiful, he thought. Her eyes were brilliant, steady. Her hands didn't tremble as they locked with his, but he thought he could almost feel the nervous beating of her heart through his fingertips. Her cheeks were pale, as smooth and white as porcelain.

He thought of the shepherdess, of how he had wanted to touch it as a child but had been afraid, lest his hands grow clumsy. He brought her hands to his lips. He would not be clumsy with Serena.

He kissed her and filled himself with the flavor alone. Though their time together now would be short, he treated the moment as if it could last for hours. With slow, tortuous nibbles he had her breath quickening. His tongue moistened and traced, then lured hers into a lazy duel that made her heart swell and thunder in her breast. Tentatively at first, she ran her hands along his coat, as if making certain his body was warm and real beneath. Murmuring something against her mouth, he began to shrug out of it. Her own shyness surprised her. She fought it back as she helped him strip it off, and as she fumbled with the buttons of his waistcoat.

He found it almost unbearably arousing to have her inexperienced hands undress him. With his eyes closed he traced kisses over her brow, her temples, her jaw, while his body tensed and hardened from the hesitant movements of her fingers. It was torture of the most exquisite kind. He realized that he was moving slowly not only for Serena and her innocence but for himself. Every instant, every heartbeat they shared here would be remembered.

She tugged off his shirt, her gaze skimming down over his bare flesh as delicately as her fingertips did. Slowly, almost afraid her hand might pass through him, she reached out to touch.

They were still kneeling, their bodies swaying closer, their breath mingling as mouth was drawn to mouth. Her mind began to whirl as she stroked her hands over him. His skin was smooth, while the muscles beneath were hard. She felt awe, as well as excitement, wonder, as well as nerves. Who would have thought a man could feel beautiful?

The sun warmed his skin as it poured over the little patch of ground they had chosen. Birds trilled in the wood beyond. On the far side of the lake, deer came quietly to drink.

As he nuzzled her neck, she felt herself go weak. She thought she knew what was to follow, but the pleasure was more than she had ever dreamed it could be.

His hands were very sure as they cupped her breasts, dragging a moan out of her as the rough material shifted and rubbed over her skin. In submission, in acceptance, in demand, her back arched and her head fell back, leaving him free to plunder. She felt his mouth cover her, nipping and sucking through the material. The tingling started deep within her stomach and spread until her body seemed alive with nerves. Then what had gone before vanished from her mind as he peeled the chemise aside and found her flesh.

She cried out in surprise and pleasure, her hands reaching for his shoulders and gripping for balance. Yet she felt as though she were falling still.

She shuddered against him, strained against him, confused, delighted, desperate for more. What she had offered, she had offered of her own free will. What she gave now, she gave without thought, without reason. When she tumbled back on the blanket, she was stripped of defenses and open to whatever commands he might give.

He had to fight back the first sharp-edged need to take. It was like a knife turning slowly in his gut. Her arms were wrapped around him, her breasts, small and white, shivering at each touch. He saw that her eyes were clouded, not with fear, no longer with confusion, but with newly awakened passions. If he were to take her now, as his body begged to, she would open for him.

But the need in his heart beat as strong as the need in his loins. He would give her more than she had asked, perhaps more than either of them could understand.

"I've dreamed of this, Serena." His voice was low as he bent his head for the next kiss. "I've dreamed of undressing you like this." He slipped the chemise from her. Now only the breeze and Brigham caressed her. "Of touching what no man has touched." He skimmed a fingertip up her thigh and watched her mouth tremble open in speechless pleasure.

"Brigham. I want you."

"And you shall have me, my love." He circled the rigid point of her breast with his tongue, then drew it slowly, almost painfully, into his mouth. "Before you do, there is much, much more."

If she could have spoken again, she would have said it was impossible. Her body seemed sated already, sensation rolling over sensation, shudder wracked by shudder. Then he began.

The eyes that had begun to close flew open in stunned awakening. Her hips arched up, meeting his questing lips just before the first flood of terrifying pleasure poured through her. Gasping, she groped for him, only to find her damp palms sliding off his skin as he moved over her, lighting fires where he willed.

The roaring in her ears prevented her from hearing herself call his name again and again. But he heard. Nothing he had heard before or would hear again would ever sound quite so sweet. She moved under him, bucking, twisting, trembling as he found and exploited new secrets. The dark taste of passion filled his mouth, driving him to find more, to give more.

Her skin was hot and damp wherever he touched, making him mad with thoughts of how she would be when he filled her. Could she know how weak she made him, how completely she satisfied him? His mind teemed with thoughts of her, memories he knew would follow him until he died. Each time he took a breath he drew in the scent of her skin, sheened now with her passion and his. No other woman would ever tempt him again, because no other woman would be Serena.

She wanted to beg him to stop. She wanted to beg him never to stop. Each breath she dragged into her lungs seemed to clog there until she feared she would die from lack of air or the surplus of it. Her eyes filled with tears, not from sorrow or regret but from the ache of a beauty so great she knew she could never describe it. Her strength ebbed and flowed, rushing into her like wildfire, then pouring out like a waterfall. But weak or strong, she had never known pleasure so huge. In some corner of her brain she wanted to know if he felt the same. But each time she began to ask, he would touch her again and send her thoughts spinning into a void of sensation.

When his lips came back to hers, she tasted desperation on them. Wanting to soothe, she answered with her heart, pulling him close.

He slipped into her, fighting with every fiber of his being to take her gently, struggling against every urge to plunge in to his own satisfaction. Sweat pooled at the base of his spine. The muscles in his arms quivered as he braced over her and watched, as he had dreamed of watching, her face as he made her his.

She cried out, but not in pain. Perhaps there was pain, but it was so smothered in pleasure that she couldn't feel it. Only him. She could feel only him as he moved into her, became part of her. With her eyes open and focused on his, she matched his rhythm. Slow...beautifully, gloriously slow. The moment when they joined would be savored, like the finest of old wines, the purest of promises.

He bent to take her lips again and swallowed her sigh. He could feel her pulse around him as clearly as he could feel her hands stroke down his back. When he thrust deep inside her, she arched and the sigh became a moan. Now it was she who changed the rhythm and he who followed. It no longer mattered who was rider, who was ridden, as they raced together. His last thought as his pleasure burst into her was that he had found home.

She wasn't certain she would ever move again, or that she would ever wish to. Her skin was cooling now that the heat of passion had faded into a softer glow of contentment. They lay tangled in the blanket, with the shadows growing long around them. His face was buried in her hair, his hand cupped loosely at her breast.

How much time had passed she couldn't be sure. She knew the sun was no longer high overhead, but there was a timelessness she needed to cling to for just a little longer.

It was almost possible, if she kept her eyes closed and refused to think, to believe it would always be like this. With the afternoon shimmering around them, the woods quiet but for the call of birds, it was difficult to believe that politics and war could pull them apart.

She loved as she had never thought to love, in a way she hadn't known was possible. If only it could all be as simple as a blanket spread beside the water.

"I love you, Rena."

She opened her eyes to see that he was watching her. "Aye. I know you do. And I love you." She traced her fingers along his face as if to memorize it. "I wish we could stay like this."

"We'll be like this again. Soon."

She shifted away from him to reach for her chemise.

"Can you doubt that? Now?"

It was more important than ever to keep her voice steady. She loved him too much, much too much, to beg him to stay. She began to lace up her bodice. "I know that you love me, and that you wish it could be so. I know that what we shared here will never be shared with anyone else."

"You don't think I'll come back." He dragged his shirt on and wondered how any one woman could pull so many emotions from his heart.

She touched his hand. She had no regrets, and she needed him to understand that. "I think if you come back, you'll come for the sake of the Prince. It's right that you should."

"I see." He began to dress methodically. "So you believe what happened here between us will be forgotten when I reach London."

"No." She stopped struggling with her own buttons and reached for him. "No, I believe what happened here will be remembered always. When I'm very old and I feel the first hint of spring I'll think of today and of you."

The anger came quickly, making him dig his fingers into her arms. "Do you think that's enough for me? If you do, you're either very stupid or mad."

"It's all there can be—" she began, but her words slipped down her throat as he shook her.

"When I come back to Scotland, I come for you. Make no mistake, Serena. And when this war is over, I'll take you with me."

"If I had only myself to think of, I would go." She clutched at his coat, willing him to understand. "Can't you see that I would die slowly with the shame to my family?"

"No, by God, I can't see that being my wife would bring your family shame."

"Your wife?" She could barely whisper the words, then jerked back as if he had slapped her. "Marriage?"

"Of course marriage. What did you think—?" Then he saw, and saw clearly, just what it was she believed he was asking her. His anger turned inward until it was a dull heat in the pit of his stomach. "Is this what you thought I meant the last time we were here?" he demanded. "Is this what you needed to think through?" His laugh was quick and humorless. "You think highly of me, Serena."

"I..." Because her legs were weak, she sank limply onto a rock. "I thought...I understood that men took mistresses, and..."

"And so they do," he said curtly. "And so I have, but only a dim-witted fool would have thought I was offering you anything but my heart and my name."

"How was I supposed to know you meant marriage?" She sprang up to face him again. "You never said so."

"I've already spoken with your father." His voice was stiff as he snatched up the plaid.

"You've spoken with my father?" she repeated, measuring each word. "You spoke with my father without ever speaking to me?"

"It's proper to ask your father's permission."

"The devil with proper." She grabbed the blanket from him. "You had no right going behind my back to him without ever saying a word to me."

He took a long look at her tumbled hair, at her lips, still swollen from his. "I believe I did more than say a word to you, Serena."

She flushed, then marched over to toss the blanket over her horse. "I'm not so green that I think what has passed here always leads to marriage." She might have struggled into the saddle if Brigham hadn't whirled her around.

"Do you think I'm in the habit of seducing virgins and then making them my mistresses?"

"I don't know your habits."

"Then know this," he began as the horse danced skittishly aside. "I intend you for my wife."

"You intend. *You* intend." She shoved him away. "Perhaps in England you can bully, my lord, but here I have some say in my life. And I say I won't marry you, and you must be mad to think it."

"Did you lie when you said you love me?" he demanded.

"No. No, but—" The words were lost as his lips crushed down on hers.

"Then you lie when you say you won't be my wife."

"I can't be," she said desperately. "How can I leave here and go with you to England?"

His fingers tensed on her arms. "So, it comes down to that once more."

"You must see, you must, how it would be." She began to speak very fast, taking his arms, as well, willing him to understand. "I would live there because I loved you, because you asked it of me, and end by bringing shame on both of us. You would hate me before a year had passed. I'm not meant to be an earl's wife, Brigham."

"An English earl," he corrected.

She took the time to draw a deep breath. "I'm a laird's daughter, it's true, but I'm not fool enough to believe that's enough. I would hate being trapped in London when I want to ride through the hills. You yourself have told me more than once that I'm not a lady. I'll never be one. I would make a poor wife for the earl of Ashburn.''

"Then you will make a poor one, but you will be my wife."

"No." She dried her cheeks with her knuckles. "I will not."

"You'll have no choice, Rena, when I go to your father and tell him I've compromised you."

The tears stopped, to be replaced by shock, then fury. "You wouldn't dare."

"I would," he said grimly.

"He would kill you."

Brigham only raised a brow. Beneath them, his eyes were dark and growing cold. Men he had faced in battle would have recognized the look. "I believe the father is not quite so bloodthirsty as the daughter." Before she could speak again, he lifted her into the saddle. "If you refuse to marry me because you love me, then you will marry me because you are commanded."

"I would rather marry a two-headed toad."

He launched himself into his saddle beside her. "But you will marry me, my dear, smiling or weeping. My journey to London should give you time to think sensibly. I will speak with your father and make arrangements when I return.''

After sending him a furious look, Serena kicked her heels. She hoped he broke his neck on the ride to London.

And when he left the following morning, she wept her own broken heart into her pillow.

Chapter Ten

He had missed London, the pace of it, the look of it, the smell of it. Most of his life had been spent there or at the graceful old manor home of his ancestors in the country. He was well-known in polite society and had no trouble finding company for a game of cards at one of the fashionable clubs or interesting conversation over dinner. Mothers of marriageable daughters made certain to include the wealthy earl of Ashburn on their guest lists.

He had been six weeks in town, and spring was at its best. His own garden, one of the finest in the city, boasted vistas of lush lawns and colorful blossoms. The rain that had drummed almost incessantly as April had begun had worked its magic and was now replaced by balmy golden days that lured pretty women in their silk dresses and feathered hats into the parks and shops.

There were balls and assemblies, card parties and levees. A man with his title, his reputation and his purse could have a comfortable life here with little inconvenience and much pleasure.

He had indeed missed London. It was his home. It had taken him much less than six weeks to discover that it was no longer his heart.

That was in Scotland now. Not a day passed that he didn't think of the hard Highland winter or of how Serena had warmed it. As he looked out at the crowded streets and the strollers in their walking coats and hats of the latest fashion, he wondered what spring was like in Glenroe. And whether Serena ever sat by the lake and thought of him.

He would have gone back weeks earlier, but his work for the Prince was taking longer than had been thought, and the results were less satisfactory than anyone had foreseen.

The Jacobites in England were great in number, but the number among them who showed eagerness to raise their sword for the untried Prince was much less. On Lord George's advice, Brigham had spoken to many groups, giving them an outline of the mood of the Highland clans and conveying what communications he had received from the Prince himself. He had ridden as far as Manchester, and had held a council as close as his own drawing room.

Each was as risky as the other. The government was uneasy, and the rumor of war with France louder than ever. Stuart sympathizers would not be suffered gladly, and active supporters would be imprisoned, at best. Memories of public executions and deportations were still fresh.

After six weeks he had the hope, but only the hope, that if Charles could act quickly, and begin his campaign, his English followers would join him.

They had so much to lose, Brigham thought. How well he knew it. Homes, lands, titles. It was a difficult thing to fight for something as distant as a cause when you gambled your name and your fortune, as well as your life.

Turning, he studied the portrait of his grandmother. His decision had already been made. Perhaps it had been made when he had still been a schoolboy, his head on her knee as she wove tales of exiled kings and a fight for justice.

It was dangerous to tarry much longer in London. The government had a way of uncovering rebels and dealing with them with nasty efficiency. Thus far, Brigham's name had kept him above suspicion, but he knew rumors were flying. Now that war with France was once more inevitable, so was talk of a new Jacobite uprising.

Brigham had never hidden his travels to France, to Italy, to Scotland. If anyone decided to shift the blocks of his last few years around, they would come up with a very interesting pattern.

So he must leave, Brigham thought, kicking a smoldering log in the dying fire. This time, he would go alone and under the cover of night. When he returned to London next, it would be with Serena. And they would stand where he stood now and toast the true king and his regent.

He returned to Scotland for the Prince, as Serena had said. But he also returned to claim what was his. Rebellion aside, there was one battle he was determined to win.

Hours later, as Brigham was preparing to leave for a quiet evening at his club, his sober-faced butler intercepted him.

"Yes, Beeton?"

"Your pardon, my lord." Beeton was so old one could almost hear the creak of his bones as he bowed. "The earl of Whitesmouth requests a word with you. It seems to be a matter of some urgency."

"Then show him up." Brigham grimaced as Parkins fussed over his coat, looking for any sign of lint. "Leave off, man. You'll drive me to a fit."

"I only desire my lord to show himself to his best advantage."

"Some of the female persuasion would argue that to do that I must strip." When Parkins remained stone-faced, Brigham merely sighed. "You're a singularly humorless fellow, Parkins. God knows why I keep you."

"Brig." The earl of Whitesmouth, a small, smooth-faced man only a few years Brigham's senior, strode into the room, then pulled up short at the sight of the valet. It only took a glance to see that Whitesmouth was highly agitated.

"That will be all for this evening, Parkins." As if he had all the time in the world, Brigham crossed to the table by the bedroom fire and poured wine into two glasses. He waited until he heard the adjoining door click quietly shut. "What is it, Johnny?"

"We have trouble, Brig." He accepted the glass, and downed the contents in one swallow.

"I surmised as much. Of what nature?"

Steadier for the drink, Whitesmouth continued. "That pea-brained Miltway drank himself into a stupor with his mistress this afternoon and opened his mouth too wide for any of us to be comfortable."

After taking a long breath, Brigham sipped and gestured to a chair. "Did he name names?"

"We can't be sure, but it seems likely he spilled at least a few. Yours being the most obvious."

"And his mistress... She's the redheaded dancer?"

"The hair on her head's red," Whitesmouth stated crudely. "She's a knowing little package, Brigham, a bit too old and too experienced for a stripling like Miltway. Trouble is, the young idiot has more money than brains."

Miltway's romantic liaisons were the last of Brigham's concerns. "Will she keep quiet, for a bribe?"

"It's too late for that. That's why I've come. She's already passed on some of the information, enough that Miltway's been arrested."

Brigham swore viciously. "Young fool."

"The odds are keen that you'll be questioned, Brigham. If you have anything incriminating—"

"I am not that young," Brigham interrupted as he began to think ahead. "Nor such a fool." He paused a moment, wanting to be certain his decision was made logically and not on impulse. "And you, Johnny? Will you be able to cover yourself?"

"I have urgent business on my estate." The earl of Whitesmouth grinned. "In fact, I have been in route several hours already."

"The Prince will do well with men like you."

Whitesmouth poured a second drink and toasted his friend. "And you?"

"I'm for Scotland. Tonight."

"Flight now will show your hand, Brig. Are you ready for that?"

"I'm weary of pretense. I stand for the Prince."

"Then I'll wish you a safe journey, and wait for word from you."

"God willing, I shall send it soon." He picked up his gloves again. "I know you've run a risk by coming to tell me when you could have been on your way. I shan't forget it."

"The Prince has my pledge, as well," Whitesmouth reminded him. "I pray you won't tarry too long."

"Only long enough. Have you told anyone else about Miltway's indiscretion?"

"That's a cool way of putting it," Whitesmouth muttered. "I thought it best to come to you directly."

Brigham nodded. "I'll spend a few hours at the club as I had planned and make certain word is passed. You'd best get out of London before someone notes that you are not indeed en route to your estate.

"On my way." Whitesmouth picked up his hat. "One warning, Brig. The elector's son, Cumberland. Don't take him lightly. It's true he's young, but his eyes are cold and his ambition hot."

The club held many faces familiar to Brigham. Games were being played, bottles already draining. He was greeted cheerfully enough and invited to join groups at cards or dice. Making easy excuses, he strolled over to the fire to share a bottle of burgundy with Viscount Leighton.

"No urge to try your luck tonight, Ashburn?"

"Not at cards." Behind them, someone complained bitterly about the fall of the dice. "It's a fair night," Brigham said mildly. "One well suited for traveling."

Leighton sipped, and though his eyes met Brigham's, they gave away nothing. "Indeed. There is always talk of storms to the north."

"I have a feeling there will be a storm here sooner." The dice game grew noisier. Brigham took advantage of the noise to lean forward and pour more wine in the glasses. "Miltway confided his political leanings to his mistress and has been arrested."

Leighton said something unflattering about Miltway under his breath, then settled back. "How loose a tongue has he?"

"I can't be sure, but there are some who should be put on guard."

Leighton toyed with the diamond pinned to the lace at his throat. He was fond of such trinkets, and was often taken for a man who preferred a soft life. Like Brigham, he had made his decision to back the Prince coolly and without reservation.

"Consider it done, my dear. Do you wish for company on your journey?"

Brigham was tempted. Viscount Leighton, with his pink waistcoats and perfumed hands, might have looked like a self-indulgent fop, but there was no one Brigham would have chosen over him in a fight. "Not at the moment."

"Then shall we drink to fair weather?" Leighton lifted his glass, then gave a mildly annoyed glance over Brigham's shoulder. "I believe we should patronize another club, my dear Ashburn. This establishment has begun to open its doors to anyone."

Brigham glanced around idly to the game. He recognized the man holding the bank, and most of the others. But there was a thin man leaning on the table, a sulky look in his eyes, a half-filled glass by his elbow. He was not taking his losses in a manner acceptable to polite society.

"Don't know him." Brigham sipped again, thinking that he might never again sit cozily by the fire in this club and drink with a friend.

"I've had the dubious pleasure." Leighton took out a snuffbox. "An officer. I believe he's off to cross swords with the French quite soon, which should make the ladies sigh. However, I am told that he is not in favor with our ladies any longer, despite the romantic figure he attempts to cut."

With a laugh, Brigham prepared to take his leave. "Perhaps it has something to do with his lack of manners."

"Perhaps it has something to do with his treatment of Alice Beesley when she was unfortunate enough to be his mistress."

Brigham raised a brow, but was still only vaguely curious. The game was growing louder yet, the hour later, and he still needed Parkins to pack his bag. "The lovely Mrs. Beesley is a dim-witted piece, but from what I'm told, quite amiable."

"Standish apparently thought she wasn't amiable enough and took a riding crop to her."

Brigham's eyes registered distaste as he glanced over again. "There is something particularly foul about a man who..." He trailed off and his fingers tightened on his glass. "Did you say Standish?"

"I did. A colonel, I believe. He earned a particularly nasty reputation in the Porteous scandal in '35." Leighton flicked a flake of snuff from his sleeve. "It seems he quite enjoyed sacking and burning and looting. I believe that's why he was promoted."

"He would have been a captain in '35."

"Possibly." Interest flickered in Leighton's eyes. "Do you know him after all?"

"Yes." Brigham remembered well Coll's story of Captain Standish and the rape of his mother, the houses burned, the defenseless crofters routed. And Serena. He rose, and though his eyes were cold, there was nothing of his temper in his voice. "I believe we should become better acquainted. I fancy a game after all, Leighton."

"It grows late, Ashburn."

Brigham smiled. "Indeed it does."

Nothing was easier than joining the game. Within twenty minutes he had bought the bank. His luck held, and as fate or justice would have it, so did Standish's. The colonel continued to lose and, egged on by Brigham's mild disdain, he bet heavily. By midnight, there were only three left in the game. Brigham signaled for more wine as he sprawled easily in his chair. He had deliberately matched drink for drink with Standish. Brigham had no intention of killing a man whose faculties were less sharp than his own.

"The dice appear to dislike you this evening, Colonel."

"Or they like others too well."

Standish's words were blurred by drink and bitterness. He was a man who required greater sums of money than his soldier's pay to back his lust for gambling, and his equal lust for a place in society. Tonight his bitterness stemmed from a failure to achieve either. His offer for a well-endowed— both physically and financially—young lady had been turned down only that afternoon. Standish was certain the bitch Beesley had gone whining to whom-ever would listen. She'd been a whore, he thought as he swilled down more wine. A man had a right to treat a whore however he chose.

"Get on with it," he ordered, then counted the fall of Brigham's dice. Snatching up the dice box, he threw and fell short.

"Pity." Brigham smiled and drank.

"I don't care to have the bank switched so late in the game. It spoils the luck."

"Yours seemed poor all evening, Colonel." Brigham continued to smile, but the look in his eyes had driven more than one man away from the game. "Perhaps you consider it unpatriotic that I'm fleecing a royal dragoon, but here we are only men, after all."

"Did we come to play or to talk?" Standish demanded, signaling impa-tiently for more wine.

"In a *gentlemen's* club," Brigham replied, coloring his words with con-tempt, "we do both. But then Colonel, perhaps you don't often find yourself in the company of gentlemen."

The third player decided the game was a bit too uneasy for his taste. Several of the other patrons had stopped what they were doing to look, and to listen. Other games were abandoned as men began to loiter around the table. Standish's face reddened. He wasn't certain, but he thought he had been insulted.

"I spend most of my time fighting for the king, not lounging in clubs."

"Of course." Brigham tossed again, and again topped the colonel's roll. "Which explains why you are inept at polite games of chance."

"You seem a bit too skilled, my lord. The dice have fallen for you since you took your seat."

"Have they?" Brigham glanced up to raise a brow at Leighton, who was idly swirling a drink of his own. "Have they indeed?"

"You know damn well they have. It seems more than luck to me."

Brigham fingered the lace at his throat. Behind them the club fell into uncomfortable silence. "Does it? Perhaps you'll enlighten me by telling me what it seems to you."

Standish had lost more than he could afford to, drunk more than was wise. He looked across at Brigham and hated him for being what and who he was. Aristocrats, he thought, and wanted to spit. It was for wastrels like this that soldiers fought and died.

"Enlighten everyone. Break the dice."

The silence roared into murmurs. Someone leaned over to tug on Brigham's sleeve. "He's drunk, Ashburn, and not worth it."

"Are you?" Still smiling, Brigham leaned forward. "Are you drunk, Standish?"

"I am not." He was beyond drunk now. As he sat he felt every eye on him. Staring at him, he thought. Popinjays and fops with their titles and smooth manners. They thought him beneath them because he had taken a whip to a whore. He'd like to take a whip to all of them, he thought, tossing back the rest of his wine. "I'm sober enough to know the dice don't fall for only one man unless they're meant to."

Brigham waved a hand toward the dice, but his eyes were sharp as steel. "Break them, by all means."

There was a rush of protests, a flurry of movements. Brigham ignored both and kept his eyes on Standish. It pleased him a great deal to see the sweat begin to pearl on the colonel's forehead.

"My lord, I pray you won't act rashly. This isn't necessary." The proprietor had brought the hammer as requested, but stood casting worried glances from Brigham to Standish.

"I assure you it's quite necessary." When the proprietor hesitated, Brigham whipped his rapier gaze up. "Break them."

With an unsteady hand, the proprietor did as he was bid. There was silence again as the hammer smashed down, showing the dice to be clean. Standish only stared at the pieces that lay on the green baize. Tricked, he thought. Somehow the bastards had tricked him. He wished them dead, all of them, every one of the pale-faced, soft-voiced bastards.

"You seem to be out of wine, Colonel." And Brigham tossed the contents of his glass in Standish's face.

Standish leaped up, wine dripping down his cheeks like blood. Drink and humiliation had done its work well. He would have drawn his sword if others hadn't stepped in to hold his arms. Brigham never moved from where he sat sprawled in his chair.

"You will meet me, sir."

Brigham examined his cuff to be certain none of the wine had spattered it. "Naturally. Leighton, my dear, you will stand for me?"

Leighton took a pinch of snuff. "Of course."

* * *

Just before dawn they stood in a meadow a few minutes' ride from the city. There was a mist nearly ankle high, and the sky was purple and starless, as it was caught between night and day. Leighton let out a weary sigh as he watched Brigham turn back his lace.

"You have your reasons, I suppose, dear boy."

"I have them."

Leighton frowned at the rising sun. "I trust they are good enough to delay your trip."

He thought of Serena, of the look on her face when she had spoken of her mother's rape. He thought of Fiona, with her small, slender hands. "They are."

"The man is a pig, of course." Leighton frowned again, this time down at the moisture the dew had transferred to his gleaming boot. "Still, it hardly seems reason enough to stand about in a damp field at this hour. But if you must, you must. Do you intend to kill him?"

Brigham flexed his fingers. "I do."

"Be quick about it, Ashburn. This business has postponed my breakfast." So saying, he strolled off to confer with Standish's second, a young officer who was pale with both fear and excitement at the idea of a duel. The swords were judged acceptable. Brigham took one, letting his hand mold to the hilt, weighing it as though he had a mind to purchase it rather than draw blood.

Standish stood ready, even eager. The sword was his weapon. Ashburn wouldn't be the first he had killed with it, nor would he be the last. Though he might, Standish thought as he remembered the stares and murmurs of the night, be the most pleasurable. He had no doubt that he would cut down the young prig quickly and ride home in triumph.

They made their bows. Eyes locked. Sword touched sword in salute. Then the quiet meadow rang with the crash of steel against steel.

Brigham measured his opponent from the first thrust. Standish was no fool with a sword, had obviously been well-trained and had kept himself in fighting trim. But his style was a bit too aggressive. Brigham parried, putting Serena out of his mind. He preferred to fight emotionlessly, using that as a weapon, as well as his blade.

The ground was rich with dew, and the mist silenced the slide and fall of boots. There was only the song of metal slicing over metal as the birds quieted. Their swords slid from tip to hilt as they came in close. Their breath mingled like that of lovers through the deadly cross of blades.

"You are handy with a sword, Colonel," Brigham said as they drew apart to circle. "My compliments."

"Handy enough to slice your heart, Ashburn."

"We shall see." The blades kissed again, once, twice, three times. "But I don't suppose you required a sword when you raped Lady MacGregor."

Puzzlement broke Standish's concentration, but he managed to block Brigham's thrust before the sword could run home. His brow darkened as he realized he had been led to this duel like a mongrel on a leash.

"One doesn't rape a whore." He attacked, fueled by a drumming rage. "What is the Scots bitch to you?"

Brigham's wrist whipped the sword up. "You shall die wondering."

They fought in silence now, Brigham cold as Highland ice, Standish hot with rage and confusion. Blades hissed and rang, competing now with the sound of labored breathing. In a daring move, Standish feinted, kissed his sword off Brigham's, sliced in *contre écart*. A red stain bloomed on Brigham's shoulder.

A cooler head might have used the wound to his advantage. Standish saw only the blood, and with the smell of it scented victory. He came in hard, judging himself moments away from triumph. Brigham countered thrust after thrust, biding his time as the blood dripped down his arm and into the thinning mist. He pulled back a fraction, an instant, laying his chest bare. The light of victory came into Standish's eyes as he leaped forward to open Brigham's heart.

With a bright flash of metal, Brigham knocked the sword aside moments before it pierced him. With a speed Leighton would claim later made the blade a blur, he twisted and plunged the point into the colonel's chest. Standish was dead before Brigham had pulled the point free.

Beside the pale-faced soldier, Leighton examined the body. "Well, you've killed him, Ashburn. Best be on your way while I deal with the mess."

"My thanks." Brigham handed Leighton the sword, hilt first.

"Shall I bind up your hurts, as well?"

With faint amusement, Brigham glanced over to his horse. Beside it, the estimable Parkins sat on another. "My valet will see to it."

Serena awoke just before dawn. She hadn't slept well for the past week, ever since a dream from which she had woken with her heart hammering. She had been sure then, somehow, that Brigham was in danger.

Even now, the moment of fear haunted her, adding to the ache she had lived with since he'd left. But that was foolish, she told herself. He was in London, safe. With a sigh, she sat up, knowing sleep was impossible. He was in London, she repeated. He might as well have been worlds away.

For a little while she had allowed herself to believe he would come back, as he'd said he would. Then the weeks had passed and she had stopped looking down the path at the sound of horses. Coll and Maggie had been married more than a week. It had been at their wedding that Serena had finally allowed hope to die. If he hadn't come back for Coll's wedding, he wasn't coming back.

She had known it, Serena reminded herself as she washed and dressed. When she had given herself to him on the banks of the loch, she had known it. And had sworn there would be no regrets. She had known, she told herself now as she bound back her hair. She had known, and she had been given everything she could have wanted.

Except that the afternoon she had spent in Brigham's arms hadn't made her quicken. She had hoped, though she had known it mad, that she would find herself with Brigham's child.

That wasn't to be. All she had left were her memories.

Still, she had her family, her home. It helped fill the gaps. She was strong enough to live her life without him. She might never be truly happy again, but she would live and she would be content.

The morning chores eased her mind and kept it from drifting. She worked alone, or with the women of her family. For them, and for the sake of her own pride, she kept her spirits up. There would be no moping, no pining, for Serena MacGregor. Whenever she was tempted to fall into depression, she reminded herself that she had had one golden afternoon.

It was early evening when she slipped away. Her mother and Maggie were sorting thread and Gwen was visiting one of the sick in the village. Dressed in her breeches, she avoided everyone but Malcolm, whom she bribed with a piece of hard candy.

She rode for the loch. It was an indulgence, right or wrong, that occasionally she allowed herself. Whenever time allowed, she went there to sit on the bank and dream a little. And remember. It brought Brigham closer to her. As close, Serena knew, as he would ever be. He was gone. Back to London, where he belonged.

Now spring was here in all its glory. Flowers waved in the gentle breeze, trees were ripe with green, green leaves. The sunlight dappled through, making pretty patterns on the soft path. Young deer walked through the forest.

By the loch the ground was springy and warm, though the water would be frigid for weeks yet, and would carry a chill all through the summer. Content from the ride, she lay on the grassy knoll to read a little, and dream. It was solitude she had wanted, and it was serenity she found. From somewhere to the west, like mourning, came the haunting call of a greenshank.

Dog violets grew, pale blue and delicate, beside her. She plucked a few, threading them idly through her hair while she studied the glassy calm of the lake. On the rocks above, heather grew like purple stars. Its fragile scent drifted to her. Farther up, the crags had been worn sheer by rain and time. There was little that could grow there, and to Serena, their very starkness made them beautiful. They were like fortresses, guarding the eastern verge of the loch.

She wished Brigham could see this spot, this very special spot, now, when the wind was kind and the water so blue it made your eyes sting.

Pillowing her head on her arm, she closed her eyes and dreamed of him.

It felt as though a butterfly had landed on her cheek. Dozing, Serena brushed it lazily away. She didn't want to wake, not just yet, and find herself alone. Soon enough she would have to go back and give up the hours she had stolen for herself. Not yet, she thought as she curled into her self. For just a little while longer, she would lie here and dream of what might have been.

She sighed, groggy with sleep, as she felt something—the butterfly—brush over her lips. She smiled a little, thinking how sweet that was, how it warmed her. Her body stretched against the gentle fingers of the breeze. Like a lover's hands, she thought. Like Brigham's. Her sigh was quiet and drowsily aroused. Her breasts tingled under it, and seemed to fill. All along her body, her blood seemed to rush to the surface. In response, her lips parted.

"Look at me, Serena. Look at me when I kiss you."

She obeyed automatically, her mind still trapped in the dream, her body heating from it. Dazed, she saw Brigham's eyes looking into hers as her mouth was captured in a kiss that was much too urgent, much too powerful, for any dream.

"My God, how I've missed you." He dragged her closer. "Every day, I swear it, every hour."

Could this be real? Her mind swam as fiercely as her blood as she wrapped her arms tight around him. "Brigham?" She held on, terrified to let go and find him vanished. "Is it really you? Kiss me again," she demanded before he could speak. "And again and again."

He did as she asked, his hands dragging through her hair, streaming down her body until they were both shuddering. He wanted to tell her how he had felt when he had stopped his horse and had seen her sleeping, sleeping where they had first come together. No one had ever looked more beautiful than his Serena, lying in her men's breeches with her head pillowed on her arm and flowers scattered in her hair.

But he couldn't find the words, and if he had, she would never have let them be spoken. Her mouth was hungry as it fused to his. When he had loved her before she had been fragile, a little afraid. Now she was all passion, all demand. Her fingers pulled and dragged at his clothes as if she couldn't bear to have anything between them. Though he murmured to her, wanting to show some gentleness on this, their first meeting in so many long weeks, she burned like a fire in his arms.

Unable to resist, he tugged the men's clothes aside and found his woman.

It was as it had been before, she thought. And more, so much more. His hands and mouth were everywhere, torturing, delighting. Her skin was covered with a moist sheen and nothing else as he pleasured both of them. Whatever shyness she had felt when she had first given herself to him was eclipsed now by a need so sharp, so desperate, that she touched and tasted in places that made him gasp in amazement and passion. She drew him down to her, reveling in the scent of him—in some way the same as it had been on their very first meeting. Sweat, horse, blood. It spun in her head, touching off primitive urges, the darkest desires.

"Name of God, Rena." He could barely speak. She was taking him places he had never been, places he had never known existed. No other woman had mastered him in this way, not the most experienced French courtesan, not the most worldly British flower. He was learning from the Scots wildcat more of love and lust than he had thought possible.

The blood was hammering in his brain. There was pain, exquisite, terrifying pain. The control with which he lived his life, with which he raised a sword or fired a pistol, was gone as if it had never existed. He dragged her against him, his fingers raking through her hair, bruising her soft flesh.

"Now, for pity's sake." He plunged into her, going deep. Her nails dug into his back as she cried out, but she was moving with him, driving her hips up to meet each thrust. With her head thrown back, she gasped for air. In some part of her brain she knew this was something like dying. Then there was no thought at all. Though her eyes flew open, she saw nothing, nothing but a white flash as her body went rigid.

The aftershocks of pleasure wracked her body even as her hands fell limply to the ground. Her vision was misted—it seemed only more of the dream. But Brigham lay, warm and solid, over her. And he was...he was trembling, she realized with a kind of wonder. It was not only she who was left weak and vulnerable, but he, as well.

"You came back," she murmured, and found the strength to lift her hand to his hair.

"I said I would." He shifted to kiss her again, but softly now. "I love you, Serena. Nothing could have stopped me from coming back to you."

She framed his face with her hands to study it. He meant it, she realized.

Seeing the truth only made her more uncertain of what to do. "You were gone so long. No word."

"Sending word would have put too many at risk. The storm's coming, Rena."

"Aye. And you'll—" She broke off as she noted blood on her fingers. "Brig, you're hurt." She scrambled up to her knees to fret over the soaked bandage on his shoulder. "What happened? You were attacked? Campbells!"

"No." He had to laugh at the way she snarled the rival clan's name. "A little business in London before I left. It's nothing, Serena."

But she was already ripping the cuff from his shirt to make a fresh bandage. Brigham sighed, knowing Parkins would make him pay, but he sat meekly and let her tend his wound.

"A sword," she said.

"A scratch. We won't talk of it now. The sun's going down."

"Oh." She blinked, noting for the first time how much time had passed. "I have to go back. How did you find me here?"

"I could say I followed my heart, which I would have. But Malcolm told me you'd ridden out."

A few flowers clung yet to her hair, and her hair was all that covered her breasts. She looked like a witch or a queen or a goddess. He could only be certain that she was all he needed. He grabbed her hands. The intensity was back in his eyes, dark, demanding.

"Tell me, Rena."

"I love you, Brigham." She brought his hand to her cheek. "More than I can say."

"And you'll marry me." When her eyes dropped from his, he erupted. "Damn it, woman. You say you love me, you all but kill me with passion, then you go skittish when I speak of making you my wife."

"I have told you I cannot."

"I have told you you will." He picked up his ruined shirt and slipped it gingerly over his shoulder, which was just beginning to ache. "I shall speak with your father."

"No." Her head shot up quickly. Trying to think, she pushed the hair back from her face. How could they have come so far and be back where they had begun? "I beg you not to."

"What choice do you leave me?" He pulled her shirt down over her head, struggling for patience when she jerked away from him to dress herself. "I love you, Rena, and I have no intention of living my life without you."

"Then I'll ask for time." She looked at him then and knew she had to resolve what was in her heart and what was in her head. "There is so much to be done, Brigham. So much that will be happening around us, to us. When the war begins, you'll go, and I shall only wait. Give me time. Give us both time to deal with what has to be."

"Only so much, Serena. And only because, in the end, I'll leave you no choice."

Chapter Eleven

Serena was right. Things were happening around them that would shape the destiny not only of two lovers, but of the whole of Scotland.

Within days of Brigham's arrival at Glenroe, the French dealt the English a crushing defeat at Fontenoy. Though Charles's, and many of the Jacobites' hopes rose with it, Louis of France still withheld his support from the rebellion. Charles had hoped to ride on the glory that surrounded the French victory, to gain much-needed impetus for his cause; once again, however, he was left to his own devices.

But this time he moved. Brigham was both confidant and informer. He knew to the day when Charles, with money raised by the pawning of his mother's rubies, fitted out the frigate *Doutelle* and a ship of the line, the *Elizabeth*. While the push in the Highlands, and in England, went on for support, Charles Edward, the Bonnie Prince, set sail from Nantes for Scotland and his destiny.

It was high summer when word came that the Prince was on his way. The *Elizabeth*, with its store of men and weapons, was chased back to port by British pursuers, but the *Doutelle*, with Charles aboard, sailed on towards the Scottish coast, where preparations were being made to greet him.

"My father says I cannot go." Malcolm, sulking in the stables, frowned up at Brigham. "He's says I'm too young, but I'm not."

The boy had just passed his eleventh birthday, Brigham thought, but prudently held back from mentioning it. "Coll goes, as do I."

"I know." Malcolm glared at the toe of his grubby boot and thought it the height of injustice. "Because I'm the youngest, I'm treated like a bairn."

"Would your father trust his home and his family to a bairn?" Brigham asked gently. "When your father leaves with his men, there will be no MacGregor in MacGregor House, but for you. Who will protect the women if you ride with us?"

"Serena," he said easily, and he spoke no less than the truth.

"Would you leave your sister alone to protect the family name and honor?"

The boy moved a shoulder, but began to think on it. "She is a better shot with a pistol than I, or Coll, really, though he wouldn't like to say so." This news brought Brigham's brow up. "But I'm better with a bow."

"She will need you." He dropped a hand on Malcolm's tousled hair. "We will all need you. With you here, we needn't worry that the women are safe."

Because he was still young enough to know what it was to be a boy, he sat on the mound of hay beside Malcolm. "I can tell you this, Malcolm, a man never goes easily to war, but he goes with a lighter heart if he knows his women are protected."

"I won't let harm come to them." Idly Malcolm fingered the dagger at his belt. For a moment, Brigham thought he looked too much a man.

"I know, as your father knows. If the time comes when Glenroe is no longer safe, you will take them up into the hills."

"Aye." The idea made Malcolm brighten a bit. "I'll see that they have food and shelter. Especially Maggie."

"Why especially Maggie?"

"Because of the bairn." His fingers slid away from his dagger. "She's to have one, you know."

For a moment, Brigham only stared. Then, with a laugh, he shook his head. "No, I didn't. How do you?"

"I heard Mrs. Drummond say so. She said Maggie's not sure she's increasing yet, but Mrs. Drummond was sure and there'd be a new wee bairn by next spring."

"Keep your ear to the ground, do you, my lad?"

"Aye." This time Malcolm grinned. "I know Gwen and Maggie are always talking about how you'll be marrying Serena. Will you be marrying her, Brig?"

"I will." He ruffled the boy's hair. "But she doesn't know it yet."

"Then you'll be a MacGregor."

"To an extent. Serena will be a Langston."

"A Langston. Will she like it?"

Brigham's eyes lost their amusement. "She'll grow used to it. Now, if you've a mind to take that ride, we'd best be off."

Always cheered by the idea of his horses, Malcolm jumped up. "Did you know that Parkins is courting Mrs. Drummond?"

"Good God." Brigham stopped in the act of leading out his horse and turned to the boy. "Someone should plug those ears of yours." Malcolm only laughed, and Brigham, unable to do otherwise, put a hand on the boy's shoulder again. "Is he really?"

"Brought her flowers yesterday."

"Sweet Jesus."

From the window of the parlor she was supposed to be dusting, Serena watched them ride off. How wonderful he looked, so tall, so straight. She leaned out the window so that she could watch him until he was out of sight.

He wouldn't wait much longer. Those had been his words the last time they had stolen an hour together by the loch. He wanted her wedded, and properly bedded. He wanted to make her Lady Ashburn of Ashburn Manor. Lady Ashburn of London society. The idea was nothing less than terrifying.

She looked down at herself now, at her dress of pale blue homespun and at the dusty apron that covered it. Her feet were bare—something Fiona would have sighed over. Lady Ashburn would never run over the moors or through the forest in bare feet. Lady Ashburn would probably never run.

Her hands. Serena turned them this way and that, examining the backs and the palms critically. They were smooth enough, she supposed. Because her mother insisted she rub lotion into them every night. But they weren't lady's hands any more than hers was a lady's heart.

But God, she loved him. She understood now that the heart could indeed speak louder than the head. English or not, she would be his. She had even come to know that she would leave her beloved Scotland behind for his England rather than live without him. And yet...

How could she marry a man who deserved the finest of ladies? Even her mother had thrown up her hands at Serena's attempts to learn the spinet. She couldn't do fancy work with her needle, only the most basic stitches. She could run a home, to be sure, but she knew from Coll that Brigham's house in London and his manor in the country were a far cry from what she was used to. She would make a mess of it, but even that she could almost bear. It was knowing how poorly she had dealt with her one brush with society—the brief months she had spent in the convent school.

She had nothing to say to the kind of women who spent their days shopping for the right shade of ribbon and making social calls. A few weeks of that life and she would go not-so-quietly mad, and once she had, Brigham would hate her.

We can't change what we are, she thought. Brigham could no more stay here in the Highlands and live her life than she could go with him to England and live his.

And yet... She had begun to see that living without him would be no life at all.

"Serena."

She turned quickly to see her mother in the doorway.

"I'm nearly done," she said, flourishing her dusting cloth again. "I was daydreaming."

Fiona shut the doors at her back. "Sit down, Serena."

Fiona used that quiet but concerned tone of voice rarely. Usually it meant that she was worried or annoyed. As Serena moved to comply, she searched her mind for any infraction. True, she'd been wearing the breeches a bit too freely on her rides, but her mother usually overlooked that. She had torn the skirt of the new gray dress, but Gwen had mended it so that it hardly showed at all.

Serena sat, pulling the cloth between her fingers. "Have I done something to upset you?"

"You're troubled," Fiona began. "I had thought it was because Brigham had gone and you were missing him. But he's been back for several weeks now and you're troubled still."

Serena tucked her bare feet under the hem of her skirt as her fingers knotted and unknotted the cloth. "I'm not troubled really. It's only that I'm thinking about what will happen after the Prince comes."

That was true, Fiona thought, but not all the truth. "There was a time you would talk to me, Serena."

"I don't know what to say."

Gently Fiona laid a hand on hers. "What's in your heart."

"I love him." Serena slid to the floor to lay her head in her mother's lap. "Mama, I love him and it hurts so terribly."

"I know it does, my darling." She stroked Serena's hair and felt the pang in her own heart that only a mother understands. "To love a man is great misery and great joy."

"Why?" There was passion in Serena's eyes and voice as she lifted her face. "Why must it bring misery?"

Fiona gave a little sigh and wished there could be a simple answer. "Because once the heart opens, it feels everything."

"I didn't want to love him," Serena murmured. "Now I can do nothing else."

"And he loves you?"

"Aye." She closed her eyes, comforted by the familiar scent of lavender in the folds of her mother's skirts. "I don't think he wanted to, either."

"You know he has asked your father for your hand?"

"Aye."

"And that your father, after long thought and consideration, has given his consent."

This she hadn't known. Serena lifted her head, and her cheeks were pale. "But I can't marry him. Don't you see? I can't."

With a frown in her eyes, Fiona caught Serena's face in her hands. From what source did this fear written so plainly on her daughter's face spring? "No, I don't see, Rena. You know well your father would never force you to marry a man you didn't want. But did you not just tell me you loved Brigham and that your love is returned?"

"I do love him, too much to marry him, too much not to. Oh, Mama, how much I would give him frightens me."

Fiona saw a bit clearer now, and she smiled. "Poor wee lamb. You're not the first to have these fears, nor will you be the last. I understand when you say you love him too much *not* to marry him. But how can you love him too much to marry him?"

"I don't want to be Lady Ashburn."

Fiona blinked, surprised by the vehemence in her daughter's words. "Because he's English?"

"Aye— No. No, because I don't want to be a countess."

"It's a good family. An honorable one."

"It's the title, Mama. Even the sound of it frightens me. Lady Ashburn would live in England, grandly. She would know how to dress fashionably, how to behave with dignity, how to serve beautiful dinners and laugh at the cleverest wits."

"Well. I never thought to see the day that Ian MacGregor's wildcat cowered in a corner and whined."

The color rose sharply in Serena's cheeks. "I am afraid, I'll admit it." She rose, locking her fingers tightly together. "But I'm not only afraid for my own sake. I would go, I would try, I would be determined to be the kind of wife Brigham needs, to be the best Lady Ashburn ever to rule in Ashburn Manor. And I would hate it. Never to be free, never to have a moment with the space to breathe. But there's more." She paused a moment, wanting to choose her words so that she would be understood. "If Brigham loves me, he loves *me*, as I am. Would he love the woman I would have to become to be his wife?"

Fiona was silent for a long moment. The girl had surely become a woman, with a woman's mind, a woman's heart and a woman's fears. "You've given this a great deal of thought."

"I've hardly thought of anything else for weeks. He will have his way, of that I'm sure. But I've come to wonder if we might not both be sorry for it."

"Think of this. If he loves you, for yourself, then he would not want you to pretend to be what you are not, nor would he ask you to."

"I would rather lose him than shame him."

"I could tell you you will do neither," Fiona said wearily as she rose. "But you must learn it for yourself. But I want to tell you one more thing." Now it was Fiona who linked her hands together. "There's been gossip in the kitchen." Her mouth twitched slightly at Serena's expression. "Aye, Parkins and Mrs. Drummond. I chanced to overhear while working in the kitchen garden."

"Aye, Mother?" Serena managed, barely able to smother a giggle. The idea of her mother eavesdropping on the valet and the cook was almost too ludicrous.

"It seems on the morning he left London, Brigham fought a duel with an officer of the government army. An officer called Standish."

At this, all humor drained from Serena's face, along with all her color. "Brigham." She remembered the wound on his shoulder, the one he had steadfastly refused to discuss. "Standish," she said in a whisper as the name came home. She saw him, as she had seen him almost ten years before, bringing his hand against her mother's face. "Dear God, how did it happen? Why did it happen?"

"I know only that the duel was fought and Standish is dead. God help me, I'm glad of it. The man you love avenged my honor, and I will never forget it."

"Nor will I," Serena murmured.

She went to him that night. The hour was late, the house quiet. After pushing open his door, she saw him with the moonlight and the candlelight tangled around him while he sat at the desk by the window penning a letter. The air coming through the open window was hot and still, so he had stripped to his breeches, leaving his shirt hung casually over the back of the chair.

It was only an instant before he glanced up and saw her, only an instant that she could look at him unobserved. But the instant flashed into her mind and was sealed there to make a memory as precious as a kiss.

The light fell over his skin, making her think of the marble statues Coll had described from his trip to Italy. Statues of gods and warriors. His hair, thick and dark, was tied back from his face and mussed a bit, as though he had worried it with his hand. His eyes were dark, as well, holding a combination she recognized as concentration and concern.

Her heart began to dance in her breast as she stood in the doorway. This was the man she loved, a man of action and loyalty. A man both reckless and deliberate, a man of arrogance and of compassion. A man of honor.

He looked up, and saw her. In the woods beyond an owl hooted, the sound rising on the air and fading like a ghost. He set the quill down and rose even as she shut the door at her back. The movement stirred the air and sent the flame and its shadow wavering.

"Serena?"

"I needed to see you alone."

He released a difficult knot of breath. It took great care and great restraint not to cross to her and gather her up. She wore only a thin white linen nightdress, and had left her hair unbound to fall in a wild mass over her shoulders and down her back. "You should not have come here like this."

"I know." She moistened her lips. "I tried to sleep, but couldn't. You are leaving tomorrow."

"Yes." The intensity in his eyes softened, as did his voice. "My love, do I have to tell you again that I'll come back?"

Tears threatened, but she willed them away. She would not leave him with the image of a weak, weeping woman. "No, but I have a need to tell you that I will wait. And I would be proud to be your wife when you come back to me."

For a moment he said nothing, only stared, as if trying to read her face and be certain he had not misheard her. She stood, her hands folded. But she wasn't meek. Her eyes held fire, her chin was up. Now he crossed to her to take one of her hands in his.

"Has your father commanded you?"

"No, the decision is mine, only mine."

It was the answer he wanted, the one he had hoped for. Gently he brushed his lips over her knuckles. "I will make you happy, Rena. On my honor."

"I will be the wife you need." Somehow, she thought within her heart. "I swear it."

He bent to kiss her brow. "You *are* the wife I need, my love. And the woman." Stepping back, he drew the emerald from his finger. "This ring has been worn by a Langston for more than a hundred years. I ask you to keep it for me until I return and give you another." He slipped it onto her finger. Serena curled her hand automatically to keep it there. "I shall give you another ring as soon as God allows, and my name, as well."

"Oh, Brigham, be safe." She threw herself into his arms. It was harder, much harder, to fight these tears than any others she had known. "If I lost you now, I couldn't bear to live. Know that if you bleed, I bleed, and take care."

"What's this?" With a light laugh he caressed her hair, but it was difficult to ignore the press of her thinly clad body against his. "Never say you worry about me, Rena."

"I will say it," she murmured against his shoulder. "If you allow yourself to be killed, I shall hate you forever."

"Then I will take great care to stay alive. Go now, before you make me feel too much alive."

She gave a weak laugh. "I fear I have done that already, my lord." She shifted wantonly to prove there were no secrets between them. She had only to rise to her toes to fit herself unerringly against him. Desire to desire. "Does being near me do that to you?"

"All too often." His own laugh was strained as he fought off the drugging power of her scent, of her shape.

"I'm glad." She lifted her head to look up at him, and her smile was wicked. "Very glad."

She made him laugh again. "You've flowered in front of my eyes, Rena.

Under my hands." He kissed her, gently, though her lips tempted him. "I wonder if there is a more precious gift a woman can give a man."

"I would give you another tonight." She drew his head down to hers. Her kiss was not so gentle. With it, she felt his body tense. "I would share your bed, Brig, your love and your sleep. No," she murmured against his lips before he could speak. "Don't tell me why it should not be, only show me why it must." She dragged her hands up his back to tangle her fingers in his hair while her lips moved restlessly on his. "Love me, Brigham. Love me so that I can live on it in all the empty days to come."

He couldn't deny her. He could no longer deny himself. Her body trembled against his, no longer from fear, no longer from doubt, but only from need. With a muffled oath, he swept her into his arms. He would be leaving at dawn. Between then and now he could give her, give them, a few perfect hours.

Her body was fluid in his arms, cool, soft, languid. Her eyes were as rich, as hot, as the flash of emerald that had passed from his finger to hers. She kept her arms around his neck as he lowered her to the bed, so that he came down with her. Then, with his hands braced on either side of her head, he began to make love to her face with his mouth alone.

She thought she could float away on this kind of sweetness. It was like a cloud, delicate and dreamy. Her body felt light and free as her lips met his again and again in a slow, luxurious dance. Another minuet, she thought. Elegant, harmonious and beautiful. With a sigh she felt him slip the night-dress from her, then heard his quick intake of breath as he discovered for himself that she wore nothing beneath it.

"You are so lovely." He touched his lips to the pulse of her throat. "Here," he murmured as his fingertips brushed her breasts. "Here." And again, as his light, clever hands moved over her: "Here."

Giddiness speared through the languor. Giddiness and delight. "Is that why you fell in love with me, *Sassenach*? For my body?"

He drew himself up far enough for a long, lazy study. "It was a great influence."

Flushed, she laughed and pinched him. Then her laughter turned into a moan as he dipped his head and streaked his tongue over a hardening nipple.

"I love all of you, Serena. Your temper, your mind, your heart, and oh, yes..." His teeth closed teasingly over the peak. "Your body."

"Show me," she demanded breathlessly.

He showed her, with tenderness, with ardor, with restraint and with desperation. Every emotion they had shared became part of that endless night of loving. There were new ways. He guided her, delighted by the eagerness with which she learned, the passion with which she gave and received. There was no shyness in her. She came to him with a trust so complete that that alone nearly dragged him over the edge.

Skin grew slick in the airless night. Not a breeze stirred through the window. High above the hills, thunder rumbled. Closer, in the forest, the owl hunted. Its scream of triumph melded with the scream of its prey. The candle flickered and guttered out.

They were aware of nothing but each other, nothing but the world they made on the soft mattress.

She made him weak, and then she made him strong. She made him laugh, and then she made him groan. He was breathless, sated, then as eager to devour her as a man starving.

In the deepest part of the night they slept briefly, only to wake with the need spiraling high once more.

There was no part of her he couldn't make ache or tremble. She could only hear her skin sing as he touched. Her body grew heavy with pleasure as it built and built to roll through her like the thunder in the distant hills. Then she was light, weightless, agilely skimming over him like a fantasy. Energy poured through her, molten.

She rose over him, her hair silvered with dying moonlight, her skin sheened with damp, her face pale with an exhaustion she had yet to feel. She took him into her, arching her back as pleasure raced through her like delirium. The fever of it boiled under her skin until her hips moved like lightning. His name sobbed through her lips as she drove them both higher. Lost, she dragged her hands up her body, over her trembling stomach, up to her breasts, then down again until they met his.

At last she slid bonelessly down, her breath shuddering out, to lie in his arms.

"I wonder," she said when she could speak again, "if it is always like this. It makes me see how one might kill for love."

"For love." He shifted so that he could hold her yet closer. "It is not always like this. For me, it has only been like this with you."

She turned her head so that she could see his face. The light was nearly gone in that hour before day begins to break through. "Truly?"

He brought their joined hands to his lips. "Truly."

She smiled a little, pleased. "If you take a mistress after we wed, I will kill her. Then you. But I will kill you more horribly."

He laughed, then took a quick bite at her lower lip. "Well I believe it. Even if I were tempted, you leave me too exhausted for a mistress."

"If I believed you were too tempted, I would leave you inadequate for a mistress." She slid a hand up his thigh meaningfully.

He started to laugh again, but her bland expression had him lifting a brow. "By God, I think you would. Should I remind you that your pleasure would be, ah, cut off, as well?"

"The sacrifice would be great." She trailed her fingers over him, delighted when he shuddered. "The satisfaction is greater."

"Perhaps I should think twice about taking a jealous hellcat to wife."

The humor fled from her eyes. "You should. But I have come to know you will not."

"No. There is only one woman for me." He kissed her again before shifting her comfortably into the crook of his arm. "One day I will take you to Ashburn Manor and show you what is mine, what is ours, what shall be our children's. It's beautiful, Rena, graceful, timeless. Already I can picture you in the bed where I was born."

She started to protest, but her fingers grazed over the pucker of skin on his shoulder where his wound was still healing. "Then our first child will be born there." She turned her face into his throat. "Oh, Brigham, I want your child inside me soon."

Stunned, and deeply moved, he lifted her face to his again. "My God, you humble me. We shall have a dozen children if you like, be they all as bad-tempered as their mother.''

That made her smile again. "Or as arrogant as their father.'' She relaxed against him again. Their time was nearly at an end. Already she could sense a faint lessening of the darkness. There had been a time for loving. Now was the time for truths.

"Brigham, there is something I need to ask you.''

"At this moment, you could ask me anything.''

"Why did you fight the English soldier, the one called Standish?''

The surprise came first, then the quick realization that Parkins and Mrs. Drummond gossiped as well as courted. "It was a matter of honor... He accused me of using weighted dice.''

She said nothing for a moment, then braced herself on her elbow to watch his face. "Why do you lie to me?''

"I don't lie. He lost, lost more, then decided there must have been a reason for it other than his lack of luck.''

"Are you telling me you didn't know who he was? What he was...to me?''

"I knew who he was." He had hoped to keep the matter to himself. Since that was not to be, he decided to make his explanations quickly and be done with it. "One might say I encouraged him to make an accusation so that a duel would be fought.''

Her eyes were very intense. "Why?''

"It was also a matter of honor.''

Serena closed her eyes. Then, lifting his sword hand, she kissed it, almost reverently. "Thank you.''

"Thanks are not necessary for killing a vicious dog." But he tensed even as she held his hand against her cheek. "You knew of this. Is that why you came to me tonight, why you agreed to be my wife?''

"Aye." When he started to pull away, she held him only tighter. "Don't. Let me say it all. It wasn't for gratitude that I came, though I am grateful. It wasn't for obligation, though I owe you a debt that can never be paid.''

"You owe me nothing.''

"Everything," she said passionately. "When I dream now of that night, when I see my mother's eyes after he had done with her, when I hear in my mind the way she wept, I will know that he is dead, and that he died by your hand. Knowing that, there is nothing I would deny you.''

"I didn't kill him for your gratitude or to put you under obligation." His voice was stiff. "I want you as my wife, Serena, intend to have you, but not because you feel you owe a debt.''

"I know that." She knelt beside him and putting her arms around him, buried her face in his neck. "Did I not tell you already that I come to you willingly? Can you doubt it after what we've shared?'' She pressed her lips against his skin, then skimmed them up to his. "When I was told of the duel, of his death, I was glad, afraid, confused. Tonight, I lay in bed and it all came so clear. It was not your fight, my love, not your family, not your mother. But you made it so. He might have killed you.''

"You have a poor opinion of my skill with a sword.''

Shaking her head, she drew back a little. He could see by her face that she would not be put off lightly. "I bound your wound. Your blood was on my hand, as my mother's was that night so many years ago." She held it, palm out. "You bled for my family. I will remember that until the day I die. I loved you before, Brigham. I had already accepted I would love no other. But tonight I came to see that you had honored my family as a man honors his own. I shall honor yours, if you'll let me."

He took the hand she held out to him and turned it over so that the emerald lay dark upon her finger. "I leave you with my heart, Serena. When I return, I'll give you my name, as well."

She opened her arms to him. "For tonight, give me your love once more."

Chapter Twelve

Prince Charles set his royal feet on the thin soil of Scotland in high summer, but not, as he and many others had hoped, in triumph. He was advised by MacDonald of Boisdale as he landed on the island of Eriskay to go home. His reply was terse, and telling.

"I am come home."

From Eriskay, he and the seven men who had sailed with him traveled to the mainland. There, too, the Jacobites were filled more with concern than enthusiasm. Support was slow in coming, but Charles sent out letters to the Highland chiefs. Cameron of Lochiel was among them, and though his support was given reluctantly, and perhaps with a heavy heart, it was given.

So it passed that on August 19, in the year 1745, before some nine hundred loyal men, the standard was raised at Glenfinnan. Charles's father was proclaimed James VIII of Scotland and James III of England, with the young Prince as regent.

The small force moved eastward, gathering strength. The clans rallied, words were pledged, and men bade goodbye to their women and joined the march.

Brigham's journeys through Scotland with Ian and with Coll had given him a knowledge of the land. They were able to make good time, ironically enough on one of the roads built to discourage Highland rebellion. Using this, and the rugged hills for cover, they avoided the government garrisons at Fort William and Fort Augustus.

Spirits were high, the men as rough and ready as their land. It had only taken, as Brigham had always imagined, the energy and force of the young Prince to bind them together. When men thought of the battles ahead, they thought not of their mortality but of victory, and of a justice that had been denied them too long.

Some were young; Brigham saw the future in their eager faces, in the way they laughed and looked at the Prince, who wore the dress of the Highlands and had fastened a white cockade, the symbol of his house, on his blue bonnet.

Some were old, and there the past could be seen, the ageless pride, the battles already lost and won. They looked to the Prince, with his fresh Stuart blood, as the glue that would hold the clans together.

But old or young, eager or heavyhearted, Charles swept them along by the force of his personality alone. This was his time, and his place. He meant to make his mark.

The weather held fine, the breezes warm. It was said by some that God Himself had blessed the rebellion. For a time, it seemed so. The men and weapons that had been lost to the Jacobites when the *Elizabeth* had turned back were forgotten. Peat was plentiful for fires, and the water was fresh from icy mountain streams. The pipes were played, whiskey was drunk, and by night the men slept the good sleep men do when they begin an adventure.

It was to Brigham that word came that a government army had been dispatched north, headed by General Sir John Cope. Brigham took the news directly to the Prince as the men broke camp and prepared for the day's march. Brigham watched the full, almost girlish mouth curve up into a smile that was very much a man's.

"So we shall fight, at last."

"It appears so, Your Highness."

The morning was warm, with the soft, watery light of Scotland gaining strength. The camp carried the scent of horses and soldiers and smoke. The rugged hills were softened now by a springy spread of heather. A golden eagle, early to the hunt, crested overhead.

"It seems a good day to fight," Charles murmured as he studied Brigham's face. "You would prefer we had Lord George with us."

"Lord George is an excellent field commander, your Highness."

"Indeed. But we have O'Sullivan." Charles gestured toward the Irish soldier of fortune who was organizing the men for the day's journey.

Brigham already had doubts in that quarter. He didn't question the Irishman's loyalty to the Prince, but he felt there was more flash than caution. "If we are engaged, we shall fight."

"I look forward to it." Charles fingered the hilt of his sword as he gazed around him. He felt something for this land, something deep and true. When he was king, he would see that Scotland and her people were rewarded. "It's been a long journey, Brigham, a far distance from Louis's court and all those pretty faces."

"A long journey, Your Highness," Brigham agreed. "But one well worth the making."

"I should tell you that there were tears on some of those pretty faces when you left. Have you taken time to break hearts in Scotland, as well?"

"There is only one face for me now, sire, and one heart I will take great care not to break."

The prince's dark eyes were alight with amusement. "Well, well, it appears the dashing Lord Ashburn has fallen for a Highland lassie. Tell me, *mon ami*, is she as pretty as the luscious Anne-Marie?"

Brigham managed a wry grin. "I would beg Your Highness to make no comparisons, particularly in front of the Highland lassie. She has a rare temper."

"Does she?" With a delighted laugh, Charles signaled for his mount. "I am most anxious to meet her and see what manner of woman snared the most sought-after man at the French court."

The pipes sounded along the road, but Cope's troops were never seen. Word came that he had detoured to Inverness. The road to Edinburgh lay open to the rebels. Three thousand strong, they captured Perth after a short, vicious battle. Victorious, they continued their drive south, engaging and routing two regiments of dragoons.

The fighting seemed to fuel the rebels. Here at last was action instead of talk, deeds instead of plans. With sword and pipe, shield and ax, they were like a fury. Survivors would spread tales of their maniacal skill and daring that themselves would serve as a weapon.

Joined by Lord George Murray at Perth, they entered Edinburgh and took it for their own.

The city was in a panic. News of the invasion had preceded the Highland forces, and rumors flew about barbarians, cannibals and butchers. The city guard had fled, and while Edinburgh slept a party of Camerons rushed the sentries, and control was gained.

Under the Prince's command, there was no looting, no pillaging. The people of Edinburgh were given justice and compassion, as was due the subjects of the true king.

It was only a month after the standard had been raised at Glenfinnan and James had been proclaimed king, and his son and regent was preparing to open a royal court at Holyrood House.

Coll was beside Brigham when the Prince rode his gray gelding into Holyrood Park. A crowd had gathered to watch him. Shouts and cheers followed them, for the people saw their heart's delight in the young man in his tartan shortcoat and blue bonnet. Perhaps he was not yet England's Prince, but he was theirs.

"Listen to them." Coll leaned forward in the saddle and grinned. "Here is our first real victory, Brigham, and by God, it has a good feel."

Brigham steadied his mount as he maneuvered through the narrow, crowded streets. "I'll swear he could drive them to London now with only a word. I can only hope the supplies and men we need will arrive before it comes time."

"We could be outnumbered ten to one today and never taste defeat. It would be as it was at Perth and, aye, at Coltbridge." The early-autumn breeze drifted, making Coll grimace. "But in God's name, this place is filthy. Give me the open Highlands and the hills. How does a man breathe," he wondered, "without the room to draw air?"

Edinburgh was packed with houses and shops, some still fashioned of mud and wood. The stone buildings rose high, like aeries, with the fronts four or five stories high, and the backs often stretching nine or ten stories down the perilously steep hills.

"Worse than Paris," Brigham agreed. The stench drifted out from crowded lanes, and waste and garbage clogged the alleys, but the people, cheering the Prince, seemed oblivious to it all.

Above the slums, the filth of the alleys and the dirt of the streets was the Royal Mile. Edinburgh Castle, majestic, already glamorous with age and history, guarded one end of that great street. Where its slope ended was Holyrood House, where palace and abbey stood together elegantly poised before the rough crags. It had already been the scene, time after time, of turbulence and passion. Mary, Queen of Scots, had been its most famous and doomed inhabitant. She had lived there, marrying her cousin Henry Stewart of Darnley in Holyrood Abbey, and seeing her lover Rizzio murdered by him in the little supper room of her own apartments. Her son James had been born in the castle, and had survived a troubled and turbulent boyhood to become king of England, as well as Scotland.

It was here, at this site of pomp and intrigue that James's great-great grandson Charles would hold his court, bringing Holyrood House to life once more.

He rode toward the palace that had once housed his ancestors. Dismounting, he walked slowly under the archway, to appear moments later in the window of his new apartments, waving to the shouts of the crowd.

Edinburgh held the Prince, and he held Edinburgh.

He was to prove this only days later, when Cope moved his troops south.

Primed, even eager, the Jacobites met the government army east of the city at Prestonpans. Red-coated dragoons faced the Highlanders, who were dressed for battle in kilts or close-fitting trews. Brigham, with a leather shield in one hand and his sword in the other, joined the MacGregors. For a moment the field was eerily silent, with only the hollow sound of the pipes rising into the misty air. Like the heartbeats of men, Brigham thought, men who were willing to die. Opposing standards waved, caught by the early breeze.

The first charge sent birds wheeling and screaming up the sky. Men on foot met with a thunderous crash of sword and ax. Here, as they had on the route south, the Scots fought like demons, hacking with blades, pressing on even when bloody. As had happened before, the English infantry couldn't withstand the violence of the Highland charge. The red line wavered and broke.

The cavalry surged forward, vicious hooves striking, claymores glinting. Brigham ignored the cries and curses around him as he met his man. A shot rang whistling past his ear, but his eyes never lost their icy determination. The Campbell on the road from London would have recognized it. Brigham was a man who was willing to die but confident he would not.

Smoke from cannon and mortar grew thick, so that men on both sides fought in a fog. The heat of battle set sweat pouring as freely as blood so that the stench of both stung the air. Already carrion birds circled overhead, lured by the battle sounds.

As Brigham maneuvered his mount through what was left of the English lines, he could see the white cockades of the Jacobites and the plaids of MacGregors, MacDonalds, Camerons. Some fell around him, victims of bayonets or swords. Again and again the ground exploded where mortars struck, flinging out rock and dirt and deadly metal. Men screamed as they were struck down. Others died in silence.

Within ten minutes, the battle was over. Dragoons sought safety in flight and raced to the concealing hills on horse or on foot. Blood streaked the thin grass and stained the gray rock. The bodies of the dead and wounded lay sprawled on the ground. That day the pipes played in victory, and the standard of the House of Stuart was held high.

"Why do we stay snug in Edinburgh when we should be marching toward London?" Coll demanded as he strode out into the courtyard at Holyrood, a plaid wrapped around his shoulders to ward off the chilly dusk.

For once Brigham could only agree with Coll's impatience to be doing. They had been nearly three weeks at Charles's newly established court. The court itself was very glamorous, with levees and councils in the palace, but the Prince had not forgotten his men and so divided his time between Holyrood and the camp at Duddingston. Morale was good, though there was more than one man among them who would have agreed with Coll's sentiments.

Balls and receptions could wait.

"Victory at Prestonpans earned us more support." Brigham flicked his cloak back, welcoming the damp evening air. "I doubt we tarry here much longer."

"Councils," Coll grumbled. "Every blessed day we have another council. If there's a problem here, my lad, it's between Lord George and O'Sullivan. I'll swear, if one says black, the other before God will vow it to be white."

"I know." It was a matter that caused Brigham no little concern. "I'll tell you true, Coll, O'Sullivan worries me. I prefer a commander a bit steadier, one who is less interested in routs than in overall victory."

"We can have neither if we dally here in court."

Brigham smiled, but he was looking out into the lowering night. "You miss your Highlands, Coll, and your wife."

"Aye. It's been barely two months since we left Glenroe, but we had little time together. With the bairn coming, I worry."

"A man's entitled to worry about the ones he loves."

"There's many a man with us who knows once the march south begins it could be a year before we see our homes and families again." Because he had no wish to fall into a black mood, Coll slapped Brigham on the shoulder. "At least there's plenty here for you to enjoy. The women are bonny. I wonder that you don't pick out a wench to charm. I'd swear you've broken a dozen hearts with your indifference these past few weeks."

"You could say I've something on my mind." Someone, Brigham thought. The only one. "What do you say we crack a bottle and find a game?" He turned at Coll's nod of assent, and together they started back across the courtyard.

Brigham noticed the woman step through the shadowy archway, but his gaze skimmed over her and passed without interest. He had taken only three steps when he stopped, turning slowly, deliberately, to stare. The light was fading quickly, and he could see only that she was tall and very slender. A plaid was draped over her head and shoulders. She might have been a servant, or one of the ladies of the court taking the air. He wondered why a stranger should remind him so achingly of his porcelain shepherdess.

And though he couldn't see her face, he was certain she was staring at him as intently as he stared at her.

The leap of attraction was unexpected. Annoyed with himself, Brigham turned again and continued on. Inexplicably, he was compelled to stop, to turn yet again. She was still there, standing in the fading light, her hands folded, her head held high.

"What the devil's wrong with you?" Coll stopped and turned himself. Spotting the figure in the archway, he grinned. "Well, if that's all. I don't suppose you'll want to dice with me now."

"No, I..." Brigham let his words trail off as the woman lifted her hands to slip the plaid from her head. The last of the light fell over her hair. Like sunset, it gleamed.

"Serena?" He could only stare. She took a step toward him, and he saw her face, and that she was smiling. His boots rang against stone as he strode across the courtyard. Before she could say his name, he swept her up into his arms, then around and around in dizzying circles.

"So that's the way of it," Coll murmured as he watched his friend drag his sister close for a long, bruising kiss.

"Why are you here? How did you come?" Then Brigham kissed her again and swallowed her answer.

"Give way, man." Coll plucked Serena from Brigham's arms, kissed her hard, then set her on her feet. "What are you doing in Edinburgh, and where's Maggie?"

"She's here." Breathless, Serena found herself swung back against Brigham's side. "And Mother and Gwen and Malcolm, as well." She reached out to give Coll's beard a sisterly tug. "The Prince invited us to court. We arrived almost an hour ago, but didn't know where to find you."

"Maggie's here? Is she well? Where is she?" With his usual impatience, Coll turned on his heel and strode off to see for himself.

"Brigham—"

"Say nothing." He combed his hands through her hair, delighted with the feel of it, the scent of it. "Say nothing," he repeated, and lowered his head.

He held her like that, mouth to mouth, body to body, while the shadows deepened. The weeks of separation melted away. Restless, his hands moved down her back, over her hips, up to her face, while his lips, heated with desire, had her moaning and straining against him.

"Beautiful, always more beautiful, Serena. A man could die from missing you."

"I thought of you every day, and prayed. When we heard of the battles, I nearly went mad waiting for your letters telling me you were safe." At last she drew away to look at him. Because he and Coll had ridden in from camp, he had yet to change to his court dress. With some relief, Serena noted that he was the same man who had ridden away from Glenroe nearly three months before.

"I was afraid you'd change somehow, being here." She moistened her lips as she looked back toward the buildings. Nothing she had ever seen was more magnificent than the palace, with its towers and steeples with lights flickering behind its tall windows. "Everything here is so splendid. The palace, the abbey."

"Wherever I am, nothing changes between us, Rena."

She moved back into his arms to rest her head on his shoulder. "I was afraid it would. I prayed every day for you to be safe. And I prayed every day that you wouldn't seek comfort in the arms of another woman."

He laughed and kissed her hair. "I shan't ask which you prayed for with more fervor. My love, there is no one else. Can be no one else. Tonight I shall find more than comfort in your arms."

She smiled as she turned her lips to his cheek. "Would that we could. In truth, next to finding you safe, my dearest desire was to spend a night loving you."

"Then I shall see to it that you have both your desires."

She kissed him again and chuckled. "I'm to share a chamber with Gwen. It would be as unseemly, my lord, for you to come to my bed as it would for me to search the corridors for yours."

"Tonight you share my chamber, as my wife."

Her mouth opened in surprise as she stepped out of his arms. "That's impossible."

"It is very possible," he corrected. "And it shall be." Without giving her a chance to speak, he pulled her through the archway.

The Prince was in his apartments, preparing for that evening's entertainment. Though Brigham's request for an audience at that hour surprised him, he granted it.

"Your Highness." Brigham bowed as he entered Charles's sitting room.

"Good evening, Brigham. Madam," he said as Serena sank into a curtsy. She would kill Brigham, she thought, for dragging her before the Prince without even a chance to wash off the travel dirt or take a comb to her hair. "You would be Miss MacGregor." Charles drew Serena to her feet and kissed her hand. "It is easy to see why Lord Ashburn no longer notices the ladies at court."

"Your Highness. It was good of you to allow me and my family to come."

"I owe the MacGregors a great deal. They have stood behind my father, and behind me. Such loyalty is priceless. Will you sit?" He led her to a chair himself.

She had never seen a room like this one. The high ceiling was festooned with swirls and clusters of fruits and flowers, and from its center hung a dripping chandelier. Murals ran along the walls depicting Stuart victories in battle. A fire crackled in the hearth beside her chair. Music lay open on a harpsichord in the center of the room.

"Sire, I have a favor I would ask."

Charles sat, then gestured Brigham to a chair. "I am sure I owe you more than one."

"There is no debt for loyalty, Your Highness."

Charles's eyes softened. Serena saw then why he was called the Bonnie Prince. It wasn't just his face and form, it was his heart. "No, but there can be gratitude. What would you ask of me?"

"I would wed Miss MacGregor."

Charles's smile spread as he tapped his fingertips on his knee. "I had already surmised as much. Shall I tell you, Miss MacGregor, that in Paris Lord Ashburn was very generous with the ladies at court? At Holyrood House he has proved most selfish."

Serena kept her hands folded primly in her lap. "I believe Lord Ashburn is a wise warrior, sir. He has some knowledge of the fierce and terrible temper of Clan MacGregor."

Highly entertained, Charles laughed. "So, I shall wish you well. Perhaps you would care to be married here, at court."

"Yes, sir, and tonight," Brigham said.

Now Charles's pale brows rose. "Tonight, Brigham? Such haste is..." He let his words trail off as he glanced at Serena again. The firelight played seductively over her hair. "...understandable," he decided. "Do you have the MacGregor's permission?"

"Yes, sir."

"Well, then. You are both Catholic?" Receiving nods, he thought it through. "The abbey is convenient. There is a matter of the banns and so forth, but I believe if a man cannot deal with such matters, he can hardly hope to win a throne.'' He rose, bringing both Serena and Brigham to their feet. ''I will see you wed tonight.''

Pale, not at all certain she wasn't dreaming, Serena found her parents in their chamber.

''Serena.'' Fiona sighed over the fact that her daughter still wore her traveling suit. ''You must change. The Prince's court is no place for muddy boots and soiled skirts.''

''Mama, I am to be wed.''

''Devil, lass.'' Ian kissed her tumbled hair. ''We're aware of that.''

''Tonight.''

''Tonight?'' Fiona rose from her chair. ''But how—?''

''Brigham went to the Prince. He took me, like this.'' Serena spread her muddy skirts, knowing her mother would understand her feelings on the matter.

''I see,'' Fiona murmured.

''And he, they...'' She looked from her mother to her father, then back again. ''Mama.''

''Is it your wish to marry him?''

She hesitated, feeling the old doubts well up. Instinctively she lifted a hand to her breast. On a heavy chain under her bodice was the emerald Brigham had given her. ''Aye,'' she managed. ''But it has all happened so fast.'' He would be leaving again, she thought. Leaving to fight. ''Aye,'' she said, her voice stronger. ''There is nothing I want more than to belong to him.''

Fiona slipped an arm around Serena's shoulders. ''Then we have much to do. Leave us, please, Ian, and send a servant for Maggie and Gwen.''

''Tossing me out, are you, my lady?''

Fiona held out a hand to him, even as Serena reached for his other. ''I fear you would have a strong dislike for the woman's work that must be done in the next few hours.''

''Aye, I'll go willingly.'' He paused a moment to draw Serena close. ''You have always made me proud. Tonight I give you to another man, and you will take his name. But you will always be a MacGregor.'' He kissed her. ''Royal is our race, Serena, and rightly.''

There was no time to think, and certainly no time to dwell on the enormity of what she would do before the night was over. Servants rushed in and out of the chambers with jugs of hot water that Fiona scented delicately for her daughter's bath. Gwen and Maggie chattered as they took out seams and sewed new ones on the dress Serena would wear to be married.

''It's romantic,'' Gwen said as she scanned her stitches with a critical eye.

''It's madness.'' Maggie glanced over, knowing Serena was soaking behind the screen. ''Rena must have woven strong magic to make Brigham hurry so. He must not be so stuffy as I once thought.''

''Imagine.'' Gwen shifted the ivory satin delicately. ''Going to the Prince. We never had a chance to unpack from the journey before we're changing Mother's ball gown into Serena's wedding gown.''

Maggie sat back, touching a hand to the mound of her belly. The baby she carried always became more active at night. The unpacking would have to wait, she thought, just as she and Coll would have to wait to have a proper reunion. She stifled a giggle as she remembered how he had roared when they had been interrupted just as they had started to become reacquainted. She looked over as Serena emerged, wrapped in towels, her skin and hair dripping.

"The dress will be beautiful," Maggie told her, blinking back tears at the thought of the wedding. "And so will you."

"By the fire," Fiona ordered, armed with a brush. Knowing the trembles had nothing to do with a chill, Fiona began to soothe her daughter as she dried her hair. "A woman's wedding is one of her most precious memories. Years from now, when you look back, what seems now like a dream will be very clear."

"Should I be so afraid?"

Fiona reached over Serena's shoulder to take her hand. "I almost think the more you love, the sharper the fear."

Serena gave a weak laugh. "Then I must love him more than I knew."

"I could not wish a better man for you, Rena. When the fighting is done, you will have a good life together."

"In England," Serena managed.

Fiona began to stroke with the brush as she had so many times before. Her hands were gentle as she thought of this small pleasure that would soon be denied her.

"When I married your father, I left my family and my home. I had grown up with the sound of the sea, the smell of it. As a girl I would climb the cliffs and watch the waves break on the rocks below. The forest of Glenroe was foreign to me, and frightening. I wasn't sure I could bear being so far away from everything I had known and loved."

"How did you?"

"By loving your father more."

They left her hair loose so that it streamed like candlelight down her back. The bodice of the gown was snug, skimming her breasts, leaving them to rise softly above as a resting place for a rope of pearls. The sleeves belled out, sheening down to her wrists. There was a glimmer of pearls on the skirt where it flared over hoops and petticoats. At the waist was a sash gathered up with a clutch of the palest pink wild roses. With her heart hammering, Serena stepped into the abbey.

It was a place of legends, of joy and despair, and of miracles. There she would be wed.

He was waiting for her. In the wavering light of lamps and candles, she walked to him. She had always thought he was at his most elegant in black, but she had never seen him look more handsome. Silver buttons glinted, adding richness to the severe cut of his coat. For the first time since she had known him, he wore a wig. The soft white added romance to his face, contrasting royally with the dark gray of his eyes.

She didn't see the Prince, or the pews filled with the lords and ladies who had come to watch the ceremony. She only saw Brigham.

When her hand touched his, it stopped trembling. Together, they faced the priest and pledged.

The clock struck midnight.

The Prince had decided that a wedding, however hurried, deserved a celebration. Within minutes after becoming Lady Ashburn, Serena found herself being led to the picture gallery of the palace, where Charles had given his first grand ball on the night he had taken the city.

The long, wide room was already filled with music. Serena was kissed and congratulated by strangers, envied by the ladies, studied by the men. Her head was reeling by the time she was handed her first glass of champagne. She sipped and felt the bubbles burst on her tongue.

Exercising his privilege, Charles claimed her for a dance. "You make a lovely bride, Lady Ashburn."

Lady Ashburn.

"Thank you, Your Highness. How can I thank you for making this possible?"

"Your husband is of great value to me, my lady, as a soldier and as a friend."

Her husband.

"You have his loyalty, sir, and mine, both as a Langston and as a MacGregor."

Brigham claimed her when the dance had ended, fending off complaints by others who would have partnered the new bride.

"You are enjoying yourself, my love?"

"Aye." Ridiculous to be shy, she thought, but she felt herself color as she smiled at him. He looked different in the wig, with the flash of jewels, she thought. Not at all like a man who would toss her over his shoulder and threaten to dump her in a loch. He looked as glamorous as the Prince himself. And nearly as much a stranger. "It's a beautiful room."

"You see the portraits?" he asked, leading her gently by the elbow for a closer look. "There are eighty-nine, Scottish monarchs all. I'm told they were commissioned by Charles II, though he never once entered Holyrood House, in fact never returned to Scotland after the Restoration."

She knew her history, she thought irritably, but tried to show an interest. "Aye. This is Robert the Bruce, a fierce soldier and well-loved king."

"I should have known a woman as well-read as you would know her history and her politics." He leaned close to her ear. "What do you know about military strategy?"

"Military strategy?"

"Ah, so there is something yet I might teach you." Before she could answer, he pulled her roughly through a doorway. She had only time for a muffled squeal before he swept her into his arms and began to race along a corridor.

"What are you doing? You've gone mad again."

"I'm escaping." As the music faded behind them, he slowed his pace. "And I went mad from the moment you walked into the abbey. Let them dance and drink. I'm taking my wife to bed."

He mounted a staircase, not even bothering to nod at a servant who, wide-eyed, bowed himself out of the way. With Serena still in his arms, he kicked the door to his chamber open, then kicked it closed again behind them. Without ceremony, he dropped Serena on the bed.

She tried to look indignant. "Is that a way to treat your new bride, my lord?"

"I haven't even begun." Turning he shot the bolt on the door.

"I might have wanted another dance or two," she said, smoothing her palm over the bed.

"Oh, I intend to dance with you, be sure of it. From now till dawn and after."

She gave him a cheeky grin. "There's dancing, *Sassenach*, and there's dancing."

"Aye," he said, mocking her. "It's not the minuet I have in mind."

She smoothed the rumpled skirt of her gown. "What is it you have in mind, then?" She lifted her brow as she assessed him and wondered that he didn't hear how fast and loud her heart was beating. "Gwen thinks you're romantic. I doubt she'll continue to think so when I tell her how you dropped me on the bed like a sack of meal."

"Romance?" He lighted the candles that stood beside the bed. "Is that what you want, Rena?"

She moved a nearly bare shoulder. "It's what Gwen dreams of."

"But not you?" With a little laugh, he shrugged out of his coat and tossed it over a chair in a manner that would have made Parkins shudder. "A woman's entitled to romance on her wedding night." He surprised her by kneeling on the bed and slipping off her shoes. "I had no chance to tell you how magnificent you looked standing beside me in the lamplight of the abbey. Or of how, when I saw you there, every dream I have ever had came true."

"I thought you looked like a prince," she murmured, then shivered when he ran his fingertips along the arch of her foot.

"Tonight I'm only a man in love with his wife." He brushed his lips over her ankle. The scent of her bath clung to it and spun seductively in his head. "Bewitched by her." Slowly he skimmed his mouth along her calf to trace the pulse at the back of her knee. "Enslaved by her."

"I was afraid." She reached for him, gathering him close. "From the moment I stepped inside the nave I was afraid." Then she sighed as he ran kisses along the edge of her bodice, moistening and heating her skin.

"Are you still?" With sure fingers he unfastened her gown, then watched as it dropped silently to her waist.

"No. I stopped being afraid when you picked me up and ran with me through the corridors." She smiled, and her hands were as confident as his as she pushed the waistcoat from his shoulders. "That was when I knew you were my Brigham again."

"I am always yours, Rena." He lowered her gently to the bed and showed her how true his words were.

Chapter Thirteen

They were three more weeks at court. Nothing could have been more splendid than Prince Charles's Holyrood. The food was sumptuous, as was the music, the entertainment, the people. It was a gold and gleaming time, when the great halls echoed with laughter and dancing, when frivolous games and affairs of the heart were played with equal abandon.

From all over the country came elegantly dressed men in their powdered wigs, and glamorously gowned women to flirt with them. Holyrood was gay and glittering, and in it Charles lived those weeks a true prince. It was a place and a time that would never be forgotten.

Serena watched Brigham meld into this world he had been born for, while she, fueled by determination more than by confidence, adjusted to the life of beauty and glamour.

There were new rules to learn, a new pattern to the days and the nights. Here, at the first court to grace Scotland in many years, Serena discovered what it was to be Lady Ashburn. There were servants to attend her whether she wanted them or not. Because of Brigham's position, they were given a gracious chamber hung with tapestries and appointed with elegant furnishings. She met more people in a matter of weeks than she had in the whole of her life, many of whom had come out of curiosity, but more still who had come out of loyalty.

Court life continued to make her uneasy, and often impatient, but the people who comprised it made her proud of her heritage, and her husband.

Serena had the first true inkling of Brigham's wealth when he presented her with the Langston emeralds. With the help of his contacts in London he had them transported from Ashburn Manor and gave them to Serena less than a week after they had exchanged vows.

The necklace was as stately as its name and glimmered with stones as green as the lawns of his estate. It was matched with a bracelet and ear bobs that made Maggie's jaw drop. To accent them, Brigham commissioned a dressmaker. Serena found herself gowned in silks and satins, in soft lawns and wispy lace. She discovered what it was like to wear diamonds in her hair and scent her skin with the finest of French perfumes.

She would have given it all for a week alone with Brigham in a Highland croft.

It was impossible not to enjoy the splendor, impossible not to revel a little in the envious glances of other ladies as she was escorted into a room by

Brigham. She wore the gowns and the jewels, dressed her hair and felt beautiful. But as the days passed, she couldn't shake the sensation that it was all like a dream. The lights, the glamour, the tinkling laughter of women, the sweeping bows of men, her own easy relationship with the Prince.

But the nights were real. Serena clung to them as tightly as she clung to Brigham in the privacy of their marriage bed. She knew it was temporary, and that its continuation was in God's hands. It was only a matter of time before Brigham would leave. They did not speak of it. There was no need to speak of what they both understood. If force of will alone could bring him back safely to her, she could be content.

At night she could be his wife freely, in heart, mind and body. By day she often felt like an impostor, masquerading in fashionable gowns as a lady while in her heart she remained a product of the Highlands, longing to kilt up her skirts and race through the autumn trees surrounding the park as the wind tore the leaves from the branches for a dizzying dance. Instead, she walked sedately with the other women while the men held council or rode to the camp.

Because she loved, she put her heart and soul into being the kind of wife she thought Brigham should have. She sat, desperately struggling to be attentive, through musical evenings. Though she found it absurd, she never complained about the necessity to change from a morning dress to an afternoon dress, then again for evening. Only once, when she was sure she wouldn't be noticed, did she accompany Malcolm to the stables to admire the horses.

She envied her young brother the freedom to take wild rides, but set her teeth and determined to enjoy her own demure ones.

"Do this, do that," she muttered as she paced alone in her bedchamber. "Don't do this, don't do that." Swearing, she kicked a chair with the toe of the pretty slipper that matched her violet morning dress. "A body could go mad trying to remember the rules, then madder still trying to live by them."

With a hiss of breath she dropped down into the chair, skirts billowing. She wanted the loch, the peace of it. She didn't just want to look out at the hills and crags. She wanted to climb them. She wanted her breeches, she thought, and her boots. She wanted...

Sighing, she braced her elbows on her knees and cupped her face in her hands. Not an attitude suitable for Lady Ashburn, but Serena didn't feel like Lady Ashburn at the moment. She was being selfish and ungrateful, she told herself. Brigham was giving her things many another women would have swooned over. He was promising her the kind of life only a fool would toss aside.

And she was a fool, Serena decided, because she would have done just that if it wouldn't have meant losing Brigham, as well. Living with dignity and propriety was a small price to pay for love. But oh, she had nearly botched it a dozen times already, and they had only been married three weeks.

She heard the door open and popped up like a spring, smoothing her skirts. A breath of relief escaped when she saw that it was Brigham. She would have hated for a servant to gossip below stairs about how Lady Ashburn sulked in her room with her elbows on her knees.

Brigham lifted a brow when he saw her. He would have sworn she grew

more beautiful each day, though he did wish from time to time that she could
wear her hair loose and free so that he could bury his hands in it at will.

"I thought you were going for a walk with your sister and Maggie."

"I was just getting ready." Automatically she reached up to pat her hair,
afraid her pacing had loosened the careful arrangement. "I didn't expect you
back until much later. Is the council over?"

"Yes. You look exquisite, Rena. Like a wild violet."

With a laugh that was half sob, she raced into his arms. "Oh, Brig, I love
you. I love you so much."

"What's this?" he murmured as she pressed her face against his neck.
"Are you crying?"

"No—aye, a little. It's only that whenever I see you I love you more than
the last time."

"Then I'll take care to leave and come back several times each day."

"Don't laugh at me."

"And risk fatal injury?" He tilted her head back so that he could kiss her
properly. "No, my dear, I shan't laugh at you."

She saw it in his eyes, and knew then that she had seen it the moment he
had come into the room. The courage she had promised herself she would
show wavered, but she willed it back. "It's time, isn't it?"

He brought her hand to his lips. "Come, sit."

"There is no need," she said steadily. "Just tell me."

"We march in a matter of days. Tomorrow you must leave for Glenroe."

Her cheeks paled, but her voice remained strong. "I would stay until you
go."

"I would go with an easier mind if I knew you were safe at Glenroe. The
journey will take longer because of Maggie."

She knew he was right, knew it was necessary, and tried to live with it.
"You march to London?"

"God willing."

With a nod, she stepped back, but she kept his hand in hers. "The fight
is mine, as well as yours, doubly so now that I am your wife. I would go
with you, if you would let me."

"No. Do you think I see my wife as a camp follower?" The look, the
very familiar look, in her eyes warned him to change tactics. "Your family
needs you, Serena."

What of my needs? The words sprang to her tongue and were bitten back.
She would do him no good by following him into battle. She looked at her
hand and cursed the fact that it was too weak to wield a sword, to protect
him as he would protect her.

"You're right. I know. I will wait for you."

"I take you with me. Here." He brought their joined hands to his heart.
"There is something I would ask of you. If things go wrong—" She shook
her head, but a look from him stopped her urgent protest. "There is a chest
in my chamber, and a strongbox. In the box is gold and enough jewels to
buy your safety and that of your family. In the chest is something more
precious that I would have you keep."

"What is it?"

He traced a fingertip along her cheekbone, remembering. "You will know
when you see it."

"I won't forget, but there will be no need. You will come back." She smiled. "Remember, you have promised to show me Ashburn Manor."

"I remember."

Lifting her hands, she began to undo the tiny buttons at her bodice.

"What are you doing?

Smiling still, she let the dress open. "What I am not doing is going for a walk with my sister." She undid the satin sash at her waist. "Is it improper to seduce one's husband at this hour?"

"Probably." He grinned as she tugged the coat from his shoulders. "But we shall keep it our secret."

They made love on the elegantly skirted bed, under the high canopy, with the sun coming strong through the windows. The proper morning dress lay discarded in billows of violet. She knelt beside him, slender, with the light playing over her skin as she drew the pins from her hair. Heavily, in a glory of flame-tipped gold, it fell over her naked shoulders and breasts. Brigham reached for it, wrapped it once, twice, around his wrists as if to imprison himself, then drew her slowly down to him.

Their bodies fit.

They both remembered the loch, and another sun-drenched morning filled with love and passions. The memory of it, and thoughts of the cloudy, uncertain future brought them gently together. Selflessly they gave to each other, beautifully they received.

With a sigh, he slipped into her. With a murmur, their lips met and clung. Together they showed one another a new level of pleasure, one that could be reached only through the purity and the passions of unconditional love.

It was the first of November when the march finally began. Many, Brigham among them, had urged the Prince to begin the campaign earlier, moving on the advantage they had gained by taking Edinburgh. Instead, Charles had continued to hope for active support from France. Money had indeed come, and supplies, but no men. Charles put his own strength at eight thousand, with three hundred horses. He knew that he must make one decisive stroke, bringing victory or defeat in a short time. As before, he decided the best strategy was a bold one.

Charles had a high opinion of his troops, as did the English. A few months before, the young Prince's ambitions and his ragtag troops of rugged Highlanders had been laughed at: Then he had swept down on Edinburgh. His early victories, and the flair with which he had brought defeat to the English had the uneasy government recalling more and more troops from Flanders, sending them to Field Marshal Wade in Newcastle.

Still, as the Stuart army marched into Lancaster under the leadership of Lord George Murray, they met with little resistance. But the celebration there might have been was offset by the disappointing number of English Jacobites who had rallied.

Near a hot fire on a cold night, Brigham sat with Whitesmouth, who had ridden from Manchester to join the cause. Men warmed themselves with whiskey and wrapped themselves in plaids against the keening wind.

"We should have attacked Wade's forces." Whitesmouth tipped his flask. "Now they've called the elector's fat son Cumberland in haste, and he's advancing through the Midlands. How many are we, Brig? Four, five thousand?''

"At best.'' Brigham accepted the flask but only stared into the fire. "The Prince is pushed two ways by Murray and O'Sullivan. Each decision comes only after agonizing debate. If you want the truth, Johnny, we lost our momentum in Edinburgh. We may never get it back.''

"But you stay?''

"He has my oath.''

They sat another moment in silence, listening to the wind crying over the hills. "You know that some of the Scots are drifting off, going quietly back to their glens and hills.''

"I know it.''

Only that day, Ian and other chiefs had spoken together. They meant to hold their men. Brigham wondered if they, or anyone, fully understood that the brilliant victories of their outnumbered and ill-equipped army had been won because the men hadn't simply been ordered to fight, but had fought with their hearts. Once the heart was lost, so would be the cause.

With a shake of his head, he shifted his thoughts to practical matters. "We reach Derby tomorrow. If we hit London quickly, thoroughly, we could still see the king on the throne.'' He sipped then, as someone began to play a mournful tune on the pipes. "We've yet to be beaten. From what news you bring, there is panic in the city and the elector prepares to leave for Hanover.''

"There may he stay,'' Whitesmouth mumbled. "My God, it's cold.''

"In the north the wind has an edge as sharp and as sweet as a blade.''

"If luck is with us, you'll be back to your wife and her Highlands by the new year.''

Brigham drank again, but in his heart he knew it would take more than luck.

In Derby, with London only 130 miles away, Charles held his council of war.

Snow fell fitfully outside as the men rounded the table. A gloom was in the room, both from the leaden light and on the faces of men. There was a good fire, but over its crackle and hiss the sound of the icy wind could still be heard.

"Gentlemen.'' Charles spread his fine hands in front of him. "I seek advice from you who have pledged to my father. It is boldness we need, and unity.''

His dark eyes scanned the room, lighting briefly on each man. Murray was there, and the man whom Murray considered a thorn in his side, O'Sullivan. Brigham watched, holding his silence, as the Prince continued to speak.

"We know that three government troops threaten to converge on us, and morale among the men is suffering. A thrust, rapier-sharp, at the capital— now, while we still remember our victories—is surely our move.''

"Your Highness.'' Murray waited, then was given permission to speak. "The advice I must offer is caution. We are poorly equipped and greatly outnumbered. If we withdraw to the Highlands, take the winter to plan a new campaign that would launch in spring, we might rally those men we have already lost and draw fresh supplies from France.''

"Such counsel is the counsel of despair," Charles said. "I can see nothing but ruin and destruction coming to us if we should retreat."

"Withdraw," Murray corrected, and was joined by the assent of other advisers. "Our rebellion is young, but it must not be impulsive."

Charles listened, shutting his eyes a moment as one after another of the men who stood with him echoed Murray's sentiments. Prudence, patience, caution. Only O'Sullivan preached attack, using flattery and reckless promises in his attempt to sway the Prince.

All at once, Charles sprang up from his chair, scattering the maps and documents spread out in front of him. "What say you?" he demanded of Brigham.

Brigham knew that, militarily, Murray's advice was sound. But he remembered his own thoughts as he had sat with Whitesmouth by the fire. If they withdrew now, the heart of the rebellion would be lost. For once, perhaps for the only time, his thoughts marched in step with O'Sullivan's.

"With respect, Your Highness, if the choice was mine I would march to London at daybreak and seize the moment."

"The heart says to fight, Your Highness," one of the advisers put in, closely echoing Brigham's thoughts. "But in war, one must heed the head, as well. If we ride to London as we are, our losses could be immeasurable."

"Or our triumph great," Charles interrupted passionately. "Are we women who cover our heads at the first sign of snow or who think of only warming our tired feet by the fire? Withdraw, retreat." He swung back toward Murray, eyes furious. "It is one and the same. I wonder if you have a mind to betray me."

"I have only a mind to see you and our cause succeed," Murray said quietly. "You are a prince, sire. I am but a soldier and must speak as one who knows his troops and the way of war."

The argument continued, but long before it was finished, Brigham saw how it would be. The Prince, never strong of purpose when faced with dissension among his advisers, was being forced to heed Murray's words of caution. On December 6, the decision to retreat was taken.

The road back to Scotland was long, and the men dispirited. It was as Brigham had feared. When a halt was called to the exuberant, aggressive advance that had given the clans such power since the previous summer, the heart went out of the rebellion. Men might still talk of another invasion in the following year, but all believed in their secret hearts that they would never march south again.

They fell back behind the Scottish border and took Glasgow, though the city was openly hostile. The men, frustrated and disillusioned, might have taken that Christmas day to loot and sack, had not Cameron of Lochiel's cool head and compassion dissuaded them.

Stirling surrendered just as reinforcements, men, stores and ammunition arrived from France. It started to seem as if the right decision had been made, but if Charles now believed Lord George had been correct, he never spoke of it.

The Prince's numbers were again on the increase as more clans came to him, pledging heart and sword and men. But there were MacKenzies and MacLeods, MacKays and Munroes who followed the elector's colors.

They fought again, south of Stirling, in the purple winter's dusk, Scot fighting Scot, as well as English. Again they tasted victory, but with it came grief, as Ian MacGregor fell to an enemy blade.

He lingered through the night. Men who ride in battle need not be told when wounds are mortal. Brigham knew it as he sat beside the old man with the night wind flapping at the tent.

He thought of Serena and how she had laughed when the big bear of a MacGregor had swung her around and around in her night robe. He thought of riding with Ian through the winter wind and of sharing a bottle of port near a great fire. Now, approaching death seemed to have stolen both size and strength so that he was only an old, fragile man. Still, his hair glowed rich and red in the pale glow of the lamp.

"Your mother..." Ian began, reaching for Coll's hand.

"I'll care for her." They were men who loved each other too well to pretend there would be a tomorrow.

"Aye." Ian's breath hissed in and out, like wind through an empty husk of wheat. "The bairn—my only regret is I won't see the bairn."

"He shall carry your name," Coll vowed. "He shall know the man who was his grandsire."

There was a faint smile on Ian's mouth, though his lips were the color of ashes. "Brigham."

"I'm here, sir."

Because his vision was fading, Ian concentrated on the voice. "Don't tame my wildcat. She would die from it. You and Coll will tend to little Gwen and Malcolm. Keep them safe."

"My word on it."

"My sword—" Ian struggled for another breath. "My sword to Malcolm. Coll, you have your own."

"He shall have it." Coll bent over Ian's hand. "Papa."

"We were right to fight. It will not be for naught." He opened his eyes for the last time. "Royal is our race, lad." He managed a final fierce grin. "We are MacGregors despite them."

There were men dispatched to bear the body back to Glenroe, but Coll refused to go with them. "He would have me stay with the Prince," Coll told Brigham as they stood out in the bitter sleet. "That he died here, with our backs turned to London."

"It's not finished, Coll."

Coll turned his head. There was grief in his eyes, and also a bright anger. "No, by God, it's not."

The men of the clans grew dispirited, as it seemed ever clearer that the invasion of England was fast petering out into a holding action. Desertions had become frequent, and the decision was made to consolidate forces in the north of Scotland. But the leaders continue to bicker, even after the rebels forded the icy waters of the Forth and marched north up the Great Glen. For seven weeks that winter, Charles made his base in Inverness. Inactivity again took its toll, dwindling the numbers of the so recently replenished troops. There were short, sporadic, often bitter little battles during those weeks. The Jacobites were again victorious in the taking of Fort Augustus, that hated English stronghold at the heart of the Highlands, but the men longed for a decisive victory and for home. Meanwhile, Cumberland massed his forces. It seemed the winter would never end.

* * *

It was snowing when Serena stood by her father's grave. He had come back to them nearly a month before, and all Glenroe had wept. Her own tears fell freely as she longed for him, for the thunderous sound of his voice, for the crushing strength of his arms and the laughter in his eyes.

She wanted to cry out. Serena much preferred fury to tears, but the anger had drained out of her. There was only a sorrow, a deep, abiding grief that stirred in her heart even as the child she now carried stirred in her womb.

It was the helplessness, she thought, that made a body weak and the heart brittle. No amount of work or temper or love could bring her father back or take the dull pain out of her mother's eyes. Men fought, and women grieved.

She closed her eyes and let the snow fall stinging to her cheeks. There must be more, she thought, more than waiting and mourning. She had already lost one man she loved. How would she go on if she lost another?

The rebellion, she thought with the first flash of fire she had felt in weeks. The damned rebellion was…was right, she realized, pushing the heels of her hands over her face to dry them. It was right and it was just. If people believed strongly, they should be willing to fight, and to die. Her father had said so, and had stood unwaveringly by his words. How could she do less?

"I miss you so," she murmured. "And I'm afraid. There's the child now, you see. Your grandchild." She smoothed a hand over the slight slope of her belly. "There was nothing I could do to save you, just as there's nothing I can do to protect Brigham or Coll. I wish— Oh Papa, I'm with child and part of me still wishes I could be a man so I could pick up a sword for you." She searched in her pockets until her fingers closed over the handkerchief Brigham had given her so many months before. She laid it on her cheek, using it as a talisman to bring him clearly to mind. "Is he safe? He doesn't even know we made a child between us. I would go to him." She felt the baby quicken. "But I can't. I can't protect and fight for him, but I can protect and fight for the child."

"Rena?"

She turned to see Malcolm standing a little way off. Snow fell in sheets between them, but she could see the quiver of his lips and the sheen of tears in his eyes. Wordlessly she opened her arms to him.

While he wept, she held him, finding comfort somehow in comforting another. He had been so brave, she remembered, standing so straight, holding their mother's arm while the priest had said the last words over their father's grave. He'd been a man then. Now he was a little boy.

"I hate the English." His voice was muffled against her shawl.

"I know. Mother would say hate is not Christian, but sometimes I think there is a time for hate, just as there is a time for love. And there is a time, my love, to let go of it."

"He was a fierce warrior."

"Aye." She was able to smile now as she drew him back to study his tear-streaked face. "Do you not think, Malcolm, that a fierce warrior might prefer to die fighting for what he believes?"

"They had retreated," Malcolm said bitterly, and Serena saw a glimpse of Coll in his eyes.

"Aye." The letter she had received from Brigham had explained the maneuver, his dissatisfaction with it and the growing dissent in the ranks. "I don't understand the strategy of generals, Malcolm, but I do know that whether the Prince is victor or vanquished, nothing will ever be the same.''

"I want to go to Inverness and join.''

"Malcolm—''

"I have Father's sword,'' he interrupted, passion darkening his eyes. "I can use it. I will use it to avenge him and support the Prince. I am not a child.''

She looked at him then. The little boy who had run weeping into her arms was a man again. He stood as high as her shoulder, his jaw firm, his hand clenched on the hilt of his dagger. He could go, Serena realized with a flutter of fear.

"No, you are not a child, and I believe you could raise Father's sword like a man. I will not stop you if your heart tells you to go, but I would ask that you think of Mother, of Gwen and Maggie.''

"You can care for them.''

"Aye, I would try, but every day the child within me grows.'' She took his hand in hers. It was stiff and cold and surprisingly strong. "And I'm afraid. I can't tell Mother or the others, but I'm afraid. When I grow as big as Maggie, how will I be able to keep them safe if the English come? I don't ask you not to fight, Malcolm, nor do I tell you you're a child. But I will ask you to be a man and fight here.''

Torn, he turned back to stare down at her father's grave. The snow lay over it in a soft white blanket. "Father would have wanted me to stay.''

Relief coursed through her, but she only touched his shoulder. "Aye. There is no disgrace in staying behind, not when it's the right thing.''

"It's hard.''

"I know.'' Now she slipped her arm around him. "Believe me, Malcolm, I know. There are things we can do,'' she murmured, thinking aloud. "When the snow stops. If the Prince's troops are as close as Inverness, the English will not be far behind. We cannot fight in Glenroe, there are too few of us, and almost all women and children.''

"You think the English will come here?'' he demanded, half eager, half terrified.

"I begin to believe it. Did word not come to us that there was a battle at Moy Hall?''

"And the English were routed,'' Malcolm reminded her.

"But it is too close. If we cannot defend, then we protect. You and I will find a place in the hills and prepare it. Food, supplies, blankets, weapons.'' She thought of the strongbox. "We will plan, Malcolm, as warriors plan.''

"I know a place, a cave.''

"You will take me there tomorrow.''

Brigham rode hard. Though it was nearly April, the weather remained cold, with snow often whipped up by the hateful wind. He commanded a handful of weary, hungry men. This foraging party, like others that had been sent out from Inverness, went in search of much-needed food and supplies. One of their greatest hopes, a captured government sloop renamed *Prince Charles*, had been retaken by the enemy off the Kyle of Tongue, and her desperately looked-for funds were now in the hands of the enemy.

Brigham's party had found more than oats and venison. They had discovered news. The duke of Cumberland, the elector's second son, lay in Aberdeen with a well-armed, well-fed army of twice their strength. He had received a powerful reinforcement of five thousand German soldiers, who remained in Dornoch, blocking the route south. The word came that Cumberland was beginning his advance on Inverness.

Hooves thudded on the layer of snow still covering the road. The men rode mostly in silence, edgy with hunger and fatigue. They wanted a meal and the cold comfort of sleep.

Redcoats were spotted to the west. With a quick signal, Brigham halted his troops and scanned the distance. They were outnumbered nearly two to one, and the dragoons looked fresh. He had a choice. They could run, or they could fight. Turning his horse, he took a hard look at his men.

"We can make the hills and lose them, or we can meet them here on the road, with the rocks to their backs."

"We fight." One man fingered his sword. Then another and another added his voice. The dragoons had already spurred into a gallop. Brigham flashed a grin. It was the answer he'd wanted.

"Then let's show them the faces of king's men." Wheeling his horse, he led the charge.

There was something fierce and chilling about a Highland charge. They rode as if they rode into hell, screaming in Gaelic and brandishing blades. Wall met wall, and the lonely hills echoed with the fury. Around Brigham men fought like demons and fell dying from the slice and hack of steel. Snow ran red.

It was unlike him to allow his emotions to surface in battle. Here, after weeks of frustration and anger, he let himself go, cutting through the line of oncoming dragoons like a man gone mad. He saw no faces, only that nameless entity known as the enemy. His sword whipped out, severing flesh as he dragged his horse right, then left, then right again.

They drove the dragoons onto the rocks, pursuing them mercilessly. Weeks of waiting had worked like a cancer that came rising to the surface to eat away at the civilized veneer.

When they were done five Jacobites lay dead or dying alongside a dozen dragoons. The rest of the government troop had fled over the rocks like rabbits.

"After them, lads," one of the Highlanders shouted. Brigham swung his horse to block the next charge.

"For what purpose?" He dismounted to clean his blade in the snow. "We've done what we've done. Now we tend to our own." A foot away, a man moaned. Sheathing his weapon, Brigham went to him. "The English dead will be buried. Our own dead and wounded will be taken back to Inverness."

"Leave the English for the kites."

Brigham's head whipped around. His eyes had lost their fever and were cold again as they studied the blood-spattered face of the hefty Scot who had spoken. "We are not animals. We bury the dead, friend or enemy."

In the end, the English dead were given cairns. The ground was too hard for graves.

The men were still weary, still hungry, when they turned their mounts toward Inverness. They rode slowly, burdened by their wounded. With each long mile, Brigham thought of how close the dragoons had been to Glenroe.

Chapter Fourteen

In the chill of April, the drums sounded and the pipes were played. In Inverness, the army readied for battle. Only twelve miles away, Cumberland had pitched camp.

"I do not like the ground." Once more, Murray stood as Charles's adviser, but the rift between them that the retreat had caused had never fully healed. "Drumossie Moor is well suited to the tactics of the English army, but not to ours. Your Highness..." Perhaps because he knew Charles had yet to forgive him for the retreat north, Murray chose his words with care. "This wide, bare moor might as well have been designed for the maneuvers of Cumberland's infantry, and I tell you there could never be a more improper ground for Highlanders."

"Do we withdraw again?" O'Sullivan put in. He was as loyal as Murray, as brave a soldier, but he lacked the hardheaded military sense of the Englishman. "Your Highness, have not the Highlanders proved themselves fierce and fearsome warriors, as you have proven a canny general? Again and again you have beaten back the English."

"Here we are not simply outnumbered." Murray turned his back on O'Sullivan and appealed to the prince. "The ground itself is the most terrible weapon. If we withdraw north again, across Nairn Water—"

"We shall stand to meet Cumberland." Charles, his eyes cool, his hands neatly folded, watched his most trusted men. "We shall not run again. Through the winter we have waited." And the wait, he knew, had disillusioned and disgruntled his men. It might have been that more than O'Sullivan's flattery or his own impatience that swayed him. "We wait no longer. Quartermaster-General O'Sullivan has chosen the ground, and we shall fight."

Murray's eyes met Brigham's briefly. They had already discussed the Prince's decision. "Your Highness, if your mind is made up, may I propose a maneuver that may strengthen our advantage?"

"If it does not include a retreat, my lord."

Color stained Murray's cheeks, but he continued. "Today is the duke's birthday, and his men will celebrate it. They will be drunk as beggars. A surprise night attack could turn the tide."

The Prince considered. "I find this interesting. Continue."

"Two columns of men," Murray began, using candlesticks to illustrate. "They would close in in a pincer movement, coming into camp from both sides and cutting down the size of Cumberland's army while they sleep off the effects of the birthday brandy.''

"A good plan," the Prince murmured, excitement once more kindling his eyes. "The duke should celebrate well, for the celebration will be short-lived.''

They marched. Men with no more than a single biscuit in their bellies set out to cover the twelve miles in the dark and the unrelieved cold. The plan was a good one, but the men sent to accomplish it were tired and hungry. Once, twice, then yet again, they lost direction and heart, until they were no more than a group wandering.

On horseback, the sun newly up, Brigham and Coll watched them return to camp.

"My God," the Scot muttered. "We've come to this."

With his own fatigue weighing on him, Brigham shifted in the saddle. Men exhausted from the march and grinding hunger dropped to the ground, many nodding off to sleep in the park of Culloden House or near the road. Others grumbled, even as the Prince rode among them.

Turning his head, Brigham looked out on Drumossie Moor. It was wide and bare, skimmed now with early frost and a thin, shifting mist. To Brigham, it might have been a parade ground for Cumberland's infantry. To the north, across the river called Nairn, the ground was broken and hilly. There Murray would have chosen to stand. And there, Brigham thought, there would have been a chance for victory.

But O'Sullivan had the Prince's ear now, and there was no turning back.

"It ends here," Brigham said softly. "For better or worse." In the east, the sun struggled sluggishly to life, trapped behind churning clouds. Spurring his horse, he rode through the camp. "On your feet!" he shouted. "Will you sleep until you wake with your throats cut? Can you not hear the English drums beating to arms?''

Dragging themselves up, men began to gather in their clans. Artillery was manned. What rations were left were passed among the troops, but they served only to leave stomachs edgy and empty. With pike and ax, gun and scythe, they rallied under the standard. MacGregors and MacDonalds, Camerons and Chisholms, Mackintoshes and Robertsons and more. They were five thousand, hungry, ill-equipped, held only by the cause that still bound them together.

Charles looked every bit the prince as he rode up and down their lines in his tartan coat and cockaded bonnet. They were his men, and the oath he had sworn to them was no less than that they had sworn him.

Across the moor, they watched the enemy advance. They were in three columns that slowly and smoothly swung into line. As Charles had done, the duke, pudgy in his red coat, a black cockade pinned to his tricorn, rode along encouraging his men.

There was the sound of drum and pipe, and the empty hum of wind that whipped sleet into the faces of the Jacobites. The first shots were fired by Jacobite guns. They were answered, and devastatingly.

As the first cannon exploded near Culloden House, Maggie arched against a contraction. They were coming quickly, powerfully. Her body, weakened by the full night of labor, was wracked with pain her mind no longer registered. Over and over she cried out for Coll.

"Poor lass, poor lass." Mrs Drummond brought fresh water and linen to the bedchamber. "Such a wee thing she is."

"There, darling, there." Fiona bathed Maggie's streaming face. "Mrs. Drummond, another log on the fire, please. We need it warm when the baby comes."

"Wood's nearly gone."

Fiona only nodded. "We'll use what we have. Gwen?"

"The babe's breech, Mother." Gwen straightened a moment to ease the strain in her back. "Maggie's so small."

Serena, one hand holding Maggie's, laid the other protectively over the child growing inside her own womb. "Can you save them, save them both?"

"God willing." Gwen wiped the sweat from her face with the sleeve of her dress.

"Lady MacGregor, I can tell Parkins to find more wood." Mrs. Drummond's wide face creased with concern as Maggie cried out with the next pain. She had birthed and lost two babies of her own. "A man ought to be good for something other than planting a seed in a woman."

Too tired to disapprove of the sentiment, Fiona nodded. "Please, Mrs. Drummond. Tell him we'd be grateful to him."

"Coll." Maggie sobbed, turning her head from side to side. Her eyes focused on Serena. "Rena?"

"Aye, my love, I'm here. We're all here."

"Coll. I want Coll."

"I know. I know you do." Serena kissed Maggie's limp hand. "He'll be back soon." Her own baby kicked, making her wonder if in a few months she would find herself confined, calling out Brigham's name over waves of pain, all the while knowing he wasn't there to answer. "Gwen says you must rest between the pains, gather your strength back."

"I try. Should it take so long?" Weakly she turned her head back to Gwen. "Tell me the truth, please. Is something wrong with the babe?"

For a split second Gwen debated lying. But though she was young still, she had already seen that women dealt best with the truth, no matter how frightening. "He's turned wrong, Maggie. I know what to do, but it won't be a simple birth."

"Am I going to die?" There was no desperation in Maggie's question, only a need for truth. As difficult as it was, Gwen had already made her decision. If she had to choose, she would save Maggie and lose the child. Before she could speak, the next contraction hit, bringing Maggie, exhausted as she was, rearing up.

"Oh, God. My baby, don't let my baby die. Swear it to me. Swear it."

"No one's going to die." Serena squeezed her hand hard, so hard it cut through the other pain and had Maggie quieting. "No one's going to die," she repeated. "Because you're going to fight. When the pain comes you're going to scream it out if need be, but you're not going to give up. Mac-Gregors don't give up."

The round shot of the government artillery cut huge holes in the Jacobite lines. Their own guns could only answer ineffectually as men fell like slain deer. Wind blew smoke and sleet back in their faces while they stood and suffered the slaughter of their ranks. Even with their lines running six deep, the cannonfire broke through and brought writhing, miserable death.

"Sweet Jesus, why won't they give the order to charge?" Coll, his face blackened with smoke, looked with desperate eyes at the carnage. "Will they have us stand here and be cut down to the last man before we raise a sword?"

Brigham swung around and galloped for the right wing, driving hard through the smoke and fire. "In the name of God," he cried when he faced the Prince, "give us the command to charge. We die like dogs."

"What are you saying? We wait for Cumberland to attack."

"You can't see what the cannons have done to your front lines. If you wait for Cumberland, you wait in vain. He won't attack as long as his guns can murder from a distance. We haven't their range, and sweet Lord, we're dying."

Charles began to dismiss him, for indeed his position was such that he had no clear view of the murderous skill of Cumberland's artillery, but at that moment, Murray himself rode to the Prince with the request.

"Give the command," Charles agreed.

The messenger was sent, but was felled by a cannonball before he could reach the ranks. Seeing it, Brigham continued the drive himself, shouting the order "Claymore" over the cheers and oaths of the men.

The center of the line moved first, racing like wild stags across the moor, and fell upon the dragoons, swinging broadsword and scythe. It would be written that the Highlanders came like wolves, desperate for blood, fearless in spirit. But they were only men, and many were cut down by bayonet and dagger.

If the English had run in front of a Highland assault before, they had now learned. In a canny and merciless maneuver, the dragoons shifted lines to catch the charging Scots in a sweeping and deadly rifle volley.

The Highland charge continued, but the ground itself, as predicted, served the English. A hail of bullets split the line. Still, it seemed for an instant as though their combined strength would crumble Cumberland's ranks, as the English were forced back to the next line of defense. But that second line held, pouring devastating fire onto the raging Highlanders. They fell, men heaping onto men so that those who still stood were forced to crawl over the bodies of their comrades.

Still the guns thundered, scattering grapeshot now—canisters full of nails and lead balls and iron scrap—like hideous rain.

The well-trained dragoons held their ground, one rank firing while the next reloaded so that the hail of bullets was unending. But still the clansmen pressed on.

Grapeshot blasted against Brigham's shield, scoring his arm and shoulder as he fought his way over the dead and wounded and through the duke's line. He saw James MacGregor, Rob Roy's impetuous son, driving his men through the living wall of English troops. His own eyes stung from the smoke that blurred his vision. Ice was in his veins as he hacked and sliced his way towards the back of Cumberland's line. Through the fog, he saw that Murray had preceded him, his hat and wig blown off during the battle. Only then did the confusion surrounding them start to come clear.

True, their right wing had cut through, taking down the dragoons in the press of their charge. But elsewhere, the Jacobites were in tatters. The MacDonalds had taken fearful punishment as they tried to lure the dragoons into attack with short, daring rushes, for the men facing them down had stood their ground and fired unrelentingly.

In a desperate move, Brigham wheeled back, determined to fight his way through yet again and rally what men who could.

He saw Coll, legs planted, claymore and dirk whistling viciously as he fought off three red-coated English. Without hesitation, Brigham went to his aid.

This was no romantic duel at dawn, but a sweaty, grunting fight for life. The wound Brigham had already received was oozing blood, and his dagger hand was slippery. Smoke billowed, clogging the lungs, even as the sleet continued to fall.

Only small, sporadic skirmishes remained in the area around them. The Jacobites were still fighting wildly but were being forced back over the moor, which was already strewn with dead and wounded. The wall of men that had once been strong on the right wing had been broken, allowing the red-coated cavalry to storm through and threaten the retreating men.

But the bigger defeat meant little at that moment to Coll and Brigham, who fought back-to-back, outnumbered in their personal war as surely as the whole of the Prince's army had been outnumbered by Cumberland's. Coll took a hit to the thigh, but the gash went almost unfelt as he continued to lash out with his weapon. Behind him, Brigham whirled and struck before another blow hit home. With this small personal victory, both men turned and began the race over the littered, smoke-covered moor.

"My God, they've destroyed us." Breathless and bleeding, Coll scanned the carnage. It was a picture a man would never forget, a glimpse of hell steaming with smoke and stinking of blood. "There must have been ten thousand of them." He saw, as they broke into a pocket of clear air, a dragoon brutally mutilating the body of an already-dead clansman. With a lionlike roar, Coll fell on him.

"Enough. Sweet Jesus." Brigham dragged him off. "There's nothing more we can do here but die. The cause is lost, Coll; the rebellion is over." But Coll was like a madman, sword raised, ready to use it on the first man who crossed his path. "Think. Glenroe is close, too close. We have to get back, get the family out."

"Maggie." Only at his father's death had Coll felt so much like weeping. "Aye, you've the right of it."

They began again, swords at the ready. Here and there could still be heard the volley of shots and the screams. They had nearly reached the hills when a chance twist of his head showed Brigham the wounded dragoon lifting his musket and taking unsteady aim.

There was time only to shove Coll out of the line of the fire. Brigham felt the ball slam into his body, felt its roaring, hideous pain.

He fell on the edge of Drumossie Moor, in the place that came to be known as Culloden.

Numb, nearly asleep on her feet, Serena burst out of the house to drag in cold, fresh air. There were wars only women knew, and she had fought such a war. They had been nearly two nights in the desperate battle to bring

Maggie's child out of her womb and into the world. There had been blood and sweat and pain she had never imagined. The boy had come, feet first, into the world, leaving his mother wavering between life and death.

Now it was nearly dusk, and Gwen had said that Maggie would live. Serena could only remember those first thin, wailing cries. Maggie had heard them, too, before she had fainted from exhaustion and loss of blood.

Here, outside, the light was soft with approaching evening. To the west the first stars had shivered themselves into life, luring a lone owl. Serena felt its call pierce through her.

"Oh, Brigham." She wrapped her arms around the slope of her own belly. "I need you."

"Serena?"

She turned, narrowing her eyes to focus as a figure limped out of the shadows. "Rob? Rob MacGregor?" Then she saw him fully, his doublet streaked with blood, his hair matted with dirt and sweat, and his eyes, his wild eyes. "What happened to you? My God." She reached for him as he stumbled at her feet.

"The battle. The English. They've killed us, Serena. Killed us."

"Brigham." She snatched at his torn shirt. "Brigham. Where is he? Is he safe? In the name of pity, tell me, where is Brigham?"

"I don't know. So many dead, so many." He wept into her skirts, broken. He had once been young, idealistic, fond of fancy waistcoats and pretty girls. "My father, my brothers, all dead. I saw them fall. And old MacLean, too, and young David Mackintosh. Slaughtered." The horror of it showed in his eyes when he lifted his face. "Even when we ran they slaughtered us like pigs."

"Did you see Brigham?" she said desperately, shaking him as he sobbed against her. "And Coll. Did you see them?"

"Aye. I saw them, but there was smoke, so much smoke, and the guns never stopped. Even when it was over it didn't stop. I saw—I saw them killing women, and children. There was a farmer and his son plowing. The dragoons rode over them, stabbing and stabbing. I was hiding, and I saw the wounded on the field. They murdered them with clubs."

"No." Again she wrapped her arms around her unborn child as she began to rock back and forth. "No."

"A man would put down his weapons in surrender and still be shot down like a dog. They came after us. There were bodies along the road, hundreds, we couldn't even bury our dead."

"When? When was the battle fought?"

"Yesterday." With a choked sob, he wiped his eyes. "Only yesterday."

He was safe. She had to believe that Brigham was safe. How could she move, how could she act, if she thought him dead? He was not dead, she told herself as she slowly rose. She would not let him be dead. She looked to the house, where the candles were already lighted for evening. She had a family to protect.

"Will they come here, Rob?"

"They are hunting us down like animals." Recovered, he spit on the ground. "My shame is that I did not kill a dozen more instead of running."

"Sometimes you run so you can fight again." She remembered him as he had been, and knew that he would never be that way again. In pity, she put her arms around him. "Your mother?"

"I haven't gone to her yet. I don't know how I can tell her."

"Tell her that her men died bravely in the service of the true king, then get her and the other women into the hills." She looked down the path to where the shadows fell over a thin frost. "This time, when the English come to burn, there will be no women to rape."

Inside the house, she sought out Gwen. The fear she felt for Brigham was trapped in the back of her mind. For her own sanity, and for the sake of her family, she wouldn't allow it to break free. Over and over, like a chant, her thoughts ran on.

He was alive. He would come back.

"Gwen." Taking her sister's hand, Serena drew her from Maggie's bedside. "How is she?"

"Weak." Gwen was teetering on the brink of exhaustion herself. "I wish I knew more. There is still so much to learn."

"No one could have done more than you. You saved her, and the bairn."

Gwen, her eyes still clouded with fatigue, looked back toward the bed where Maggie slept. "I was afraid."

"We all were."

"Even you?" Gwen smiled and pressed her sister's hand. "You seemed so fearless, so confident. Well, the worst is over. The bairn is healthy, miraculously so." She sighed, allowing herself to think for the first time of her own bed. "A few weeks of rest and care and Maggie will regain her strength."

"How soon can she be moved?"

"Moved?" Gwen paused in the act of adjusting the fillet that held back her hair. "Why, Serena?"

Maggie murmured in her sleep. With a gesture, Serena brought Gwen outside into the hallway. "I've just seen Rob MacGregor."

"Rob? But—"

"There was a battle, Gwen. It was bad, very bad."

"Coll?" Gwen managed after a moment. "Brigham?"

"Rob didn't know. But he told me that our troops were routed and that the English are pursuing the survivors."

"We can hide them. Rob, and whoever else comes. Surely if the English come and find us only women alone they will leave again."

"Do you forget what happened before when we were only women and the English came?"

"That was only one man," Gwen said in a desperate whisper.

"Listen to me." Serena put her hands on Gwen's shoulders and struggled to speak calmly. "Rob told me. He said it was like madness. He said the dragoons murdered the wounded, that they struck down women and children. If they come here before the madness is passed they will kill us all, even Maggie and the bairn."

"We may kill her if we move her."

"Better that than have her butchered at the hands of the English. Gather together what she and the child will need. We daren't wait to move longer than first light."

"Rena, what of you and your child?"

A light came into her eyes that had nothing to do with fear. Had her father seen it, he would have smiled. "We will survive, and we will remember."

With her own words drumming in her ears, she walked downstairs. In the kitchen, her mother was preparing a tray of broth and bread.

"Serena, I thought you would rest. Go now, get to your bed. As soon as I have seen Gwen eat this, I shall be certain she does the same."

"Mama, we must talk."

"Maggie?" Fiona said immediately. "The babe?"

"No, Gwen tells me they do well enough." She turned her head so that her eyes met Mrs. Drummond's, then Parkins's. "We must all talk. Where is Malcolm?"

"In the stables, my lady," Parkins told her. "Tending the horses."

With a nod, Serena led her mother to a chair at the table. "Is there tea, Mrs. Drummond? Enough for all of us?"

"Aye." Silently she poured the cups, then took a seat when Serena gestured.

"There is news," Serena said, and told them.

At first light, they took what they could carry. Parkins laid Maggie as gently as he could in the litter he had fashioned. She bit back her moans, and though she tried, she was too weak yet to hold the baby. The journey into the hills was slow and nearly silent, with Malcolm leading the way.

At the top of a ridge, where the first early flowers were pushing their way through the thin soil, Fiona stopped. The forest where she had come as a bride spread beneath, shimmering behind a thin, morning mist. At the top of the rise stood the house where she had lived with Ian, given birth to her children.

As she stood, the breeze rippled her plaid but left her cheeks colorless and her eyes dull.

"We will come back, Mother." Serena slipped an arm around her mother's waist and laid her head on Fiona's shoulder. "They will not take our home."

"So much of my life is there, Serena, and my heart. When they brought your father back, I thought my life had ended, as well. But it has not." She took a long breath. Her slender shoulders straightened. Her head came up. "Aye, the MacGregors will come back to Glenroe."

They stood a moment longer, watching the blue slate house glimmer in the strengthening sunlight.

They reached the cave two hours later. Malcolm and Serena had already laid by wood and peat for the fire. They had blankets and stores from the kitchen, medicines and milk drawn fresh that morning. Hidden behind rocks was the chest that held Brigham's shepherdess and a miniature of his grandmother, and his strongbox. Serena set her grandfather's claymore at the entrance to the cave and checked the pistols and ammunition.

Gwen tended Maggie while Fiona soothed the baby they already called young Ian.

"Can you fire a pistol, Parkins?" Serena asked.

"Yes, Lady Ashburn, should it become necessary."

Despite her fatigue, she grinned. He had used the same tone of voice he might have if she had asked him if he knew how to remove a wine stain from lace. "Perhaps you would take this one?"

"Very well, my lady." He took the pistol with a slight bow.

"You are more than you seem, Parkins." She thought of the competent manner with which he had fashioned the litter, and of the way he had pulled it and its fragile burden over the rough ground. "I begin to see why Lord Ashburn keeps you close. You have been with him long?"

"I have been in service with the Langstons for many years, my lady." When she only nodded and stared at the mouth of the cave, he softened. "He will come back to us, my lady."

Tears threatened, but only one managed to escape before she blinked them back. "I would give him a son this first time, Parkins. What was his father's given name?"

"It was Daniel, my lady."

"Daniel." She was able to smile again. "We shall name him Daniel, and he will be brave enough to walk into the lion's den." She turned her smile up to Parkins. "He shall be the next earl of Ashburn, and one day he shall walk through Glenroe."

"Will you rest now, Lady Ashburn? The journey has tired you more than you know."

"Aye, in a moment." She turned to be certain the others were busy. "When Brigham and my brother return, they will not know where to find us. It will be necessary for one of us to go down every few hours and watch for them. You and Malcolm and I will take shifts."

"No, my lady."

Her mouth opened, then shut, then opened again. "No?"

"No, my lady, I could not in good conscience permit you to travel again. My master would not hear of it."

"Your master has nothing to say about it. Both he and Coll will need to be led to this place."

"And so they shall be. Young Malcolm and I will arrange it. You and the other women will remain here."

Her face, pale and bruised with fatigue, set into stubborn lines. "I will not sit in this bloody cave and wait when I can be of use to my husband."

Parkins merely spread a blanket over her. "I fear I must insist, Lady Ashburn. My lord would demand it."

Serena merely scowled at him. "I wonder that Lord Ashburn didn't dismiss you years ago."

"Yes, my lady," Parkins said comfortably. "So he has said himself many times. I will bring you a cup of milk."

She slept. She had the pistol at one hand and the sword at the other, but her dreams were peaceful and filled with Brigham. She could see him clearly, almost clearly enough to touch him as he smiled at her. Her hand was in his, and she could all but feel the warmth of his flesh as they danced together under dappled sunlight near the riverbank. He wore the gleaming black and silver, and she the ivory satin seeded with pearls.

They were alone, gloriously alone, with only the rippling rush of water and the call of the birds for music. Their faces were close, then closer, then close enough to kiss as they continued to step and sway with the dance.

He was so handsome, her tall English lover with the dashing rebel's heart. His kiss was so sweet, so gentle, like one of greeting or of farewell.

Then she saw the blood staining his coat, seeping through it to dampen her hand as she reached for him. The blood was real, real enough that she could feel the warmth of it on her skin. But when she tried to take him into her arms, he faded until she stood alone on the banks of the river, with the only sound the high call of a warbler searching for its mate.

She woke with Brigham's name on her lips and her heart thundering. Fighting for air, she lifted her trembling hand and found no blood. Slowly, struggling to separate dream from reality, she pressed the hand to her heart. It wasn't a warbler she heard, but an eagle. It wasn't the song of the river, but the moan of the wind.

He was alive, she told herself, and laid a hand over the mound of her stomach as if to reassure her child that its father was safe. Almost immediately she heard the whimper of the baby already born. Wearily she rose to make her way to the back of the cave. With Fiona's help, Maggie held young Ian to her breast, where he sucked lustily.

"Serena." Maggie's voice was thin and her cheeks still deathly pale, but her smile was sweet. "He grows stronger every hour," she murmured, and lifted a hand to stroke his downy head. "Soon you'll have your own."

"He's beautiful." With a little sigh, Serena sat beside her. "God was good enough to give him your looks instead of his father's."

Maggie laughed, settled comfortably in the crook of Fiona's arm. "I didn't know I could love anyone as much as Coll. But now I do."

"I know the journey was difficult for you. How do you feel?"

"Weak. I hate feeling so weak and helpless."

Serena stroked her cheek. "A man doesn't fall in love with a packhorse, you know."

This time Maggie's laugh was a little stronger. "If some girl tries that trick with my little Ian, I'll scratch her eyes out."

"Of course, but you'll be sure to teach it to your daughters."

"Oh, aye." Maggie shut her eyes. "I'm so tired."

"Just sleep," Fiona murmured. "When the bairn's had his fill, we'll tend him."

"Will Coll come soon?"

Over Maggie's drooping head, Fiona's eyes met Serena's. "Aye." Fiona's voice was soothing. "Very soon. He'll be so proud of you for giving him a son."

Serena gathered up the dozing baby as Fiona settled Maggie among the blankets. "So tiny." Serena swaddled Ian and laid him to sleep. "It always seems a miracle."

"It is." Fiona looked to the far side of the cave to where Gwen lay curled in exhausted sleep. "Each child is a miracle. There is always death, Serena; there is always grief and loss. Without the promise of new life, we couldn't bear it."

Serena asked now what she had not been brave enough to ask before. "Do you think they're dead?"

"I pray they live." Fiona took Serena's hands in hers. "And I will pray every moment until we know. You must eat," she said briskly. "For yourself and the child."

"Aye, but..." She let her words trail off as she glanced around the cave. "Where is Malcolm?"

"With Parkins. They left soon after you went to sleep. Down for more supplies."

Frowning, Serena started to accept the bowl Mrs. Drummond offered.

"Don't you fret about them, lassie, my Parkins knows what he's about."

"Aye, he is a good man, Mrs. Drummond, a steady one."

A becoming blush glowed in the widow's cheeks. "We are to be wed."

"I am happy for you." She stopped, her fingers tightening on the bowl. "Do you hear that?" she whispered as she set the bowl down.

"I hear nothing." But Fiona's heart had risen into her throat.

"Someone's coming. Stay to the back of the cave. See that Ian makes no sound."

"Serena."

But even as Fiona reached for her, Serena was moving quietly to the cave opening. Ice ran through her veins, freezing her fear and making her strong. She would kill if God showed her no other way, and she would kill well.

With a steady hand, she picked up the pistol, then the sword. If the English had come, they would find women alone, but they would not find women defenseless. Behind her, Mrs. Drummond gripped a carving knife.

As the footsteps came closer, there could be no doubt the cave would be seen. Holding both weapons, Serena stepped out of the cave and prepared to do battle. The sun fell over her, striking her eyes so that she narrowed them even as she leveled the pistol.

"Still a hellcat, I see."

Brigham, supported by Coll and Parkins, managed to grin at her as he was half carried over the broken ground. The light shone over his blood-streaked coat and breeches.

"Oh, sweet God." Laying the weapons down, Serena ran to him.

Her face swam in front of his eyes as he struggled to speak again. He could only manage her name before darkness closed in on him and smothered the pain.

Chapter Fifteen

"How bad is it?" Serena knelt on the floor of the cave beside Brigham while Gwen examined his wounds. The fear had returned, drying her mouth to dust.

Wordlessly Gwen probed Brigham's side where the ball was lodged. A few feet away, Fiona dressed the gash in Coll's leg while he stared in wonder at his son.

"The shot was meant for me." Coll clung to Maggie's hand. The fire in his leg was a dull, almost dreamy pain beneath his exhaustion. He was alive, beside his beloved wife and firstborn son while his friend lay bleeding from a bullet that had been meant for him. "He stepped in front of it, took it. We were trying to fight our way into the hills. We'd lost, everything was lost. We were separated from our regiment. I thought—at first I thought him dead."

"You brought him back." Serena looked up, gripping a blood-soaked cloth.

"Aye." Coll turned his face into his wife's hair. Wanting to smell only the sweetness of it and not the stench of death and battle.

He would never be able to describe the events of the last day and night. But he would always remember the desperation he had felt when he had carried Brigham into the hills. He would remember hiding like a wild dog and binding the wounds as best he could while the English searched the rocks and heather. He had hidden in the lee of a rock, too weak to cross the stretch of moor to a barn. There, lying in scrub with Brigham unconscious beside him, he had seen the soldiers come and set fire to the building. And he had heard the screams of the wounded who had hidden within.

He had made the rest of the miles to Glenroe mostly at night, supporting Brigham when he was conscious, carrying him when he was not.

"We were afraid for you," he managed after a moment. "Afraid the English would come before we could warn you."

"The bullet must come out right away." Gwen pressed a cloth against the wound as all eyes turned toward her. "We must find a doctor."

"There is no doctor." Serena felt the hysteria bubbling up and fought to control it. Had he been given back to her only so that she could watch him die? "If we searched for one, we would only bring the English down on us."

"I know the risk," Gwen began.

"They would kill him." Serena spoke flatly. "As an English nobleman, they would be doubly harsh. They would heal his wound only to keep him alive for execution. You must take it out."

"I've never done anything like this." Gwen closed a hand over Serena's arm. "I lack the skill and the knowledge. I would kill him in trying to save him."

Panic fluttered. Beneath her hands, Brigham moaned and stirred. "Better he die with us, here." Her eyes were grim as she looked down at Brigham. "If you won't try, I will do it myself."

"My lady." Parkins's voice was as expressionless as ever as he stepped forward. "I will remove the ball, with Miss MacGregor's assistance."

"You? Can you?" Serena gave a brittle laugh. "We're not talking about starching lace, man."

"I have done it once before, my lady. That is once more than you. And Lord Ashburn is my master," he said stiffly. "I will tend him. He will need to be held." Parkins turned his gaze to Coll.

"I will hold him." Serena leaned over Brigham's body, as if to shield him. "And God help you if the knife slips."

They built a fire and turned a blade in it until the tip glowed red. When Brigham surfaced, Gwen held a bowl of medicine heavily laced with poppies to his lips. Sweat poured down his face no matter how diligently Serena wiped his skin with a cool cloth.

"Sit with Maggie and Mother, Rena," Coll said quietly. "Let me hold him down."

"No. This is for me to do." She braced herself over Brigham, clasping her hands on his arms, then lifted her face to Parkins. "I know you will have to hurt him, but for mercy's sake, be quick."

The valet had stripped off his coat and rolled back his sleeves to reveal thin, spindly arms. Serena closed her eyes a moment. She was putting her love, her life, into the hands of a man who looked able to do no more than shine boots. Opening them again, she studied the valet's face. Steady. She had called him so herself. Loyal. More than loyal, she realized. As a man could love another, he loved Brigham. With a prayer, she nodded for Parkins to begin. And watched the knife cut into her husband's flesh.

Even dazed by the drug, Brigham stiffened. Serena used all her strength to press him down even as she murmured to him, nonsense, endearments, promises. She watched the knife go deeper and ignored the rolling of her stomach.

As the pain of the knife sliced through the swoon and the drug, Brigham began to fight. Coll tried to take Serena's place, but she snarled him away and summoned all her strength.

There was no sound in the cave but for Brigham's harsh breathing and the low crackle of the fire. But the air was charged with silent prayers, said with a unity that made them as strong as a novena. Serena watched her husband's blood stain the floor of the cave and his face go ashen. In her prayers, she begged to take some of his pain into herself and spare him.

"I've found it." Sweat streamed down Parkins's face as he probed for the ball. In his heart he prayed that his master would faint and escape the pain. But his thin hand was steady. Slowly, terrified of causing more damage, he began to guide the bullet out. "Keep him still, my lady."

"Get the damn thing out." She shot a furious look at Parkins as Brigham moaned and struggled under her confining hands. "He suffers."

She watched, her breathing harsh and unsteady, as Parkins pried the small ball of metal from Brigham's flesh. Before Parkins could release the breath he had been holding, Gwen was taking over.

"We must stop the bleeding. He can't lose much more and live." Competently she began to pack the wound. "Mama, will you see to his arm and shoulder? They are less severe, but look ugly. Mrs. Drummond, my medicines."

As Brigham went limp again, Serena leaned back. Her arms and back were trembling with the pressure. Carefully, mindful now of the child, she made herself relax. "How can I help?"

Gwen glanced up only briefly from her work. Serena's face was as pale as Brigham's. "By getting air. Please, leave this to me."

With a nod, Serena rose and moved slowly to the mouth of the cave. It was nearly dusk again, she noted. How quickly the time had passed. And how strangely. A year before it had been Brigham, carrying a wounded Coll. Now it was Brigham who lay near death. The time between seemed like a dream, filled with love and passion, laughter and weeping.

She could see the hills going purple in the lowering light. The land, she thought. Would they now lose even that? They had fought, they had died. Coll had told her that their father's last words had been "It will not be for naught." But the man she loved lay wounded and the land they had fought for was no longer hers.

"Lady Ashburn?"

Blinking, Serena brought herself back. She was Lady Ashburn. She was a MacGregor. She laid a hand over her stomach as the child within kicked. A new life. A new hope. No, she thought, she would not say it had been for naught.

"Aye?"

"I thought you might enjoy a hot drink."

She turned, nearly smiling at the formal tone of Parkins's voice. He was wearing his coat again, and the perspiring, intense man who had removed a bullet might never have been. "Thank you, Parkins." She took the cup and let the liquid soothe her raw throat. "I would like to apologize for speaking to you as I did."

"Pray do not consider it, my lady. You were distraught."

Serena lifted her hand to her face as she was caught between tears and laughter. "Aye. Distraught. You have a steady hand, Parkins. A steady heart."

"I have always strived to, my lady."

She let out a long breath, swiping at her face with her knuckles. "Have you a handkerchief, as well?"

"Of course, Lady Ashburn." With a slight bow, Parkins offered one of sensible cloth.

"Parkins, you have served Lord Ashburn today, and you have also served me. There may be a time when you require a favor of me. You have only to ask."

"My service was given without condition, my lady."

"Aye." She took his hand, causing him to color a bit. "I know it. The boon is still yours when you need it." She offered him back the damp hand-kerchief. "I will go sit with my husband now."

The wind picked up and howled like a wild beast. It fought its way through the blanket over the cave opening and sent the flames of the low fire dancing. In its shrieks, Serena heard what her ancestors would have called the spirits in the hills. They laughed and moaned and mumbled. She felt no fear of them.

She watched Brigham through the night, unable to sleep even when Gwen pleaded with her. The fire burned through him, so hot at times Serena feared it would eat him alive. Sometimes he spoke, in rambling sporadic sentences that told her he was reliving the battle. Through his words, she saw more clearly than ever how complete the slaughter had been. Once he spoke to his grandmother, telling her despairingly of the dreams that had been shattered by the English guns.

He called for Serena, and would be soothed for a time by her murmurs and by her hand, cool on his brow. He would wake again, delirious, certain that the English had found her.

"I will sit with him, Serena." Fiona knelt beside her, laying a comforting arm over her shoulders. "You need rest, for yourself and your child."

"I cannot leave him, Mama." Serena wrung out a cool cloth and stroked it over Brigham's pale face. "I am easier here than I would be if I tried to sleep. Just looking at him helps somehow. Sometimes he opens his eyes and looks at me. He knows I'm with him."

"Then sleep here, for just a little while. Put your head in my lap as you did when you were a girl."

With Fiona's gentle persuasion, Serena curled up on the floor of the cave. Reaching out, she covered Brigham's hand with her own.

"He is beautiful, is he not, Mama?"

With a little smile, Fiona stroked her daughter's hair. "Aye, he is beau-tiful."

"Our baby will look like him, with those fine gray eyes and strong mouth." She closed her eyes and listened to the fearless song of the wind. "I loved him, I think, almost from the first. I was afraid. That was foolish."

Fiona continued to soothe and stroke as Serena's words grew slurred with sleep. "Love is often foolish."

"The child is moving," she murmured, smiling as she drifted off. "Brigham's child."

Brigham's dreams were unrelenting. Sometimes he was back on the moor, trapped in the smoke and fury of battle. Men died agonizing deaths around him, some by his own hand. He could smell the blood and the acrid scent of gunpowder. He could hear the pipes and drums and the unrelenting boom of artillery.

Then he was limping through the hills, the fire in his side and the mist over his brain. He thought he smelt burning—wood and flesh—and heard screams echoing in his head.

Just when he knew he would scream himself from the sound of it, it stopped. Serena stood beside him, wearing a white dress that glittered over her skin, her hair falling like melted gold.

Sometimes when he opened his eyes he would see her, so clearly that he could make out the smudges of sleeplessness under her eyes. Then his weighted lids would close again and he would be pitched back onto the battlefield.

For three days he drifted between consciousness and unconsciousness, often delirious. He knew nothing of the little world that had been conceived within the cave, or of the comings and goings of its people. He heard voices, but had not the strength to understand or to answer. Once, when he floated to the surface, it was dark and he thought he heard a woman's quiet weeping. Another time, he heard the thin cry of a baby.

At the end of three days he fell into a deep, dreamless sleep, a sleep as peaceful as death.

Waking was something like being born, confusing, painful, helpless. The light burned his eyes, though it was dim in the rear of the cave. Weakly he shut them again and tried to orient himself with sounds and smells.

There was earth and smoke and, oddly, a smell of cooking food. There was also the sickly scent of poppies that spoke of sickness. He heard murmurs. With the patience of the weak he lay still until he began to make them out.

Coll. Gwen. Malcolm. Relief poured through him nearly as strongly as the delirium. If they were here and safe, so was Serena. He opened his eyes again, wincing at the light. He was gathering his strength to speak when he heard a rustle beside him.

She was there, sitting with her knees curled up close, her back against a wall of rock. Her hair had fallen forward, almost curtaining her face. A wave of love all but drained him.

"Rena," he murmured, and reached to touch.

She woke immediately. Emotions raced across her face as she shifted close to run her hands over his face. It was cool, blessedly cool. "Brigham." She lowered her lips to his. "You've come back to me."

There was so much to tell him, so much to hear. At first Brigham was only strong enough to stay awake for an hour at a time. The memory of the battle was clear, but that of the aftermath was, mercifully, a blur to him. There had been pain, a hotter, sharper one than the throbbing ache he felt now. He remembered being dragged and lifted and carried. There had been cool water poured down his burning throat. Once he remembered coming out of a half swoon when he and Coll had stumbled across six bodies.

Gradually, at his insistence, the gaps were filled in. He listened grimly, his fury and disgust at Cumberland's atrocities offset only by the joy of having Serena and his unborn child close to him.

"This place won't be safe for long." Brigham sat braced against the wall of the cave, his face still pale in the dim light. It had been two days since he had come out of that fever. "We need to move as soon as possible, toward the coast."

"You're not strong enough." Serena kept his hand in hers. A part of her wanted to stay snug in the cave and forget there was a world outside.

In answer, he brought their joined hands to his lips. But his eyes were hard and focused. He would be damned if he would see her forced to give birth in a cave. "I think we could seek help from my kin on Skye." He looked at Gwen. "How soon will Maggie and the baby be fit enough to travel?"

"In a day or two, but you—"

"I'll be ready."

"You'll be ready when we say you are," Serena cut in.

A trace of the old arrogance flickered into his eyes. "You've grown tyrannical since I last saw you, madam."

She smiled and touched her lips to his. "I have always been a tyrant, *Sassenach*. Rest now," she urged as she settled a blanket over him. "When your strength returns we shall go anywhere you choose."

His eyes became very intense, and her smile wavered. "I may hold you to that, Rena."

"Just rest." The weariness in his voice made her ache. He had left her a strong, seemingly invincible man. He had come back to her inches from death. She would not risk losing him to his own stubbornness. "Perhaps Coll and Malcolm will bring back meat." She lay beside him, stroking his brow as he drifted off, and wondering why her brothers tarried so long.

They had seen the smoke from the ridge. Sprawled on their bellies, Coll and Malcolm looked down at Glenroe. The English had come again, bringing their fire and their hate. Already the crofts lay in ruins, their thatched roofs gone. MacGregor House was alight, and flames flickered out of broken windows.

"Damn them," Coll murmured over and over as he pounded a fist against the rock. "Damn them all."

"Why do they burn our houses?" Malcolm was ashamed of the tears and hastened to wipe them away. "What need is there to destroy our homes? The stables," he said suddenly, and would have risen up if Coll hadn't restrained him.

"They would have taken the horses, lad."

Malcolm pressed his face to the rock, caught between childish tears and a man's fury. "Will they go now, and leave us?"

Coll remembered the carnage surrounding the battlefield. "I think they will hunt the hills. We must get back to the cave."

Serena lay quietly, listening to the comforting domestic sounds. Young Ian was suckling again, and Maggie hummed to him. Mrs. Drummond and Parkins murmured over the preparation of a meal, easily as if they were still gossiping in the kitchen. Near Maggie, Fiona worked with a spindle, peacefully spinning what would one day be made into a blanket for her grandchild. Gwen fussed with her jars and pots of medicine.

They were all together at last, together and safe. One day, when the English grew tired of raping Scotland and returned over the border, they would go back down to Glenroe. She would make Brigham happy there somehow, make him forget the glittering life he had led in London. They would build a house of their own near the loch.

Smiling, Serena shifted away to let Brigham sleep. She had a passing thought to look out and see if she could spot her brothers returning, but even as she stood, she heard the sound of someone moving near the mouth of the cave. Words of greeting were on the tip of her tongue, but then she stopped. Neither Coll nor Malcolm would have a need to come so cautiously. With a hand that had gone suddenly cold, she reached for the pistol.

A shadow blocked out the light at the mouth of the cave. Then she saw with a sickening lurch of her heart the glint of metal and the telling red of the coat.

The soldier straightened, his sword raised, as he took quick stock of his find. Serena noted that his coat and his face were streaked with dirt and soot. There was a look of triumph in his eyes, and an unmistakable glint in them when he spotted Gwen.

Without a word, and with no thought of mercy, he advanced on Parkins. Serena lifted the pistol and fired. He stumbled back, blank surprise showing in his face the instant before he crumpled to the ground. Thinking only of defending what was hers, Serena gripped the hilt of her grandfather's claymore. Another soldier broke in. Even as she raised the sword, she felt a hand close over hers. Brigham was beside her. The soldier, teeth bared, charged forward, leading with his bayonet. Another shot rang out, felling him. Parkins stood, his rail-thin body shielding Mrs. Drummond's, the pistol still smoking in his hand.

"Reload," Brigham ordered, thrusting Serena behind him as another dragoon pushed into the cave. The redcoat didn't advance, only stood stiffly for an instant before falling headfirst. There was an arrow quivering in his back.

Breathing through his teeth, Brigham rushed out of the cave. There were two more. Coll was fighting one, sword to sword, as he maneuvered desperately to shield Malcolm with his body. The other dragoon advanced on the young boy, who held an empty bow as a useless defense.

With a shout, Brigham lunged. The pain exploded afresh in his side, almost blinding him. The dragoon swung around, but raised his sword again over Malcolm's head.

Serena fired the freshly loaded pistol from the mouth of the cave and sent a ball into his heart.

It was over in minutes. Five dragoons lay dead, but the sanctuary of the cave was ended.

They moved at dusk, heading west. Two of the horses the dragoons had tethered were Malcolm's own. They took shifts, riding, walking. When it was possible, they sheltered in mud huts or with the cattle. Highland hospitality was as it had always been. Through the people they met they learned of Cumberland, who was already known as the Butcher. The persecution was unbearable, and the search for the Prince through the heather unrelenting.

Houses were in ruin; cattle and horses and sheep had been driven off. The Highlanders, never rich, faced starvation. Still, they hid their Prince and any fugitive who asked for shelter.

Progress was slow, with each day bringing its own dangers. Thousands of troops had been engaged to find the Prince. It was June before they were able to sail from the mainland to Skye, where they were taken in by the MacDonalds of Sleat.

"It's as beautiful as she said it was," Brigham murmured as he stood with Serena on the lush green grass of a small slope and looked out at Uig Bay. "My grandmother told me how she ran through the grass as a girl and watched the boats."

"It is beautiful." The breeze was kind against her face. "Everything is beautiful now that we're all together and safe."

For how long? Brigham wondered. There were troops here, as well. The sea was being patrolled. There were rumors that the Prince was near. If he was, the English would be on his heels. A way had to be devised for the Prince to return to France or Italy. But more personally, and more importantly, Serena and the child had to be kept safe.

He had thought of little else during the days of his recovery, during the nights they had traveled like outcasts through the hills of Scotland. He could not now return to England and give Serena what was rightfully hers as Lady Ashburn. Nor could he, though she had yet to accept it, return to Glenroe for years to come.

"Sit with me, Serena."

"Gladly." She laughed a little as he helped her settle what had become a cumbersome weight. "I shall never be able to face a cow again."

"You've never looked more beautiful."

"You lie." She grinned and turned her face for a kiss. "But the truth wouldn't earn you a kiss." With her head on his shoulder, she looked out at the bay. The sun scattered over it, edging the blue with gold, like a lady's ball gown. "It is beautiful here, Brig. I'm glad you had the chance to see the land where your grandmother grew up. That we had the chance to see it together." With a little sound of discomfort, she rested a hand on her stomach.

"Do you feel unwell?"

"No, better every day since we've come here." It was true, spiritually. She didn't want to tell him how poorly she had begun to feel physically. Only that morning the ache in her back, and the pressure, had nearly kept her in bed. "Your grandmother's people have been so kind to us."

"I know. I shall always be grateful to them, and all the others who gave us shelter." His eyes clouded as he looked down over the water. "It is difficult to understand how they could give shelter so freely to an Englishman."

"How can you speak so?" There was genuine anger in her voice as she gripped his arm. "It was not your England that has murdered Scotland. It was, is, Cumberland and his thirst for blood, his need to destroy. It is he who has laid waste to the glens."

"And in London he is cheered like a hero."

"Listen to me." Her grip gentled as she reached for his hand. "There was a time I blamed all for the wrongs of a few. As you love me, don't do the same." With a smile, she moved his hand over her belly. "Our child carries English blood. I am proud of it."

He brought her close a moment, just to hold her. "Again you humble me." They remained as they were, sitting close, clinging to the hope that had come even out of loss. "You know, if I am found here, what will happen to the MacDonalds?"

It was cowardly, but she didn't want to think of it. "You will not be found."

"I cannot run forever, Rena, nor continue to endanger friend and stranger."

She plucked nervously at the turf. It was so green and smelled so sweet. "I know, but what choice do we have? The Prince is still hunted. I know you worry for him."

"I do, but I also worry for you and our child." When she started to reassure him, he gripped her hands. "I will never forget that last day in the cave, the way you were forced to defend me, to kill for me and your family."

"I did what needed to be done, what you would have done. All those months I felt useless because I could do nothing. That day, things changed. A woman might not join the rebellion on a battlefield, but a woman can protect what she loves."

"I will tell you in truth that I have never loved you more than I did that day, when you held a sword and a pistol in your hands." He kissed them, then looked steadily into her eyes. "Can you understand that I wanted to give you beauty, not a life of fear and running? I wanted to give you what was mine, but is mine no longer."

"Brigham—"

"No, wait. There is something I must ask you. You said you would go with me wherever I chose. Will you?"

She felt a little pain ripple through her, but nodded. "Aye."

"Will you leave Scotland, Rena, and travel with me to the New World? I cannot give you all that I once promised, though we won't be poor. So many of the things I wanted for you will be left behind. You will be only Mrs. Langston, and the land and the people will be strange to you, to both of us. I know what I ask you to give up, but perhaps one day we can return."

"Ssh." Overcome, she wrapped her arms around him. "Don't you know I would ride into hell with you if you asked?"

"I don't ask you to ride into hell, but I know what I ask you and what promises I break."

"You promised only to love me, and to come back to me. You have done both." She shook her head before he could speak. "You must listen, and try to understand. The weeks I had with you at court were beautiful, but only because we were together. I have never needed such things, Brigham. The title means nothing to me, nor do the balls or the gowns. Only you." With a watery laugh, she pulled back. "Every day at Holyrood I worried that I would make a mistake and embarrass you, that you would see you had made a grave error in judgment in taking me for Lady Ashburn."

"What nonsense is this?"

"I shall never be an easy aristocrat, Brigham. I was afraid you would ask me to go to France, to court."

His eyes narrowed as he studied her. "Your life would be easier there, as it was in Edinburgh."

"And I would have to pretend to be a lady while I longed for my breeches and a fast ride."

"You would rather go to America with only a chest of gold and a dream?"

She framed his face with her hands. "England was yours and Scotland mine. We've lost them. Together we will make our own."

"I love you, Rena. More than my life."

"Brigham, the child—"

"Shall be happy. I swear it."

"Sooner than we think," she managed. At his expression, she managed another laugh, then winced. "Oh, I think he has my impatience. I need Gwen, Brigham, and Mother."

"But you said it would be a few weeks yet."

"It's not what I say." She held a hand over her belly as it hardened with a contraction. "It's what he says."

She caught her breath, then giggled when he swept her awkwardly into his arms. "Brigham, there is no need. I'll break your back."

At that moment she felt weightless. "Madam," he said with a trace of mockery. "Have a little faith."

Epilogue

Near the last day of June, fourteen months after he had raised his standard, Prince Charles landed near Mugston House on the Isle of Skye. He was disguised as the lady's maid of Flora MacDonald, a young woman who risked her life to travel with him and see him to safety.

He had missed capture by a hairbreadth, but had lost neither his ambition nor his eagerness. Nor had he lost his air of romance. He left Flora with a lock of his hair and the wish that they might meet again, at the Court of St. James.

Brigham saw him briefly. They spoke as they had often spoken in the past, with ease and mutual respect. Charles did not, though the hope was in his heart, ask Brigham to join him on the journey to France.

"You will miss him," Serena said as they stood in their bedchamber at Mugston House.

"I will miss him as a man, and I will grieve for the loss of what might have been." He gathered her close, holding her newly slim body against his. "It was he and his cause that brought me to you. We did not win, Rena, but I have only to look at you, and my son, to know that neither did we lose." With his arm around her, he turned to look down at the child they had christened Daniel. "It is as your father said, love. It has not been for naught." He pressed his lips to hers, lingering over the kiss, drawing out the passion, the love and the trust. "Are you ready?"

With a nod, she picked up her traveling cloak. "If only Mother and Coll and Maggie would go with us."

"They need to stay, as we need to go." He waited as she gathered up the child. "You will have Gwen and Malcolm."

"I know. I only wish..."

"There will be a MacGregor in Glenroe again, Serena. And we will come back."

She looked at him. The sun was streaming through the window at his back. He was as he had been when she had first seen him, dark, stunningly handsome, a little reckless. It made her smile even as the baby stirred against her. "There will be a Langston at Ashburn Manor again. Daniel will come back, or his children will. They will have their place there, and in the Highlands."

He lifted the chest that held the little Dresden shepherdess. One day he would give it to his son. He had bent to kiss her again when there was a knock on the door.

"Your pardon, my lord."

"What is it, Parkins?"

"We will lose the tide."

"Very well." He gestured to the other cases. "And Parkins, must I remind you that you are to address me as Mr. Langston now?"

Parkins hefted the cases in his thin arms. He had asked his favor of his lady, and he and the new Mrs. Parkins were traveling to America. "No, my lord," he said mildly, and proceeded them.

Over Brigham's oath, Serena laughed and walked out with the baby. "You will always be Lord Ashburn, *Sassenach*. Come." She held out a hand to him. "We are going home."

* * * * *

Reckless Love

ELIZABETH
LOWELL

Chapter One

Heart pounding, body flattened to the hot earth, Janna Wayland peered down the brush-covered slopes and watched the tall stranger run naked between a double line of Cascabel's renegade Ute warriors.

He'll never make it, Janna thought. Her heart turned over in pity for the man as blow after blow rained onto his powerful body, staggering him, sending him to his knees. *No matter how big or how strong he looks from here, they'll kill him. They always kill the white men they catch.*

Crimson streaks appeared on the man's broad back as he struggled to his feet and began to run once more, doubled over in pain, lurching from side to side between the two lines of half-drunk warriors. When he reached the end of the gauntlet he straightened unexpectedly and surged forward, his legs driving hard, his head up, running with the power and grace of a wild stallion.

The laughing, jeering Utes remained unconcerned about their prey's apparent escape. Other men had run the gauntlet before. Most of them never reached the end before being knocked unconscious and clubbed to death. The few prisoners who managed to survive the gauntlet had provided great sport for the renegades as they tracked their bleeding quarry through the rugged canyons, plateaus and mountains of the lower Utah Territory. Whether they found their prisoner a hundred yards away or a mile, the end was always the same—torture and a death that was no more merciful than the red-rock desert itself.

Go to the left, Janna prayed, her slender body vibrating with intensity. *Don't take the first side canyon that offers itself. It's a death trap. Go left. Left!*

As though he heard her silent pleas, the man passed up the brush-choked entrance of a small ravine and ran on. For a few more moments Janna watched him through her spyglass, assuring herself that he was running in the correct direction. Despite the crimson blood staining his skin, the man ran smoothly, powerfully. Janna's breath caught and then wedged in her throat as she watched the stranger run. Every line of his body proclaimed his determination to survive. She had seen nothing so beautiful in her life, not even Lucifer, the black stallion every man pursued and every shaman said no man would catch.

The stranger disappeared around a bend in the dry wash, still running hard. Janna collapsed the spyglass, stuffed it into her hip pocket and began wiggling backward out of the brush that had concealed her from the warriors below. As she moved, she automatically smoothed out signs of her passage and replaced stones or twigs that her body overturned. She had survived for years alone in Indian country by being very, very careful to leave few traces of her presence.

Once Janna was out of sight of the warriors below—and of the guard on the rimrock at the head of Raven Canyon, where Cascabel's renegades had their camp—she began running on a roundabout course that skirted one of the many prows of rock that jutted out from the sloping base of Black Plateau. She crossed a dry wash by leaping from boulder to boulder, leaving no trace of her passage. Then she set off on a course that she hoped would cut across the stranger's trail within a few hundred yards.

If he got that far.

Despite her urgency, Janna used every bit of cover along the way, for she could do the man no good if she were caught by renegades herself. After five minutes she stopped, held her breath and listened. She heard nothing to suggest that the renegades had begun pursuing the stranger. Hope rose a little higher in her heart. She resumed running, moving with the grace and silence of fire skimming over the land. It was the silence of her movement as well as the rich auburn blaze of her hair that had caused the natives to call her Shadow of Fire.

Just before Janna reached another dry wash, she saw the stranger's trail. She veered left, following him, wondering which hiding place the man had chosen of all those offered by the tiny finger canyons and rugged rock formations that riddled the base of the plateau. Not that hiding would do him much good. He tried to conceal his trail, but he was bleeding so much that every few feet bright crimson drops proclaimed his passage.

Janna slowed and began rubbing out the telltale drops, using sand or dirt or brush, whatever was near at hand. When his blood trail began to climb up the slope, she noted with approval that the man had passed up obvious hiding places where the renegades would be sure to look. In spite of injuries and the certain knowledge of pursuit, the man hadn't panicked. Like the elusive Lucifer, the stranger relied on intelligence as well as raw strength for his survival.

Yet it was the man's determination that impressed Janna while she followed his twisting trail up the steep, rocky flank of the plateau. She realized that he was hiding in the most unexpected manner. He was taking a route up the plateau's north face that was so difficult the warriors wouldn't believe their prey could possibly have gone that way. The renegades would search the easier escape routes first, perhaps wasting enough time that darkness would fall before the stranger was discovered.

It was a long chance, but it was the only one he had, and he had been smart and tough enough to take it.

Janna redoubled her efforts, moving quickly, wiping out signs of the man, doing everything she could to help him elude the warriors who were sure to follow. The farther up the flank of the plateau she climbed, the more her admiration for the stranger's determination and stamina increased. She began to hope that he knew of an ancient footpath to the top of the plateau, a path that had been abandoned by the Indians, who now rode horses.

The farther up she climbed, the more she allowed herself to believe that the stranger would make it to the top. Up there was water, cover, game, all

that a man would need to survive. Up there she could hide him easily, care
for his wounds, nurse him if he required it.

Hopes high, Janna levered herself over a rockfall, only to find a stone cliff
cutting off all possibility of advance or escape. At the base of the cliff, piñon
and rocks grew in equal profusion.

There was no one in sight.

But there was no way out of the rugged little canyon except the way he
had come, and she certainly hadn't seen anything bigger than a rabbit. He
had to be somewhere in the piñon- and rock-filled hollow behind the landslide—unless he had spread spectral wings and flown from this trap like a
shaman.

A frisson went over Janna's skin at the thought. If any man could have
flown like a pagan god, this one could have. He had taken a beating that
would have killed most men, then he had run three miles and threaded his
way to the head of a nameless rocky canyon over land that had tried even
Janna's skill.

Don't be foolish, Janna told herself firmly. *He's as human as you are.
You've looked at enough of his blood in the last mile to swear to that on a
stack of Bibles as tall as God.*

Intently Janna stared at every foot of the sloping hollow. Despite her sharp
eyes, it took two circuits of the ground before she spotted the stranger lying
facedown amid the low, ragged piñon branches. She approached him cautiously, unwilling to make any unnecessary sound by calling out to him.
Besides, he could be playing possum, waiting for her to get within reach of
those powerful hands. He wouldn't expect to be followed by anyone but a
renegade Indian out to kill him.

A few minutes of silent observation convinced Janna that the stranger
wasn't lying in ambush. He was too still for too long. Janna began to fear
that the man was dead. He lay utterly motionless, his limbs at very awkward
angles, his skin covered by blood and dirt. In fact it was the slow welling of
blood from his wounds that told her he was still alive. She crawled beneath
piñon boughs until she was close enough to put her mouth next to his ear.

"I'm a friend. Do you hear me? I'm a friend."

The man didn't move.

"Mister?" Janna whispered, touching his naked shoulder, shaking him
lightly, calling to him in her low, husky voice.

There was no sign that he heard.

Carefully Janna sat on her heels next to the man, letting fragrant piñon
boughs brush over her. She slid her hand around his neck until she could
press against the jugular...and breathed out. Her first impression was of fiery
heat, then of the strength in his muscular neck, and then finally she felt the
slow, somewhat ragged beating of his heart. From the size of the lump on
the side of his head, she was surprised that he had remained conscious long
enough to get this far.

"You're not going another inch, are you?" she asked very softly.

The man didn't disagree.

With gentle fingers Janna probed his head wound. Though it was puffy,
there was no softness of crushed bone beneath. Nor was blood pooling in
the dirt anywhere around his big body, which meant that none of his wounds
were bleeding him to death.

Once Janna assured herself of that, she didn't waste any more time checking injuries. The stranger's extraordinary efforts had ended up defeated by a
dead end against a stone cliff, but his original plan was still good—take such
a difficult route up the side of the plateau that Cascabel wouldn't think to
look there for an injured man. All Janna had to do was backtrack, thoroughly
wiping out the man's trail as she went. Then she would lay a false trail in
another direction and sneak back up to the stranger to make sure that he kept
quiet until Cascabel tired of the game and went back to camp.

Slowly Janna worked back down the man's trail, doing a thorough job this
time of removing all signs that anyone had come this way. Where blood had
fallen onto loose stone, she picked up the stained rock and substituted another
of like size. Where the man's feet had disturbed earth, she brushed it flat
once more and sifted dust and plant debris over the surface.

She worked in this manner past several places where he could have chosen
other routes to the left or right, up the slope or down. When she came to
another place where he had a choice of directions, she pulled a knife from
the sheath at her waist, gritted her teeth and cut her arm until blood flowed.

Using her own blood, Janna laid a false trail, concealed it so hastily that
it could be detected readily by a warrior with sharp eyes, and began a long,
slanting descent to the base of the plateau, heading away from the renegades'
camp. As she went, she made more obvious attempts to conceal her direction
each time there was a logical choice in routes to make. The closer to Mustang
Canyon she came, the less blood she left behind, for she wanted to suggest
to the renegades that their quarry wasn't badly wounded; that, in fact, he was
bleeding less and less with each moment. Hopefully, when the blood spoor
disappeared, the Indians wouldn't be suspicious.

Just as Janna reached the broad mouth of Mustang Canyon, she heard
Cascabel's men. They were behind her—and they had just discovered the
trail of their prey.

Chapter Two

Trapped by Mustang Canyon's high rock walls, the cries of the renegades echoed eerily, making Janna feel surrounded. She redoubled her speed, running hard toward the head of the wide, deep canyon. As she ran, she pulled the bandanna from her neck and wrapped her arm so that no more drops of blood would fall to the ground.

By the time Janna found the tiny side canyon she had been headed for, she was breathing raggedly. Even so, she took great care to mask her trail when she turned into the twisting slot that opened onto the floor of Mustang Canyon. The feeder canyon she had chosen was extremely deep and narrow. The creek that lay in the tiny canyon's bottom was dry, for it carried water only in the wet season or after summer cloudbursts.

No more than six feet wide as it opened onto Mustang Canyon's broad floor, the slot was a hundred feet deep. Only if the sun were directly overhead did any light reach the bottom of the finger canyon. Thirty feet up the sides were marks of previous floods—brush and small trees wedged into crevices, water stains, small boulders perched precariously in water-smoothed hollows. The floor of the feeder canyon was a dry wash paved with boulders and fine deposits of silt and dried mud, all of which angled steeply back into the body of the plateau.

Leaving no trace of her passage, Janna leaped from boulder to boulder up the slot canyon's floor until it became so narrow that she couldn't extend both arms out from her sides at the same time. At this point the top of the canyon—which was the surface of the plateau itself—was only fifty feet away. Farther on, when the red stone walls pressed in even more tightly, she turned sideways, put her back against one wall and her feet against the opposite wall and inched up the chimneylike opening. The top was only thirty feet away, but her progress was dangerously slow. If one of Cascabel's men should happen into the tiny side canyon, she would be discovered within minutes.

In the distance came shouts from the renegades. Janna ignored them, concentrating only on climbing out of the slot canyon and onto the relative safety of the plateau beyond. By the time she reached the top, she was trembling with the effort of levering her body up the narrow opening. She heaved herself over the edge and lay flat, breathing in great gasps, trembling all over and stinging from the scrapes and cuts she had gotten from the stone walls.

What am I complaining about? she asked herself tartly. *He suffered a lot worse and kept going. And if I don't do the same, he's going to come to and thrash around and groan and Cascabel will find him and spend the next four days torturing him to death.*

The thought galvanized Janna. The stranger was too strong and too courageous for her to permit him to die at Cascabel's cruel hands. She pushed herself to her feet and began trotting across the top of Black Plateau, whose rumpled forests, meadows, and crumbling edges she knew as well as any human being ever had. The plateau was part of the summer grazing territory of Lucifer's band.

Janna had spent five years following Lucifer's band, caring for the sick or the lame, taming those animals that hungered for human companionship or easy food, leaving free those horses that could not accept anything from man's hand, even safety. One of those horses had become Janna's only companion in the plateau's wildness, coming to her freely, staying with her willingly, carrying her on wild rides across the rugged land. It was that horse Janna hoped to find now. The band often grazed this part of the plateau in the afternoon.

She found Lucifer and his harem grazing along one of the plateau's many green meadows, some of which ran like a winding river of grass between thick pine forests. A tiny creek trickled down the center of the sinuous meadow.

Janna lifted her hands to her mouth. Moments later a hawk's wild cry keened over the meadow. She called three times, then went to one of the small caches she had scattered across the plateau and surrounding countryside for the times when Cascabel amused himself by pursuing her. From the cache she took a canteen, a handful of rawhide thongs, a leather pouch that was full of various herbs, a blanket and a small leather drawstring bag that contained some of the gold that Mad Jack insisted was her father's share of his gold mine. As her father had been dead for five years, Mad Jack simply paid her instead.

After a moment of hesitation, Janna removed a knife as well, the last item in the small cache. It took just seconds and a few lengths of rawhide thongs to transform the blanket into a makeshift pack. She slung the pack diagonally across her back and looked over to where the wild horses grazed. Lucifer was staring in her direction with pricked ears, but he was not alarmed. Though he had never permitted her to come within fifty feet of him, he no longer ran from or threatened to attack her. He had come to accept Janna as a particularly slow and awkward horse that showed up from time to time carrying delicacies such as rock salt and grain—certainly no threat to his band despite the man odor that accompanied her.

By the time Janna filled her canteen at the small stream, one of Lucifer's mares had come over at a trot, whinnying a welcome. Zebra was dust colored with black mane, tail, stockings, ears, muzzle, and a black stripe down her back. Cowboys called such horses zebra duns and prized them above all others for stamina, intelligence, and the natural camouflage that allowed them to pass unnoticed where other horses would be spotted by hostile Indians or equally hostile outlaws.

"Hello, Zebra," Janna said, smiling and stroking the dust-colored mare's velvety black muzzle. "Ready for a run? It won't be far today. Just a few miles."

Zebra nudged her muzzle against Janna with enough force to stagger her. She grabbed a handful of mane and swung onto Zebra's back. A light touch of Janna's heels sent the mare into a canter, which rapidly became a gallop. Guided only by Janna's hands, heels and voice, the mare took a slanting course across a corner of the plateau, then plunged down the hair-raising trail used by the wild horses to climb up or down the plateau's north side.

This particular route was one of the most difficult ways to ascend or descend the plateau. That was why Janna chose the route. To her knowledge, none of Cascabel's men had ever used it. They gained access to the plateau through one of the two western trails or from the southern edge, leaving the northern and eastern areas of the plateau pretty much alone. That suited Janna very well; a slot canyon that opened up from the plateau's eastern face was as close to a home as she could ever remember having.

Twenty minutes after Zebra attacked the precipitous trail down into Mustang Canyon, she slid to the canyon's floor and stretched out for a good run. Janna let her go until she was as close to the stranger's hiding place as she could come without making her destination obvious.

"That's it girl. Whoa, Zebra. This is where I get off."

Reluctantly Zebra slowed. Janna leaped off and smacked the mare lightly on her dust-colored haunch to send her on her way.

The mare didn't budge.

"Go on," Janna said, smacking Zebra again. "I don't have time to play anymore today. Next time, I promise."

Abruptly the mare's head went up and her nostrils flared. She stood motionless, drinking the wind and staring off down the canyon. Janna didn't need any more warning; she faded back into the rocks and clumps of brush. Zebra stood for a few moments more, then quietly withdrew back up the canyon. Within minutes she was all but invisible, protected by her natural camouflage.

Moving quickly, silently, camouflaged by her own dusty clothes and earth-colored hat, Janna retreated along the canyon bottom until she could turn and climb up to the small hollow. Wiping out her traces as she went, she approached the stranger's hiding place from a different, even steeper angle, scrambled over the rock slide at the hollow's entrance and immediately looked toward the tangle of piñons and rocks at the base of the cliff.

The stranger was gone.

Janna ran across the hollow and went into the piñons on her hands and knees. There was blood still fresh on the ground, as well as signs that the man had dragged himself deeper into cover. She followed his trail, wiping it out as she went, crumbling and scattering earth and the debris that piled up beneath the piñons. She found him in a dense thicket that crowded up against the cliff. Bloody handprints on the stone told her that he had tried to climb, only to fall. He lay where he had fallen, facedown in the dirt, his hands still reaching toward stone as though he would awaken at any moment and try to climb once more.

She bit her lip against unaccustomed tears, feeling as she had once when she had found a cougar with its paw wedged into a crack in the rocks. She hadn't been able to approach the cat until it was nearly dead with thirst. Only then had she been able to free it—but she would never forget the agony of waiting for the magnificent cat to weaken enough to allow her close.

"Pobrecito," Janna murmured, touching the man's arm as she settled into place beside him. *Poor little one.*

The swell of firm muscle beneath her fingers reminded Janna that the man was hardly little; he was as powerful as the cougar had been, and perhaps as dangerous. He had shown a frightening determination to survive, driving himself beyond all reason or hope. Perhaps he was like Cascabel, whose ability to endure pain was legendary. As was his cruelty.

Was this man also cruel? Had it been savage cunning and coldness that had driven him to survive rather than unusual intelligence and courage and determination?

Shouts floated up from the canyon bottom as renegades called to one another, searching for the man who had run their gauntlet and then disappeared like a shaman into the air itself. Janna shrugged out of her pack, untied the rawhide thongs and spread the army blanket over the stranger. An instant later she removed it. The solid color was too noticeable in the dappled light and shadow of the piñons. As long as there was any chance of Cascabel finding the hollow, the man was better off camouflaged by random patterns of dirt and dried blood.

Slowly, silently, Janna shifted position until she was sitting next to the man, his face turned toward her. She looked at him intently, trying to guess what kind of man lay beneath the bruises and dirt. If she hadn't already had ample evidence of his strength, his body would have convinced her of his power. His shoulders were as wide as the length of an ax handle, his back was a broad wedge tapering to narrow hips, and his legs were long, well muscled, and covered in black hair that was repeated in the small of his back and beneath his arms.

Gradually Janna realized that the stranger was very handsome and intensely male. There was a regularity of feature in his face that was pleasing. His forehead was broad, his eyes were set well apart and thickly lashed, his cheekbones were high and well defined beneath the black beard stubble, his nose was straight, his mustache was well trimmed, and his jaw fully reflected the determination he had already shown. She wondered whether his eyes were dark or light, but his skin gave no clue. Faint lines of laughter or concentration radiated out from the corners of his eyes. Beneath the dust and blood, his hair was thick, slightly curly, and the color of a raven's wing. His hair tempted her to run her fingers through it, testing its depth and texture.

More voices floated up from the canyon, freezing Janna in the act of reaching out to stroke the stranger's hair. Cascabel's men were closer now—much too close. They must have seen past her efforts to obscure the trail.

The man's eyes opened. They were a deep, crystalline green, and they burned with the savage light of his determination to live. Instantly Janna put her fingers over his lips and shook her head. Her other hand pressed down on his back, urging him not to move. He nodded his understanding that he must not speak or make any motion that might give away their hiding place.

Frozen, barely breathing, they waited and listened to the sounds of Cascabel's renegades searching the rugged land for their prey.

Gradually the sounds withdrew. Apparently the Indians hadn't believed that their wounded prey could climb the steep side of the canyon. When the voices failed to come back again, the man let out a long, broken breath and fell unconscious again.

Janna bent and stroked the stranger's hair in a silent reassurance meant to soothe the animal awareness that had awakened him at the first sound of pursuers. She understood the kind of life that resulted in a division of the mind where part slept and part stood guard. It was how she slept, alertly, waking often to listen to the small sounds of mice and coyote, the call of an owl and branches rustling against the wind. She accepted the dangers of a wild land, thinking no more about their presence than she did that of the sun or the wind or the brilliant silver moon.

After it had been silent for an hour, Janna cautiously opened the leather pouch she had brought. One by one she unwrapped the herbs she had collected at different times and places as she roamed the Utah Territory. Some of the herbs had already been made into unguents. Others were whole. Working quickly and quietly, she treated the wounds she could reach without disturbing the stranger's sleep. His feet were a collection of cuts, thorns and bruises. She cleaned the cuts, removed the thorns, applied a thick layer of healing herbs and wrapped his feet in strips she cut from the blanket. Not once did he stir or show any signs of waking. His stillness would have worried her had it not been for the strong, even beating of his heart and his rhythmic breathing.

When Janna could do no more for the stranger, she pulled the blanket over him, sat next to him and watched the sky catch fire from the dying sun. She loved the silent blaze of beauty, the incandescence and the transformation of the sky. It made her believe that anything was possible—anything—even her fierce, silent hope of someday having a home where she could sleep without always waking alone.

Only when it was full dark and the last star had glittered into life did Janna put her arms around her knees, lower her forehead to them and sleep, waking every few minutes to listen to the small sounds of the living night and the breathing of the man who trusted her enough to sleep naked and weaponless at her feet.

Chapter Three

Tyrell MacKenzie awoke feeling as though he had slept beneath a herd of stampeding steers. Despite the pain lancing through his head with every heartbeat, he didn't groan or cry out; his instincts were screaming at him that he had to be silent and hide. The Civil War had taught Ty to trust those instincts. He opened one eye a bare slit, just enough to see without revealing the fact that he had returned to consciousness.

A pair of moccasins was only inches away from his face.

Instantly memories flooded through Ty's pain-hazed mind—Cascabel and his renegades and a gauntlet of clubs that had seemed to go on forever. Somehow he had gotten through it and then he had run and run until he thought his chest would burst, but he had kept on running and trying to find a place where he could go to ground before the Indians tracked him down and killed him.

Another memory came to Ty, that of a thin boy with ragged clothes and steady gray eyes warning him to be silent. Ty opened his eyes a bit more and saw that the moccasins belonged to the boy rather than to one of Cascabel's killers. The boy had his head on his knees and was hugging his long legs against his body as though still trying to ward off the chill of a night spent in the open.

The angle and direction of the sunlight slanting between the towering black thunderheads told Ty that it was early afternoon rather than early morning, which meant that he had slept through yesterday afternoon, all of the hours of darkness, and most of the day, as well. He was surprised that the cold hadn't awakened him during the night. Even though it was still August, the countryside wasn't particularly warm once the sun set behind Black Plateau.

The boy turned his head until his chin rested on his knees. Ty found himself staring into the clear gray eyes he remembered. Such a steady glance was unusual in a boy so young that he wouldn't need a razor for a few years. But then, Ty had seen what war did to children. The ones who survived were old far beyond their years.

The youth raised his index finger to his lips in a signal for Ty not to make a sound. Ty nodded slightly and watched while the boy eased through the underbrush with the silence of an Indian. Despite the aches of his bruised and beaten body, Ty didn't shift position. That was another thing the war had taught him. The man who moved first died first.

While Ty waited for the youth to return from reconnoitering, he noticed that there was a blanket covering his body, protecting him against the chilly air. From the look of the corner covering his arm, the blanket was as ragged as the boy's clothes. Ty realized that the blanket must belong to the boy, who obviously had stood guard throughout the cold night and the long day as well, protecting a helpless stranger, giving him the only cover.

Hell of a kid, Ty thought. *Wonder what he's doing out here alone?*

It was the last thought Ty had before he drifted off into a pain-filled, fitful sleep.

He was still dozing when Janna returned through the brush as silently as she had come. Even so, his eyes opened. Like a wild animal, he had sensed that he was no longer alone.

"You can move around, but we can't leave yet," Janna said in a low voice. "Cascabel and his men are still searching for you, but they're on the east side of Black Plateau."

"Then you better get out while you can," Ty said hoarsely. He shifted position with cautious movements, grimaced with pain and kept moving anyway. He had to find out what his body would be good for if he had to run again. And he would have to run if Cascabel were still searching. "I left a trail a blind man could follow."

"I know," Janna said softly. "I wiped it out as I followed you."

"Won't do any good," Ty said in a low voice that was more like a groan. He forced himself into an upright position despite dizziness and the excruciating pain in his head. "Once Cascabel sobers up, he'll find your sign. He could track a snake over solid rock. Go on, kid. Get out while you can."

Janna saw the stranger's pallor and the sudden sweat that covered his face. She wanted to tell him to lie down, not to move, not to cause himself any more pain; but she knew that he might have to move, to run, to hide. Better that they find out now how much strength he had so that they could plan for his weakness rather than being caught by surprise.

"I laid a false trail to a blind keyhole canyon way back up Mustang Canyon," she said softly. "Then I climbed out. I'd stopped bleeding by then, so I didn't leave any sign of where I went."

"Bleeding?" Ty looked up, focusing on the boy with difficulty because pain had turned the world to red and black. "Are you hurt?"

"I cut myself," Janna said as she unwrapped the bandanna from her arm. "Cascabel knew you were bleeding. If there weren't any sign of blood, he wouldn't believe the trail was yours."

The last turn of the bandanna was stuck to Janna's skin by dried blood. She moistened the cloth with a small amount of water from the canteen, gritted her teeth and pulled the bandanna free. The cut oozed blood for a moment, then stopped. There was no sign of infection, but she dug in the leather pouch and sprinkled more herb powder over the cut anyway.

"You all right?" Ty asked thickly.

Janna looked up and smiled. "Sure. Papa always told me that cuts from a sharp knife heal better than cuts from a dull one, so I keep my knives sharp. See? No sign of infection."

Ty looked at the long red line on the back of the unmuscular forearm and realized that the boy had deliberately cut himself in order to leave a trail of blood for Cascabel to follow.

"Your papa raised a brave boy," Ty said.

Janna's head came up sharply. She was on the edge of saying that her father had raised a brave *girl*, when she caught herself. Other people had mistaken her for a boy since her father had died, especially after she had done everything she could to foster the impression. She bound her breasts with turn after turn of cloth to flatten and conceal her feminine curves. For the same reason she wore her father's old shirts, which were much too big, and his old pants rode low on her hips, hiding the pronounced inward curve of her waist. She wore her hair in thick Indian braids stuffed beneath a man's hat, which was also too big for her.

Being taken for a boy had proven useful when Janna went to the few ranches around to trade her writing and reading skills for food, or when she went to town to spend a bit of Mad Jack's gold on store-bought clothes or rare, precious books. Being a boy gave her a freedom of movement that was denied to girls. Because she loved freedom as much as any mustang ever born, she had always been relieved when strangers assumed she was a boy.

Yet it galled Janna that this particular stranger had mistaken her sex. Her first reaction was to make him look beyond the clothes to the woman beneath. Her second reaction was that that would be a really stupid thing to do.

Her third reaction was a repeat of her first.

"Your papa didn't do badly, either," Janna said finally. "Cascabel has killed more men than you have fingers and toes."

"Don't know about the toes," Ty said, smiling crookedly as he sat upright and examined his feet. The sight of the bandages made him look quickly at Janna.

"Oh, you've still got ten of them," she said. "A bit raw, but otherwise intact. It's going to hurt like the devil to walk on them, though."

Ty hissed softly through his teeth as he crossed his legs and sat Indian-style. "Don't have to wait until I walk. Hurts like hell right now."

Janna said nothing because her mouth had gone dry. When he had sat up and crossed his legs, the blanket had fallen away, revealing a broad, bloody chest and muscular torso. Crisp black hair swirled around his flat nipples, gathered in the center line of his body and curled down to his loins. There the hair became thick and lush as it fanned out, defining and emphasizing the essential difference between male and female.

Abruptly Janna looked away and forced herself to drag air into her aching lungs, wondering if she were going to faint.

Why am I being such a goose? she asked herself fiercely. *I've seen naked men before.*

But somehow cowboys washing off in lonely water holes and dancing Indians wearing little more than strings and flapping squares of cloth weren't the same as the powerful man sitting naked and unconcerned just a few feet away from her.

"Hey, kid," Ty said softly. "You sure you're all right? You look kind of pale."

Janna swallowed hard, twice. "I'm fine," she said huskily. "And my name is…Jan, not 'kid.'"

"Jan, huh?" Ty said, unwrapping his right foot carefully. "My mother's father was called Jan. He was a big Swede with a laugh you could hear in the next county. Mama used to say I took after him."

"Well, you're big enough," Janna said dryly, "but I'd keep a tight rein on the laughing until Cascabel gives up."

Ty hissed an obscenity under his breath when the strip of blanket refused to come off the sole of his foot. After a moment he added, "My name's Ty MacKenzie." He looked up at the long-legged, thin youth and smiled. "As for big, don't worry, ki—Jan. You'll start putting on height and muscle about the same time you think you need to shave."

"And pigs will fly," Janna muttered beneath her breath.

Ty heard anyway. He smiled widely and gave Janna a brotherly pat on the knee. "I felt the same way when I was your age. Thought I'd never catch up with my older brother, Logan, but I finally did. Well, almost. No one's as big as Logan. I've had one hell of a lot more luck with the ladies, though," Ty added with a wink.

The news didn't sweeten Janna's temper. She could well imagine that women would swoon over a cleaned-up version of Tyrell MacKenzie, because the beaten, dirty, naked version was giving her pulse a severe case of the jump and flutters. And that irritated her, because she was certain that she hadn't had the least effect on Ty's pulse.

You'll start putting on height and muscle about the same time you think you need to shave.

Grimly Janna told herself that one day she would think back on this and laugh. Someday, but definitely not today.

A small sound from Ty made Janna glance up—way up, all the way to his eyes, which were narrowed against pain. He was sweating again and his hands were pressed against his forehead as though to keep it from flying apart. Instantly she forgot her pique at not being recognized as a woman and reached to help him.

"Lie down on your back," she said, pushing against Ty's chest and supporting his head at the same time.

It was like pushing against a sun-warmed cliff.

"If you lie down, it will be easier for me to tend your cuts," Janna pointed out. "I could only get to your back last night. If I don't clean up your front, you'll get infected and feverish and be no more use in a fight than a half-starved kitten."

Ty shook his head slowly, then grimaced again.

"How's your stomach?" Janna asked, giving up for the moment on making him lie down. With deft fingers she rewrapped the bandage on his right foot. "Do you feel sick?"

"No."

She stared into the crystalline green of his eyes. Both of his pupils were the same size.

"Look into the sun for a second," she said.

Ty gave Janna a long look, then glanced overhead, where a piece of sun was peeking between thunderheads. When he looked away, she stared at his pupils intently. Both of them had contracted in response to the sun's light.

"Well? Do I have a concussion?" he asked, his voice low and amused.

"With a skull as thick as yours, I doubt it," she retorted.

"Is that a professional opinion, doctor?"

"Pa was the doctor, but he taught me a lot before he died." Janna looked at Ty's pupils again, fascinated by the clear midnight circles surrounded by such a gemlike green. "It's a good thing Indians collect scalps, not eyes. Yours would be a real prize."

Ty blinked, laughed softly, then made a low sound of pain as his own laughter hit his skull like a hammer.

"You sure your stomach is all right?" she asked.

"Yes," he said through clenched teeth. "Why?"

"You should drink to replace the blood you lost, but if you're going to throw up there's no point in wasting water. The nearest seep is a quarter mile from Cascabel's camp."

Silently Ty took the canteen Janna held out to him. He drank slowly, savoring the cool glide of water over his tongue and down his throat. After several long swallows he reluctantly lowered the canteen and handed it back. Janna shook her head, refusing the canteen. "Unless you're nauseated, drink more."

"What about you?" he asked.

"You need it more than I do."

Ty hesitated, then took a few more swallows and handed the canteen back.

"Here, chew on this while I clean the cuts on your chest," Janna said.

As she spoke, she dug a piece of beef jerky from her shirt pocket. Ty took the tough strip of dried meat, automatically reached to his waist for a knife with which to cut off a bite and realized all over again that he was naked. Before he could say anything, Janna handed him the long-bladed hunting knife she had taken from the cache. He tested the edge, nodded approvingly and sliced off a chunk of jerky with a swift, controlled motion that spoke of real expertise in using knives.

Janna cut off the cleanest corner of the blanket she could find, moistened it carefully with water from the canteen and reached toward the broad expanse of Ty's chest. At the last instant she hesitated.

"This will hurt."

Ty gave her a sidelong, amused glance. "Boy, there isn't a square inch of me that doesn't hurt."

Boy.

The corners of Janna's mouth turned down in displeasure, but her hands were careful as he cleaned the blood-encrusted cuts on Ty's chest. Two of them were ragged, puffy and already inflamed. She bit her lip against the pain she knew she must be causing Ty despite all her care.

"Sorry," she whispered helplessly when he grimaced.

Ty heard the distress in the youthful voice and felt like gathering that slender body into his arms and giving comfort. The thought both surprised him and made him uncomfortable. He definitely wasn't the type of man who liked boys. Abruptly he grabbed the narrow wrists and held them away from his body.

"That's good enough," he said brusquely.

"But I'm not fin—"

Janna's words ended as though cut off by a knife. Into the taut silence came the sound of a rock bouncing and rolling down the slope.

Ty's hands shifted with shocking speed. In an instant Janna found herself jerked over his body and then jammed between his broad back and the face of the cliff.

Naked and weaponless but for the knife, Ty waited to see what scrambled up over the rockfall and into the piñon-filled hollow.

Chapter Four

A soft nicker floated through the air as a horse scrambled over the last of the rockfall and into the hollow.

"What the hell?" whispered Ty.

Janna peeked over his back. "Zebra!"

"Boy, can't you tell a horse from a zebra!"

"Better than you can tell a girl from a boy," Janna muttered.

"What?"

"Let me out," she said, pushing against Ty's back.

"Ouch!"

Instantly Janna lifted her hand and apologized. Ty grunted and moved aside so that she could crawl out over his legs. Zebra walked up to the edge of the piñon grove, pushed her head in and nickered again.

"Hello, girl," Janna said softly, rubbing the velvet muzzle. "Did you get lonesome without me?"

Zebra whuffled over Janna's fingers, nudged her hands, and kept a wary eye on Ty all the while. When he moved, her head came up and her nostrils flared.

"Be still," Janna said. "She's not used to people."

"What does she think you are?"

"A bad-smelling horse."

Ty laughed softly. The sound made Zebra's ears twitch. He began talking in a gentle, low voice.

"You've got a better nose than my daddy's best hound ever did," he said. Without looking aside he asked Janna, "How long have you owned her?"

"I don't."

"What?"

"I don't own her. She likes me, that's all. Some horses enjoy people, if you approach them the right way."

"And some horses damn near get people killed," Ty said. "I was about ten seconds away from dropping my loop on Lucifer's neck when Cascabel jumped me."

Janna's heart hesitated, then beat faster. Despite Lucifer's refusal to approach her, she thought of him somehow as her own horse. "How did you get so close to him?"

"I'm a fair tracker when I'm not half-dead," Ty said dryly.

"The shamans say that no mortal man will ever capture Lucifer. He's a spirit horse."

Ty shook his head. "That old boy is pure flesh and blood, and he sires the best colts I've seen west of the Mississippi. Lucifer's my ticket to the future that the Civil War took away from the MacKenzie family. With him I'm going to found the kind of herd that my daddy always wanted. He would have had it, too, except for the war. The four MacKenzie brothers rode off to battle on his best horses. They saved our lives more than once."

Janna saw Ty's mouth harden. He shrugged as though to throw off unhappy memories. Into the silence came the rumble of distant thunder and the scrape of branches stirring beneath a wind that smelled of moisture.

"Hope it rains soon," Ty said, looking up at the massed thunderheads. "Otherwise that big dog's tracks are going to lead Cascabel right to us."

"It will rain."

The confidence in Janna's voice made Ty turn and look at her intently.

"How do you know?" he asked.

"I just...know," she said slowly. "I've lived with the land so long that I know a lot of its secrets."

"Such as?"

"Such as—when the air over the Fire range gets an odd sort of crystal shine to it and then clouds form, it always rains about two hours before sundown. It rains hard and cold and sudden, like an ocean turned upside down and pouring back to earth. After an hour or two some of the finger canyons run twenty feet deep with water." Janna pushed away the mare's muzzle and looked at Ty. "Are you still dizzy?"

Ty wasn't surprised that his occasional dizziness had been noticed. He was discovering that not much escaped those clear gray eyes.

"Some," he admitted. "It comes and goes."

"Do you think you can get over that rockfall if I help?"

"Count on it, with or without your help."

Janna looked at the determined lines of Ty's face and the latent power in his big body and hoped he was right. The rocky hollow had been useful, but it would become a lethal trap the instant Cascabel scrambled up and found his prey. The sooner they left, the better it would be.

There was only one haven Janna could think of. It lay on the southeast side of Black Plateau, at the edge of Cascabel's ill-defined territory. It was a spirit place avoided by Indians, whose legends told of a time when the mountain had roared in anguish and split open and thick red blood had gushed forth, spirit blood that made everything burn, even stone itself. When the blood finally cooled it had become the dark, rough rock that gave Black Plateau its name. There, at the foot of ancient lava flows and sandstone cliffs, Janna had found a keyhole canyon snaking back into the solid body of the plateau. Once past the narrow entrance, the canyon widened out into a parklike area that was thick with grass and sparkling with sweet water. It was there she wintered, secure in the knowledge that no warriors or outlaws would see her tracks in the snow.

It had been her secret place, as close to a home as she had ever known. She had shared it with no one. The thought of sharing it with Ty made her feel odd. Yet there really was no other choice.

"Soon as I get you patched up," Janna said, turning to her bag of herbs, "we'll go to a keyhole canyon I know about. Nobody else has any idea that it exists, except maybe Mad Jack, and he hardly counts."

"Mad Jack? I thought he was a legend."

"He's old enough to be one."

"You've actually seen him?"

Janna dug out the herbal paste she had made during the long hours of daylight while Ty had slept. "Yes, I've seen him," she said, and began dabbing the paste on the worst of Ty's cuts.

"I've heard he has a gold mine hidden somewhere on Black Plateau."

Her hands paused, then resumed slathering on medication. "Whatever Mad Jack has or doesn't have is his business."

Ty's black eyebrows lifted at Janna's curt words. "Ouch! Watch it, boy, that's not stone you're poking."

"Sorry," she said in a tight voice.

For several moments Ty watched the gray eyes that refused to meet his.

"Hey," he said finally, catching Janna's chin in his big hand, forcing her to meet his eyes. "I'm not going to hurt that old man no matter how much gold he might have found. I'm not a thief or a raider. I'm not going to build my future on bloodstained gold."

Janna searched the green eyes that were so close to hers and saw no evasion. She remembered Ty telling her to leave him and save herself, and she remembered how he had put his own body between her and whatever danger might have been coming into the hollow. Abruptly she felt ashamed of her suspicions.

"I'm sorry," Janna said. "It's just that I've had men follow me out of town when I buy supplies with a bit of gold I've found here and there. It's usually easy enough to lose the men, but it hasn't given me a very kind opinion of human nature."

The surge of anger Ty felt at the thought of a child having to lose white men in the rocks as though they were Indian renegades surprised him. So did the protectiveness he felt toward this particular child. Uneasily it occurred to Ty that beneath the shapeless old hat and the random smears of dirt, the youth's face was…extraordinary.

My God, I've seen women a hell of a lot less beautiful than this boy. Maybe the men weren't following gold, after all.

Ty snatched his hand back as though he had been burned. The sudden movement made Zebra shy away violently.

"That damn horse is as spooky as a mustang," he said, rubbing his hand against his chest as though to remove the tactile memory of soft skin and delicate bone structure.

Janna blinked, wondering what had made Ty so irritable. She wished that he would put his hand beneath her chin again. His palm was warm and firm, his fingers were long and gentle, and it had been years since she had felt a comforting touch from another human being.

"Zebra is a mustang," Janna said huskily. "When she's not with me, she runs free."

Ty's head turned toward the mare with renewed interest. He studied her carefully, especially her hooves. They had been trimmed by stony ground rather than by a pair of steel nippers. She was sleek without being fat, strong without being big. Nowhere did she show the marks of man—no brand, no ear notch, no shoes, no rubbed places on her hide where bridle or saddle had rested.

"Do you ride her?" he asked.

"Sometimes, when it's safe."

"When is that?"

"When Cascabel isn't around," Janna said simply. "He's been around a lot the past six months, which is why Zebra is so lonesome. I guess the Army is making life hard for Cascabel."

"Or Black Hawk is tired of being blamed for Cascabel's raids and is clamping down," Ty said. "Black Hawk is a war chief and a leader. Cascabel is a butcher and a raider. Hell, I'm surprised that renegade hasn't tracked you down and cooked you over a slow fire just for the sport of it."

Janna shrugged off the implicit question. She had no intention of telling Ty that to most Utes she was Shadow of Fire, *una bruja*, a witch who walked with spirits. Ty thought of her as a boy, which was both irritating and quite useful—especially as long as he was sitting around stark naked while she rubbed medicine into his cuts.

The renewed realization of Ty's nudity brought heightened color to Janna's cheeks. It took every bit of her willpower to keep her hands from trembling as she smoothed the herb paste over his skin.

Ty noticed the fine tremor in the slender fingers and swore under his breath.

"Sorry, boy. I didn't mean to scare you," he said gruffly. "Once we get free of Cascabel, I'll take you to the Army post at Sweetwater. You'll be safe there."

Janna shook her head and said nothing, concentrating on keeping her hands from revealing the uncertain state of her emotions.

"Don't be silly," Ty said. "You might have survived out here in the past, but it's different now. The Army has been fighting Black Hawk for nearly three years, since the end of the Civil War. They've had a bellyful of fighting Utes. There will be a big campaign before winter. The Army figures to have it all wrapped up by Thanksgiving and to have Cascabel's ears in the bargain. Between Black Hawk and the soldiers fighting each other, and Cascabel killing everything that moves, it won't be safe for man nor beast here, much less a boy who's as skinny as a willow switch."

"If it's so dangerous, why are you here?"

"Lucifer," Ty said simply. "I figured this was my best chance. Once the Utes are quiet, every man with an eye for prime horseflesh will be trying for that stallion. Even if no one gets him, sure as hell some money-hungry mustanger will put a bullet through his black head just to get at his colts." Ty looked at Zebra again. "He sired her, didn't he?"

"Yes."

"It shows in her long legs and well-shaped head. The barb blood in Lucifer comes through no matter what he breeds with. Does she run with his bunch?"

"Yes."

"How did you get close to her?"

Janna wiped her fingers on her pants as she looked critically at Ty's cuts. "Her mother was a runaway ranch horse. She liked salt and grain and human company. Zebra grew up with me petting her. There are others like her in Lucifer's bunch. They accept me. After a time, so do some of the true mustangs. I take care of their cuts and scrapes and scratch the places they can't reach, and they tell me when there are men around. That's how I've kept away from Cascabel. Lucifer can smell him a mile off.''

"Does Lucifer let you pet him?'' Ty asked intently.

"He's as wild as a storm wind,'' Janna said, not answering the question.

"So is that one,'' Ty said, looking at Zebra, "but she followed your trail like a tame old hound dog. Will the next horse through that gap be Lucifer?''

"No. I've survived by being inconspicuous. Anyone standing next to Lucifer would be as conspicuous as lightning.''

Thunder belled suddenly, but Ty didn't look away from Janna's face.

"Have you ever tried to get close to Lucifer?''

"No.''

"Why not? Is he a killer?''

Janna shrugged. "Wouldn't you try to kill a man who wanted to put you in a cage?''

"Horses have been bred by men for thousands and thousands of years. It's a partnership, like men and dogs.''

"Not to a lot of men.''

"Those same men are cruel to other men. I'm not. I don't fight for the pleasure of it, but to get the job done.''

Janna looked at her knife, which Ty kept within easy reach at all times. She remembered how he had held the knife—as a weapon, not as a tool. There was no doubt in her mind that he could "get the job done'' better than any man she had ever seen, except Cascabel.

The realization should have frightened her, for despite Ty's injuries he was far stronger than she was. Yet she was no more frightened of him than she was of Lucifer. In the past her instincts had proven to be very good at picking up the presence of senseless viciousness or cruelty; she sensed none in either Ty or the big black stallion so many men longed to own.

But what if I'm wrong this time? What if Ty is just another man greedy for whatever he can get from those weaker than he is?

There was no answer to Janna's silent question but the obvious one—if she took Ty to her private refuge and discovered there that she had been wrong about his essential decency, she would have made the worst mistake of her life.

And probably the last, as well.

Chapter Five

The sudden downpour of cold rain was like a blow. In spite of that, the rain was welcome, for it would wash away Ty and Janna's trail.

"Ready?" Janna asked.

Ty nodded grimly. He was still angry at having lost the battle of the shrinking blanket. Over his objections Janna had cut the blanket up into a breechcloth, bandages for his bruised ribs and a makeshift poncho. He hadn't objected to the breechcloth, had given in on the bandages, but had been damned if he would wear a blanket while a child ran around with no more protection against the thunderstorm than a ragged shirt and pants.

Yet here he was, wearing the blanket; and there the kid was, wearing only a shirt and pants.

"Stubborn as a Missouri mule," Ty snarled, but his words were drowned out by thunder.

Zebra took the lightning, thunder and pelting rain with the indifference of a horse born and raised out in the open. She watched with interest as Ty and Janna negotiated the rocky rubble at the head of the hollow. While the mustang wasn't completely relaxed around Ty, she no longer shied at his every movement.

It was a good thing. Ty made some very sudden movements as he clawed over the rockfall, hobbled by his injuries and the increasing slickness of the rocks. Though he said nothing, he was grateful that his ribs were bound, despite the fact that it made breathing deeply impossible. He was also grateful for the small, surprisingly strong hands that helped to lever him over the tricky places—although he had nearly yelped with surprise the first time he had received a firm boost from behind.

Janna passed Ty just beneath the crest of the rockfall. She motioned with her hand for him to wait. When he sank into a sitting position, she peered through a crevice between two rocks. All but the first two hundred feet of the slope was veiled in sheets of rain. In the stretch of land that she could see, nothing moved but rain itself. She turned and went back to Ty.

"How do your feet feel?"

He gave her a slanting glance. "You saw them. How do you think they feel?"

"Worse than your ribs and better than your head," Janna said succinctly.

Ty grunted and began to struggle to his feet once more.

She bent, put both of her hands around his right arm just beneath his shoulder and steadied him as he came to his feet. The hissing intake of his breath, the pallor of his skin and the clenched iron of the muscles beneath her hands told Janna just how painful it was for Ty to stand on his raw feet. There was no help for it, though. There would never be a better time to exit the hollow without attracting Cascabel's notice.

By the time Janna and Ty had climbed up and over the rockfall, both of them were sweating in spite of the cold rain pouring over their bodies. Though Ty was breathing hard and fast, he didn't suggest a rest. The slope was too exposed. One of Cascabel's renegades—or a bolt of lightning—could find them at any moment.

Behind Ty and Janna came the clatter and slide of stones as the mustang scrambled over a slope Ty would have sworn a donkey would refuse. But then, he had watched in disbelief while Lucifer's band took worse countryside at a dead run in order to escape from men, including one Tyrell MacKenzie. The horses that weren't fast enough were caught. The remainder ran free to give birth to another generation of fleet, agile mustangs.

When the steepest part of the slope had been negotiated, Janna stopped and looked over her shoulder. Zebra was following close behind, watching the humans' progress with interest, pausing from time to time to sniff the strange mixture of sweat and herbal odors that Ty gave off. On the whole, the mare was rather intrigued by his smell.

"She likes you," Janna said.

"She ought to. I smell like the warm mash Daddy used to give his favorite brood mares."

Janna smiled. "Can you ride bareback?"

Ty gave Janna a disbelieving look. "What do you think I am, a greenhorn? Of course I can ride bareback."

"Let me rephrase that. Can you ride Zebra without a saddle or a bridle?"

"Boy," Ty said, shifting his position in a vain attempt to ease the searing pain in his feet and the throbbing in his head and ribs, "this is a piss poor time for me to be breaking a mustang."

"I've ridden Zebra a lot. She likes it."

Ty looked skeptical.

Janna made an exasperated sound, dropped her hold on Ty and went to the mare. She grabbed a double handful of thick mane and swung onto Zebra's back. The horse didn't even switch her tail, much less offer to buck. When Janna urged her forward until she stood next to Ty, the mustang responded as placidly as a plow horse.

"Pet her," Janna said.

Zebra flinched at the strange hand reaching up to her neck, but Ty's low, reassuring voice and gentle touch soon calmed the mare. After a few minutes she sighed and lowered her head until she could use Ty's chest as a shield against the cold rain. Smiling slightly despite his pain, he rubbed the base of the mare's ears, scratching all the itchy spots a horse couldn't reach for itself.

As Janna watched Ty's big, careful hands caressing the mare so skillfully, an odd feeling shimmered in the pit of her stomach. She wondered what it would be like if he stroked her half as gently as he was stroking Zebra. The thought brought a tingling that spread out from her stomach to her fingertips, making her shiver. With a quick motion she slid off the horse. In her haste she landed so close to Ty that she had to catch her balance against his bare, rain-chilled thigh. Instantly she snatched back her hand.

"I'll help you on," Janna said, then added quickly, "I know you could do it alone, but there's no point in putting any more strain on your ribs than you have to."

"Five will get you ten that your mustang bucks me off into the rocks," Ty said.

"She's never bucked with me."

"She's never had a man on her back instead of a skinny boy."

Boy.

"Listen," Janna said through gritted teeth, very tired of hearing herself described as a boy, "it's at least twenty miles to my winter camp. You can walk, you can ride, or you can freeze to death right here while you make smart remarks about my lack of muscle."

"Easy, girl," Ty said softly.

For an instant Janna thought he was talking to her; then she realized that he had taken a good grip on Zebra's mane and was looking over his shoulder toward the "skinny boy."

"Well?" Ty asked. "You waiting for me to freeze to death?"

"Don't tempt me," Janna muttered.

She braced herself, cupped her hands to make a stirrup and prepared to help Ty onto the mare. A few seconds later Janna was looking up at him in surprise. He had moved so quickly that she had barely felt his weight before it was gone. Zebra looked around in surprise as well, for she had been expecting Janna's light weight. But instead of mounting the horse, Janna stood with her hand on Zebra's muzzle in a steady pressure that was a signal to stand quietly. The mare snorted uneasily, then stood still, adjusting to the strange weight on her back.

"You're very quick for such a big man," Janna said.

For the space of a few breaths Ty was in too much pain to answer. When he did look down he had to fight the impulse to cup his hand caressingly beneath that delicate chin. The eyes looking back up at him were as clear as rain and a lot warmer...the eyes of a woman experiencing the slow unfolding of desire.

Pain is making me crazy, Ty told himself in disgust. *That's a boy looking up at me, not a girl, and he's got a bad case of hero worship. Poor kid must be lonely as hell, living with only wild horses for companionship.*

"And you owe me ten dollars," Janna added.

"What?"

"Zebra didn't buck you off into the rocks."

"You'll have to collect from Cascabel. He stole my money along with my hat, boots, guns and clothes."

"And your horse."

Ty's mouth flattened. "He shot Blackbird out from under me. That was the only way Cascabel caught me. Blackbird was half-thoroughbred and all heart."

"I'm sorry," Janna said, resting her hand on Ty's leg in an impulsive gesture of comfort.

At first touch his skin was cold, yet within moments the vital heat of him flowed up and warmed her palm. After a time Janna realized she was staring up at Ty, and had been for too long. She snatched back her hand and turned away, heading down the steep slope to the flatter land beyond the plateau's face. She would have to take a looping route to her secret canyon, for the base of the plateau itself was too rugged to travel along in anything approaching a straight line.

Zebra followed Janna without guidance, which was just as well. After the first four miles Ty was no longer in shape to give directions. The pounding in his head alternated with twisting strikes of agony from his ribs. The blanket was some protection against cold, but not nearly enough. He was shivering before a mile had passed beneath the mustang's agile, untrimmed hooves.

During the first hours Janna turned and looked over her shoulder every few minutes to reassure herself that Ty was all right. The farther they went, the more he slumped over Zebra's neck. Janna kept on going because there was no other choice. She had to get Ty to a place of safety.

Rain pelted down in an unceasing, cold barrage. Behind the clouds the sun slowly set, its passage marked only by a gradual lowering of the level of light. A wind sprang up soon after sunset, tearing apart the storm until only brief, hard showers remained. Through great rents in the clouds a brilliant half-moon shone forth. The wind concealed and then revealed the moon again, weaving intricate patterns of darkness and light.

Shivering, tired, worried about Ty's strength and his ability to endure any more pain, Janna forced herself to keep going, knowing that that was all she could do to help him. She walked quickly despite her own weariness, using the familiar silhouettes of buttes and mesas looming against the night sky as her landmarks. The moon had crossed more than half of its arc before she stopped and looked toward the bulky, ragged outline of the plateau whose north and east flanks she had been skirting through the long hours of darkness.

The long, sloping outwash plain glittered with rills and shallow streams as Black Plateau shed water from the recent storm. A branch of that network of shifting, gleaming temporary streams led to her hidden canyon. She hoped that there would be enough water in that temporary stream to hide her tracks, but not so much that it would be dangerous to go through the narrow slot that led to the concealed valley. She hoped, but she had no way of knowing until she got there. Everything depended on how much rain had fallen on this side of Black Plateau.

Until now Janna had made little effort to conceal her trail, hoping that the violent, intermittent showers would wash out enough of her tracks to confuse any pursuer. But now she was within four miles of her hidden valley. She could take no chance that a wandering renegade would come across her tracks and follow them to the tiny slot carved by time and water into the side of Black Plateau.

Resolutely Janna turned toward the nearest shallow wash and began wading. Zebra watched, then calmly paced alongside—beyond the reach of water. Janna waded farther out. Zebra kept walking along the edge of the runoff stream. Finally Janna waded back toward the horse.

"Ty?"

There was no answer.

For an instant Janna's heart stopped. She ran up and saw Ty slumped over Zebra's neck, his hands twisted into her mane. He seemed to be asleep.

"Ty?" she asked, pressing against his arm. "Zebra has to walk in the water."

Slowly he straightened. She looked up at him anxiously. As she watched, he began to slump again. Obviously he wouldn't be able to guide the mustang. Nor could Janna lead her; she had never put a rope on Zebra, so the mare wouldn't have the least idea how to respond.

"I hope you don't mind riding double," Janna said to Zebra. "Stand quiet, girl. It will be a big load for you, but it's the only way I'll be able to hide your tracks."

Janna grabbed the horse's long mane in her left hand and tried to swing around Ty and up onto the mare's back. It was an awkward mount that was saved from disaster only when Ty wrapped his arm around Janna and heaved her into place. The groan that ripped through him at the effort told her more than she wanted to know about the condition of his ribs.

Zebra sidestepped, almost unseating both riders. Janna spoke reassuringly and sat very still, letting the mare become accustomed to the added weight. When Zebra settled down, Janna nudged her lightly with her heels. The horse moved awkwardly for a few minutes, then settled back into her normal rhythmic walk. Ty slumped forward once more, keeping his seat by instinct, experience and sheer determination.

"Hang on, Ty. We're almost there."

It was a lie, but it was more helpful than the truth, which was that they had a lot of hard going left—and no assurance at all that the slot wouldn't be choked with floodwaters when they finally arrived.

Chapter Six

Ty awoke with the sun shining right onto his face and the familiar sound of a horse cropping grass nearby. As he turned to check on Blackbird, pain brought back all the memories—his horse's death and his own capture, Cascabel and the gauntlet, pain and running endlessly, and the gray-eyed waif who had patched up his wounds. Vaguely Ty remembered getting on a zebra dun and riding until he was quite certain he had died and gone to hell.

Except that this wasn't hell. True enough, the overhang he lay beneath was hot red stone, but the canyon floor was lush with the kind of vegetation that only came from water. Definitely not a flaming hell. In fact, with the sun's warmth and the lazy humming of insects and the calling of birds, this could only be a slice of heaven.

Automatically Ty sat up to have a better look around. Pain and dizziness struck, chaining him in place, forcing him to revise his opinion of where he was. Eyes closed, his weight braced on his elbows, he decided that the valley might be in heaven, but his body was indeed in hell.

"Lie down, Ty. You've been sick."

He opened his eyes. Gray eyes watched him with concern. Without thinking, Ty shifted his weight until he could raise his hand to touch the cheek that was so close to his. The skin was smooth and fine grained, as soft as an angel's wing.

"It's all right," he said fuzzily. "I'm fine now."

"Lie down," Janna said, pressing against his bare shoulders.

It did no good. He remained as he was, propped half-upright on his elbow.

"Please, Ty," Janna said, her voice husky with emotion. "Lie down. The fever's broken and you're much better, but you need to rest."

"Thirsty," he mumbled.

Instantly Janna grabbed a canteen, poured a stream of amber, herbal-smelling tea into a tin cup and helped Ty to drink. The taste of the liquid brought back other memories. He had drunk from this cup many times, with slender hands holding him upright and then easing him back down and stroking him until he fell once more into feverish sleep.

Sighing deeply, Ty allowed Janna to help him to lie down again.

"How long?" he asked.

"How long have we been here?"

He nodded slightly.

"Four days."

His eyes opened.

"You've been sick," Janna explained. "You caught a chill riding through the rain. That, plus your injuries from the gauntlet..." Her voice died. Automatically she reached forward and brushed back the slightly curly lock of black hair that had fallen over Ty's forehead.

Ty flinched from the touch and looked Janna over with narrowed green eyes. "You don't look so good yourself. You're skinnier than ever. If you don't take better care of yourself, you'll never get tall and put on muscle."

"Not all men are built like a side of beef," Janna retorted, hurt because Ty had refused her touch. She reached into the herb pouch, brought out a twist of paper and sprinkled the white powder into another cup of the herbal tea. "Here. Drink this."

"What is it?"

"Poison."

"Fresh as paint, aren't you, boy?"

"You're half-right," Janna muttered, but she said it so softly that Ty couldn't hear. She silently vowed that she would make him see which half of the truth he knew—and that he would be crazy with desire before he figured it out.

Ty drank the contents of the cup, grimaced and gave his companion a green-eyed glare. "Tastes like horse piss."

"I'll take your word for it, having never tasted that particular liquid."

Ty laughed, grabbed his left side and groaned. "Damn. Feels like a mule kicked me."

"It won't be so bad in a few minutes," she said, standing up. "Then I'll unwrap the bandages and take another look."

"Where are you going?"

"To check on the soup."

The thought of food made Ty's salivary glands contract in anticipation.

"Hungry?" she asked wryly, recognizing the look.

"I could eat a horse."

"Then I'd better warn Zebra to stay away from you."

"That old pony would be too tough to eat," Ty drawled, smiling slowly as he relaxed against the folded blankets beneath him.

Janna watched from a distance while Ty's eyelids closed and the taut lines around his eyes relaxed as he drifted into sleep. Only then did she return to his side, kneel and pull up the blanket so that his shoulders were covered once more. Even with the overhang of red rock to reflect back the sun's heat, she was afraid of his catching another chill. She didn't know what she would do if he became ill again. She was exhausted from broken sleep or no sleep at all, and from worrying that she had helped Ty to escape from renegades only to kill him by dragging him through a cold rain into the secret valley.

These had been the longest days of Janna's life since her father had died five years before, leaving his fourteen-year-old daughter orphaned and alone at a muddy water hole in southern Arizona. Watching Ty battle injury and fever had drained Janna's very soul. He had been so hot, then drenched in cold sweat, then hot and restless once more, calling out names of people she didn't know, fighting battles she had never heard of, crying out in anguish over dead comrades. She had tried to soothe and comfort him, had held him close in the cold hours before dawn, had bathed his big body in cool water when he was too hot and had warmed him with her own heat when he was too cold.

And now Ty flinched from her touch.

Don't be foolish, Janna told herself as she watched Ty sleep for a few moments longer. *He doesn't remember anything. He thinks you're a skinny boy. No wonder he didn't want you petting him.* And then, *How can he be so blasted blind as not to see past these clothes?*

As Janna went to the small campfire to check on the soup, she couldn't help wondering if Ty would have responded differently if he had known she was a girl.

Her intense desire that he see her as a woman caught her on the raw. She knew she was becoming too attached to the stranger whom chance had dropped into her life. As soon as Ty was healed he would leave with as little warning as he had come, going off to pursue his own dreams. He was just one more man hungry for gold or for the glory of being the person to tame the spirit horse known as Lucifer.

And he was too damned thickheaded to see past the skinny boy to the lonely woman.

Lonely?

Janna's hand froze in the act of stirring the soup. She had been alone for years but had never thought of herself as lonely. The horses had been her companions, the wind her music, the land her mentor, and her father's books had opened a hundred worlds of the mind to her. If she found herself yearning for another human voice, she had gone into Sweetwater or Hat Rock or Indian Springs. Each time she went into any of the outposts of civilization, she had left after only a few hours, driven out by the greedy eyes of the men who watched her pay for her purchases with tiny pieces of raw gold—men who, unlike Ty, had sometimes seen past Janna's boyish appearance.

Gloomily Janna studied the soup as it bubbled and announced its readiness in the blended fragrances of meat, herbs and vegetables. She poured some soup into her steep-sided tin plate and waited until it cooled somewhat. When she was sure the soup wouldn't burn Ty's mouth, she picked up her spoon and went to the overhang.

He was still asleep, yet there was an indefinable change in his body that told her Ty was healing even as she watched. He was much stronger than her consumptive father had been. Though Ty's bruises were spectacular, they were already smaller than they had been a few days before. The flesh covering his ribs was no longer swollen. Nor was his head where a club had struck.

Thick muscles and an even thicker skull, Janna told herself sarcastically.

As though he knew he were being watched, Ty opened his eyes. Their jeweled green clarity both reassured and disturbed Janna. She was glad that he was no longer dazed by fever, yet being the focus of those eyes was a bit unnerving. He might have been just one more gold- and horse-hungry man, but he had the strength, intelligence and determination to succeed where other men never got past the point of daydreaming.

"Are you still hungry?" Janna asked, her voice low and husky.

"Did you cook up poor old Zebra for me?"

The slow smile that followed Ty's words made Janna's nerve endings shimmer. Even covered with beard stubble and lying flat on his back, Ty was one of the most handsome men she had ever seen.

"No," Janna said, smiling in return. "She was too big for my pot." With unconscious grace, Janna sank to her knees next to Ty, balancing the tin plate in her hands without spilling a drop. "A few weeks back I traded a packet of dried herbs, three letters and a reading of *A Midsummer Night's Dream* for thirty pounds of jerked beef."

Ty blinked. "I beg your pardon?"

Janna laughed softly. "I'll tell you while I feed you soup. Can you sit up?"

Cautiously, then with greater assurance, Ty sat up. He started to say that he could feed himself before he realized that he was light-headed. He propped his back against the gently sloping stone cliff that was both wall and, eventually, ceiling to the natural shelter. The blanket covering him slid from his shoulders, down his chest, and finally rumpled across his lap.

Janna's pulse gave an odd little skip at the sight of the dark, masculine patterns of hair curling out from beneath Ty's bandages and down his muscular body. The temptation to trace those patterns with her fingertips was almost overwhelming.

Don't be a goose, she told herself firmly. *I've been washing, feeding and caring for Ty like a baby for four days. I've seen him wearing nothing but sunlight and soapy water, so why on earth am I getting all foolish and shivery now?*

Because he's awake now, that's why.

Ty looked down at his own body, wondering why he was being stared at. What he saw made him wince. Spreading out from beneath his rib bandage were bruises every color of the rainbow, but the predominant hues were black and blue with garish flourishes of green.

"I'm a sight, aren't I?" Ty asked wryly. "Looks worse than it feels, though. Whatever medicine you've been using works real well."

Janna closed her eyes for an instant, then looked only at the plate of soup in her hands. The surface of the liquid was disturbed by delicate rings, the result of the almost invisible trembling of her hands while she had looked at Ty.

"Don't go all pale on me now, boy. You must have seen worse than me."

Boy.

And thank God for it, Janna reminded herself instantly. *I have no more sense than a handful of sand when he looks at me and smiles that slow, devil-take-it smile.*

But, God, I do wish he knew I was a woman!

She took a deep, secret breath and brought her scattering emotions under control.

"Ready?" she asked, dipping the spoon into the soup.

"I was born ready."

She put the spoon into Ty's mouth, felt the gentle resistance of lips and tongue cleaning the spoon, and nearly dropped the plate of soup. He didn't notice, for the taste of the soup had surprised him.

"That's good."

"You needn't sound so shocked," she muttered.

"After that horse piss you've been feeding me, I didn't know what to expect."

"That was medicine. This is food."

"Food's the best medicine save one for what ails a man."

"Oh? What's the best?"

Ty smiled slowly. "When you're a man you won't have to ask."

The spoon clicked rather forcefully against Ty's teeth.

"Sorry," Janna said with transparent insincerity.

"Don't look so surly, boy. I felt the same way you did when I was your age. You'll grow into manhood with time."

"How old do you think I am?"

"Oh...thirteen?"

"Don't try to be kind," she said between her teeth.

"Hell, boy, you look closer to twelve with those soft cheeks and fine bones, and you know it. But that will begin to change about the time your voice cracks. It just takes time."

Janna knew that there would never be enough time in the whole world for her to grow into a man, but she had just enough common sense and self-control to keep that revealing bit of truth to herself. With steady motions she shoveled soup into Ty's mouth.

"You trying to drown me?" he asked, taking the soup from her. "I'll feed myself, thanks." He crunched through a pale root of some kind, started to ask what it was, then decided not to. The first thing a man on the trail learned was that if it tastes good, don't ask what it is. Just be grateful and eat fast. "What's this about herbs and Shakespeare and letters?" he asked between mouthfuls of soup.

"My father and I used to divide up a play and read parts to each other. It helped to pass the time on the trail. I still have a trunk of his books," Janna said, helplessly watching the tip of Ty's tongue lick up stray drops of broth. "When I need supplies, I'll go to the Lazy A or the Circle G and write letters for the cowhands. Most of them can't read anything but brands, so I'll also read whatever letters they've saved up until someone like me happens by."

Ty looked at the thick, dark lashes, crystalline eyes and delicately structured face of the youth who was much too pretty for Ty's comfort. "Where did you go to school?" he asked roughly.

"On the front seat of a buckboard. Papa had a university degree and a case of wanderlust."

"What about your mother?"

"She died when I was three. Papa told me her body just wasn't up to the demands of her spirit."

The spoon hesitated on the way to Ty's mouth. He pinned Janna with an intense glance. "When did your Daddy die?"

Janna paused for an instant, thinking quickly. If she told Ty her father had died five years before, he would ask how a kid under ten had survived on his own. If she told Ty that she was nineteen, he would realize that the only way a nineteen-year-old boy could lack a deep voice and a beard shadow and muscles was if said boy were a girl wearing men's clothing. She wanted Ty to figure that out for himself—the hard way.

"Papa died a few seasons back," she said casually. "You lose track of time living alone."

"You've lived alone since then?" Ty asked, startled. "The whole time?"
Janna nodded.

"Don't you have any kin?"

"No."

"Wouldn't any of the townspeople let you trade room and board for work?"

"I don't like towns."

"Surely one of the ranches would take you on as a cook's helper or fence rider. Hell, if you can tame a mustang, there isn't a ranch anywhere that wouldn't take you on as a mustanger," Ty added, disturbed at the thought of an orphaned child wandering homeless over the land. "You could make a decent living catching and breaking horses for the rough string."

"I don't catch mustangs," Janna said flatly. "Too many of them refuse to eat once they're caught. I've seen them starve to death looking over a corral fence with glazed eyes."

"Most mustangs accept men."

Janna simply shook her head. "I won't take a mustang's freedom. I've gentled a few ranch-bred horses for women's mounts or for kids, but that's all."

"Sometimes a man has to do things he doesn't want to in order to survive," Ty said, his eyes narrowed against painful memories.

"I've been lucky so far," Janna said quietly. "More soup?"

Slowly, as though called back from a distance, Ty focused on Janna. "Thanks, I'd like that," he said, handing over the plate. "While I eat, would you mind reading to me?"

"Not at all. Anything in particular you want to hear?"

"Do you have *Romeo and Juliet*?"

"Yes."

"Then read to me about a woman more beautiful than the dawn." Ty closed his eyes and smiled. "A well-bred lady of silk, softer than a summer breeze, with pale hair and skin whiter than magnolias, and delicate hands that have never done anything more harsh than coax Chopin from a huge grand piano..."

"What's her name?" Janna asked tightly

"Who?"

"The silk lady you're describing."

"Silver MacKenzie, my brother's wife." Ty's eyes opened, clear and hard. "But there are other women like her in England. I'm going to get one."

Abruptly Janna came to her feet. She returned a few minutes later with a heavy book tucked under her left arm and carrying a bowl of soup with her right hand. She gave Ty the soup, opened the worn book to *Romeo and Juliet*, Act II, Scene II, and began to read:

"'But, soft! What light through yonder window breaks?

It is the East, and Juliet is the sun...'"

Chapter Seven

That day set the pattern for the next two weeks. When Janna thought Ty had been pushing himself too hard in his efforts to regain full strength, she would bring out the Bible or the Shakespearean plays or the poetry of Dante, Milton or Pope, and she would read aloud. Ty saw through what she was doing, but didn't object. He had too much fun teasing "the boy" over the real meaning of the words in *The Song of Solomon* or Pope's *The Rape of the Lock*.

"Read that verse to me again," Ty said, smiling. "You ran over it so fast I missed most of the words."

Janna tilted her head down to the worn pages of the Bible and muttered, "'Vanity of vanities…all *is* vanity.'"

"That's Ecclesiastes," Ty drawled. "You were reading *The Song of Solomon* and a woman was talking about her sweetheart. 'My beloved is gone down into his garden, to the beds of spices, to feed in the gardens…' Now what do you suppose that really means, boy?"

"He was hungry," Janna said succinctly.

"Ah, but for what?" Ty asked, stretching. "When you know the answer, you'll be a man no matter what your size or age."

Janna looked at Ty's long, muscular arms and the smooth give-and-take of his skin over his chest and torso and vowed again that she would go into Sweetwater first thing tomorrow and get Ty some clothes. She wasn't going to be able to look at him running around in a breechcloth much longer without reaching out and running her hands over all that tempting masculine hide.

The thought of Ty's shocked expression if she gave in to temptation restored her humor. It would be worth almost anything to see him shocked. Until that time came, she would have to be satisfied with watching his unease when she leaned too close or casually brushed against him, making him uncomfortable because of "the boy's" closeness.

When Ty saw Janna's full lips curve into a slow, almost hidden smile, he felt a jolt of something uncomfortably close to desire lance through him.

That boy is too damned feminine for my self-respect, much less for my peace of mind. I think I'd better take another long soak in that hot pool in the head of the valley. Doubt that it will take the starch out of me, though. I haven't been this hungry since I was fourteen. Dammit, but I need a woman.

Disgusted with himself, Ty came to his feet in a muscular rush. Janna was so surprised by the abrupt movement that she dropped the book she was holding. A sheet of paper that had been held safely between the pages fluttered out. Ty scooped it up before Janna could. He looked at the paper and let out a low whistle of admiration.

"Now there is a real lady," Ty said, gazing at the drawing of a woman in long, formal dress and elaborately coiffed hair. "Elegance like that is damned rare. Where did you get this?"

"Papa drew it when Mother was alive."

"This is your mother?"

Janna nodded.

"I see where you get your fine bones and..."

Ty's voice died. There was no point in telling the kid that his mouth would have done credit to a courtesan and his eyes were too big and too expressive to belong to a boy of any age. So Ty kept his mind on the drawing and off the fey creature whose skin and hair smelled like a meadow drenched in sunshine and warmth.

"Your daddy was a lucky man," Ty said after looking at the drawing for a long time. "This is a woman to dream on. All silk and sweet softness. After I catch Lucifer and build my own horse herd, I'm going to Europe and court a fine lady just like this. I'll marry her and bring her home, and we'll raise strong sons and silky daughters."

"Silk doesn't last long on the frontier," Janna said stiffly.

Ty laughed. "That's why I'm going to build my fortune first. I'd never ask a true lady to live in a dirt-floored shack and ruin her soft hands on scrub brushes and the like."

Janna looked at her hands. While not rough, they weren't exactly silky, either. "Soft isn't everything."

Ty shook his head, seeing only his dream. "It is in a woman. I'll have my silken lady or I'll have none at all for longer than it takes to pleasure myself."

The words sliced into Janna like knives, wounding her. The pain she felt shocked her, and the rage, and the sense of...betrayal.

"What makes you think that a silken woman would have a man like you?" Janna asked coolly.

Ty smiled to himself. "Women kind of take to me, especially when I'm cleaned up a bit."

"Huh," she sniffed. "I don't think there's enough cleaning time between now and Christmas to make any fancy woman look at you twice."

Before Ty could say anything, Zebra whinnied in alarm. Even as he turned toward the sound, Ty yanked Janna to the ground and pulled out the hunting knife he wore at his waist. An instant later his big body half covered hers, pinning her against the earth.

"Don't move," Ty breathed against Janna's ear, his voice a mere thread of sound.

Janna nodded slightly. She felt Ty's weight shift as he rolled aside. There was a flash of tanned skin in the tall grass, a suggestion of movement in the streamside willows, and then nothing more. Ty had vanished. A shiver went over Janna as she realized how very quick Ty was now that he was well, and how powerful. She thought of wiggling backward until she was in better cover, then discarded the idea. Ty would expect her to be where he had left her—and he would attack anything that moved anywhere else. That thought was enough to rivet her in place.

The willows slid soundlessly past Ty's nearly naked body as he eased through the streamside thickets. The creek was no more than a few feet wide and still slightly warm from its birth in a hot springs back at the head of the small valley, a place where lava and red rock and lush greenery entwined in a steamy Eden whose water contained a sulfurous whiff of hell.

Nothing moved in the willows around Ty, nor was there any sound of birds. The silence was a warning in itself. Normally small birds darted and sang in the valley, enjoying the rare presence of water in a dry land. If the wildlife were quiet, it meant that an intruder was nearby.

Fifty yards away, belly-deep in grass, Zebra snorted. The sound was followed by a drumroll of hooves as the mare fled. The mustang's flight told Ty that the intruder was either a cougar or a man. Nothing else would have sent the horse racing away in fear. Without disturbing the thick screen of willow branches, Ty looked out into the valley. Zebra was standing seventy yards away with every muscle quivering and poised for flight. Her head was high and her black ears were pricked forward. She was looking at something that was well downstream from Ty.

Something just came out of the slot. Which direction is the intruder going, girl? Is he going for the hot springs at the north end or the Indian ruins at the south end?

Motionless, Ty watched the mare, knowing that she would track the intruder better than he ever would have been able to with mere human senses. Zebra kept her head and ears up, watching something that he couldn't see. Slowly her head turned toward Ty.

All right. The intruder is coming toward me.

Mentally Ty reviewed the small, irregularly shaped valley. Barely more than a mile long, never more than a quarter of a mile wide, the valley was walled in by red sandstone on one side and black lava on the other. The hot springs at the north end fed the small stream. Other watercourses joined the stream at various points of the valley, but they held water only after heavy rains, when cliffs wore lacy waterfalls that were as beautiful as they were short-lived.

Ty decided that the best point for an ambush was right where he was. A very faint trail wound between the edge of the willows and the ancient lava flow that all but cut the valley in two. Anything trying to reach the head of the valley would be forced to walk between the willow thicket and the cliff. All Ty had to do was be very still and watch what passed within reach.

Motionless, poised for attack, Ty waited as he had waited too many times before.

Wish Logan were here. A man's unprotected back gets real itchy at times like this.

But Logan was in Wyoming with Silver. As for his other brothers, the last Ty had heard, both Case and Duncan were looking for gold with Blue Wolf, trying to repair the MacKenzie family fortunes and make a future for themselves. At least, that's what Duncan was doing. No one but God—more likely, the devil—knew what went on in Case's mind. Fighting in the war had closed Ty's youngest brother up tighter than bark on a tree.

A few minutes later Ty heard the faint sounds of a man's progress through the tall grass. When the sounds passed the willows where Ty hid, he came out in a silent rush. One arm hooked around the intruder's neck from behind as the knife sliced upward in a lethal arc.

At the last instant Ty realized that the man was old and unarmed. He pulled the knife aside.

"Who are you?" Ty asked quietly, holding the blade across the man's throat.

"John Turner. And I'm right glad you ain't an Injun or a bandit. I'd be dead by now."

Ty didn't bother to make welcoming sounds. "Walk ahead of me toward that red cliff. Don't hesitate or turn around. If you make a wrong move I'll kill you."

Chapter Eight

Ty followed close behind the intruder, but not so close that a sudden turn and lunge would have caught him off guard. A few minutes later they walked up to the edge of Janna's hidden camp.

"All right, kid. Come on out," Ty said.

Janna stood up. "How many times do I have to tell you that my name isn't kid, it's—oh, hello, Jack. Did you run out of stomach medicine already?"

The old man didn't answer, because Ty's knife was resting once more against his throat.

"You told me your name was John Turner," Ty said.

"'Tis, but most folks call me Mad Jack."

Ty looked over at Janna.

She nodded. "It's all right, Ty. Jack was Papa's friend."

Ty lowered the knife. Mad Jack turned and spat a thin stream of brown liquid toward a nearby bush.

"Her pa staked me We was partners," Mad Jack said, shifting the cud of tobacco to the other side of his mouth. "He cashed in his chips a few years back, but I ain't done with the game yet." He looked at Janna. "Brung you some more gold, but you wasn't in any of the old places."

"It wasn't safe anymore. Cascabel's new camp was too close."

"Yeah, them pony soldiers have made that old rattlesnake's life pure hell this summer." Mad Jack shucked off his backpack, untied a flap and pulled out a fat leather bag that fit in his hand. "Figured you'd need to lay in some winter supplies. From the size of your young buck, I shoulda brung two pokes of gold."

"How has your stomach been?" Janna asked hurriedly, wanting to get off the subject of her "young buck."

"Middlin'," Mad Jack said, shifting the wad of tobacco again. "How 'bout you, Janna? You be all right? You come early to your winter-over place."

"Ty was injured," Janna said. She glanced briefly at him and prayed without much hope that he would ignore the difference between the names Janna and Jan. "He ran Cascabel's gauntlet and got away."

Mad Jack turned and looked at Ty as though for the first time. "So you're the one, huh?" The old man's chuckle was a dry, rustling sound. "Made Cascabel the laughing-stock of the Utes. Black Hawk ever finds you, he'll like as not give you a medal 'fore he lifts your hair. How'd you hitch up with Janna?''

The second time Ty heard the name Janna, he knew it hadn't been a slip of the old prospector's tongue. Ty turned and looked at the "boy" with narrowed green eyes. After an instant the "boy" began to study the ground as though it were alive and likely to start nibbling on toes at any instant.

"Janna, huh?" Ty asked. "Is that your real name, kid?"

She threw him a quick, sideways glance, looked away and nodded very slightly.

Ty's right hand flashed out as he yanked off the floppy old hat Janna always wore. Two long, thick, Indian-style braids fell down her back. The braids were tied with leather thongs. An Indian band went around her forehead and tied in back, keeping any stray locks from escaping the hat's confinement. Her hair was a dark auburn that shimmered with unexpected fire whenever her head moved. In contrast with the darkness of her hair, the pale, crystalline depths of her eyes looked as brilliant as diamonds. The delicacy of her bone structure and the fine-grained texture of her skin seemed to taunt him for his blindness.

"Well, kid," drawled Ty, narrow eyed, furious with himself for having been deceived and with her for having deceived him, "I'll say this—you made a prettier boy than you do a girl."

Mad Jack's rustling chuckle did nothing to make Ty feel better. He flipped the hat over Janna's head and pulled down hard, covering her to her nostrils.

"Fooled ya, did she?" Mad Jack asked, slapping his hands together in pleasure. "Don't feel bad, son. That's a right clever gal. She's got the Indians believing she a *bruja*—a witch—and the mustangs believing she's just a funny kind of two-legged horse."

Ty grunted.

"'Course," Mad Jack continued, looking at Ty's nearly bare, tanned body, "a body what runs around near naked and sneaks up on folks might be accused of tryin' to make folks think he's an Injun. Might also explain why a young lady might want to be taken fer a boy."

"Lady?" Ty asked sardonically, looking up and down Janna's ragged length. "That might indeed be a female, Jack, but it sure as hell isn't a lady. A lady wouldn't be caught dead in that outfit."

Janna ignored the hurt caused by Ty's caustic comments and let her anger bubble forth instead. She turned to Mad Jack and spoke in the cool, cultured voice that her father had taught her was appropriate for reading Shakespeare.

"Of course, you have to understand that Ty is an expert on ladies. You can tell that just by looking at him. Note the fashionably cut pants and the spotless linen shirt. His suit coat is obviously handmade from the finest blend of silk and wool. His boots are fine examples of craftsmanship raised to the level of art. His own skin couldn't fit him better."

Long before Janna had finished her sarcastic summary of Ty's attire, Mad Jack was laughing so hard he nearly swallowed his cud of tobacco. Ty's smile was a bleak warning curve carved out of the blackness of his beard.

"There's more to a man than his clothes," Ty said.

"But not to a woman, hmm?"

"Kid, you don't have enough curves to be a woman." Ty turned away before Janna could say anything more. "I'm going to the Tub," he said, using Janna's nickname for the deep pool in which they both bathed—separately. "Don't worry about hurrying along to scrub my back. I can reach it just fine."

Careful to show no expression at all, Janna watched Ty stalk from the camp. Then she turned and began preparing an herbal tea for Mad Jack.

"Sorry, gal," Mad Jack said, watching her work. "If I'd thunk about it, I wouldn't've opened my trap. You want I should stay with you?"

Janna shook her head. "It's not necessary. I know how restless you get after you've been in camp for a few hours. Ty's mad, but he'll get over it."

"That wasn't what I meant. Now that he knows you're a female, maybe you won't be wanting to be alone with him."

"There won't be any problem," Janna said unhappily. "You heard him. He thinks I'm about as appealing as a fence post." She shrugged, trying to appear casual about her lack of feminine allure.

Mad Jack's faded eyes watched Janna shrewdly. "And you be kinda wishin' it was otherwise," he said after a moment.

She opened her mouth to object forcefully, then realized there was no point in denying the truth, no matter how painful that truth might be.

"Yes, I'd like to be attractive to him. What woman wouldn't? He's all man," Janna said. She added a pinch of herbs to the tiny pot. "And he's a good man. Even when he was half out of his head with pain, his first instinct was still to protect me rather than himself. He'd never force himself on me." She grimaced and added wryly, "Not that he'd ever have the chance. I'd probably say yes so quick it would make his head spin."

Mad Jack hesitated, then sighed. "Gal, I don't know how much your pa told you about babies and such, but more women have spent their lives wishin' they'd said no than otherwise. When the urge is ridin' a man, he'll talk sweet as molasses and promise things he has no damn intention of giving."

"Ty wouldn't lie to me like that."

"You can't rightly call it lyin'. When a man's crotch is aching, he don't know lies from truth," Mad Jack said bluntly. "It's natural. If menfolk stood around wonderin' what was right instead of doin' what come natural like, there wouldn't be enough babies to keep the world goin'."

Janna made a neutral sound and stirred the herbal tea. Despite the faint suggestion of red on his weathered face, Mad Jack forged ahead with his warning about the undependable nature of men.

"What I'm tryin' to say," Mad Jack muttered as he dug around in his stained shirt pocket for a plug of tobacco, "is that's a big stud hoss you found, and he's getting right healthy again. He'll be waking up hard as stone of a mornin' and he'll be lookin' for a soft place to ease what's aching."

Janna ducked her head, grateful for the floppy brim of the hat, which concealed her face. She didn't know whether to throw the steaming tea at Mad Jack or to hug him for trying to do what he was obviously ill-suited to do, which was to be a Dutch uncle to a girl who had no family.

"Now, I know I'm being too blunt," Mad Jack continued doggedly, "but dammit, gal, you ain't got no womenfolk to warn you about a man's ways. Next thing you know, you'll be gettin' fat, and I can tell you flat out it won't be from nothing you et."

"Your tea is ready."

"Gal, you understand what I been sayin'?"

"I know where babies come from and how they get there, if that's what you mean," Janna said succinctly.

"That's what I mean," Mad Jack mumbled.

Janna glanced up and made an irritated sound as she saw Mad Jack sawing away on a plug of tobacco with his pocketknife. "No wonder your stomach is as sour as last month's milk. That stuff would gag a skunk."

Dry laughter denied her words. "I'm at the age when a good chew is my only comfort. That and finding a mite of gold here and there. I done right well for myself since your pa died. I been thinking 'bout it, and I done decided. I want you to take some gold and get shuck of this place."

The immediate objections that came to Janna's lips were overridden by Mad Jack, who didn't stop speaking even while he pushed a chunk of tobacco into his mouth and started chewing with gusto.

"Now you just listen to me, gal. Territory's gettin' too damn crowded. One of these days the wrong man's going to cut your trail, the kind of man what don't care about sweet talkin' or protecting or any damn thing but his own pleasure. And I don't mean just renegades, neither. Some of them pony soldiers is as bad as Injuns, an' the scum selling rifles to Cascabel is no better than him."

Mad Jack looked at Janna as she worked gracefully over the fire, every line of her body proclaiming both her femininity and her unwillingness to listen to his advice.

"It's gettin' too damn dangerous out here for any woman a'tall, even one wearing men's clothes. You be too good a woman to go to waste out here alone."

"I've done fine for five years."

He snorted. "Fine, huh? Look at you, thin as a mare nursing two foals. You want to get a man, you gotta put meat on them bones."

"My mother wasn't built like a butter churn," Janna muttered. "Papa didn't mind one bit."

And neither had Ty, if his reaction to the drawing were any guide.

Mad Jack cursed under his breath and tried another tack. "Don't you get lonesome chasing mustangs and living so small you barely cast a shadow?"

"Do you?" Janna countered.

"Hell, I'm different. I'm a man and you ain't, never mind the clothes you wear. Don't you want a man of your own an' kids to pester you?"

Janna didn't answer, because the answer was too painful. Until she had found Ty, she hadn't really understood what life had to offer. Then she had met him—and now she knew the meaning of the word *lonely*.

"The mustangs are all I have," she said.

"And they're all you'll ever have if'n you don't leave."

"If I leave, I'll have nothing," Janna said matter-of-factly. "I'm not the kind of woman to catch a man's eye. Ty has made that real plain, and he's the 'stud hoss' who should know." She shrugged, concealing her unhappiness. "I'd rather live with mustangs than cook at a boardinghouse where men grab at me when they think nobody's looking."

"But—"

"I'm staying, and that's that."

Chapter Nine

The Tub's slick-walled pool was far enough from its hot-spring source to have lost the scalding edge of its temperature and nearly all of its sulfurous smell. The water was a clear, pale blue that steamed gently in the cool hours of night and gleamed invitingly all the time. Though safe to drink, the water was too hot for plants to grow in it. Nothing but sand and stone ringed the pool. The high mineral content of the water had decorated the rock it touched with a smooth, creamy-yellow veneer of deposits that had rounded off all the rough edges of the native stone, making a hard but nonetheless comfortable place for Ty to soak out the last legacy of Cascabel's cruel gauntlet.

Usually Ty enjoyed the soothing heat of the pool, but not today. Today he simmered from more than the temperature of the water. Knowing that "the boy" was a girl made him want to turn Janna over his knee and paddle her until she learned some manners. When he thought how she had let him run around wearing nothing more than a few rags of blanket...

A flush spread beneath the dark hair on Ty's chest and face. The realization that he was embarrassed infuriated him. It was hardly a case of his never having been nearly or even completely naked around a woman; of all the MacKenzie brothers, Ty had been the one who had caught women's eye from the time he was old enough to shave. What bothered Ty was that he must have shocked Janna more than once. The thought of a girl of her tender years being subjected repeatedly to a full-grown man's nakedness made Ty very uncomfortable.

She must have been dying of embarrassment, but she never let on. She just kept on washing me when I was delirious and putting medicine all over me and reading to me while I teased her in a way I never would have teased a girl. A woman, maybe, but not a girl. Why, she can't be much more than...
Abruptly Ty sat up straight on the stone ledge, sending water cascading off his body. *Just how old is she? And how innocent?*

Ty remembered the look of desire he had once seen in Janna's eyes. Instantly he squelched the thought. He was nearly thirty. He had no damned business even looking at a thirteen-year-old, no matter how soft her cheeks were or how her gray eyes warmed while she looked at him when she thought he wouldn't notice. Beside , boy or girl, at thirteen a case of hero worship was still a case of hero worship.

If she was, indeed, thirteen.

She can't be much older than that. I may be blind but I'm not dead. If she had breasts, I'd have noticed. Or hips, for that matter. Even under those flapping, flopping, ridiculous clothes, I'd have noticed...wouldn't I?

Hell, yes, of course I would have.

The reassuring thought made Ty settle back into the pool. A kid was still a kid, no matter what the sex. As for his own body's urgent woman-hunger, that was just a sign of his returned health. It had nothing to do with a gray-eyed waif whose delicate hands had touched nearly every aching inch of his body.

But it was the aching inches she hadn't touched that were driving him crazy.

"Dammit!" Ty exploded, coming out of the water with a lunge.

He stood dripping on the stone rim of the pool, furious with himself and the world in general, and with one Janna Wayland in particular. Viciously he scrubbed his breechcloth on the rocks, wrung it out and put it on, concealing the rigid evidence of his hunger.

Then he turned around and got right back into the Tub again. This time he remembered the bar of camp soap that Janna always left in a nearby niche. Cursing steadily, he began washing himself from head to newly healed feet. When he was finished he rinsed thoroughly, adjusted the uncomfortably tight breechcloth once more and stalked back to camp.

Janna was calmly tying twists of greenery to branches she had laid between two tall forked sticks. The stems of the plants turned slowly in the sun and wind as the leaves gave up their moisture. In a week or two the herbs would be ready to store whole or to crumble and pound into a powder from which she would make lotions, pastes, potions and other varieties of medicine.

"How do your feet feel?" Janna asked without looking up from her work.

"Like feet. Where's Mad Jack?"

"Gone."

"What?"

"He was worried when he didn't find me in any of the usual places, so—"

"Where are the usual places?" Ty interrupted.

"Wherever Lucifer's herd is. Once Jack found out I was all right, he went back."

"To where?"

"Wherever his mine is."

Ty reached to readjust the breechcloth again, remembered that Janna wasn't a boy and snatched back his hands, cursing.

"Do you think that zebra dun of yours would take me to Sweetwater?"

"I don't know. She likes you well enough, but she doesn't like towns at all."

"You two make a fine pair," Ty muttered, combing through his wet hair with long fingers.

"Catch."

Reflexively Ty's hand flashed out and grabbed the small leather poke Janna had pulled from her baggy pants pocket.

"What's this?" he asked.

"Mad Jack's gold. You'll need it when you get to town. Or were you planning to work off whatever you buy?"

"I can't take gold from a thirteen-year-old girl."

Janna looked up briefly before she went back to arranging herbs for drying. "You aren't."

"What?"

"You aren't taking gold from a thirteen-year-old. I'm nineteen. I only told you I was thirteen so that you wouldn't suspect I was a woman."

"Sugar," drawled Ty, giving Janna a thorough up-and-down look, "you could have walked naked past me and I wouldn't have suspected anything at all. You're the least female female I've ever seen."

Janna's fingers tightened on the herbs as the barb went home, but she was determined not to show that she'd been hurt.

"Thank you," she said huskily. "I just took a leaf from Cascabel's book—hide in plain sight. The pony soldiers caught him way down south last year. He escaped from them. They went looking for him, expecting to run him down easily because there was no cover around. It was flat land with only a scattering of stunted mesquite. No place for a rabbit to hide, much less a man."

Ty listened in spite of his anger at having been deceived. As he listened, he tried to figure out why Janna's voice was so appealing to him. Finally he realized that she no longer was trying to conceal her voice's essentially feminine nature, a faintly husky music that tantalized his senses.

And she was nineteen, not thirteen.

Stop it, Ty told himself fiercely. *She's all alone in the world. Any man who would take advantage of that isn't worthy of the name.*

"Because the soldiers knew there was no place to hide, they didn't look," Janna continued. "Cascabel is as shrewd as Satan. He knew that the best place to hide is in plain sight, where no one would ever look. So when he was convinced that he couldn't outrun the soldiers and they would catch him in the open, he rolled in the dust, grabbed some mesquite branches and sat very still. The branches didn't cover him, but they gave the soldiers something familiar to look at—something they would never look at twice. And they didn't," Janna concluded. "They rode right by Cascabel, maybe a hundred feet away, and never saw him."

"Probably because Cascabel looks a hell of a lot more like a mesquite bush than you look like a woman."

"That's your opinion," Janna retorted, "but we both know how trustworthy your eyes are, don't we?"

Ty saw the reaction that Janna tried to hide. He smiled, feeling better than he had since he realized how badly he had been fooled. If his brothers ever found out what had happened, they would ride him until he screamed for mercy. Ty had always been the one the MacKenzie men turned to for advice on the pursuit and pleasuring of the fair sex.

He laughed aloud and felt his temper sweeten with every passing second. He was going to get some of his own back from the gray-eyed chameleon, and he was going to enjoy himself thoroughly in the process. She would rue the day she had fooled him into believing she was an effeminate boy.

"If you'd been any kind of a woman," Ty drawled very slowly, "I'd feel right ashamed of being fooled. But seeing as how you only *say* you're a girl, and I'm too much of a gentleman to ask you to prove it…I guess I'll just have to keep my doubts to myself."

"You? A gentleman?" Janna asked in rising tones of disbelief. She looked pointedly at his half-grown beard and soggy breechcloth. "From what I can see—and there's darn little I *can't* see—you look like a savage."

Ty's laugh wasn't quite so heartfelt this time. "Oh, I know I'm a gentleman for a fact, *boy*. And so do a lot of real ladies."

Mentally Janna compared herself to the sketch of her mother—loose, ragged clothes against stylish swirls of silk, Indian braids against carefully coiffed curls. The comparison was simply too painful. So was the fact that Ty had been taken with her mother's image and couldn't have been more blunt about the daughter's lack of feminine allure.

Unshed tears clawed at the back of Janna's eyelids, but the thought that Ty might catch her crying appalled her. Without a word she dusted off her hands and brushed past Ty, refusing even to look at him, knowing that for all her scathing comments to the contrary, his eyes were uncomfortably sharp when it came to assessing her mood.

When Janna was at the edge of the grassy area of the valley, she cupped her hands to her mouth and called out to Zebra, using the keening cry of a hawk. To human ears there was almost no difference in the sounds—to Zebra, it was a call as clear as a trumpet's. Within moments the mare was cantering through the grass towards Janna.

"Hello, pretty girl," Janna murmured. She stroked the mare's neck and pulled weeds from her long mane and tail. "Show me your hooves."

She worked slowly around the horse, touching each fetlock. Zebra presented each of her hooves in turn, standing patiently while Janna used a short, pointed stick to worry loose any mud or debris that had become caught between the hard outer hoof and the softer frog at the center.

"It would be easier with a steel hoof pick," Ty said.

Janna barely controlled a start. On the meadow grass Ty's bare feet had made no more sound than a shadow.

"If I bought a pick, people would wonder what I was planning to use it on. Only one other human being knows that I've tamed..." Janna's voice died when she realized that Ty as well as Mad Jack knew that she mingled with Lucifer's herd. "Could it be our secret?" she asked as she looked at Ty, her voice aching with restraint. "It's bad enough that I turn up from time to time with raw gold. If some of the men around here knew that I could get close to Lucifer, they'd hunt me down like a mad dog and use me to get their hands on him."

Ty looked at the face turned up toward him in silent pleading and felt as though he had been kicked in the stomach. The idea of using Janna to get close to Lucifer had been in the back of his mind since he had realized that Zebra was part of the big black stallion's harem.

They'd hunt me down like a mad dog and use me...

Before Ty realized what he was doing, he cupped Janna's chin reassuringly in his hand.

"I won't tell anyone," he said quietly. "I promise you, Janna. And I won't use you. I want that stud and I plan to have him—but not like that, not by making you feel you had betrayed a trust."

The heat of Janna's tears on his hand shocked Ty, but not as much as the butterfly softness of her lips brushing over his skin for an instant before she turned away.

"Thank you," she said huskily, her face hidden while she resumed working over Zebra's hoof. "And I'm sorry about what I said earlier. You're very much a gentleman, no matter what you're wearing."

Ty closed his eyes and fought against the tremor of sensation that was spreading out from the palm of his hand to the pit of his stomach and from there to the soles of his feet. Before he could prevent himself, he had lifted his hand to his lips. The taste of Janna's tears went to his head more quickly than a shot of whiskey, making him draw in a sharp breath.

You've been without a woman too long, he told himself as he fought to control a combination of tenderness and raw desire.

Yes—and the name of the cure is Janna Wayland.

"No," Ty said aloud harshly.

"What?" Janna said, looking up.

Ty wasn't watching her. He was standing rigid, his face drawn as though in pain. When she spoke, he opened his eyes. She wanted to protest the shadows she saw there, but he was already speaking.

"I'm not what you think," Ty said, his voice rough. "I'm too woman hungry to be a gentleman. Don't trust me, Janna. Don't trust me at all."

Chapter Ten

Under Janna's watchful eyes, Ty sprang onto Zebra's back with a flowing, catlike motion. The mare flicked her ears backward, then forward, accepting Ty as her rider without a fuss.

"I told you she wouldn't object," Janna said. "You've ridden her before."

"Don't remind me," he said. "I've had nightmares about that ride every night since." He leaned down and offered Janna his left arm. "Grab just above the elbow with your left hand, pretend I'm a piece of mane and swing up behind me."

Janna followed Ty's instructions and found herself whisked aboard Zebra with breathtaking ease. She lifted her hand instantly, too conscious of the heat and power of Ty's bare arm. She found herself confronted by an expanse of naked shoulders that seemed to block out half the world.

"H-how is your back healing?" she asked.

"You tell me," Ty said dryly. "You can see it better than I can."

She bit her lip, irritated by her inane question and his goading response. On the other hand, asking that question had been safer than following her original impulse, which had been to run her hands over his tanned, supple skin. Taking a deep breath, Janna forced herself to concentrate on the shadow bruises and faint, thin lines of red that marked recently healed cuts. She traced the longest line with delicate fingertips. He flinched as though she had used a whip on him.

"Don't do that," he snapped.

"I'm sorry. I didn't know it was still painful. It looks healed."

Ty's lips flattened, but he said nothing to correct Janna's assumption that it had been pain rather than pleasure that had made his body jerk. Her fingertips had been like that single touch from her lips, a brush of warmth and a shivering hint of the feminine sensuality concealed beneath men's clothing.

"When we get back from town, I'll put more salve on," Janna continued.

His mouth opened to object, but he closed it without making a sound. The temptation to feel her soothing hands on his body was simply too great for him to deny himself the opportunity of being cared for by Janna.

Silently Ty nudged Zebra with his left heel. The mare turned obediently and headed toward the cleft in the rocks that surrounded the tiny valley. Each motion of the horse's buttocks, combined with the natural forward slope of Zebra's back, gently moved Janna toward Ty's warm body. He flinched again when the brim of her floppy hat touched his skin.

"Sorry," muttered Janna, pulling her head back.

He grunted.

Zebra kept on walking and Janna kept sliding closer to Ty. Before they came to the cleft that led from the valley, she was flush against his body. Only by leaning back at an awkward angle could she prevent her hat—or her lips—from brushing against his skin.

The fifth time Janna felt compelled to apologize for the contact she could not avoid, she wriggled away from Ty until she could put her hands on the horse's back between their bodies. Cautiously she pushed herself backward a fraction of an inch at a time, not wanting to alarm Zebra.

As Janna's weight settled farther back on the mare's spine, her tail swished in warning, sending a stinging veil of hair across Ty's naked calf.

"Damn, what is her tail made of—nettles?"

Janna didn't answer. Instead, she eased herself backward another inch, then two.

Zebra balked and humped her back in warning.

"What's wrong with her?" Ty asked, turning to look over his shoulder at Janna. "What the hell are you doing way back there? Don't you know a horse's kidneys and flanks are sensitive? Or maybe you're trying to get us both bucked off in the dirt?"

"I was trying not to hurt your back."

"My back? My back is just fi—" Abruptly Ty remembered what he had said about his back being hurt by Janna's light touch. "I'll live," he said grimly. "Scoot on up here where you belong before this mustang bucks us both off."

"I'd rather not," Janna said through stiff lips.

Ty kicked his right leg over Zebra's neck and slid off onto the ground. "Get up there where you belong," he said in a curt voice. "I'll walk."

"No, I'll walk," Janna said, dismounting in a rush, landing very close to Ty. "I'm used to it. Besides, I haven't been hurt and you have."

"I'm all healed up."

"But you said your back—"

"Get on that mustang before I lose my temper," Ty said flatly, cutting across Janna's protest.

"Lose your temper? Impossible. You'd have to find it first."

Ty glared into Janna's gray eyes. She didn't flinch. With a hissed curse he grabbed her and dumped her on her stomach across Zebra's back. He had plenty of time to regret the impulsive act. Janna's scramble to right herself and assume a normal riding position pulled the fabric of her pants tightly across her buttocks, revealing to him for the first time the unmistakable curves of a woman's hips.

At that instant Ty abandoned all thought of climbing on Zebra behind Janna. The feel of those soft curves rubbing between his thighs and against his aching male flesh would quickly drive him crazy.

Cursing steadily beneath his breath, Ty reached up to drag Janna off the mare. He told himself it was an accident that his hands shaped Janna's buttocks on the way to pulling her down, and he knew that it was a lie. He could have pulled on Janna's feet or even her knees. He didn't have to grab her hips and sink his fingers into her resilient flesh, sending a wave of heat through his body.

Even as Ty withdrew his hands, he wondered if he had been as wrong about Janna's breasts as he had been about her hips—she had more than enough curves to fill a man's hungry hands. The realization that the ride into town would probably tell him just how soft and tempting her breasts were was enough to make Ty groan and swear even more. The amount of control he had to exert to drag his hands away from Janna's body shocked him. He had never been the kind of man who grabbed at what a woman wouldn't freely offer to him.

"Stand still," Ty said harshly as Janna twisted against him, trying to regain her balance.

"Now listen, you son of—"

A broad, hard palm covered Janna's mouth. Green eyes stared into furious gray ones.

"No, you listen to me, *boy*," snarled Ty. "We're going to get on that horse and you're going to ride far enough forward that Zebra's spine isn't hurt. She's a good-sized mare, but carrying double is still a lot of weight for her, especially when one of her riders is my size."

Janna stopped fighting. She hadn't thought that her foolish scooting about might have hurt Zebra. With a small cry she turned toward the mare. The horse looked back at her with an equine's patience for crazy humans.

"I'll walk," Janna said.

"Like hell you will. It's too far."

"I've walked a lot farther in a morning."

"And left footprints every step of the way. If you take time to hide your trail, it'll take a week to get to town. If you don't hide your trail, the next man through that gap won't be Mad Jack. It will be Cascabel."

There was a moment of silence while Janna digested the unpleasant truth of what Ty was saying. Signs left by an untrimmed, unshod horse wouldn't attract much attention, particularly after they crossed their trail with that of any of the several wild horse herds in the area. Tracks left by a trimmed, shod horse, or a human, would bring down Cascabel quicker than the strike of his namesake reptile—the rattlesnake.

"It won't hurt Zebra to carry double," Ty said, "especially without a saddle. Just don't ride so far back."

"What about you? I don't want to hurt your back, either."

He closed his eyes so as not to see the unhappiness in Janna's at the thought of hurting anything, even the man who was presently making her life very difficult.

"I'm ticklish, that's all," Ty said grimly. "My back is fine."

"Oh."

Ty swung up onto Zebra, helped Janna swing up behind him and gritted his teeth at the feel of her breath against his naked skin. When Zebra walked once more to the cleft that led out of the valley, the gentle rubbing pressure of Janna's thighs against his own was an even worse distraction than the heat of her breath washing over his spine.

Think of her as a boy.

Ty tried. All he could think of was the lush resilience of Janna's hips. The smooth, curving heat of them could never have belonged to a boy.

Be grateful she doesn't have big breasts to rub against you.

Ty tried to be grateful. All he could think of was pulling off Janna's tentlike shirt and finding out just how soft her breasts were, and if her nipples were as pink as her tongue, and if they would pout hungrily for his mouth.

The reflexive tightening of Ty's body in response to his thoughts was communicated to Zebra. Sensing his agitation without understanding its source, she began to shy at the breeze stirring through the belly-deep grass as though it were a yellow-eyed cougar stalking her.

Janna talked to the mare in a soothing, husky voice that worked on Ty's aroused senses like repeated, silky caresses. He clenched his teeth when she shifted position and leaned around him in order to stroke Zebra's neck soothingly.

"I don't know what's wrong with her," Janna said, keeping her voice low and reassuring. "She's only like this when there are Indians or cougars around. I haven't seen any sign of cats in the valley. Maybe Mad Jack didn't cover his trail out of here well enough and Cascabel followed it."

"Doubt it," Ty said in a clipped voice. "That old man has been outsmarting trackers for more years than I've been alive. Zebra's probably just nervous about having two riders."

Janna made a sound that had no meaning except to soothe the restive mustang.

By the time they approached the slit in the cliffs that surrounded the valley, Zebra no longer shied at every shadow, Janna had relaxed so that she no longer jerked back from the inevitable contact with Ty's nearly naked body— and Ty's jaw ached from being clenched against the hot sensations radiating through his body from every accidental, brushing contact with Janna.

And it seemed that she touched him everywhere, except in those places where he ached to the point of pain.

Chapter Eleven

Silently Ty endured the continual brush of Janna's body against his as they went toward the cleft. They rode alongside the stream until it spread out into a small slough and vanished, leaving not even a trickle to enter the stone slot that was the valley's only outlet. There was nothing about the mouth of the cleft to suggest that it was any different from the hundreds of other narrow, barren gouges in the eroded flanks of the huge plateau. That, and the fact that the narrow, twisting passage was both difficult and uninviting for a horse, were why the valley had remained Janna's secret.

The slit in the rocks looked like the entrance to hell, but Ty watched it approach with a feeling of relief. When the opening was thirty yards away, he could bear Janna's unintentional sensual torment no longer. With a feeling of relief, he slid off Zebra and away from the fiery brush of Janna's body.

"Wait here," Ty said curtly. "I'll check out the trail."

He was gone before Janna could put her objections into words.

Inside the cleft it was cool, damp, dusky. A few shallow pools left by recent rain showers reflected the dark red, oddly stained cliffs that towered above the floor of the narrow canyon. Overhead the sky was reduced to a thin blue string thrown carelessly between the cliffs. In the places where black lava replaced sandstone, the cleft darkened until it was both somber and eerie, as though night had condensed and taken a solid form on the face of the land itself.

There were no tracks at all in the dry watercourse, not even those of wildlife. Ty wasn't surprised by the lack of animal signs. He had expected to find nothing. Wild animals had an instinctive abhorrence of small openings, of being trapped somewhere that lacked room to run or places to hide. What did surprise Ty was that Mad Jack had left no more trail than if he had flown from the secret valley.

In fact, Ty found it impossible to believe that Mad Jack had gone through the cleft at all.

The passage itself was familiar to Ty. He had made it a point to familiarize himself with the slit that was the difference between the valley being a haven for them or a trap with no exit. Yet each time he walked the cleft he felt a deepening admiration for Janna, who had found and used a passage whose secret had been lost to the Indians for hundreds of years, perhaps even thousands. He doubted that any Indian had used the cleft at all since the coming of the horse several hundred years before.

Or perhaps the valley hadn't been lost by the Indians but simply avoided as a spirit place where mortal men shouldn't go, a place of the People who Came Before. Within the twilight confines of the slot canyon, it would be very easy to imagine malevolent spirits waiting in ambush for anything foolish enough to stray inside the black stone jaws.

The narrowest point of the cleft was not at the entrance to the valley but about a third of the way toward the open land beyond. At the stricture, both canyon walls were of a dense, black, fine-grained stone that cracked in long parallel columns. Water had polished the stone into a slick, shiny mass that, with the addition of a layer of fine mud, was almost as slippery as ice. Unlike Mad Jack, Janna had never found a way to avoid leaving tracks over that segment of the slot, which was why she had always taken on the passage just before or just after a rain, when any tracks she left would be washed completely away by the runoff stream.

That was another thing Ty admired. Few people who knew the country would have had the courage to test the stone slit when clouds massed over the plateau and water was running down its sides in rushing veils. Fewer people still would have had the skill to read the land and weather correctly enough to survive negotiating the narrow slot. He wondered how many times Janna had waited, eyeing the muddy rush of water and calculating her best chance to pass through without leaving a sign or being drowned.

Warily Ty looked up the uneven walls where debris lodged twenty or thirty feet higher than his head. The thought of the risk Janna had taken to get him into the hidden valley made sweat start on his body. He remembered the black clouds, the pelting rain…and nothing more. He only knew that she had taken an enormous risk while getting him to a safe place to heal. In fact, she had taken one hell of a risk for him, period, since the first moment she had begun wiping out his trail so that Cascabel would lose his prey. If the renegade ever found out how his prisoner had truly escaped, Janna's life wouldn't be worth a handful of cold spit.

Ty half walked, half slid over the cleft's slick bottom. Once he was past the place where black walls pinched in, the cleft opened out slightly again. He moved quickly, leaving very little trace of his passage. There was no other sign of life within the steep canyon. When the gloom brightened, announcing the end of the slot, Ty went to the deepest area of shadow and eased forward until he could look over the fan of debris that washed down from the plateau's edge, creating a sloping skirt that led to the flatlands beyond.

For several minutes Ty remained motionless, studying the landscape for any sign of movement. There was no motion but the ragged race of cloud shadows over the earth. No bird was startled into flight. No raven scolded an intruder in hoarse tones. No shape of man or horse separated from cover to ghost over the land. If there were anyone about, he was even better hidden than Ty.

After ten minutes Ty withdrew from the entrance to the slot and returned to Janna. She was waiting precisely where he had left her, for she knew the importance of keeping the secret of the slit canyon and the hidden valley beyond.

"All clear," Ty said, answering the question in Janna's eyes. "Nothing has been in or out since the last shower."

Even though Janna had expected nothing else, she couldn't conceal her relief. Without the secret valley she would have no place to hide, no sanctuary in which to live during the wild country's cold winters.

Ty saw Janna's relief, guessed at its source and had to restrain himself from telling her not to worry, she wasn't going to have to spend another winter hiding in the valley, she was leaving Indian country and that was that. But he said nothing, because she would have argued with him, and arguing against the inevitable was a waste of time. As far as he was concerned, it was inevitable that Janna would no longer live alone. No white woman should have to exist like a savage, fearful of every shadow and without even the company of other human beings when danger threatened.

Ty had decided that he would take Janna to Sweetwater or Hat Rock or Santa Fe or even all the way to Denver, if it came to that. It was the least he could do for the orphan girl who had saved his life.

To Ty's surprise, Janna slid down from Zebra and walked to the cleft. As always, the mare followed her.

"Aren't you going to ride?" he asked.

"Too dangerous. That narrow stretch must still be slick from the last rain."

"We rode in double that way."

"Someone had to keep you astride Zebra. We'll mount after the canyon widens again."

Ty didn't argue. No matter how important it might be not to leave human footprints, he had dreaded the thought of going over the slippery black rock while mounted bareback and double on an unbroken mustang.

In the end it was the very narrowness of the canyon that kept Ty from falling. He simply levered himself along by acting as though he were trying to push the two sides of the canyon farther apart with his hands. Janna, more accustomed to the tricky stretch, knew where there were handholds and niches to use in maintaining her balance. Zebra had the advantage of four feet—if one slipped, there were three to take its place.

"How did you manage on horseback?" Ty asked as he reached a wider point in the slit and Janna came alongside.

"There was no other choice."

He thought about that for a moment, then nodded slowly, understanding that that was how Janna had managed to survive out here on her own: she believed that there was no other choice.

But there was.

"With all your books, you could be a teacher," Ty said as he swung aboard Zebra once more and scraped his knee against the canyon wall in the process.

Janna grabbed his arm and swung up behind him. "Not enough kids except in towns."

"So?"

"I don't like towns. They seem to bring out the worst in people."

Ty opened his mouth to argue, realized that he agreed with Janna and felt trapped. "Not all the time," he muttered.

She shrugged. "Maybe I just bring out the worst in towns."

"Do you really plan on spending the rest of your life out here?" he demanded.

"Unless you keep your voice down, the rest of my life won't amount to more than a few hours," Janna said dryly. "These walls make a dropped pin echo like a landslide."

Ty turned around and glared at her but said nothing more, except for a muffled word or two when his legs scraped against narrow points in the cleft. Janna's slender legs were in no such danger, and in any case were enveloped by protective folds of cloth. Even so, Ty had an acute appreciation of the warm flesh beneath the folds, especially when she rubbed against him as she adjusted to Zebra's motions.

Cautiously Ty urged Zebra out of the cleft, keeping to shadows and high brush wherever possible, trying to break up the telltale silhouette of horse and rider. They had gone no more than a mile when they cut across tracks left by a group of unshod ponies. The horses had moved in a bunch, not stopping to graze or to drink from the few puddles that remained after the previous thunderstorm. From the distance between sets of prints, Janna guessed that the horses had been cantering.

"That's Cascabel's horse," Janna said in a low voice.

She pointed to a set of larger hoofprints that had been all but obliterated by the rest of the group. Though the horse had once been shod, it had no shoes any longer. All that remained were vague traces of nail holes around the rim of the untrimmed hooves.

"He stole two Kentucky horses from an officer at the fort over by Split-rock Springs," she continued. "One of the horses used to be the fastest horse in Utah Territory."

"Used to be? What happened?"

"Cascabel ran it to death trying to catch Lucifer. He takes better care of the second horse. It won't last much longer, though. It's a paddock horse, bred for grooming and grain. All it has out here is grass and a big renegade with a whip."

"Yeah, and that big renegade is too damn close for comfort."

Janna chewed silently on her lip for a moment before agreeing. "Yes. This is only the third time I've found his tracks on the east side of Black Plateau. I wonder what happened to make him come this far. The ranches he usually raids are in the opposite direction."

"I'll bet the soldiers are closing in. They have a real mission where Cascabel is concerned. They're going to see him hang or know the reason why."

She closed her eyes and shook her head, trying to throw off the uneasy feeling that had been growing in her day by day since the beginning of the summer, when she had discovered that Cascabel had been forced to move his camp. He had chosen to make his new camp on the Raven Creek watershed, a place that was perilously close to Mustang Canyon. Whether Black Hawk had driven Cascabel south, or the soldiers had, or Lucifer had lured him to the red buttes and high plateau and brooding Fire Mountains, it didn't matter. Janna knew that she couldn't remain hidden for long once so many eyes started scrutinizing every shadow.

Yet she couldn't leave, either. She had no place to go. A woman alone among men was the subject of snickers and speculation and blunt offers of sex in exchange for money or safety. The closest thing she had to a home was the wild land itself. She couldn't bear to lose it and her freedom in the same blow.

Unfortunately, it was becoming clear that she had no other choice.

Silently Janna guided Zebra in a circuitous route to Sweetwater. When Ty realized where they were going, he turned questioningly to her.

"Hat Rock is closer," he said.

"I know. I went to Sweetwater last time."

"So?"

"So Joe Troon won't be looking for me there."

"What?"

"I never go to the same town or ranch twice in a row," Janna explained. "Except for the hidden valley, I never go to the same places at the same time of year or in the same order. If you don't have a pattern, no one can guess where you're going to be and lay a trap for you."

Ty sensed the apprehension behind Janna's calm words. "Did this Troon character try to trap you?"

"Once or twice."

"Why?"

"Mad Jack's mine, Lucifer or..." Janna's voice died as she remembered overhearing Troon bragging about how he would break her in right and then sell her south to a Mexican whorehouse after she led him to Lucifer and Mad Jack's gold mine. She cleared her throat. "I didn't wait around to find out."

The surge of anger and adrenaline that went through Ty's body surprised him, but it didn't keep him from demanding roughly, "Did he lay a hand on you?"

"He never even saw me that time," Janna said evasively. "I hung back in the brush and listened long enough to figure out how he had found me, and then I swore never to be predictable again. I haven't been, either."

"You said you follow Lucifer's bunch in the summertime."

"Yes."

"Then you're predictable. Every mustanger knows Lucifer's territory. All any man would have to do is to lie in wait at the water holes his herd uses. Lucifer is fast enough to get away from that kind of ambush. You aren't."

"Cascabel is keeping the mustangers away."

"He didn't keep me away. Nothing will. I'm going to have that stud no matter what. I need him too badly to let a few renegades get in my way."

"You plan to use Lucifer to buy your silken lady?"

"Yes," Ty said, his voice flat, inflexible. "The war took everything but my life and my dreams. I'll have that silken lady or die trying."

Janna held herself tightly, trying not to flinch against the pain she felt.

"Then you understand," she said huskily.

"What?"

"You understand why I can't live in a town as a kitchen maid or a saloon girl. I have my own dream."

There was a surprised silence while Ty digested the idea that the ragged waif had a goal beyond simple survival. "What is it?"

Shaking her head, eyes tightly closed, Janna said nothing. There was no point in telling Ty that she had begun to dream of having him turn to her and discover within her the silken lady he sought. It was a dream that would never come true and she was practical enough to know it.

But it was the most compelling dream Janna had ever had. She could no more turn away from it than she could transform herself into the lady of Ty's dreams.

Chapter Twelve

A mile outside of town, Ty shifted his weight and spoke softly to the mare. Zebra stopped obediently no more than two feet from a clump of boulders and brush.

"Get down," Ty said, handing Janna the big knife she had given him. "I'll be back as quick as I can."

"I'm going with you."

"No."

"But—"

"No!" Hearing the roughness in his own voice, Ty winced. "Janna, it isn't safe. If you're seen with me on a mustang—"

"We'll tell them you tamed her," Janna interrupted quickly.

"They'd have to be dumb as a stump to believe that," he retorted. "I'm going to have enough trouble making them believe I survived without help as it is. You know damn good and well if Cascabel finds out you were responsible for making him the laughingstock of the Utah Territory, he'll come after you until he gets you and cooks you over a slow fire."

Without another word Janna slid down from Zebra. She vanished into concealment between one breath and the next. For a moment Ty couldn't believe that she had ever been with him at all. An odd feeling shot through him, loneliness and desire combined into a yearning that was like nothing he had ever known.

"Janna?" he called softly.

Nothing answered but branches stirring beneath a rain-bearing wind. The scent of moisture reminded Ty of the urgency of the situation. They had to be back at the hidden valley before the storm broke or they would spend a miserable night out in the open, unable even to have a fire to warm them for fear of giving away their presence.

Thunder rumbled in the distance, causing Zebra to throw up her head and snort. Ears pricked, nostrils flared, the horse sniffed the wind.

"Easy, girl," Ty murmured. "It's just the summer rains."

He slid from Zebra's back, landed lightly and pulled off his breechcloth. His foot wrappings came off next. After he poked the scraps of blanket into an opening between two boulders, he turned east and began working his way over the rocky surface of the land toward a wagon trail a half mile beyond. He was very careful not to leave any signs of his passage, for he had been into Sweetwater once before, riding Blackbird and armed with two pistols, a rifle and a shotgun. He had been glad for each weapon; the only thing sweet about the town was the name and the tiny spring that bubbled to the surface nearby, watering stock and men alike without regard to their individual natures.

As Ty walked toward town, he wished heartily for one of the new repeating carbines that loaded as fast as they fired. Even a pistol would have been nice. Two revolvers and extra cylinders loaded with bullets would have made him feel a lot better about going in among the canted shacks.

Though Janna seemed not to realize it, Sweetwater was an outlaw hangout, and the two ranches she bought supplies from had a reputation for branding "loose" cattle that was known from the Red River to Logan MacKenzie's ranch in Wyoming. Some of the Lazy A's and Circle G's cowhands were doubtless reasonably honest men who had been forced to make a living any way they could after the Civil War had ruined their farms and homes. Other cowhands on those ranches were men who would have been raiders in heaven itself, because they plain enjoyed riding roughshod over people weaker than themselves.

How the hell did Janna ever survive out here? Ty asked himself for the hundredth time as he walked quietly into the collection of ramshackle, weathered shacks that constituted one of the few towns within several hundred miles.

No answer came back to Ty but the obvious one, the uncomfortable memory of women in a war-ravaged land, women selling themselves for bread or a blanket, women who in peacetime wouldn't have dreamed of letting a man touch them outside the boundaries of love and marriage.

Is that how you survived after your father died, Janna? Did you sell yourself until you had the skill and the strength to survive alone?

Again there was no answer but the obvious one. She had survived. The thought of Janna's soft body lying beneath rutting men both sickened and angered Ty; for a woman to sell herself like that in order to survive was simply another kind of rape.

In the past, Ty had surprised more than one woman caught within the ruins of war by giving her food or shelter or blankets and taking nothing in return. He would never forget one girl's combined look of shock, relief and gratitude when he had refused her thin, bruised body as payment for a plate of beans. She had eaten quickly and then had vanished into the night as though afraid he would change his mind and take her after all.

And when Ty had finally fought his way home, he had discovered that his sister, Cassie, hadn't been so fortunate in the strange men who had crossed her path. Taken by raiders, she had been a captive until she became too ill to service the men; then she had been abandoned to die. She would have, too, if Logan and Silver hadn't caught up with her and gentled her back into sanity and health.

Ty's grim thoughts were a match for the town that he finally reached. There were no men loitering in front of Sweetwater Mercantile when Ty walked by. There were no horses tied to broken railings. No dogs slept in sun-warmed dust. The first person Ty saw was a boy who was emptying slops out the saloon's back door. The boy took one look at Ty and ducked back inside. Instants later the door creaked open again. The bartender stood with a shotgun cradled in his thick hands. A single glance took in Ty's muscular, naked body covered with healing bruises.

"Well, you be big enough and the right color," the bartender said. "Maybe you be Tyrell MacKenzie."

Ty nodded slowly.

The bartender stepped aside. "Come on in. Name's Ned. A breed by the name of Blue Wolf was looking for you 'bout two weeks back."

When he heard Blue Wolf's name, Ty almost laughed aloud. "Wondered how long it would take him to catch up with me."

"Friend of yours?"

"Yeah."

"Good thing, too. From the look of that buck, he'd make a powerful bad enemy. He's damn near as big as Cascabel and white-man smart into the bargain. Talks English better than me."

"He's a dead shot, too."

Ned grunted, reached behind the door and pulled a ragged shirt off a nail. He threw the cloth to Ty. "Wrap up and sit down."

Within moments Ty had the shirt wrapped around his hips and between his legs in a semblance of a breechcloth. He sat down, enjoying the unfamiliar sensation of a chair after months on the trail. Ned went to a sooty corner of the small room and pulled a pot off a broken-legged stove. He wiped a spoon on his britches, stuck it into the pot and shoved it in front of Ty.

"Reckon you're hungry."

Ty wasn't, but admitting that would raise too many questions, so he dug into the cold beans and ate quickly, trying not to remember how much better Janna's food had been. Cleaner, too. Living in the camp with the hot springs had spoiled him. A bath every day, clean dishes, and clean company. It would take him a long time to get used to the smell of a sty like Ned's saloon.

"Thanks," Ty said, shoving away the empty pot.

"Smoke?"

Ty shook his head. "Gave it up the night I saw a man get killed lighting a pipe when he should have been holding still and looking out for enemies."

Ned grinned, revealing teeth about the color the beans had been. "Yep, war can be hard on a man. Worse 'n robbin' banks or rustlin'."

The oblique question about his past was ignored by Ty.

"Don't mean to jaw your arm off," Ned said quickly, "but it's been nothin' but me and Johnny for two weeks now. Rest of 'em went to the fort. Old Cascabel's got 'em pissin' their britches. Hear tell he killed two white men a week ago."

"I wouldn't know about that. I've been too busy hiding and healing. Did Blue Wolf say when he'd be back here?"

Ned opened a stone jug and thumped it onto the table. "Don't know as he's comin' back. I told him you'd been took by Cascabel. He said you wouldn't stay took. Left a poke of gold for you over to the fort. Said you'd be needful of it when you got shuck of Cascabel. From the look of you, he was right."

"Did he say where he was going?"

"He was meetin' up with your brothers north of here. Looking for gold." Ned grunted. "Probably'll find it, too, if'n Black Hawk don't lift their hair first."

"With Wolf on scout, no one will even know they're around." Ty paused, then added casually, "When my brothers come back here looking for me—and they will—tell them I headed for Mexico. I'm going to finish healing up in some *señorita*'s bed."

Ned's smile was as crooked as a dog's hind leg as he absorbed Ty's gentle message: Ty might be naked and alone, but if he were killed his brothers would come hunting for the killer. So Ned poured cloudy liquid from the jar into a dirty tin cup and put it in front of Ty.

"Drink up."

"If it's all the same, I'd rather have water," Ty said. "My daddy always told me not to mix liquor with an empty stomach or a knot on the head."

Ned chuckled, picked up the cup and drained it. His harshly expelled breath made Ty glad there wasn't an open flame nearby. Sure as hell, the alcohol on Ned's breath would have caught fire and burned down the saloon.

"Damn, but that's good 'shine," Ned said, wiping water from his eyes. "A man couldn't get from dawn to dusk without it."

Ty could have gotten from birth to death without moonshine, but he said nothing. He had known a lot like Ned, men for whom the savage bite of homemade liquor was the sole joy of life. With outward patience, Ty waited while Ned's hands stroked the cold curves of the stone jar, lifted it and shook it to gauge the amount of liquor left within.

"You say you and the boy are the only ones left in Sweetwater?" Ty asked after a few moments.

Ned poured another half cup of pale liquid, belched and sat down opposite Ty. Though it was daytime, the interior of the saloon was gloomy. If there had ever been glass windows in the slanting walls, the panes had long since been replaced by oiled paper.

"Yep. Just me and that useless whelp. He's so scared he's gonna run off first time I turn my back." Ned took another swig of liquor, shuddered deliciously and sighed. "And Joe Troon. That sidewinder ain't never far off. Used to keep a Mex gal stashed somewhere off in the rimrock to the north, but she run off with Cascabel's renegades. Ol' Troon's real lonely these days, less'n he caught that *bruja* again."

"What?"

"That red-haired gal the renegades call Sombra, cuz she leaves no more sign than a shadow. Lives with the mustangs, and she's a wild 'un just like them." Ned took another huge swallow, grimaced and sighed out the fumes. "Troon had her once a few years ago but she got away. Gals don't cotton much to Joe Troon. Mean as a spring bear, and that's gospel. Wish he'd kept her, though. I get right tired of squaws."

When Ty understood that the *bruja* under discussion was Janna, it was all he could do not to hurl himself over the table and hammer the half-drunk bartender into the floor.

"But now Troon's decided to make hisself rich off of that old black stud," Ned continued. "He took his rifle and went to Black Plateau. Gonna crease that stud bastard, break him and take his colts while every white man in the territory is too scared to butt in."

Ty grimaced. "Creasing is a chancy thing. A lot more horses are killed than caught that way."

"One mean stud more or less won't make no never mind in this world.

If'n it was me, I'd kill the stud, grab the best colts and light a shuck clean out of the territory before the Army finds Cascabel and the whole shootin' match goes up in smoke.''

Ty thought of Lucifer as he had last seen the stallion—ears pricked, neck arched, muscles gleaming and sliding beneath a shiny black hide. The thought of someone killing that much animal just to grab his colts made Ty both disgusted and angry. But he had no doubt that Troon would do just that, if he got to Lucifer first.

"Is the mercantile closed?" Ty asked, interrupting Ned's monologue.

"What? Oh, you mean the Preacher's store. Naw, he didn't close up when he went to the fort. Ain't no man would steal from him. Sooner steal from Satan hisself. Even the renegades leave the Preacher alone. Cunning as a coon and snake-mean into the bargain. Troon gave up on the red-haired gal after the Preacher told him to leave her be. See, she gave him a Bible once. So when you see her again, you tell her it's safe to come into Sweetwater. Troon won't bother her."

A cold breath of caution shivered over Ty's skin. The bartender was no more drunk than Ty was.

"Who?" Ty asked, scratching his beard.

"The red-haired gal."

"Don't know her. She live around here?"

Ned squinted at Ty with pale, watery eyes. "Nobody knows where she lives. 'Cept maybe you. She pulled your tail out of a mighty tight crack."

"Mister, the only crack my tail has been in lately was with Cascabel's renegades, and I got shuck of them by running my feet to the bone, hiding in brush, drinking rainwater and eating snakes. Not a one of them had red hair."

Ned stared at Ty for a long time and then nodded slowly. "If that's the way you want it, mister, that's the way it is."

"Wanting has nothing to do with it," Ty drawled coolly, standing up. "I'm telling you the way it was. Thanks for the beans. I'm going over to the Preacher's store. I'll leave a list of what I take. He can get his payment out of the gold Blue Wolf left at the fort."

"I'll tell Preacher when I see him."

"You do that." Ty started for the door, feeling an acute need for fresh air, then realized he wasn't through with Ned yet. "I need to buy a horse."

"The Circle G has right fine horseflesh. Best in the territory. Course, if'n a man was to ride one out of the territory, he might run into a cowpoke what lost a horse just like it."

Ty smiled wryly as he got the message. "I'll settle for a town horse."

"Ain't none," Ned said succinctly. "Took 'em all to the fort."

"Where's the closest homestead that might have an animal to sell?"

"Ain't none left for a hundred miles, 'cept renegade camps and wherever that redheaded gal lives. But you don't know nothin' about her, so it don't help you none."

Ty shrugged. "I'll find a horse between here and Mexico. Thanks for the beans, Ned."

The door shut behind Ty, but he still felt Ned's narrow, calculating eyes boring into his naked back. It made Ty's spine itch and his palms ache for the cool feel of an army rifle.

Janna didn't know it, but she wasn't coming back to Sweetwater again. Ever.

Chapter Thirteen

Janna awoke when a man rose up from the ground in front of her, blocking out the sun with his body. She was grabbing for her knife when Zebra snorted and the man turned and sunlight caught the emerald glint of his eyes.

Hardly recognizing Ty beneath his store-bought clothes, Janna could do no more than stare. The slate-gray shirt and hat, black bandanna, and black pants emphasized Ty's size and masculine grace. He looked as handsome as sin and twice as hard. His beard was shaved off, leaving his face clean but for a midnight slash of mustache that heightened the pronounced planes of his cheekbones and made his teeth gleam whitely. In that instant, with fright still vibrating in her body and her defenses awry, Janna's response to him was so intense that she could scarcely breathe.

"Ty?" she asked huskily. "Is that really you?"

"You better hope it is," Ty snapped. "What the hell were you doing asleep? It could have been Joe Troon who cut your trail rather than me. Or maybe you'd like to be kept by him again?"

Janna's heart was beating too rapidly for her to make sense out of Ty's words. "You scared the life out of me, sneaking up like that!"

"Sneaking up? Hell's bells, Janna, you expect Cascabel to march in here with a band playing 'Onward Christian Soldiers'?" Ty demanded. "You should have been on guard and seen me coming half a mile away!"

"Zebra was on guard," Janna said, standing and wiping her palms on her baggy pants. "Yell at her. She must have recognized your smell and not made a fuss."

Ty looked over at the mustang. Zebra was cropping at wisps of dry grass, lifting her head to scent the wind, then relaxing once more for a few moments before sniffing the wind again.

"Scented me, huh?" Ty said, feeling his anger slide away as he realized that Janna had been well guarded after all. "Are you saying I need some more time in your hot spring?"

"Ask Zebra. Her nose is better than mine," Janna retorted, forcing herself to look away from the hard, handsome planes of Ty's face. She closed her eyes, braced her fists in the small of her back and knuckled the tight muscles. "Lordy, there was a root beneath me the size of my arm. No matter how I lay I couldn't avoid it."

Whatever Ty had been going to say was forgotten beneath the impact of the supple reach and sway of Janna's body while she worked out the kinks of lying in cover for several hours.

"Here," he said gruffly. "This will help."

Janna's eyes flew open when she felt Ty's strong hands knead down her spine to her hips and back up again, lingering at the curve of her waist, rubbing the muscles in the small of her back, then caressing her waist once more before probing at the bands of cloth that wrapped her rib cage beneath her shirt. When he discovered the knotted muscle in her shoulder, he pressed down firmly, smoothing away the knot, making her knees loosen with relief.

"Oh, that feels good," Janna said huskily, her voice catching with pure pleasure. "Yes, there. Ahhh… You're unraveling me like a snagged mitten."

With a low sigh that was almost a moan of pleasure, Janna let her head slowly drop back until it rested on Ty's chest. His hands hesitated as his heart slammed suddenly, sending blood rushing through his body, making him feel both heavy and powerful. Taking a discreet, deep breath, he resumed the leisurely, gentle massaging of Janna's back. Each murmur of her pleasure was like flames licking over him, tightening every muscle in his big body, flushing him with sensual heat.

The piñon-and-sunshine smell of Janna's hair intoxicated Ty. The curve of her neck above her clothes tantalized him. The sounds she made inflamed him. He wanted to bend over and taste the clean skin rising above her collar; then he wanted to peel her clothes away and taste soft skin that had never seen the sun. Yet she felt so fragile beneath his big hands, almost frail.

She's just a girl, Ty reminded himself harshly.

The memory of what Ned had said about Joe Troon and Janna went into Ty like a knife.

Poor little thing, Ty thought, moving his hands up to her shoulders and rubbing very gently before he released her with a reluctance he couldn't disguise. *She's known little of kindness from men. I can't take advantage of her just because she comes undone at a gentle touch.*

Janna turned her head, brushing her lips lightly over Ty's fingers as they moved away from her shoulder.

"Thank you," she murmured, her eyes closed and her voice a sigh of pleasure. "That felt as good as sunlight on a cold day."

Head still turned toward Ty, Janna opened her eyes—and felt her breath wedge tightly in her throat. He was so close, his eyes a glittering green that was both beautiful and savage. Tiny shards of black acted to deepen and define the vivid green surrounding the pupils. The dark gleam at the center of his eyes was repeated in the dense midnight of his eyelashes. His pulse beat full and strong at his temple and his lips were a flat line, as though he were angry or in pain.

"Ty? Did…did everything go all right in Sweetwater?"

Janna's question sounded very far away to Ty. Slowly he realized that he was staring into the depths of her rain-clear eyes while his fingertips traced and retraced the soft curve of her cheek.

"You're never going back there, Janna. That damned greasy bartender…" Ty's voice died. He could think of no delicate way to put into words what he had seen in Ned's eyes when he talked about women.

"Ned?" Janna asked, shrugging. "I stay out of his way. I'm careful never to be in town more than a few minutes at a time. Even if someone sees me, the Preacher makes sure I'm left alone.''

"The Preacher pulled up stakes and went to the fort along with everybody else except Ned. Renegades from all over the territory are drifting down to Black Plateau to join Cascabel.''

She frowned. "Why would Ned stay in town? Nothing in his dingy old shack is worth dying for.''

"Before Cascabel caught me, I spent some time in Hat Rock. The folks there think Ned is the one selling guns to the Indians. If that's true, he wouldn't be too worried about getting his hair cut by a renegade barber.''

"Pity,'' she said. "He could use a trim.''

Ty smiled and Janna's stomach did a little dip and curtsy. She looked away hastily.

"Guess we'd better get back to Black Plateau,'' she said, clearing her throat. "It will be—''

"You're going to the fort,'' Ty interrupted.

"What?''

"It's too dangerous for a woman out here. On the way in to Sweetwater I cut the trail of three different groups of Indians. Two or three braves to a group. No sign of women or kids.''

"Utes?''

Ty shrugged. "If they are, they're renegades. Black Hawk is trying to keep a short rein on his young warriors.''

"Where were the tracks headed?''

"Sweetwater,'' Ty said succinctly. "I'll bet they bought rifles from Ned and then hit the trail for Cascabel's new camp.''

Frowning, Janna looked at the sky over toward Black Plateau. The thunderheads were a solid, blue-black mass that trailed dark curtains of rain. The Fire Mountains had been buried in storm clouds when Ty left for town, which meant that several hours of rain had fallen on top of Black Plateau. The finger canyons would be filling with runoff before too long.

"Don't even think about it,'' Ty said, following Janna's glance. "The crack leading to your camp is probably up to a horse's fetlocks by now. Even if Zebra galloped all the way back, the water would be hock-high for sure. Chest-high, more than likely. But it wouldn't matter.''

"It wouldn't?'' Janna asked, surprised.

"Hell, no. We'd be dead before we got there, picked off by renegades and staked out for the ants to eat.''

"But—''

"Dammit, Janna, don't you see? Cascabel must have passed the word that he's getting ready for one last push. Every renegade Indian west of the Mississippi is jumping reservation, stealing a horse and riding hard for Black Plateau. The only safe place for you is at the fort.''

"For me?'' she questioned.

Ty nodded tightly.

"What about you?'' she asked.

"I'm going after Lucifer.''

"What makes you think Cascabel won't get you?''

"If he does, that's my problem.''

"Then we agree.''

"We do?" asked Ty, surprised.

"We do. We'd better get going. I know a good place to camp on the northeast slope of the plateau."

"The fort is to the west of the plateau. Won't you be taking us the long way around?"

"I'm not going to the fort."

"The hell you aren't."

"That wasn't our agreement," Janna said quickly.

"What?"

"Our agreement was that it's your problem if Cascabel gets you, correct?"

"Yes."

"Then it follows that it's my problem if Cascabel gets me."

Ty opened his mouth, closed it, grabbed Janna in his powerful hands and lifted her until she was at eye level with him.

"You," he said coldly, "are going to the fort if I have to tie you and carry you belly down over my saddle."

"You don't have a saddle."

"Janna—"

"No," she interrupted. "You can tie me up and haul me from one end of the territory to the other, but the second you turn your back or take off the ropes I'll be gone to Black Plateau."

Ty looked into Janna's unflinching gray eyes and knew that she meant every word. Her body might have been slender but her will was fully the equal of his own.

Ty looked from Janna's wide gray eyes to her lips flushed with heat and life. He could think of many, many things he would like to do at that moment, but none would be quite as sweet as sliding his tongue into her mouth until he could taste nothing but her, feel nothing but her, know nothing but her.

Yet he shouldn't even touch her. Even if she didn't have the sense to realize it, she was a nearly helpless girl whose life was at risk every hour she spent running free with her mustangs.

"What am I going to do with you?" he asked huskily.

"Same thing I'm going to do with you," she retorted.

Ty smiled slowly. "What are you going to do with me?" he asked, his voice deep, his mouth frankly sensual.

"Hunt L-Lucifer," Janna said, stammering slightly, wondering what had given Ty's green eyes their sudden heat and intensity.

"I thought you didn't want to help anyone catch Lucifer."

"I said 'hunt,' not 'catch.'"

"Little one, what I hunt, I catch."

Janna tried to breathe, couldn't, and tried again. "Ty..." she said, her voice ragged.

The word sounded more like a sigh than a name. She licked her lips and prepared to try again.

Ty's hands tightened almost painfully around Janna's rib cage as he watched the pink tip of her tongue appear and disappear, leaving behind lips that were moist, soft and inviting. Knowing he shouldn't, unable to help himself, he slowly brought Janna closer to his own mouth.

Just beyond the shelter of the brush, Zebra threw up her head and pricked her ears, staring upwind. Her nostrils flared, fluttered and flared again. Abruptly her ears flattened to her head.

Ty dropped to the ground, taking Janna with him.

Moments later, no more than two hundred feet away, a group of four Indian warriors rode out of a shallow ravine.

Chapter Fourteen

Stomach on the hard, uneven ground, Janna lay wedged between a boulder on one side and Ty's body on the other. Very slowly she turned her head until she could see beneath Ty's chin. He had a pistol in his left hand and was easing his right hand toward another boulder, where he had propped his new carbine before he woke her up. From the corner of her eye she saw his long fingers wrap around the stock of the weapon. Without making a sound he lifted the carbine and slowly, slowly eased it into firing position at his shoulder.

Screened by brush and rocks, Janna and Ty watched the warriors cross a small rise and angle back toward the cover of another dry wash. For long minutes after the Indians vanished, Ty lay unmoving. The weight of his body ensured that Janna stayed motionless, as well. Not until Zebra snorted, rubbed her muzzle against her knee and then resumed grazing did Ty release Janna. Even so, when he spoke to her, he laid his lips against her ear, and his voice was a mere thread of sound.

"Ready to go to the fort now?"

Janna turned until she could see his eyes, so close they all but filled her world.

"No," she said distinctly.

"You're a fool, Janna Wayland."

"Then so are you."

"I'm a man."

"You support my argument," she shot back in a fierce whisper.

Thunder broke and rumbled over the land.

"We should go as far as we can before the storm breaks," Ty said. "That way our tracks will be washed away before any wandering renegades can find us." He came to his feet, pulling Janna after him. "Get on Zebra. I'll ride behind you."

Janna swung up on the mare and looked back at Ty. He was shrugging on a big, heavy backpack stuffed with clothes, bedding and supplies. The carbine was strapped to the back of the pack, muzzle down, riding in what would have been a saddle holster if Ty had had a saddle; but he didn't. He was his own pack mule for the moment.

Ty handed Janna an oilskin slicker, jerked his new hat into place and swung up behind her, heavy backpack and all.

Fat, cold drops of rain began to fall.

"Put on the slicker," he said.

"What about you?"

"Put on the damned slicker!"

Janna shook out the drab, canvas-colored cloth, saw that it was no more than a tarpaulin with a slit for a man's head, and promptly widened the slit with her knife.

"What are you doing?" Ty demanded.

"Making it big enough for two. Hang on to your hat."

Janna turned around enough to pull the slicker over Ty's head. Facing forward again, she put her own head through the slit and tucked flapping folds beneath her legs. Ty's motions told her that he was doing the same thing, although while he did it, he was muttering a lot of words she preferred not to overhear.

When Janna settled into place to ride, she realized that she was sitting quite close to Ty. In fact, she couldn't have been sitting closer unless she had been on his lap rather than surrounded by it. She felt the rub of his thighs along hers, the small movements of his hips and the supple swaying of his torso as he adjusted his body to Zebra's stride. Janna was doing the same— rocking slightly, rubbing gently, swaying, cocooned in oilcloth and wrapped in warmth.

Once she got used to the novelty of being so close to Ty, she realized that it was deliciously warm and comfortable, except for the shivery sensations that uncurled along her nerve endings at odd moments when his hands brushed her thighs or his breath rushed over her neck. And even those un- expected quivers of heat within her body were—intriguing. With an uncon- scious sound of pleasure, she settled more deeply into the warmth and mus- cular resilience of Ty's body.

Ty set his teeth until his jaw ached, barely resisting the impulse to rip off the oilcloth and free himself from the innocent, incendiary rock and sway of Janna's body. The wind gusted, bringing cold splashes of sensation that only made the shared intimacy of the oilcloth more vivid.

After a time it began to rain in earnest, as though the descending sun had somehow freed the water drops from their cloud prisons. The oilcloth turned away much of the rain, but not all. Although it became increasingly damp beneath the poncho, neither Janna nor Ty suggested stopping, for there was no cover nearby worthy of mention. When lightning bolts became closer and more frequent, Janna said something that Ty couldn't catch. He bent forward, bringing his mouth against her ear.

"What?"

She turned toward him, so close that her warm breath washed over his lips. "Hang on."

The belling of thunder drowned out Ty's response, which was just as well. Instinctively his legs clamped around Zebra's barrel as the mare went from a walk to a gallop. The rhythmic rocking motion intensified the friction of Janna's body rubbing against Ty's. The resulting heat was a bittersweet pain. Each time the mare climbed a small rise, Janna's buttocks pressed more snugly into his lap, stroking his aroused flesh. Each time the mare descended, he slid harder against Janna, their bodies separated by only a few folds of cloth, until he wanted nothing more than to imprison her hips in his hands and move with her until he burst.

"How much farther?" asked Ty through gritted teeth.

"Two miles."

Ty wondered if he would survive. He couldn't decide if the stimulation would have been easier to bear at half the pace and twice the time of suffering, or if twice the stimulation and half the time was indeed the easier course.

Oblivious to Ty's masculine discomfort, Janna guided Zebra into what looked like a simple thickening of brush. It turned out to be a narrow trail snaking up the base of a nameless mesa. Soon Ty had to reach around Janna and grab the mare's mane with both hands to keep his slippery seat.

Partway up the mesa, the trail ended in a shallow overhang of red rock stained with streaks of very dark brown. There was no way out and no other trail but the one they had just come up. Obviously this was the shelter Janna had chosen.

Ty didn't wait for an invitation to dismount. He ducked out of the shared slicker and slid from Zebra's back, barely biting off a savage word when the shock of landing jolted through his aroused body. He eyed the narrow shelter with a mixture of relief and anger. There was just enough room for the mustang and two people to stay reasonably dry—if the mustang weren't restless and the two people occupied the same space at the same time.

Bitterly Ty told himself that at least staying warm without a fire wouldn't be a problem. All he had to do was look at Janna, or even think about looking at her, and his new pants fit way too tightly. He told himself that it was because the pants were too small, and he knew he lied. He could count his heartbeats in the hard flesh that had risen between his legs, and every beat made him want to draw up in pain.

What the hell is the matter with me? he asked himself savagely. *I've never gotten this hot over a full-grown woman wearing silk and perfume. Why am I getting in a lather over a ragged little waif with no more curves than a fence rail?*

The only answer that came to Ty was the memory of Janna's uninhibited response when he had rubbed her back. If such an impersonal touch made her breath shiver and break, what would happen if he touched her the way he wanted to, no holds barred, nothing between them but the sensual heat of their bodies?

Biting back a curse, Ty fought to subdue the demands of his own flesh. He forced himself to ignore the sexual urgency that grew greater with each of his rapid heartbeats, reminding him that he was very much a man and that Janna, despite her ragged men's clothes and slender body, was way too much woman for his comfort.

Without a word to Janna, Ty began exploring the dimensions of the ledge that would be his prison for the night. From the corner of her eyes, Janna watched Ty prowl while she dismounted and checked Zebra's hooves for stones. There were none. She caressed the mare's curious, nudging nose for a few minutes, tugging from time to time on the horse's soft lips in a gentle kind of teasing that Zebra enjoyed as much as Janna did.

"Go find dinner," Janna said finally, pushing Zebra's velvet muzzle away.

Apparently the mare had grazed enough while waiting for Ty to return. She showed no inclination to go back down the steep trail to look for food.

"Then get out of the way," Janna said, exasperated.

Zebra looked at her.

Janna laced her fingers in the mare's mane and tugged. Obediently Zebra moved forward, allowing herself to be led to the opposite end of the ledge, where it angled down to the nearly invisible trail.

"It's all yours, girl."

Thunder rumbled heavily, making the ground quiver. Zebra flicked her ears and sighed.

"Have you ever hobbled her?" Ty asked, eyeing the narrow space they all had to share.

Janna shook her head.

"Hope to hell she doesn't walk in her sleep," he muttered, unloading his backpack. The burden hit the ground with a *thump* that spoke eloquently of weight.

"We spent three days up here in the spring, when Cascabel was trying to catch Lucifer," Janna said. "Zebra never stepped on me once. I think she has me confused with a foal. When I lie down to sleep, she'll move off to graze, but she always keeps her eye on the place where I'm sleeping. If anything happens, she gives me a warning."

"Are all your mustangs like that?"

She shook her head again. "No, just Zebra. Most of the time she really likes my company."

"Most of the time?"

"When she's in season, she stays close to Lucifer and I stay away."

Ty glanced over at Zebra. "Is she in season now?"

"It's early. But if she isn't pregnant by winter, it won't be Lucifer's fault," Janna said dryly.

Ty's smile gleamed for an instant and he drawled, "I'm sure Lucifer takes good care of his mares. I'm surprised he lets her wander, though."

"He's too busy running from men and driving off other stallions to worry about a stubborn bunch quitter. Besides, he's figured out that Zebra always comes back."

"How long have you been following Lucifer's bunch?"

"Since Pa died."

"Has Lucifer always kept to the same territory?"

"It's bigger than it was in the beginning, but otherwise Lucifer is like all wild animals. He sticks to what he knows is safe unless he's forced to change. When that happens, he goes into hiding with just a few of his wildest mares."

"Do you know where he goes?"

Janna gave Ty an unhappy look and said nothing. He knew that she was protecting the big stud's secrets. He didn't blame her, but he intended to have those secrets just the same.

"You know Joe Troon," Ty said. "How good a shot is he?"

The change of subject surprised Janna. "Pretty good, unless he's been drinking. Then he's only fair."

"Is he a good tracker?"

"Not as good as you or me."

"You're sure?"

"Once he spent a whole afternoon looking for me, and I was only fifteen feet away most of the time."

Ty closed his eyes against the sudden rush of adrenaline that came when he thought of Janna alone, hiding in the brush, and a man like Troon searching for her with tight britches and pure lust in his blood.

"Can Troon get within rifle range of Lucifer?"

Janna froze. "What are you saying?"

"Ned told me that Troon took his rifle and went hunting. He's going to crease Lucifer. Unless Troon is a damn fine shot, he'll end up killing Lucifer by mistake."

A shudder ran through Janna's clenched body. Her greatest fear had been that some greedy mustanger would give up trying to catch the elusive stallion and simply kill him instead, thereby making the job of capturing the herd much easier.

"If Troon catches the mustangs in one of the pocket canyons, he could shoot from the cliffs above. But Lucifer's been chased so much lately that he's stayed away from the east side of Black Plateau. He's pushed north and west, into the slick rock country that only the Indians know."

"Will he stay there?"

Janna wanted to say yes, but she knew Lucifer too well. He had been driven from his preferred range in the past; he had always returned to Black Plateau, often with new mares he had run off from ranches or other wild herds. The stone canyons, year-round seeps and untrammeled space of the land spreading out from the plateau seemed to have an indelible allure for the big stallion. Year after year he returned, no matter how hard man chased him. But this time he would be chased by bullets that even his strong legs couldn't outrun.

The thought was unbearable to Janna. There was only one way she might be able to prevent Lucifer's death—by betraying him to a man who wouldn't use a gun.

Janna looked up into Ty's steady green glance and prayed that she was making the right decision.

"The best grazing and water for a hundred miles in any direction is around Black Plateau," she said, her mouth dry. "I know every seep, every bit of cover, every place where grass grows lush and thick. I'll take you to each secret place until we find Lucifer, but first you have to promise me one thing."

The unhappiness and determination in Janna's face made Ty wish for a moment that he had never heard of the big black stallion. But he had heard of Lucifer, and so had every other man from the Rio Grande to the Snake River. The stallion's time as a free-ranging mustang was rapidly coming to an end, and Janna knew it as well as Ty did. That was why she was blinking back tears and trying to speak.

"I'll be as gentle as possible with him," Ty said in a low voice, taking Janna's hand between his own. "I don't want to break Lucifer's spirit. I just want to breed him with some fine mares. I'll take him to Logan's ranch in Wyoming and let him run with the remuda while I build my own ranch. For Lucifer, it will be almost as good as running free down here. He'll be safe, Janna. No man will come after him with a rifle or a whip.

"And if he can't accept capture," Ty continued, stroking Janna's hand with his fingertips, "I'll turn Lucifer loose myself. I'd rather that he die free than live in a cage with eyes as dull as stones. Is that what you wanted me to promise?"

She drew a shaking breath. "Thank you, but I already knew those things about you or I'd never have spoken in the first place and offered to help you."

"Then is it money you want? I don't have much, but I'll be glad to—"

"No," she interrupted swiftly. "I'd never take money for Lucifer. I want you to promise that you'll let me try to gentle him first. I couldn't bear to see him brought down by a rope and broken by force."

Ty thought of the stallion's raw power and his hard, flashing hooves. "No. It's much too dangerous."

For a long moment Janna looked at Ty's face. The dying rays of the sun revealed a determination as great as her own. Without a word she eased her hand from his grasp, tossed the rain poncho aside and went about smoothing out a place to sleep for the night. As she worked Ty watched her in silence, wondering what she was thinking.

Finally the lightning barrage ended, leaving only a hard, steady rain. Ty looked over at Janna, who was half-reclining against the stone wall. In the darkness he couldn't be sure whether she was asleep. He thought she was.

"Janna?" he called softly.

No answer came.

Ty pulled on the rain poncho and walked from the protection of the ledge. If he had been camping with one of his brothers, he wouldn't have gone more than ten feet before relieving himself. As it was, he went considerably farther.

When he came back Janna was gone.

Chapter Fifteen

⟨⟨⟨⟨⟨⟨⟨⟨⟨

The cold rain made Janna shiver and long for the bedroll she had left in her winter camp, but no matter how much it rained, she didn't stop to find shelter from the downpour. As long as it rained her tracks would be washed out. Besides, she was less than three miles from one of her Black Plateau caches. By morning she would be warm and dry and sleeping in a place no man would ever find.

Not even Ty MacKenzie.

When the clouds finally dissolved into streamers of mist buffeted by a playful wind, Janna was beginning to wish she hadn't left Zebra behind. But she hadn't been able to bring herself to leave Ty afoot in a land teeming with Indian renegades. Zebra would at least take him as far as the thousand hidden canyons and secret springs of Black Plateau before she trotted off to look for Lucifer's herd once more.

And Janna had no doubt that it would be toward Black Plateau that Ty headed, rather than toward the safety of the fort. He wouldn't leave the territory until he had what he had come for—Lucifer.

The cold light of a new moon gave small illumination and less comfort to Janna as she walked steadily toward the dark bulk of the plateau, which rose from the land until it shut out the stars along the horizon. When she could see the faint notch she called Wind Gap, she turned west. Alternately running and walking, she came closer to the place that was as much a home as she had ever had.

In the darkness before dawn, it took Janna three tries to find the mound of broken boulders where she had stashed a spare canteen, blanket, knife and matches. The blanket was mouse chewed and musty but dry. She wrapped it around her and filled her canteen from a hole that had been worn in solid stone, creating a bowl that held rainwater after a storm.

Canteen and knife on her hip, dry matches in her shirt pocket, Janna climbed farther up the canyon until she came to a place where water from runoff streams had long ago worn out a room-size hole in the canyon wall. Water no longer reached the hollow; even in the highest flood it remained safe and dry. By the time she scrambled up the last steep pitch of rock to the east-facing hollow, Janna was trembling with hunger, cold and exhaustion.

Because the wind was from the north, only the hardest gusts reached her. She thought longingly of the hot spring in her winter camp, and of sunlight and of beds fragrant with piñon. Then she thought of the warmth of Ty's big body, and the sweet friction of his chest against her back, his thighs against her thighs, his arms like warm steel around her as he hung on to Zebra's long·mane.

The curious, fluttering warmth returned to the pit of Janna's stomach, making her shiver with something more than cold. She remembered Ty's strength, the feel of his flexed muscle when he had lifted her and she had balanced herself by hanging on to his arms. The memory made her palms tingle as though she had been rubbing them along his sleeves. She thought of the strained, intent look on his face when he had bent down to her in the thicket where he had startled her from a deep sleep; and she wondered what would have happened if Zebra hadn't scented the renegades on the wind, ending the hushed expectancy of the moment.

After a time Janna finally fell asleep. Her dreams were as restless as the wind.

Ty slept until the wind swept the sky free of clouds, allowing the moon's narrow silver smile to illuminate the land.

"How about it, girl?" Ty said very softly. "You afraid of the dark?"

Zebra tugged impatiently against the hand restraining her nose. She wanted to be free to go down the trail.

"Yeah, that's what I thought. Which will you go after, Janna or that big black stud?"

Zebra snorted.

"Well, I'll tell you, girl," Ty said, swinging onto the mare's warm back, "I hope it's Janna. When I find her, I'm going to..."

Ty's voice faded. He didn't know what he was going to do when he found Janna. His dreams had left him restive and aroused, and as surly as a bear with a broken tooth. He was furious that Janna had slipped out into the stormy night without so much as a makeshift poncho to turn away the rain. No matter how many times he told himself that she had earned whatever her stubbornness brought her—or that she was obviously able to take care of herself in any case—the thought of her being wet and cold and hungry haunted him.

"Hell, why didn't she at least ride you?" muttered Ty to the horse. "Did she figure your tracks wouldn't wash out well enough? Or did she figure you would run off and I'd follow and miss her tracks completely?"

Zebra didn't even pause at the sound of her rider's muttered questions. She picked her way down the slope with the swift, clean poise that only a mustang could achieve over the rugged land.

Ty didn't bother trying to guide Zebra. He didn't know where he was going. Besides, in the dark the mare's senses were much more acute than his own. His only advantage over the mustang was his brain.

Some advantage, Ty told himself sardonically. *I can't even outwit a slip of a girl.*

The thought didn't improve his disposition. Nor did the fact that every time he closed his eyes, he saw the utter stillness of Janna's face when he had refused to promise that she would be the one to capture Lucifer.

Hellfire and damnation, Ty seethed silently. *What kind of a man does she think I am to let her risk her scrawny little ass fighting that stud?*

A vivid memory of Janna's body condensed in Ty's mind, reminding him that her bottom wasn't scrawny at all. It had been smooth and resilient beneath his hands when he had pulled her from the horse. Her hips had curved enticingly below her slender waist, curves that sheltered feminine secrets, curves that invited a man's hands to follow them, then his mouth, his lips, his tongue....

Ty shifted to relieve the pressure on his burgeoning, hardening flesh. He ached with every heartbeat, an ache that had become all too familiar since his mind had discovered what his body had known all along: Janna was a woman, not a boy.

Did she know how much I wanted her? Is that why she ran out into the storm?

Uneasiness flattened Ty's mouth into a hard line. Janna had saved his life, risking her own in the process. The thought that he, however unintentionally, had driven her away from the protection he could offer in this troubled land made him disgusted with himself and his unruly body.

Ty's reaction to Janna baffled him. He had never pursued women in the past; he had never had to. They came to him like moths to a naked flame. He took what they offered, gave them pleasure in return and avoided virgins because he was determined not to marry until he could have a fine silk lady for a wife. He had made no secret of his intention to remain free, but the women who came to him either hadn't believed him or hadn't cared.

But none of them ran from me, by God. Hell, often as not I was running from them!

The cold wind swirled down from Black Plateau's rumpled heights, reminding Ty of how miserable Janna must be—on foot, no real jacket and probably soaking wet, as well. He glared out at the pale rose dawn as though it were responsible for all that had gone wrong since he had been within moments of catching the big black stud, only to find himself caught by Cascabel instead.

The dawn sky passed from pale pink to a pale, rain-scrubbed blue. There was little real warmth in the early-morning sun, but as Zebra trotted toward the crest of a long rise, the light was strong enough to allow Ty to find out where he was. He halted Zebra just below the top of the rise, dug a new spyglass out of his backpack and looked out over his trail. Nothing moved behind him but a few ravens flying blackly through the hushed air.

Ty shifted position, looking to the right and the left. It was the same everywhere he could see. Nothing moving. He couldn't have been more alone if he had been the first man on earth.

Zebra snorted and shifted her weight, telling Ty that she wanted to be on her way.

"Easy girl. Let me look around."

No matter where Ty looked, the countryside was daunting. It was also beautiful to anyone who appreciated the naked form of mountains and mesas, stone pinnacles and steep canyons, long crests and ridges of rocks devoid of gentle greenery. The plants that existed were spread out over the rugged countryside so thinly that the stone substructure of the land was visible in many places. Against the deepening blue of the sky, rock ridges and cliffs and gorges gleamed in every color from white through pink to rusty red and black. On the lower slopes juniper stood out like deep green flames burning at random on the fantastic rock formations.

The only familiar-looking part of the landscape to someone who hadn't been born west of the Mississippi was the pile of stone known as Black Plateau; from a distance, it rather resembled a ruined mountain. Other than that, the stark combination of sheer red or white cliffs and rumpled rivers of black lava were like nothing Ty had ever seen. He could still remember the excitement and visceral sense of danger that the land had called forth from him at first look. Harsh, beautiful, beguiling in its secrets and its surprises, the vast country threatened his body even as it compelled his soul.

Frowning, Ty looked out over the land behind him once more, letting his gaze go slightly unfocused. Even using that old hunter's trick to reveal movement in a vast landscape, Ty saw nothing new. If Janna were somewhere behind him, he couldn't see her. Nor could he see any renegades, soldiers, mustangs or rabbits. He put the spyglass away.

"All right, girl. Let's go."

Zebra moved out smartly, hurrying over the crest of the rise as though she understood that to silhouette herself against the sky was to ask for unwanted attention. The mustang had taken a straight line beginning at the place where they had sheltered from the worst of the rain and ending at the long, broken line of cliffs that marked the eastern margin of Black Plateau. Ty knew of no way up onto the plateau from the east side, unless there was a game trail. In any case, he wouldn't want to try such a path riding bareback on a mustang that might take a notion to unload him at any time.

"I can ride you or track you," Ty muttered. "Which would be better?"

If personal safety were the most important consideration, Ty knew he should let the mustang go and track her. But he wasn't worried about his own safety half as much as he was about finding Janna quickly; and for speed, riding beat tracking six ways from Sunday. If Zebra unloaded him, then he could worry about tracking her through the afternoon thunderstorms that occurred as often as not in the canyon country. Until then, he would stay with her like a cactus thorn and hope to get to Janna before she caught lung fever from running around in the rain.

And Ty would also hope that Troon poured enough rotgut down his throat to ruin his aim, so that Lucifer lived to be captured by Tyrell MacKenzie.

Chapter Sixteen

The track was as perfect and as unexpected as a diamond in a handful of mud.

"Whoa, Zebra."

Ty might as well have saved his breath. Zebra had already stopped and lowered her nose to the footprint. She sucked in air, blew it out and sucked it in again. Unlike the mare, Ty didn't have to rely on his sense of smell; he had no doubt that the line of slender footprints was Janna's. What baffled him was that the tracks appeared from nowhere and vanished within thirty feet.

Bruja. Witch.

Skin shifted and prickled on Ty's neck. He wasn't a superstitious man, but it was easier to believe in witches than it was to believe that something as generous and gentle as Janna had survived unaided in this land.

Atop Zebra, Ty quartered the land where the prints had vanished. Beyond them he spotted a narrow tongue of stone coming in from the right. The toe of the last track was more heavily imprinted, as though Janna had dug into the wet ground in the act of leaping toward the stone. Zebra whuffed over the stone tongue for a minute before she looked back at Ty as though to ask, *Well, what now?*

"Good question," Ty muttered.

The runner of rock led to a rugged, narrow ridge that was nothing but wind-smoothed stone. Someone as agile as Janna might have been able to use the ridge as a trail, but it would be rough going for the mustang and her rider.

Like all good hunters, Ty had learned long ago that tracks weren't the only way to follow prey. A better way was to know where the prey was going. He had seen the dismay and fear in Janna's face at the thought of Lucifer being hunted with a rifle. It took no particular prescience on Ty's part to decide that she would head for Lucifer by the shortest possible route. Unfortunately, nothing of the country ahead of him looked passable by man, much less by horse.

Then Ty remembered what Janna had said: *I know every seep, every bit of cover, every place where grass grows lush and thick.*

Sitting motionless, Ty looked at the land ahead of him. It wasn't simply luck that had led him to cut across Janna's trail. In fact, luck had had little to do with it. Despite the vastness of the land itself, there were relatively few places where people and animals could move freely, and fewer still where they could pass from one mesa or canyon to another. The jutting mesas, deep stone ravines, and unfailing ruggedness of the land limited movement to the broad washes between Black Plateau and the mesas or to snaking around the plateau itself. Everything—deer, wild horses, Indians, cattle and cowhands alike—was forced to follow pretty much the same course over the face of the land.

Hiding was another matter entirely. There were literally thousands of places for a person to hide. But eventually every rabbit had to come out into the open to find water or to find food or simply to find a safer place to hide.

Janna was no different.

Janna bit her lip and tugged her hat lower over her auburn hair, concealing any telltale flash of color. The sun's heat had strengthened to the point that cold was no longer a problem for her. Her canteen took care of her thirst. Her stomach, however, was unhappy. It reminded her ceaselessly that it was past time for breakfast and lunch, not to mention that she hadn't had so much as a snack after her midnight walk in the rain.

Yet hunger wasn't Janna's biggest problem. Ty was. Barely a half mile away, he sat on stone outcropping that gave him a commanding view of the countryside. A rugged piñon that grew in the crevices gave concealment to his body; if Janna hadn't caught a glimpse of movement when he had climbed up to his present position, she would never have spotted him in time to go to ground.

Now she was trapped. She had to move across bare rock in order to get to the sole path up Black Plateau's steep eastern side. The instant she broke cover Ty would be on her like a hungry coyote on a rabbit.

Why didn't you just ride Zebra up onto the plateau when she became restless? Janna silently demanded of Ty. *Why did you turn her loose? She could lead you to Lucifer as fast as I could, so why are you staked out over there looking for me instead of for that stallion?*

Nothing answered Janna's silent questions. She shifted her weight carefully, rubbing her hip where a loose rock had been digging into tender flesh. With an impatient sound she turned her head just enough to look across the distance separating her from Ty.

He was still there.

Ordinarily Janna would simply have settled deeper into cover and outwaited her hunter. She had done it many times before, when Cascabel's men had come across her tracks and given chase. Always her patience had proven to be greater than that of her pursuers.

But no longer. Janna's patience was evaporating even more quickly than rain puddles beneath the hot sun. Every minute she stayed in hiding was one minute closer to Lucifer for Joe Troon. The thought was agony to Janna, especially when she knew that she wasn't in any real danger from Ty. Even if he caught her, he wouldn't beat or rape or torture her. In fact, Janna couldn't think of anything painful he would be likely to do to her, except to remind her of how far she was from his ideal of a silken lady.

The thought deepened the unhappy downward curve of Janna's mouth. Beyond being certain that she didn't stand out against the rugged landscape, she had never thought much about her appearance one way or another. Now she did. Seeing Ty in his new clothes with his cheeks smooth shaven had driven home to her just how handsome he was, and by how great a margin she missed being the fragile silken lady who could attract and hold him.

Janna looked across the wild land at Ty and admitted to herself how much she wanted to be his dream. And at the same time she admitted to herself how impossible it was for her to be that dream.

If she had been the silken lady of Ty's desire, she would have died at the same lonely water hole her father had, for there had been no one to depend on but herself. If she hadn't died there, she would certainly have starved, because she would not have been able to catch and kill her own food. Instead of feeling wretched because she was self-sufficient, she should be thanking God for her ability to adjust to the harsh demands of surviving in the wild land.

Do I really want to be all soft and useless just so I can attract Ty? she asked herself scornfully.

Yes.

The prompt, honest reply didn't improve Janna's humor. She glared out across the ground separating Ty from herself.

If I'd been all simpering and soft in the head, Cascabel would have tracked Ty down and killed him. But did Ty ever think of that? No. He just mooned over a will-o'-the-wisp that would probably faint combing tangles out of her own hair.

Janna glared across the space separating herself from Ty. *Move, dammit! I've got better things to do even if you don't.*

Ty remained in place.

Another half hour crawled by, marked by no more motion than that of the shadows responding to the slow arc of the sun across the empty sky. Ravens called across empty ravines. Rabbits nibbled on brush. Lizards whisked across hot rock, towing the racing black shape of their shadows behind. A hawk circled overhead, sending its keening cry to the earth like a thrown lance. Janna felt like calling out in return, venting her growing frustration.

Another sound came—a rifle shot rather than the call of a hawk. The sound was distant and wasn't repeated.

Three things occurred to Janna simultaneously. The first was that no white man was crazy enough to call down the attention of Cascabel's renegades by shooting at game. The second was that Joe Troon had taken a shot at Lucifer. The third was that Ty would be looking in the direction of the shot rather than at the open space between herself and the route up the east side of Black Plateau.

No sooner had the thought occurred than Janna acted. She popped out of the crevice in which she had hidden and began running swiftly.

Ty had heard the sound of the rifle shot at the same instant Janna did. Like her, he had thought of several things simultaneously while he strained to hear other shots and heard only the wind. But he didn't look in the direction of the shot. He knew that whatever had happened or was happening over there was too far away for him to affect. His attention never wavered from the broken land between himself and the plateau.

He spotted Janna instantly. He had spent the past few hours memorizing the possible approaches to the vague trail he had spotted up onto Black Plateau, so he didn't even hesitate to choose his own route. He came to his feet and hit top speed within a few strides, running hard and fast and clean, covering ground with a devouring speed, closing in on Janna with a diagonal course.

Janna caught the motion from the corner of her eye, recognized Ty and redoubled her own efforts to reach the plateau trail. It was as though she were standing still. She had seen Ty run once before, but he had been injured then, reeling from the effects of running Cascabel's gauntlet. Ty wasn't injured now. He ran with the speed of a wolf, closing the space between himself and his prey with every leaping stride.

One instant Janna was in full flight—the next instant she was brought down on the hard earth. Only it wasn't the ground she fell upon, it was Ty, who had turned as he grabbed her so that it would be his body that took the impact of the unforgiving land.

Even so, Janna was knocked breathless. By the time she could react, it was too late. She was flat on her back, pinned to the hot earth by the weight of Ty's big body. He caught her wrists and held them above her head, imprisoned in his hands.

"Don't you think it's time that you and I had a little chat?" Ty drawled.

"Let go of me!"

"Promise you won't run?"

Janna twisted abruptly, trying to throw Ty off. He simply settled a bit more heavily onto her body.

"I'm bigger than you are, if you hadn't noticed," Ty said. "A little thing like you doesn't have a chance against a man of any size, much less one as big as I am."

Janna started calling Ty the same names her father had used when the wagon mule wouldn't move. "You misbegotten whelp of a cross-eyed cow and the stupidest stud son of a bitch that God ever—"

A big hand clamped over Janna's mouth, cutting off the flow of her invective.

"Didn't anybody ever tell you a girl shouldn't use such language?"

The muffled sounds from beneath Ty's hand told him that Janna wasn't listening to him. She flailed against his shoulder and chin with the hand he had freed in order to cover her mouth. He lifted that hand and grabbed her wrist again.

"Bastard son of a one-legged whore and a one-eyed, flea-brained—"

Abruptly Ty's hard mouth covered Janna's. Her lips were open, her breath hot, the taste of her as fresh as rain. He shuddered heavily and thrust his tongue deep into her mouth again and again, wanting to devour her.

The fierceness of Ty's mouth and the wild penetration of his tongue shocked Janna into complete stillness. She trembled helplessly, overpowered by his strength and by her awareness of his body moving over hers, rubbing urgently, as though he were trying to push her into the ground.

Janna couldn't move, couldn't breathe, and still the contact went on and on, his big body crushing hers, showing her how futile it was to fight him. She tried to speak and found she couldn't even do that. Twisting, writhing, she tried to fight him but he was too big, his body was everywhere; she was as helpless as a mouse caught in the talons of a hawk.

Chapter Seventeen

When Ty finally tore his mouth away and stared down at Janna, he was breathing in deep, ragged bursts and her pupils were wide, dark, enormous, magnified by tears.

"Don't you ever run from me again," Ty said, his voice hoarse and his eyes almost black from the dilation of his pupils.

Janna felt the violent shudder that shook his body, felt the quick force of his breaths against the tears on her cheeks, felt the savage power of his clenched muscles. She should have been terrified, yet at some deep, subconscious level she knew that Ty wouldn't truly hurt her. Even so, she trembled, not understanding the feelings that were coursing through her body—and through his.

"You can let me g-go," she said shakily. "I w-won't run."

For the space of several breaths there was only silence and the wild glitter of Ty's eyes. Abruptly he let go of Janna and rolled aside into a sitting position, drawing his legs up to his body as though he were in pain.

"Christ," Ty said through clenched teeth. "I'm sorry, little one. I've never forced myself on a woman in my life."

Janna let out one long, ragged breath and then another. "It's all right."

"Like hell it is," he snarled. He turned his head and looked at her with eyes as hard as stone. "You don't belong out here, Janna Wayland. You're a walking temptation to every man who sees you all alone and unprotected. I'm going to take you to the fort and that's final."

"If you do that, Joe Troon will kill Lucifer, assuming he hasn't already. That could have been the rifle shot we heard."

Ty said something savage beneath his breath, then added, "You don't understand."

"No, it's you who doesn't understand," Janna said quickly. "At the fort or in any town or at one of the ranches, I'm a girl without kin, fit only for washing clothes or dishes or feeding men or...well, you know." Janna shook her head fiercely. "I don't want that. Out here I'm free of their sly looks and pawing hands. The only man out here is you, and you don't think of me that way."

"I don't? What the hell do you think just happened?" Ty demanded, hardly able to believe his ears.

"I made you mad and you got even." Janna shrugged. "So what? I've taken a lot worse from men and survived."

Ty started to ask what Janna meant, then realized that he didn't want to know. He had heard his sister's broken cries when she relived in nightmare the time of her captivity at the hands of white raiders. The thought of Janna being brutalized like that was unendurable. She was so fierce in her desire for freedom, so terrifyingly fragile beneath the heavy clothes that muffled her.

"God," Ty groaned, putting his head in his hands, hating himself. "Janna...little one...I didn't mean to hurt you."

"But you didn't." She looked at him anxiously when he didn't respond. She put her hand on his wrist where the shirt ended and his warm flesh began. "Ty? Honest. You scared me a little and confused me a lot, but you didn't hurt me at all. And I've changed my mind. I'll help you get Lucifer before Joe Troon does."

For a long moment Ty stared at the hand resting on his wrist. The fingers were long and delicate, gently browned by the sun, the nails beautifully formed and pink with health, the skin supple and warm. He wanted to pick up that feminine hand and kiss the hollow of her palm, lick the sensitive skin between her fingers, bite gently at the pad of flesh at the base of her thumb until her breath broke and her hand curled around his touch like a sleeping flower....

"Stop looking at me like that," Janna said, snatching her fingers back. "I know my hand isn't lily-white and soft and stinking of perfume, but it's a good hand all the same. It helped to save your stupid masculine hide, remember?"

Ty opened his mouth to tell Janna that she had misunderstood, that he had been thinking how alluring her hand was rather than the opposite. At the last instant common sense held his tongue in check. She refused to leave the country, and he couldn't leave until he had Lucifer. He needed her help with the stallion and she needed him to guard her back; but he was so woman hungry that he barely trusted himself to keep his hands off her. Keeping her irritated with him would go a long way toward maintaining a safe distance between them. Knowing what her experience with men must have been like, he simply couldn't have lived with himself if Janna thought he were demanding sex in return for safety or anything else he could give her.

"And I've been trying to thank you for saving my hide by saving yours in return," Ty drawled, "but to hell with it. You want to run around here risking your scrawny little self, you go right ahead. Me? I'm just thanking God that He made you so damned unappealing to men. Any other woman and I'd be tempted to find out what was beneath all the rough clothes. But you? You're like a baby quail, all eyes and mouth and frizzled features. With you I'm as safe from the temptations of the flesh as any monk in a monastery."

"Why, you—"

Ty's hand shot out, covering Janna's mouth and cutting off her words.

"You should be down on your knees thanking God that I feel that way," Ty said savagely. "If I ever put my hands on you, it wouldn't be violins and roses. I'm too woman hungry to stop short of taking what I need. And that's all it would be. Taking. No promises, no soft words, no wedding vows, nothing but male hunger and a handy female."

Janna heard every word but only cared about Ty's admission that he was woman hungry. It gave her the weapon she needed. It appeared that her efforts at proving she was a woman had been having some effect.

She smiled rather bitterly and decided that she would make him eat every one of his cutting words about her lack of womanly allure. From that moment on she would redouble her efforts to remind him that she was a woman and he was a hungry man. She would bring him to his knees with desire...and then she would laugh in his face and walk away, leaving him as miserable and unhappy as she was now.

"Now that we understand each other," Janna said tightly, "could we possibly get going so that Joe Troon doesn't kill Lucifer before we can stop him?"

Ty told himself that the hurt and anger he saw in Janna's eyes were better than the bigger hurt that would come if he couldn't keep his hands off her. From what he had heard, at best she had been roughly treated by men; at worst she had been brutalized. If he took advantage of her, he would be no better than Joe Troon.

Ty told himself that, but he wasn't sure he believed it. He would be gentle with Janna even if it killed him...wouldn't he? Surely he would. He wasn't an animal to take what a woman wouldn't freely give him.

Oh, sure. I'm a real Southern gentleman. That's why I was grinding Janna beneath me into the dirt as though I'd never had a woman and never would unless I had her right there. I can't trust myself with her any farther than I can throw myself uphill.

Ty looked at Janna's gray eyes watching him with too many shadows, waiting for his answer.

"Hell of an idea," Ty said curtly. "Wait here while I get my pack."

Janna watched him get up and leave without a backward look. She didn't move. She knew that he was testing her, finding out if he could trust her. If she were going to run off at the first opportunity, better that he discover her untrustworthiness now than when it came time for her turn at night guard while he slept. Approving his pragmatism almost as much as she approved his lithe, muscular stride, Janna watched until Ty disappeared. She waited for his return without moving one inch from her cross-legged position on the ground.

When Ty returned and saw Janna precisely where he had left her, he understood her silent message: he could trust her. He nodded approvingly and held out his hand to help Janna to her feet.

It was the opportunity she had been waiting for. She allowed herself to be pulled upright, then stumbled and fell against Ty's body, letting him take her full weight. His arms closed around her automatically, supporting her.

The impact of Janna's weight was negligible to a man of Ty's size, but the warmth of her body wasn't. When his arms tightened around her to keep her upright, he knew a lightning stroke of pleasure at how perfectly she fit against him. Supple, slender, smelling of piñon, she was like an armful of sunlight.

"Janna? What's wrong?"

For a moment longer she savored the delicious warmth and strength of Ty's body before she slowly began to take her own weight again. Even then, she held on to his muscular arms, bracing herself against his strength.

"Sorry," Janna said, eyes downcast as she flexed her fingers into the swell of Ty's biceps and very slowly released him. "I guess I'm a little...hungry."

Ty was glad Janna wasn't looking at him when she confessed her hunger, because she would have seen the naked statement of his own need in the tension of his face. In the next instant he understood that Janna wasn't talking about the elemental hunger of sex but the equally basic hunger of the stomach. Hers was growling audibly as she rested her cheek against his chest, leaning as though she were too tired to stand entirely by herself. He smiled despite the desire snaking through his loins. He tapped the bridge of Janna's nose gently with his index finger.

"Poor little baby bird," Ty said sympathetically. "Come on. As soon as we get in better cover, I'll feed you."

His voice was a deep rumble beneath Janna's cheek, but the indulgence in his tone was unmistakable. *Baby bird.* Her mouth drew down unhappily. Her attempt to arouse desire in him had resulted in a brotherly pat. The temptation to bite the hard, warm chest that lay beneath her cheek almost overwhelmed her. She sensed that would have been a serious mistake in her campaign of "accidental" seduction, so she contented herself with pushing away from the shelter offered by Ty's arms.

"Thank you," Janna said politely. "I'm fine now."

She turned away and began walking quickly toward the rugged wall of black lava and red sandstone that formed the east face of Black Plateau. Ty stood and watched the almost concealed sway of Janna's hips beneath the men's clothing and prayed that she would find Lucifer and find him very soon; the more he looked at Janna, the harder it became to ignore her unconscious, utterly feminine allure.

Yet he had to ignore it. He had to forget how good it had felt to rock his hips hard against the softness beneath her clothes.

He had to...but he couldn't.

Chapter Eighteen

Anger helped Janna to hold to a good pace despite her growling stomach. Without looking back to see how Ty was doing with his heavy pack, she attacked the steep, winding trail that led to the top of Black Plateau. As she climbed, she looked for signs of anyone else using the trail.

She found no traces of man and very little of beast. There were no signs that anything had used the trail recently other than herself. There were no hoofprints in the rare patches of dirt, nor scars where hooves had slipped or scraped across stone. She had never seen signs of any hoofed animal on the trail except occasional deer—and once, just once, tracks that indicated that Lucifer had skidded down over the precipitous path in order to shake off mustangers who had gotten too close.

The idea of any horse taking the trail down the plateau's east face made Janna's heart stop. She herself used the route only when she was afoot and wanted to go to Sweetwater by the shortest possible route. There were other, safer routes up onto the plateau. One route was on the north side, one on the south, and there were several on the western side. All of them were far easier than the eastern trail.

Climbing at a rapid rate, Janna worked her way up the trail until it dipped into one of the many runoff ravines that channeled the plateau's east face. Safe from observation from any angle but directly overhead, Janna sat on a stone seat and awaited Ty's arrival. She didn't wait long. He had walked only far enough behind her to avoid the shower of pebbles disturbed by her passage.

Ty grunted and shucked off the heavy pack, using it as a seat while his breathing returned to normal.

"Hell of a path," he said after a bit. "I didn't see any sign of Zebra coming up, but she sure headed straight here like she had something in mind."

"She did—avoiding a river of black rock about a quarter mile south of here," Janna explained. "It's too rough to climb over. To avoid it, you have to go several miles away from the plateau until the rock sinks into the dirt, or you have to climb partway up the east face of the plateau to go around the head of the rock river. That's what Zebra usually does. Then she goes up onto the top by the southern route, which is easy."

For several minutes there was silence while Ty looked out over the land from his new perspective, checking his memories against Janna's words.

"Does the lava flow—the river of black rock—begin there?" he asked, pointing to what looked like a dusty black creek running out from the base of the plateau.

Janna leaned out to look, taking the opportunity to brush against Ty's outstretched arm.

"Yes."

Ty grunted. "I can see why Zebra goes around it. A lot of jagged rock and nothing much else."

He looked for a time longer, waiting for Janna to withdraw the tantalizing brush of her body. She didn't. He shifted slightly, ending the intimacy, for his blood was still running hotly. Even worse, he suspected that it was going to be a permanent condition around the ragged, too-feminine waif.

"How deep are those canyons?" Ty asked, pointing toward the shadows that looked rather like a network of black lightning fanning out from the base of the plateau.

For a few moments Janna considered moving closer to Ty in order to brush against him again, but then she decided against it. Next time she would choose her moment better, so that retreat would be impossible. In a place as narrow as this crevice, she shouldn't have to wait long for her opportunity.

"The canyons are deep enough that the wild horses go around them," Janna said. "The countryside is full of ravines and washes and canyons like that. Most of them are dry, but nearly every butte and mesa has at least a tiny seep or rock tanks that hold water almost year-round. Black Plateau is different. It's big enough to have water all year up top as well as seeps and springs at the base. That's why there's so much grass and game."

Saying nothing, Ty smoothed a patch of dirt with his hand, then began drawing on the surface with his fingertip. Knowing that the plateau was Lucifer's preferred range, Ty had spent weeks scouting the area before he had decided on the best way to capture the wild stallion. Unfortunately Ty had ended up captured by Indians before he could try out his plan. Janna, however, had spent years on and around Black Plateau. If there were anything wrong with Ty's plan, she would spot it.

"This outline is Black Plateau," he said, pointing to the very rough rectangle he had drawn in the dirt. He added sides to the rectangle, showing depth as well as area. Only the western side remained untouched, suggesting the relative flatness where the plateau's surface blended into the rumpled front of the Fire Mountains. "From what I've seen, the closer you get to Black Plateau from the east, the steeper and deeper the canyons, gullies and ravines get."

Janna shifted position, brushing against Ty's thigh as she did so. When she leaned forward to look at what he had drawn, she braced her hand on his thigh. Ty's hand, which was drawing lines in the dirt, jerked. He said something beneath his breath and changed position until Janna's hand was no longer resting on his thigh.

"That's right," she said. "The plateau's east face rises very steeply from the flatlands." She leaned forward again, and again braced herself on Ty's leg, ignoring his attempts to evade her touch. "Black Plateau is really part of the Fire Mountains," she added, drawing a series of pyramids along the plateau's western flank to represent the mountains. "According to Indian legends, the spirits fought each other until the earth cracked and bled and everything the blood touched became fire. Long after the earth healed, the angry spirits roared and spit fire among the peaks of the Fire range, and sometimes new blood flowed over the plateau and dripped down into the desert, where it turned into black rocks. The angry spirits still live beneath the earth around here, turning water so hot that there are springs that cook food faster than a campfire.''

Ty tried to concentrate on Janna's words, but the presence of her hand on his leg was burning hotter than anything in the Indian legend. He would have retreated to the side again if he could have. He couldn't. The crevice in the plateau's side where they had taken shelter was simply too small. He was up against a black boulder right now—and her hand had slipped around to the inside of his thigh. She was so involved in the map he had drawn that she didn't seem to notice.

Talk about being between a rock and a hard place... Ty told himself, disgusted because the hard place was in his own lap. He pulled off his hat and dumped it between his legs, hiding the growing evidence of his discomfort in the only way he could.

"There are two good trails up on top of the plateau on its western side," Janna continued, flexing her fingers slightly as she shifted position. Now that she had discovered it, the heat and resilience of Ty's leg fascinated her. "The first trail is here, about two miles from the southern boundary. It's called the Long View Trail." She leaned down and forward until her ribs brushed Ty's leg as she marked the trail on the map he had drawn in the dirt. "That's the easiest way up. The Indians have used it for as long as anyone can remember. The second trail is here." She made another mark. "The trails are about twenty miles apart as the crow flies. Walking it doubles the distance. The second route up is called Raven Creek Trail. It isn't as easy as the Long View Trail, and it doesn't lead immediately to water or good grazing, so Raven Creek Trail isn't used except by Indian hunting parties."

"Or war parties?"

Janna nodded. "Cascabel has his camp at the base of the plateau, where Raven Creek empties into Santos Wash. Mustang Canyon," she added, pointing to the northern edge of the plateau, where a large notch had been cut into the stone foundations of the land, "is here. There's good grazing all year and a trail to the top of the plateau that only deer and mustangs use, and occasional crazy mustangers."

"And you?"

She smiled. "And me. But Zebra grew up on that trail. Sometimes I think her mama was a goat. Zebra is as surefooted as one. Besides, most of the time I get off and walk. There's one slick rock patch that gives me nightmares."

Ty smiled thinly. "You? Nightmares?" he scoffed. "You're too tough to be afraid of anything."

Janna said nothing, though she couldn't help remembering all the nights after her father had died when she had jumped at the smallest sound, biting off screams that would have given away her position rather than summoning the help she needed. Even years later, certain combinations of sounds and smells could set her heart to hammering hard enough to break her ribs.

"Is your keyhole canyon about here?" asked Ty, pointing to a place near the southeast corner of the plateau.

"Yes."

Steadfastly ignoring the gentle crowding pressure of Janna's body, Ty looked at the map and mentally began turning the plateau's neat edges into a fringe of varying lengths, for that was closer to the truth of the landscape. The plateau's north, east and south edges were fringed with sheer-sided stone promontories and cliffs, as well as canyons and ravines of varying sizes and depths; and the larger canyons had side canyons, which in turn branched into finger canyons, which branched into runoff crevices.

The result was a maze in which a person could stand on one canyon edge and look at the opposite edge only a few thousand feet away—and it would take a day of circling around to get to the other side. Most of the hundreds of nameless canyons that fringed the plateau were blind; ultimately they had only one outlet, and that was down onto the flatlands rather than up onto the top of Black Plateau itself.

"Do you know of any other trails up to the top?" Ty asked, marking the ones Janna had already mentioned. "What about all these fringe canyons? Could a man on foot climb out of some of them and up onto the plateau itself?"

Janna shrugged. "Ask Mad Jack the next time you see him. He knows things about Black Plateau that even the Indians don't. But the canyons I've seen end in sheer cliffs, the kind you'd have to be crazy or running for your life to try to climb."

"Does Lucifer graze in blind canyons?"

"The biggest ones, yes. The narrow ones, never. Some mustangers must have trapped him once. He won't even go near the entrance of any canyon that isn't at least a quarter mile across. He's smart and wild as they come."

"No wonder he's still running loose," Ty said, admiration and disgust mixed equally in his voice. "I was lucky to get as close as I did before Cascabel nailed me. What are the chances of startling Lucifer and getting him to run headlong into a small blind canyon before he knows what's happening?"

"It's been tried by every mustanger who ever came here."

Ty didn't ask what the result had been. He didn't need to. The stallion still ran free.

"No wonder Troon decided to try creasing that black devil," Ty muttered.

Janna thought of the rifle shot they had heard and bit her lip.

Ty saw and had to look away. The idea of gently biting Janna's lip himself was too tempting. In fact, everything about her was too tempting. Though she was no longer leaning over to add marks to his rough map, her hand was still resting on his leg, sending heat spreading out in all directions through his body, tantalizing him with how close those slender fingers were to the very part of him that ached for her touch.

Cursing silently, viciously, Ty tried to ease away from the intimate contact. Half an inch away he came flat up against the crevice's stony limits. Close beside him, Janna's stomach growled audibly in the taut silence, reminding Ty that she hadn't eaten since they had left Keyhole Canyon yesterday morning.

"Scoot over so I can reach my pack," Ty muttered.

Even if Janna didn't move, the pack was within a long arm's length of Ty—if he were willing to press against her in order to increase his reach.

She gave him a sideways look and decided not to point out how close the pack was. Without a word she eased backward and to the side an inch or two.

"More."

Ty's curt command irritated Janna. "Haven't you noticed? There's not much room in this crack."

"Yeah, and you're taking up at least three-quarters of it," he retorted. "Quit crowding me."

"Crowding you? My God, you'd think I had fleas or something," Janna muttered beneath her breath. "Seeing as how you're the one who's been to Ned's saloon recently, you're more likely to have fleas than—"

"Janna," Ty interrupted, his voice threatening. "Move!"

"All right, all right, I'm moving." She pushed herself to the far side of the crevice and hugged the wall as though there were a cliff inches away from her feet. "This better?"

Ty snarled something Janna chose not to hear. A pocketknife appeared in his hand. He grabbed his pack and began rummaging through it. A few moments later he pulled out a tin can. He punched the point of the blade twice into the top of the can. The second time he rotated the knife, making a wider opening. He handed the can to Janna.

"Here. Drink this."

Janna lifted the can, tilted, sipped and made a sound of disbelief as the thick, sweet, peach-flavored liquid trickled across her tongue. She took two long, slow swallows before she reluctantly handed the can back to Ty. He refused to take it with a shake of his head.

"Finish it," he said.

"I can't do that. Preacher charges a dollar a can for his peaches."

A look at Janna's clear eyes told Ty that arguing over the peaches would be futile. He took the can, drank two small sips and handed it back over.

"Your turn," he said flatly.

She said nothing, but she took the can and drank slowly, savoring each drop. Her undisguised pleasure made Ty smile with the knowledge that he had given her a real treat. He had spent more than enough time on the trail to know how much a person began craving something sweet and succulent after weeks or months of dried meat and biscuits and beans.

The can was passed back and forth several times, and each time Ty swore that the metal became warmer to his touch. He tried not to think about the lips that had been pressed against the rim before his own lips drank. In fact, he was doing fine at controlling the direction of his thoughts until Janna tipped the can up and waited for several seconds for the last sweet drop to fall from the rim onto the tip of her outstretched tongue. The temptation to suck that drop from her tongue with his own lips was so great that he had to turn away.

"Now what?" she asked, holding the can under Ty's nose.

Hell of a question, he thought savagely. *Wish I had an answer I could live with.*

Using swift, vicious strokes of the pocketknife, Ty cut the lid from the rim, speared a peach half and held it out to Janna. She took the lush golden fruit with her fingertips, ate with delicate greed and waited her turn for another. They traded turns eating until only one piece of fruit was left, a piece

that stubbornly eluded Ty's knife. Finally he speared it and held it out to
Janna. As she slid the fruit from the knife blade she sensed Ty's intense
interest. She looked up to find him watching her mouth. His eyes were a
smoky green that made frissons of heat race over her skin. Without thinking
she took a bite of the succulent fruit and held out the remainder to him with
her fingertips.

"Your turn," she said huskily.

For a long, aching moment Ty looked at the sweetness dripping from
Janna's slender fingers. Then he stood up in a controlled surge of power,
grabbed his pack and strode out of the crevice without a word.

Chapter Nineteen

A late-afternoon storm had swept across Black Plateau, making the rocks and trees shine as though freshly polished. The slanting golden light transformed the winding meadow into a river of glistening gold. Once Janna would have felt the beauty of the land like a balm over her hungry soul; today she only saw what was absent rather than what was present. Lying on her stomach, using a row of evergreen seedlings for cover, she scanned the length of the long meadow in front of her once more, staring through the spyglass until her arms trembled with fatigue.

Ty didn't bother to go over the land again with his own glass. He knew he would see what he and Janna had seen for the past five days—grass and water and wind in abundance, but no Lucifer standing guard over his herd. Cascabel's renegades had been present, however. They were the reason that Ty and Janna had had to tiptoe around the plateau like thieves, able to get only as close to the mustangs as the tracks they had made yesterday or even the day before.

"I don't understand it," Janna said, finally lowering the spyglass and wiggling backward deeper beneath the cover of the pines that grew right to the meadow's edge. "Even if Lucifer had been caught, wouldn't we at least see some of his herd wandering around? No mustanger is going to want the older mares or the spring foals. Besides, we haven't seen or heard any sign of Troon or any other mustanger since we came up the east trail."

"Except for that flurry of rifle shots yesterday," Ty said. "That didn't sound like the hunting parties we've been hearing. Troon could have run afoul of Cascabel."

Janna frowned and said reluctantly, "I suppose I should scout Cascabel's camp."

"What?" Ty asked, astonished.

"That's how I found you," she explained. "I heard gunfire, ran over, saw where the tracks of two shod horses were crossed by a bunch of unshod Indian ponies. The ponies turned to follow your horses and so did I. Eventually the tracks led to Cascabel's camp. I couldn't get to you right away to free you, so I hid and waited for a chance to help. It finally came when you got through the gauntlet and were still able to run."

Ty thought of the danger Janna had risked to save a total stranger and shook his head in wonder. That deceptively slender body hid a lot of plain old courage, but there was no need to spend it on a swamp Yankee like Joe Troon.

"Is Troon a friend of yours?" Ty asked.

Janna gave Ty a startled look. "Joe Troon? I wouldn't cry one tear at his funeral," she said in a low, flat voice. "In fact, he..."

Her voice died. She didn't like to remember the time Troon had trapped her and started stripping off her clothes before she managed to break free and run. He had spent hours searching for her. The whole time he had yelled just what he would do when he caught her.

The combination of fear and dislike on Janna's face told Ty more than he wanted to know about Janna and Joe Troon.

"Janna," Ty said softly, pulling her out of her unhappy memories, "from what I've heard in towns where I bought my supplies, Troon is a drunk, a thief, a coward, a woman beater and a back shooter. He deserves whatever Cascabel feels like giving to him. Besides, you don't even know if Troon has been captured. He could be back in Sweetwater right now, getting drunk on Ned's rotgut. There's no point in either of us risking our butt to scout a renegade camp for a no-good bit of swamp gas like Joe Troon."

"I know," Janna said. "I just hate to think of anyone caught by Cascabel. He's so cruel."

Ty shrugged. "Cascabel doesn't see it that way. He's a warrior who has stood up to the worst the country, the pony soldiers and his fellow Indians can offer in the way of punishment. He's never given quarter and he's never asked for it. And he never will."

"You sound like you admire him."

There was a long silence before Ty shrugged again. "I don't like him, but I do respect him. He's one hell of a fighter, no matter what the weapon or situation. He has knowledge of how to use the land and his limited arms to his own advantage that many a general would envy."

"Do you have any idea what he does to the captives who don't escape?"

"Yes," Ty said succinctly. "I didn't say I admired him, Janna. But I learned in the war that honor and good table manners don't have a damned thing to do with survival. Cascabel is a survivor. Black Hawk knows it. He hasn't pressed a confrontation because he hopes that the U.S. Army will take care of the renegades for him."

"Black Hawk is lucky that Cascabel hasn't lured the whole tribe away from him," Janna grumbled. "Cascabel must have half of Black Hawk's warriors down here by now, and they're still coming in by twos and threes every day."

"Cascabel is half-Apache. The elders in the Ute tribe would never let him be a headman. As for the younger men, they still believe that they're invincible. They haven't had time to learn that the same army that flattened the South sure as hell won't have too tough a time ironing out a few renegade wrinkles in the Utah Territory."

Janna started to speak, then caught a flash of movement at the far edge of the meadow. Ty had seen the movement, too. As one they flattened completely to the earth, taking advantage of every bit of cover offered by the slight depression in which they had lain to watch the meadow.

Four hundred feet away, five Indians rode out into the wide river of meadow grass that wound between the two evergreen forests. The men rode boldly, without bothering about cover or the possibility of ambush, because they knew that Cascabel ruled Black Plateau. The only reason they weren't laughing and talking among themselves was that human voices carried a long way in the plateau's primal silence, and the deer they were hunting had excellent hearing.

Peering cautiously through the dense screen of evergreen boughs, spyglass shielded so that it wouldn't give away their position by reflecting a flash of light, Ty watched the hunting party ride along the margin of forest and meadow. Usually in any group of Indians, barely half the men were armed with carbines, rifles or pistols, and there were rarely more than a few rounds of ammunition for each weapon. Part of the problem for the Indians in getting arms was simply that it was illegal to sell weapons or ammunition to Indians. What they couldn't take as the spoils of war they had to buy from crooked white traders.

But most of the problem the Indians had in staying well armed was that none of the tribes had any experience in the care and repair of machines or in the art of making reliable bullets. The weapons they acquired through war or bribery quickly became useless either because of lack of ammunition or because of mechanical failure.

Cascabel's men were well outfitted. As well as the traditional bow and arrows, each man had a carbine and a leather pouch bulging with ammunition. Ty was relieved to see that the carbines were single-shot weapons of the type that had lost the Civil War for the South. None of the five Indians had a weapon that could compete with the new Winchester carbine he had discovered in an otherwise empty box at the store Preacher had rather hastily abandoned. Ty's new carbine was the type of weapon Johnny Rebs had enviously insisted that a Yank "loaded on Sunday and fired all week long." With his new Winchester, Ty could reload as fast as he could fire, an advantage the Indians didn't have unless they used their bows and arrows.

Ty went over the details of the Indians' gear with the experienced eye of a man to whom such knowledge had meant the difference between continued life and premature death. The presence of good weapons explained some of Cascabel's allure for young warriors—on a reservation, these men would have barely enough to eat, no weapons beyond what they could make with their own hands, and no freedom to roam in search of game. With Cascabel, the young men would have a chance to gain personal fame as warriors, they would be well fed and well armed, and they could live the roving life celebrated in tribal legends.

The fact that the young men would also find themselves the target of every white man with a gun simply added spice to the Indians' lives. After all, there weren't that many white men.

Ty knew that the situation would change, even if the Indians didn't. Since the end of the Civil War, footloose and disenfranchised white men had pressed west in greater and greater numbers. Most of them had already been in shooting battles, so the prospect of occasional skirmishes with Indians wasn't much of a deterrent. Ty himself was one of those men, as were his brothers. There were hundreds and thousands more men like the MacKenzies, drawn by the West's wild horizons and seductive promises of a better life for anyone who had the courage and stamina to withstand the hardships. Not all the promises of the new land would be kept, but each man was certain that, for him, the dreams would indeed come true.

And a lot of those men would be armed with repeating rifles and carbines and as many bullets as they could wear without dragging their belts down to their boot tops. The Indians would take some of those weapons and put them to deadly use, but more white men would come west, and then more and more, and their superior arms would always be enough to offset the Indians' superior knowledge of the land.

Ty had no doubt about the eventual outcome of the battle between Indian and white; he just wasn't sure he would be alive to share in the celebration when the renegades were defeated.

Abruptly the five Indians stopped their mounts. One of the warriors leaped from his horse, landed lightly and sat on his heels while he examined something on the ground. After a time he stood again, walked a few steps and then bent over the ground once more, looking at everything from a different angle.

Ty lay without moving, going over in his mind once more what he would do if he and Janna were discovered. With his new carbine he could cause as much damage in one minute as ten men with single-shot guns. Even allowing for the fact that he hadn't had time to accustom himself to the Winchester's action, he should be able to put two warriors out of the fight before the others took cover. That would give Janna plenty of time to slip away while he played cat and mouse with the remaining warriors. With a little luck, he might even get away himself.

With a lot of luck, he and Janna wouldn't be discovered in the first place.

When the warrior finally remounted and the five continued along the far edge of the meadow without looking in the direction where Janna and Ty lay concealed, he breathed a quiet sigh of relief. He had known some men who loved fighting and killing. He wasn't one of them. He was quite pleased to see the Indians disappear into the trees without a single shot having been fired from his shiny new carbine.

Neither Ty nor Janna stirred from their prone position. Something had piqued the Indians' curiosity enough to deflect them from their original course of hunting. If the curiosity were quickly satisfied, the Indians would come back to the meadow and resume hunting deer.

Besides, Janna was lying quite close to Ty, able to feel him all along her right side, able to move subtly against him, reminding him of her presence. She had done a lot of that in the past five days, leaning over him by the campfire, brushing his hand when she gave him a plate of food, tripping and falling against him when the trail permitted it.

She had seen the green intensity of his glance and had known that her presence was felt, but she was no longer certain that she would laugh and walk away if she brought him to his knees with desire. The thought of being close to him, truly close, brought her to her own knees with an answering desire that burned just beneath her skin, silently reaching out to him even as his own male heat radiated out to her, caressing and calling to her.

The bronze light of very late afternoon burnished the meadow. Soon deer would be emerging from cover to feed. At first they would graze only along the western margin of the meadow, where the descending sun pushed thick shadows out of the dense pines. As the shadows stretched across the grassy clearing, the deer would follow until finally the meadow would be dotted by graceful shapes grazing upon moon-silvered grass.

That was when it would be safest for Ty and Janna to move, when the much more acute senses of the deer would give warning of other men roaming around in the night. Not that Ty expected to run across any Indians on the move in full darkness, but he had learned that allowing for the unexpected was the best way to survive life's lethal little surprises.

Besides, it was very pleasant to lie in the warm aftermath of day on a thick bed of pine needles and listen to birds settling into cover for the night, calling and singing to one another as though they had a lifetime of information to pass on and only a few minutes until the last golden sunlight faded, bringing with it darkness and night.

It was also pleasant to feel Janna's warm body pressed against his left side.

After a moment's thought, Ty conceded to himself that perhaps pleasant wasn't the right word to describe the combination of sensuous heat and mental torture she had inflicted on him in the past days. He couldn't turn around but she was there, touching him in the most casual ways, never forward or aggressive, just...*there*. Always. A smile or a fleeting brush of her body over his, a look from gray eyes as clear as springwater, a soft laugh that made his loins tighten. He sensed that she was getting even with him for belittling her feminine allure, but he couldn't prove it. There was always a logical reason for her touches.

And her touches were driving him crazy, sending fire licking over his skin, heat whispering to him, telling him that beneath those flapping clothes was a woman. With each second that passed, the chance of the Indians returning became less likely, and the fragrance of her body became more compelling. He sensed each of her breaths, knew that she felt him as well, and he wanted nothing more than to turn toward her and mold her along the aching length of his body.

Ty kept remembering that single, penetrating kiss he had given to Janna. He could recall the feeling of her body beneath his with a vividness that sent blood rushing hotly, hardening his male flesh until it ached.

But she hadn't enjoyed that kiss. She had taken it as a punishment.

Yet it was Ty who was being punished. He owed Janna his life. He had sworn to himself that he wouldn't repay that debt by frightening or hurting her as other men had. The only way he could keep his promise to himself was to keep his hungry hands off her. And his hungry mouth. And most of all, his hungry—

"Ty?" Janna whispered softly.

Her body was shaking. So was her voice. Though she made no more noise than a sigh, Ty heard her. He heard every breath she took, saw every time she licked her lips, tasted her in his memory. He didn't know how much longer he would be able to admire her without touching the easy sway of her hips as she led him along the plateau's secret byways.

"Ty?" she said, a bit more loudly.

"What?" he groaned, wondering how much longer he could lie next to her without grabbing her.

"There's a snake crawling along my leg."

Chapter Twenty

"**D**on't move."

Ty knew as soon as he whispered the urgent words that his command was unnecessary—Janna knew better than to make a sudden move around a snake. She also must know that all she had to do was lie quietly until the snake slithered off into the late afternoon and she would be all right.

"Can you see the snake?" he whispered.

Janna's answer was more a whimper than a "no."

"Just stay quiet," he repeated. "The snake isn't interested in you and he won't be as long as you don't move."

But Janna couldn't remain still. Tremors of sheer terror were rippling through her. She could face almost anything without losing her head, but not a snake. She remembered all too well the nightmare of awakening to her father's shouts and frantic flailing about as he tried to shake off the rattlesnake that had crawled into his bedroll. He had been bitten on his feet and his calf, his wrist and his cheek.

At the time they had been deep in Indian country, chasing one of her father's dreams of gold. There had been no one to help. None of the herbs or balms or potions her father knew had managed to pull the poison out of his body. Nor had lancing the oozing wounds helped.

She would never forget the endless death throes of the big snake after she had cut off its triangular head with her sheath knife. Nor would she forget the long days of her father's agony and delirium before he finally died.

Without realizing it, Janna began whimpering softly with every shallow breath she took. Ty heard and realized that she wouldn't be able to lie still until the snake moved on in search of its normal evening meal of mice or young rabbit. She was terrified. In the grip of such mindless fear she might scream, and then the snake would be the least of their worries.

"Janna," Ty whispered urgently. "You'll be all right. Just lie still. I'll take care of it. Whatever happens, *don't move.*"

The increasingly violent trembling of Janna's body was her only answer.

Slowly Ty eased onto his right side, lifted himself on his elbow and reached to his waist for his sheath knife. The way he and Janna were lying, he had no choice except to use his left hand, but that fact didn't slow him down. The first thing the elder MacKenzie had taught his boys was that a left-handed knife fighter had an advantage in a brawl, and a two-handed fighter would win every time.

Ty's movements and Janna's trembling had made the snake freeze in place as it tried to decide whether the movement represented food or danger or simply a neutral presence such as the wind. In the dying light the motionless snake blended so well with its surroundings that Ty had a hard time seeing it. When he did, he swore silently.

It was a timber rattlesnake, and it was as thick around as his forearm. There would be enough venom stored up in that big mouth to kill a man, much less a girl the size of Janna.

When nothing came of Janna's quaking movements, the rattler lowered its head and continued on its evening hunt. The snake was so close that Ty could easily make out the flickering tongue and the triangular head darting from side to side with the forward motion of the coils. He could even distinguish the third "eye" that identified the deadly pit viper.

The rattlesnake's body made an odd rubbing-rustling sound as it progressed slowly along the length of Janna's pant leg. Ty watched with the poised patience of a predator, knowing that he had no choice but to wait for an opening. Until the snake's head was drawn away from Janna's body by the sinuous movements of reptilian coils, there was nothing Ty could do that the snake couldn't do quicker—and it would be Janna rather than Ty who suffered from any miscalculation on his part.

Speaking softly and reassuringly to Janna, telling her that there was nothing to fear, Ty waited until the snake's undulating forward motion finally pulled its head to the left, away from Janna's leg. Ty struck swiftly, cleanly, severing the rattlesnake's head from its body. Then he struck again with savage speed, using the knife point to pick up the deadly head and fling it far away from Janna. He grabbed the writhing coils and threw them away, as well. Then he went down beside Janna and pulled her into his arms.

"It's all right, little one," Ty whispered, holding her shaking body. "It's all right. The rattlesnake is dead."

The soothing rumble of Ty's voice and the gentle stroking of his hands over Janna's back calmed her more than his words. Unable to control the trembling of her own body, she clung to him, whispering incoherently about a water hole and a rattlesnake that had struck again and again, and the long days and nights before her father had finally died.

When Ty finally understood what Janna was saying, emotion went through him like a burst of dark lightning. He couldn't bear the thought of Janna alone with her dying father, watching him swell and blacken as the poison slowly destroyed his flesh. It could so easily have been her bedroll the snake had chosen, her tender skin pierced by fangs, her life draining away between labored breaths; and then Ty never would have known Janna, never held her, never breathed kisses over her tear-streaked face.

The realization of how close he had come to losing Janna caused a surge of emotion that was both tender and fierce. The thought of almost having been deprived of her presence made it impossible to deny himself the sweet luxury of holding her now.

The warmth and comfort of Ty's big hands rubbing slowly down Janna's back gradually penetrated her panic. His gentle, brushing kisses brought heat back to skin that had been chilled by fear. Turning her face up to his lips, she gave a long, shaky sigh and snuggled even closer to him, needing the reassurance of his body in a way that she couldn't put into words. Nor did she have to. He needed her physical proximity in the same way, the warm pressure of her body against his telling him that they both were alive and safe.

When Ty's arms tightened around Janna and he whispered her name, her hands crept up his chest to his stubble-roughened cheeks and beyond. Her fingers sought the thick black hair she longed to caress as she had in the days when he had been too ill to object to her touch. She slid her hands beneath his hat, dislodging it, and she shivered with pleasure when her fingers knew again the silky textures and fullness of his hair. She moved her hands slowly, flexing them gently, caressing him and the sensitive skin between her fingers at the same time.

The intimate, changing pressure of Janna's hands on Ty's scalp made his breath catch, break and emerge as an almost silent groan. He moved his head slowly, increasing the pressure of her caressing hands, and the sound he made seemed to Janna more like a purr from a very large cat than any noise a man might make. Smiling, she closed her eyes and concentrated on the delicious sensations radiating out from her hands to envelop her whole body.

Janna's small, almost secret smile was irresistible to Ty. Knowing he shouldn't, unable to help himself and no longer caring, he bent his head until he could trace the curve of her mouth with the tip of his tongue. The unexpected caress startled a soft cry from her.

"Hush," Ty breathed against her lips, moving his head slowly from side to side, gentling her with soft kisses. "You're all right, little one. You're safe with me. I won't let anything hurt you."

Janna parted her lips to explain that she wasn't frightened any longer, but the gentle glide of Ty's tongue into her mouth stole from her both the ability and the desire to speak. This was totally unlike the kiss he had given her before. His mouth was seductive rather than demanding, his tongue tempting rather than overwhelming. The sliding, hot, almost secret touches were unbearably sweet. Without realizing it, she began to return his caresses. At first the movements of her tongue were tentative, but when his arms tightened, bringing her even closer to his body, she knew that he was enjoying the kiss as much as she was.

Ty felt the hesitant touch of Janna's tongue as though it were a soft flame. The knowledge that she wasn't frightened of him both reassured Ty and tightened every muscle in his body with the anticipation and hunger that had been growing in him since he had first looked through a haze of pain into her clear, compassionate eyes. Even though he had been beaten, bloodied, half-dead with exhaustion, some elemental male level of awareness within himself had seen past her clothes and recognized the essential female presence beneath.

"Janna," Ty sighed. He nuzzled her lips, trying to part them again, knowing he shouldn't. He was too hungry, blood rushing too hotly, the aftermath of danger and adrenaline mixed wildly with his need of her. "Let me kiss you, really kiss you. It won't be like the other time. I won't hurt you," he whispered, licking her lips gently, feeling her tremble. "Do you trust me not to hurt you?"

The sweet glide of Ty's tongue over Janna's sensitized lips made her shiver again. She knew that her moment had finally arrived, the moment when she could get even with him for making fun of her lack of allure. He wanted her now. He couldn't deny it. It was there in the tension of his body, in his ragged breath, in the heat of his flesh hard against her hip.

Trembling, she breathed her answer into his mouth, tasting him. "I trust you."

With gentle, inevitable movements of his head, Ty fitted his mouth more deeply to Janna's. She felt herself tasted and enjoyed in the sensuous rhythm of penetration and retreat, advance and withdrawal, the cycle repeated endlessly, like flames dancing up from a campfire. Each caressing movement of their joined mouths brought more and more pleasure until her whole body trembled in anticipation of the next touch, the next intimate tasting, the next languid tangling of warm tongues.

Heat stole beneath Janna's skin, flushing her face, shortening her breath. Bubbles of sensation grew slowly inside her, expanding with each warm movement of Ty's tongue until she shivered and a bubble burst, drenching her with golden heat; and then pleasure gathered again, burst sweetly, made her shiver and moan Ty's name. The slender hands buried in Ty's hair flexed and relaxed in the same rhythms of Janna's tongue—seeking, stroking, finding, mating with the slow, deep motions he had taught her.

The sensuous, searching caresses brought a violent hardening of Ty's flesh that both shocked and dismayed him, telling him that he was very close to the edge of his self-control. With an effort he turned aside from Janna's mouth.

"Little one," he whispered, grabbing her hands, stilling them. "Don't."

When Janna felt Ty's withdrawal, she was unable to control a soft cry of protest. "I thought—I thought you wanted—"

Her voice broke. She didn't try to speak again; the loss of his warmth was devastating to her. Even the hushed light of dusk couldn't conceal the hurt twisting through her at his abrupt rejection. Just as she gathered herself to turn away from him, he shifted his hands and pinned her in place.

"Hell yes, I want you!" Ty whispered fiercely, looming over Janna. "I want your hands all over me. I want to take off your clothes and put my hands all over you, and then I want to open your legs and slide into that soft body of yours and feel you take every bit of me. I want it so much I couldn't stand up straight right now to save my soul."

The look of stunned disbelief on Janna's face made Ty want to laugh and swear at the same time.

"Can't you feel me shaking?" he demanded, barely remembering to keep his voice low. "Do you think it's because of that fool snake? Hell, I've eaten bigger snakes than that and looked around for seconds. It's you that's making me shake. You've been driving me crazy since I first came to after hiding from Cascabel and saw your beautiful gray eyes watching me."

"You th-thought I was a boy," Janna accused in a low voice.

"I thought you were too damned sexy, girl *or* boy, because my britches had a better grip on the truth than my eyes did. My eyes kept telling me that you were a boy and I was some kind of crazy to get all hot and bothered when you touched me. My britches kept telling me that you were as female as they come and I was some kind of moron not to peel off your clothes and get better acquainted."

The hands that had been tightly gripping Janna eased and began rubbing her shoulders with gentle, circular motions.

"I know you've been hurt in the past," Ty said, his voice low, carrying no farther than her ears. "And I want you so bad that I can't even think, but I would cut off my fingers rather than hurt you. And the way you were kissing me..." He closed his eyes as a sensual echo resonated through his body, tightening his loins until he had to clench his teeth against the bittersweet ache. "Do you want me, little one?"

Janna tried to speak but she had no breath. Her heart was wedged in her throat, blocking the passage of air. Seeing Ty's need turned her inside out. She wanted to hold his head against her body and comb her fingers soothingly through his hair; and she wanted to kiss and be kissed again, teasing his tongue with her own and tasting him in a slow, secret kind of dance that made pleasure expand and softly burst deep within her body. Her need to experience that again was so great it was pain.

Was that what was drawing Ty's face into taut lines? Did he feel the same aching need?

"Ty?" she whispered.

His eyes opened. In the fading light they were a green as deep as the forest itself.

"I..." Janna's voice died. She licked her lips and felt the sudden tension in Ty's body as his glance followed her tongue. "Did you like kissing me?"

Ty almost laughed in the instant before he remembered that any knowledge Janna had of men was brief and brutal.

"Yes," Ty murmured, brushing his open mouth over hers. "I liked it. Did you?"

He felt her breath hesitate, catch, then flow over his face in a sweet sigh of agreement. Smiling, he gently caught her lower lip between his teeth, testing the warmth and resilience of her flesh. She went very still in the instant before she trembled and made a small sound.

"I'm sorry," Ty said, releasing her. "I didn't mean to frighten you."

"You didn't," Janna said quickly. "I don't know what's wrong. It just felt so good it made something burst inside me and I went all shivery. I'm sorry."

Ty's breath caught and his eyes narrowed in sensual response to her words. Whatever might have happened to Janna in the past, she was a total innocent when it came to the pleasure a woman could find in the arms of a loving man. The thought of teaching Janna the secrets hidden within her body made Ty feel hot, heavy, thoroughly masculine.

"Don't be sorry," he said huskily. "I like knowing that I've pleased you."

"You do?" she whispered, looking at his lips, wanting to taste him again, to feel his tongue moving within her mouth.

"Yes." Ty smiled and nuzzled the slanting line of Janna's cheekbones until he came to the silky edge of her hair. He stripped off her hat and headband, untied the rawhide thongs holding her braids and unraveled them until his hands were full of the cool fire of her hair. He made an inarticulate sound of pleasure as he searched blindly with his mouth for the tempting curves of her ear. "I want to please you, little one. Will you tell me if I do?"

"Y-yes."

"Yes," Ty breathed as he found Janna's ear with the tip of his tongue, teased the rim and then penetrated the hidden, sensitive core.

Frissons of pleasure tightened Janna's skin, sending telltale parades of goose bumps up and down her arms. She made a startled sound and her hands tightened on Ty's shirt in sensual reflex. When his tongue repeated the penetration again and then again, she felt a sensation like wires tightening deep within her body, making her feel languid and restless at the same time.

"More?" Ty whispered, biting Janna's ear delicately.

He felt her helpless shiver of response and his lips shifted into a very masculine smile of approval and triumph. Before she could speak he softly devoured her ear, his tongue pressing into its core with the same rhythmic movements that had made pleasure swell and burst within her before. Her husky, barely audible moan made him feel as though he were being bathed in golden fire.

With a swift movement of his head Ty captured Janna's mouth. There was no surprise this time when his tongue slid between her teeth, filling her mouth with the taste and feel and textures of his hungry kiss. She answered him by spearing her fingers into his hair and holding his mouth hard upon her own, moaning softly at the sensual heat of him, wanting to take that heat within her own body. The rhythmic caress of tongue against tongue was reinforced by the unconscious movements of her body against his as she tried to ease the heaviness and aching that had condensed in her tightly bound breasts and between her restless legs.

Making a sound halfway between a curse and a prayer, Ty gently disengaged from Janna's hot embrace.

"Before you ask," he said, breathing quickly, audibly, keeping his voice low, "I liked having your body rubbing over mine. I liked it too damn much. I don't want to hurt you, little one. That means we have to take it slow for a bit longer, until you're ready." He closed his eyes and wondered how the hell he would manage it. "Which means that you'll have to give me a minute or two to catch my breath."

"Can I talk while you breathe?" she asked hesitantly, keeping her voice as low as his.

Ty laughed softly despite the savage ache between his legs. Leaning down, he brushed his lips over Janna's mouth, tasting her with a single quick stroke of his tongue before straightening and smiling down at her.

"What do you want to talk about?" he murmured.

"I wish it were darker. Then you wouldn't see me blush when I ask you."

"I'm glad it isn't darker," Ty whispered, nibbling on her chin. "I want to see you, blushes and all. Especially the 'all.' What's your question?"

"Will it—will you hurt me?"

"Oh, God," Ty whispered, gathering Janna into his arms and rocking her gently against his body. "No, little one," he said, kissing her hair, her ear, her flushed cheek, her eyelids, her lips, butterfly brushes that reassured her as no words could have. "If I go slow and you try to relax and not be afraid, it won't hurt you at all. And I'll go slow, Janna. I'll go slow if it kills me."

Slowly her arms came up and around his neck. She pressed her face against the hot skin at the opening of Ty's shirt.

"Will going slow spoil it for you?" Janna whispered. "I don't want to make it bad for you. I want to please you, Ty. I want that so much I ache."

"Going slow won't spoil it. In fact, it can make it so good you feel like dying."

"It can?"

Janna's voice was husky with the conflicting emotions racing through her, passion and nervousness and a hunger to touch and be touched that was completely new to her.

"It can," Ty said. "At least, that's what I'm told. I've never known that kind of pleasure myself."

Janna tried to speak but had no voice. She licked her lips and tilted her head back until she could look into the darkly luminous green of Ty's eyes.

"I want to pleasure you like that," she whispered. "Will you teach me how?"

Chapter Twenty-One

The husky intensity of Janna's voice and her honesty made Ty want to ravish and cherish her in the same instant. The thought of teaching her how to tease and ease and pleasure him was more heady than any liquor he had ever drunk. He traced the lines of her face with his fingertips before caressing the taut curve of her neck and the warm flesh inside her collar. Inevitably his fingers found and undid the first button of her shirt. He bent and pressed his lips against the pulse beating rapidly just beneath her skin.

"Janna," Ty said, breathing her name as much as saying it, "I hope to God I can set fire to you half as hot as you set fire to me. If I can, we'll burn down the whole damn plateau."

"Is that—is that good?"

"Ask me tomorrow," he said, barely stifling a groan as he felt the leap and quickening of her pulse at the touch of his tongue.

Then Ty could deny himself no longer the minor consummation of Janna's mouth. He kissed her slowly, deeply, hungrily, as he finished unbuttoning her shirt. When the cloth parted he expected to find the warmth of her flesh beneath. Instead he found thick layers of fabric and no buttons at all. Even after he took Janna's arms out of the sleeves of her shirt, he could see no way of removing the layers of cloth that bound her.

"What the hell?" muttered Ty.

Belatedly Janna realized that her shirt was unbuttoned and Ty was looking at the wrapping she used to flatten her breasts, disguising her feminine outline.

"Do you sew yourself into that thing?" Ty asked, giving her a crooked smile that made her toes curl.

Janna laughed helplessly, torn between embarrassment and the delicious feeling of having Ty's hands caressing her bare arms. His palms stroked her from her wrists to her shoulders, caressing her inner arms with his long fingers. As he softly probed, he discovered the place beneath her left arm where she tucked in the tail of the cloth, securing the wrapping.

"So that's how you do it."

Pulling the end of the cloth free, Ty turned it back upon itself several times, rolling it loosely. When he had unrolled the fabric across her chest and under her other arm, he put his hand just below Janna's shoulder blades and arched her back enough that he could reach beneath, continuing the slow unwrapping.

With each complete circuit of her body, an inch of previously hidden skin was revealed. Both the cloth and her skin had an elusive fragrance that was a compound of herbs and wildflowers and warm femininity that made his head spin. When he could bear it no longer, he bent and kissed the smooth band of flesh he had just unwrapped.

The feel of Ty's lips skimming below her collarbone made Janna tremble. She slid her hands into his thick hair and rubbed his scalp, smiling when she felt the answering movement of his response. After a few moments the temptation of her still-covered breasts overcame Ty and he resumed unwrapping the long length of cloth.

Gradually the pressure of Janna's bindings eased as more and more layers of fabric were removed. As always, the relief was exquisite. She arched her back, trying to make the unwrapping go more quickly, eager to be able to breathe easily once more, to be free of the cloth restraints.

Ty refused to be rushed, for he was finding an unexpected, intensely sensual pleasure in the slow revelation of Janna's body. As the turns of fabric moved down her chest, the first curves of her breasts were unveiled. There were long lines of red pressed into her skin, legacy of the tight bindings. He smoothed his thumb over the lines as though to erase them, then brushed his lips over the marks and traced them with the tip of his tongue.

Eyes closed, Janna made soft sounds of pleasure as Ty soothed her skin. She was still breathless from the unexpected caress of his tongue when he arched her back, lifting her so that the cloth could unwind beneath her. He circled her body once and then twice, three times; and then the unwrapping stopped again. But instead of gently lowering her to the ground as he had before, he held her suspended over his powerful forearm, the graceful line of her back like a drawn bow. Slowly Janna opened her eyes and saw Ty staring at her as though what he saw was totally unexpected.

And it was. He never would have guessed at the presence of full, firm curves and lush pink tips hidden beneath turn after turn of tight cloth.

"Ty?" Janna whispered, not understanding why he was so still, so intent. "What's wrong?"

He looked up and her eyes widened at the harsh lines of his face.

"Don't ever," Ty said distinctly, "punish yourself like that again."

Before Janna could speak he bent over her breasts and soothed each mark that had been left by the cloth, working from the first smooth swell of flesh toward the deep pink crowns. The feel of his tongue laving the small marks the bindings had left was indescribable. She wanted to twist slowly in his arms like a flame, offering every bit of her breasts to his mouth. When he came to the margin between the satin of her skin and the velvet of her nipple, he circled her with exquisite care, ignoring her startled cry and her broken breath and the fingers tightening reflexively in his hair.

And then Ty could bear the temptation no longer. He took Janna's offering into his mouth, sucking on the velvet nipple until it was tight and hard, and still he tugged on her with slow, sensual rhythms that made small cries ripple from her.

When the nipple could be drawn out no more, he slowly released it, admiring the taut, glistening peak. He cupped the breast in his hand and made tight circles with his palm, rubbing the hard nipple as he bent and caressed her other breast with lips and tongue, drawing her out, shaping her, pulling sensuously until her breath was quick and broken with the lightning strokes of sensation streaking through her body.

Dizzy, breathless, lost in a hushed, shimmering world she had never known existed, Janna felt pleasure expand and burst and radiate through her. Ty felt it too, the flush of sensual heat spreading beneath her skin, the small movements of her hips as she sought the pressure of his body, the tiny cries when his teeth and tongue brought new heat to her.

Finally Ty lifted his head, releasing the nipple he had so lovingly shaped. Janna whimpered very softly, wanting more of the pleasure that had grown in her with each movement of his mouth. She opened her gray eyes and looked at him with silent pleading.

"More?" Ty asked, smiling, his voice as heavy as the blood beating in his veins.

Janna shivered helplessly as Ty's hand closed over one of her breasts and slowly pleasured her.

"Yes," she whispered.

He smiled, enjoying her open pleasure and the growing flush of arousal beneath her skin. "Where else would you like to be kissed?"

The shocked look that came to Janna's face told Ty that she had never thought about such things.

"Never mind, little one," Ty said. He circled the erect tip of each breast with his tongue and whispered, "I'll think of something."

With a speed and power that surprised Janna, Ty turned and lay on his back and in the same movement lifted her, pulling her over his body like a living blanket. When her hips pressed against the hard ridge of flesh that waited impatiently beneath the thick cloth of his pants, he made a low sound of pleasure-pain.

Not understanding, Janna pulled away. Ty's legs parted and her own legs sank between his. He moved quickly, lifting his legs just enough to trap hers beneath, twining his legs with hers at the ankles, forcing their bodies into an intimate match, hard against soft, consummation no more than a few layers of cloth away.

"Unbutton my shirt," Ty said in a thick voice. "You'll like the feel of my bare skin against your breasts. And so will I."

The slight movement of Janna's body when she reached for Ty's collar button made her hips rock against the hot cradle he had made for her between his legs. He groaned in a kind of exquisite agony, for he had never needed a woman so much as he needed Janna at that instant.

"Again," he whispered. "Move against me just once more. Just once."

Hesitantly Janna moved her hips against Ty again, feeling the hard bulge of his erection like a brand against her abdomen. The sound he made deep in his throat could have come from agony or undiluted pleasure. His hand came between their bodies. Unerringly he found the most sensitive part of her and pressed, rocking his hips slowly beneath her. The sudden heat that radiated out from his hand made her gasp. His name came from her lips in a husky, urgent, questioning cry.

"Yes," Ty said, his voice low and thick. "You can feel it, too, can't you?" Gently he released Janna's ankles and lifted her into a sitting position astride his waist. Her breath caught and her hips moved helplessly as he teased her nipples again with his fingertips. "It's going to be good. It's going to be so damn good. Unbutton my shirt, sugar. I want to feel your hands on my bare skin.''

With fingers that trembled, Janna undid the buttons on Ty's shirt. She had seen him naked before, but it hadn't affected her one-tenth as much as watching his powerful body emerge from the shirt. In the dusk, the curling pelt of black hair was very distinct, as was the dark center line of his body where the hair narrowed to pencil width and vanished behind his belt. The heat and resilience of him were as alluring as his dark smile. With catlike pleasure Janna kneaded the muscular flesh she had so often bathed or medicated but had never caressed.

And she had wanted to. She realized that now. She understood that her hands had quivered to know every texture of Ty, the satin smoothness where skin stretched over muscle, the power inherent in him, the thick silk of his chest hair, the finer silk of the hair beneath his arms, the flat disk and hard nubbin of his nipples. Just as she had become lost in the discovery of her own body beneath his mouth, she became lost in the discovery of his body beneath her hands.

Ty watched Janna through eyes narrowed with passion. Her transparent pleasure in exploring his body was violently exciting to him. It was unlike anything he had ever known. It put him on an exquisite rack, which pulled him in two conflicting directions. Part of him wanted to grab Janna and thrust into her and end the pulsing ache of his body.

And part of him wanted to keep his hands off her and learn more about himself and her and the sweet torment of being suspended between anticipation and ecstasy.

Again and again Janna's fingers combed through the hair covering Ty's chest, tracing his nipples and then following the quickly narrowing pelt down to the cold of his belt buckle. She knew that slim line of hair would continue down his body for a hand span and then radiate out into a thick, curling thatch. She wanted to see that too, to run her hands over him without any boundaries on the touching. She wanted that so much she couldn't breathe.

Not stopping to think or to question, Janna reached for Ty's belt buckle.

"Not yet," he said huskily, grabbing Janna's hands and pulling them back up to the safer territory of his chest. "It will be too quick that way. I want to enjoy you first."

"I thought you had enjoyed me," she whispered, bending to kiss his hands.

His smile made her heart turn over. "Just part of you, sugar. There's some very sweet territory I haven't unwrapped yet, much less enjoyed."

Ty reversed their positions with one of the swift, powerful movements that always caught Janna off guard but no longer frightened her. Whatever came next, she was certain Ty would be careful with her. She lay quietly, watching him as he knelt at her feet and removed her knee-high moccasins and his own boots with quick motions. He tugged open his belt but left his pants untouched. When he unfastened Janna's belt she trembled.

"It's all right," Ty said, kissing Janna's lips. "I won't hurt you."

Janna took a shaky breath and nodded. "I know. It's just…''

Before she could explain that she had never been naked in front of anyone, it was too late. Her ability to speak deserted her as leather slipped from the buckle with an easy movement of Ty's hand. Without the belt, her oversize men's pants slid easily from her body, and with them her underpants.

When Janna lay completely nude before Ty, his breath came out in a slow, unraveling groan.

"It's like seeing a satin butterfly emerge from a mud cocoon," Ty whispered, running his fingertips over the pale curves and velvet shadows of Janna's body.

When he reached the dark delta at the base of her torso, she made a surprised sound and moved as though to evade his hand, pressing her legs together reflexively.

"Hush, little one," Ty murmured, kissing her lips. "I know you've been hurt there but I won't hurt you. I know how delicate you are, how soft, how warm. Even you don't know how soft you can be or how warm. Let me show you."

"What d-do you want me to do?" Janna's voice broke as she shivered in a combination of nervousness and surprise at the presence of Ty's fingers searching gently through the dense triangle of hair that shielded her most sensitive flesh.

"Don't be so stiff. I won't hurt you," Ty murmured. He kissed Janna coaxingly until her lips parted and he could love her with slow, deep strokes of his tongue. He lifted his mouth and whispered against her lips. "Open your legs just a little, sugar, just a little. I'll be very gentle."

His voice became a husky sigh of triumph and discovery when Janna relaxed enough to allow his fingertip to skim over the soft, hot folds between her legs.

"Just a little more," Ty whispered, caressing her, seeking the heated well of her femininity, finding just its soft, burning edges. But it was enough. It told him that her blood was running as hotly and hungrily as his own. He probed lightly and was rewarded by a hint of the smooth, sultry sheath that awaited him. "My beautiful satin butterfly," he said huskily. "So hot, so sleek. Open a little more for me, butterfly. I won't force you. I just want to love all of you. Let me..."

Janna tried to speak but her voice broke over Ty's name. The gliding, skimming caress of his finger had changed into a gentle penetration that took her breath away. He bent to her mouth and his tongue echoed the tender movements of his hand between her legs. The heat and tension that had been gathering deep within her body flared suddenly, wildly, claiming her in a gentle convulsion that took her wholly by surprise.

But not Ty. He had been coaxing Janna toward just such a minor peak of ecstasy since he had first discovered the sensuality hidden within her body. He repeated the twin, gentle assaults on her body, his tongue gliding over hers in a deep kiss as his finger slid between her legs in a slow, teasing dance of penetration and withdrawal that brought soft whimpers from her throat. Passion shimmered and burst within her again, heat and pleasure overflowing.

Janna moaned softly as Ty withdrew from her sultry center and caressed the bud of her passion with fingertips still slick from her own response. Heat speared through her, tightening her body. She cried out into his mouth and her hips moved beneath his hand, asking for something she had never known. She sensed his hesitation, felt as much as heard him groan, and bit back a cry of protest when he withdrew his caressing hand.

"Hush, little one," Ty murmured, freeing himself of his clothes in a few swift movements. "It won't be long."

"Ty?"

"I'm right here," he said, gently pressing Janna's legs farther apart, making room for himself.

Delicately he teased the nub he had coaxed from her soft, humid folds. She trembled and her knees flexed instinctively, allowing him greater access to her body. Her passionate response spilled over him as he probed her softness with his own aching flesh. The moist, welcoming heat of her body was unmistakable, a silent command that he come deeply within her; but she was so tight that he was afraid of hurting her.

Shivering with the harshness of his self-imposed restraint, Ty began taking Janna as gradually as evening took the day. Her eyes opened in sensual surprise and she looked up into the face of the man who was slowly, so slowly, becoming part of her. Each time the pressure of him within her became almost painful, he sensed it, withdrew and gradually came to her again.

The exquisitely gentle penetration made waves of heat gather and burst within her, showering him with her pleasure. She heard him groan and push more deeply inside and then felt the harsh tension shaking his body as he forced himself to stop.

"You're a virgin!"

Chapter Twenty-Two

Ty's accusing voice was hoarse as he fought against his deepest needs and tried to force himself to retreat from Janna's moist, clinging heat. But he couldn't. He wanted only to continue taking her a bit at a time; and when he caressed her to ecstasy once more he wanted to thrust past the frail barrier separating their bodies from total unity. She would feel no pain at the instant he took her because she would be too deeply enmeshed in her climax to know or care that for the first time in her life a man would be fully sheathed within her.

Virgin.

"Christ," Ty groaned, "if I'd known, I never would have touched you."

"Then I'm glad you didn't know," Janna said huskily. She shivered and melted over him again, moving her hips helplessly, in the grip of a passion she had never expected and had no idea how to control. All she wanted was more of him, more of the sweet friction as she stretched around him. "I want this, Ty. Please. You're not hurting me. I love...feeling you." She moved her hips slowly, caressing him and herself in the same motion. "Oh, that's so good," she whispered raggedly, rocking, moving as much as he would allow, "but it's not enough...not...enough."

"Stop it!" Ty said roughly as he felt the last shreds of his self-control slipping away. "You're a virgin!"

Janna's nails dug into the flexed power of Ty's buttocks and her body twisted wildly beneath his as she whispered again and again that what he had given her was good but not enough. With each movement she became more seductive, more demanding, more welcoming, so hot and sleek that he found himself pressing again and yet again at the fragile flesh that barred total consummation.

Ty groaned and forced himself to move just slightly while his fingers sought and claimed the slick, delicate nub of Janna's passion. He controlled the instinctive rocking of her hips by settling more of his weight between her legs, pinning her in place while he caressed her, bringing her closer and closer to ecstasy.

When he felt the sudden mist of passion flush her skin and her breath broke and her cries came quickly, rising urgently, he covered her mouth with his own and began to move again within her, trying to hold back from the elemental consummation that awaited him in the depths of her virginal body. A groan racked him as he thought what it would be like to sheathe every bit of his need in her, to pierce her virginity and feel her pleasure flow over him in a hot, ecstatic rain.

And then it was happening, the hot rain and the sheathing, ecstasy bursting with each movement of Ty's hips; and Janna wept at the perfection as he let go of control and locked himself so deeply within her that she felt the certainty of his climax as the most intimate kind of caress, a pulsing presence that sent her spinning into ecstasy once again, her body caressing him rhythmically in the quivering aftermath of his own release.

Janna's tiny, ecstatic cries pierced Ty like golden needles, reaching past the flesh to the soul beneath. Violent pleasure racked him until his muscles stood out like iron. The endless, shuddering release that followed overwhelmed him. Unable to see, unable to think, unable to speak, he spent himself again and again in the virgin who had touched a part of him no other woman ever had.

When Ty was at last quiet once more, Janna clung to his powerful, sweat-slicked body, savoring the intimacy of lying beneath him and feeling him inside her as evening condensed soundlessly into night around them. She hadn't known what to expect from the act of love, but she hadn't anticipated anything so hot, so sweet, so violently complete.

"I love you," Janna whispered, kissing Ty's shoulder.

The words were very soft, barely a whisper, but Ty heard them. A combination of guilt and anger raced through him when he remembered the irrevocable instant when he had taken Janna's virginity. Silently he raged at himself and his baffling lack of control where she was concerned. He had been able to keep himself tightly reined while he seduced her, yet he hadn't been able to pull back after he had discovered she was a virgin.

He didn't understand that. He should have been able to turn away from her; she wasn't the first woman to try that particular marital trap. He had eluded the others in the past, and those girls had been much more accomplished in their snares and lures.

But Janna had been a handful of fire and beauty, and her ecstatic cries as he pierced her virginity would haunt Ty until he died.

"I never should have taken you," he said in a low, bitter voice.

Janna's gently stroking hands became still. "Why?"

"Because I discovered that you were a virgin and I had no intention of marrying you, that's why. But I had a lot of help getting past your innocence, didn't I? First you tell me you're not a virgin—"

"I never said that," Janna interrupted in a fierce whisper.

"What about when you ran and I brought you down and kissed you too hard, and you said you'd taken a lot worse from men and survived?"

"I only meant that you hadn't really hurt me. And you hadn't."

"What about Joe Troon?"

"What about him?"

"Ned said that Troon 'kept' you for a while."

"Ned is a drunk and a liar. Troon caught me but he never kept me."

"Well, sugar, you sure as hell didn't act like any virgin I'd ever met. Ever since I came to after Cascabel's gauntlet you've been rubbing up against me and sighing and smiling and looking at me out of those smoky gray eyes like I'd spilled honey in my lap and you couldn't wait to lick off every bit of it," Ty said in a low, angry voice. "It would have served you right if I'd backed you up against a tree, opened my pants and had you standing up like the lowest kind of camp follower.''

Janna thought of the ways she had tormented Ty without truly understanding the elemental force of his need...and her own. The thought of how often she had smiled when he had turned away to hide the evidence of his arousal made her ashamed now.

"I'm so sorry," Janna said, touching Ty's face tentatively. "I didn't know what I was doing to you. I didn't know the power of what you were fighting, how much you needed me."

"It was a woman I needed, not you," snarled Ty, jerking away from Janna's gentle touch.

All the movement accomplished was to remind him that he was still held within the satin sheath of her body; and she felt even better now than in his hottest memories. He told himself to roll aside, to separate himself from her, but his body refused to respond. He was drinking her heat, growing inside her, and his blood was beating heavily, urging his hips to move in primal rhythms.

"Virgin," Ty said, and it was a curse. "But you wanted it as much as I did, didn't you? Hell, you damn near burned me alive with your cries and your hips sliding, pushing me deeper and deeper..."

Ty shuddered unexpectedly, memories bursting inside him, sensuality lancing through his body, tightening him, making him feel every bit of the hot perfection of being locked inside Janna.

The knowledge of his own helpless response to her shocked Ty. He shouldn't feel this way. The sweat wasn't dry on his body from the first time he had taken her. He shouldn't want her again the way he did right now— need knotting his guts, his body hard and heavy and hot, filled to bursting once more.

He fought to remain still, not to respond, not to move, but the knowledge of the ecstatic consummation he would find within Janna's body was too new, too overwhelming for him to deny or control it. With a low, raw cry, he fought against the lure of her, but even as he cried out he was moving slowly, surrendering himself to her one hard inch at a time.

Janna's breath caught as Ty deliberately measured himself within her once, then twice, then three times. She didn't understand his rejection of her apology or his anger with her, but she understood the need that was making him tremble; it was her own need, doubling and redoubling with each heartbeat, a flame burning up from their joined bodies, heat delicately melting and ravenously devouring her at the same time. She shivered and arched beneath him in sensual abandon.

Ty groaned and felt fire eat ever more deeply into him, burning away thought, burning away reluctance, leaving only the elemental union of male and female, a joining that was deeper than flesh, hotter than desire, two living flames leaping higher as they touched, overlapped, entwined. He swore in a mingling of awe and savage triumph as he felt his lover's fluid grace rise to match his own savage need.

"Satin...butterfly," Ty said hoarsely, more accusation than affection in his voice. "Did you think that I'd marry you once I found what it was like to have you?"

He thrust his tongue into Janna's mouth, muffling whatever her answer might have been. Before the kiss ended she was moaning softly and moving in languid counterpart to the slow, circular dance of his hips.

"It won't work," he said, his breath coming quickly, heavily. "I'll take every bit of your body. I'll give you every bit of my body in return. But that's all. Just two bodies giving and taking. Do you hear me?"

Janna moaned brokenly and closed herself around him in a deep, instinctive caress.

"Do you hear me?" Ty demanded, clenching himself against the unbearable seduction of her body.

"Yes," she whispered. Her hips lifted slightly, then circled, seducing him, loving him. "I heard you the first time you told me in the valley."

"What?"

Ty's past words echoed cruelly within Janna's mind: *I'll have my silken lady or I'll have none at all for longer than it takes to pleasure myself.*

"I know that I'm not the silken lady of your dreams," Janna said, her voice a whisper of unquenchable hope and a foretaste of despair. "You're pleasuring yourself. That's all."

Ty didn't argue or protest her words.

Janna had expected no more, yet she had to bite her lip not to protest aloud the emotions tearing through her, passion and grief and the shivering precursors of wild ecstasy. When Ty moved within her again, she wept silently, grateful that it was too dark for him to see her tears, feeling his breath as cool, quickening gusts over her wet cheeks.

"But you still want me?" Ty persisted. "No games, no secret plans, no regrets?" He locked their bodies together suddenly, a joining so deep and hot and complete that it tore a low cry from his throat, a cry that was her name. He rocked against her with tiny, intense motions, burning up, buried in fire and wanting it, all of it, *burning*. "Do you still want this?"

"I want..." Janna whispered, but could say no more because tears drowned her voice and the truth was too bitter to speak aloud. She wanted to be loved by him in all ways, not just one.

"Janna?" Ty asked, holding himself motionless but for the helpless shuddering of his aroused body. "Answer me!"

She tried to move, to take from him what he was withholding. It was impossible. He was too strong, too skilled, and she loved him.

"Yes, damn you," she whispered achingly. "Yes!"

Ty heard only the agreement, not the pain. He let out his pent breath in a ragged groan.

"I need you," he said in a low voice. His hips began to move in quickening rhythms as shudder after shudder of tension went through his powerful body. "God help me, I've never needed any woman like this."

Janna heard the bafflement and strain in Ty's voice and felt herself swept up in his overwhelming need. Crying silently, loving him and knowing that he would love no one but the silken lady of his dreams, Janna took all that Ty could give to her of himself and in return gave all of herself that he would take.

The sensual generosity of Janna's response washed over Ty, bathing both of them in fire. She heard his broken groan, felt the power of him within her redouble, felt the hungry, rhythmic penetration as his body drove against hers again and again and again. His urgency excited her, overwhelmed her, shattered her, and still he moved hard within her, drinking her rippling cries, rocking, rocking, rocking…burning, she was burning and there was no end to the wild, consuming flames.

Janna's breath broke and a low cry was torn from her throat as she surrendered to savage ecstasy. Ty drank that cry and silently asked more of her, fierce in his demands of her body, wanting something he couldn't name, driving into her as though she were the last woman he would ever have, wanting at some deep, inarticulate level of his consciousness to leave his imprint upon her very soul.

Her legs twisted around his waist and her body shivered, her mouth bit into his, her nails scored his back; and he smiled and spoke dark words to her as he slipped his arms beneath her knees and slowly pulled her legs up his body, over his shoulders, opening her to him fully.

With deep, shuddering pleasure Ty drove again and again into the satin heat of Janna's body, smothering her abandoned cries with his mouth, penetrating her completely, repeatedly, powerfully, until she was racked by ecstasy; and still his potent movements continued, as though he would become a part of her or die in the effort. She thought she could know no greater pleasure without dying, and she tried to tell him but suddenly she had no voice, no will, for she was transfixed by a savage rapture.

Janna would have screamed her pleasure then, heedless of the danger, but Ty's mouth was consuming hers. He took the ecstatic scream into himself as passionate convulsions swept his body, burning him to his soul, ecstasy racking him with every heartbeat.

And he thought he was dying as he poured himself into her wildly shivering, welcoming body.

Chapter Twenty-Three

Utterly spent, Ty groaned softly and laid his head next to Janna's. He kissed her very gently, feeling an almost overwhelming tenderness toward the woman who had accepted him without restraint or regret or promises, bringing him the most intense, consuming union he had ever known.

When his lips brushed her cheek he tasted tears. The thought that his ecstasy had caused Janna hurt made pain lance harshly through Ty, an agony as surprising to him as the endless, hot, violent upwelling of his need for her had been.

"I'm sorry," Ty said, kissing Janna's face blindly, gently, finding everywhere the taste of tears. "Little one, I'm sorry. I didn't mean to hurt you."

Janna tried to answer but could not, for emotion had closed her throat.

Ty held her, rocking her in his arms, hating himself for hurting the girl who had saved his life at such great risk to her own.

"I owe you so much more than this..." he whispered, and he was haunted by the silken lady of whom he had dreamed so long, the wife who would be the greatest adornment of the life he would build to replace what war had taken away. "Oh God, what have I done to you, to myself?"

Janna shook her head silently, fighting for control of herself, not understanding what had caused the pain in Ty's voice. After a few moments she was able to speak.

"You didn't hurt me."

"Like hell I didn't."

"Ty, you didn't. I felt nothing but pleasure."

He heard Janna's words, felt her hands stroking his hair, soothing him, and felt a cold rush of self-contempt. He had wanted her, he had taken her despite her innocence, and in doing so he had left her suited only for the life of a prostitute or a nun.

"You're so innocent. My God, you don't even understand what has happened, do you?"

"I understand that you didn't hurt me."

"I didn't hurt..." Ty's laughter was low and as harsh as the guilt clawing at him. His hands tightened on Janna as he realized the extent of his folly. "You little fool, I ruined you! You have no family, no profession, no wealth. All you had of value for a husband was your virginity, and now that's gone. I've left you suited to be nothing except a man's mistress, but you lack the social graces for even that profession. You'll end up locked in a nun's cage or you'll be the toy of many men, not one."

Janna flinched and tried to draw away from Ty's cruel summation of her value as a woman, a mate, but she was too securely held to retreat. He drew her closer, not even noticing her futile attempts to free herself from his embrace.

"Never mind, little one," Ty said, his voice low and empty, echoing with despair at the death of his personal dream, the silken lady who now would forever be beyond his reach. "It was my fault, not yours. I'll marry you as soon as we get to the fort."

It took Janna a minute to absorb what he had said, what he had implied—and when she understood, she was wild with hurt.

"Like burning hell you'll marry me," Janna said in a low, savage voice.

"What?"

"I may be suited only to be a saloon girl, but I keep my word."

"Janna, I didn't mean—" Ty began, only to be cut off.

"No! I said that I wouldn't ask for any promises or have any regrets or any secret plans," she whispered angrily, telling herself that hopes weren't the same as plans.

Not that it mattered. Ty had taken care of the hopes, as well. *No family. No profession. No wealth. No social graces.* And no emotion in his voice but guilt and despair and anger at being trapped into marrying such a poor specimen of femininity.

"I've never trapped a living thing in my life," she said fiercely, "and I'll be damned to hell for eternity if I take your freedom now. Do you hear me, Tyrell MacKenzie? Do you?"

"You didn't take my freedom. I gave it away the same way men always have, thinking with my crotch instead of my brain."

"You can have it right back—freedom, brain, crotch, all of it! I want nothing that isn't freely given."

"The world doesn't work that way, sugar," Ty said wearily, releasing Janna and rolling over onto his back. "The only virgin a decent man takes is the girl who becomes his wife. We'll be married as soon as—"

"They'll be picking cotton in hell before I marry you," Janna interrupted, her voice shaking, her body cold and empty without him.

It was as though Ty hadn't heard. "I'm responsible for you. I live up to my responsibilities."

"I'm responsible for myself. I've lived on my own for five years. I can do it for another—"

"Christ!" hissed Ty, cutting Janna off. "Are you so naive that you don't know you could get pregnant after this? How would you take care of yourself, much less a baby, too?" He waited, but there was no answer except the small sounds Janna made as she searched for her clothes in the darkness. "We'll be married at the fort and you'll stay there while I hunt for Lucifer."

"No."

"Janna—oh, the hell with it," Ty whispered harshly. "We'll be married at the fort and then we'll hunt Lucifer together. Does that satisfy you?"

"No."

Janna thrust an arm through a shirtsleeve and fished around for the other opening. Even if it hadn't been dark, the tears streaming down her face would have blinded her. None of her emotions showed in her constrained whisper, for which she was grateful. Having marriage offered to her out of guilt was bad enough; having it offered to her out of pity would be unbearable.

"Janna, be reasonable. I'll need Lucifer to build a good horse herd," Ty said as patiently as he could manage. "Otherwise I'll have no way to take care of my family."

"I said I'd help you catch Lucifer and I will. Marriage was no part of the bargain."

Ty's patience evaporated. With uncanny speed he grabbed Janna, flattened her beneath him once more and began whispering furiously.

"Listen to me, you little fool. You have no idea how the world works."

"Then teach me," she whispered defiantly. "Teach me how to please a man, how to be good enough to be a mistress rather than a whore. That's all I ask of you. Education, not marriage."

"But if you're preg—" he began.

"I stopped bleeding two days ago," she interrupted. "There's little chance you've made me pregnant."

Ty should have been relieved, but the scent and feel of Janna beneath him was driving everything else from his mind. Even as he told himself he must be crazy, he realized that he wanted her again.

"This time, yes," he agreed huskily, "but what about the next time I take you, and the next, and the times after that? Because if I'm around you, I'll take you every damned chance I get." His hand slid down her body until he could feel once more her intimate heat. "Satin butterfly," he whispered, unable to control the faint trembling of his fingers as he skimmed the edges of her softness. "Don't you understand yet? When I see you, hear you, smell you, touch you, taste you..."

A threadlike groan vibrated through Ty. "You're killing me. I can't leave you alone if I'm around you. I can't live with myself if I get you pregnant. And I need you around so that I can track down Lucifer before he gets killed or this whole damned territory blows up in our faces. We have to get married, Janna. There's no other way."

"No."

Janna clamped her legs together, trying to deny Ty the softness only he had ever touched.

It was futile. All she succeeded in doing was imprisoning his hand between her thighs. He made a sound of pleasure and despair as one finger slid gently into her and he felt her sleek, humid warmth surrounding him once more.

"I won't marry you," Janna whispered, her breath breaking. "Do you hear me? I won't spend my life having you look at me and long for a silken lady."

Ty hesitated, then slowly probed Janna's sensuous warmth. "I hear you. But what are we going to do about this? I meant what I said, little one. Having had you, I can't leave you alone."

She tried not to give voice to her pleasure, but a husky sound escaped her lips. "Teach me. That's all I ask of you. A mistress, not a whore."

The words went into Ty like knives, twisting even as they sliced into him. "I can't live with that. It's not enough. You deserve much more. Come back to Wyoming with me," he said in a low voice, caressing Janna because he was helpless to stop. "Silver and Cassie can teach you how to sit and speak and smile like a lady. They'll teach you how to dress and I'll see that you have enough dowry to attract a good man, a man who won't berate you for what I took from you. Then you'll be a married woman, Janna, not any man's mistress or every man's whore.''

"I'll marry no man," she whispered. "Ever."

"Janna..."

Her only answer was a husky cry and her warmth reaching out to Ty, silently promising oblivion within her body. The heat and scent of her filled his nostrils, sending a wave of desire through him. Suddenly he wanted to bend down and immerse himself in Janna, tasting her essence, drinking the very secrets of her body. The thought shocked him, for he had never wanted that kind of intimacy with a woman before.

"You're so sweet to touch," Ty whispered, stroking Janna with slow, hidden motions. "I never knew a woman could be so responsive, so perfect. Satin butterfly, more beautiful to me each time I touch you."

"Ty..." Janna said, moaning his name softly, feeling her tumultuous emotions condense into pure burning desire.

She knew she should tell him to stop but she was unable to form the words. She wanted his touch too much. She had never known such ravishing closeness with anyone, had never even dreamed it was possible. The knowledge that he, too, found something special in her made it impossible to turn away from his need.

Ty heard the telltale break and quickening of Janna's breath and didn't know whether to curse or laugh as he felt himself hardening, succumbing to her sleek satin trap once more. She was a handful of fire, a sensuous dream, so recently a virgin and yet so generous and unafraid as a lover.

Janna's small hands found his in the darkness and she held them motionless, trying to still the secret movements within her body.

"Stop," she whispered, yet even as she spoke she felt her own heat overflowing in silent contradiction.

"Why?" Ty murmured, slowly penetrating and withdrawing from her body despite her clinging fingers. "Am I hurting you?"

"N-no."

To Ty the sensual break and shiver of Janna's voice was as arousing as her heat welling up at his touch.

"You're too innocent to understand how rare you are, how extraordinary this is," he whispered, feeling the vital hardening of his flesh as he bent down to her. "But I'm not innocent. I know. I'd agree to anything in order to keep on touching you. I've never been like this with any woman. *Bruja*, sweet fire witch. You burn me alive and I tremble and spend myself within you...and then you renew me with a breath, a kiss, a touch.''

Janna whispered Ty's name helplessly, moved beyond words that she could affect him so deeply.

"Renew me," Ty whispered, lifting her hand and kissing it before placing it over his swelling male flesh.

She felt the helpless, sensuous jerk of his body as her fingers curled around him in answer to the pressure of his own hands.

"Teach me?" she whispered.

"Yes," he said. "Every chance I get. All the way from here to Wyoming. And then—''

"No," she interrupted, arching up to meet him. "No tomorrows. Just teach me. Teach me now."

He started to speak, then forgot what he was going to say when her hands moved.

"Like this?" Janna whispered, measuring and caressing him with the same slow, sensuous motion.

"Sweet...God...yes," Ty said. His whole body tightened and moved with her hands in a sinuous dance that made him tremble. He lowered his head until he could feel her breath against his lips. "And like this," he whispered, fitting first his body and then his mouth to hers, thrusting deeply into her generous warmth. "And this...and *this*..."

Even as Janna shivered and softly cried out, Ty bent and drank ecstasy from her lips, sinking wholly into her, wondering who was the teacher and who the student in the hushed intimacy of the meadow night.

Chapter Twenty-Four

The brutal crack of rifle fire at the northwest end of Raven Creek's meadow jerked Janna and Ty awake in a heart-pounding instant.

Neither one moved.

No more sounds came. After a few minutes Ty eased away from Janna, grabbed his carbine and crawled to a vantage point where he could look out across the meadow. There was nothing in sight. A moment later he sensed Janna coming up behind him. He turned and shook his head. She retreated as silently as she had come. So did he.

Without talking, they withdrew to the place where they had slept. Ty reached for his backpack at the same instant that Janna reached for the cloth she had used to bind her breasts. Although she and Ty had been forced by the cold to put on their clothes in the hours before dawn, he hadn't allowed her to wrap up in the cloth again. Instead, he had curled spoon fashion along her back, slid his hands up beneath her loose shirt and caressed her gently until they both fell asleep.

As soon as Janna's fingers closed on the binding, she realized that she wasn't going to be allowed to use it this morning, either. Ty snatched the cloth from her fingers, rolled it tightly and jammed it into his backpack. Then he pulled her to her feet.

"I'd kiss you," he said very softly, looking hungrily at her mouth, "but if I did, I'd undress you and lie between your legs again. That wouldn't be a very smart thing to do right now."

Janna's mind agreed, but her body swayed hungrily toward Ty. He let go of her as though he had grabbed something too hot to hold. Saying nothing, Janna turned and began threading through the forest, circling toward the northeast corner of the meadow. After a few minutes she looked at Ty and gestured toward the meadow. He nodded. Together they walked, then crawled and finally wiggled snake fashion toward the edge of the meadow.

In the clear yellow light of morning, the signs were unmistakable—a group of unshod horses had grazed the meadow within the past few days. The presence of small hoofprints and diminutive manure piles told Ty and Janna that the horses were wild, for hunting or raiding parties didn't use mares whose foals were unweaned. Overlaid on the random tracks of grazing animals were those of a shod horse walking across the meadow and into the dense pine forest beyond. It was those prints that had attracted the Indian hunting party the previous night.

"Troon," Janna whispered, looking at the prints.

"How can you tell?"

"See how worn the shoe is on the left front hoof? Troon's too cheap to get his horse shod regularly."

"Wasn't bothering to hide his trail, was he?" Ty muttered.

"He was probably drunk."

"Then he's probably dead. Was it Lucifer's bunch he was following?"

"I can't tell from the tracks around here. I'd have to go to the center and check the muddy spots along Raven Creek. Besides, Lucifer never mixes with his herd when the mares graze. If this is his bunch, his tracks will be off to the side somewhere."

Both Janna and Ty looked out over the empty, inviting meadow that Troon had crossed sometime yesterday. The ground beneath their bodies was still slightly damp with dew, but they were in no hurry to stand up and expose themselves to any watchers who might have been posted by the meadow. Raven Creek's watershed had become all but overrun by Cascabel and his growing band of renegades.

Ty's hard green eyes searched the boundary between forest and meadow, seeking any sign that Indians were about. Birds called and flew naturally, landed in low branches or on the meadow itself. No bird flew up with a startled outcry, indicating that danger lay hidden somewhere around Raven Creek's meadow itself.

Janna watched the area as carefully as Ty. She saw nothing that should disturb her, yet she was reluctant to cross the meadow in pursuit of either Lucifer's tracks or those of Joe Troon. She looked at Ty and gestured toward the meadow in silent question. He shook his head in a slow negative. She didn't disagree. Together they eased backward deeper into the small trees and sun-hungry bushes that ringed the meadow. When both of them were within the cover of the forest once more, Ty gestured for Janna to choose the best route around to the opposite side of the meadow.

Moving quickly and quietly, Janna set off into the forest. Within the fragrant, hushed cover beneath the trees, the going became easier. The tall pines screened out much of the sunlight, making it impossible for plants to thrive on the forest floor. Even so, fallen trees and branches forced Janna to make many small detours. Every few minutes she stopped and stood motionless, watching and listening to the forest with the consummate grace and stillness of a wild deer.

Ty never became impatient with Janna's detours or her seemingly random stops. Watching her blend with the land was a pleasure for him. Though he took second to few people in his ability to track or to hunt, Ty knew that here on Black Plateau, Janna was at home in a way that only a wild animal could equal.

It's a good thing she didn't get up here before I found her, Ty thought as he watched Janna merge with the shadows beneath the trees. *I never would have caught her.*

Part of Ty wondered if that wouldn't have been better for both of them, but even as the question occurred to him he denied it. The thought of never having known such intense, consuming pleasure was unbearable to him. Memories of the night before licked like scented fire over his body. For an instant he savored the sensuous rush of images, tasted again in memory

Janna's mouth and breasts, felt again the tightness of her body as she accepted him into her satin heat. Then he put memories aside with a skill he had learned during the war, dividing his mind into compartments like a dresser; and like a man dressing, he had learned to open only the drawer that contained what he needed at the moment.

Making no sound, Janna walked forward once more, a gray-eyed shadow among shadows. With an unconscious movement Ty shifted his carbine into carrying position again, holding his right hand around the stock in such a way that it would take only an instant to pull the trigger and keeping the muzzle pointed so that an accidental firing wouldn't hit anyone in front of him. The buttoned pocket of his wool shirt bulged with a box of bullets. Similar boxes made his backpack heavier than its size would have indicated.

He didn't notice the extra weight, much less complain of it. There had been too many times in the past when he would have sold his soul for extra ammunition. He felt the same way about the beef jerky that he was chewing on at the moment—it might have been tougher than leather, unsalted and stone dry, but it was food and he had been hungry too many times in the past to be fussy about what he ate now.

The wind breathed softly over Janna and Ty, bringing with it the smell of pine resin and sun. Off in the distance a raven jeered at something concealed within pine boughs. Janna and Ty froze as one. The raven's harsh cries rang in the silence, then faded as the bird flew farther away. Both of them remained motionless, wondering if it had been another bird or a man that had disturbed the crow.

The breeze sighed over Janna's face, stirring wisps of auburn hair. The delicate brushing movement reminded her of Ty's gentleness when he had first taken her into his arms to calm her after her encounter with the snake. An odd frisson of sensation raced through Janna's body from her breasts to her thighs as she remembered what had followed the first soft kisses.

And on the heels of hot memories came the icy knowledge that Ty was hers for only a short time, just long enough to find and tame Lucifer. Then Ty would go in search of the silken lady he was determined to have. A yearning to be that lady twisted through Janna with such painful intensity that she couldn't breathe.

Don't be a fool, she told herself harshly. *I know all about silk purses and sows' ears. A man like Ty does, too. He was raised in a grand house with servants and tutors and people to tell him how to speak and eat and dress and write a fine hand. I had my father and a wagon seat and a trunk full of old books. I can read and write...and that's all. If I ever wore a dress, I've forgotten what it feels like. The only shoes I remember having are the moccasins I make for myself. The only perfume I know is what I make from crushed flowers. The only salves I have are for healing, not for making me beautiful. The only thing my hands are good for is surviving, not for playing grand songs on a piano.*

Then Janna remembered one other thing her hands had proven to be good for—arousing Ty until he was as hot and hard as sun-warmed stone. If she closed her eyes she could still feel him changing within her grasp, becoming full and tight and heavy, moving blindly between her hands, seeking more of her.

Will he want me like that again tonight, nothing but the two of us locked together and pleasure like a fire burning between us?

Without thinking, Janna turned and looked over her shoulder where she knew Ty would be. He was standing as motionless as she was, and he was watching her with eyes that glittered like green gems. She sensed in that moment that he knew her thoughts, her memories, for they were his thoughts, his memories.

The breeze blew softly, caressing Janna's face. Ty could see the stirring of soft auburn hair. He knew what those silky wisps felt like on his lips, knew what her skin tasted like along her hairline, knew that she trembled when the tip of his tongue traced her ear or found the pulse beating in her neck. And he knew from the sudden, slight parting of her lips that she was remembering what it had felt like to have his tongue slide between her teeth to probe and caress the passionate softness of her mouth.

Janna made no sound as she turned away from Ty, but he knew why she had retreated. If they had looked at each other for even one more second, he would have pulled her down to the ground and taken her and to hell with the risk. It would have been worth it to die of ecstasy and then to be reborn and die again, sheathed so perfectly within her body.

The small, normal sounds of the forest surrounded Janna as she moved from shadow to shadow, all senses alert. A squirrel scolded a trespassing cousin, two ravens called as they flew overhead, and needles whispered secretively as they combed through the erratic breeze. Through the massed, dark trunks and dead lower branches of the pines, Janna caught occasional views of the sunny meadow.

There were game trails crisscrossing the forest and the meadow itself. Whenever Janna came to such a path, she stopped and read the signs left by passing animals. The damp earth held tracks for a long time, telling of the passage of deer and coyote, cougar and bear, men and horses. The first few game trails were little more than faint threads winding around deadfalls and between trees. The fourth path she discovered was much more obvious, for it was frequently used by wild horses. The trail began at the west end of the meadow and took a reasonably straight line toward the northwest corner of the plateau, where Raven Creek cut through the land on its way to joining the warm, shallow waters of Santos Wash—and Cascabel's sprawling renegade camp guarding the northwest approach to the plateau.

Suddenly Janna went to her knees, her heart pounding. There, alongside the main trail, was a partial track left by a large, unshod horse.

"Lucifer," she said, spreading her fingers, measuring the huge print.

"Are you sure?" Ty asked, quickly kneeling beside her. "There's not much of a track to go on."

"No other horse but Cascabel's is so big. But there's no sign that this horse has ever been shod, and Cascabel's has "

Silently Ty began casting for a sign on either side of the trail. He wasn't long in finding it.

"Janna."

She came to her feet instantly and ran to his side.

"He was coming out of the meadow and something spooked him," Ty said softly, pointing to the place where Lucifer's hooves had dug abruptly into the trail, gouging out clots of dirt and debris as he sprang to one side. "He took off running through the trees."

Janna looked from the churned earth to the forest beyond. A faint trail of disturbed pine needles showed as lighter marks against the forest floor. She bent and studied the damp, undisturbed ground and the tracks themselves.

And then she saw the blood.

Joe Troon took off with his rifle. Swore he was going to crease or kill Lucifer.

With a trembling hand she touched the blood spoor. It was neither fresh nor old.

"The tracks were left within the past few hours," Ty said.

"So was the blood."

Janna sensed rather than saw Ty's head jerk toward her. Within seconds he was squatting on his heels next to her, rubbing a bit of the dark, thumbnail-size spot between his fingers. He stared at the results and cursed the man who hadn't drunk enough to miss entirely.

"I'll bet it happened just after dawn," Ty said.

"We heard more than one shot."

Ty grunted. "There's more than one renegade riding around here looking for trouble. Maybe one of them found Joe Troon."

Ty rubbed his hand clean on his pants and stood. The idea of the magnificent stallion slowly bleeding to death made him sick. But before they followed Lucifer's trail, they had to know if it were Joe Troon or a renegade party they were likely to run into.

"I'm going to cast around back toward the meadow and see if I can find what spooked Lucifer," Ty said. "You follow his tracks. I'll follow you. If you lose the trail, stay put until I catch up." He looked into her clear eyes. "Do you want the carbine?"

She shook her head. "Keep it. I haven't shot a long gun in years. Snares or a bow and arrow are much more quiet for hunting game."

"At least take my pistol."

Janna hesitated, then gave in. She wouldn't do either Ty or herself much good if she stumbled across renegades and all she had to throw at them was a handful of pine needles.

Frowning uneasily, Ty watched Janna push his big revolver behind her belt. He knew it was irrational of him not to want to leave her alone—after all, she had survived for years on her own in this very country—but he still didn't like it.

"You're coming with me," he said without warning.

Startled, she looked up. "Why?"

"My backbone is itchy as all hell, that's why, and I'm a man who listens to my instincts."

"Lucifer's bleeding. If I hurry—"

"A few minutes more or less won't make much difference," Ty interrupted. "Besides, there's no way we can be sure that it was a bullet that hurt him. Could have been a sharp branch he shied into. Could have been another horse. I've seen him fight more than one eager stud and they both walked away dripping blood." Ty turned back toward the meadow. "Hurry up. We're wasting time talking when we could be tracking."

Mouth open, Janna watched Ty trot off along the game trail, covering ground at a good clip while looking for signs of other horses or other men. If he noticed that she wasn't following, he gave no indication of it.

Without a word Janna turned and began running in a different direction, following the trail Lucifer had left during his panicked flight away from the meadow.

Chapter Twenty-Five

Head down, his attention focused on the wild horse trail, Ty trotted rapidly through the forest toward the meadow. Tracks and signs abounded, but he could see without slowing that nothing was less than a few days old. He was looking for much fresher marks.

He found them less than two hundred feet from the meadow itself.

The empty rye bottle glittered on top of the pine needles. The bottle hadn't been there long, for when Ty picked it up and sniffed, the smell of alcohol was strong in his nostrils. Nearby was a tree stained with urine from chest high to the ground. There were hoof tracks left by a shod horse next to the tree.

From that point the trail was easy to reconstruct. Troon—for Ty was certain that the empty bottle had belonged to Joe Troon rather than to a solitary Indian—had been relieving himself from the saddle when something had surprised him.

"I'll bet he was hot on Lucifer's trail and had to piss so bad that his back teeth were floating," Ty said very softly, believing that Janna was right behind. "So there he was, still in the saddle and pissing up a storm when he saw Lucifer through the trees, dropped everything and grabbed for his rifle. Lord, what a mess that must have been."

When Janna made no comment, Ty turned and looked at his own trail. Janna was nowhere in sight.

The uneasiness that had been riding Ty crystallized in an instant of stabbing fear. He ignored his first impulse, which was to backtrack along his own trail until he found Janna. That would take too long, for he had come nearly half a mile. Obviously Troon's trail and Lucifer's crossed somewhere ahead. If Ty followed one and Janna followed the other, they would meet much quicker than if he retraced his own tracks and then hers, as well.

If both of them were really lucky, none of Cascabel's renegades would ride over to find the cause of the single rifle shot. But Ty really didn't expect that kind of luck.

Swearing savagely to himself, he began trotting along the trail left by the shod horse. Within ten yards he spotted the brass from a spent cartridge gleaming among pine needles. The shine of the metal told Ty that the cartridge hadn't been long out of a rifle barrel. He had no doubt that it was the debris of the shot that had awakened Janna and himself less than half an hour ago. He also had no doubt what the intended target had been.

You drunken, greedy swine. If you've murdered that stallion I'll roast you over a slow fire and serve you to Cascabel with an apple in your mouth.

Rifle shots split the silence, followed by the wild cries of Indian renegades hot on a human trail. Fear splintered through Ty like black lightning, for the sounds were coming from ahead and off to his right, where Troon's trail was going, where Lucifer would have gone if he had followed a straight course through the forest—and where Janna would be if she had been able to follow Lucifer's trail.

Ty had no doubt that Janna could track Lucifer anywhere the stallion could go.

Running swiftly and silently, Ty traced the twisting progress of Troon's horse through the forest. The animal had been moving at a hard gallop, a pace that was foolhardy under the conditions. Stirrups left gashes across tree trunks where the horse had zigzagged between pines. Farther down the trail low-growing limbs showed signs of recent damage. Bruised clusters of needles were scattered everywhere. A man's battered hat was tangled among the branches.

Ty had no doubt that he would find blood if he wanted to stop and check the bark on the limb that was wearing Troon's hat, but at the moment it wasn't Troon's blood that interested Ty. It was the palm-sized splotches that had suddenly appeared along with the hoofprints of a huge, unshod horse.

Lucifer.

Like the rifle cartridge, the blood hadn't been exposed to air for more than a half hour. The spots glistened darkly in the shade and were near-crimson markers in the occasional patches of sun. From their position, they could only have come from the stallion.

Breathing easily, running quietly, Ty followed the bloody trail. He knew that he should be sneaking from tree to tree in the thinning forest. He knew that at the very least he should be hunting cover in case he literally ran up on the heels of the renegades. He also knew that Janna was somewhere up ahead alone, armed with a pistol good for six shots and no spare cylinders or ammunition within reach. He didn't know how many renegades there were, but he doubted that six shots would get the job done.

Janna's too clever to be spotted by renegades. She'll go to ground and pull the hole in after her. They'll never find her.

The reassuring thought was interrupted by a flurry of rifle fire. The sounds came from ahead, but much farther to the right than Ty would have expected from the trail he was following. Either Lucifer or Troon—or both—must be hoping to escape by making a break for the steep northern edge of the plateau.

There were a few more sporadic shots and eager cries, then silence. Ty ran harder and told himself it was good that he hadn't heard any pistol shots, for that meant Janna hadn't been spotted. He refused to consider that it could also mean she had fallen in the first outbreak of shooting before she even had a chance to defend herself. He simply ran harder, carrying his carbine as though it were a pistol, finger on the trigger, ready to shoot and fire on the instant.

The hoofprints, which had been a mixture of shod and unshod, abruptly diverged. The unshod prints continued without interruption. The shod hoofprints veered starkly to the right. Ty had no doubt that he was seeing traces of the instant when the renegades had spotted Troon; the prints of Troon's horse were inches deep in the ground at the point where the horse had dug in and spun away from the renegades. Troon had chosen to flee along the rumpled, downward sloping land that led to the plateau's northern edge. There the land was rocky, broken, full of clefts and hollows and sheer-sided ravines where a man could hope to hide.

If Troon were lucky, he might even survive. Ty hoped he didn't. Any man who would shoot at a horse like Lucifer out of greed deserved to die. Without a further thought, Ty veered off after the stallion, leaving Troon to whatever fate luck and the renegades would visit upon him.

The stallion's tracks showed no sudden gouges or changes in direction as Troon's had. When the renegades had spotted Troon, apparently Lucifer hadn't been within sight. The wild horse had cannily chosen a route that looped back toward the eastern end of Raven Creek's long, winding meadow. From there Lucifer could head for the northeast edge of the plateau and slide on his black hocks down into Mustang Canyon or he could run southeast and then straight south, using the entire surface of the plateau, losing himself among the pines, meadows, ridges and ravines that covered the land's rugged surface.

Assuming, of course, that Lucifer was in any shape for a long, hard run. It was an assumption Ty wasn't prepared to make. The stallion's tracks were becoming closer together. His strides were shortening as though he were winded, and the blood splotches were bigger and more frequent. Part of the horse's slowed progress might have been simply that the land was broken and rolling here, with more uphill than down as Lucifer headed straight toward the eastern lip of the plateau. And the shortening strides might also have been the result of injury.

Ty remembered Janna saying that she had once seen signs that Lucifer had skidded down the steep trail on the plateau's east edge in order to evade mustangers. He wondered if the stallion had remembered his past success and was laboring toward the east trail in hope of another such escape.

But Ty didn't think Lucifer would make it. The path on the east face was too far, too steep, and the blood sign along the stallion's trail was almost continuous now. The land here was steep, rising sharply into one of the many low ridges that marked the plateau's rumpled surface.

I hope they catch you, Troon. I hope they cut off your—

Ty's bitter thoughts of vengeance were wiped from his mind the instant he saw over the crest of the ridge to the land below. Less than a quarter mile away, Janna was running flat out down the slope. Her course paralleled a narrow, steep ravine that cut into the body of the ridge. Lucifer was forty feet ahead of her, veering toward the ravine as though he were planning to jump it, but it was too wide a leap for an injured horse. A half mile off to the right, all but concealed in another fold of land, a dust cloud of renegades was in wild pursuit of Joe Troon, who apparently had abandoned the idea of making a run to the northwest and Raven Creek Trail. Instead he was spurring his horse toward the east, leading the renegades toward Janna, who couldn't see them yet but almost certainly could hear their chilling cries.

Turn around and hide, Janna! Go to ground, Ty commanded silently. *Don't get yourself caught trying to help Lucifer.*

The stallion reached the edge of the ravine and threw himself toward the far side. His forelegs found purchase on the opposite bank of the ravine, but his left rear leg gave way when it should have provided support. He was too weak to struggle over the lip to safety. Kicking and screaming in a mixture of fear, pain and rage, the black horse skidded and rolled into the narrow, brush-choked bottom of the ravine twenty feet below. There he lay on his side, thrashing wildly in a futile attempt to regain his feet and scramble to safety.

Without pausing, Janna threw herself over the edge of the ravine, hurtling down into the tangle of brush and flailing hooves.

There was only one way Ty could save Janna from being injured or killed by the trapped stallion. Even as he whipped the carbine to his shoulder and took aim at Lucifer's beautiful black head, he saw hooves glance off Janna's body. At the precise instant he let out his breath and took the last of the slack from the trigger, Janna's back appeared in the gun sight. She had thrown herself over the stallion's head, pinning it to the earth, ensuring that the horse wouldn't be able to struggle to his feet.

Get out of there, you little fool! Ty screamed silently. *You can't hold him. He'll beat you to death with those big hooves.*

The ravine Lucifer was trapped in was a long crease running down the side of the ridge at whose top Ty waited. It would be an easy shot, no more than three hundred feet. He had made more difficult shots with a pistol. A savage fusillade of shots and triumphant shouts came from the direction of Troon and the renegades. Ty's attention never wavered from the bottom of the ravine, nor did the tension of his finger lift on the trigger.

A man's screams told Ty that either Troon or a renegade had just been wounded. Ty's glance remained fixed on the ravine bottom where Janna struggled to master the big horse. Ty knew that sooner or later Lucifer's struggles to free his head would throw Janna aside. When that happened, Ty's finger would tighten on the trigger and the stallion would die.

What the hell...?

Janna had one knee pinning the stallion's muzzle to the ground and the other knee just behind his ears. She was literally kneeling on the horse and ripping her shirt off at the same time.

A crescendo of triumphant whoops and shots told Ty that the chase was over for Joe Troon. Ty still didn't look up from the ravine; he wouldn't have walked across a street to aid the man who had captured Janna once and bragged to a bartender about what he would do when he caught her again. As far as Ty was concerned, Troon had gone looking for trouble and he had found more than he wanted. It often happened that way to a man who drank too much and thought too little. Ty's only regret was that Troon hadn't bought it sooner, before he had led the renegades back to within a quarter mile of Janna.

Over the carbine's steel barrel, Ty watched while Janna turned her torn shirt into a makeshift blindfold and struggled to secure it around Lucifer's eyes. Abruptly the stallion stopped thrashing around. With rapid movements Janna whipped a few turns of cloth around the horse's muzzle. When she was finished, Lucifer could open his mouth no more than an inch. She bent over him once more, holding him down while she stroked his lathered neck.

Ty could see the shudders of fear that rippled over the stallion with each stroke of Janna's hand. Ty could also see that the horse was no longer a danger to her; blindfolded, muzzled, pinned in place by Janna's weight, Lucifer was all but helpless.

Very slowly Ty eased his finger off the trigger and sank down behind the cover of a piñon tree that clung to the rocky ridge top. Screened by dark green branches, Ty pulled out his spyglass and looked off to the right. A single glance confirmed what his ears had already told him: Joe Troon had made his last mistake.

Ty looked around carefully and decided that he had the best position from which to protect the ravine. Pulling his hat down firmly, he chose a comfortable shooting position, shrugged out of his pack and put two open boxes of ammunition within easy reach. Stomach against the hard earth, green eyes sighting down the carbine's metal barrel, Ty settled in to wait and see if the renegades were going to come toward the ravine when they were finished looting and mutilating Troon's body.

Chapter Twenty-Six

"Easy now, boy. Easy...easy."

The ceaseless murmur of Janna's soft voice and the gentle pressure of her hands finally penetrated the stallion's pain and panic. With a long, groaning sigh, Lucifer stopped fighting. Janna rewarded him by shifting her knee from his muzzle to the ground, praising him with a flow of sentences and nonsense sounds, knowing that it was her voice rather than the meaning of her words that reached past the horse's fear.

Very slowly Janna slid her other knee from Lucifer's neck, leaving him able to lift his head, which was the first thing a horse did before it came to its feet. Lucifer made no attempt to take advantage of his freedom in order to stand up. As Janna had hoped, the blindfold held him more quietly and more surely than any rope could have. Even so, she reluctantly bound his left hind foot to his right foreleg. When she began cleaning and treating the bullet wound on his left rear leg, she didn't want him to lash out at the pain. She was already bruised enough as it was. A broken bone wouldn't do either of them any good.

Ignoring her own pain, Janna kept one hand constantly on Lucifer's head, talking incessantly and softly, letting him know where she was. When his ears were no longer flattened against his head, Janna leaned over and snaked her own makeshift backpack to a place within easy reach. While she sorted one-handed through her herbs and salves, she told herself that Ty was all right, that the shots had been from Troon or the renegades, not from Ty's carbine, that he and she were safe even though they were separate....

"God, please let him be safe," Janna prayed softly, stroking the powerful, lathered neck of the stallion.

Though Lucifer was no longer fighting her, he groaned with each heaving breath he took, for the cloth muzzle restricted his breathing. In the silence, the sound of the horse's labored breaths were like thunder. After a few minutes Janna opened her pocketknife and cut the cloth free, allowing the stallion to open his mouth and nostrils fully. Immediately his breathing eased.

"You weren't going to bite me anyway, were you?" Janna murmured, stroking Lucifer's nose.

The stallion's ears flicked but didn't flatten against his head. He was too tired, too weak or simply not fearful enough to attack Janna.

Wondering if anyone had been attracted by the stallion's labored breathing, Janna glanced anxiously up and down the crease in the earth that was their only hiding place. She heard no one approaching. Nor did she see any movement along the ravine's rim.

It was just as well, for there was no way to hide from anyone. The brush through which Lucifer had fallen had been bruised and broken beyond all hope of concealment from any trackers. Nor was there any real cover within the ravine itself. Janna had no illusions about what her chances of escape would be if the renegades found her in the bottom of the ravine with the wounded, blindfolded stallion.

After a last look at the rim of the ravine, Janna pulled out Ty's big pistol, rotated the cylinder off the empty chamber and cocked the hammer so that all it would take was a quick pull on the trigger to fire the gun. Very carefully she laid the weapon out of the way yet within easy reach. Then she turned back to Lucifer.

"This is going to hurt," Janna said in a low, calm voice, "but you're going to be a gentleman about it, aren't you?"

She wet the last torn piece of her shirt with water from her canteen and went to work cleaning the long furrow Troon's bullet had left on Lucifer's haunch. The blindfolded stallion shuddered and his ears flattened, but he made no attempt to turn and bite Janna while she worked over him. She praised the horse in soothing tones that revealed neither her own pain from her bruises nor her growing fear that Ty hadn't been able to evade the renegades.

Lucifer flinched and made a high, involuntary sound as Janna cleaned a part of the wound that had picked up dirt in his slide down into the ravine.

"Easy, boy, easy...yes, I know it hurts, but you won't heal right without help. That's it...that's it...gently...just lie still and let me help you."

The low, husky voice and endless ripple of words mesmerized Lucifer. His ears flicked and swiveled, following Janna's voice when she turned from her backpack to the wound on his haunch.

"I think it looks a lot worse than it is," Janna murmured as she rinsed out her rag and poured more water into its folds. "It's deep and it bled a lot, but the bullet didn't sever any tendons or muscles. You're going to be sore and grouchy as a boiled cat for a while, and you'll limp for a time and you'll have a scar on your pretty black hide forever, but you'll heal clean and sound. In a few weeks you'll be up and running after your mares.

"And you'll have a lot of running to do, won't you? Those mares will be scattered from hell to breakfast, as Papa would have said. I'll bet that chestnut stud you ran off last year is stealing your mares as fast as he finds them."

Lucifer flicked his ears, sucked in a long breath through his flaring nostrils and blew out, then took in another great breath.

"Easy now, boy. Easy...easy... I know it hurts but there's no help for it."

Janna reached for her backpack again and winced. Her left arm was beginning to stiffen. By the time she was finished doctoring Lucifer, she'd have to start in on herself. With only one hand, it was going to be difficult.

Ty, where are you? Are you all right? Did you get away? Are you lying wounded and—

"Don't think about it!" Janna said aloud, her voice so savage that Lucifer, startled, tossed his head.

"Easy, boy," she murmured, immediately adjusting her voice to be soothing once more. "There's nothing to worry about. Ty is quick and strong and smart. If he got away from Cascabel he can get away from a bunch of hurrahing renegades who were looking for a man on horseback, not one on foot. Besides, I'll never get a better chance to tame you," she said, stroking the mustang's barrel, where lather was slowly drying. "If you accept me, you'll accept Ty, and then he'll have a start on his dream, a fine stallion to found a herd that will bring money enough to buy a lady of silk and softness."

Janna's mouth turned down in an unhappy line, but her hand continued its gentle motions and her voice remained soothing.

"Anyway, boy, if I leave you and go looking for a man who is probably quite safe, who will take care of you in three days or four, when your wound gets infected and you get so weak you can hardly stand?"

Lucifer's head came up suddenly and his ears pricked forward so tightly that they almost touched at the tips. His nostrils flared widely as he took in quantities of air and sifted it for the scent of danger.

Watching him closely, Janna reached for the pistol. Being blindfolded was no particular handicap for the stallion when it came to recognizing danger— a horse's ears and sense of smell were far superior to his eyes. But when it came to dealing with danger, a blind horse was all but helpless.

Janna looked in the direction that Lucifer's ears were pointing. All she saw was the steep side of the gully and the brushy slope rising to the ridge top beyond. She hesitated, trying to decide whether it would be less dangerous to crawl up out of the ravine and look around or to simply lie low and hope that whatever Lucifer sensed wouldn't sense them in return.

Before she could make up her mind, Janna heard what was attracting the horse's attention. There was a faint chorus of yips and howls and cries followed by the distant thunder of galloping horses and the crack of rifle fire. The sounds became louder as the renegades galloped closer to the ravine. For a few horrible minutes Janna was certain that the renegades were going to race straight up the slope above the ravine—and then she and Lucifer would be utterly exposed, with no place to hide and no way to flee.

The sounds peaked and slowly died as the Indians galloped off to the northwest, where Cascabel had his camp.

Heart pounding, Janna set aside the pistol she had grabbed and went back to tending Lucifer with hands that insisted on trembling at the very instant she most needed them to be still. She watched Lucifer's ears as she worked on his wound, for she knew that his hearing was superior to hers.

"I hope they're not coming back," she said softly, stroking the horse's hot flank as she examined the long furrow left by the bullet. "Well, Lucifer, if you were a man I'd pour some witch hazel in that wound to keep it clean. But witch hazel stings like the very devil and I don't have any way of telling you to hold still and not make any noise, so—"

Janna froze and stopped speaking as Lucifer's ears flicked forward again. Concentrating intently, she heard the faintest of scraping sounds, as though a boot or a moccasin had rubbed over loose rock, or perhaps it was no more than the friction of a low branch against the ground. Then came silence. A few moments later there was another sound, but this time that of cloth sliding over brush. Or was it simply wind bending the spring brush and releasing it again?

The silence continued with no more interruptions. Very slowly Janna reached for the pistol again, listening so intently that she ached. She didn't breathe, she didn't think, she simply bent every bit of her will toward hearing as much as possible. The stallion remained motionless as well, his ears pricked, his nostrils flared, waiting for the wind to tell him whether to fight or freeze or flee whatever danger existed beyond the ravine.

"Janna?"

At first the whisper was so soft that she thought she had imagined it.

"Janna? Are you all right?"

"Ty? Is that you?"

"Hell, no," Ty said in disgust. "It's Joe Troon's ghost come to haunt you. Stand back. I'm coming down."

A pebble rolled down the side of the ravine, then another and another as Ty chose speed over caution in his descent. Crossing the open spots from the top of the ridge to the gully's edge had taken years off his life span, even though there was no reason for him to think that the renegades would come back right away. Nor was there any reason to think that they would *not*. The sooner he was under even the minimal cover of the gully, the better he would feel.

Janna watched Ty skid down the last steep pitch into the ravine. He braced himself on a dead piñon trunk, looked toward her and smiled in a way that made her heart turn over.

"Sugar," Ty drawled, "you are a sight for sore eyes."

His glance moved over her like hands, reminding her that she was naked from the waist up. Blushing, she crossed her arms over her breasts but couldn't conceal the pink tide rising beneath her skin.

Ty's breath caught and then stayed in his throat at the picture Janna made, the pale perfection of her body rising from the loose masculine pants. Her arms were too slender to hide the full curves of her breasts. The hint of deep rose nipples nestled shyly in the bend of her elbows.

"Ty...don't."

"Don't what?"

"Look at me like that."

"Like what?" he said huskily. "Like I spent most of the night licking and love biting and kissing those beautiful white breasts?"

Janna couldn't conceal the shiver of sensual response that went through her at Ty's words.

"Put your arms down, sugar. Let me see if you remember, too."

Very slowly Janna's arms dropped away, revealing breasts whose rosy tips had drawn and hardened at his look, his words, her memories.

"God," breathed Ty, shutting his eyes, knowing that it didn't matter, the vision was already burned into his memory. Blindly he dug into his backpack, found the roll of cloth he had refused to let her wear, and dropped the cloth on her lap. "Here. Wrap up before you make me forget where we are. Do it fast, little one. A man never wants a woman so much as when he's come close to dying."

"Does it work that way for a woman, too?" Janna asked as she snatched the cloth and began wrapping it over her breasts.

"I don't know. How do you feel right now?"

"Shivery. Feverish. Restless. And then you looked at me and I felt hot and full where you had touched me...and yet empty at the same time."

"Then it works the same for a woman, if the woman is like you," Ty said, trying to control the heavy beat of his blood. "Satin butterfly. God, you don't know how much I want to love you right now. I saw Lucifer jump and fall into the ravine and then you threw yourself after him and I couldn't get a clean shot at his head and—"

"What?" Janna interrupted, appalled. "Why did you want to shoot Lucifer? He isn't that badly injured."

"I know. That's why I was afraid he'd beat you to death with those big hooves."

"You would have killed him to save me?"

Ty's eyelids snapped open. "Hell, yes! What kind of a man do you think I am?"

Janna tried to speak, couldn't find the words and concentrated on wrapping herself tightly.

"For the love of God," Ty said in a low voice. "Just because I seduced you doesn't mean that I'm the kind of bastard who would leave you to be killed when I could have saved you!"

"That isn't what I meant. It's just that...that..."

"What?" Ty demanded angrily.

"I'm surprised you would have killed Lucifer without hesitation, that's all," Janna said, her voice shaking. "Lucifer is your best chance of building a fine horse herd. He's your best hope of getting enough money to buy your silken lady. He's the beginning of your dreams. He's...everything. And I'm..." She drew in a deep breath, looked away from Ty's harsh, closed expression and continued quietly. "I'm not your blood or your fiancée or anything but a...a temporary convenience. Why should you kill your dream for me?" She glanced quickly at him. "But thank you, Ty. It's the nicest thing anyone has ever done for me."

Chapter Twenty-Seven

"How bad is he hurt?" Ty asked.

Janna jumped in surprise. It was the first thing Ty had said to her in the hour since she had thanked him for being prepared to sacrifice his dream in order to save her life.

After that, Ty had gone to Lucifer's head, knelt and put himself between the horse's teeth and Janna. He had spoken gently to the stallion, stroking Lucifer's powerful neck with slow sweeps of his hand until the horse relaxed and accepted the strange voice and touch. Except for those murmured reassurances to the big horse, Ty had said nothing as he watched Janna tend Lucifer. Ty moved only to stroke the stallion or to hand her a packet from her leather pouch or to rinse the rag she was using to clean Lucifer's cuts and abrasions.

"He's strong. He'll be fine," Janna said, smiling tentatively at Ty.

"That's not what I asked. I've treated horses for sprains and stones in their shoes and colic and such, but bullet wounds are new to me. It's not a deep wound, but I've seen men die of shock with wounds not much worse than that. Do you think Lucifer can walk?"

Janna turned and reached for the stallion's muzzle, only to have Ty quickly intervene.

"I can't answer your question until I've looked at Lucifer's mouth," she explained.

Ty gave Janna an odd look and reluctantly moved aside. She bent over the stallion's muzzle and spoke in low, even tones as her fingers lifted his upper lip. His ears flattened warningly and he jerked his head away. Patiently Janna worked over him until he tolerated her fingers around his mouth without laying back his ears.

"What the hell are you doing?" Ty asked quietly.

"Papa said you can tell a lot about men or animals by the color of their gums. Lucifer was real pale when I first checked him, but he's nice and pink now. He'll be able to walk as soon as I untie his feet, but it would be better if he didn't move around much. That wound will start to bleed all over again at the first bit of strain."

Ty looked at the long gash on Lucifer's haunch and muttered something beneath his breath.

"What?" asked Janna.

"We can't stay here. Those renegades could come back or some of their friends could come prowling to see if anything was missed the first time around. Lucifer left a trail a blind man could follow.'' Ty glanced at the sky overhead. ''No rain today and probably not any tonight, either. And if there was enough rain to wash out the trail, we'd be washed right out of this gully, too. There's no food, no water and no cover worth mentioning. The sooner we get out of here the longer we'll all live.''

Janna looked unhappily at the stallion but didn't argue with Ty. What he had said was true and she knew it as well as he did. She just didn't want to have to force the wounded stallion to walk.

''I wish he were human,'' Janna said. ''It would be so much easier if we could explain to him.''

''How far do you think he can go?''

''As far as he wants to, I guess.''

''He moved fast enough getting here,'' Ty said dryly.

''He was running scared then. I've seen frightened mustangs gallop on sprained ankles and pulled hamstrings, but as soon as they stop running, they're finished. They can barely hobble until they heal.''

Ty said nothing. He had seen men in the heat of battle run on a foot that had been shot off; after the battle, those same men couldn't even crawl.

''The sooner we get going the better our chances are,'' Ty said finally. ''At the very least we've got to get to decent cover and wipe out as much of our trail as we can. Do you know any place near the meadow?''

Janna shook her head. ''Not where a horse could hide long enough to heal. The only place Lucifer would be safe is my keyhole canyon, and I don't know if he'd make it that far. By the time we got over to the Mustang Canyon trail and down into the canyon and then clear out away from the plateau to the Santos Wash trail...'' She shook her head again. ''It's a long way from there to my winter camp.''

''And the renegades are real thick in Santos Wash,'' Ty added. ''We've got no choice, Janna. We'll have to take Lucifer down the east face of the plateau. From there it's only a few hours to your hidden canyon.''

Janna's objections died before they were spoken. She had come to the same conclusion Ty had; she just hadn't wanted to believe it was their best chance. The thought of taking the injured stallion down the precipitous eastern edge of the plateau, and from there through the tortuous slot canyon, made her want to cry out in protest.

But it was their best hope of keeping Lucifer—and themselves—safe while his bullet wound healed.

''I know how you feel about restraining a horse, so I won't ask you to do it,'' Ty said firmly. ''I don't think Lucifer's going to take too kindly to it, either, but there's no damn choice.'' He looked at Janna. ''Get your medicine bag packed and stand lookout up on the ridge.''

''I'll help you with Lucifer.''

''There's not room enough for two of us.''

''But I'm used to mustangs.''

''You're used to coaxing mares into gentleness when they have all the room in the world to run. Lucifer is a stud and trapped and hurting and probably of no mind to be meek about wearing his first hackamore. I don't blame him a bit. I'll be as gentle with him as I can, but I want you a long way away when I pull off that blindfold. Besides, someone has to stand watch. That someone is going to be you.''

Janna looked into the crystalline green of Ty's eyes and knew that arguing would get her nowhere. "I'll bet you were an officer in the war between the North and the South.''

Ty looked surprised, then smiled. "You bet right, sugar. Now shag your lovely butt up onto that ridge. If you see something you don't like, give me that hawk cry you use to call Zebra. And don't forget my pistol.''

Without a word Janna tucked Ty's pistol in place behind her belt and began climbing out of the ravine. When she was safely up on the rim, Ty turned to Lucifer once more.

"Well, boy, it's time to find out if all your piss and vinegar is combined with common sense, or if you're outlaw through and through.''

Speaking gently and reassuringly, Ty reached into his backpack and pulled out a pair of sheepskin-lined leather hobbles that he had taken from the Preacher's store in hope of just such an opportunity to use them. When the hobbles were in place on Lucifer's front legs, Ty cut through the cloth that joined the stallion's hind and foreleg. Lucifer quivered but made no attempt to lash out with his newly unbound feet. Ty stroked the horse's barrel and talked soothingly until the stallion's black hide no longer twitched and trembled with each touch.

"You did real well, boy. I'm beginning to think you're as smart as you are handsome.''

Ty went to the backpack for the length of braided rawhide and the steel ring he had also bought. A few quick loops, turns and knots transformed the ring and rawhide into a workable hackamore.

"You're not going to like this, but you'll get used to it. Easy, son. Easy now." As Ty spoke, he slipped the makeshift hackamore onto the stallion's head.

Lucifer snorted and began trembling again as soon as he felt the rawhide against his skin. Patiently Ty rubbed the horse's head and neck and ears, accustoming him to the pressure of human hands and hackamore on his head. Lucifer calmed quickly this time, as though he were losing the ability to become alarmed—or questioned the necessity for alarm—at each new thing that happened. Ty hoped that it was common sense rather than weakness that was calming the stallion, but he wouldn't know until he got Lucifer up on his feet how much strength the wound had cost the horse.

"Well, son, this is the test. Now you just lie still and show me what a gentleman you are underneath all that bone and muscle and wildness.''

With slow, smooth motions, Ty eased the blindfold down Lucifer's nose until the horse could see again. For a moment the stallion made no movement, then his ears flattened and he tried to lunge to his feet. Instantly Ty pinned the horse's muzzle to the ground and held it there, all the while talking soothingly and petting the rigid muscles of the stallion's neck as he struggled to get to his feet and flee.

Ty never knew how long it took to get through Lucifer's fear to the rational animal beneath. He only knew that he was sweating as hard as the stallion before Lucifer finally stopped struggling and allowed himself to be calmed by the voice and hands whose gentleness had never varied throughout the pitched, silent struggle.

"How the hell did she ever hold you long enough to get the blindfold on?" Ty wondered aloud as he and Lucifer eyed each other warily. "Or were you just used to her smell?"

The stallion's dark, dark eyes regarded Ty with an intelligence that was almost tangible. There was no malevolence, no sense of a feral eagerness to find an opening and strike. There was simply an alertness that had been bred into the horse's very bones and had been honed by living in the wild.

"Wonder who your mammy was, and your daddy, too. They sure as hell weren't bangtail ridge runners. You've a lot of the great barb in you, and maybe some Tennessee walking horse thrown in. My daddy would have traded every stud he ever owned to get his hands on you, and he would have considered it a bargain at twice the price. You're all horse, Lucifer. And you're mine now."

Lucifer's ears flicked and his eyes followed each motion Ty made.

"Well, you're half mine," Ty amended. "There's a certain stubborn girl who owns a piece of you whether she admits it or not. But don't worry, son. If you can't take the tame life, I'll set you free just like I promised. I don't mind telling you, though, I hope I don't have to. I left some fine mares with Logan. I'd love to take you up to Wyoming and keep you long enough to have at least one crop of foals from you."

While Ty talked he began to shift his weight off the stallion's muzzle a bit at a time until very little was left to hold the horse down.

"Ready to try getting up again? Slowly, son, slowly. Real nice and gentle. You lunge around this little gully and you're going to hurt both of us."

Once Lucifer realized that his head was free, he rolled off his side and got his feet underneath him. He quickly learned that the same man who could pin his muzzle to the ground could also help getting him to his feet with a few judicious pulls on the halter rope. Very shortly the stallion was standing again, unblindfolded and trembling all over at the strangeness of being close to a man.

"I was right. You're as smart as you are handsome. It's a shame you ran loose so long. You would have been a fine partner for a man, but after all these years I doubt you'd accept a rider. But that's all right, son," Ty said, slowly coiling the rawhide lead rope until he was right next to Lucifer's head. "I don't need to strut and show off how grand I am by breaking you. There are a thousand horses I can ride, but you're the only one I want covering my mares."

The words meant nothing to the stallion, but Ty's calm voice and gentle, confident hands did. Lucifer gave a long snort and stopped rolling his eyes and flinching at every touch. Slowly he was accepting the fact that although man in general had been his enemy in the past, this particular man was different. Lucifer had been pinned and blinded and helpless, but the man hadn't attacked him. Obviously he wasn't going to, either.

As the stallion slowly relaxed, Ty let out a long, quiet breath. "You're going to make it easy on both of us, aren't you? I'm sure glad that bullet and a few miles of running took the starch out of you. I've got a feeling you wouldn't have ' een nearly so civilized about this if I'd caught you fresh. But then, if you'd been fresh, we'd never have caught you, would we? The Lord works in strange ways, Lucifer. I'm glad He saw fit to give you to us, if only for long enough to heal you and set you free."

Ty stood and praised the stallion for a long time, until at last the horse let wariness slide away and weariness claim his big body. With a huge sigh, Lucifer allowed his head to drop until it all but rested against Ty's chest. Standing three-legged, favoring his injured hip, the stallion took no more notice of Ty than if he had been a foal.

Slowly Ty bent until he could release the hobbles on Lucifer's front legs. The stallion's shoulder muscles flinched and rippled as though shaking off flies, but that was all the notice he took of being free.

"That's real good, son," Ty murmured, stroking the stallion's black hide. "Now let's see if you're going to try to kill me the first time I tug on that hackamore."

Chapter Twenty-Eight

As Ty slowly tightened the lead rope, Janna watched with breath held and her hands so tightly clenched around the spyglass that her fingers ached.

"Be good, Lucifer," she prayed. "Don't go crazy and hurt Ty when that hackamore gets tight."

Lucifer's head came up sharply when the hackamore began to exert pressure behind his ears and across his upper neck. He snorted and shook his head, but the gradually increasing pressure didn't diminish. Trembling, sweating nervously, ears swiveling forward and then away from the man's gentle voice, the stallion tried to understand what was happening, how to meet the new threat. When he attempted to back away from the pressure, it got sharply worse. When he stood still, it got slowly worse.

But when he limped forward, the pressure lifted.

"That's it," Ty murmured, slacking off on the lead rope immediately. He petted Lucifer, praising the horse with voice and hands. "Let's try a few more steps, son. We've got a long way to go before we're safe."

It didn't take Lucifer more than a few minutes to understand that a pressure urging him forward meant walk forward and a pressure across the bridge of his nose meant stop.

"You're not an outlaw at all, are you?" Ty asked softly, stroking the horse's powerful, sweaty neck. "Men have chased you, but thank God no man ever had a chance to ruin you with rough handling."

Lucifer flicked his ears as he followed the calm sounds of Ty's voice while the man backed up, paying out lead rope as he went.

"All right, son. It's time to get you out of this hole." Slowly Ty tightened the lead rope. "Come on. That's it...that's it. One step at a time, that's all." His mouth flattened as he saw the stallion's painful progress. "That hip sure is sore, isn't it?" Ty said in a low voice. "Well, son, it's going to get worse before it gets better, I'm afraid. But you'll live, God willing."

Ty coaxed the limping stallion along the bottom of the ravine until they came to a place he had spotted from the ridge above, a place where the sides of the gully were less steep. Ty climbed halfway out, turned and began applying a steady pressure on the lead rope once more.

"Up you go. It will be easier to walk once you're on sort of level land again. Come on...come on...don't go all mulish on me now, son. It's not as steep as it looks."

Lucifer disliked the idea of climbing the gully, but he disliked the slowly tightening vise of the hackamore even more. Suddenly he lunged forward, taking the side of the ravine in a hurtling rush. Ty leaped aside just in time to avoid being trampled and scrambled up the slope after the stallion. Once on top, Lucifer came to a stop and stood three-legged, trembling from nervousness and pain.

Janna left her lookout place on the ridge and ran down to meet Ty, slowing to a walk for the last few yards so as not to frighten Lucifer.

"No one in sight," she said quietly.

"All right." Ty lifted his hat, wiped his forehead and resettled the hat with a hard tug. "How's your arm?"

Surprised that Ty had noticed, Janna hesitated and then shrugged. "Better than Lucifer's haunch."

"Hand over your pack."

She tried not to wince as he helped her out of the rawhide straps, but she couldn't conceal her left arm's growing soreness. With gentle fingertips he traced the dark bruise where one of Lucifer's hooves had struck a glancing blow.

"Any numbness?" Ty asked.

She shook her head.

"All your fingers work?"

Silently she wiggled each of them in turn.

"Can you scout for us?" Ty asked, releasing her arm, caressing her all the way to her fingertips.

Suddenly breathless, Janna nodded.

"Cat got your tongue?"

She smiled and stuck her tongue out at Ty.

"Is that a promise?" he drawled. He smiled and touched her lips with his fingertip. "Stick it out again, sugar."

"I don't think—"

That was as far as Janna got before Ty bent and took what she had promised to him a moment before. Surprise stiffened Janna for an instant before she sighed and invited Ty into the softness and warmth of her mouth. Almost shyly she touched his tongue with her own, retreated, then returned to touch fleetingly again and again, until there was no more retreat, just two mouths in a seething, seamless mating.

When Ty finally lifted his head he was breathing too hard, but he was smiling.

"It occurred to me when that stallion was doing his best to trample me into the dirt," Ty said, "that a man shouldn't die without tasting a woman on his lips. You taste good, like Christmas and Thanksgiving and my birthday all rolled into one. And if you don't turn around and get busy scouting, I'm going to be walking bent over double and in damn near as much pain as Lucifer."

Janna smiled up at Ty, showing him the same near shyness with which she had begun their kiss. His eyelids lowered and desire changed his expression, making it both harder and more sensual. For an instant she thought that he was going to kiss her again, and she longed for it. Then he reached out, turned her around and swatted her lightly on the rear. She would have said something about the trail she was going to take to the east, but the swat had ended with Ty's hand tracing the curve of her buttocks with loving care and suddenly she found herself breathless and aching.

"I'll head east and a little bit south unless you come and tell me otherwise," Ty said. Quickly he removed a handful of bullets from his pistol belt. "Take these."

The bullets felt smooth, cool and heavy in Janna's hand. She put them in her pocket and prayed she wouldn't need them. While she could shoot a pistol, she couldn't hit much at any range greater than a few hundred feet. If she were forced to use the weapon at all, its greatest benefit would probably be as a warning to Ty that he had better take cover.

And he would need that warning. Unable to hide his tracks, forced by Lucifer's injury to go slowly and to take the easiest—and therefore most open—way available, Ty would be a sitting duck in a pond surrounded by hunters. Both he and Janna knew it.

Janna set off to the southeast at a steady trot. Her knee-high moccasins made almost no sound over pine needles and grasses, and she left few marks of her passage. She ran without pausing except to listen for any wind-carried conversations or for the sound of distant gunfire. She heard nothing but the normal calling of birds, the scolding of squirrels, and the restless murmuring of the wind as it tried to herd together enough clouds for a storm.

Behind her, Ty talked to the black stallion, praising him as he limped over the land. For his part, Lucifer moved as quickly as he could. A lifetime of running from man had given the stallion a relentless wariness that worked to Ty's benefit; the horse was as intent upon reaching a safe place as Ty was. And like Ty, the stallion knew instinctively that safety wasn't to be had in the wide-open spaces of the plateau. Space was useful only if you could outrun your enemies. At the moment, Lucifer couldn't outrun anything that was worth fleeing from in the first place.

Initially Ty walked ahead of Lucifer, encouraging him with a steady pressure on the hackamore. After the first hour, the horse no longer needed to be reminded that he was supposed to keep walking. When Ty moved, so did Lucifer. When Ty stood, Lucifer stood. When Ty walked, Lucifer walked with his head even with Ty's left shoulder. The hackamore's lead rope remained slack.

"You're some kind of special," Ty said, talking to Lucifer as they walked. "You're as gentle as a lady's hack. Makes me wonder if maybe you weren't paddock raised and then got free somehow. Of course, it simply could be that we both want the same thing right now—a safe place to hide. You might be a lot harder to get along with if you wanted one thing and I wanted another."

Lucifer's only answer was a brisk swish of his long black tail as he drove off flies attracted to his wound. Ty checked the gash, saw that it was bleeding again and knew that nothing could be done for it.

"Better a wound that bleeds than one that festers," Ty reminded himself, drawing on his battlefield experience. "As long as it doesn't bleed too much."

He kept an eye on the stallion's injury. After a few miles it became apparent that the bleeding was more of a steady oozing than a serious flow.

Janna, using her spyglass, had reassured herself on the same subject; Lucifer was bleeding, but it wasn't a problem yet. Despite his limp he was moving at a good walking pace. With luck they would reach the edge of the plateau before dark. Otherwise they would have to find a place to sleep, because nothing short of the most extreme emergency would force Janna to take on the east trail in full darkness while leading an unbroken, injured mustang.

Ignoring the steady throbbing of her arm, Janna trotted across the plateau's wild surface, scouting both for enemies and for the easiest, quickest way to reach the trail down the east face. She used what cover she could find but didn't waste time trying to be invisible. It was more important that Lucifer and Ty reach the east edge of the plateau before dark than that she leave no trail.

As the day wore on, Janna ranged farther and farther ahead, checking on Ty and Lucifer less and less often. They had agreed that if she didn't check back before Ty reached the east rim, he would take Lucifer down the trail and keep on going toward the keyhole canyon. He was reluctant to stop for a rest, much less for a whole night, because he knew that Lucifer would stiffen up badly once he stopped moving.

By the time Janna reached the last, long fold of land that lay between her and the eastern edge of the plateau, it was late afternoon. She climbed the long ridge at a diagonal, heading for two tall pines. From the top she knew she would be able to see out across several hundred square miles of plateau, including the eastern edge and a bit of the low country beyond. She hoped that she would see only the usual things—pines, grass, sky, rivers of black rock spilling down ragged slopes, wild horses grazing, perhaps even an antelope or two. What she hoped *not* to see was any sign of man.

Just below the crest, Janna dropped to her stomach and wormed her way up until she could see over without giving away her own presence to anyone who might be on the other side. The first thing she saw was a hawk patrolling just below the ridge top. The second thing she saw was Zebra grazing with a scattering of Lucifer's mares.

Immediately Janna put her hands to her mouth. A hawk's wild cry floated from her lips. Zebra's head came up, her ears pricked and her nostrils flared. A soaring hawk cried in fierce answer to Janna's call, but Zebra didn't even turn her head toward the bird. Janna's high, keening cry came again. Zebra spun and cantered eagerly toward the ridge, whinnying her welcome.

"Hello, girl," Janna said, standing up, as pleased as the mare was. "Did you know that you're the answer to a prayer? Now I'll be able to cover three times the ground and not have to worry about tracks."

Zebra nickered and whuffled and pushed her head against Janna's body, nearly knocking her off her feet.

"I hope you're as eager for a run as you look, because you're going to get one. Hold still, girl. My arm is as stiff as an old man's knees."

Janna's mount wasn't very elegant, but she managed to finish right side up on the mare, which was all that counted.

"Come on, girl, let's check on your lord and master."

Eagerly Zebra responded to the pressure of Janna's heels. Cantering swiftly, the horse ate up the distance between Janna and Ty. Janna guided the horse in a long, looping curve, wanting to check more of the land on the way back to Ty. The mare sped quickly through the open country, going from tree shadow to full sun and back again, a kaleidoscope of light and darkness flowing over horse and rider, and always the earth flying beneath the mare's hooves.

Janna was only a few minutes away from where she had left Ty when she saw the renegades.

Chapter Twenty-Nine

Zebra spun aside and leaped into a full gallop in the same motion. Janna didn't try to slow or turn the horse back toward the place where Ty was. She simply grabbed a double handful of flying black mane and bent over the mare's neck, urging her on to greater speed. Behind her the Indians shouted and fired a few shots as they gave chase.

Janna had ridden Zebra at a gallop before, but nothing like this frantic pace. The mare's speed would have been frightening to Janna if it hadn't been for the fact that she was fleeing an even greater danger. As it was, Janna flattened down against Zebra's sleek, driving body, urging greater speed and trying to make herself as light a burden as possible.

Zebra stretched out her neck and ran as though fleeing hell. The force of the wind raking over Janna's eyes made tears stream down her face. Her hat was ripped from her head. One of the chin strings snapped and the hat sailed away. Soon her braids had unraveled and her long hair was streaming out behind her like darkly burning, wind-whipped flames.

The sudden appearance of Janna's distinctive hair cooled the urgency of the chase for the Indians. There was little sport and even less glory or booty in capturing a homeless girl. There were also the uncomfortable whispers about the true nature of that girl. *Bruja.* Witch. Shadow of Flame. That was what she looked like as she bent over the wild horse she rode with neither bridle nor saddle, her body all but lost in the flying mane and her own unbound hair streaming behind her in the wind like a warning flag.

And surely only a spirit horse ridden by a spirit woman could be so fleet.

Janna didn't try to guide Zebra, for the mare knew the plateau's twists and turns and traps as well as Janna did. All that she cared about was that the horse was racing away from the eastern trail and therefore away from Ty and the injured stallion. She made no attempt to use the revolver that was digging into her body as she rode the wildly galloping horse. Drawing the weapon would have been difficult enough; shooting accurately would have been impossible.

With every passing minute it became more obvious that Zebra was outrunning the renegades. Well fed, well rested, carrying only Janna's insignificant weight, Zebra not only had more speed than the renegades' horses, she had more stamina, as well. After a few miles the renegades became certain that they were spending their horses in a losing cause. First two warriors dropped out of the chase, then a third, then a fourth, until finally only one man still pursued the bright banner of Janna's hair. Finally he, too, gave up and stopped whipping his laboring horse.

Zebra knew before Janna did that the chase was over. Even so, the mare kept galloping for a time, putting more distance between herself and her pursuers. Janna sensed the difference in Zebra's pace and knew that the immediate danger had passed. Cautiously she shifted her grip on the mane, wiped her eyes and looked over her shoulder. There was nothing behind her but Zebra's tracks across an empty land.

When Zebra breasted a ridge, Janna urged the mare into the cover of some trees and then checked her trail very carefully, using the spyglass. The renegades weren't anywhere to be seen. What she could see of the land ahead of her looked equally empty.

For a few minutes Janna considered the various ways and means of hiding Zebra's tracks in order to confuse any followers. Every way she thought of, including dismounting and letting the mare go free once more, would make it impossible for Janna to get to the east rim of the plateau before dark. She would have to keep Zebra with her and count on the mare's speed to thwart any more pursuit.

"All right, girl," Janna said, "let's go back and see if Ty and Lucifer are all right."

At a touch from her rider, the mustang turned and began cantering at an angle to her old trail. Though Janna watched warily, she saw no sign that any human had been along recently. Wild horses grazed undisturbed until Zebra appeared, and then the horses spun and raced away. Janna urged Zebra to detour into the three groups of horses she found, mixing the mare's tracks with those of her mustang kin, making it all but impossible for anyone to follow Janna from that point on.

By the time Janna spotted Ty and Lucifer, it was midafternoon and she was only a mile from the eastern trail. Clouds that had been frail and white earlier in the day had matured into towering, seething billows, which were creamy on their curving tops and blue-black on their flat bottoms. The Fire Mountains were already obscured beneath dense clouds. Distant thunder rumbled down from the invisible peaks. Soon the plateau would be engulfed by sound and fury and tiny, icy hammer blows of rain. Lightning would strike the plateau's promontories and lone trees would run the risk of being transformed into torches.

It would be no different for a man caught in the open on the exposed, eastern face of the plateau. If they hoped to get down the east trail today, they would have to move quickly.

As though sensing her rider's urgency, Zebra cantered to the edge of the plateau. There, wind and rain had unraveled the land into countless crevices, gullies, ravines and canyons. There, at the head of an insignificant ravine, began the sole path down the plateau's rugged east face. There, too, were Ty and Lucifer.

Ty didn't wait for Janna to dismount. Before Zebra had come to a full stop, he plucked Janna off and held her close while the two horses nickered and nuzzled each other in friendly greeting.

"What the hell happened to you?" Ty demanded harshly, but the hands stroking her unbound hair were gentle.

"I found Zebra and we were coming back to check on you and we popped up over a rise and found a bunch of renegades." Janna felt Ty's arms tighten abruptly.

"I knew it," he said, his voice rough. "I heard those damned shots and I just *knew*."

"The renegades were as surprised as I was," Janna said, trying to reassure Ty. "They only got off a few shots before I was out of range. None of the bullets even came close."

"Then how did you lose your hat?"

"Wind," Janna said succinctly. "Zebra ran like hell let out for a holiday. I couldn't see for the tears in my eyes."

Ty thought of the rugged land and the wild mustang and Janna riding her with no stirrups to support and balance her, no bridle to help her control her mount, nothing to help her stay in place if the horse should stumble; and injury or death awaiting her if she fell.

"Dammit, Janna...!"

Ty's voice trailed off. He knew that it was unreasonable of him to be angry with her for having been in danger. She could no more help her position in the wild land than he could.

"This can't go on," Ty said beneath his breath. "I've got to get you to a place where you'll be safe."

Thunder muttered across the plateau, reminding Ty that danger wore many faces, and another one was looking at them right now. Reluctantly he turned and measured the hair-raising trail that awaited the injured stallion.

The path began at the head of a narrow ravine that rapidly branched sideways and downward, threading a tortuous zigzag route across the crumbling east face of the plateau. After the first quarter mile the path became less steep. After a mile the trail merged with the sloping outwash plain that began several thousand feet below the plateau itself. At that point the path became no worse than any other game trail in the rugged land.

But that first quarter mile was a nightmare, and the last three quarters were little better. It had been difficult enough to scramble up onto the plateau via that trail. Climbing down was always more dangerous. Ty didn't see how they were going to negotiate the steep path without losing the tug-of-war with gravity and falling a long, long way down.

"The first part is the hardest," Janna said.

"Is that supposed to make me feel better?"

"Well, it shouldn't make you feel worse."

For an instant Ty's smile flashed whitely beneath his black mustache. He brushed his lips over Janna's answering smile before he released her.

"Keep Zebra back until Lucifer is through with the worst of it," Ty said. "I'm going to have enough trouble staying out from under the stallion's hooves. I sure don't need to be looking over my shoulder for the mare, too." He turned to Lucifer and pulled gently on the hackamore's lead rope. "Come on, son. Might as well get it over with. As my daddy used to say, 'We can't dance and it's too wet to plow.'"

Lucifer walked to the beginning of the path, looked down the slope and refused to take another step.

"Don't blame you a bit," Ty said soothingly, "but it has to be done." He increased the pressure on the lead rope. "Come on, you big black stud.

Show Janna what a well-behaved gentleman you've become during our walk today."

The stallion's head came up sharply, counteracting the pressure that tended to pull him toward the steep, dangerous path. Thunder rolled and muttered. A freshening wind brought with it the scent of rain, warning that the possibility of a storm grew greater with every passing minute.

"Come on," Ty said, increasing the pressure on the lead rope until he could pull no harder. "If you think that little bit of a path looks rough now, wait until it's raining fit to put out the fires of hell. When that happens we want to be long gone from here."

Lucifer's ears went back as he set himself more firmly, pulling hard against the pressure on the hackamore.

"Your daddy must have been Satan's own black mule," Ty said, but his tone was still mild and reassuring. "Come on, son. You heard the lady. The first part is the hardest. After that it's as easy as licking honey off a spoon."

Lucifer's ears flattened against his head.

Ty had several choices. He could keep pulling and hope the stallion would give up. He could keep pulling and have Janna make a loud noise, stampeding the stallion over the rim—and right onto Ty. Or he could lure the stallion onto the trail using the oldest bait of all.

"Janna, do you think that cat-footed mare of yours will go down this trail?"

"I don't know. It's worth a try."

"Easy, son," Ty said as he went up to Lucifer and put pressure on the horse's black nose to make him back up. "If you don't want to be first you'll just have to get out of the way and let your lady show you how easy it is."

Lucifer willingly backed away from the trail. Wind gusted suddenly, bringing with it a foretaste of the chilly storm. The stallion pricked his ears and snorted, feeling an instinctive urge to seek shelter.

Ty wrapped the lead rope and secured it around Lucifer's neck, freeing his own hands and at the same time making sure that the stallion didn't get all tangled up in loose rope. When Ty was finished he led the stallion aside, making room for Janna and Zebra to approach the rough path. When Zebra was pointed in the right direction—straight down—Janna smacked the mare on her warm haunch.

"Down you go," she said hopefully.

Zebra turned and looked at Janna.

"Shoo, girl! Go on, get on down that trail. Get!"

The mustang shook her head as though ridding herself of persistent flies. Deliberately she backed away from the trail.

"Dammit," Ty said. "Maybe if we—Janna, don't!"

It was too late. Janna had already darted around in front of Zebra and started down the trail herself. She picked her way down the first steep pitch, found a relatively secure place to stand and turned to call to Zebra.

"No," Ty said urgently. "Don't take the trail in front of Zebra. If she slips she'll roll right on over you and leave you flatter than a shadow!"

"I'll stay out of her way," Janna said, but her voice was tight. She knew even better than Ty the danger of being on the downhill side of a horse on a precipitous slope. "Come on, girl. Point those black hooves in this direction. Come to me, Zebra. Come on."

As always, Janna's coaxing murmur and her outstretched hands intrigued the mare. She edged as far forward as she could without committing herself to the trail. Neck outstretched, nostrils flaring, ears pricked forward, Zebra leaned toward Janna. Her hooves, however, remained firmly planted.

Without hesitation, Janna retreated farther down the trail. When she reached another relatively level patch of ground, she was fifty feet away. She put her hands to her mouth and a hawk's wild cry floated up. Zebra nickered nervously and shifted her feet. The hawk cry came again, reminding the mare of all the times she had answered the call and found Janna waiting with her backpack full of treats.

One of the mare's black hooves lifted, then set down barely a few inches away. Another hoof lifted. Another few inches gained. Ears pricked, skin flinching nervously, Zebra literally inched her way down the trail. Janna melted away in front of the mustang, calling softly, praising Zebra with every breath.

As Ty watched, his body ran with sweat. A single hesitation, a loose stone, any miscalculation on the mare's part and Janna quickly would be engulfed in a flailing, lethal windmill of horse and human flesh. There was no place for her to leap aside, no place to hide. If Zebra fell, Janna would be killed.

Unknowingly Ty prayed in low tones, never lifting his glance from Zebra's mincing progress, feeling as though his soul were being drawn on a rack.

If you get out of this alive, Janna, Ty vowed silently, *I'll make sure you stay out of danger if I have to tie you up and stuff you in my backpack and never let you out.*

Lucifer whickered nervously, calling to Zebra. The mare ignored him, intent on the trail and on the girl who kept retreating down the dangerously steep slope. The stallion's next call was louder and more urgent but it had no more effect than the first. He whinnied imperiously. Zebra's ears swiveled and her tail swished. She lifted her head to look, began slipping and sat down on her haunches. For the space of several breaths the mare simply remained motionless, then she slowly gathered herself and resumed her inching progress down the trail.

The stallion's barrel swelled as he took in air for another whinny.

"Shut up, son," Ty said.

Long, powerful fingers closed gently and completely over the stallion's nostrils, making it impossible for the horse to whinny. Lucifer threw up his head but Ty hung on, talking calmly the whole time.

"Yelling at her won't do any good right now," Ty assured the stallion. "That little mare no more listens to you than Janna listens to me. Later I'll be glad to let you give your woman a royal chewing out—and I plan to do the same to mine—but first let's get them to a safe place."

The firm hands and reassuring voice held Lucifer quiet, though his half-flattened ears told anyone who cared to look that the stallion wasn't very happy about the situation.

Ty didn't notice. The farther the mare got down the trail, the more impossible it seemed that a horse had descended it at all. But Zebra had. The evidence was everywhere, in clumps of dirt gouged out by hooves and in hoofprints elongated by skids. Beneath his breath Ty counted out the steps remaining on the last steep pitch before the trail leveled out to the point where Zebra didn't have to go down half-sitting and braced on her stiffened forelegs.

"Seven, six, fi—"

Zebra skidded the last fifteen feet and then stood quietly, absorbing Janna's praise. Ty let out a long breath as he released his grip on Lucifer's muzzle.

"All right, son. It's our turn. And this time I'm not taking no for an answer."

Chapter Thirty

Lucifer went to the edge of the plateau, whinnied loudly and was answered by Zebra. He whinnied again. Zebra looked up the steep path but didn't move one step in the stallion's direction.

"She's not about to scramble up to you," Ty said calmly. He stood to the side of Lucifer's head and pulled steadily forward on the hackamore. "If you want her, you're going to have to do it the hard way."

The stallion stood at the trailhead, laid back his ears...and began climbing down.

Janna found it more unnerving to watch Ty descend alongside the stallion's big hooves than it had been for her to climb down the plateau's face in front of Zebra. The first quarter mile was especially dangerous, for there really wasn't enough room for Ty to stand alongside the horse on the path without being under Lucifer's feet half the time.

Let go, Ty. Let Lucifer do it alone, Janna urged silently. *He won't back out now. He can't. The only thing he can do is keep coming down and he knows it.*

Snorting, mincing, sliding, sweating, the muscles in his injured leg trembling at the strain, the stallion negotiated the first quarter mile with surprising speed. More than once it was Ty's timely jerk on the hackamore that saved Lucifer from a fall by levering his head up, which helped the horse to regain control when his feet started sliding. Under normal conditions the mustang's own agility would have been sufficient to get him down the trail, but his injury made the difficult footing all but impossible had it not been for Ty's help.

Without warning the stallion's injured leg gave way and he lost his footing. Ty threw all his muscle behind the hackamore, forcing Lucifer back onto his haunches. Front legs braced, hooves digging into the path, the horse slid about twenty feet before he came to a stop. Sitting up like a big black hound, the stallion sweated nervously while displaced pebbles bounced and rattled down the slope. Right beside him, Ty sweated just as hard. It had been much too close to disaster. Someone with less strength than Ty wouldn't have been able to prevent the horse from falling.

Janna held her fist against her teeth as she forced back a scream. Ty had taken a terrible gamble, for if his weight and leverage hadn't been enough to counteract gravity, he would have been swept away with Lucifer in a long, lethal fall.

"That's it, son," Ty said, his voice soothing despite the hammer blows of his own heart. "You rest and get your wind back. That old leg just keeps fooling you. You expect it to be there for you and it isn't, not the way you need it to be. That's the problem with strength. You get to counting on it and then it lets you down. So use your head instead. You can't just rush the path and scramble and slide and get it over with the way you would if you had your usual muscle and coordination. You have to take it nice and slow."

When Lucifer's skin no longer rippled with nervous reaction, Ty gradually released his pressure on the hackamore. Gingerly the stallion shifted his weight forward and began descending once more. As though he had understood Ty's words, the mustang moved more slowly now, demanding less of his injured leg.

Even so, by the time Lucifer reached the end of the steepest portion of the path, Janna was trembling with a fear she had never known for herself. When both man and horse were on safe ground, she let out a shaky breath and ran to Ty, throwing herself at him, holding on to him with fierce strength despite her bruised arm.

"I was so frightened," Janna said against Ty's neck. "All I could think of was what would happen if Lucifer got to sliding too fast or lost his footing completely and you couldn't get out of the way in time."

Ty's arms closed around Janna, lifting her off her feet. "The same thought occurred to me about every other step," he said roughly, "but worst of all was watching you stand in front of Zebra and knowing there wasn't a damn thing I could do if things went to hell." He held Janna hard and close, savoring the feel of her in his arms, her living warmth and resilience and the sweet rush of her breath against his neck. "God, little one, it's good to be alive and holding you."

A cool wind swirled down the plateau's face, trailing the sound of thunder behind. Reluctantly Ty released Janna and set her back on her feet. A moment later he fished the crumpled rain poncho from his backpack. Without a word he tugged the waterproof folds over Janna.

"That should do it," he said. "Now let's get off this exposed slope before lightning has better luck at killing us than that damn trail did."

With the casual strength that kept surprising Janna, Ty tossed her onto Zebra's back.

"Don't wait for me. Just get off the slope," Ty said to Janna. He stepped back and smacked Zebra lightly on her haunch. "Get to it, horse. And you keep your rider hair side up or I'll skin you for a sofa covering."

Zebra took to the path again with an eagerness that said more plainly than words that the mustang understood the danger of being caught out in the open during a storm. Lucifer was just as eager to see the last of the exposed trail leading from the foot of the plateau to the lowlands beyond, but his injury forced a slower pace. Limping heavily, the stallion started off down the rocky decline.

Out in the distance to the east, blue-black buttes and localized thunderstorms were intermixed with golden cataracts of light where sunshine poured through gaps between squall lines. Overhead, lightning played through the massed clouds and the wind increased in power.

By the time Lucifer and Ty reached the place where the plateau merged with the lower canyon lands beyond, the last luminous shafts of sunlight had slowly merged with the thunderstorm gathering overhead, leaving behind an odd, sourceless gloaming that made every feature of the land stand forth as though outlined in pale gold. The effect lasted for only a few minutes, until the first sweeping veils of rain came down, blending sky and land into one seamless whole. Lightning danced across the land on incandescent feet, while thunder rumbled behind its shimmering, elusive mistress.

"Well, son," Ty said, pulling his hat down tighter against the wind and pelting rain, "this cloud's silver lining is that no self-respecting renegade is going to be out chasing around in the rain."

If that fact cheered Lucifer, the horse didn't show it. He limped along with his ears half-laid-back in warning of his surly temper. Ty felt the same way himself. With luck the storm would turn out to be a small, fast-moving squall line. Without luck, the rain would last for hours. With bad luck, the slot leading into Janna's hidden canyon would be too deep with runoff water from the thunderstorm for them to enter and they would have to spend another night in the open.

Janna was worrying about the same thing. If she were alone, she would have hurried Zebra toward the miles-distant slot. But she wasn't alone, and despite Lucifer's best efforts, his shuffling, painful walk meant that it would be several hours before they reached the haven of her hidden canyon.

The rain quickly limited visibility to a few hundred yards, making scouting both impossible and unnecessary. Janna turned Zebra and retraced her steps until she saw Lucifer and Ty. She slid off Zebra and fell into step beside Ty.

"Go ahead on to the canyon," he said. "No sense in you catching your death out in the rain."

"It will be dark an hour before you get to the slot. You'll miss it. Besides, you know how it is with misery. I was feeling like a little company."

Ty thought of objecting more forcefully to Janna's presence but didn't. Part of him agreed with her that he would have trouble finding the narrow slot in the dark in the rain, because the only other time he had been through it from this direction he had been more dead than alive. But the real reason he didn't object was that he enjoyed having Janna beside him, her fingers laced through his, their hands slowly warming with shared body heat.

"Janna?" Ty asked after a long time of rain and silence, voicing a thought that had been nagging at him for hours.

"Yes?"

"Why did you risk your life holding on to Lucifer in that ravine?"

"I didn't want Troon to get him again."

"But you heard the renegades. You had to figure that Troon was as good as dead. You could have let Lucifer go, but you didn't. You hung on despite the danger to yourself."

Janna said nothing.

"Sugar? Why?"

"I promised you a chance to gentle Lucifer," Janna said simply. "There would never be a better chance than in that small ravine."

Ty swore very softly. "I thought it was something crazy like that. Listen to me. You're free of that promise you made. Do you hear me? If Lucifer decides to take off in twelve different directions, that's my problem, not yours. You just get the hell out of the way where you won't get hurt." Ty waited but she said nothing. "Janna?"

"I heard you."

"Do I have your word that if Lucifer bolts or goes loco, you'll get out of the way instead of trying to help?"

"Ty—"

"Give me your word," he interrupted, "or so help me God I'll turn around right now and walk back to Wyoming and to hell with that damned black stud."

"But he's your future, the only way you'll get a chance to buy your silken—"

Ty interrupted with a burst of language that was both savage and obscene. It was a mile before Janna had the courage to break the silence that had followed.

"I promise," she said finally. "I don't understand why you won't let me help you, but—"

"You don't understand?" Ty demanded fiercely, cutting off Janna's words once more. "You must have a damned poor opinion of me if you think I'd build my dream on top of your dead body!"

"I never meant anything like that!" Janna said instantly, shocked that Ty had misunderstood her words. "I know you'd never do something that awful. You're much too kind and gentle and generous."

Ty's laughter was as harsh as his swearing had been, for he knew that a man who was kind or gentle or generous wouldn't have eased his violent hunger at the cost of Janna's innocence. But Ty had done just that and now she was no longer innocent...and worst of all, he couldn't bring himself to truly repent his action. The ecstasy he had known within Janna's body was too great, too consuming, to ever be repudiated.

If he had it to do all over again, he would no more be able to preserve Janna's virginity than he had been the first time. She was wildness and grace and elemental fire, and he was a man who had hungered a lifetime for all three without knowing it. She had sensed his needs, given herself to him and had required nothing of him in return. Not one damn thing.

And he felt the silken strands of her innocence and generosity twining more tightly around him with each moment, binding him.

"Do you do it on purpose?" Ty demanded angrily.

"What?"

"Give everything and ask nothing and thereby chain me to you tighter than any steel manacles could."

Janna felt as though she had been struck. The cold rain that had been making her miserable became her friend, for it hid the tears and disappointment she was too tired to conceal. When Ty had swept her up in his arms and held her as fiercely as she had held him, she had begun to hope that he cared more for her than simply as a sexual convenience. When he had held her hand and walked in companionable silence with her through the storm, she had been certain that he cared for her.

What she hadn't realized was that he would resent that caring, and her.

"Well, you're by God going to take something from me," Ty continued. "Lucifer is half yours."

"I don't want him."

"I didn't want you to risk your neck, either," Ty shot back, "and a lot of good my wanting did me."

Janna jerked her hand free of his. "Did you ever think that the reason I didn't ask for anything from you was that there was nothing you had that I wanted?"

"Nothing?" Ty asked sardonically. "You could have fooled me."

The tone of his voice told Janna that he was remembering her hands caressing him, her lips clinging, her hips lifting in silent pleading that his body join with hers. Shame coursed through her.

"Don't worry," she said, her voice strained. "You won't have to lose any sleep on my account tonight. I won't seduce you again."

"Seduce me? Is that what you think happened? You seduced me?" Ty laughed. "Sugar, you don't have the least idea how to seduce a man. A woman seduces a man with rustling silks and secret smiles and accidental touches of her soft, perfumed hands. She seduces a man with her conversation and the sweet music of her voice when she greets her guests for a fancy ball. She seduces a man by knowing fine wines and elegant food, and by her special grace when she enters a room knowing he'll be there." Ty shook his head and added, "You well and truly bedded me, but you sure as hell didn't seduce me."

Janna remembered what Ty had said about her last night…*suited to be nothing except a man's mistress, but you lack the social graces for even that profession.*

Without a word Janna turned away from Ty and swung onto Zebra's warm back, ignoring the pain that mounting the horse without aid gave to her bruised arm.

"Janna? What the hell…?"

She didn't answer. Her heels urged Zebra forward until Janna could see and hear only the rain.

Chapter Thirty-One

"Come on, it's just a little bit farther," Ty said to the stallion, hoping he wasn't lying. Neither Ty's voice nor the steady pressure he put on the hackamore revealed the weariness that had settled into the marrow of his bones, turning his muscles to sand.

For a moment Ty was afraid that the stallion wouldn't respond, but the pressure on the hackamore eased abruptly as the horse resumed his awkward walking gait.

"That's it, son," Ty said encouragingly. "She said the slot was at the top of a little rise."

And that was all Janna had said through the long hours of intermittent rain and wind. When it wasn't raining she rode far ahead of Ty and Lucifer. When it rained she rode in close enough that her tracks were always clear for Ty to follow. When it became dark she rode closer still, ensuring that Lucifer wouldn't get lost.

Ty was certain that it was the stallion's welfare rather than his own that concerned Janna. Not once since she had mounted Zebra had she said anything to Ty. He missed her conversation. In the past weeks he had become accustomed to her insights into the land and its animals, her uninhibited response to the wind and sun, and her shy smile when he touched her. He missed her laughter when she talked about hiding from Cascabel in the same way the renegade had once hidden from the soldiers—out in plain sight. Ty missed the snippets of plays and poetry and essays she liked to talk about with him, drawing from him the missing parts of her education. Most of all he missed the warm, companionable silence they had shared while they walked hand in hand in the cold rain.

The silence Ty and Janna had shared since she had ridden off was anything but companionable. It was as chill and empty as the night.

"Maybe you can tell me," Ty said to Lucifer. "Why would a woman get all upset because I told her it isn't her fault that she's not a virgin anymore? Because it sure as hell isn't her fault. Janna didn't have the faintest idea of what waited for her at the end of that primrose path. She could no more have known when to say no to me than she could have walked down the plateau trail carrying Zebra on her back.

"But I knew where we were going. I knew the first time I kissed Janna that I should stop myself right there or I wouldn't be able to quit short of burying myself in that sweet young body. But I didn't stop. I wanted her the way a river in flood wants the sea. Just plain unstoppable. And God help me, I still want her just like that.

"I knew what I was doing every inch of the way...and it was every inch the best I've ever had. I'll die remembering the beautiful sounds she made while I was inside her, pleasuring her with my whole body."

Ty's voice thickened as memories poured through him in an incandescent tide. Despite his exhaustion, his blood beat heavily at the thought of being sheathed within Janna's fire and softness once more.

"She didn't have a chance to refuse me," Ty continued, his voice rough. "Not a single damned chance in hell. It should have made her feel better to know that what happened was my fault, not hers.

"So why won't she speak to me?"

Lucifer didn't have any answer for Ty. Not that he had expected one. If the stallion had known how to handle the supposedly weaker sex, Zebra wouldn't have been racing around the plateau with Janna for the past few years. Muttering to himself, Ty walked up the rise, urging the limping stallion along with a steady pressure on the hackamore.

At last a low nicker came floating out of the darkness in front of them. Lucifer nickered in return. No verbal welcome came to Ty, however. Nor did Janna say anything when she dismounted and walked around the stallion. Frowning, peering into the coldly brilliant moonlight that had replaced the wind-frayed clouds, she tried to gauge Lucifer's condition.

"Is there too much water in the slot for us to get through?" Ty asked.

"No."

He waited, but Janna had nothing more to say on that subject—or any other, apparently. At least, not to him. But it seemed she had nothing against talking to the stallion.

"You poor, brave creature. You've really been put through it today, haven't you?" Janna said in a gentle voice as she reached out to pet Lucifer.

Ty opened his mouth to warn Janna that the stallion was feeling surly as hell, but the words died on his tongue when Lucifer whickered softly and stretched his muzzle out to Janna's hands. Slender fingers stroked his muzzle and cheeks, then searched through the stallion's thick, shaggy forelock until she found the bony knob between his ears. She slid her fingers beneath the hackamore and rubbed away the unaccustomed feel of the leather.

Lucifer let out a breath that was almost a groan and put his forehead against Janna's chest, offering himself to her touch with a trust that first shocked Ty, then moved him, making his throat close around all the emotions he had no words to describe. Seeing the stallion's gentle surrender reminded Ty of the ancient myth of the unicorn and virgin. But as Ty watched Janna, he wondered if it weren't some elemental feminine quality that had attracted the unicorn to the girl, rather than her supposedly virginal state.

That poor unicorn never had a chance, Ty told himself silently. *He was born to lay his head in that one maiden's lap and be captive to her gentle hands.*

The insight made Ty very restless. Though Janna had done nothing to hold him, he felt himself somehow confined, caught in an invisible net, tied with silken threads; and each thread was a shared caress, a shared smile, a shared word, until one thread became thousands woven into an unbreakable bond, and the silken snare was complete.

"Ready, boy?" Janna asked quietly. "It's going to be hard on your poor leg, but it's the last thing I'll ask of you until you're healed."

Janna turned and walked toward Zebra. Lucifer followed, silently urging Ty forward with a pressure on the lead rope he still held. The reversal in their roles gave Ty a moment of sardonic amusement. He wondered what would happen if he tied the rope around the stallion's neck and then turned and walked away, leaving everything behind.

I'll tell you what would happen, Ty thought to himself. *You'd spend the night hungry and freezing your butt off in the cold and Lucifer would spend it belly-deep in food with Janna's warm hands petting him. So who do you think is smarter—you or that stallion?*

With a muttered curse Ty followed Lucifer over the wet, rocky ground to the invisible opening in the plateau's wall. The face of the plateau at this point was made of broken ranks of sheer rocky cliffs punctuated by dark mounds of black lava. As though to make up for the precipitous nature of the land, the cliffs were only a tenth of the height of the heavily eroded wall Janna and Ty had descended earlier.

Even so, Janna had discovered no trail up onto the plateau itself from this area. If she wanted to go back up on top, she had to walk much farther south, following the ragged edge of the plateau as it rose and fell until she reached the gentle southern ascent. That would have been a full day's ride on a good horse. The east path, while steep, was only a few hours by foot.

Ahead of Ty both horses stopped abruptly. Zebra snorted nervously when Janna waded into the water gushing from the slot, but the mare didn't balk. She followed Janna into the ankle-deep runoff stream, for she had done this before and not been hurt by the experience. Lucifer hesitated, lowered his head and smelled the water, then limped into the stream in the manner of an animal who was too exhausted at the moment to do more than go where he was led.

Inside the slot, moonlight was reduced to a pale glimmering over the surface of the water. The horses were better off than the humans, both by reason of four legs and the superior night vision of equines. Even with those advantages, the horses didn't have an easy time of it. Janna, with her greater experience in negotiating the slot, managed not to slip and fall more than twice. Ty fell four times and considered himself fortunate that it wasn't a lot worse.

When they emerged into the valley, humans and animals alike were soaked by a combination of rain, runoff water and sweat.

"That's it, girl," Janna said tiredly, slapping the mare on her muscular haunch. "We're home."

Zebra trotted off into the moonlight, heading for the sweet grass and clover she had discovered on her previous visit. Ty considered hobbling Lucifer, then rejected the idea. Even if the stallion wanted to leave Zebra, Lucifer was too tired to take on the slot again. With a few smooth motions Ty removed the hackamore. When it was off, he rubbed away all the marks the leather had left on the horse's head. Lucifer leaned into the touch, obviously enjoying it.

"Yeah, I know. It doesn't take long to get spoiled, does it?" murmured Ty, thinking of Janna and the night before. "Tomorrow I'll give you a good rubdown, but right now you need food more than you need petting. Go follow Zebra, son. She knows where all the sweet things are in this place.''

After Ty removed his hand, it took a moment for the stallion to realize that he was free. When he did, he snorted, shook his head and limped off after Zebra. Ty looked away just in time to see Janna vanish into the willows that grew alongside the stream.

By the time Ty got to the cliff overhang Janna called home, a small glow of flame was expanding into the darkness. Sitting on her heels next to the fire, Janna fed in fuel from the supply she kept dry in one corner of the overhang. Once the fire took hold she added wet wood from the pile that was stacked beyond the protection of the rock.

Only when water was warming over the fire did Janna turn away and go to the small trunk she had laboriously tugged through the slot three years before, when she had discovered the secret canyon. Most of the trunk was filled with books. A small part of it was taken up with the last of her father's clothes. Only one ragged shirt remained, one pair of Sunday pants, three socks and the moccasins she had traded medicines for last spring.

''I took three shirts from Preacher's store. Do you want one of them?''

The sound of Ty's voice startled Janna. She hadn't realized that he was in camp. But there he was, standing on the other side of the fire, stretching muscles that were tired from carrying the heavy backpack that now rested against the stone cliff. Ty peeled off his hat and slapped it against his thigh, driving water from the hat rim in a fine spray.

''No,'' Janna said, turning away from Ty again, refusing more than his offer of a shirt.

She unlaced her soggy moccasins and set them aside to dry. With cold hands she worked beneath the poncho, unwinding the cloth that bound her breasts. The motions sent stabbing pains through her bruised arm. She set her teeth and continued. She had suffered worse injuries in the past; she would probably suffer more in the future.

Ty didn't bother to ask if Janna wanted any help, for he knew she would refuse him. Without a word he lifted the cumbersome poncho from Janna's shoulders and threw it aside. The sight of the bruise on her arm made his breath come in with an audible hiss. Even though experience told Ty that the bruise looked much worse than it actually was, he hated seeing the dark shadow of pain on her skin.

''Don't you have something for that?'' he asked.

''Yes.''

Janna tried to step away. Ty's hands closed around her lower arms in a grip that was gentle but unshakable.

''Hold still, sugar. Let me help you.''

Afraid to trust her voice, Janna shook her head in a negative.

''Yes,'' Ty countered instantly. ''You've patched me up often enough. Now it's your turn to be patched.''

Janna looked up into Ty's glance. His eyes were very dark yet alive with flames reflected from the campfire. The warmth of his hands on her chilled skin was shocking, but not as shocking as the heat that uncurled in her loins at the thought of being cared for by him. She shivered in a combination of cold and remembered desire.

And she hated it, both the memory and the desire, hated wanting a man whose feelings for her teetered between pity and contempt, lust and indifference.

"You're chilled through and through," Ty said, frowning as he saw Janna shiver violently. With quick motions he began unwrapping the cloth that bound her chest. "Where's the medicine you need?"

She shook her head, refusing him, refusing her memories, refusing everything.

"Janna, what in hell is the matter with you?"

Ty didn't wait for an answer. Janna felt cloth being stripped from her body by his big hands. Suddenly she couldn't bear the thought of her naked breasts being revealed to Ty again. He would touch them, kiss them, and the heat that was spreading from the pit of her stomach would flare up, burning away everything, even the knowledge that she loved a man who loved only his own dream...and she was not that dream.

With an inarticulate cry Janna tried to push away Ty's hands. It was like pushing on warm stone.

"It's too late to be shy," he said flatly, ignoring her attempts to stop him from unwrapping her breasts. "Hold still while I get this wet stuff off you."

"Let go of me."

The quality of Janna's voice was chilling. Ty's hands froze in the act of unwrapping her.

"Janna, what's wrong?"

His voice was gentle but Janna didn't hear that, or the emotions churning just beneath his control. She heard only her own memories, Ty's voice echoing and reechoing in her mind as he listed all her shortcomings as a woman— nothing to offer a husband, too unskilled to be a mistress, good only for the male need that built up inexorably when no other woman was around.

"Little one?" Ty asked, tipping Janna's chin up and brushing a kiss over her lips. They were as cold as her voice had been. "What did I do to make you so angry with me?"

When he would have kissed her again, she jerked her head away. "Don't touch me. I don't feel like being your whore tonight."

Chapter Thirty-Two

Ty's tightly held emotions exploded into a fury that was unlike any he had ever felt. He stopped trying to peel off layers of wet cloth and grabbed Janna's shoulders instead.

"Don't say something like that about yourself! Do you hear me, Janna Wayland? *You are not a whore!*"

Angry, ashamed, defiant, Janna stood shivering within Ty's grasp. "Just what would you call it?"

"We're...lovers."

"I don't think so," she said distinctly. "To be someone's lover suggests a certain affection mixed in with the lust. I'm not your lover. I'm a convenience until you take Lucifer and go off to buy your silk—"

"Don't say it," Ty interrupted savagely. "I'm sick to death of having those words flung in my face."

"Then stop flinging them in mine."

"I've never—"

"The hell you haven't!" Janna interrupted, her voice as savage as his. "'I'll have my silken lady or I'll have none at all for longer than it takes to pleasure myself,'" Janna quoted, each word clipped. "'You're the least female female I've ever seen.' Then you said that Cascabel looked more like a mesquite bush than I looked like a woman, and the comparisons didn't stop after you had me, either. You couldn't wait to tell me that it was a woman you'd needed, not me."

Janna's voice broke, then steadied as words rushed out. "And then you told me that my virginity was all I had to offer to a husband because I had no family, no profession, no money. You said that you had ruined me, because now I wasn't good enough to be a wife and wasn't educated enough to be a mistress and that meant that I wasn't good enough to be anything but a 'toy of many men, not one.' That's a whore in any man's language."

"Janna—my God, I never meant—"

"I'm not finished," she said, cutting across Ty's shocked words. "Or maybe I should say *you're* not finished. You've had a lot to say about my shortcomings as a woman. As woman hungry as you were, I couldn't even seduce you. You said, 'Sugar, you don't have the least idea how to seduce a man. A woman seduces a man with rustling silks and—'"

Ty's hand clamped across Janna's mouth, cutting off her bitter recitation of his words.

"You don't understand," Ty said urgently. "I didn't mean any of that to belittle you. Especially after we made love."

The mute defiance of Janna's eyes and the hot rain of her tears said that she had understood him all too well.

"Janna," he whispered, kissing her eyelashes, tasting her tears, "please believe me. I never meant the words as an insult to you. You're a young girl alone in the world and I seduced you, knowing I shouldn't. That's all the words meant. My shortcomings, Janna, not yours."

She trembled as she felt Ty's caresses and soft words stripping away her anger, revealing the despair that was the other side of her fury. Nothing he had said or could say would change the heartbreaking reality: she was not the silken lady of her lover's dreams.

"Do you believe me?" Ty asked, the words as soft as the repeated brush of his lips over Janna's eyelids, her cheeks, her mouth. "I never meant to belittle you. Satin butterfly...believe me...I never meant..."

Gentle words became tender kisses, which lingered and deepened until Ty's tongue touched Janna's for just an instant. Then he withdrew.

"You're so cold you're shivering," he said huskily.

With a volatile mixture of despair and tenderness and desire, Janna waited for Ty to suggest the obvious way to warm her.

Ty looked from Janna's clear, fathomless eyes to the fire whose flames were licking against a huge wall of stone. "And that fire has a lot of rock to warm before it will do us any good." Suddenly he smiled. "But there's a better way."

Janna's answering smile was bittersweet as Ty's hands went to the soggy material that was still wrapped around her breasts. She could refuse him when she was in the grip of anger, but she could never refuse the man who had kissed her so gently just moments before.

When Ty saw the sad acceptance of Janna's smile, he felt as though a knife were turning within his body. He knew that he could have her now, that she would give herself to him once more with all the sensual generosity that had been such a marvel each time he had experienced it; but this time, after the shattering ecstasy had passed, she would believe herself a whore once again.

Nothing he could say would change her mind, for he had said too much already, heedlessly, not knowing that his words were wounding her. He had never meant to strip her pride away. But he had, and he finally knew it.

Too late.

Janna felt the world tilt as Ty picked her up and carried her away from the fire. She made a startled sound and threw her arms around his neck.

"It's all right, Janna. I won't drop you."

Although Ty's voice was as gentle as his kisses had been, in the moonlight his face was a portrait composed of harsh planes and angles, and the line of his mouth was as sad as Janna's had been. At first the clammy fabric of his shirt made Janna shiver with renewed chill. Caught between two bodies, the cloth quickly warmed, and so did she.

Neither of them spoke while Ty walked down the path that led to the hot spring. As the stone ramparts closed in and the valley narrowed, the temperature rose due to the heat radiated by the hottest pool. Ty stopped well short of the first pool, choosing instead the one they called the Tub. There he knelt and lowered Janna into the water without bothering to remove the rest of her clothes. She made a long sound of pleasure as the water's heat penetrated the chill that had come from hours of riding through the storm with only the haphazard protection of the poncho to turn aside the cold rain.

"That feels wonderful," Janna murmured.

With a sigh she sank up to her chin in the water, all but disappearing beneath the veils of steam lifting from the pool's surface. Automatically she searched out the water-smoothed ledge that she usually half floated and half lay on while she soaked in the pool's heated water. Closing her eyes, she eased down the ledge to make room for Ty to join her. When minutes passed and there was no splash or displacement of water from his entry into the pool, she opened her eyes.

She was alone.

"Ty?" she called softly.

No one answered.

"Ty?" This time Janna's call was louder. "There's room here for both of us. You don't have to wait to get warm."

Words that Janna couldn't distinguish came from the direction of camp. She listened intently but no other sounds came. She started to get out of the pool, only to begin shivering immediately. Experience told her if she stayed in the pool for a long enough time her body would absorb so much heat that the walk back to the campfire wouldn't chill her, even in the middle of winter.

Janna took off her remaining clothes, slid back into the pool and let the hot water claim her body once more. Eyes closed, half-floating in the gently flowing water, she wondered why Ty hadn't gotten into the pool with her. Surely he had to be as cold as she was, for he hadn't even had the protection of the makeshift poncho against the rain and wind.

Gradually Janna realized that she was no longer alone. She opened her eyes and saw Ty sitting cross-legged at the edge of the pool, fully clothed, smiling as he watched her. She didn't know that her answering, half-shy smile was another knife of regret turning within him; she only knew that for an instant he looked so sad that tears burned behind her eyes.

"Ty?"

"I'm here, little one."

Janna didn't hesitate or withdraw when Ty bent over the pool. She turned her face toward him, expecting to be pulled into his arms for a kiss that was as steamy and deep as the hot spring itself.

"Close your eyes and hold your breath," he said huskily.

She blinked in surprise, then did as he asked.

"Now go under the water."

Saying nothing, Janna moved down the ledge until she slipped beneath the veils of mist and water. When she surfaced again Ty was waiting for her with a mound of soft, fragrant soap in his palm. The haunting scent of summer roses expanded through the steamy air.

"No wonder your backpack was so heavy I could hardly drag it," Janna said. "You must have cleaned Preacher out."

The white curve of Ty's smile gleamed in the moonlight. "It had been a long time since I'd been in a store with a poke of gold to spend."

Soon Ty's strong fingers were working the soap through Janna's hair until soft mounds of lather gathered and dropped to the water, only to float away downstream like tiny ghost ships in the moonlight. Janna closed her eyes and luxuriated in the unprecedented pleasure of having someone wash her hair.

"Ready to hold your breath again?"

She nodded even as she sank beneath the gently steaming water once more. When she emerged he was waiting with more fragrant soap. He lathered her hair again, working slowly, enjoying the feel and scent of the soap, savoring the pleased curve he had brought to her lips, a smile that was untinged by sadness. It was many minutes before his fingers reluctantly released her soft, rose-scented hair.

"Hold your breath."

Smiling, Janna held her breath and slipped into the pool's seamless embrace. When she came up again her hair was free of soap, yet the fragrance of roses lingered. Ty inhaled deeply, letting the scent caress his senses. He dipped into the pot of soft soap once more before he began washing the rest of Janna as gently as though she were a child. The hard rise of her nipples beneath his palms told Ty that she was a woman, not a child, but he forced himself to continue bathing her without lingering over the breasts that were silently begging for his caresses.

Ty's hands didn't hesitate in their slippery travel from her ribs to her hips. He tried to bathe her sleek legs with the same, almost impersonal touch he had used on her shoulders. He succeeded until he came to the triangle of hair that was glittering midnight now but had been brushed by fire in the hushed twilight when he had first undressed her.

As Ty's long fingers began washing the warm mound at the apex of Janna's thighs, she trembled and made a broken sound.

"Hush, little one," he murmured, ignoring the doubled beating of his own heart. "At least you won't have to hold your breath to rinse off. I'll be able to do it for you."

Janna's answering smile lasted only an instant before the intimacy of Ty's touch called another small cry from her lips. He made the same kind of meaningless, reassuring, almost purring sound he had so often used on Lucifer.

"It's all right," he said softly. "I'm not going to take you again. I'm just bathing you. Do you mind that so very much?"

"It's...no one has ever..."

Janna's words fragmented into an involuntary sound of pleasure as Ty's fingers moved between her legs, washing and setting fire to her in the same sliding motions.

Despite his fierce desire, Ty's smile was gentle. "I'm glad. I've never bathed a woman before." He started to add that he had never wanted to, but Janna cried out and he remembered the past night, her innocence ripped away, and his repeated, urgent penetrations of her untouched body. "Are you sore, darling? Am I hurting you now?"

Janna tried to speak, couldn't and shook her head instead, sending wavelets lapping against the sandy rim of the pool.

"Are you sure?"

She nodded, making more tiny waves.

"Cat got your tongue?"

The lazy, sensual humor in Ty's voice made Janna smile just before she stuck out her tongue. As she had hoped, he pulled her halfway from the pool even as he bent to kiss her; and the kiss was what she had longed for, a sharing as hot and deep as the pool itself.

"I'm getting you wet," Janna said when Ty finally released her, letting her slide back into the heated water.

"The rain already took care of that. Open your legs, satin butterfly. I don't want to leave any soap on that soft, soft skin."

The swirling motions of the water as Ty rinsed Janna made heat shimmer up through her body. She smelled the haunting fragrance of roses again when Ty scooped a bit more soap onto his palm.

"Wash your hair once for cleanliness, twice for beauty. Isn't that what mothers tell their daughters?" Ty asked.

"Is that what mothers tell daughters?"

"Yes."

"Yes," Janna whispered, shivering in anticipation.

Again Ty's hand slid and pleasured, skimming over Janna, sensitizing her until her breath was a husky sigh. When he pressed apart her thighs, she gave herself willingly, shivering with each hot swirl of water rinsing her, crying out helplessly when his finger began to ease into her warmth. Instantly he stopped.

"Was that a cry of pain?" Ty asked huskily.

"No."

The word became a moan as he stole tenderly into Janna. The satin flutter of her response tore a barely throttled groan from him. He didn't know how he had borne being without her all the long hours of the day—or how he would be able to bear not having her again day and night without end.

"Satin butterfly," Ty whispered, withdrawing from Janna, his hand trembling.

He lifted her from the water and laid her in the center of the blanket he had brought back to the pool. Steam rose from her body even as it did from the water itself, veiling her in silver mist. He folded over the sides of the blanket until she was covered snugly. With long, leisurely sweeps of his hands over the blanket, he dried her. When she would have helped, he captured her hands, kissed them and tucked them along her sides beneath the blanket once more.

"Let me," he said huskily, peeling back the edges of the blanket until her nipples were just barely uncovered.

"Yes," Janna whispered, feeling herself tighten as she remembered the pleasure of Ty's mouth loving her.

But it was his hands that came to her breasts, caressed them, plucked at their rosy tips until her back arched in response to the currents of pleasure pouring through her. She closed her eyes and gave herself to the shimmering sensations her lover's hands called from her body. Her teeth sank into her lower lip, biting back the cries that came when his mouth caught one nipple and suckled until a bubble of pleasure burst within her. When his hands skimmed down her body and pressed between her legs, she shifted, allowing him the freedom of her body.

Janna's reward was a love bite that made pleasure expand through her until she could hold no more and sultry heat overflowed, merging her scent with that of roses. Ty groaned beneath the redoubled violence of his own arousal. He would have given his soul to take her while she melted around him, but he knew it wasn't his soul that would be forfeited. It would be hers.

Janna trembled as Ty kissed and licked and nuzzled the length of her torso, smoothing her legs apart as he had in the pool. This time there were no hot swirls of water to caress her, only the heat and textures of her lover teasing the humid softness that his fingertips had first discovered.

The first gliding touch of Ty's tongue brought a startled cry from Janna. It was answered by a reassuring murmur and a kiss both tender and hotly intimate. She tried to say his name, but all that came out was a whimper of shock and pleasure. She started to sit up, only to be impaled by a shaft of ecstasy when her lover captured and teased the violently sensitive nub that had been hidden between soft folds of skin. A sound came from deep in her throat, protest and extraordinary pleasure combined.

Ty's hands flexed, holding Janna captive and sensuously kneading her thighs at the same time.

"Don't pull away," he said in a low voice. "I won't hurt you. I just want to...love you." Slowly he turned his head from side to side, caressing Janna with his breath, his stubble-roughened cheeks, his mouth. "You're so sweet, so soft, so warm. I'll be gentle with you. Let me..."

Janna didn't answer, for the hunger and passionate intimacy of Ty's caresses had taken from her the ability to think, to form words, to speak. Her breathing disintegrated into ragged gasps as she felt her body begin a slow, sensual unraveling that had no end, no beginning, just a timeless, ravishing moment in which pleasure burst and grew and burst again, incandescent sensations rippling through her body until she moaned and moved helplessly, totally captive to the man and the ultimate instant of pleasure.

And still the moment and the unraveling and the sweet ravishment continued. Ty's name burst from Janna's lips in a cry of protest and pleasure, for she hadn't known that ecstasy was the mythic phoenix, rising newborn from the steamy ashes of sensual completion. She rose with the phoenix, spiraling higher and higher until she screamed at the violent currents of pleasure searing through her, burning through flesh and her mind, leaving her soul as naked as her body.

And then he touched her so perfectly, so gently, so hotly that she wept his name and died.

For a long time Ty held Janna's trembling body against his own, ignoring the violent demands of his own hunger, stroking her slowly until she could take a breath that didn't fragment with the aftershocks of ecstasy. When she stirred and sighed and began sliding from ecstasy into sleep, he tilted her face up and brushed her lips with his own.

"You're not a whore, Janna Wayland."

Chapter Thirty-Three

Lucifer cantered across the valley toward Ty and Janna. His ears were pricked alertly, his tail was held up like a black banner and his stride was both muscular and effortless. It was only in the chill of morning that he walked stiffly, revealing the injury that was almost, but not quite, healed.

"Hard to believe he's the same horse that stumbled into this valley three weeks ago," Janna said.

"More like a month," Ty corrected.

She said nothing, although she knew that it had been precisely twenty-four days since Ty had carried her to the steamy pool and then had brought such intense, exquisite pleasure to her. Twenty-four days, each one longer than the one before, because he hadn't touched her since then. Not once. Not even in the most casual way. It was as though she stood behind an invisible wall too thick and too high for him to reach across.

Lucifer came to a stop a few feet away from Janna and Ty, tossed his elegant black head and watched both of them. Then he nickered a soft welcome and stretched his neck toward Ty's hands. Janna smiled to see the big stallion's trust. Although he often looked to her to be petted, it was to Ty the stallion came first. An unusual, deep bond had been forged between man and horse on the painful trip from the plateau to the keyhole valley. The bond had been reinforced in the weeks that followed, weeks when Janna had deliberately stayed away from Lucifer much of the time, wanting it to be Ty whose touch and voice and medicines both healed and tamed the stallion.

With a hunger Janna couldn't conceal, she watched Ty's long-fingered hands smooth over Lucifer's black coat. She didn't realize how much her stare revealed until she sensed Ty's attention and looked up to find him watching her in the same way that she had watched him. Hastily she looked away, not knowing what else to do, unable to slow the sudden hammering of her heart.

Each time she had begun to think Ty didn't want her anymore, she would turn around suddenly and see him watching her with hunger blazing in his green eyes. Yet he never moved toward her, always away. He would not touch her.

You're not a whore, Janna Wayland.

The words Ty had spoken that first night in the valley echoed in Janna's soul every hour of every day. She believed Ty, but it was the way he had made love to her that had instilled that belief; without his healing touch, the words would have been but a thin balm over a deep wound.

When a week had gone by and Ty had made no move to touch Janna in any way, she had tried to tell him that she understood why he couldn't love her, that she had accepted not being his dream, that it was all right if he touched her, that she wanted to be his lover; but he had turned away and walked out into the meadow, leaving her alone, ignoring the words she called after him in her futile attempt to make him understand that she wanted him without vows or pledges or guarantees of anything beyond a sharing of selves within the hushed stone boundaries of the secret valley.

He still would not touch her.

Janna would have tried to seduce Ty, but she didn't know how. She had no silks to wear, no grand home in which to throw parties, no room to enter gracefully knowing that he waited within to see her. She knew nothing about such civilized rituals of seduction. She only knew that she awoke in the middle of the night with her hands clenched into fists and her body on fire and her heart beating so harshly that her head felt as though it would split with the pain and force of her rushing blood.

But that wasn't the worst.

The worst was the emptiness growing inside Janna, the feeling of having lost something unspeakably rare and beautiful. It was the certainty that where she had once gone through life alone and content, now she would go through life alone and lonely. She was doomed to remember a time when she had touched love and had had it slide like sunlight through her outstretched fingers, leaving bleak night behind to pool in her palms until it overflowed and kept on overflowing, consuming the remaining light, consuming her.

A velvety muzzle nudged Janna gently, then more insistently. She started and realized that she had been staring at Ty once more, her breath held in anticipation of…something. Yet there was nothing to anticipate now but one more day, one day worse than yesterday, more light sliding through her outstretched fingers, more darkness pooling in her empty soul.

With a stifled cry Janna looked away from Ty again. She tried to make herself breathe deeply. It was impossible. Her body was so taut that she vibrated like a bow being drawn by too powerful an archer, the wood bent so harshly that breakage was only a breath away…so she refused to breathe.

I can't be with Ty like this. I can't bear it. It's worse than being alone. It's like watching Papa die all over again, all the life, all the possibilities, all the laughter, all the love, everything sliding away beyond my reach.

Something thumped soundly against Janna's chest. She made a startled noise and looked down. The thump had come from Zebra's muzzle. The mare was getting impatient for her mistress's attention.

"H-hello, girl," Janna said, stammering slightly, unable to prevent the telltale trembling.

The catch in Janna's voice made Ty feel as though a knife had flicked over an open wound. Like her body, her voice said that she wanted him until she shook with it. He wanted her in the same way, wanted her until he felt as if his guts were being drawn through the eye of a red-hot needle.

And he wouldn't take her.

"Easy, son," Ty said, making his voice as gentle as he could under the circumstances.

Lucifer eyed Ty warily, telling the man that his attempt to be reassuring hadn't been very convincing.

"Let's take a look at that wound," Ty murmured, smoothing his hands over the stallion's warm hide. "Easy, son, easy. I'm not going to hurt you."

The echo of Ty's reassurances to Janna by the pool pierced the silence between the two of them with uneasiness. He refused to look at her, knowing that if he did he would see in her eyes the sweet, consuming wildfire of her passion. He had never touched a woman as he had Janna that night; even the memory of it brought an almost shocked disbelief...and a searing hunger to know her that way again, to bathe in her like a warm pool, washing away the impurities of the years in which he hadn't known that he could touch his own soul by soaring deep within Janna's sensual generosity.

"You'll have a scar," Ty said tightly, looking at Lucifer's haunch, "but that's little enough for a bullet wound to leave as a calling card."

Silently Ty wondered what wound would be left on his own life by the much softer, much more agonizing brush of a satin butterfly's wings.

"Soon Lucifer will be strong enough to go to Wyoming," Janna said, speaking her worst fear aloud.

"Yes." Ty's tone was curt. "You won't be able to take much except clothes, but your books should be safe enough here. When things settle down in the territory, you can..." His voice died. "I'll see that you get your books. I'll see that you get everything you need for the kind of life you deserve."

Janna turned away from Ty, hiding her face, not letting him see in her expression the decision she had made not to go to Wyoming. She really had no choice but to stay. Instinctively she knew it would be easier to live alone in the valley than anywhere on earth with Ty always within reach, never touching her.

"Janna?" he asked roughly.

After a few seconds she said calmly, "I'll do what has to be done."

It sounded like agreement, yet...

Ty stared at the back of Janna's head and wished that he could read her mind as easily as she seemed to read the animals and the clouds. And himself.

"The sooner we start, the better," he said.

Janna said nothing.

"We should get out of here before the Army decides to move against Cascabel."

She nodded as though they were discussing nothing more important than the shape of distant clouds.

"We'll have to take it slow until I can find a horse to ride. Even if Lucifer would accept me as a rider—which I doubt—he should have another week or so without any strain." Ty waited. Janna said nothing. "Janna?"

Auburn hair flashed in the sun as she turned to face him. Her eyes were as clear as rain—and haunted by elusive shadows.

"Yes, it would be better for Lucifer not to have to take the strain of a rider for a few more days."

"That's not what I meant and you know it."

Janna hesitated, then shrugged. "The first days will be slow and dangerous. Walking is always slower than riding."

"You're coming with me," Ty said bluntly.

"Of course. Lucifer would never leave the valley without Zebra," Janna said, turning away again, stroking the mare's dust-colored hide with loving hands.

"And Zebra won't leave the valley without you," Ty said.

"She never has before."

Ty's scalp prickled. Every instinct he had told him that Janna was sliding away from him, eluding his attempts to hold her nearby. She was vanishing as he watched.

"Say it," he demanded.

"Say what?"

"Say that you're coming to Wyoming with me."

Janna closed her eyes. Hidden beneath Zebra's mane, her hands clenched into fists. "I'm leaving the valley with you."

"And you're coming to Wyoming with me."

"Don't."

"Don't what?"

"Force me to lie to you."

"What does that mean? You can't stay here forever and you know it!"

"I can't stay on your brother's ranch in Wyoming, either."

"You won't have to stay there forever."

"Just long enough to set a marriage snare for some man who's too stupid to know the difference between true silk and an ordinary sow's ear?" Janna offered bitterly.

"Dammit, that's not what I said!"

"You don't have to say it. I did." She swung onto Zebra's back with a quick motion that was eloquent of wild emotions barely restrained. "I promised to help you get your stallion. You promised to teach me how to please a man. Those promises were made and kept on Black Plateau. Wyoming was no part of it."

Abruptly Zebra exploded into a gallop.

In seething silence Ty watched while the mare swept toward the far end of the valley where Indian ruins slowly eroded back into the stony land from which they had come. Janna had spent a lot of time in the ancient place since they had brought the stallion into the valley. Ty had thought Janna's sudden interest in the ruins was an attempt to remove Zebra's distracting presence while he spent hours with Lucifer, accustoming the wild stallion to a man's voice and touch.

But now Ty suspected that Janna had been trying to wean Lucifer of Zebra's company so that the stallion wouldn't balk at being separated when the time came for Ty to head for Wyoming—without Janna.

"It won't work!" Ty called savagely. "You're coming to Wyoming with me if I have to tie you over Zebra's back like a sack of grain!"

Nothing answered Ty but the drumroll of thunder from the mare's speedy, fleeing hooves.

Ty's words echoed mockingly in his own ears. He knew that all Janna had to do was ride off while he slept or worked with Lucifer. On foot he couldn't catch her. Even if she didn't ride Zebra, Ty wasn't much better off. Black Plateau was an open book to Janna; she could hide among its countless ravines the way a shadow could hide among the thousand shades of night.

He would find her eventually, of course. Assuming Cascabel didn't find them first.

Chapter Thirty-Four

The stallion's clarion call resonated through the valley, echoing and reechoing from stone walls, telling anything with ears that an enemy had appeared in the tiny, concealed Eden.

Ty dropped his dinner plate, grabbed his carbine and sprinted for the willows. Within seconds he was under cover, but he didn't slow his speed. Running, twisting around slender limbs, leaping roots and rocks, heedless of noise, Ty raced toward the entrance of the valley.

When he arrived at the edge of the willows' dense cover, he stopped and watched the meadow for signs of man. Nothing moved near the cleft, which was the valley's only access to the outer world. Carbine at his shoulder, Ty stared down the metal barrel at the expanse of grass. Nothing moved in the emptiness but the wind.

Lucifer's wild, savage call to arms came again, making the skin of Ty's scalp ripple in primal response. The stallion was far up the valley, out of sight in the narrow bend where the Indian ruins were hidden. Neither Zebra nor Janna was in sight.

Desperately Ty wanted to call out to Janna and reassure himself that she was safe. He kept silent. He didn't want her to give away her position to a skulking renegade.

Ty had no doubt that the stallion's savage cry had been triggered by the presence of a strange human being. In the weeks since he had come to the valley, Ty had never seen signs of anything larger than a rabbit within the valley itself. Of all the animals in the vast land, only man had the curiosity— or the need—to follow the narrow, winding slot through stone-lined darkness into the canyon's sunlight.

Stay down in the ruins, Janna, Ty prayed silently. *You'll be safe there. The Indians avoid the spirit places.*

The birds that usually wheeled and darted over the meadow were silent and hidden. Ty's narrowed glance raked the valley again, looking for any sign of the intruder.

Suddenly Lucifer burst out from the area of the ruins into the larger meadow. Zebra was running at his side. When the stallion dug in and stopped, the mare kept galloping, stopping only when she was several hundred feet beyond. Lucifer reared and screamed again, hooves slashing the air, putting himself between the mare and whatever danger threatened.

As the stallion's feral challenge faded, the cry of a hawk soared above the silence, followed by Janna's voice calling what could have been Ty's name. He turned toward the sound. Over the metal barrel of the carbine, he saw Janna coming from the area of the ruins. A man was walking behind her. Reflexively Ty took slack from the trigger, let out his breath and waited for the trail to turn, giving him a view of the stranger.

It was Mad Jack.

Gently Ty's finger eased from the trigger as he lowered the carbine from his shoulder. When he emerged from the cover of the willows and trotted out into the open and across the meadow, Lucifer neighed shrilly, as though to warn him of danger. Ty turned aside long enough to reassure the stallion.

"Thanks for the warning, but it's just a crazy old prospector," Ty said, talking soothingly to the stallion.

Lucifer snorted and stamped nervously but permitted Ty to stroke his neck. Even then the stallion never stopped watching the two figures that were coming out of the ruins. When the people began walking toward him, Lucifer spun and ran away, sweeping Zebra before him. Ty turned and waited for Janna and Mad Jack.

"Right fine lookout you have there," Mad Jack said, holding out his hand for Ty to shake.

Smiling, Ty took the old man's hand. He was surprised at how fine Mad Jack's bones were beneath his scarred, leathery skin. The prospector's grip was a quick, light pressure, as though any more would be painful.

"Run out of stomach medicine again?" Ty asked, although he suspected that medicine was the last thing on the other man's mind.

Mad Jack laughed. He knew what Ty was thinking—that he had come to check up on Janna, not to replenish his supply of medicine.

"You be half-right, son. I come to check on my gal."

"Well, you can see that she's bright eyed and bushy tailed," Ty said dryly.

Mad Jack's faded eyes appraised Janna with a frankness that made her flush.

"You be right," he said, fishing in his pocket for his chewing tobacco. "'Course, mares in foal look right sassy for the first few months, too."

"Don't beat around the bush," Janna said in a combination of embarrassment and exasperation. "Just say anything that's on what passes for your mind."

"I make it a habit to do just that. So are you?"

"Am I...?"

"Pregnant."

Red flags burned on Janna's cheeks. "Jack!"

"Well, are you?"

"No."

"You sure?"

"Yes," she said succinctly. "As sure as I am that water runs downhill."

Jack rubbed his face and sighed. "Well, durn it all anyway. That's gonna fuss things up considerable."

"Have you been drinking?" Janna demanded.

"No." He sliced off a big hunk of tobacco, stuffed it in his mouth and said, "I been thinkin', which is a horse of another color entirely. Both of 'em make my head hurt, I'll give you that."

"What," Ty asked, "is going on?"

"Mad Jack has been thinking," Janna said. "That's a serious matter."

"Damn straight it is," Jack agreed. "Last time I got to thinkin', I took old Jimbo—he was my mule—out of the traces, hiked my leg across his back and headed west. Nary a word to my wife since then, nor my kids, neither. Thinkin' is right hard on a man."

"Sounds like it wasn't real easy on your wife, either," Ty said dryly.

"That's what I got to thinkin' about," Mad Jack agreed. "I been pokin' in rocks for years, tryin' to find the one glory hole what's got my name on it. Well, I don't rightly think I'm gonna find it this side of heaven and more 'n likely I'm a-headed straight for hell." Jack spit, wiped his mouth and continued. "Now, ol' Charity—that's my wife—probably died of some woman's complaint or another by now, but my kids was right healthy grasshoppers. Some of 'em are bound to be alive, or their kids. An' that's why I'm unhappy that you ain't pregnant," he added, pointing at Janna.

Ty looked sideways at Janna. She was watching Mad Jack as though he had just sprouted horns or wings or both.

"I don't understand," she said flatly.

"Hell, gal, it's as plain as the color of the sky. I got gold to give to my kids, an' I ain't gonna leave this here country and you can't get out the gold alone, an' if you ain't pregnant, you ain't got no stud hoss to protect you, an' my gold won't get delivered an' my kids won't know their pappy ever thought about 'em."

Janna opened her mouth. Nothing came out. She swallowed and tried again, but it was too late. Ty was already speaking.

"Let me be sure I understand," Ty said smoothly, seizing the opportunity with both hands. "You have gold you want taken to your children. You thought if Janna were pregnant, we'd be leaving the valley and we could deliver the gold to the fort for you."

Mad Jack frowned. "I had in mind something more…friendly like than the fort. See, I ain't sure where my kin are no more. Now, if'n I go hire some man at the fort I don't know from Adam's off ox, how can I be sure my gold gets to my kin once I turn my back?"

Ty tried to say something. It was impossible. Mad Jack had been thinking, and the result of that unusual exercise had made the future clear to him.

"I can't be sure," Mad Jack said forcefully, answering his own question. "But if'n I give the gold to a friend, I can rest easy. You get my drift, son? Now, you ain't my friend. No offense, just the God's truth. Janna here, she's my friend. If'n she told me she'd get the gold to my kids, I know she would or die trying.

"And that's the crux of the matter. She's game but she ain't real big. Ain't mean, neither. Carryin' gold needs someone who's mountain big and snake mean."

"Like me?" Ty suggested.

"Yep."

"But I'm not your friend. No offense."

"None taken, son. It's the God's truth. But if'n you was Janna's man, an' she took the gold, you'd go along to protect her. Then she'd be safe and the gold, too. But she ain't pregnant so you ain't her man an' that means my gold ain't got no man protectin' it once it leaves here."

"The fact that I'm *not* pregnant should reassure you that Ty is an honorable man," Janna pointed out quickly. "If he agreed to take your gold, you could be sure that he wouldn't keep it for himself."

Mad Jack made a sound that was a cross between a mutter and a snort. "Hell's bells, gal, if you ain't pregnant, it ain't because you was sayin' no, it's because he weren't askin'. That may say somethin' about his honor right enough, but it sure as hellfire don't reassure me none about his manly, er, notions."

A wave of scarlet humiliation went up Janna's face as she realized that Mad Jack knew how much she had wanted Ty to notice her as a woman. When the blood ebbed Janna was very pale. All that kept her from turning and walking away was the need she sensed in Mad Jack, a need that was driving the old man far beyond the boundaries of even his customary bluntness. She looked at the prospector's face and saw the yellowish pallor underlying the weathered skin. Although he had always been wiry, now he seemed almost frail. He looked...desperate.

Thinking could be hard on a man, especially when he was old and ill and had only one chance to right past wrongs.

Janna gathered her courage, ignored her own raw feelings and touched Mad Jack's arm reassuringly. "There's nothing wrong with Ty's sense of honor or his 'notions' or anything else," she said with a fierce kind of calm. "He took what I was offering and decided it wasn't for him, that's all."

"Janna—" Ty began.

"What?" she demanded, interrupting without looking away from the old man. "I didn't say it as fancy or as long-winded as Ty did, but that doesn't change what happened, does it? I wanted him. He took me. He doesn't want me anymore. It's an old story. From the books I've read, I'd say it's the oldest story on earth. But that doesn't mean one single thing against Ty's honor, Jack. He didn't lie to me, not even the way you said a woman-hungry man would. No pretty words, no fancy promises, nothing but Ty and me and the night."

Mad Jack was quiet for a long moment before he sighed and patted Janna's hand. "I'm sorry, gal."

"Don't be. I'm not. When I go back and read that trunk full of books again this winter, I'll understand them better. That's nothing to be sorry over. It will make spring come faster for me. Then Zebra will have a foal for me to fuss over and by the end of summer I'll be riding Zebra again and we'll fly over the plateau like a hawk's shadow and then autumn lighting will come again and thunder and the mustangs' breath will be like earthbound clouds and snow will turn the night silver and I'll make up stories about the shadows my campfire throws against the stone cliff, people and places and memories coming to life..." Janna's voice faded into a whisper. "Don't be sorry."

Ty tried to speak and found he had no voice. Janna's words were in his own throat, crowding out speech, filling him until he ached. He clenched his teeth against a sadness as piercing as it was unexpected.

"You can't stay," Ty said hoarsely.

It was as though he hadn't spoken. Janna didn't look away from the old prospector, who was watching her and shaking his head slowly.

"He's speakin' God's truth," Mad Jack said. "You can't stay here, gal. Not no more. I been thinkin' about that, too. Spent a lot of time on it. A lot of my gold belongs to you."

"Don't be ridic—" began Janna.

"No, young'un," Mad Jack said, cutting across her objections. "You jest button up and listen to an old man what's seen more of this here world's good an' bad than you have. Your pappy gave me money more times than either of us counted."

"And you've given us gold as long as I can remember," Janna said quickly.

Mad Jack grunted. "What about the time you found me all broke up at the bottom of a gulch and you set my bones and patched me up and you were no more than a kid in men's britches? You saved my life, you keep my stomach from eatin' a hole in itself, and you listen to my stories no matter how often I tell 'em. Half my gold is yours and that's flat. Should of give it to you years ago so you could get out and get a life for yourself, but I liked knowin' there was one soul in this godforsaken land that wouldn't kill me for my gold."

"Thank you, but I enjoyed your company as much as you enjoyed mine," Janna said. "Any gold you have is yours."

"You ain't been listening, gal. It ain't safe for you here no more." Mad Jack turned to Ty. "Beggars can't be choosers, son. I got a proposition. You be willin' to listen?"

"I'm willing."

"This here gal is game, but game ain't gonna get the job done. Injuns been comin' into the country like rain. Soldiers' scouts been comin', too. Everybody's sayin' that the Army is gonna clean out that rattlesnake's nest once an' for all. Cascabel's been fastin' an' prayin' up a storm. A few days back a vision come to him. He's gonna lead his renegades to a big victory— but not until Janna's hair hangs from his war lance."

Ty's whole body changed subtly, as though Cascabel himself had just appeared at the slot entrance to the valley. Mad Jack measured the change and smiled beneath his ragged beard; Ty might not be Janna's man, but he wasn't about to go off and leave her to fend for herself against the likes of Cascabel.

"Well, she was right about the honor," Mad Jack said. "An' I'll take her word about the rest of you bein' man enough. Here's the deal, son. You get her out of here and to a safe place, and my gold with her, and a quarter of my gold is yours."

"Keep your money, old man," Ty said savagely. "I'll get Janna out of here and to a safe place. You've got my word on it."

Mad Jack chewed for a few moments, turned aside and spat a brown stream into the grass. Turning back, he wiped his beard on his frayed shirtsleeves.

"Suit yerself. Just so's you get her shuck of this place, and my gold with her. She'll need her quarter so's she won't have to marry no mean lard-butt town widower nor sell her company to strangers just to put beans on the table."

"I'm not going to leave just because you—" Janna began hotly.

"Shut yer mouth, gal," Mad Jack said, giving her a fierce glare. "You ain't dumb so don't get to actin' like it. Only reason Cascabel ain't caught you is he ain't took a hard notion before now. Well, he done been took somethin' fierce. Long as that evil son of a rattlesnake is alive, this country ain't safe for chick nor child."

Janna closed her eyes and fought against the ice condensing in her stomach. "Are you sure that Cascabel is after my hair?"

"Dead sure. Sound carries right good in some of these canyons. He bragged on his intentions to Ned."

"The saloon keeper?" Ty asked. "What was he doing with Cascabel?"

"Sellin' rifles, same as always. But don't worry, son. He won't be doin' it no more. He upped the ante once too often. Cascabel took Ned's rifles, then he took his liver, lights and hair."

Janna shuddered.

Mad Jack turned aside, spat and straightened, pinning Ty with a shrewd glance. "You break that stud hoss yet?"

"No."

"Better get to it, son. Man on foot carryin' gold ain't gonna do nothin' out there but die."

Chapter Thirty-Five

"**M**y God." Ty knelt in the dirt and gritty dust of the ruins and looked up at Janna for a long moment. With hands that were none too steady, he refastened the old saddlebags. "It's gold. All of it. Sweet Jesus. When Mad Jack talked about gold, I thought he meant a few pokes, not two big saddlebags jammed full to overflowing." Ty looked at his hands as though hardly able to believe the wealth that they had held. "Pure. Gold."

Ty lifted the bags and stood with a grunt of effort. Janna watched him with wide gray eyes. His words had meant little to her. Even the sight of the gold hadn't made it seem real to her; but watching the saddlebags make Ty's muscular arms bunch and quiver made the gold's weight all too real. She had tested that male strength, seen Ty's power and stamina and determination; and she knew that it wouldn't be enough.

Man on foot carryin' gold ain't gonna do nothin' out there but die.

"You can't take it all," Janna said.

"Doesn't weigh much more than you," Ty said, "but dead weight is the hardest kind to carry." He shook his head in continuing disbelief. "When I get back to camp and get my hands on that crazy old man, I'm going to ask him how the hell he got these saddlebags into the valley."

"Maybe he's been bringing the gold in a poke at a time."

Ty grunted. "If so, he didn't leave any more tracks between here and the slot than the wind. Anyhow, it doesn't matter. I'm not taking a quarter of his gold and he's not staying behind to get spitted and roasted by Cascabel. Like it or not, that old man's coming out with us."

Janna didn't argue or point out the difficulties in taking a third person when there was only one horse to ride. She felt as Ty did about leaving Mad Jack behind.

Finally Janna had realized that staying in the valley was the equivalent of a death sentence. Mad Jack was correct: the only reason she had been safe during the past years was that she had been more trouble to track down than she was worth to Cascabel. That was no longer true. Cascabel now believed that she was all that was standing between himself and the conquest of the Utah Territory.

Unhappily Janna followed Ty as he picked his way out of the crumbling ruins that filled the small side canyon. Once out in the meadow again, the walking was easier. Lucifer and Zebra waited out in the middle of the grass. The stallion was restive. He kept watching the willows that fringed the valley as though he expected a predator to leap out. Zebra was calmly grazing, not nearly as upset by Mad Jack's presence as Lucifer was.

"We could rig a surcingle for Zebra," Janna said, spotting the mare. "That way she could carry the saddlebags and your pack while we walked."

Ty gave her a sideways look that was little more than a flash of green.

"Zebra can't carry both of us and the gold, too," Janna pointed out.

"She can carry you and the gold if it comes to that. All you have to do is get her used to a hackamore and a surcingle."

"But what about you?"

"That's my problem."

White teeth sank into Janna's lower lip as she bit off her retort. She closed her eyes and silently asked for Lucifer's forgiveness. But there was really no choice. If he could be broken to ride, it had to be done.

"Be as gentle with Lucifer as you can," she said in a low voice, "but don't hurt yourself in the process, Ty. Promise me that you'll be careful. He's so strong and so quick." She looked at the stallion standing poised in the meadow, his big body rippling with strength, his ears erect, his head up, sniffing the wind. "And he's so wild. Much wilder than Zebra."

"Not with you. He comes up and puts his head in your hands like a big hound."

"Then why won't you let me be the one to break him?" Janna's voice was tightened by fear and exasperation. She and Ty had argued about just this thing since the moment Mad Jack had pointed out that a man on foot didn't have much chance of surviving.

"God save me from stubborn women," muttered Ty. "I've spent the last half hour telling you why. That stud's big enough to buck you into next week and you know it. I sure as hell know it! You're quick and determined as they come, but that's no substitute for sheer strength if Lucifer goes crazy the first time he feels a rider's weight."

Impatiently Ty shifted the slippery leather connecting the saddlebags. When the bags were in a more secure position over his shoulder he continued his argument. "Besides, you'll have your hands full talking Zebra into a hackamore and surcingle. She's not going to like that belly strap worth a damn. I'm going to rig stirrups for you, too. She won't like those, either, but it's only way you and that old man stand a chance of staying on if we have to run for it. One of you has to be stuck on tight enough so the other has something to hang on to."

Janna opened her mouth to object but didn't. She had lost this argument, too, and she knew it. She hadn't wanted to put restraints on Zebra, yet there was little rational choice. If their lives were going to depend on their mounts, the riders had to have more than intangible communication with their horses. Particularly if she and Mad Jack were going to be riding double.

"Once we get to Wyoming, you can go back to riding Zebra any way you want," Ty said. "Hell, you can let her run wild again for all of me. But not until then, Janna. Not until you're safe."

Closing her eyes, she nodded in defeat. "I know."

Ty gave Janna a surprised look. He had expected a fierce battle over the necessity of introducing any real control over Zebra. Janna's unhappy expression told him just how much the concession cost her. Without thinking about his vow not to touch her again, he took Janna's hand and squeezed it gently.

"It's all right, sugar. Even with a hackamore and surcingle, you aren't forcing Zebra to obey you. You aren't strong enough to force an animal her size. Anytime Zebra lets you up on her back, it's because she wants you there. All the hackamore will do is make sure Zebra knows where you want her to go. After that, it's up to her. It's always that way, no matter what kind of tack the horse wears. Cooperation, not coercion."

The feel of Ty's palm sliding over her own as they walked was like being brushed by gentle lightning. Janna's whole body tingled with the simple pleasure of his touch.

"Thank you," she said, blinking back sudden tears.

"For what?"

"For making me feel better about putting a hackamore on Zebra. And—" Janna squeezed his hand in return "—for understanding. It's frightening having to give up the only home I've ever known."

Knowing he shouldn't, unable to prevent himself, Ty lifted Janna's hand to his face. The long weeks during which he hadn't shaved had softened his beard to the texture of coarse silk. He rubbed his cheek against her palm, inhaled her scent and called himself twelve kinds of fool for not touching her in the past four weeks—and fifty kinds of fool for touching her now.

She wasn't a whore or a convenience. She was a woman who appealed to him more with every moment he spent in her company. Her sensuality was like quicksand, luring him deeper and deeper until he was trapped beyond hope of escape. But she didn't mean to be a trap any more than he meant to be trapped. He was sure of it. That was what made her feminine allure all the more irresistible.

With aching tenderness Ty kissed Janna's palm before he forced himself to let go of her hand. The loss of her touch was a physical pain. The realization appalled him.

God in heaven. I'm as stupid as that damned unicorn being drawn to his captivity and not able to pull away to save his life, much less his freedom.

Abruptly Ty shifted the heavy gold to his other shoulder, using the saddlebags as a barrier between himself and Janna. She barely noticed. She was still caught in the instant when his hand had been sharply withdrawn. It had been like having her sense of balance betray her on a steep trail, leaving her floundering. She looked at Ty questioningly, only to see a forbidding expression that promised unhappiness for anyone asking questions of a personal nature, especially questions such as *Why haven't you touched me? Why did you touch me just now? Why did you stop as though you could no longer bear my touch?*

"Will you take the gold on Lucifer?" Janna asked after a silence. She forced her voice to be almost normal, although her palm still felt his caresses as though Ty's beard had been black flames burning through her flesh to the bone beneath.

"He's strong enough to take the gold and me both and still run rings around any other horse."

"Then you'll have to use a surcingle on him, too, either for stirrups or to hold the saddlebags in place or both."

"The thought had occurred to me," Ty said dryly. "First time he feels that strap bite into his barrel should be real interesting."

Ty shifted the gold on his shoulder again and said no more. In silence they continued toward the camp beneath the red stone overhang. Janna felt no need to speak, for the simple reason that there was little more to say. Either Lucifer would accept a rider or he wouldn't. If he didn't, the odds for survival against Cascabel were too small to be called even a long shot.

"We have to talk Mad Jack into leaving the gold behind," Janna said finally.

Ty had been thinking the same thing. He also had been thinking about how he would feel in Mad Jack's shoes—old, ill, eaten up with guilt for past mistakes, seeing one chance to make it all right and die with a clean conscience.

"It's his shot at heaven," Ty said.

"It's our ticket straight to hell."

"Try convincing him."

"I'm going to do just that."

Janna's chin came up and she quickened her pace, leaving Ty behind. But when she strode into camp, all that was there of Mad Jack was a piece of paper held down by a stone. On the paper he had painfully written the closest town to the farm he had abandoned so many years ago. Beneath that were the names of his five children.

"Jack!" Janna called. "Wait! Come back!"

No voice answered her. She turned and sprinted toward the meadow.

"What's wrong?" Ty demanded.

"He's gone!"

"That crafty old son of a bitch." Ty swore and dropped the heavy saddlebags with a thump. "He knew what would happen when we found out how much gold there was to haul out of here. He took our promise to get his gold to his children and then he ran like the hounds of hell were after him."

Janna raised her hands to her mouth. A hawk's wild cry keened across the meadow. Zebra's head came up and she began trotting toward them.

"What are you going to do?" Ty asked.

"Find him. He's too old to have gotten far in this short a time."

Ty all but threw Janna up on top of Zebra. Instants later the mare was galloping on a long diagonal that would end at the narrow entrance to the valley.

By the time they arrived at the slot, Zebra was beginning to sweat both from the pace and from the urgency she sensed in her rider. Janna flung herself off the mare and ran to the twilight shadow of the slot canyon.

Heedless of the uncertain footing, she plunged forward. She didn't call Mad Jack's name, however; she didn't want the call to echo where it might be overheard by passing renegades.

No more than fifty feet into the slot, Janna sensed that something was wrong. She froze in place, wondering what her instincts were trying to tell her.

There was no unexpected sound. No unexpected scent. No moving shadows. No sign that she wasn't alone.

"That's what's wrong," Janna whispered. "There's no sign at all!"

She went onto her hands and knees, but no matter how hard she examined the ground, the only traces of any passage over the dry stream course were those she herself had just left.

Zebra's head flew up in surprise when Janna hurtled back into the valley from the slot.

"Easy, girl. Easy," Janna said breathlessly.

She swung onto the mare. Within moments a rhythmic thunder was again rolling from beneath Zebra's hooves. When she galloped past Lucifer, he lifted his head for an instant, then resumed biting off succulent mouthfuls of grass, undisturbed by the pair racing by. In past summers, Zebra and Janna often had galloped around while he grazed.

"Well?" Ty demanded when the mare galloped into the campsite.

"He's still in the valley. You take the left side and I'll take the right."

Ty looked out over the meadow. "Waste of time. He's not here."

"That's impossible. There's not one mark in that little slot canyon that I didn't put there myself. He's still here."

"Then he's between us and Lucifer."

Janna looked to the place where the stallion grazed no more than a hundred feet away. There wasn't enough cover to hide a rabbit, much less a man.

"Why do you say that?" she asked.

"Wind is from that direction. Lucifer stopped testing the wind and settled down to graze about ten minutes ago."

Janna's urgency drained from her, leaving her deflated. If the stallion didn't scent Mad Jack it was because Mad Jack wasn't around to be scented.

Grimly Janna looked at the heavy saddlebags, an old man's legacy to a life he had abandoned years before. It was too heavy a burden—but it was theirs to bear. Her only consolation was that Ty's share, plus her own, should be enough to buy his dream. She didn't know how much silken ladies cost on the open market, but surely sixty pounds of gold would be enough.

Ty's expression as he looked at the saddlebags was every bit as grim as Janna's. His consolation, however, was different. He figured that Janna's thirty pounds of gold, plus his thirty, would be more than enough to ensure that she would never have to submit her soft body to any man in order to survive.

Chapter Thirty-Six

Lucifer's ears flattened and he screamed his displeasure, lashing out with his hind feet. Ty made no attempt to hold the mustang. He just ducked and ran for cover. The stallion exploded into wicked bucking as he tried to dislodge the surcingle Ty had cut from the buffalo robe in Janna's trunk. When bucking didn't work, the stallion tried outrunning the strap and the flapping rope stirrups.

By the time Lucifer realized that he couldn't outrun the contraption clinging to his back—and that he wasn't being attacked by whatever was on him— the stallion's neck and flanks were white with lather and he was breathing hard. Janna wasn't surprised at the horse's signs of exertion; Lucifer had been racing flat out around the valley for nearly half an hour.

"Lord, but that's one strong horse," she said.

Ty grunted. He wasn't looking forward to the next part of the stallion's education, the part when he felt a man's weight on his back for the first time. Ty approached the big mustang slowly, speaking in a low voice.

"Yeah, I know, it's a hell of a world when you can't outrun all of life's traps and entanglements. But it isn't as bad as it seems to you right now," Ty murmured, stroking the stallion. "Ask Zebra. She took to the surcingle and stirrups like the good-hearted lady she is."

Lucifer snorted and butted his head against Ty as though to draw the man's attention to the irritation caused by the unwanted straps.

"Sorry, son. I'll rub away the itches but I'm not taking off that surcingle. I had enough trouble getting the damned thing on you in the first place."

Janna had a hard time not saying a heartfelt "amen." Watching Ty risk his life under Lucifer's hooves in the process of getting the surcingle in place had been the most difficult thing she had ever done. She had both admired Ty's gentle persistence and regretted ever asking him not to use restraints on the powerful stallion.

Ty continued petting and talking to Lucifer until the horse calmed down. Gradually Ty's strokes became different. He leaned hard on his hands as he moved them over the horse, concentrating mainly on the portion of Lucifer's back just behind the withers, where a man would ride. At first the stallion moved away from the pressure. Ty followed, talking patiently, leaning gently and then with more force, trying to accustom the mustang to his weight.

Again, Janna watched the process with a combination of anxiety and admiration. Most of the men she had known would have snubbed Lucifer's nose to a post, twisted his ear in one hand and then climbed aboard in a rush. Once the rider was in the saddle, the horse would have been released and spurs would have begun raking tender hide. The bucking that would have followed was inevitable. So was the fact that some horses broken that way weren't trustworthy. They tended to wait until the rider was relaxed and then unload him with a few wicked twists of their body.

Yet Ty had to be able to trust Lucifer with his life, and he had promised Janna to treat the stallion as gently as possible and still get the job done.

Breath came in sharply and then stuck in Janna's throat while she watched Ty shift his weight until his boots no longer touched the ground. Lucifer moved nervously, turned around in a circle rapidly several times, then accepted the fact that Ty's soothing voice was coming from a new direction. After a few minutes the stallion began grazing rather irritably, ignoring the fact that Ty was draped belly down over his back.

By the time two more hours passed, Ty had gotten Lucifer to the point of not flinching or even particularly noticing when Ty's weight shifted from the ground to the horse's back. Janna had seen Ty creep into position, moving so slowly that every muscle stood out as he balanced against gravity and the mustang's wary, mincing steps. When Ty finally eased from his stomach to a rider's normal seat, Janna wanted to shout a cheer. All that kept her quiet was an even bigger desire not to spook the mustang.

For the stallion's part, Lucifer simply twitched his ears and kept grazing when Ty sat upright. The horse's whole stance proclaimed that the bizarre actions of his human companion no longer disturbed him.

Elation spread through Ty when he felt the calm strength of the stallion beneath him. More than ever, Ty was certain that Lucifer had been gently bred, raised by humans, and then had escaped from his owners to run free before any brand of ownership had been put on his shiny black hide.

"You're a beauty," Ty murmured, praising the stallion with voice and hands. "Does part of you know that you were born and bred to be a man's friend?"

Lucifer lipped grass casually, stopping every few minutes to sniff the wind. Ty made no attempt to guide the stallion with the hackamore. He simply sat and let the mustang graze in a normal manner. When Lucifer moved in the course of grazing, he walked a bit awkwardly at first, unaccustomed to the weight settled just behind his withers. But by the time the sun was tracing the last part of its downward arc in the west, Lucifer was moving with his former confidence, adjusting automatically to the presence of a rider. Occasionally he would turn and sniff Ty's boot as though to say, "What, are you still here? Well, never mind. You're not in the way."

Ty's answer was always the same, praise and a hand stroking sleek muscles. When Lucifer responded to a firm, steady pull on the hackamore by turning in that direction, the praise and the pats were redoubled. When the pulls were accompanied by gentle nudges with Ty's heels, Lucifer learned to move forward. When the pressure on the hackamore was a steady pull backward, the stallion learned to stop.

"That's it for now, son," Ty said, sliding carefully from Lucifer's back. "You get the rest of the day off."

The stallion snorted and sidestepped at the release of the pressure from his back, but that was all. When Ty raised his hands and tied the hackamore lead rope securely around the black neck, Lucifer didn't even flinch.

"You're a shining wonder," Ty murmured.

Lucifer promptly put his head against Ty's chest and rubbed hard, trying to dislodge the hackamore. Laughing softly, Ty began soothing away the itches that came from wearing leather against hot, sweaty hide.

"Sorry, son. I'm going to leave all this gear in place. It won't hurt you and it will save me a hell of a lot of trouble come tomorrow, when the lessons resume. But right now you've earned a good graze and I've earned some time in the Tub. Get along, son. Go over and berate Zebra about the crazy humans she sicced on you."

A few minutes later Janna looked up from sorting herbs and saw that Lucifer was riderless. For a moment her heart turned over in fear. Then she realized that Ty had probably dismounted of his own accord, giving both himself and Lucifer a rest. Janna turned back to her herbs, testing the leaves' dryness. Fragrances both pungent and mild rose from the rustling herbs as she set some aside to be taken from the valley and designated others to be made into tinctures or lotions or balms. She knew that she wouldn't have time to properly prepare more than a fraction of the herbs and seeds she had collected, but that didn't stop her. Working with them gave her hands something to do besides remember how it had felt to touch Ty and her mind something to do besides think about leaving the valley behind...and then leaving Ty behind, as well.

Stop thinking about it, Janna told herself urgently. *And don't think about Mad Jack probably being sick or Cascabel probably waiting to kill me. Don't think about anything but these herbs. I can't affect Mad Jack or Ty or that cruel renegade. I can make lotions, though. I can make a batch of stomach medicine and leave it behind. I can do the same with the other medicines. I can do anything I want while I'm still here.*

Except seduce Ty.

Herbs and seeds tangled and fell to the ground as Janna's hands jerked at the thought of seducing Ty. She bit back unhappy words and picked up the mess. The second time she thought of making love with Ty the same thing happened. Her fingers were just too shaky to deal with anything as finicky as preparing medicines.

"Well, I can at least get some of that sulfur water from the high spring," she muttered to herself. "Surely that shouldn't be too difficult for my clumsy hands."

Janna grabbed a small metal pot and set off toward the Tub. In the past weeks the trail had become rather well beaten. Both she and Ty loved to float in the warm water and watch the clouds change shape overhead. They did their floating alone, but the thought of what had happened the one time she and Ty had been together in the Tub nearly made Janna drop the small pot. She would have given a great deal to be allowed again to touch Ty so tenderly, so intimately, so wildly. Just once more.

Just once before they left the valley and never saw each other again.

When Janna entered the narrowest part of the valley, the hot springs' steamy silence brought an onslaught of memories. The lush profusion of soft-leaved plants, the sparkling condensation of water on black rock, the vague sulfur odor underlying that of earth and sun and greenery, everything com bined in her mind to create a dizzying mixture of memory and desire.

And then she saw Ty rise out of the nearest pool and stand naked on the sandy shore. Silver streamers of mist lifted from his hot skin, moving as he moved, their fragile grace in sharp contrast to the bunch and ripple of his powerful muscles. Unable to move, Janna simply stared at Ty, transfixed by the pagan beauty of the man, memorizing every pattern of water curling down through the dark hair of his chest and torso and thighs.

Janna didn't have to look at Ty's face to know that he had seen her. The visible evidence of his maleness stirred into life, growing rapidly, insistently, rising from its dark nest of hair as inevitably as Ty had risen from the steaming pool.

The pot Janna carried made a sharp sound as she dropped it onto a rock. She didn't even hear the noise. She had attention for nothing but the man who stood naked before her. Without knowing it she began walking to him.

The expression on Janna's face was the most potent aphrodisiac Ty had ever known. A savage, elemental need twisted through him, black lightning tightening his body until he could barely speak; and with the lightning came an even blacker despair. He had fought so hard to keep from touching Janna, from taking her, from making her feel like a convenience with no value beyond the passionate moment. He had lain awake night after night in the willows, his body on fire, his mind determined not to allow himself the surcease he knew waited within her generous, sensuous body. But he had also known that whatever private hell of deprivation he suffered would be worth it if he never again had to listen to Janna describe herself as a whore.

Yet there she was, inches from him, and her gray eyes blazed with reflections of the need that burned within him.

"Janna," Ty said hoarsely. "No."

Chapter Thirty-Seven

Janna's slim fingers covered Ty's lips, preventing him from saying any more.

"It's all right," she murmured. "I just want to..." Whatever Janna was attempting to say was lost temporarily when she bent her head and kissed the hard swell of Ty's biceps. "Yes," she breathed, shivering with the exquisite pleasure of brushing her lips over his naked arm. "Let me..."

When the tip of Janna's tongue traced the shadow line between Ty's arm and the flexed muscles of his chest, he made a sound as though he were in pain; yet she knew that it was need, not pain, that had dragged the sound from his body. The cry sent piercing needles of pleasure through Janna, making her tremble with the intensity of her response. She turned her head and found the dark, flat disk of Ty's nipple with her tongue and lightly raked the erect nub with her teeth.

Ty's hands closed suddenly around Janna's upper arms as though to push her away, but the attempt never was made. His hands refused to take the commands of his mind. He simply couldn't force himself to push her away. He had wanted her too much for too long. He held her closer and shuddered as though each gliding caress from her tongue was a harsh blow rather than the most tender kind of caress.

"Yes," Janna whispered, feeling the lightning strokes of desire racking the man she loved. "Yes, you need this. You need..." She shivered and her teeth pressing into the hard muscles of his torso became less gentle. "You need to...be tasted. And I need to taste you. Please, Ty. Let me. Please."

Janna didn't wait for an answer before she flowed down his body. The flesh beneath her caressing mouth was hot, misted with sweat, tasting of salt and passion and the indefinable flavor of masculinity. Touching Ty was a pleasure so great it was nearly pain. A shivering ripple of sound came from her lips, for she had dreamed of being given the gift of his body once more.

Ty's clenched thigh muscles barely gave beneath the testing of Janna's teeth. Feeling the intense strokes of desire that shook him with each of her moist caresses was intensely arousing to her, but she was too consumed by her sensual explorations to realize that her own body was as hot as his. She only knew that bursts of pleasure went through her when she rubbed her breasts over his hard thighs and brushed her cheeks over the rigid evidence of his desire.

"Janna," Ty said raggedly. His voice when she turned her head and her lips brushed over him in a caress that nearly undid him. "Sweet God, you're killing me. Love, don't, I've never...you'll make me..."

The intimate touch of Janna's tongue was a liquid fire that burned away Ty's words, burned away his thoughts, burned away everything but the incandescent instant when she first tasted him.

Speech unraveled into a cry that was torn from deep in Ty's throat. The harsh sound made Janna stop. She looked up. The green blaze of his eyes made her tremble.

"Did I hurt you?"

"No."

"But you...cried out," she said hesitantly.

"So did you when I touched you that way."

Janna's eyes half clouded as sensual memories burst inside her, drenching her with heat. She looked at Ty and remembered what it had been like to feel his mouth loving her, enthralling her, devouring her in steamy intimacy. She looked again at the potent male flesh that had felt so hard and smooth and intriguing to her tongue just a moment ago.

"Don't," Ty said huskily, biting back a raw sound of need. "You'll make me lose control."

"But I'm not even touching you," she whispered.

"You are in your mind. And in mine. Satin butterfly, hot and sleek and perfect. When you took me into your body it was like being taken into a fiery paradise. You burned me to my soul. You're still burning in my soul, burning in my body, everything burning. You don't know what you do to me."

Ty saw Janna's shivering response to his words and thought he would lose what little control remained to him.

"You burned me the same way," she said, touching him with the tip of her tongue. "I'm still burning."

Restlessly Janna stroked her hands over Ty's clenched leg muscles, trying to tell him something for which she had no words, seeking something she couldn't name. One of her hands caressed the inside of his thigh until she could go no higher. She felt him shudder, heard his ripping intake of breath and knew she had found another way to touch him with fiery paradise. Fascinated by the tangible variation between his body and her own, she caressed the very different flesh suspended so tightly between his thighs.

Ty watched Janna with eyes that were no more than green slits set against the stark tension of his face. He had thought he could want her no more without losing control. He had been wrong. He wanted her more now than he ever had; yet he made no move to take her, for he was learning more about himself and her with every instant, every caress, each sweet glide of her tongue as she discovered the changing textures of his masculinity.

The sight of Janna loving him, enjoying him, pleasuring him and herself at the same time was unlike anything Ty had ever known. Slowly his legs gave way, unable to bear the weight of his passion any longer. He sank to his knees, then onto the grass; and she moved with him, loving him in silence, displaying that love with every caress.

When her mouth circled him, accepting and cherishing him with a shattering intimacy, a cry was ripped from him once again. This time she didn't stop loving his hot flesh, for she knew that he had but given voice to the savage, overwhelming pleasure that was shaking his body.

"*Janna...*"

Her answer was silent, a changing pressure of her mouth that dragged a hoarse sound of ecstasy from his throat. He tried to tell her what she was doing to him, consuming and renewing him with each clinging movement of her lips and tongue. Despite his efforts no words came, for he had none to describe the shattering beauty of being loved without inhibition, without bonds, without expectations, nothing but the sultry heat of her mouth cherishing him.

"Janna," he said hoarsely. "Don't. I'm going to..." Words became a groan of ecstasy dragged from Ty as his hips moved in helpless need. "For the love of God...stop."

"Am I hurting you?" Janna asked, knowing the answer, wanting to hear it anyway.

Ty laughed brokenly, then made a low sound when her hands and mouth slid over him once more, caressing him, burning through his control, burning him alive.

"Love...stop. I can't take any more without losing control."

He felt the shiver that overtook Janna in the instant before she stroked him and whispered, "Yes, I'd like that."

Ty clenched against the pulses of ecstasy that were bursting through his body, not knowing how to give himself in that elemental way.

"Please," Janna whispered. She touched the tip of her tongue to the blunt masculine flesh that was no longer a mystery to her. "You taste like life itself."

Watching her, Ty made an anguished sound as he fought the tide of ecstasy that was surging through him. Deep within his soul he realized that he would never forget the picture she made as she loved him with a generosity that was a kind of ecstasy in itself, a giving and a taking that became a profound sharing he had never imagined possible. She accepted and cherished him without restraint, teaching him that he had known nothing of true intimacy before he had known Janna.

Ty felt his control being stripped away with each loving instant, each sweet and wild caress. Pleasure convulsed him, shaking his body and soul with each primal pulse of rapture; and the word he cried out at the shattering peak of ecstasy was Janna's name. The cry pierced her soul, bringing tears that were both hot and sweet, an overflowing of her joy in the certainty that she had given the man she loved such intense pleasure.

When Ty could again control his own body, he caught Janna between his hands and pulled her into his arms, needing the feel of her close to him. She closed her eyes and held him as strongly as he was holding her, savoring the closeness and the sound of her name repeated over and over by her lover as the aftermath of ecstasy shuddered through his powerful body. When he finally tilted her face up to his own, she smiled and nuzzled against the masculine lips, which were resilient and soft and...insistent.

"Ty?"

Her husky voice was like a caress on his hot skin.

"I need to be part of you," he said simply. His hand slid from Janna's cheek, skimmed down her shirtfront, below her waist, seeking and finding the soft mound at the apex of her thighs. He made a deep sound of discovery and satisfaction when he felt the sultry heat of her. "And you need me, too. I can feel it even through all the clothes you use to conceal your beauty. My own satin butterfly, waiting to be freed of your cocoon."

The pressure of Ty's strong hand cupping her so deliberately made a shimmering tension gather in the pit of Janna's stomach.

"You need me, butterfly," Ty said, flexing his hand, feeling Janna's alluring heat calling to him. He bent to take her lips, then stopped just short of that goal. "You need me, but do you want me, too?"

Janna tried to answer. All that came out was a breathless sound when Ty's tongue touched her lips and she realized how hungry she was for his kiss. Vaguely she felt a shifting pressure at her waist, but she barely noticed, for Ty's teeth had caught her lower lip and were holding it captive for the slow probing of his tongue. He released her soft lip by tiny increments.

"Do you want me?" he asked huskily while his hand flicked open buttons, pushed aside cloth, slid beneath fabric, seeking her feminine core. "Will you let me undress you, touch you, tease you until you're hot and wild and you can't breathe without calling my name?"

Janna couldn't answer, for his hand had claimed her and the blind searching of his fingertip was making her tremble in anticipation of the ecstasy she would know again at her lover's hands.

"Janna," Ty said in a low voice. "Tell me what you want."

"Touch me," she said raggedly.

"I'm already touching you."

She shivered and shifted her legs unconsciously, silently telling him what she wanted.

"Say it," he whispered. "I want to hear it. I need to know that I'm giving you something as sweet and powerful as you gave to me."

"I...I..."

Janna turned her face against Ty's chest in a gesture of trust and shyness that made him smile despite the need clenching fiercely within him. She had been so abandoned in her seduction of him a few moments before that he had forgotten she was new to sensuous play.

"Then I'll tell you what pleases me," Ty said, and as he spoke, his fingertip barely brushed the dark auburn triangle that both defined and concealed Janna's softness. "I love seeing you this way, with your clothes opened and your breasts bare and my hand between your beautiful thighs. I love watching your nipples rise and tighten even though nothing of me is touching you but my words. I love watching your breath shorten and your legs move restlessly until you open for me, asking that I touch what no other man has."

Smiling with frank sensuality, Ty watched the effect of his words on Janna. He encouraged her movements with teasing hesitations and tiny touches on her breasts, her navel, the heavy auburn silk at the apex of her thighs; and she moved beneath his touch, response and plea at once.

"Yes, like that. Just like that," Ty said, his voice thickening. His hands moved, caressing and revealing her in the same motions. "I love parting your soft lips and sliding into you. So warm..."

A ragged cry came from Janna as she felt a bubble of sensation expand wildly within her and then burst, heat spilling over at her lover's words, his touch, his clear enjoyment of her body.

"Yes, I love that, too," Ty said.

He advanced then withdrew his touch from her, teasing her and pleasuring her in the same motions, feeling the increase in her heat and softness with each caress. His voice changed with the heavy running of his own blood, becoming dark, deep, as elemental as the endless hunger he felt for the woman whose body became his at a touch.

"The way you respond to me makes me feel like a god. Hot satin butterfly..." Ty's voice broke as he felt the sudden constriction in Janna's satin depths, heard her breath hesitate and then come out in a low moan. "Love," he whispered, bending down to her, "tell me what you need. I'll give it to you, all of it, and then I'll begin all over once more, touching you, pleasuring you again and again until neither one of us has the strength to speak...if that's what you want. Tell me what you want."

Ty's name came from Janna's lips in a ripple of small cries marking the rings of pleasure expanding and bursting sweetly within her body. Blindly her hands moved over his hot skin until she found the flesh that she had come to know so intimately. He was hard and smooth to her touch, as tight as though it had been weeks rather than minutes since he had known release. Having tangible proof of her ability to affect Ty was like another kind of caress, deep and hot and unbearably sweet.

"I want you," Janna said, her voice breaking beneath an unexpected, wild burst of pleasure at feeling him so thick and heavy in her hands. "I want to be joined so closely with you that I can feel each heartbeat, each pulse of life..."

Her words shattered into rippling sounds, tiny cries called from her very core as Ty swept her loose pants from her body and merged their bodies with a single powerful motion, giving her all that she had asked for and more, for he had wanted the joining as intensely as she had.

The swift fulfillment was like lightning searching through Janna's flesh, creating an incandescent network of fire, burning through to her soul. She didn't know that she called Ty's name even as ecstasy transfixed her, but he knew. He heard his own name, felt the satin convulsions deep within her body, and he smiled in a mixture of triumph and passionate restraint as he bent to drink from her lips the taste of ecstasy.

Only when the last of Janna's cries had faded and the final echoes of passionate release had stilled in her body did Ty begin the slow dance of love, penetration and withdrawal, sliding deeply, retreating, sheathing himself within her once more, retreating, sheathing.

Janna's body gave no warning; suddenly she was in the grip of something unknown, something hot and vital coiling relentlessly within her, tighter with each movement, tension dragging breath from her lungs and strength from her limbs.

"*Ty.*"

His answer was an even more complete sheathing followed by husky laughter when he felt Janna's back arch in helpless reflex to his presence deep within her body. Her cries unraveled into a moan as she joined with Ty in the sinuous dance of love, her body driven by the pressure coiling within her. He encouraged her with dark words whispered into her ear and the strength of his arm circling beneath her hips, sealing their bodies tightly together. He felt the tension vibrating within her satin depths as surely as she did; the realization that she was poised on the brink of violent rapture slammed through him, nearly wrenching away his own control.

Ty fought against his own climax, dragging himself back from the brink. He didn't want release yet. Not before he had drunk the wine of Janna's passion to the last glorious drop.

The feel of her nails against his buttocks was like being burned by sensual fire. He groaned and gave her what she was demanding, what she needed, the elemental joining of his body to hers, no barriers, no calculation, nothing but heat and sweet friction and the driving rhythms of life.

The tightness within Janna increased until she would have screamed, but her voice was paralyzed. Her body twisted and her legs wrapped around Ty's lean hips as she strained toward something she both feared and needed, something so powerful that having it might destroy her; but not having it would certainly destroy her. She began to call Ty's name with each breath, broken sounds; she was being pulled apart by the tension that had no end, no release, nothing but a need that drove her relentlessly higher.

And then the tension doubled and redoubled with each heartbeat. She screamed his name and burst into a thousand blazing pieces, each one of them a separate ecstasy consuming her all the way to her soul.

Ty held Janna and himself, drinking her passion, feeling her climax to the marrow of his bones and beyond, kissing her with both gentleness and hunger, holding himself still despite the tension still hammering in his body with each breath, each heartbeat; and he didn't move because he wanted it to last forever.

There had never been a woman for him like Janna. He had learned in a twilight meadow on Black Plateau Janna's rare gift for ecstasy. Now he was driven to learn the boundaries of that gift. He began to move again, caressing and probing and filling her once more, each motion inciting flesh still quivering from the height of sensual stimulation and wild release.

"Ty?" she asked, opening dazed eyes.

"Yes," he said, bending down to Janna's mouth. "To the last drop of passion. Until we can't breathe. Until we die."

Chapter Thirty-Eight

Janna looked at the stone overhang that had been the only home she had ever had. Only scattered ashes remained of the campfire that had always been carefully tended. The pots and pans had been washed, upended and set aside. The trunk had been filled with herbs that would discourage insects or mice from settling in. All that she had kept out was a small pack consisting of her bedroll, herb pouch and canteen…and the sketch of her mother, a silken lady who hadn't survived the rigors of frontier life.

"We'll be able to get the books once the Army takes care of Cascabel," Ty said, putting his arm around Janna.

For an instant Janna leaned against Ty, savoring his strength and the knowledge that for once she didn't have to stand alone. Then she straightened and smiled up at him, but she said nothing about their coming back to the secret valley. If she kept her portion of Mad Jack's gold, she could build a home anywhere she wished, save one—wherever Ty was. That she would not do. She had been lucky enough to have her dream of a home made possible. The fact that she now wished for Ty to share that dream was unfortunate, but it was her misfortune, not his. She had taken advantage of his natural woman-hunger by teasing him until he was beside himself with need. She hadn't realized the power of the weapon she had turned on him. He had tried to resist, but he hadn't been able to, not entirely. That was her fault, not his.

Especially yesterday, when she had thrown herself at him with utter abandon, touching him in ways that made it impossible for him to turn away. Even now the memories made her tremble with the aftershocks of what he and she had shared.

But to Janna, her wantonness was no reason for Ty to give up his own dream. Requiring him to give up his deepest desire just because he had been the first man to show her ecstasy; that would be an act of hatred, not of love…and she loved Ty so much it felt as though she were being pulled apart by claws of ice and fire and night.

Silken lady, wherever you are, whoever you are, be kind to the man I love. Give him the dream he has wanted for so many years.

"Janna?" Ty asked, his throat aching with the sadness he felt twisting through her, the bleak shadow of night just beneath her sunny smile. "We'll come back. I prom—"

She put her fingers over his lips, sealing in the unwanted promise before it could be spoken. "It's all right," she said. "I knew I would have to leave someday. Someday...is today."

Ty lifted Janna's hand and pressed a kiss into her palm. "Wyoming is beautiful, too. If you don't like it there we can go anywhere."

Tears Janna couldn't conceal came to her eyes. Ty's words were agony to her, for they weren't the words she had longed so much to hear, the words he only spoke to her in her dreams, the words his silken lady would someday hear from his lips.

I love you.

But Ty didn't love Janna. He was amused by her, he liked her, and he was enthralled by her sensuality without realizing that passion's wellspring was her own deep love for him. He talked about their future together, but it was a future decreed by his unbending sense of honor and duty, not his desire to make Janna his mate, his lifetime companion, the mother of his children.

Honor and duty weren't love. Neither was kindness. Janna would rather live the rest of her life in the wild than watch Ty become bitter and ground down by regrets for the freedom and the dream he had lost.

And Janna would rather die than live to see the day when Ty stood like a captive mustang, his head down and his eyes as dead as stones.

"Go ahead and cry," Ty said, folding Janna into his arms, rocking her. "It's all right, sugar. It's all right. You'll have the home you've dreamed of if it's the last thing I do. It's the very least that I owe you."

Janna closed her eyes to conceal the wave of pain his words had caused. Very gently she brushed her lips over his shirtfront, savoring for the last time his heat, his scent, his strength, the male vitality that radiated from him.

"You owe me nothing at all."

Ty's laugh was harsh and humorless. "Like hell I don't. You saved my life, and all I've done since then is take from you. When I think of you throwing yourself under Lucifer's hooves just to catch him for me, I..."

Ty's words faded into a hoarse sound. Strong arms tightened almost painfully around Janna, as though Ty were trying to convince himself that she was all right despite all the dangers she had endured for him.

"I didn't catch Lucifer to make you feel obligated to me," Janna said quietly. "I did it so Lucifer wouldn't be killed by some greedy mustanger or be caught by a man too cruel to do anything but make Lucifer into a killer. You were the one who gentled Lucifer. You were the one who taught him to trust a man. Without that, what I did would have been worse than useless. Thank yourself for Lucifer, not me."

Ty tilted up Janna's chin and stared at her translucent gray eyes. "You really believe that, don't you?"

"I know it. *You don't owe me anything.* Not for your life, not for Lucifer, and not for the pleasure we shared. Not one damn thing. Once we get to the fort we're quits. You're as free as Lucifer once was. And so am I."

A chill came over Ty, making his skin tighten and move in primitive reflex. Janna's voice was calm and precise, lacking in emotion, as bleak as the darkness underlying her smile. She was systematically pulling away from him, cutting the ties that had grown silently, powerfully between them during the time they had spent in the hidden valley.

"No."

Ty said nothing more, just the single word denying what Janna had said.

Before she could say anything in argument, Ty turned away and whistled shrilly.

Moments later Lucifer came trotting over and began lipping at Ty's shirt in search of the pinch of salt Ty often had hidden in a twist of paper. There was no salt today, simply the voice and hands Lucifer had come to enjoy.

Ty petted the stallion for a few moments before he picked up the heavy saddlebags Mad Jack had left behind. Ty had cut slits in the leather that joined the saddlebags. Through the slits he had threaded the surcingle. Once the strap had been tightened, the saddlebags would stay in place on the stallion's back.

Lucifer didn't care for the surcingle around his barrel, but he had become accustomed to it. He did nothing more than briefly lay back his ears when the strap tightened just behind his front legs. Ty praised the stallion, shrugged his own backpack into place and vaulted onto the mustang's back. It was a heavy load Lucifer was carrying, but Ty wasn't worried. Lucifer was an unusually powerful horse. Even if Ty had added a saddle to the load, the stallion wouldn't have been overburdened for normal travel.

"I'll scout the area beyond the slot," Ty said. "Get Zebra over there and wait for my signal."

"Ty, I won't let you—"

"Let me? *Let* me!" he interrupted, furious. "To hell with 'letting'! You listen to me and you listen good. You might be pregnant. If you think I'll run off and leave an orphaned girl who could be carrying my child to fend for herself in Indian country, there's no damned point in even talking to you! I'll try hammering my message through that thick skull of yours after we get to the fort. Maybe by then I'll have cooled down or you'll have grown up. Until then, shut up and stop distracting me or neither one of us will live to see tomorrow."

Lucifer leaped into a canter before Janna had a chance to speak, even if she had been able to think of something to say.

By the time the stallion reached the exit to the valley, Ty had gotten his temper under control. He didn't permit himself to think about Janna and the immediate past, only about Cascabel and the immediate future.

Ty dismounted and looked at the area right in front of the cleft. No new tracks marked the meadow. A vague, telltale trail had been worn through the grass despite his and Janna's efforts never to take the same way twice into the cleft.

It doesn't matter now. By the time we come back the grass will have regrown. And when we do come back, we won't have to try to live so small we don't even cast shadows.

Beyond the ghostly paths there were no signs that anything had ever passed through the cleft to the outer world. Ty picked his way over the narrow watercourse and through the shadowed slot between rock walls. The afternoon light glowed overhead, telling him that the sky was nearly cloudless. Until the sun went down they would be vulnerable to discovery, for there would be no rain to conceal their presence while they crossed the wild land.

Yet they had no choice but to move in daylight. There was simply too much risk that one of the horses would injure itself scrambling over the cleft's treacherous watercourse in the dark. Besides, even if they got through the slot safely at night and then traveled until dawn, they would still be deep within Cascabel's preferred range when the sun once more rose, exposing them to discovery.

Their best chance was to sneak out of the slot and take a long, looping approach to the fort, hoping that Cascabel would have been driven to the southern edges of his territory while the two of them traversed the northern part. The fort itself was a hard three-day ride, and there was no haven short of the stockade walls.

Standing well back from the sunlit exit to the cleft, Ty pulled out his spyglass and examined as much of the land as he could see beyond the stone walls. A quick look showed nothing. A long look showed no more. A point-by-point survey revealed no sign of renegades.

Wish my backbone didn't itch.

But it did, and Ty wasn't going to ignore his instincts. There was danger out there. His job was to find out where and how much. Unconsciously he fingered the hilt of the big knife he always carried at his belt. He waited for fifteen minutes, then lifted the spyglass and studied the land again. Again he saw nothing to alarm him. He took off his backpack, checked the load in his carbine, grabbed a box of bullets and went out to have a closer look at the land.

He was no more than thirty feet from the cleft when he cut the trail of three unshod ponies. The hoofprints stayed together and marked a purposeful course, telling Ty that the horses had been ridden; they had not been grazing at random as wild horses would. The horses had come out of Cascabel's usual territory.

As Ty followed the traces he hoped that the Army had been successful in driving the renegades away. That hope died when he saw other tracks meet those that he was following. The two sets of tracks mingled, then split once more, heading in all directions, as though the riders had exchanged information and had then separated and gone to search for something.

Ty had a terrible suspicion that what the renegades were searching for was a *bruja* called Janna Wayland.

Keeping to cover as much as possible, crawling when he had to, walking when he could, Ty followed the tracks that crisscrossed the flatlands in front of the cleft. Everything he saw brought him to the same conclusion: the renegades were going to beat the bushes and ravines until their auburn-haired quarry burst from cover. Then they would run her down and bring her back to Cascabel. There would be medicine chants and dances, celebrations of past victories and future coups; and then Cascabel would lead his renegades into war with Janna's long hair hanging from his lance like a flag, proving to the world that his spirit was the greatest one moving over the wild face of the land.

For a moment Ty considered simply sneaking back to the cleft and waiting until Cascabel got tired of searching for his elusive quarry. That was what Janna had done in the past—hide. But in the past, Cascabel hadn't been so determined to catch her. If Ty and Janna retreated to the valley and then were found, they would be trapped in a stone bottle with no chance of escape. Better that they take their chances in the open.

Retreating silently back toward the cleft, Ty made a brief side trip to the top of a rise. From there he hoped to get a better view of the rugged land they had to cross. Just before he reached the edge of the rise, he took off his hat and went down on his stomach, presenting as little human silhouette as possible.

An instant later Ty was glad he had taken the trouble to be very cautious. On the far side of the rise, four warriors sat on their heels, arguing and gesticulating abruptly as they divided up the area to be searched for the Shadow of Flame, the witch who had been stealing Cascabel's spirit. Just beyond the warriors, seven horses grazed on whatever was within reach.

Four renegades. Seven horses. And my backbone is on fire.

The only warning Ty had was a slight whisper of sound behind him. He rolled onto his back and lashed out with his booted feet as the renegade attacked.

Chapter Thirty-Nine

Ty's kick knocked the air from the Indian's lungs, preventing him from crying out and alerting the others. Even so, Ty had no sooner put his hand on his knife hilt than the renegade was on his knees and trying to bring his rifle to bear. Ty threw himself forward, pinning the Indian to the ground with a hard forearm across his throat. A knife flashed and blood burst silently into sunlight. The renegade jerked once, twice, and then lay motionless.

For a few instants it was all Ty could do to breathe despite the screaming of his instincts that the danger had just begun, not ended, and he should be running rather than lying half-stunned. He rolled off the dead renegade and began collecting himself, relying on the survival reflexes he had learned in war. He cleaned his knife blade and put it back in its sheath. He picked up the carbine, checked it for dirt or mechanical damage, found none and made sure the weapon was ready for instant use.

Only then did Ty retreat silently, pausing long enough to close the dead warrior's eyes.

Ashes to ashes, dust to dust... And may God have mercy on both our souls.

Three hundred feet away Janna sank slowly to her knees, feeling as though her own heart had burst. The barrel of the pistol she was holding clanked softly against stone. She took a deep breath, then another, trying to quiet her body's trembling as she watched Ty glide from brush to boulder, retreating toward the cleft's uncertain shelter.

It had been nerve stretching for Janna to stay within the slot's narrow shadow, knowing as she did from Ty's actions that he must have cut the trail of renegades. She had been watching him for the past half hour while he reconnoitered. Her eyes ached from staring out and trying to guess what Ty was reading from various signs crisscrossing the earth.

Then an Indian had risen up out of the very ground and launched himself at Ty, choosing the greater glory of personal combat to the sure kill offered by picking off Ty with a rifle. Even though the range had been too far for Janna to use the pistol with real accuracy, she had reached for the gun. The fight had ended before she could even lift the weapon above her waist to take aim. She had never seen a man so quick as Ty, or so deadly in that quickness. She realized at that instant just how much of his strength he held in check when he was with her.

And Ty could have died despite all his power and speed, his blood a crimson stain bursting from his body to be drunk by the thirsty earth. All that was Ty, the passion and the laughter, the anger and the sensual teasing, the silence and the silken dream, all of it gone between one breath and the next.

Janna watched each of Ty's movements hungrily, needing the reassurance that he was alive. She scanned the land behind him as well, and she did it from over the barrel of the pistol, wanting to be able to shoot quickly at anything she saw.

Despite Janna's alertness, she didn't see the second renegade until the sun glinted off a rifle barrel as the warrior shifted position to shoot at Ty. Not even bothering to aim, Janna triggered a shot in the direction of the Indian.

At the sound of the shot, Ty dived for cover in a shallow ditch left behind by storm water fanning out from the cleft's narrow mouth. A few instants later he had his hat off and his carbine barrel resting on the lip of the ditch as he searched for the source of the attack. He didn't have to search long. The Indian shifted his aim again, sending more sunlight off his rifle barrel and drawing another shot from the cleft.

Janna's second bullet came much closer than the first had. The renegade's answering shot sent rock chips flying not four feet from her.

Despite the heavy pack Ty wore, he was up and sprinting for the next bit of cover while the renegade reloaded. Ty halfway expected to draw more fire from the other Indians, but none came. He hit the dirt a second before Janna fired at the rifle barrel that was once more poking out from a low mound of rocks and brush. The sharper *crack* of a rifle shot occurred a split second after Janna triggered her pistol.

Ty scrambled up and began running again, counting off the seconds he had before he must throw himself to the ground again. As intently as a hawk, Janna watched the cover that concealed the renegade. Steadying the heavy pistol with both hands, she waited for the renegade to reload and poke the rifle barrel out again, giving her a target.

Suddenly a flash of human movement off to the side caught Janna's eye. She screamed at Ty to take cover as she spun to the left and fired. Two rifle shots rang out, kicking dirt just in front of Ty. He flattened out into another shallow runoff ditch while Janna fired a shot at the orginal attacker.

Five, Ty counted silently to himself. *That's it. She has to reload.*

The pistol in Janna's hand clicked loudly twice before she realized that she was out of ammunition.

"Reload!" yelled Ty without looking away from his right, where the new attacker was hidden. *Come on, come on,* he silently urged the second renegade. *Show yourself.*

Reloading was much easier said than done for Janna. White lipped, she worked to eject the spent casings, fumble bullets from her pocket and shove them one by one into the six waiting chambers. This time she wouldn't leave one chamber empty as a precaution against accidentally discharging the revolver; she wanted all six shots and she wanted them right now.

But first she had to get the bullets into the chambers.

Four hundred feet away and ᴛᴏ the right of Ty, a thrown pebble bounced harshly on the hard ground. Knowing it was a feint, Ty fired in that direction anyway, then turned quickly toward the position of the first attacker.

Come and get it, he urged silently.

As Ty had hoped, the first renegade assumed he was facing an enemy armed with a single-shot rifle. The Indian broke cover and stood up, striving for a clean shot before his prey could reload or find better cover. Smoke puffed from Ty's carbine and the renegade died before he could even realize what had gone wrong. Ty levered another bullet into the firing chamber even as he whipped around to confront the second renegade, who had had time to reload and was taking aim.

Ty threw himself to the side, spoiling both his own shot and the renegade's. Ty's second and third shots were dead on target. He rolled to a new position of cover and waited. No more shots came. Either the other renegades hadn't had time to take position yet or the speed with which Ty could "reload" and fire his carbine had made them cautious.

"Janna," called Ty. "Are you all right?"

"Yes." Her voice was oddly thinned but strong.

"Tell me when you've reloaded."

Swearing shockingly, Janna worked at the unfamiliar task of putting cold, slippery bullets into the warm cylinder. She dropped two bullets before she managed to get all six chambers full. Cocking the revolver, she looked out over the land once more.

"Ready," she called.

"I'm coming in from your right."

"Go!"

An instant later Ty was on his feet and running toward the slot, dodging and turning every few seconds, doing everything he could to spoil a hunter's aim. Janna's gray eyes scanned the countryside to the left of the slot, alert for any sign of movement. At the edge of her side vision she watched Ty's long-legged stride eat up the distance between himself and safety.

Only twenty yards to cover. Then ten, then—

There was no time to warn Ty, no time to aim, no time to do anything but fire at almost point-blank range as a renegade sprang from cover just outside the cleft and came at Janna with a knife. Her first shot was wild. Her second shot hit the renegade's shoulder a glancing blow, knocking him backward. The third and fourth shots were Ty's. No more were needed.

"Get back," Ty said harshly, dragging Janna farther inside the cleft. "There are three more out there and God knows how many will come in at the sound of the shots."

Breathing hard, Ty shrugged out of his backpack and took up a position just inside the slot. He began refilling the carbine with quick, sure motions. As he worked he looked up every few instants to scan the landscape. What he saw made him swear tonelessly. There was a distant swirl of dust, which was probably a rider going off for reinforcements. One of the remaining renegades was taking up a position that would cover the mouth of the cleft.

The second Indian wasn't in sight, but he was within rifle range, as a screaming, whining, ricocheting bullet proved. Rock chips exploded, showering Ty with dust and stinging shards.

"Get farther back," he yelled as he blinked his eyes and took aim.

Ty fired several times at the most likely patches of cover from which the renegade might be shooting. Then he lowered his carbine and waited. A few moments later another shot whined past. This time he saw where it had come from. He answered instantly with closely spaced shots, sending bullets raking through the cover. There was a startled yell, then silence. Methodically Ty shoved bullets into the carbine's magazine, replacing those he had spent.

No more shots came.

"Janna?"

"I'm back here," she said.

The odd acoustics of the canyon made her sound close, though she was thirty feet away.

"We're going to have to get out on foot and try to steal horses from the Indians," Ty said.

Janna had arrived at the same conclusion. Getting Lucifer and Zebra out without being spotted by the Indians would be impossible.

"There's no moon tonight," Ty continued without looking away from the bit of cover where the Indian had hidden. "We'll go out an hour after full dark. Try to get some sleep until then."

"What about you?"

"I'll guard the entrance."

"But the ricochets—"

"If I get out of range of a ricochet," Ty interrupted impatiently, "I won't be able to see the mouth of the slot to guard it." Ty's expression softened for a moment when he looked at Janna. "Don't look so worried, sugar. He doesn't have a very good angle from where he is. I'll be all right."

Turning back to the slot, Ty fired six times in rapid succession, stitching bullets on either side of the place where the renegade had taken cover, forcing anyone who might still be in range to get down and stay down. Janna hesitated, then went quickly to Ty. She threw her arms around him and hugged him fiercely. He returned the embrace with a strength and a yearning that made tears burn against Janna's eyelids. In tones too soft for him to hear, she whispered her love against his neck before she turned away and retreated toward the meadow.

But Ty had heard Janna's words. For an instant he closed his eyes and felt the exquisite pain of having been given a gift he didn't deserve.

With automatic motions Ty propped his backpack against a stone, sat on his heels and loaded the carbine to full capacity once more. The angle of the shadows on the canyon walls told him that he had several hours to wait until sunset came, much less full dark.

Leaning against the wall, carbine at the ready, Ty tried to convince himself that when dawn came he and Janna would still be alive.

Chapter Forty

The meadow's sunlight seemed blinding after the cool, dim passage into the secret valley. Janna stood on the edge of the opening and sent a hawk's wild cry into the still air. A second call brought Zebra at a trot, her head high, her ears pricked. Lucifer followed after the mare, for the two horses had become inseparable during the weeks when the stallion was healing.

Janna mounted Zebra quickly and turned the mare toward the ancient ruins where Mad Jack had hidden his gold. She had never pried into the old prospector's secrets before—but then, she had never been trapped in a stone bottle before, either.

"Jack must have had a way in and out of this valley without coming through the slot," Janna said aloud to Zebra, "because I never saw a mark in that creek bed. If he had been coming and going from my end of the valley, I'd have heard him or you would have or Lucifer would have."

Zebra flicked her ears back and forth, enjoying the sound of Janna's voice.

"But you didn't hear Jack, and that old man was too weak to carry more than a few pounds of gold at a time, which means there was a lot of coming and going before those saddlebags were full. He had to have left some kind of trail, somewhere. He just had to."

And Janna had until dark to find it.

She urged Zebra into a canter, watching the rocky walls and lava flows, probing light and shadow for any sign of a faint trail. The valley narrowed in at the south end, where the ruins were. Beyond ascertaining that there was a clear spring welling up at the base of the ramparts that were just before the ruins, Janna had never really explored this part of the valley. The ruins were eerie by daylight and unsettling by night. She much preferred the clean reach of the stone overhang at the opposite end of the valley to the cramped and broken rooms of a people long dead.

But Janna wasn't looking for a campsite now, or even for temporary shelter. She was looking for the ancient trails that the vanished Indians must have left if they came and went from their home by any route other than the dark cleft. It was possible that the Indians might have built their fortress in a blind valley with only one exit, but Janna doubted it. A tribe that took so much trouble to hide its home was a cautious people, and cautious people knew that the only difference between a fortress and a trap was a bolt hole.

In the country outside the valley, Janna had spotted ancient trails in the past simply by standing on a ridge and allowing her eyes to go slightly unfocused. When she lost the finest edge of visual acuity, other patterns came to light, vague lines and odd shadows. Most often they were simply random lines in a wild land, but sometimes they were ghost trails no longer used by man.

Crisscrossing the area around the ruins, Janna searched for any trail, new or old. She found nothing on the ground but grass, brush, rocks, sunlight and signs of her own passage. She urged Zebra farther into the ruins. The angle of the sun made shadows spill out from crumbling stone rooms, as though darkness had breached stone dams and was welling up to fill the valley beyond.

A frisson of uneasiness ran through Janna. She had always avoided the ruins in the hours beyond midafternoon, when the descending sun played odd tricks with light and shadow and stone. All that drove her farther into the ruins now was the certainty that nothing a ghostly Indian had to offer could be worse than what waited beyond the cleft in the form of flesh-and-blood renegades.

No matter how Janna focused her eyes or didn't, tilted her head or held it straight, narrowed her eyelids or widened them until her eyes ached, she saw nothing on the ground to suggest an ancient, forgotten trail. Working out from the room in which Mad Jack had stored his gold, she quartered the open space. She found nothing she could be sure was Mad Jack's sign rather than her own or a random displacement of pebbles.

The farther back into the ruins Janna went, the narrower the canyon became. Stone rubble covered the ground. At first she assumed the rocky debris was the result of stones falling from the surrounding cliffs, but the farther back into the narrow throat of the canyon she went, the more she was struck by an odd thing—in some places the rubble looked as though it once had been level, as though broad steps or narrow terraces had once climbed up the throat of the valley.

With growing excitement Janna followed the frayed remnants of what might once have been a well-built path snaking back and up the broken ramparts of stone that surrounded the hidden valley. Behind Zebra a pebble rolled under Lucifer's feet. The mare snorted and shied at the sound, giving vent to her nervousness at being asked to take a trail that showed every evidence of getting more and more narrow while going nowhere at all.

"Easy, girl," Janna said soothingly, stroking the mare. "There's nothing around but you, me, Lucifer and a lot of rock. The shadows just look scary, that's all. There's nothing in them but air."

Under Janna's urging Zebra climbed the steepening path. The farther along she went, the more Janna's hopes sank. What had once looked like a wide path was rapidly degenerating into a jumble of stone that resembled nothing so much as the debris that always built up at the foot of stone cliffs.

Janna's hopes sank when Zebra scrambled around a tight corner and was confronted by a rock wall. Nothing that in any way resembled a trail broke the sheer rise of stone. Apparently Janna had been following a random chute paved with fallen rocks rather than a ghost path left by an ancient people.

For a long time she simply sat, staring at the end of her carefully constructed and entirely false logic of hope. However Mad Jack might have come into the valley, it wasn't this way; and this had been by far the best hope of finding his path. The other possibilities—the random ravines and slender runoff gullies and crevices that opened into the narrowest end of the valley where Janna was—were much less likely to lead to the top of the plateau than the ground she had just covered.

But Janna had no choice except to try the other possibilities. No matter how small they were, they were better than the chance of sneaking past Cascabel and his renegades while they were camped outside the valley's only exit like a horde of hungry cats waiting at a mouse hole.

There was barely enough room for Zebra to turn around in order to head back where she had come from. Lucifer saw Zebra turning and followed suit. He led the retreat over the rough ground at a brisk trot, relieved to be free of the narrow passage between broken walls of stone. Zebra was equally relieved. She followed after the stallion eagerly.

They had retreated no more than a hundred feet when Janna noticed a small ravine that she hadn't seen before, for it joined at an oblique angle to the main passage and was walled off by a pediment of stone. Immediately she turned Zebra toward the side ravine. The mare tossed her head, not wanting to leave Lucifer and enter the narrow gulch.

"Come on, girl. There's nothing up this trail but stone and shadows and maybe, just maybe, a way out of here."

Zebra didn't budge.

Janna stopped using pressures of her hand to guide the mare. Instead, she pulled on the knotted hackamore reins Ty had insisted that Zebra be trained to wear. Reluctantly the mare turned away from Lucifer and walked into the gulch. Once past the rocky outcropping that guarded the ravine's narrow mouth, the passage opened out again, becoming wider than the slot where Ty waited for a renegade who was brave or foolish enough to show himself.

Janna didn't know if it were wishful thinking or truth, but it seemed to her that the new path had once been made more level by a series of broad steps composed of stony rubble, which followed the steep rise of the ravine farther and farther back into the body of the plateau. The steps, or ramps, had since largely crumbled and been washed away beneath torrential rains, but enough remained to give a mustang adequate footing.

To Janna's surprise, Lucifer followed, as though determined not to lose sight of Zebra in the midst of echoing stone ravines. The path snaked higher and higher, sometimes scrambling over stony ridges to follow a different runoff course up the broken walls that constituted the western side of the valley.

There were places where Janna was certain that rock must have been hammered away to make passage possible. In other places she was just as certain that nothing had touched the trail but wind and water, sun and storm. Then she would see gouge marks on the stone and wonder if they weren't the result of intelligence rather than past landslides.

The trail came to yet another narrowing of the branching network of runoff channels that covered the eroding face of the western ramparts of the valley. Without being urged, Zebra scrambled and lunged over the small rise, for there had been many such changes of direction in the past half mile.

There was sun shining on the rise, for they had climbed far enough to be beyond the reach of lengthening shadows. Janna shaded her eyes and looked ahead, confidently expecting to find an obvious way to proceed. She saw nothing except a lateral crack in the stone cliff, but the crack was too small

to be called a passage. Turning slowly, she looked over her trail. Her breath
came in with a sharp sound. She was nearly to the top of the stone ramparts
that surrounded her hidden valley.

"There has to be a way to get out from here," Janna said aloud as she
stroked Zebra absently.

For several minutes Janna looked at the dubious lateral crevice that angled
up and across the remaining cliff. The narrow ledge she saw might or might
not lead to the top of the plateau. If the ledge ended short of the top, she
would be stuck; there was no place for a horse to turn around. If the mustangs
entered the crack they would be committed to going up, not down.

Janna slid off Zebra, then pressed the mare's nose in a signal for her to
stay behind. Ears pricked, nostrils flared, the mustang watched her mistress
take the narrow trail. Janna looked back only once to assure herself that Zebra
wasn't going to stray.

After Janna had gone fifteen feet, she was certain that she was going the
right way. The crack became a very narrow ledge, too narrow for a horse to
pass safely. Marks that could have been left by a chisel or hammer showed
in the stone. Apparently the ancient tribe had widened and leveled a natural
split in the rock face until it became a ledge just wide enough to take a man
on foot. With overhanging rock on her left, a path no more than twenty inches
wide at her feet—and sometimes less, if the rock had crumbled away—and
a sheer drop to the valley floor on her right, she scrambled the length of the
crack.

When Janna vanished around a column of rock on the far end of the ledge
Zebra nickered as though to call a foal back to her side. When that didn't
work, the mustang neighed loudly. Lucifer added a ringing, imperious command that carried from one end of the hidden valley to the other.

Janna popped back into view, sliding and skidding down to the ledge,
desperate to calm the stallion before he alerted half of Utah Territory. Despite
the need for haste, Janna slowed to a very careful walk while she negotiated
the dangerous ledge. Zebra whickered softly in encouragement or warning,
then nuzzled Janna when she was within reach once more. Having achieved
his purpose in calling back a straying member of his band, Lucifer made no
further noise.

"Lord, what a bugle you have," Janna said to Lucifer, who ignored her
irritation. She looked back at the ledge and shook her head. "I know, that's
a scary path even for humans. I can imagine what it must look like to you.
But you didn't give me a chance to find out if the rest of the trail—if it really
is a trail—goes all the way to the top."

After a few moments spent reassuring the horses, Janna started toward the
ledge again. She had taken no more than two steps when she heard a barrage
of rifle fire.

She froze, listening intently, trying to decide where the shots were coming
from. The lighter, rhythmic barks of Ty's Winchester resolved the issue beyond a doubt. The sounds were coming from the cleft that Ty had remained
behind to guard. The Indians must have decided to try rushing the cleft's
entrance, or perhaps it was only a feint.

Either way, Janna wasn't comforted. The number of shots that were being fired told her that renegade reinforcements must have arrived. If they timed their attack carefully, they could provide cover for one another while they reloaded their rifles. But Ty was alone in the rocky cleft with no one to cover him while he reloaded.

Chapter Forty-One

The trip back down the ancient trail took much less time than the trip up had, but it seemed like an eternity to Janna. The instant it was safe to demand speed from Zebra, she kicked the mare into a hard gallop that ended only at the shadowed entrance to the cleft. Heart hammering, Janna leaped from Zebra and ran into the dark opening just as there was a renewed fusillade of rifle fire. The cleft distorted sounds, making them seem to come from nearby and far away all at once. She kept hoping to hear the carbine's lighter sound but heard only her own breath and the erratic bark of renegade rifles.

Just as Janna rounded the last bend before the exit, Ty's carbine resumed its rhythmic, rapid firing. She slowed slightly, almost dizzy with relief.

Ty heard her footsteps and looked over his shoulder. "You're supposed to be sleeping."

"Not likely with all the racket you're making," she said breathlessly.

His smile was rather grim as he turned his attention back to the land beyond the cleft. He fired quickly three times and was answered by a scattering of shots.

"I'm having a little help making noise, as you can see."

"How many?" Janna asked.

"I saw enough dust for an army, but I don't think there are more than ten rifles out there right now, and all of them are single shot."

"For these small blessings, Lord, we are thankful," Janna said beneath her breath. "I think."

Ty's smile was little more than a hard line of white beneath his black mustache. He wasn't sure that it made a difference what kind of rifles the renegades were shooting. The chance of Janna and himself slipping past the Indians—much less of stealing a horse or two on the way by—had dropped to the point that it would be frankly suicidal rather than probably suicidal to try escaping through the cleft.

But there was no other way out.

"I think I found a way out," Janna said.

Her words echoed his thought so closely that for a moment Ty wasn't sure that she really had spoken. His head snapped around.

"What did you say?"

"I think I found how Mad Jack got his gold into the ruins without our seeing him."

A movement beyond the cleft commanded Ty's attention. He turned, got off two quick shots and had the satisfaction of knowing that at least one of them had struck home. There was a flurry of return fire, then silence. As he watched the area beyond the cleft he began reloading methodically.

"How did he do it?" Ty asked.

"You know how the valley narrows out behind the ruins?"

"Yes."

"I followed it," Janna said.

"So did I about two weeks ago. It ends in a stone cliff."

"There's a ravine coming in before that."

"There are at least ten ravines 'before that,' and those ravines branch into others, which branch into others. And they all end against a stone cliff," Ty concluded flatly.

"Even the one with the ledge?" Janna asked, trying to keep the disappointment from her voice.

"What ledge?"

"The one that goes along the western lip of the valley almost to the rim."

"Are you certain?"

"I was on it until I heard rifle fire."

Slowly Ty lowered his carbine and turned toward Janna. "You said 'almost to the rim.' How close is 'almost'?"

"I don't know. Zebra started whinnying when I got out of sight and then Lucifer set up such a ruckus that I came back to calm him down. Then I heard rifle fire and was afraid they were rushing you and you didn't have anyone to cover you while you reloaded." Janna closed her eyes briefly. "I got back here as quick as I could."

"How close is almost?" Ty repeated calmly.

"A hundred feet. Maybe a hundred yards. Maybe a quarter mile. I couldn't see."

"Would you bet your life on that path going through?"

"Do we have a choice?"

"Probably not. If Cascabel isn't out there soon, he will be when word gets to him. Until then, there are at least eight able-bodied warriors and two wounded renegades under cover out there, just waiting for something to show at the cleft."

"What if we wait until dark?"

"We can try it."

"But?" Janna prodded.

"Our chances of getting out alive through that cleft are so slim they aren't worth counting," Ty said bluntly. "The same darkness that would cover our movements also covers theirs. Even now the renegades are moving in closer, finding cover, covering each other, closing in on the cleft. By dark they'll have the cork well and truly in the bottle. After that, it's just a matter of time until I run out of ammunition and they rush me."

Ty said nothing more. He didn't have to. Janna could finish his bleak line of thought as well as he could.

"There's something else to consider," Ty said. "If you can find that trail from this end, sure as God made little green apples, a renegade can find it from the other end if he has a good enough reason to go looking—and your hair is a good enough reason, thanks to Cascabel's vision."

Janna nodded unhappily. The same thought had occurred to her. "We can take the horses most of the way."

"But not all?"

"The ledge was made for men, not horses."

Ty had expected nothing more. He bent, put his arms through the straps of his heavy pack and shrugged it into place. "Let's go. We only have a few hours of light left."

Janna turned to leave, then was struck by a thought. "What happens if the Indians rush the cleft while we're still in the valley?"

"I've made the renegades real wary of showing themselves. But if they do—" Ty shrugged "—I can hold them off in the ruins almost as well as in the cleft. You'll have plenty of time to follow the path."

"If you think I'd leave you to—"

"If I tell you to take that trail," Ty interrupted flatly, *"you damn well will take that trail."*

Without another word Janna turned and began working her way rapidly back through the cleft. Ty was right on her heels. When they came out into the little valley, Zebra and Lucifer were standing nearby, watching the opening attentively. Janna mounted and waited while Ty pulled the saddlebags full of gold out of a hiding place and secured them on Lucifer's muscular back. As soon as Ty had mounted, Janna urged Zebra into a gallop.

The mustangs quickly covered the distance to the ruins. Janna didn't slow the pace until the valley narrowed and the rubble underfoot made the going too rough for any speed greater than a trot. The sounds of stones rolling beneath the horses' hooves echoed between the narrowing walls of the valley. Walking, trotting, scrambling, always pushing ahead as quickly as possible, Zebra climbed up steeper and steeper byways, urged by Janna through the twisting web of natural and man-made passages. Lucifer kept up easily despite the double load of Ty and the gold. The stallion was powerful, agile and fully recovered from his brush with Joe Troon's rifle.

More than once Ty thought that Janna had lost her way, but each time she found a path past the crumbling head of a ravine or through places where huge sheets of rock had peeled away from the ramparts and smashed to pieces against stone outcroppings farther down the cliff. When Zebra scrambled over a ridge of stone and came to a stop, Ty wondered if Janna had finally lost her way. He hoped not; he had begun to believe there was a way out of the hidden valley that had been first a haven and then a deadly trap.

Janna turned and looked back at Ty. "This is as far as the horses can go."

Before Ty could answer, Janna slid from Zebra's back, adjusted the small pack she wore and set off to traverse the narrow ledge. Ty dismounted, scrambled up the last few feet of trail and saw the ledge—and the sheer drop to the valley below.

"Sweet Jesus," he whispered.

Ty fought against an urge to call out to Janna to come back. All that made him succeed was the fear of distracting her from the trail's demands.

The sound of rifle fire drifted up from the direction of the cleft, telling Ty that the renegades were on the move once more. He turned and looked toward the east. He couldn't see the spot where the cleft opened into the meadow. He could, however, see that once the renegades spread through the valley looking for their prey, it would be just a matter of time until a warrior looked up and saw Janna poised like a fly on the wall of the valley's western ramparts.

Zebra called nervously when Janna vanished around a bulge of stone. The stallion's ringing whinny split the air, reverberating off rocky walls. Ty went back to Lucifer and clamped his hand over the horse's nostrils. The stallion shook his head but Ty only hung on harder. He spoke softly, reassuring the mustang, hoping the horse's neigh hadn't carried over the sound of rifle fire.

"Easy, boy, easy. You and Zebra are going to be on your own again in just a little bit. Until then, shut up and hold still and let me get this surcingle undone."

Lucifer snorted and backed away, tossing his head even as his nostrils flared. Ty threw himself at the stallion's head, just managing to cut off Lucifer's air before he could whinny again.

"What's wrong with you?" Ty asked soothingly. "You've never been this jumpy. Now hold still and let me get this strap off you."

Without warning Lucifer lurched forward, shouldering Ty roughly aside.

"What the hell?"

Ty regained his balance and followed Lucifer up the last few feet of trail. Ty was fast, but not fast enough. Lucifer's demanding bugle rang out. Reflexively Ty lunged for the stallion's nose. The horse shouldered him aside once more. Cursing, Ty scrambled to his feet, wondering what had gotten into Lucifer.

"Dammit, horse, where the hell do you think you're going?"

The stallion kept walking.

Then Ty looked past the stallion and realized what had happened. "God in heaven," Ty whispered.

Zebra had followed Janna out onto the ledge—and the stallion was going out right after her, determined not to be left behind.

Chapter Forty-Two

Afraid even to breathe, Ty watched Zebra and Lucifer picking their way over the narrow ledge with the delicacy of cats walking on the edge of a roof. The worst part of the trail was halfway along the ledge, where rock had crumbled away to make an already thin path even more skeletal. All that made passage possible was that the cliff at that point angled back from the vertical, rather than overhanging as it did along much of the ledge.

When Zebra reached the narrow place where rock had crumbled away, she stopped. After a moment or two her hooves shifted restively. Small pieces of rock fell away, rolling and bouncing until there was no more stone, only air. The mare froze in place, having gone forward no more than an inch or two.

"Go on," Ty said under his breath. "You can't turn around and you can't back up and you can't stay there forever. There's only one way out and that's to keep on going."

Zebra snorted. Ears pricked, she eyed the ledge ahead. Her skin rippled nervously. Sweat sprang up, darkening her pale hide around her shoulders and flanks. Trembling, she stood on the narrow ledge.

And then she tried to back up.

A hawk's wild cry keened across the rocks. The sound came once, twice, three times, coaxing and demanding in one; Janna had returned to the far side of the ledge to see what was taking Ty so long. A single glance had told her what the problem was, and how close it was coming to a disastrous solution. She began speaking to Zebra in low tones, calming the mare, praising her, promising her every treat known to man or mustang if Zebra would only take the few steps between herself and Janna.

Slowly Zebra began to move forward once more. Holding out her hands, Janna backed away, calling to the mustang, talking to her, urging her forward. Zebra followed slowly, placing each hoof precisely—and on her right side, part of each hoof rested on nothing but air.

Gradually the ledge became wider once more, allowing Zebra to move more quickly. She completed the far end of the trail in a subdued rush, barely giving Janna a chance to get out of the way.

Ty had little time to be relieved that Zebra was safe, for now it was Lucifer's turn on the crumbling stone. The stallion liked it even less than the mare, for he was bigger and the saddlebags tended to rub hard against the overhang along the first part of the ledge, pushing the horse outward and toward the sheer drop to the valley floor. Unlike Zebra, Lucifer didn't stop on the narrow section of the trail. He simply laid back his ears and placed each hoof with excruciating care, sweating nervously until his black coat shone like polished jet.

Just as he reached the far end of the ledge, a piece of stone crumbled away beneath his great weight. His right rear hoof lost purchase entirely, throwing him off balance.

Janna bit back a scream as she watched Lucifer scramble frantically to regain his balance and forward momentum. For long seconds the stallion hung poised on the brink of falling. Without stopping to think of the danger, Janna darted past Zebra, grabbed Lucifer's hackamore and pulled forward as hard as she could, hoping to tip the balance.

"Janna."

Ty's horrified whisper was barely past his lips when Lucifer clawed his way over the last of the ledge and lunged onto the wider trail, knocking Janna down and aside in his haste to reach safe footing. The stallion crowded against Zebra, nipping at her haunches, demanding that she keep going up the trail.

Ty barely noticed the narrowness of the ledge or the rub of his left shoulder against the overhang. He covered the stone pathway with reckless speed, wanting only to get to Janna. With fear like a fist in his throat, he knelt next to her and touched her cheek.

"Janna?"

She tried to speak, couldn't and fought for air.

"Take it easy, sugar," Ty said. "That fool stud knocked the breath out of you."

After a few more moments air returned to Janna in an aching rush. She breathed raggedly, then more evenly.

"Do you hurt anywhere?" Ty asked.

Janna shook her head.

"Have enough air now?"

She nodded.

"Good."

Ty bent and pulled Janna into his arms, hugging her hard, then taking her mouth in a kiss that was both savage and tender. After a long time he lifted his head.

"Don't ever do anything like that again," Ty said roughly. "Nothing's worth your life. Not the stallion. Not the gold. Not *anything*. Do you hear me, Janna Wayland?"

She nodded, more breathless from Ty's searching, hungry and gentle kiss than from her skirmish with Lucifer.

Ty looked at Janna's eyes. They were clear and warm as summer rain, radiant with emotion, and he felt his heart turn over in his chest. He closed his own eyes, unable to bear the feelings tearing through him, pulling him apart.

Two feet away from Ty's left leg, stone chips exploded, spattering both of them with shards. From the valley below came the sound of rifle fire.

Ty dragged Janna up the trail and around an outcropping of rock until they were out of view of the valley. From ahead came the sound of stones rolling and bouncing as the mustangs scrambled on up the trail.

"When you get to the top, wait ten minutes," Ty said. "If I don't come, get on Zebra and ride like hell for the fort. Don't come back, Janna. Promise me. Don't come back. There's nothing you can do here but get killed."

"Let me stay," she pleaded.

"No," he said. Then he added in a low voice, "Please, Janna. Let me feel that I've given you something. Just once. Just once for all the things you've given to me. Please."

Janna touched Ty's cheek with fingers that trembled. He turned his head and kissed her fingertips very gently.

"Now go," he said softly.

Janna turned and walked away quickly, trying not to cry. She had gone no more than a hundred feet before she heard the harsh, evenly spaced sounds of Ty's carbine firing down into the valley below.

The remaining trail to the top of the plateau was more of a scramble than a walk, for the ravine that the path followed was filled with stony debris and a few hardy evergreens. The mustangs had left ample signs to follow—broken twigs and overturned stones and shallow gouge marks along solid rock.

The few steep pitches were mercifully brief. Within fifteen minutes Janna was standing on top of the plateau. She hadn't heard any sounds of shooting for the last ten minutes as she had climbed upward. She had told herself that that was good, that it meant Ty was on his way up the trail. She also had told herself he was all right, but tears kept ruining her vision and fear made her body clench.

From where Janna stood on the plateau there was no hint that there might be a trailhead nearby, or even that the long, shallow gully she had just climbed out of was in any way different from any of hundreds of such gullies that fringed the steeper edges of the plateau.

The horses grazed nearby, wary of all sounds and shadows. All that forced Janna to mount Zebra was the memory of Ty's eyes pleading with her to be safe, and the gentle kisses that still burned on her fingertips, sealing her promise. Torn between fear and grief, rebellion and love, Janna mounted Zebra and waited, counting off the minutes.

Three minutes went by. Then five. Eight. Nine. Ten.

I'm safe enough here. It won't hurt to wait just a bit more. The mustangs will tell me if anyone else is near.

Twelve minutes. Fifteen. Seventeen.

Janna had reached eighteen when the mustangs lifted their heads and turned to watch the mouth of the gully with pricked ears and no nervousness whatsoever. Minutes later Ty came scrambling up out of the ravine.

"I told you—ten minutes," he said, breathing heavily.

"I don't know how to c-count," Janna said, trying to blink back tears and laughter at the same time.

Ty swung up on Lucifer, brought the stallion alongside Zebra and gave Janna a fierce kiss.

"Sweet liar."

Ty smacked Zebra hard on the rump, sending the mare into startled flight. Lucifer leaped to follow. Together the two mustangs settled into a ground-covering gallop. The plateau's rumpled surface flew beneath their hooves.

Twice Janna and Ty heard gunfire. Each time they veered more to the east, for the sounds were coming from the north and west. About every ten minutes

Janna would slow the pace to a canter, allowing the horses to catch their breath. Despite the itching of his backbone, Ty never complained about the slower pace. He knew that the mustangs might be called upon to outrun Indians at any moment; the horses wouldn't have a prayer if they were already blown from miles of hard running.

During the third time of resting, the distant crackling of rifle fire drifted to Janna and Ty on the wind. This time the sound was coming from the east.

"Should we—" began Janna.

She was cut off by a curt gesture from Ty. He pulled Lucifer to a stop and sat motionlessly, listening.

"Hear it?" he asked finally.

"The rifles?"

"A bugle."

Janna listened intently. She was turning to tell Ty she couldn't hear anything when the wind picked up again and she heard a faint, distant cry rising and falling.

"I hear it. It must be coming from the flatlands."

"Where's the closest place we can get a good look over the edge?" Ty asked.

"The eastern trailhead is only a few miles from here."

Janna turned Zebra and urged the mare into a gallop once more, not stopping until she came to the crumbling edge of the plateau where the trail began. Lucifer crowded up next to Zebra and looked out over the land, breathing deeply and freely, appearing for all the world as though he had barely begun to tap his strength.

Ty examined the land through his spyglass, sweeping the area slowly, searching for signs of man. Suddenly he froze and leaned forward. Six miles north and east of his present position, a small column of cavalry was charging over the land, heading south, sweeping a handful of renegades before it. Well behind the first column of soldiers, a larger one advanced at a much more sedate pace.

Ty swung the spyglass to look to the south, closer in to the plateau's edge.

"Christ almighty," Ty swore. "Cascabel's got an ambush set up where the trail goes through a ravine. That first group of renegades is the bait. He's got enough warriors hidden to slaughter the first group of pony soldiers before the rear column can get there to help."

"Can we get down in time to warn them?"

Grimly Ty looked at the trail down the east face of the plateau. It was even more precipitous than he had remembered. It was also their only hope of getting to the soldiers before Cascabel did.

"Would it do any good to tell you to stay here?" Ty asked.

"No."

"You're a fool, Janna Wayland."

Ty jerked his hat down on his forehead, settled his weight into the rope stirrups, gave a hair-raising battle cry and simultaneously booted Lucifer hard in the ribs.

The stallion lunged over the rim and was launched onto the steep trail before he had a chance to object. Front legs stiff, all but sitting on his hocks, Lucifer plunged down the first quarter mile of the trail like a great black cat. In helping the stallion not to overrun his balance, Ty braced his feet in the rope stirrups and leaned so far back that his hat brushed the horse's hard-driving rump.

When Lucifer stumbled, Ty dragged the horse's head back up with a powerful yank on the hackamore reins, restoring the stallion's balance. Surrounded by flying grit and rolling, bouncing pebbles, horse and rider hurtled down the dangerous slope.

Zebra and Janna followed before the dust had time to settle. As had the stallion, Zebra sat on her hocks and skidded down the steepest parts, sending dirt and small stones flying in every direction. Janna's braids, already frayed by the wind, came completely unraveled. Her hair rippled and swayed with every movement of the mustang, lifting like a satin pennant behind her.

When Lucifer gained the surer footing on the lower part of the trail, Ty risked a single backward look. He saw Zebra hock-deep in a boiling cloud of dirt and pebbles, and Janna's hair flying behind. The mustang spun sharply sideways, barely avoiding a stone outcropping. Janna's body moved with the mare as though she were as much a part of the mustang as mane or tail or hooves.

Lucifer galloped on down the sloping trail, taking the most difficult parts with the surefootedness of a horse accustomed to running flat out over rough country. Ty did nothing to slow the stallion's pace, for each second of delay meant one second nearer to death for the unsuspecting soldiers in the first column. As soon as the trail became more level, Ty pointed Lucifer in the general direction of the advancing column, shifted his weight forward over the horse's powerful shoulders and urged him to a faster gallop.

When Zebra came down off the last stretch of the eastern trail, she was more than a hundred yards behind Lucifer. But Janna knew the country far better than Ty. She guided Zebra on a course that avoided the roughest gullies and rocky rises. Slowly the mare began to overtake Lucifer, until finally they were running side by side, noses outstretched, tails streaming in the wind. Their riders bent low, urging the mustangs on.

Rifle fire came like a staccato punctuation to the rhythmic thunder of galloping hooves. A lone rifle slug whined past Ty's head. He grabbed a quick look to the right and saw that the Indians apparently had abandoned the idea of leading the soldiers into a trap. Instead, the renegades had turned aside to run down the great black stallion and the spirit woman whose hair was like a shadow of fire. Even Cascabel had joined the chase. Dust boiled up from the ambush site as warriors whipped their mounts to a gallop and began racing to cut off Janna and Ty from the soldiers.

Ignoring the wind raking over his eyes, Ty turned forward to stare between Lucifer's black ears, trying to gauge his distance from the column of soldiers. Much slower to respond than the renegades, the cavalry was only now beginning to change direction, pursuing their renegade quarry along the new course.

It took Ty only a few moments to see that the soldiers were moving too slowly and were too far away to help Janna and himself, whose descent from the plateau had been so swift that they were much closer to Cascabel than to the soldiers they had wanted to warn of the coming ambush. What made it worse was that the renegades who had waited in ambush were riding fresh horses, while Zebra and Lucifer had already been running hard for miles even before the hair-raising race down the eastern trail. Now the mustangs were running flat out over the rugged land, leaping ditches and small gullies, whipping through brush, urged on by their riders and by the whine of bullets.

Ty knew that even Lucifer's great heart and strength couldn't tip the balance. The soldiers were simply too far away, the renegades were too close, and even spirit horses couldn't outrun bullets. Yet all that was needed was two minutes, perhaps even just one. With one minute's edge, Janna's fleet mustang might be able to reach the soldiers' protection.

Just one minute.

Ty unslung his rifle and snapped off a few shots, knowing it was futile. Lucifer was running too hard and the country was too rough for Ty to be accurate. He hauled on the hackamore, trying to slow the stallion's headlong pace so that he could put himself between the renegades and Janna. Gradually Zebra began pulling away, but not quickly enough to suit Ty. He tried a few more shots, but each time he turned to fire he had to release the hackamore's knotted reins, which meant that Lucifer immediately leaped back into full stride.

Dammit, horse, I don't want to have to throw you to make you stop. At this speed you'd probably break your neck and I sure as hell wouldn't do much better. But we're dead meat for certain if the renegades get us.

And I'll be damned in hell before I let them get Janna.

Ty's shoulders bunched as he prepared to yank hard on one side of the hackamore, pulling Lucifer's head to the side, which would unbalance him and force him to fall.

Before Ty could jerk the rein, he heard rifle fire from ahead. He looked over Lucifer's ears and saw that a group of four horsemen had broken away from the column of soldiers. The men were firing steadily and with remarkable precision, for they had the platform of real stirrups and their horses had been trained for war. The repeating rifles the four men used made them as formidable as forty renegades armed only with single-shot weapons. The horses the four men rode were big, dark and ran like unleashed hell, leaving the cavalry behind as though the soldiers' mounts were nailed to the ground.

For the second time that day, Ty's chilling battle cry lifted above the thunder of rifles and hooves; but this was a cry of triumph rather than defiance. Those were MacKenzie horses and they were ridden by MacKenzie men and Blue Wolf.

Janna blinked wind tears from her eyes and saw the four horses running toward her, saw the smoke from rifles and knew that had caused Ty's triumphant cry: the speed of the four horses had tipped the balance. They were going to reach Ty and Janna before Cascabel did.

"We're going to make it, Zebra. We're going to make it!"

Janna's shout of joy turned to a scream as Zebra went down, somersaulting wildly, sending her rider hurtling to the ground.

Chapter Forty-Three

Before Janna hit the ground Ty was hauling back and to the right on the reins, forcing Lucifer into a hard turn. Despite the speed of Ty's reflexes, the stallion was galloping so fast that momentum alone swept them far past the place where Janna had fallen. Long before the stallion completed the turn, Zebra staggered to her feet to stand alone and trembling, favoring her left foreleg. Rifle fire erupted around her. She lunged to the side, seeking the cover of nearby piñons.

Ty saw the mare's three-legged motion and knew that she would be no help to Janna. A few yards from the mustang, Janna was struggling to her hands and knees, obviously dazed and disoriented by the force of her fall. A half mile beyond her, Cascabel and his renegades were bearing down in a cloud of dust and triumphant yells, certain that their prey was finally within their reach.

Measuring the distances involved, Ty quickly realized that Lucifer wasn't running fast enough to get Janna to safety before the Indians came within range. The stallion was straining, running with every bit of strength in his big body, but he was carrying more than three hundred pounds on his back.

Ty's knife flashed, severing the leather band that held the saddlebags full of gold on Lucifer's lathered body. The heavy pouches dropped away just as the mustang leaped a small gully. The gold vanished without a sign into the crease in the earth. Freed of the dead weight, Lucifer quickened his gallop.

"Janna!" Ty shouted. "Janna! Over here!"

Barely conscious, Janna turned toward the voice of the man she loved. She pushed hair from her eyes, forced herself to stand and saw Lucifer bearing down on her at a dead run. Ty was bent low over the horse's neck, giving the stallion all the help a rider could and at the same time calling for Lucifer's last ounce of speed.

Rifle slugs whined overhead and kicked up dirt around Janna. She noticed them only at a distance, as if through the wrong end of a spyglass, for she was concentrating on the wild stallion thundering down on her with Ty clinging like a cat to his black back.

A hundred yards behind Ty, four riders raced over the land like the horsemen of the Apocalypse, sowing destruction and death to any renegade within range of their rifles. The barrage of bullets slowed the charging Indians, who were unused to coming up against the rapid-fire rifles.

At the last possible instant, Ty twisted his right hand tightly into Lucifer's flying black mane and held his other hand out to Janna. He knew that he had to grab her and not let go—the momentum of the racing stallion would lift her quickly from the ground, allowing Ty to lever her up onto the horse's back.

"Get ready!" Ty shouted, hoping Janna could hear him.

His voice stitched between the war cries of the Indians behind Janna the erratic thunder of rifles and the drumroll of galloping hooves. She gathered herself and waited while Lucifer bore down on her like a runaway train. Despite the danger of being trampled, Janna didn't flinch or move aside, for she knew that her only hope of life lay in the man who was even now bending low over the stallion's driving body, holding his hand out to her.

Between one heartbeat and the next Janna was yanked from the ground and hurtled onto Lucifer's back just behind Ty. Automatically she scrambled for position, thrusting her arms around his waist and hanging on with all her strength while Ty hauled the mustang into a plunging, sliding turn that would take them away from the renegades. As the mustang straightened out again, Ty let out another chilling battle cry. Lucifer flattened his ears and his hooves dug out great clots of earth as he gave his riders the last bit of strength in his big body, running at a furious speed despite the additional weight he was carrying.

Ty's battle cry came back to him doubled and redoubled as the four horsemen bore down on him. They split evenly around the lathered, hard-running stallion. Each man fired steadily, making full use of the tactical superiority their repeating rifles gave. They were close enough now for accuracy, even from the back of a running horse. The relentless rain of bullets broke the first ranks of the charging renegades, which slowed those who were immediately behind and confused those who were on the sides.

A shout from the biggest MacKenzie sent all four horses into a tight turn. Soon they were galloping hard in Lucifer's wake, snapped at by sporadic rifle bullets from the disorganized melee of renegades.

There were only a few warriors who gave chase, for Cascabel had spotted the larger column of soldiers, which had been galloping hard to catch the smaller group since the first burst of rifle fire had come. Cascabel was far too shrewd to fight the Army on its own terms. An ambush was one thing; a pitched battle was another. The renegade leader turned his horse and began shouting orders. In a short time the renegades had reversed direction and were retreating at a dead run, preserving their arms and ammunition for a better battleground.

The first group of soldiers swept by Ty and then the MacKenzie brothers. Neither group broke pace. Not until the brothers were within sight of the larger Army column did they overtake Lucifer.

Knowing that it was finally safe, Ty slowed the stallion to a walk, stroked the mustang's lathered neck and praised him over and over. The biggest of the MacKenzie brothers reined in alongside.

"That's one hell of a horse you're riding. Am I to presume he's the fabled Lucifer?"

Ty's flashing grin was all the answer that was needed.

"Then that must be your famous silken lady riding postilion," the man said dryly.

Janna flinched and looked away from the tall rider's odd, golden-green eyes. She knew instantly that this man must be Ty's brother, for surely no two men could look so alike and be unrelated. Tall, powerful, dark haired— on first glance he was Ty's twin. A second glance showed the differences; a hardness of feature, a sardonic curl to the mouth, eyes that summarized what they saw with relentless pragmatism.

"Janna Wayland, meet Logan MacKenzie, my older brother," Ty said.

Janna's arms tightened around Ty's waist. She didn't speak or turn her face from its hiding place just below his shoulder blades.

"Sugar? You're all right, aren't you?"

"Yes," she said, her voice muffled. "Can we go back for Zebra?"

Logan's black eyebrows lifted at the husky, tantalizing, feminine voice issuing from such a disheveled creature.

"No. Cascabel won't keep running. He'll split his forces and double back to pick off scouts, stragglers or anything else he can get in his sights before the sun sets."

"But—"

"No," Ty said roughly, interrupting. Then, more gently, "I'm sorry, sugar. It's just too dangerous for you. Zebra will be all right. Mustangs are tough. They have to be. She was limping off to cover before you even got to your hands and knees."

"Zebra?" Logan asked mildly. "Were you keeping a zoo?"

When Janna didn't answer, Ty said, "Zebra is a mustang. Janna talked her into becoming a friend."

Logan gave Ty a slanting green glance. "'Talked' her into it?"

"That's right, big brother. Talked. No ropes. No saddle. Not even a bridle or stirrups. Just those soothing hands and that sweet, husky voice promising all kinds of things...and then delivering each and every one of them."

Logan's eyes narrowed at the seething mixture of emotions he heard in Ty's voice—affection, anger, bafflement, passion.

"Seems she caught herself more than a zebra mustang that way," Logan muttered.

If Ty heard the statement, he ignored it.

A renewed clash of rifle fire came from behind. The second column of soldiers had just come within range of the fleeing renegades. A bugle's wild song rose above the sound of shots.

"Hope whoever is leading those soldiers knows his business," Ty said. "Cascabel had an ambush laid that would have wiped out the first column before reinforcements could arrive."

"So that's why the two of you came down like your heels were on fire. Case heard something and put the glass on the cliff. He knew right away it was you."

"Surprised Blue didn't spot me first. He's got eyes that would put an eagle to shame."

"Blue was talking with the lieutenant at the time, trying to convince the damned fool that we might be galloping into an ambush."

"And?"

"Blue was told that when the lieutenant wanted a breed's advice, he'd ask for it."

Ty shook his head in silent disgust. "Well, at least he'll keep Cascabel busy long enough for Janna to get clear. Cascabel made some strong vows on the subject of her hair."

Logan looked from his brother to the auburn-haired girl who had refused to face the MacKenzies after that first brief look. Logan remembered the flash of pain he had seen in Janna's face before she turned away. He reined back slightly, leaned over and slid his hand beneath her chin. Gently, firmly, he turned her face toward himself.

"Easy, little one," Logan said soothingly. "No one's going to hurt you. I just want to be sure you're all right. That was one hell of a header you took."

Reluctantly Janna turned toward Ty's older brother. Long, surprisingly gentle fingers touched the bruised spot on her cheek and the abrasion along her jaw.

"Feeling dizzy?" he asked.

"I'm all right. No double vision. No nausea. I didn't land hard enough to get a concussion."

"She knows what she's talking about," Ty said. "Her daddy was a doctor."

Black eyebrows rose again, then Logan smiled, softening the harshness of his face. "You'll do, Janna Wayland. You'll do just fine." He turned toward the other three riders. "Listen up, boys. This lady is Janna Wayland. Janna, the big one is Blue Wolf."

"Big one?" Janna asked, looking at the men surrounding her. "Are you implying that one of you is small?"

One of the riders tipped back his head and laughed, reminding her of Ty.

"The laughing hyena is Duncan," Logan said. "The dark-eyed, mean-looking one on the chestnut horse is Blue Wolf."

"Pleased to meet you, Janna Wayland," Blue Wolf said in educated tones, and his smile refuted the very idea of "mean." He tipped his hat to her and went back to scanning the countryside for danger.

"The quiet one is Case. He's the baby of the family."

Case nodded slightly to Janna. A single look at his pale green eyes told her that Case might have been the youngest in years but not in harsh experience. There was a darkness in him that transcended words. A wave of overwhelming sadness and compassion whirled up in Janna as she looked at Ty's youngest brother.

"Hello, Case," she said softly, as though she were talking to an untamed mustang.

Ty heard the emotion in Janna's words, smiled rather grimly to himself and said in a voice too low to carry to Case, "Save your sweetness for something that appreciates it, sugar. Except for blood family, Case has all the feelings of a stone cliff."

"Why?"

"The war."

"You went to war, too."

Logan looked over at Janna. "All the MacKenzie men fought," he said. "Case is the only one who won't talk about it. Not one word. Ever. Not even with Duncan, who fought at his side most of the time. Duncan doesn't talk much, either, but it's different somehow. He still laughs. Case doesn't." Logan shook his head. "Damned shame, too. Case used to have the most wonderful laugh. People would hear him and stop and stare and then smile, and pretty soon they'd be laughing, too. No one could resist Case. He had a smile like a fallen angel.''

The clear regret on Logan's face changed Janna's opinion of him once more; despite his hard exterior, Logan was a man who cared deeply for his family. Rather wistfully, Janna wondered what it would have been like to grow up with that kind of warmth surrounding her. Her father had loved her, but in a rather distracted way, never really stopping to discover his daughter's needs and yearnings, always pursuing his own dreams and never asking about hers.

"What a sad smile," Logan said. "Is your family back there?"

"Where?"

"In Cascabel's territory."

"Not unless you could call Mad Jack family," Janna said. "Besides, he ran off rather than hang around and be dragged to the fort. He knew how mad we would be about the gold."

"Gold?" Logan asked, looking at Ty.

"More than a hundred pounds of it."

Logan whistled. "What happened?"

"He gave us half and we promised to take half to his kids."

"Where did you leave it?"

"We didn't," Janna said. "It's in those saddlebags in front of Ty."

Ty and Logan exchanged a look.

"It was too much for Lucifer to carry," Ty said. "I cut it loose."

Janna stiffened. "But that was how you were going to buy your silken la—"

"One more word, Janna Wayland," Ty interrupted savagely, "and I'm going to hand you over to that scalp-hunting renegade myself!" He took a deep breath and struggled to leash his volatile temper. "Anyway, the gold isn't lost. Soon as I'm sure that Lucifer didn't hurt himself on that run, I'm going back for the saddlebags."

Janna wasn't surprised that Ty would risk his life looking for the gold once more, but she yearned to be able to talk him out of it. Hopefully she looked over at Logan. His smile didn't comfort her—it fulfilled the sardonic promise she had first noticed in the line of his mouth.

"So Janna isn't your silken lady after all?" Logan asked Ty. "Damned white of you to save her hide anyway at the cost of all that gold."

The cold, needling edge to Logan's tone didn't escape Ty. Nor did the censure in Logan's eyes, for he had realized that Ty was Janna's lover the first time Ty had called her sugar in a soft, concerned voice.

"Drop it," Ty said flatly.

Logan's smile changed indefinably, becoming almost sympathetic as he realized Ty's dilemma. For years Ty had been pursued by the finest that southern and northern society had to offer; he had turned everyone down in his own pursuit of a dream of the perfect silken lady. Now he found himself hopelessly ensnarled with a wild, gray-eyed waif whose voice could set fire to stone.

Logan leaned over and cuffed Ty's shoulder with rough affection. "Forget the gold, little brother. I'll turn Silver loose on your uncurried mustang lady. In a few weeks you'll never know she wasn't paddock born and raised."

Janna turned her face away, trying to conceal the red tide that climbed up her face as she thought of the unbridgeable gap between silk purses and sows' ears. Eyes closed, she held on to Ty, saying goodbye to him in silence, for she knew with bittersweet certainty that he would go after the gold...and she would walk away from the MacKenzies and never look back, freeing Ty to pursue his dream.

"You planning on taking her to Wyoming?" Case asked. Like his eyes, his voice was cool, passionless. He had been watching Janna with measuring intelligence.

Ty turned and glared at Case. "Yes. You have any objections?"

"Not a one."

Ty waited.

"She doesn't want to go," Case added matter-of-factly.

"She'll go just the same."

"Is she carrying MacKenzie blood in her womb?"

If anyone else had asked that question, Ty would have beaten him into the ground. But Case wasn't anyone else. Because Case had destroyed or walled off all emotion within himself, he didn't concede its presence in anyone else.

"She could be carrying my child," Ty said tightly.

"Then she'll be in Wyoming when you get there."

With no warning Case bent over, plucked Janna from Lucifer's back and put her across his saddle.

"Ty!"

"It's all right. Case will take good care of you." Ty smiled oddly. "Don't try running from him, sugar. He's the best hunter of all of us."

Chapter Forty-Four

"They must have magic mirrors in Wyoming," Janna said, looking in disbelief at her own reflection. "That can't be me."

Silver MacKenzie smiled, touched up the dusting of rouge on Janna's cheeks and stepped back to view the results. "It's amazing what three weeks of regular food and sleep can do for a body, isn't it?"

"More like four," Janna said.

Silver's ice-blue eyes closed for an instant as she composed herself; the thought of losing Logan made her heart freeze.

"I'm sure the men are all right," Silver said firmly. "It must have been harder to find the gold than they thought, that's all. Perhaps Ty couldn't remember precisely where he cut the saddlebags loose. You left rather in a rush, from what Case said."

Janna smiled wanly. "You could say that. At least, Ty was in a rush to get away."

"Speaking of getting away…" Silver began, changing the subject eagerly.

A flush crawled up Janna's cheeks as she remembered the night after she had arrived in Wyoming. Case had dropped her rather unceremoniously at the doorstep, told Silver that Janna had come to be combed and curried like a paddock horse for Ty and that she might be carrying Ty's child. Silver had been sympathetic, Cassie had been angelic, and Janna had gone out the second-story window the first time everyone's back was turned.

The next morning a very tight-lipped Case had brought Janna back, set her on the doorstep and told her that she could give her word not to run until Ty came back or she could spend the time waiting for him trussed hand and foot like a chicken going to market.

"…now you know why men like their women dressed in yards of silk," Silver finished. She blew a wisp of moon-pale hair away from her lips as she bent and adjusted the voluminous skirt of Janna's cream silk ball gown.

"What?" asked Janna, distracted by her memories.

"We can't run worth a darn for all the hoops and flounces, that's why. The best we can manage is a serene face and a dignified, very slow exit."

Janna smiled just as Silver straightened. The older woman stared, arrested by the sight Janna made. Her dark auburn hair was piled high in deceptively simple coils, which had been threaded through with strings of pearls. Pearls circled her neck in a delicate choker whose centerpiece was a ruby that had been in Silver's family for three hundred years. Earrings of pearl and teardrop rubies hung from Janna's ears. The ball gown's off-the-shoulder style dipped to a modest point in the front. The hint of a shadow between Janna's breasts was as seductive as the lines of the ball gown were simple. A brooch of ruby and pearls was pinned at the base of the gentle décolletage. With each breath, each movement, ruby fire shimmered, echoing the secret fire of Janna's hair.

"Shadow of Flame," Silver murmured. "The renegades saw you very clearly, didn't they? You're really quite stunning. The dress looks far better on you than it ever did on me, as do the rubies."

"It's very kind of you to say so."

"The truth is rarely kind," Silver said grimly.

Janna saw the shadows of worry on Silver's face and knew that she was concerned about her husband.

"I'm sure Logan is all right," Janna said. "He's a smart, tough man."

"All the MacKenzies are smart and tough. Even the women. You'll fit in just fine."

There was silence, then Janna said huskily, "Ty wanted something different in his wife."

"Ah, yes, Ty's famous silken lady." Silver saw Janna wince. "Don't worry, he'll take one look at you and see the woman of his dreams. He may be MacKenzie stubborn but he's not stone-blind."

Tears ached behind Janna's eyes at hearing her own secret dream spoken aloud. The hope of having Ty turn to her and see his silken lady was so overpowering that she was helpless against it. That, as much as Case's threat, had held her in Wyoming.

Silver's hand rested lightly on Janna's cheek. "Does he know how much you love him?"

Janna nodded slowly and whispered, "It wasn't enough. His dream..."

"It was the war, Janna. Each MacKenzie responded to it differently. Logan wanted revenge." Silver's mouth turned down in sad remembrance. "He found it, but it wasn't what he thought it was. I think Ty will discover that silk isn't what he thought it was, either."

A call came from the front of the house. Both women froze in wild hope before they realized that it was Case greeting guests rather than Case announcing the return of Blue Wolf and the MacKenzie brothers. But Janna had to be sure. She ran to the window and looked out. The first of the guests were indeed arriving.

"I still find it hard to believe that there are lords and ladies running loose about Wyoming," Janna said.

Silver smiled wryly. "Unfortunately, it's true. What's worse, I'm related to most of them by blood or marriage." She looked out the window. "Those specimens are Cousin Henry's guests. They don't actually live in Wyoming. They just came here to hunt." She sighed and shook out the folds of her skirt so that it fell properly. "I'd better go meet them. Case has impeccable manners, but he tires of the game very quickly. I don't want Melissa to drive him away before the ball even begins. He's a marvelous dancer. Almost as good as Ty."

"I can't imagine a woman driving Case anywhere."

"It's my fault, really," Silver said as she hurried out the bedroom door, her ballgown billowing gracefully. "I made him promise not to hurt Melissa's feelings. Case takes promises very seriously. Come down as soon as you're ready, but don't be too long. Everyone is dying to meet you. Women are so rare in this place. Especially young and pretty women.''

Janna looked in the mirror for a moment longer. A stranger looked back at her, a woman not unlike her mother in elegant appearance, but a stranger all the same. Janna wondered if she would ever become used to dresses and rustling folds of cloth. Even after nearly a month, she was still aware of the muffling yards of material swathing her legs and the contrasting snugness of bodice and waist. Even if the cloth had allowed her to run, the tight waist would have made deep breathing impossible. The shoes were the hardest to bear, however. They pinched.

She looked toward the armoire, where her father's hand-me-downs hung. She had washed and mended the clothes very carefully, for they were all that she could call her own. Her moccasins were patched as well, using doeskin she had traded a few of her precious herbs to obtain. Her canteen, medicine pouch and ragged blanket roll were set aside, waiting to be picked up on a moment's notice.

Maybe I won't need them. Maybe Ty will look at me and see a woman he could love. Maybe...

With hands whose creamy softness still surprised Janna from time to time, she reached into the medicine pouch and pulled out the sketch of her mother. Broodingly Janna looked from her reflection in the mirror to the sketch and then to her reflection again.

Will what he sees please him? Will he turn to me out of love rather than duty?

After a few minutes Janna set the sketch aside and went downstairs through the huge ranch house, which had been restored after a fire had all but razed it. She walked through rooms whose furniture had been shipped from England and France and whose rugs had come from China. She barely noticed the elegant furnishings. Nor did the sparkle of crystal reflecting candle flames catch her eye. In her mind she was once again in the secret valley, where Ty was holding out his arms to her with a smile on his face and love in his eyes.

Janna went through the ritual of introductions and polite words, moving with a natural grace that enhanced the seductive rustling of silk around her body. Men were drawn to her, both because of her restrained beauty and the natural thirst of men in a rough country for that which was soft and fragile. Janna was like the ruby between her breasts—clear yet enigmatic, sparkling yet self-contained, the color of fire yet cool to the touch. When the violins played she danced with men from neighboring ranches, men both titled and common, men who shared a common interest—Janna—and a common complaint—her lack of interest in them.

"May I have this dance?"

With a subdued start, Janna focused on the man who was standing between herself and the blaze of candlelight from the buffet table. For one heart-stopping instant she thought that Ty had come back; then she realized that the familiar, broad-shouldered silhouette belonged to Case.

"Yes, of course," Janna said, extending her hand to take his.

Moments later she was whirling and turning to the stately strains of a waltz played by Silver on the grand piano. The music was rich and civilized, a brocade of sound embroidered upon the wilderness night. Case danced with the casual perfection of a cat stalking prey.

"I've been watching you," he said.

Janna looked up at his pale green eyes. "That's not necessary. I gave you my word. I'll keep that word."

He nodded. "I wasn't worried about that. I was afraid that you'd get to believing all the polite nonsense Silver's cousins and guests are pouring into your ear."

With a smile that hovered on the brink of turning upside down, Janna shook her head. "I know what I am and what I'm not," she said huskily. "I'm not the 'fairest flower ever to bloom on the western land,' among other things. Nor am I a fool. I know what men hope to gain by flattering a woman." She met Case's eyes and said evenly, "Your brother didn't lie to me in any way, even that one. He always stated quite clearly that my feminine attractions were...modest."

Case looked at the proud, unhappy set of Janna's mouth. "That doesn't sound like Ty. He always had a line of flowery speech that was the envy of every man around."

"Flowers and silk go together."

"And you weren't silk, so he saved the flowers and got right down to business, is that it?"

Janna's eyelids flickered. It was the only sign of her pain, but Case saw it. As Ty had warned her, Case was the best hunter of all the MacKenzies. Nothing escaped his cool, dispassionate eyes.

"No, I wasn't silk," Janna agreed huskily.

"But you are now."

She smiled sadly and said nothing.

One of Cousin Henry's guests cut in. Janna tried to remember his name, but nothing came to her mind except the memory of the young man's intense, hungry eyes watching the ruby brooch shift and shimmer with her breaths. She prayed for the waltz to end, freeing her.

"Are all western women so charmingly quiet?"

Janna opened her mouth to answer. Nothing came out except a soft, startled sound when the waltz ended in an abrupt jangle of notes. She looked over at the piano in time to see Silver lifted into Logan's arms for a kiss that conceded nothing to silk or ritual politeness.

"They're back!" Janna said.

She looked around frantically but saw only one tall, roughly dressed man mingling with the guests—Blue Wolf, not Ty. Then she felt a tingling all the way to her fingertips. She turned and saw Ty standing at the doorway. He was leaning against the frame, his arms crossed over his chest and his eyes narrowed. Slowly he straightened and began walking toward her. As he closed in on her, there was no welcoming smile on his bearded face. There was only anger.

"Willie," Ty said coldly, "your nanny is looking for you."

For a moment the young aristocrat holding Janna thought of taking the insult personally; then he shrugged and handed Janna over to Ty.

"Apparently this dance belongs to the rude frontiersman?"

When Janna didn't object, the man bowed and withdrew. Ty ignored him completely, having eyes only for the *bruja* who stood before him gowned in silk and shimmering with gems.

The waltz began again, played by four hands. Ty took Janna into his arms, holding her too close for propriety. He moved with the graceful, intricate, sweeping motions of an expert dancer. An equally expert partner could have followed him, but Janna was new to ball gowns and dips and whirls. Inevitably she stumbled. He took her weight, lifted her, spun her dizzyingly until she had to cling to his arms for support.

"Ty, stop, please."

"Why? Afraid those fancy Englishmen will see you holding on to me?" Ty's narrowed green eyes glittered coldly at Janna through his black eyelashes. His voice was equally icy. "Not one of those titled fops would touch you if they knew your past. When they see past the silk they'll be furious at the joke you've played on them."

"Men never look past the silk."

"I've looked, Janna Wayland. I know what's beneath all the finery—and it sure as hell isn't a fragile silken lady."

The words sank into Janna like knives, killing the last of her foolish hope. A feeling of emptiness stole through her as she realized that no matter how she dressed she would never be Ty's dream, for he would always look at her and see the ragged waif dressed in men's clothes.

Silk purse. Sow's ear. Never the twain shall meet.

Janna tried to turn away from Ty, but his fierce grip on her never wavered. She would have fought despite all the people around, but even if she had won free she would still have been trapped within swath after swath of silk. Silver had been right: men preferred silk because it prevented women from running off.

Janna was in a silken prison. There was no escape, no place of concealment for her but deep within herself. Yet even then her tears gave away her hiding place.

Case tapped Ty firmly on the shoulder. "This dance is mine."

Ty turned on his younger brother with the quickness of a cat. "Stay out of it."

"Not this time," Case said matter-of-factly. "I brought her here, forced her to stay here until you came back, and now you're spoiling the Thanksgiving ball Cassie has looked forward to all year. Your family deserves better than that, don't you think?"

Ty looked beyond Case and saw Blue Wolf starting through the throng in Ty's direction. He knew that Blue was even more protective of Cassie than Case was. Then Ty spotted Duncan and Logan closing in on him with grim expressions.

Silver began playing a waltz again. Its slow, haunting melody recalled formal summer gardens and elegant dancers glittering with gems. Calmly, Case disengaged Janna from Ty's arms. As Case whirled Janna away, he said over his shoulder, "Go take a bath. You aren't fit company for anything but a horse."

Without a word Ty turned and stalked off the dance floor, shouldering aside his brothers.

Behind him Case and Janna danced slowly, gracefully, for Case matched his demands to his partner's skill. When the final strains of the waltz dissipated among the candle flames and rainbows trapped within crystal prisms, Case and Janna were standing at the doorway. He held her hand and looked at her for a long moment.

"Cassie told me you aren't pregnant," Case said finally. "I'm sorry. A child with your grit and grace and Ty's strength and fancy speech…well, that would have been something to see."

Janna tried to smile, couldn't, and said simply, "Thank you."

"There's a fiesty zebra dun in the corral. That fool brother of mine packed more than a hundred pounds of gold all over Utah Territory for three weeks looking for that zebra mare. Sixty pounds of that gold is now in a bank waiting for you to draw on it. The MacKenzies will honor Ty's promise to see that Mad Jack's half gets to his kids."

"Half of my gold is Ty's."

Case shook his head. "No."

Janna started to object again. Case watched her with the patience of a granite cliff. She could object all she wanted and nothing would change.

When Case saw that Janna understood, he bowed to her more deeply than custom required and released her hand.

"You're free, Janna. All promises kept."

Chapter Forty-Five

The oil lamps in Janna's room turned her tears to gold, but that was the only outward sign of her unhappiness. Cream leather shoes stood neatly next to the armoire. Pale silk pantalets were folded neatly on the chair. Hoops and petticoats were hung out of the way. Earrings and necklace and brooch rested in an open, velvet-lined box. All that stood between Janna and freedom was the maddening fastenings on her ball gown. The dress had been designed for ladies who had maids in attendance, not for a mustang girl who had nothing but her own ill-trained fingers and a burning need never to see or touch or be reminded of silk again.

"Allow me."

Janna spun so quickly toward the door that candle flames bowed and trembled.

Ty stood in the doorway watching her, but he was a different man. Gone was the rough frontiersman. Ty was clean shaven except for a black mustache. He smelled of soap and wore polished black boots, black slacks and a white linen shirt whose weave was so fine it shone like silk. He looked precisely like what he was: a powerful, uncommonly handsome man who had been born and raised to wealth and fine manners, a man who had every right to require that the mother of his children be of equal refinement.

Janna turned away and said carefully, "I can manage, thank you. Please close the door on your way out."

There was silence, then the sound of a door shutting behind Janna's back. She bit her lip against the pain ripping through her body.

"A gentleman never leaves a lady in distress."

Janna froze with her hands behind her back, still reaching for the elusive fastenings that held her confined within a silken prison.

"But I'm not a lady, so your fine manners are wasted. Nor am I pregnant, so you needn't feel dutiful."

The bleakness of Janna's voice made Ty's eyes narrow. He came and stood behind her, so close that he could sense her warmth.

"Case told me," Ty said.

His nostrils flared at the fragrance of crushed roses that emanated from her skin and hair. Memories blazed for an instant in his eyes. He brushed her hands away from the fastenings that went down the back of her dress.

"You're a satin butterfly," Ty said, unfastening the dress slowly, feeling a hunger to touch her that was deeper and more complex than a desire, a hunger that tightened his body as each tiny hook silently gave way, revealing a bit more of Janna's skin. "And I'm going to release you from your cocoon."

Ty's long index finger traced the graceful centerline of Janna's back. She made a stifled sound as the dress fell away, leaving her naked. Ty had never seen anything quite so beautiful as her elegant feminine curves. He traced her spine once more, following it to the shadow crease of her hips.

"During the war, Case kept his sanity by walling off his emotions," Ty said quietly. "I kept my sanity in a different way. I swore that I would never see such ugliness again. If I survived, I vowed to surround myself with fine and fragile things that had never known even the shadow of violence and death. Every time grapeshot ripped through living flesh, every time I saw young children with empty eyes, every time one of my men died...I renewed my vow."

Eyes closed, body trembling, Janna felt the lingering caress of Ty's fingertip tracing her spine; but it was the pain in his voice that broke her heart and her control. She had loved him recklessly, without regard for the future cost. Now the future had come to demand its reckoning.

"It's all right, Ty," she said huskily. "I understand. You've earned your silken lady. I won't—"

Janna's voice shattered as Ty's hands caressed the length of her back before smoothing up her torso until her breasts were cupped in his hands.

"Run away?" Ty offered, finishing Janna's sentence for her. The feel of her nipples hardening at his lightest touch made blood rush in a torrent through his body. "That's good, because touching you makes me so damn weak that I can hardly stand, much less run after you." With aching gentleness he caressed the breasts whose textures and responsiveness never ceased to arouse him. "So soft, so warm. No, hold still, love. It's all right. We're going to be married just as soon as I find the strength to leave this room and round up a preacher."

"Ty..." Janna's throat closed around all the tears she hadn't shed, all the dreams that couldn't come true. "You have to let me go."

"Why?" His long fingers shaped her, caressed her, made her tremble with a wild longing. "You want me as much as I want you. Have I told you how much I like that? No games, no coyness, just the sweet response of your body to my touch."

Janna bit off a telltale moan and asked desperately, "Did your parents love each other?"

Ty's hands stilled in surprise. "Yes. Why?"

"Think how you would have felt if they hadn't. Think how a child would feel growing up and knowing that his father felt a combination of desire and duty and disappointment toward his mother. Your child deserves better than that. So do you. And," Janna added softly, "so do I. Seeing you, having your body but not your heart... It will break me, Ty. Is that what you want?"

Gently Ty turned Janna around. She met his eyes without evasion despite the slow, helpless welling of her tears.

"Janna," he said softly, bending down to her, "I—"

She turned her head aside and spoke quickly, interrupting Ty, words tumbling out in a desperate effort to be heard. "No. Please listen to me. Please. I may not be fine or fragile, but even mustang ladies can be broken. You said once you owed me more than you could ever repay. You can repay me now. Let me go, Ty. *Let me go before I break.*''

Eyes closed, hands clenched into fists at her side so that she wouldn't reach for the man she loved too much ever to cage, Janna waited for Ty to leave. She heard him make a hoarse sound that could have been anger or pain, sensed currents of air moving as he moved, and she trembled with the violence of her emotions.

Tears touched the sensitive skin between her breasts, and she was shocked to know how hot her own tears were. Then she felt Ty's cheek against her body, saw him kneeling at her feet, felt his arms close tightly around her waist, and she realized that the scalding tears weren't her own.

Moved beyond words, Janna stroked Ty's hair with trembling hands, feeling as though she were being torn apart. She had thought she could leave him, but every instant she was with him told her how wretched life without him would be.

"I won't let you go," Ty said finally. "Don't ask me to. Don't beg me to. I can't do it, Janna. I need you too much."

"Ty, don't," she whispered achingly, trying to still the trembling of her body, failing. "I want so much for you to have your dream."

"I dreamed of you every minute I was away. You're my dream, Janna. I went back to get that gold for you, not for myself. I couldn't close my eyes without seeing you, couldn't lick my lips without tasting you, couldn't sleep for wanting you. Then I walked into that ballroom and saw the perfect silken lady of my dreams dancing with the perfect silken man. *And I wasn't that man.* I went—crazy. I wanted very much to kill that high-nosed son of a blue-blooded bitch for even looking at you."

"But you said—you said that you'd seen past the clothes, that I wasn't a fragile silken lady."

"Yes, I'd seen past the clothes, and I thank God for it."

Ty turned his head slowly, kissing the smooth breasts that smelled of roses.

"Listen to me, Janna. There's far more to being a lady than silks and bloodlines. A true lady is more concerned with the needs of the people around her than she is with the state of her wardrobe. A true lady gives succor to the sick, laughter to the lonely, respite to the weary. And to one very, very lucky man, a true lady gives herself...and asks nothing in return but that she be allowed to give the gift of her love."

Ty smoothed his cheek between Janna's breasts, absorbing the beauty of her living warmth. "That kind of gift is so rare that it takes a man by surprise."

He kissed the velvet tips of Janna's breasts, smiled to hear her breath break and tremble even as her body did. His mouth caressed the smooth skin of her stomach and the auburn cloud at the apex of her thighs.

"My sweet satin butterfly," he said in a low voice. "Let me love you again." His hand eased between her legs and he groaned to feel her heat once more. "Janna...please, let me."

Janna's knees gave way at the first gliding penetration of his caress. Ty's arm tightened, holding her still for a searing instant while he was still within her warmth. Her breath unraveled as he slowly released her, leaving her body shimmering and without the strength to stand.

With a dark yet oddly tender smile, Ty caught Janna and came to his feet, taking the warm weight of her in his arms once more. He walked the few steps to the bed, put her on the fur coverlet and kissed her lips gently before he stepped back and unhurriedly removed his own clothes, watching her with smoldering green eyes the whole time.

When he was as naked as she, he lay next to her on the bed, gathered her against his body and kissed her as tenderly as though she were a frightened maiden. The caresses he gave her were equally restrained, almost chaste, but his words were elemental fire.

"Your body is all satin, strong and hot and sleek. You're perfect for a man who is more rawhide than silk. For me, Janna. Just for me. You are... perfect."

Janna's breath caught, then broke when Ty's hand smoothed down her body. She didn't deny him the intimate warmth he so gently sought. She could no more have refused him than she could have told her heart to stop beating. Nor could she hold back the shimmering pulse of her pleasure, the heat that welled up and overflowed at his touch; and she cried out his name with each pulse.

The evidence of Janna's need for him was an exquisite shaft of pleasure so intense that it was also pain. Ty groaned and sought her secret warmth once again, and once again she didn't deny him. Eyes closed, he bent and kissed her lips, her breasts, the taut curve of her belly, trying to tell her things for which there were no words. And then her fingers threaded lovingly through his hair and the words came to him.

"Once," Ty whispered, "I saw Lucifer go to you, put his head into your hands with such trust that I was reminded of the legend of the unicorn and the maiden. It made me...restless, baffled, angry. I felt sorry for the unicorn, trapped by his reckless love.

"And then the maiden opened her hands and let the unicorn go, for she loved the unicorn too much to hold it against its will."

Janna's fingers stilled until Ty's head shifted against her palms, asking to be stroked once more, asking to be held by her touch even as the unicorn had been held.

"The unicorn ran off and congratulated himself on his clever escape, and then..." Ty turned slowly, covering Janna's body with his own. He touched the hot center of her just once, slowly, drawing a long, broken moan from her. "And then," Ty whispered, watching Janna's eyes, "the unicorn realized what a fool he had been. There was nothing in the forest as exciting as the maiden's touch, no beauty to equal her companionship, no pleasure as deep as the ease she had given his soul. So he went running back and begged to be given the maiden's gift once more."

When Ty neither spoke nor moved to join their bodies, Janna's heart hesitated, then beat with redoubled strength.

"What did the maiden say?" she whispered.

"I don't know. Tell me, Janna. What did the maiden say to the unicorn?"

Tears magnified Janna's eyes. "I love you," she said huskily. "I'll always love you."

She felt the emotion that shuddered through Ty's strong body as he bent and kissed her tears away.

"Yes," Ty said, watching Janna's eyes. "I want you to be my wife, my mate, my woman, the mother of my children, the keeper of my heart, the light of my soul. I love you, Janna. *I love you.*"

Janna reached for Ty even as he came to her. Their bodies merged, softness and strength shared equally, defining and discovering one another in the same elemental moment. Ecstasy blazed as they lost and then found themselves, man and woman forever joined in the reckless, incandescent union known as love.

* * * * *

Dark Stranger

HEATHER GRAHAM POZZESSERE

PART I   The Stranger

Chapter One

Summer, 1862   *The Kansas/Missouri border*

The hoofbeats were the warning. The relentless, pounding hoofbeats. The sound of them sparked a sense of primal fear deep inside Kristin. Strangely, before she'd first felt the staccato rhythm through the ground, she hadn't contemplated such a danger. The day had been too ordinary, and perhaps she had been too naive. She had expected a storm, but not of the magnitude that was to come.

It began with the stillness in the air. As she came along the path through the orchards from the river, Kristin paused. The breeze had dropped. The day had gone dead still. The sudden calm gave her a strange feeling, and she searched the sky. Overhead, she saw blue, a beautiful blue. No clouds marred that endless blue.

It was the calm before the storm, she thought. Here, on the Missouri side of the Kansas-Missouri border, storms were frequent and vicious. Blue skies turned to smoke, and vicious twisters whirled out of nowhere.

Then she heard the hoofbeats.

She looked out across the plain that stretched away from the house. A tumbleweed caught by a sudden gust of wind blew across a patch of parched earth.

Bushwhackers.

The word came unbidden to her mind, and raw fear swept through her, fear and denial. Please, God, no...

Pa! Matthew, Shannon...

Kristin began to run. Her heart began to race, thundering along with the sound of the hoofbeats.

Pa was already dead, she reminded herself. They'd already come to kill him. They'd come, on a cloudless day, and they'd dragged him out in front of the house. He had drowned in a pool of his own blood while she had stood there screaming. There had been nothing, *nothing* she could do.

Matthew was safe. He'd gone off to join up with the Union Army near the Mississippi. He had said she would be safe. After all, they'd already killed Pa in his own front yard, killed him and left him bleeding.

Bleeding. They called it "bleeding Kansas," and though they were on the Missouri side of the border here, the blood ran thick and deep. The War Between the States had boiled down to a barbarian savagery here. Men did not just fall in battle here, they were cruelly, viciously executed—seized, judged and murdered. Kristin had few illusions; one side was almost as bad as the other. The dream of freedom, the dream of endless land and a life of dignity and bounty had drowned in rivers of blood. The dream was dead, and yet it seemed that

was all she had left to fight for. Her father had died for it, and they thought she
would flee, but she wouldn't. She couldn't. She had to fight. There was nothing
else to do.

Shannon.

Cold dread caught in her throat. Shannon was up at the house. Young, frightened, vulnerable.

Her feet slapped against the dry earth as the hoofbeats came closer. How
many of them were there? Maybe twenty, like the day they had come to kill
Pa? Maybe not so many. Maybe they knew that Matthew had gone off to fight
in the war and that no one remained behind but the girls, the foreman, a maid
and a few young hands. She almost felt like laughing. They'd tried to take
Samson and Delilah the last time they had come. They didn't understand that
the two were free, able to make their decisions. Pa wasn't a fanatical abolitionist;
he had just liked Samson, plain and simple, so he had freed them on the occasion
of their marriage. Little Daniel had been born free, and they'd all come here
together in search of the dream...

Kristin stumbled and fell, gasping for breath. The riders were just behind the
trees to her left. She heard screams and shouts, and she knew they were slaugh-
tering whatever cattle they could lay their hands on. This wasn't war.

This was carnage.

She staggered to her feet, smoothing back stray tendrils of hair still damp
from her early-morning swim in the river.

They could hold the attackers off. She would be prepared this time. She
wouldn't assume that some of these men would be old friends and acquaintances.
She wouldn't assume that they were human, that they knew anything about
morals or ethics or simple decency. She didn't think she would ever trust in
such things again.

Suddenly, while Kristin was still several hundred yards from the house, the
horsemen burst through the trees.

"Samson!" she screamed. "Samson! Get me Pa's six-shooter. Samson!"

Samson, a tall, dignified black man, burst through the front door. He glanced
at Kristin, then at the horsemen racing through the corn, trampling the tender
green stalks.

"Run, Miss Kristin, run!"

She could hardly breathe, could hardly speak. "Pa's Colt, get me the Colt!
Tell Shannon to get to the cellar!"

"Samson, what is it?"

Samson turned to see Shannon standing behind him in the hallway.

"Bushwhackers," he said grimly. "Where's Delilah?"

"Out back, feeding the chickens."

She was in the barn. His wife was in the barn. God, he prayed silently, give
her the good sense to stay there!

"Shannon," he told her, "you get yourself in the cellar."

She turned away, and Samson hurried back to the hallway, then paused. He
thought he'd heard something around back. When the sound wasn't repeated,
he looked out the front door again. He could see the riders, and he could see
Kristin running.

There were about twenty men, Samson reckoned. Just an offshoot of a bigger
raiding party, probably. Some of Quantrill's raiders.

Quantrill himself was a damned butcher. He sanctioned the horror, and the
death. Once upon a time he'd been friends with Gabriel McCahy, Kristin and

Shannon's father, but one of his henchmen, a man named Zeke Moreau, had wanted Kristin. She hadn't wanted anything to do with him though. She was in love with Adam Smith. But Adam was dead now, too. Dead like her pa, dead like hundreds of men.

Now Zeke Moreau was coming back. He was coming for Kristin. Samson was sure of it.

"Samson!"

Her eyes met his, desperate, pleading.

Those might be God-fearing gentlemen out there, but if they captured a black man after he had leveled a Colt at them, even in his own defense, they would skin him alive.

It didn't matter. Gabriel McCahy had been the most decent man Samson had ever met. He would lose his skin over old Gabe's daughter if he had to.

He swung around, ready to rush into the house and get the guns. Then he paused, his eyes going wide and his throat closing up, hot and dry.

Zeke Moreau was already in the house. He was standing in the hallway, on the polished oak floor, and he had a double-barrelled shotgun leveled right at Samson.

A slight sound caught Samson's attention. He turned swiftly to see that another man was holding Delilah, one arm around her waist, a hand tight against her mouth.

"Watch it, Samson," Zeke said. "Be quiet now, or I'll hang you, boy. Hang you 'til you're dead. Then I'll see that your woman and your kid wind up on the auction block down Savannah way."

Zeke Moreau smiled slowly. He was dark-haired, with a dark, curling moustache, and Samson thought he would look more at home on a riverboat with a deck of cards than he did now, standing there in chaps and a vest, holding a shotgun. He was a good-looking man, except for his eyes. Cold, pale eyes, just like Kristin had always said.

Samson smiled back. "You murdered Gabriel, didn't you?"

Zeke rested his shotgun against his thigh. Samson was a big man, a good six-foot-six, and he was all muscle. But Zeke knew Samson wasn't going to move. Not while Delilah was being held.

"Now, Zeke, Gabe was my friend. He had some bad acquaintances, and he shot off his mouth too much, but I was mighty sorry to hear what happened to him. And it hurt me, hurt me bad, to hear about young Matthew running off to join up with them Yanks."

"Samson!"

He spun around at the sound of Kristin's voice. Just as she reached the steps, her voice rose in a sudden scream.

The horsemen had reached the steps, too and Kristin was trapped. She was choking in a cloud of dust as they circled her, chasing her back into the center of their trap every time she tried to elude them.

As Samson watched, she cried out and ran again. An Appaloosa ridden by a yellow-toothed scavenger in a railroad man's frock coat cut her off completely. She turned again, and the man rode closer, reaching down to sweep her up. She clawed at him, and Samson saw the blood run down the man's cheek. Kristin cursed and swore, fighting like a tigress. The Appaloosa reared and shrieked as its rider wrenched hard on the reins. The man struck out with a whip, and Kristin fell. As Samson watched, the Appaloosa reared again and again, its hooves just missing Kristin's face.

She didn't move, didn't flinch. She just stared up at the man, hatred in her eyes.

Samson charged toward the door, but Zeke stepped up behind him, slamming his head hard with the butt of his shotgun.

Kristin cried out as she saw him fall through the doorway, blood trickling down his forehead.

Then she saw Zeke. He stepped over Samson's body and onto the porch. A man came from behind, holding Delilah. She screamed, and the man laughed, then threw her down on top of Samson. Sobbing, she held her husband.

The horses around Kristin went still, and the men fell silent.

Kristin got to her feet and stared at the man. She even managed a semblance of a smile.

"Why, Mr. Moreau, what a pleasure." Her voice dripped with sarcasm.

Zeke Moreau let out a long sigh. "Dear, dear Kristin. It just never seems to cross that little mind of yours that you're in deep trouble, girl."

"Trouble, Zeke? I'm not in any trouble. Trouble is something that's hard to handle. You're just a fly to be swatted away, nothing more."

"Look around, Kristin. You know, you've always been a real sassy piece of baggage. The boys and me, we think it's about time you paid for that. You *are* in trouble, honey. Deep trouble." He started walking toward her.

Kristin held her ground. She'd never known what it was like to hate before. Not the way she hated Zeke. Her hatred for him was fierce and intense and desperate. She stared at him and suddenly she knew why he had come, knew why he was moving slowly, why he was smiling. This was vengeance, and he meant to savor it.

She didn't give a damn. She wasn't even really frightened. She knew that she would scratch and claw and fight just as long as she was still breathing, as long as her heart was still beating. He couldn't understand that she had already won. She had won because she hated him so much that he *couldn't* really touch her.

Zeke kept walking toward her, his smile still in place. "Fight me, Kristin," he said softly. "I like it that way."

"You disgust me," she hissed. She didn't tell him that he would pay, didn't threaten revenge. There was no law to make him pay, and whatever revenge she dealt out would have to be now.

"You know, once upon a time, I wanted to marry you. Yeah, I wanted to head out to the wild, wild west and make you my wife. I wanted to hit the gold fields out in California, and then I wanted to build you a fine house on a hill and make you into a real lady."

"I am a real lady, Zeke. But you're just dirt—and no amount of gold could make you anything but."

She raised her chin slightly. There was a hard core of fear inside her, she realized. This man didn't want her to die. He wanted her to pay. He wanted her to cry out in fear, wanted her to beg for mercy, and she was afraid that he could make her do it.

Zeke would never, never be prosecuted. No matter what he did to her.

He smiled and lunged toward her, and his men hooted and called from the backs of their mounts.

Kristin screamed. Then she grabbed a handful of the loose Missouri dirt, cast it into Zeke's eyes and turned to run.

The Appaloosa came at her again, with its dead-eyed rider. She tried to escape, but the animal reared, and she had to fall and roll to avoid its hoofs.

She heard Zeke swearing and turned to see that he was almost upon her again. The dirt clung to his face, clumps of it caught in his mustache.

She leaped up and spun toward him. The catcalls and whistles from the mounted men were growing louder and more raucous.

Escape was impossible. Zeke caught hold of her arms. She slammed her fists against his chest and managed to free herself. In a frenzy, she brought up her knee with a vengeance. Zeke let out a shrill cry of pain; his hold on her eased, and she broke free.

Someone laughed and before Kristin could gain her breath the back of Zeke's hand caught her. Her head swam, and she felt his hands on her again. Wildly, she scratched and kicked and screamed. Sounds rose all around her, laughter and catcalls and cheers. Her nails connected with flesh, and she clawed deeply. Zeke swore and slapped her again, so hard that she lost her balance and she fell.

He was quick. He straddled her while her head was still spinning. The hoots and encouraging cheers were growing louder and louder.

She gathered her strength and twisted and fought anew. Zeke used his weight against her while he tried to pin her wrists to the ground. Gasping for breath, she saw that while she might be losing, Zeke's handsome face was white, except for the scratches she had left on his cheek. He was in a cold, lethal rage, and he deliberately released his hold on her to slap her again with a strength that sent her mind reeling.

She couldn't respond at first. She was only dimly aware that he had begun to tear at her clothing, that her bodice was ripped and that he was shoving up her skirt. Her mind cleared, and she screamed, then began to fight again.

Zeke looked at her grimly. Then he smiled again. "Bitch," he told her softly. He leaned against her, trying to pin her mouth in a savage kiss while his hands roamed over her.

Kristin twisted her head, tears stinging her eyes. She could probably live through the rape. What she couldn't bear was the thought that he was trying to kiss her.

She managed to bite his lower lip.

He exploded into a sound of pure rage and jerked away, a thin line of blood trickling down his chin.

"You want it violent, honey?" he snarled. "That's the way you're going to get it then. Got that, Miss High-and-Mighty?"

He hitched up her skirt and touched her bare thigh, and she braced herself for the brutality of his attack, her eyes shut tight.

Just then the world seemed to explode. Dirt spewed all around her; she tasted it on her tongue.

Her eyes flew open, and she saw that though Zeke was still posed above her he seemed as disoriented as she was.

Even the men on horseback were silent.

A hundred yards away, stood a single horseman.

He wore a railroad man's frock coat, and his hat sat low over his forehead, a plumed feather extending from it.

He carried a pair of six-shooters, holding them with seeming nonchalance. Yet one had apparently just been fired. It had caused the noise that had sounded like an explosion in the earth. Along with the six-shooters, there was a rifle shoved into his saddle pack.

His horse, a huge sleek black animal, began to move closer in a smooth walk.

Finally he paused, only a few feet away. Stunned, Kristin stared at him. Beneath the railroad coat he wore jeans and a cotton shirt and he had a scarf around his throat. He wasn't wearing the uniform of either army; he looked like a cattleman, a rancher, nothing more.

Or a gunfighter, Kristin thought, bewildered.

His face was chiseled, strong. His hair was dark, lightly dusted with gray. His mustache and beard were also silvered, and his eyes, beneath jet-black brows, were silver-gray, the color of steel.

"Get away from her, boy," the stranger commanded Zeke. His voice was deep, rich. He spoke softly, but the sound carried. It was the voice of a man accustomed to being obeyed.

"Who's gonna make me?" Zeke snarled.

It was a valid question. After all, he was surrounded by his men, and the stranger was alone.

The man tipped his hat back from his forehead. "I'm telling you one more time, boy. Get off the lady. She doesn't seem to want the attention."

The sun slipped behind a cloud. The stranger suddenly seemed no more than a silhouette, an illusion of a man, atop a giant stallion.

Zeke made a sound like a growl, and Kristin realized that he was reaching for his Colt. She inhaled to scream.

She heard a sound of agony rend the air, but it wasn't hers. Blood suddenly streamed onto her chest. In amazement, she realized Zeke had cried out, and it was Zeke whose blood was dripping down on her. The stranger's bullet had struck him in the wrist.

"Fools!" Zeke shouted to his men. "Shoot the bastard."

Kristin did scream then. Twenty men reached for their weapons, but not one of them got off a shot.

The stranger moved quickly. Like double flashes of lightning, his six-shooters spat fire, and men fell.

When the shooting stopped, the stranger dismounted. His guns were back in his gun belt, but he carried a revolver as he walked slowly toward her.

He tipped his hat to Zeke. "I don't like killing, and I do my damnedest not to shoot a man in cold blood. Now, I'm telling you again. Get away from the lady. She doesn't want the attention."

Zeke swore and got to his feet. The two men stared at one another.

"I know you from somewhere," Zeke said.

The stranger reached down and tossed Zeke his discarded Colt. "Maybe you do." He paused for just a moment, arching one dark brow. "I think you've outworn your welcome here, don't you agree?"

Zeke reached down for his hat and dusted it furiously against his thigh, staring at the stranger. "You'll get yours, friend," he promised softly.

The stranger shrugged in silence, but his eyes were eloquent.

Zeke smiled cruelly at Kristin. "You'll get yours, too, sweetheart."

"If I were you," the stranger said softly, "I'd ride out of here now, while I still could."

Furiously, Zeke slammed his hat back on his head, then headed for one of the now riderless horses. He mounted the animal and started to turn away.

"Take your refuse with you." The stranger indicated the dead and wounded bodies on the ground.

Zeke nodded to his men. A number of them tossed the dead, wounded and dying onto the skittish horses.

"You'll pay," Zeke warned the stranger again. Then his mount leaped forward and he was gone. The stranger watched as the horses galloped away. Then he turned to Kristin and she felt color flood her face as she swallowed and clutched her torn clothing. She stumbled to her feet.

"Thank you," she said simply.

He smiled, and she found herself trembling. He didn't look away gallantly. He stared at her, not disguising his bold assessment.

She moistened her lips, willing her heart to cease its erratic beating. She tried to meet his eyes.

But she couldn't, and she flushed again.

The day was still again. The sun was bright, the sky blue.

Was this the calm before the storm?

Or had some strange new storm begun? Kristin could sense something in the air, an elusive crackling, as if lightning were sizzling between them. Something tense and potent, searing into her senses.

And then he touched her, slipping his knuckles beneath her chin.

"Think you might offer a drifter a meal, Miss—"

"McCahy. Kristin McCahy," she offered softly.

"Kristin," he murmured. Then he smiled again. "I could use something to eat."

"Of course."

She couldn't stop staring at him now, searching out his eyes. She hoped fervently that he couldn't feel the way she was trembling.

He smiled again and brushed her fingers with a kiss. Kristin flushed furiously, suddenly aware that her breast was almost bare beneath her torn chemise and gown. She swallowed fiercely and covered herself.

He lowered his eyes, hiding a crooked smile. Then he indicated Samson, who was just coming to in the doorway. "I think we should see to your friend first, Kristin," he said.

Delilah stood up, trying to help Samson. "You come in, mister," she said. "I'll make you the best meal this side of the Mississippi. Miss Kristin, you get in here quick now, too. We'll get you some hot water and wash off the filth of that man."

Kristin nodded, coloring again. "Shannon?" She whispered softly to Delilah.

"Your sister's in the cellar. Things seem to be all right. Oh, yes, bless the heavens, things seem to be all right."

The stranger started toward the steps, and Kristin followed, watching his broad shoulders. But then she paused and shivered suddenly.

He had come out of nowhere, out of the dirt and dust of the plain, and he had saved her from disaster and despair.

But Zeke Moreau had ridden away alive.

And Zeke Moreau would surely ride back, once the stranger had ridden on and she was alone again.

It wasn't over. Zeke had come for her once, and he would come again. He wasn't fighting for Missouri, for the South, for the code of chivalry. He was in this to loot, to murder, to rob—and to rape. He would come back for her. He sought out his enemies when they were weak, and he would know when she was weak again.

They would have to leave, she thought. This was her home, the only home she could remember. This land was a dream, a dream realized by a poor Irish immigrant.

But that immigrant lay dead. Gabriel McCahy lay with his Kathleen in the little cemetery out back. He lay there with young Joe Jenley, who had tried to defend him. The dream was as dead as Pa.

She couldn't just give it up. She had to fight the Zeke Moreaus of the world. She just couldn't let Pa's death be in vain.

But she had fought, and she had lost.

She hadn't lost, not this time. The stranger had come.

Kristin straightened, squared her shoulders and looked after the tall, dark man who was moving up her steps with grace and ease. The man with the set of six-shooters and the shotgun. The man who had aimed with startling, uncanny precision and speed.

Who was he?

And then she knew it didn't matter, she just didn't care. Her eyes narrowed pensively.

And she followed the curious dark stranger into her house.

Chapter Two

A fire burned warmly against the midmorning chill in the enormous kitchen. Even with her head back and her eyes closed, she could imagine everything Delilah was cooking from the aromas that surrounded her over the rose scent of her bath. Slab bacon sizzled in a frying pan along with hearty scrapple. There would be flapjacks, too, with melted butter and corn syrup. Delilah was also going to cook eggs in her special way, with chunks of ham and aged cheese. They were usually careful about food these days. If Quantrill's raiders didn't come looking to steal horses and cattle—or worse—the Union side would come around needing supplies. Kristin had long ago been stripped of all her illusions about the ethics of either side. There were men on both sides who claimed to be soldiers but were nothing but thieves and murderers. This wasn't a war; it was a melee, a bloody, desperate free-for-all.

It was amazing that the family still had enough to eat. There was the secret cellar, of course. That had saved them many a time. And today it didn't matter. Today, well, today they all deserved a feast.

The stranger deserved a feast.

The kitchen door was pushed open, and Kristin sank deeper into the bubbles that flourished in the elegant brass bathtub, an inheritance from Kristin's mother, who had dragged it all the way over from Bristol, in England.

She needn't have feared. It was only Delilah. "How you doin' there, child?" she demanded. She reached into the cabinet above the water pump and pulled out a bottle of Kristin's father's best Madeira. She set the bottle and a little tray of glasses on the counter and pulled the kettle off the kitchen fire to add more steaming water to Kristin's bath.

Kristin looked into Delilah's dark eyes. "I feel like I'm never going to get clean, Delilah. Never. Not if I wash from here to doomsday."

Delilah poured out the last of the water, warming Kristin's toes. Then she straightened and set the kettle down on the hearth. She walked over to the stove to check the bacon and the scrapple. "It could have been a lot worse," she said softly, staring out the window at the now deceptively peaceful day. "Thank the Lord for small miracles." She looked back at Kristin. "You hurry up there, huh, honey?"

Kristin nodded and even managed a small smile. "Do we have a name on him yet?"

The kitchen door burst open again. Kristin shrank back and Delilah swung around. It was Shannon, looking flushed, pretty and very excited.

"Kristin! You aren't out of there yet?"

Kristin looked at her sister, and she didn't know whether to be exasperated or relieved. She was still shaken by the events of the morning, but Shannon had put them all behind her. Of course, Shannon had been down in the cellar. And that was what Kristin had wanted. It seemed that everyone here had lost their innocence. The war didn't let you just stay neutral. Man or woman, a body had to choose a side, and you survived by becoming jaded and hardened. She didn't want that for Shannon. She wanted her sister to retain a certain belief in magic, in fantasy. Shannon had turned seventeen not long ago, and she deserved to be able to believe in innocence. She was so young, so soft, so pretty. Blue-eyed and golden blond, a vision of beauty and purity. Kristin didn't think she'd ever looked like that. When she looked at herself in the mirror she knew that the lines and planes and angles of her face were hard, and that her eyes had taken on an icy edge. She knew she looked much older than eighteen.

She had aged ten years in the last two. Desperation had taught her many lessons, and she knew they showed in her face.

"I'm coming out in just a minute, Shannon," Kristin assured her sister.

"Slater," Delilah said.

"Pardon?" Kristin asked her.

"Slater." Shannon came over to the bathtub, kneeling beside it and resting her elbows on the edge. "His name is Cole Slater."

"Oh," Kristin murmured. Cole Slater. She rolled the name around in her mind. Well, that had been easy enough. Why had she thought it would be so difficult to drag the man's name out of him?

Shannon jumped to her feet. "Kristin's never coming out of this old tub. Shall I get the Madeira, Delilah?"

"Sounds like someone's got an admirer," Kristin murmured.

"I'm trying to be polite," Shannon said indignantly. She arranged the little glasses on a silver serving tray. "Honest, Kristin, he's a right courteous fellow, and he told me I shouldn't rush you, says he understands you might feel you need a long, long wash. But I think you're just plain old rude and mean. And you know what else I think? I think you're afraid of him."

Kristin narrowed her eyes at her sister, tempted to jump from the tub and throttle her. But it was far more serious than that. "I'm not afraid of Zeke Moreau, or even Bill Quantrill and all his raiders, Shannon. I just have a healthy respect for their total lack of justice and morality. I'm not afraid of this drifter, either."

"But you *are* beholden to him," Delilah reminded her softly.

"I'm sorry," Shannon murmured.

When Kristin looked at her sister, she saw the pain that welled up in her eyes, and she was sorry herself. Shannon had lived through the same horrors she had. She just wasn't the eldest. She wasn't the one with the responsibility.

She smiled at Shannon. "Bring the Madeira on in, will you please? I'll be right out."

Shannon smiled, picked up the tray and went out of the kitchen. Kristin grinned at Delilah. "Pa's Madeira, huh? You must think highly of this drifter."

Delilah sniffed as she fluffed out the clean petticoat she'd brought down from Kristin's room. She sent Kristin a quick glare. "He ain't no ordinary drifter. We both know that. And you bet I think highly of him. Moreau might—just might— have left you alive, but he'd have hanged Samson. Slater kept my husband alive and he kept me from the block at the slave market. You bet I think highly of him."

Kristin grinned. From what she remembered of her lovely and aristocratic mother, she knew Kathleen McCahy would have been shocked by such blunt language. Not Pa, though. Pa had made himself a rancher and a farmer; he'd learned all the rough edges of the frontier. He'd have laughed at the plain truth of her statement. Then he'd have been grateful to have Delilah safe and sound, because she and Samson were part of the family, too.

"Want to hand me a towel, Delilah?" Kristin said, thinking again about the stranger who had arrived among them just in the nick of time. No, he wasn't any ordinary drifter, not judging by the way he handled a weapon. What was he, then? A gunslinger from down Texas way, maybe? Perhaps he'd come from farther west—from California, maybe. Somewhere he'd learned to make an art of the use of his Colts.

He made an art of the simple act of walking, too, she thought. She shivered suddenly, remembering the silence that had followed the sudden burst of gunfire. She remembered the way his eyes had looked as he'd ordered Zeke away from her. Slate-gray eyes, steel eyes, hard and merciless. She remembered the way his frock coat had fallen along the length of his tall body, remembered his broad shoulders, remembered the way he'd looked at her. A heat that didn't come from the water seemed to flutter to life deep inside her.

It hadn't been a romantic look, she reminded herself. She knew about romantic looks. She knew about falling in love. It was easy and gentle. It was slow and beautiful. It was the way she had felt about Adam, and it was the way he had felt about her. When he had looked at her, he had looked into her eyes. He had held her hand, awkwardly at first. He had stuttered sometimes when he had spoken to her, and he had whispered tenderly to her. That was romance. That was love. She had never felt this shameful burning inside when she had been with Adam. She had been content to hold his hand. They had been content to sit and dream. She had never once imagined him...naked.

Appalled by her thoughts, she swallowed hard. She hadn't imagined any man naked, and certainly not this stranger. No, he had not given her any romantic looks. What he had given her was an assessment. It had been just as if he were studying a horse and liked what he saw, good bones and decent teeth. And then he had smiled, if not tenderly, at least with a certain gentility.

Still, the way he had looked at her...

And he had seen her nearly naked.

Color seemed to wash over her body. She rose to reach for her towel, then fell back into the water again, shamed by the way her breasts swelled and her nipples hardened. She prayed that Delilah hadn't noticed.

"You cold?" Delilah asked her.

Delilah had noticed.

Kristin quickly wrapped the big towel around herself. "A little," she lied.

"Get over by the fire. Dry off good and I'll help you get your clothes on."

Kristin nodded, rubbing her pink flesh dry. The fire warmed her, the flames nearly touching her. At least she would have an excuse for being red.

When she was finished she sank into the old rocker by the fire and Delilah brought over her corset, pantalets and stockings. Kristin quickly slid into the knit stockings and pantalets, and Delilah ordered her to hold her breath while she tied up the corset.

Kristin arched a tawny brow when she saw the dress Delilah had brought down for her. It wasn't one of her usual cotton day dresses. It was muslin, with

soft blue flowers and double rows of black-and-white lace edging along the puff
sleeves, the bodice and the hem. It was one of her best dresses.

"Delilah—"

"Put it on, child, put it on. We are celebrating here, remember?"

"Oh, yes." Kristin grinned, but then she started to shiver again. She was
afraid she was going to burst into tears. They were never going to be done with
it. They couldn't ignore it, and they couldn't accept it. Pa had been murdered,
and the same—or worse—could have happened today. Today could have been
the end of everything.

They had been saved today, but it was only temporary. Zeke would be back.

"Lordy, Lordy," Delilah said. She and Kristin hugged one another, holding
tight.

"What are we going to do?" Delilah said.

"We—we have to convince him to stay around a while," Kristin said softly.

"Think he needs a job, maybe?" Delilah said hopefully.

"Does he look like he needs a job?" Kristin said, smiling shakily as she
pulled away. She turned her back to Delilah. "Hook me up, please."

Delilah started with the hooks, sweeping Kristin's bountiful hair out of the
way. When she was done she stepped back, swirling Kristin around. She sur-
veyed her broadly, then gave her a big smile. "Miss Kristin, you're the prettiest
little thing I ever did see!"

Kristin flushed. She didn't feel pretty these days. She felt tired and old and
worn most of the time.

"Brush your hair now. Your little Chinese slippers are by the door. Slip them
on. And go out there and see what else you can find out about that man beyond
his name."

"Yes, yes," Kristin murmured. Delilah searched her pockets for a brush.
Kristin stood on tiptoes to stare into the small mirror on the kitchen door. She
combed out her hair, leaving it thick and free and a little wild. She looked too
pale, she thought. She pinched her cheeks and bit her lip. Then she thought
about the man beyond the door again and all the color she could have wanted
flooded into her face.

"Thanks," she said, handing the brush back to Delilah. Then she pushed the
door open and hurried out.

She went through the family dining room first. Ma had always wanted a dining
room, not just a table in the middle of everything else, as in so many ranch
homes. Dining rooms were very proper, Ma had thought. And it was nice, Kristin
decided now. The Chippendale table was covered with a lace cloth and with
Ma's best silver, crystal and Royal Doulton plates. The table was set for three.
The four young ranch hands they had remaining ate in the bunkhouse and she
couldn't let a stranger know that she and Shannon usually just sat down with
Samson and Delilah. Of course, they didn't use the silver or the crystal or the
Royal Doulton every day, either.

After the dining room she came to the parlor. There was another big fireplace
here, and a braided rug before it, over the hardwood floor. Large windows looked
out on the sunshine. Ma had liked things bright, even though there were heavy
velvet-and-lace curtains in crimson softened by white that could be closed at
sunset to hold in the warmth. The furniture here was elegant, a small settee, a
daybed and fine wood chairs, and a spinet that both girls had learned to play.
It was a beautiful room, meant more for a lady than for a man. Kristin knew
she would find the stranger and her sister in the next room, Pa's office and

library. That was a far more comfortable room, with rows of books, a huge oak desk and a pair of deacon's benches that drew up to the double-sided fireplace.

Kristin was right. When she came through the parlor doorway, she saw that the stranger—no, Cole, his name was Cole Slater, and she had to stop thinking of him as the stranger—was indeed in this room. It was a great room. It smelled of pipe tobacco and fine leather, and it would always remind her of her father.

Cole Slater looked good here, as if he fit the place. He'd removed his plumed hat, his spurs and his railroad coat. Kristin paused, annoyed that she was trembling again just at the sight of him. He was a handsome man, she thought, though not in any usual way. He was far from pretty, but his steel-gray eyes were arresting, and what his face lacked in actual beauty it made up in strength. It was fine-boned yet powerful, sensual yet hard. And Kristin thought that she saw still more in his face. Cole Slater was another one who had lost all his illusions. She saw it when their eyes met. She studied him, and it was several long moments before she realized that he was studying her, too.

His knee was up, and his booted foot was resting against one of the footstools that seemed to have been cast haphazardly alongside the rows of books in the study. His boots were high, like cavalry-issue boots. His trousers hugged his long legs, betraying the lean muscles there, the trim line of his hips and the contours of his strong thighs and buttocks. His shoulders were broad, and he was tightly sinewed, and yet, he gave the appearance of being lean. A tuft of dark hair showed where his shirt lay open below his throat, and Kristin thought that his chest must be heavily matted with it.

Then she saw that his gaze was resting on her chest, too, and that just the hint of a smile was playing at the corners of his mouth. She almost lowered her lashes. Almost. She kept her eyes level with his and raised her chin a fraction. Then she inclined her head toward the glass of Pa's that he held—the little pony glass seemed ridiculously small contrasted with the size of his bronzed hand and the length of his fingers—and smiled graciously. "I see that Shannon has been taking good care of you."

He grinned at Shannon, who sat on one of the deacon's benches with a happy smile glued to her features. "Your sister is a most courteous and charming hostess."

Shannon colored with pleasure at the compliment. Then she laughed and jumped to her feet with the curious combination of grace and clumsiness that always reminded Kristin of a young colt. "I'm trying, anyway," she said. "And you two haven't been properly introduced. Miss Kristin McCahy, I give you Mr. Cole Slater. Mr. Slater, my sister, Miss Kristin McCahy."

Cole Slater stepped forward. He took Kristin's hand, and his eyes met hers just before his head lowered and his lips touched her hand. "I'm charmed, Miss McCahy. Quite charmed."

"Mr. Slater," she returned. She tried to place his accent, but she couldn't. He didn't sound as if he came from the deep South, and he didn't sound as if he came from any of the New England states. He wasn't a foreigner, but he didn't speak with the twang of the midwesterner, either.

He was still holding her hand. There was a feeling of warmth where his lips had touched her flesh, and the sensation seemed to seep into her, to enter into her bloodstream and head straight for the coil of liquid heat that churned indecently near the very apex of her thighs.

She pulled her hand away.

"We really don't know how to thank you, you know," she said, remaining still and seeking out his eyes again.

"I don't want to be thanked. I stumbled along at the right moment, that's all. And I'm damned hungry, and everything cooking smells damned good. A meal will make us even."

Kristin raised a brow. "You'll forgive me if I find my life, my friends, my sister, my sanity, my—"

"Chastity?" he offered bluntly.

"My person," she returned quietly, "are worth far more than a meal."

"Well, now..." He set his empty glass down, watching her thoughtfully. "I reckon that you are worth much, much more, Miss McCahy. Still, life isn't like a trip to the dry-goods store. I don't sell my services for any price. I was glad to be here when I was needed. If I helped you—"

"You know that you helped me. You saved all of us."

"All right. I helped you. It was my pleasure."

His voice matched his eyes. It wasn't quite a baritone, but it was still deep and full of the same hard, steely confidence. A drifter, a man who knew his guns. He had faced death out there today almost callously. Where did such a man come from?

Kristin stepped back. He was a tall man, more than six feet, and she was no more than five foot two. She felt more comfortable when there was a little distance between them.

And distance helped keep her heart from pounding, helped keep her blood from racing. Dismayed, she wondered what it was about him that made her feel this way. She never had before, not even with Adam.

Of course, not even Shannon could be completely innocent here. This was a working ranch, after all. Her father's prize bulls were the most valuable possessions he had left behind, and no matter how many of their cattle were stolen, Kristin knew they could start over with the bulls. But because of them and the other animals on the ranch, none of them could escape the details of the act of procreation.

Of course, watching the bulls made it all seem horribly crude. And nearly falling prey to the likes of Zeke Moreau made the bulls look like gentlemen of quality. She had never—never—imagined that a woman could actually wonder about what it would be like with a man, think about his hands touching her, think of his lips touching places other than her mouth.

She wanted to scream. She wondered suddenly if Cole could read her mind, for he was smiling again, and his smile seemed to reach into the heart and soul and heat of her. He knew.

She scowled and spun around, forgetting that he had saved her from a fate worse than death.

"I believe the meal that is worth so much to you is just about on the table, Mr. Slater. Shannon...let's all come along, shall we?"

Cole Slater followed his hostess through the parlor and into the formal dining room, suddenly and keenly aware of the soft scent of roses wafting from her flesh.

Then he noted that the fragrant flesh was as soft and smooth and tempting as cream silk. Her hair, loose around her shoulders, was like spun gold. And her eyes were level and filled with a surprising wisdom.

She was a very beautiful woman.

Outside, not so long ago, he had seen her differently. He had seen the Missouri dirt that had clung to her, and he had seen her spirit, but he had seen someone very young then. A girl, over-powered but fighting madly. Memory had clouded his vision, and he had seen the world through a brilliant red explosion.

He should have killed the bastard. No matter what his own past, no matter his codes when it came to dealing out death, that was one bastard he should have killed. Zeke Moreau. He had recognized Cole. Well, Cole had recognized Zeke, too. Zeke was one of the creatures that had been bred here in this den of blood, creatures that could shoot an unarmed man right between the eyes without blinking.

Zeke wanted this girl bad. No, this woman, he thought, correcting himself. She really wasn't a child. What was she? Twenty, perhaps? Older? Her eyes spoke of age, and so did the grace of her movements, and the confidence with which she spoke.

She was built like a woman.

Longing, hard and desperate, like a lightning bolt out of a clear blue sky, suddenly twisted and seared into him, straight into his groin, with a red-hot heat that was even painful.

He was glad he was walking behind her and Shannon. And he was glad his button-fly trousers were tight.

He clenched his teeth as another pain sizzled and burned in the area around his heart. This was a decent woman, this girl who had fought a strong man so desperately. Decent and still innocent, he imagined—thanks to his timely arrival.

This was the kind of girl men married.

Exhaling through clenched teeth, Cole wondered if there was a bordello any-where nearby. He doubted it. There was probably a cold river somewhere, though. He would eat and then head out and hit that river.

Damn her, he thought suddenly, savagely. So she was innocent—maybe. The way she had looked at him had been too naked. He had seen too many things in her eyes. Too much that was sensual and tempting. He could have sworn she had been wondering about things that she shouldn't have been wondering about.

He would eat and then get out. And he would bear in mind that his range of experience far surpassed hers. Did she think she could play cat and mouse with him? She might not know it, but she was the mouse.

Still, when she seated herself at the head of the table, he felt the lightning again. It filled the air when she spoke. It raced through him when she lightly brushed her fingers over his hand as she reached for the butter. It filled him when their knees brushed beneath the table.

"So..." She handed him a plate of flapjacks. "Where do you hail from, Mr. Slater?"

Kristin watched as the stranger helped himself to the flapjacks. He buttered them lavishly, then poured what seemed like a gallon of syrup over them. He shoveled a forkful into his mouth, chewed and swallowed, then answered her.

"Oh, here and there."

Here and there. Kristin sat back, dissatisfied.

Delilah came into the room, bringing more coffee. "Mr. Slater," she said, filling his cup again, "can I get you anything else?"

"Thank you, Delilah, no. This is one of the finest meals I've ever had."

Delilah smiled as if someone had just given her the crown jewels. Kristin sent her a glare over Cole's bowed head as he sipped his coffee.

Delilah nudged her firmly. Kristin sighed inwardly, and her eyes answered

Delilah's unspoken question. She knew as well as Delilah that they needed Cole Slater.

"Where are you heading, Mr. Slater?" she asked.

He shrugged. "Just drifting at the moment, Miss McCahy."

"Well," Kristin toyed idly with her fork. "You certainly did drift into the right place for us this morning, sir."

He sat back, studying her in a leisurely fashion. "Well, ma'am, like I said, I'm right glad to be of service." She thought that was all he was going to say, but then he leaned forward, his elbows on the table, his steel-gray eyes on hers.

"How did you get on the wrong side of this Moreau man?" He paused again, just for a split second. "Isn't he one of Quantrill's boys?"

Kristin nodded.

Shannon explained, "She turned him down, that's what happened. Pa used to know Quantrill. The bastard—"

"Shannon!" Kristin protested.

Shannon ignored her. "They act like he's Jesus Christ come back to life, some places in the South—"

"Shannon! What would Pa say! You're supposed to be a lady!"

Shannon grimaced in exasperation and submitted reluctantly to Kristin's chastisement. "Oh, all right! But Mr. Slater, Quantrill is a bloody traitor, that's all!" She insisted. "He used to be a jayhawker out of Kansas, preying on the Southerners! Then he led a band of abolitionists down here, pretended he was spying out the terrain and turned on his own people! He got out of it by passing out a lie about his older brother being killed by jayhawkers. He didn't have an older brother, but those stupid fools fell for it!"

Kristin looked at her plate. "Quantrill is a murderer," she said softly. "But he usually leaves women alone. He won't let them be murdered."

"But Zeke would," Shannon said. "Zeke would kill anybody. He wants to kill Kristin now, just because she turned him down. She was in love with Adam, you see."

"Adam?"

"Shannon!"

"Adam, Adam Smith. Adam was like Pa. He had no stake in this war. He just wanted to be a rancher. But when the bushwhackers came and killed Pa, Adam went out with a group of jayhawkers to find Zeke's boys. Kristin didn't know about it, not until they sent her back his horse. They killed him down southwest somewhere, and we don't even know where they left his bones. At least Pa is buried out back."

Kristin felt his eyes on her again. She looked up, but that steel-hard gaze was unreadable.

"So this was no random raid here today," he said. It was a statement, not a question.

"No," Kristin admitted. She felt as if she were holding her breath. He must realize that once he left they were all at the mercy of Zeke's bushwhackers again.

"You should get out," he told her.

"What?"

"You should get out. Pack your bags, get some kind of an escort and get the hell out."

It was a cold, callous statement. But what could she say in reply? He had stumbled upon them and he had saved her, but it had happened almost by accident. He didn't owe her a thing. She already owed him.

"I can't get out. My father died for this land. I owe it to him to keep it for him."

"To keep it for what? Your father is dead, and if you stay you'll probably wind up that way, too."

"That's all you can say?"

"What do you want me to say? I can't change this war, and I can't change the truth. Trust me. I would if I could."

For the first time she heard the bitterness in his voice. She wondered briefly about his past, but then she saw that he was rising, and panic filled her. He couldn't be about to ride away.

She stood. "You're not leaving?"

He shook his head. "I saw a few cigars in your father's study. Mind if I take one out back?"

Kristin shook her head, speechless. He wasn't leaving. Not yet.

She heard his footsteps as he walked through the dining room, heard them soften as he walked over the braided rug by the stairs. A moment later she heard the back door open and close.

"Kristin, are you all right?"

Kristin saw that Shannon was watching her, grave concern in her eyes.

"You're all pale," she said.

Kristin smiled, biting her lower lip and shaking her head. She squeezed Shannon's hand. "Help Delilah with the chores, won't you?"

Shannon nodded. Kristin turned around and followed the path the stranger had taken out of the house.

He was out back, puffing on one of her father's fine Havana cigars, leaning against the corral and watching as a yearling raced along beside its mother.

He heard Kristin and turned his fathomless gray gaze on her as she approached. He waited, his eyes hooded and curious.

Kristin wasn't at all sure how to say what she had to say. She folded her hands behind her back and walked over to him with what she hoped was an easy smile. Once she had thought she had the power to charm the male of the species. Once. She had been able to laugh and tease and flirt, and at any dance she had been breathless and busy, in unending demand.

Those days seemed so long ago now. Now she felt very young, and totally unsure of herself.

She had charmed boys, she realized. This was a man.

Still, she came over to him, leaning against the wooden gate of the corral.

"It's a good ranch," she told him.

He stared at her relentlessly, she thought. He didn't let a woman use her wiles. He didn't let her smile or flirt or tease.

"It's a good ranch," he agreed.

"Did I tell you just how much we appreciate your timely arrival here?"

"Yes, you did." He hiked himself up suddenly and sat on the gate, staring down at her. "Spit it out, Miss McCahy," he demanded, his eyes hard. "You've got something to say. Say it."

"My, my, you are a discerning man," she murmured.

"Cut the simpering belle act, Kristin. It isn't your style."

She flashed him an angry glance and started to turn away.

"Stop, turn around and tell me what you want!" he ordered her. He was a man accustomed to giving commands, she realized. And he was a man accustomed to his commands being obeyed.

Well, she wasn't going to obey him. She had paused, but she straightened her shoulders now and started to walk away.

She heard his boots strike the dirt softly, but she didn't realize he had pursued her until she felt his strong hands on her shoulders, whirling her around to face him. "What do you want, Miss McCahy?" he demanded.

She felt his hands, felt his presence. It was masculine and powerful. He smelled of leather and fine Madeira and her father's fine Havana cigar. He towered over her, and she wanted to turn away, and she wanted to touch the hard planes of his face and open his shirt and see the dark mat of hair that she knew must cover his chest.

"I want you to stay."

He stared at her, his eyes wary, guarded. "I'll stay until you can get some kind of an escort out of here."

"No." Her mouth had gone very dry. She couldn't speak. She wet her lips. She felt his eyes on her mouth. "I—I want you to stay on until—until I can do something about Zeke."

"Someone needs to kill Zeke."

"Exactly."

There was a long, long pause. He released her shoulders, looking her up and down. "I see," he said. "You want me to go after Zeke and kill him for you."

Kristin didn't say anything.

"I don't kill in cold blood," he told her.

She wanted to lower her eyes. She had to force herself to keep meeting his demanding gaze.

"I—I can't leave this ranch. I can give you a job—"

"I don't want a job."

"I—" She paused, then plunged on desperately. "I can make it worth your while."

He arched a brow. Something brought a smile to his lips, and suddenly his face was arrestingly handsome. He was younger than she had thought at first, too. But then he was talking again.

"You—you're going to make it worth my while."

She nodded, wishing she could hit him, wishing he would quit staring at her so, as if she were an unproved racehorse.

"Come here," he said.

"What?"

"Come here."

"I—I am here."

"Closer."

He touched her. His hands on her shoulders, he dragged her to him. She felt the steely hardness of his body, felt its heat and vibrancy. Through his pants and through all her clothing she felt the male part of him, vital and pulsing, against the juncture of her thighs. She still stared at him, wide-eyed, speechless, her breasts crushed hard against his chest as he held her.

He smiled crudely. Then his lips touched hers.

Curiously, the touch was very, very light. She thought she might pass out from the feel of it, so startling, so appealing. His lips were molded to hers....

Then hunger soared, and his tongue pressed between her teeth, delving deep, filling her mouth. She was engulfed as his mouth moved over hers, his lips taking hers, his tongue an instrument that explored her body boldly and intimately. Her breasts seemed to swell and she felt her nipples harden and peak almost painfully against his chest. He savaged her mouth, moving his tongue as indecently as he might have moved another part of his hard body...

Something inside her exploded deliciously. Heat coursed through her, filling her. She could not meet the power of his kiss, but she had no desire to fight it. It was shameful, maybe more shameful than what had happened to her this morning.

Because she wanted it.

She savored the stream of liquid sensations that thrilled throughout her body. Her knees shook, and the coil deep inside her abdomen that was so much a part of her womanhood seemed to spiral to a peak, higher and higher. She wanted to touch him. To bring her fingers against him, exploring. To touch him as his tongue so insinuatingly invaded all the wet crevices of her mouth...

Then he released her. He released her so suddenly that she nearly fell, and he had to hold her again to steady her.

He stared down at her. Her lips were wet and swollen, and her eyes were glazed. He was furiously angry with himself.

"Worthwhile?" he asked.

Kristin's mind was reeling. What did he mean?

"You don't even know how to kiss," he told her.

"What?" she whispered, too stunned to recognize the anger rising inside her.

"I'm sorry," he said. His voice was softer now.

"Damn you!" Kristin said. "I'll make a bargain with you! If you'll just stay—"

"Stop it!" he said harshly. "I'm sorry. I just don't have the time or the patience for a silly little virgin."

"What?" She stepped back, her hands on her hips, and stared at him. The insolence of him! She wanted to scream and she wanted to cry.

"I don't want a love affair, Miss McCahy. When I do want something, it's a woman, and it seldom matters who she is, just so long as she's experienced and good at what she does. Understand?"

"Oh yes, I understand. But I need help. I need you. Doesn't that mean anything?"

"I told you, I don't want a virgin—"

"Well then, excuse me for an hour, will you?" Kristin snapped, her eyes blazing. "I'll just run on out and screw the first cowhand—oh!"

She broke off in shock as he wrenched her hard against him. "Shut up! Where the hell did you come up with language like that?" he demanded heatedly.

"Let me go! It's none of your business! It's a rough world here, Slater!" she flailed desperately against him. He didn't feel her fists, and he didn't even realize that she was kicking him.

"Don't ever let me hear you say anything like that again!"

"Who do you think you are, my father?" Kristin demanded. She was very close to bursting into tears, and she was determined not to, not here, not now— not anywhere near this drifter. He had made her feel as young and naive and foolish and lost as Shannon. "Let me go!"

"No, I'm not your father. I'm a total stranger you're trying to drag into bed," he said.

"Forget it. Just release me and—"

"You just stop, Miss McCahy!" He gave her a firm, hard shake, then another.

At last Kristin stopped fighting. Her head fell back, her hair trailing like soft gold over his fingers, her eyes twin pools of blue fire as she stared into the iron-gray hardness of his.

"Give me some time," he said to her very softly, in a tone that caused her to tremble all over again. "I'll think about your proposition."

"What?" she whispered warily.

He released her carefully. "I said, Miss McCahy, that I would think about your proposition. I'll stay tonight. I'll take my blanket out to the bunkhouse, and I'll give you an answer in the morning." He inclined his head toward her, turned on his heel and started off toward the house.

Chapter Three

When she walked back into the house, Kristin was in a cold fury. She didn't see Cole Slater anywhere, and for the moment she was heartily glad.

He had humiliated her, plain and simple. She'd been willing to sell honor, her pride, her dignity—and he hadn't even been interested in what she'd had to sell. She wished fervently that she wasn't so desperate. She'd have given her eyeteeth to tell the man that he was a filthy gunslinger, no better than all the others.

Yet even as she thought of what she'd like to be able to say to him, she realized it would be a lie. He'd saved her from Zeke, from the man who had murdered her father. She owed him.

And she'd paid, she thought drily. With humiliation.

Shannon wasn't around when Kristin reached the dining room. Delilah was there, though, humming a spiritual as she carefully picked up the fine crystal and china on the table. She glanced Kristin's way curiously and kept humming.

"Where's Shannon?" Kristin asked.

"Out feeding the chickens," Delilah said.

Kristin decided to help clear away the remains of the meal, but when her fingers clenched too tightly around a plate, Delilah rescued it from her grip. "Sorry," Kristin muttered.

"Kristin, for the sake of your mama's fine things, you go do something else here this morning, hm?"

Kristin stepped away from the table, folding her hands behind her back.

"You didn't ask where Mr. Slater had gotten himself off to," Delilah said.

"I don't care where Mr. Slater has gotten himself off to," Kristin replied sweetly.

Delilah shot her a quick glance. "The man saved our lives," she said sharply.

Kristin strode furiously across the room to look out the window. "He saved our lives...and he really doesn't give a damn."

"He's riding out?"

Kristin exhaled slowly. She could see Shannon by the barn, tossing feed to the chickens. If she had any sense she would leave. Shannon was precious to her, just as Delilah and Samson were. She should do whatever was necessary to protect them.

But the dream was precious, too. The dream and the land. And where would she go if she did leave? She could never embrace the Southern cause—she had been treated too cruelly by the bushwhackers here for that—nor could she turn against Missouri and move into Yankee territory. She wanted desperately to fight, but she was helpless.

It didn't matter where she went, Richmond, Virginia or Washington, D.C. Nowhere was life as cruel and violent as it was here on the border of "bleeding Kansas." Nowhere else did men murder each other so callously.

"Kristin?" Delilah said.

"Slater..." Kristin murmured. Her pride was wounded, she realized. She had offered up her finest prize—herself—and he had informed her crudely that he wasn't interested.

"Kristin, if you're mad at that man for something, you remember the rest of us here. You understand me, missy?" Delilah came toward her, waving a fork. Kristin tried not to smile, because Delilah was deadly serious. "Quantrill's men get ahold of us and they'll think nothing of a hanging. You saw what they did to your pa. I got a baby boy, Kristin, and—"

"Oh, Delilah, stop! I'm doing my best!" Kristin protested. She tried to smile encouragingly. She couldn't quite admit to Delilah yet that she had offered her all and that it hadn't been enough. She hadn't even tempted the man.

She clenched her teeth together. She'd like to see him desperate, his tongue hanging out. She'd like to see him pining for her and be in the position to put her nose in the air, cast him a disdainful glance and sweep right on by. Better yet, she'd like to laugh in his face. If it hadn't been for this war, she could have done just that. She could have had any rich young rancher in the territory. She could have had—

Adam. She could have had Adam. A numbing chill took hold of her. Adam had loved her so much, and so gently. Tall and blond and beautiful, with green eyes that had followed her everywhere, and an easy, tender smile.

Adam was dead. The war had come, and Adam was dead, and she had few choices. Yes, Slater had humiliated her. But part of it was the fire. Part of it was the feeling that he had embedded in her, the hot, shameful longing for something she didn't know and didn't understand. She had loved Adam, but she had never felt this way when she had been near him. Never. Cole Slater *did* frighten her. She didn't like the feelings he evoked in her. They shattered her belief in her own strength.

"Cole Slater is staying tonight," she told Delilah.

"Well, glory be!"

"No, no," Kristin said. "He's bunking with the hands for the night. He'll, uh, he'll probably be gone by morning."

"By morning?" Delilah repeated blankly. "Kristin, I don't want to suggest anything that ain't proper, but chil', I'm just sure that if you tried being friendly to the man..."

"Delilah," Kristin murmured, her sense of humor returning at last, "I'm sure I don't remember what proper is anymore. I tried. Honest to God, I tried." She shrugged. "I'm not going to do you any good around here. I'll see you in a bit, huh?"

She hurried toward the stairs, giving Delilah a quick kiss on the cheek as she passed. She felt the older woman's worried gaze follow her, but by the time she reached the landing, she had forgotten about her.

The house felt so empty now.

Delilah and Samson and their baby had the rooms on the third floor. Kristin's and Shannon's were here on the second floor. But Matthew's room was empty now, as was the big master bedroom where her father and mothers had slept.

The two guest rooms were empty, too. They hadn't entertained guests in a long, long time.

Kristin walked down the hallway, not toward her own room but toward the room that had been her parents'. She opened the door, stood there and smiled slowly. Her mother had been dead for years, but her father had been unable to part with the big Bavarian sleigh bed that his wife had so cherished. After her death he'd slept in it alone. And it was beautiful still. Delilah kept the mahogany polished and the bedding clean, as if she expected Pa to come back anytime.

Kristin walked into the room. There were giant armoires on either side of the window. One still held Pa's clothes, and the other still held her mother's.

We don't take to change easily here, Kristin thought. She smiled. It was the Irish blood, Pa had always told her. They were too sentimental. But that was good. It was good to hold on to the past. It helped keep the dream alive. Someday Pa's grandchildren would have this room. Matthew's children, probably.

If Matthew survived the war. It couldn't be easy for him, a Southern boy fighting in the Yankee army.

Kristin turned away. If Zeke Moreau had his way, none of them would survive the war. And when he was done torturing and killing, he would burn the house to the ground.

She started to close the door. Then she hesitated and turned back. She could suddenly see Cole Slater stretched out on that sleigh bed. It was a big bed, plenty big enough for his height and for the breadth of his shoulders. She could imagine him there, smiling lazily, negligently. Then suddenly, a whirlwind, a tempest of heat and fire…

She gritted her teeth, closed her eyes tightly and swore. She was sick of thinking about Cole Slater, and she was sick of remembering how grateful she had to be to a man who made her feel this way.

She slammed the door to her parents' room and hurried to her own. She threw her good dress on her bed and did likewise with her silk slippers and her corset. She slipped on a chemise, a cotton shirt, a pair of breeches and her high leather boots, and headed straight for the stables. She didn't bother with a saddle, but grabbed a bridle from a hook off the wall for Debutante and slipped into the stall to find her horse.

Debutante was an Arabian mare, a gift to Pa from one of the men he'd done business with in Chicago. She was a chestnut with white stockings, a deep dish in her nose and a tail that rode as high as the sun. Kristin loved her. She was amazed that the horse hadn't been stolen yet, but so far she had managed to have the horse out in the far pasture when the various raiding parties had swept through.

"Hello, you beautiful thing," Kristin whispered as she slipped the bit into the mare's mouth. Debutante nudged her. Kristin stroked the horse's velevety nose, then leaped on her back. Debutante nudged the stall door open, and Kristin gave her free rein as they left the stables behind.

It felt good to ride. It was good to feel the wind strike her cheeks, to feel the coolness of the air as it rushed by her. She was glad she had come bareback. She could feel the power of the animal beneath her, the rhythm of her smooth gallop, the great constriction and release of superbly toned muscle. Kristin leaned close to Debutante's neck. The horse's mane whipped back, stinging her cheeks, but she laughed with delight, glad simply to be alive.

Then Kristin realize she was being followed.

She wasn't sure how she knew she was being followed, except that there was an extra beat to the rhythm churning the earth, something that moved in discord.

She tried to look behind her. Her hair swept into her face, nearly blinding her.

There was a rider behind her. A lone figure, riding hard.

Panic seized her. She was already riding like the wind. How much harder could she drive the mare?

"Debutante! Please! We must become the wind!" She locked her knees more tightly against the animal's flanks. They were moving still faster now. The Arabian mare was swift and graceful, but the horse behind them seemed to be swifter. Either that, or Debutante's stamina was fading.

"Please!"

Kristin leaned closer to the mare's neck. She conjured up a mental image of the terrain. Adam had once owned this land. Ahead, just to the right, was a forest of tall oaks. She could elude her pursuer there.

The trees loomed before her. She raced the mare into the forest, then reined in when the trees became too dense for a gallop. She moved to the right and to the left, pushing deeper and deeper into the maze of foliage. Then she slid from the mare's back and led her onward.

Kristin's heart was pounding as she sought shelter.

If Zeke had come back, if he found her now...

She would pray for death.

But he was alone this time, she thought, praying for courage. She could fight him.

A twig snapped behind her. She spun around. She couldn't see anything, but she knew that her pursuer had dismounted, too, that he was still following her.

The branches closed above her like an arbor. The day was not bright and blue here, it was green and secretive, and the air was cold. She began to shiver.

She wasn't even armed, she realized ruefully. She was a fool. After all that had happened this morning she had ridden away from home without even a pocketknife with which to defend herself.

Kristin searched the ground and found a good solid branch.

Another twig snapped behind her. She dropped the mare's reins and crouched down against an oak. Someone was moving toward her.

Someone was behind her.

She spun around, the branch raised, determined to get in the first blow.

"Son of a bitch!" he swore.

She had gotten in the first blow—just barely. The man had raised his arm, and the branch struck it hard.

The impact sent her flying, her hair in her eyes. She landed in the dirt, and he was on top of her in an instant. She slammed her fist into his face, and heard a violent oath.

"Stop it! Kristin!"

He caught her wrists and straddled her.

She blinked and went still. It was Cole Slater.

"You!"

He rubbed his jaw. "You pack a hell of a punch."

"A hell of a punch?" she repeated. "You—you—" She was trembling with fear and with fury. She didn't mean to strike him again but she was nearly hysterical with relief, and she moved without thinking, slapping him across the face.

She knew instantly it was a mistake. His eyes narrowed, and everything about him hardened. Kristin gasped and looked around her for another weapon. Her fingers curled around a branch, and she raised it threateningly.

Cole wrenched the branch from her grasp and broke it over his knee, then pulled her roughly against his chest.

"What do you think you're doing?" he asked.

She had never seen him so furious, not even when he had gone up against Zeke and his gang of bushwhackers. Then he had seemed as cool as a spring stream. Now his eyes were the dark gray of a winter's sky, and his mouth was a white line of rage.

Kristin clenched her teeth hard, struggling to free herself from his grip. "What am I doing? You scared me to death."

He pulled her closer, and when he spoke again, his words were a mere whisper. "You're a fool, girl. After a morning like this you take off into the woods, without a word, without a care."

"I'm not a fool, and I'm not a girl, Mr. Slater, and I'd appreciate it, sir, if you would take your hands off of me."

"Oh, great. We have the grand Southern belle again."

Kristin gritted her teeth, wishing she could stem the rising tide of rage within her, rage and other emotions. He was too close. He was touching her, and she could feel the power of his anger, the strength of his body, and she was afraid of her own reactions.

"Let go of me. Just who the hell do you think you are?"

"The man who saved your life."

"I'm getting tired of eternal gratitude."

"Gratitude? A crack with a stick?"

"I didn't know it was you! Why didn't you say something? Why didn't you let me know—"

"You were running that mare a little fast for casual conversation."

"Why were you chasing me?"

"Because I was afraid you were going to get yourself in trouble."

"What were you afraid of? I thought you'd decided I wasn't worth the effort."

"I hadn't made any decisions yet. You are a girl, and you are a fool. You didn't give Moreau's men a chance to get far enough away. I didn't save you this morning for a gang rape this afternoon."

"Well, Mr. Slater, I wouldn't have been an annoying little virgin then, would I?"

Kristin was stunned when his palm connected with her cheek. Tears stung her eyes, though she wasn't really hurt. She hadn't expected his anger, and she hadn't imagined that she could humiliate herself this way again.

"Get off me!" she demanded.

"I don't want to hear it again, Kristin. Do you understand me?" He stood and reached down to help her up. She ignored his outstretched hand, determined to rise unaided, but he wouldn't even allow her to do that. He caught her arms and pulled her up. She hated him at that moment. She hated him because she needed him. And she hated him because this heat filled her at his touch, and this curious longing grew within her. She was fascinated by the scent of him, amazed by her desire to touch his face, to feel the softness of his beard....

To experience the sweeping wonder of his kiss once again.

She jerked free, and the leaves crackled under her feet as she whistled for Debutante. He followed behind her, dusting his hat off on the skirt of his coat.

"Kristin..."

She spun around. "You know, I've been wondering where you come from. You certainly aren't any Southern gentleman."

"No?" he queried. They stared at one another for a moment. Then his lips began to curl into a rueful smile. "I'm sincerely beginning to doubt that you're a Southern lady—or any kind of a lady, for that matter."

She smiled icily. She could manage it when he wasn't touching her. Then she turned away from him, squared her shoulders and walked toward her waiting mare.

"Sorry. I haven't had much time lately for the little niceties of life."

When she reached Debutante, he was there beside her. She didn't want his help, but he was determined to give it anyway. He lifted her onto the mare's back and grinned up at her.

"I may have to accept your generous offer."

"My generous offer?"

"Yes." His eyes suddenly seemed dazzling. Smoke and silver. His smile lent youth and humor to his features. He laughed. "I may have to bed you yet. To save you from yourself."

She wanted to say something. She wanted to say that her offer was no longer valid, that she would rather go to bed with Zeke and every single one of his raiders, than spend a single night with him, but the words wouldn't come. They weren't true. And it didn't matter, anyway, because he had already turned away. He picked up the reins of his big black horse and leaped upon the animal's back with the agility of long practice.

Kristin started out of the forest, heading for the house. She didn't look back. She rode ahead all the way. He rode behind her, in silence.

By the time they reached the house she was trembling again. She didn't want to see him, she didn't want to talk to him. The whole thing had been a deadly mistake. He needed to get his night's sleep and head out in the morning.

She didn't even know who the man was! she reminded herself in dismay.

When they had dismounted she spoke at last, but without looking at him. "The hands eat out in the bunkhouse at about six. Sleep well, and again, thank you for rescuing us all. I really am eternally grateful."

"Kristin—"

She ignored him and walked Debutante toward the stables. Her heart began to pound, because she imagined that he would follow her. He did not.

She didn't rub Debutante down as she should have. She led the mare into the stall and removed her bit. In a worse turmoil than she had been in when she had left, she walked to the house.

Cole Slater was no longer in the yard. Kristin walked into the house. It was silent, and the drapes were drawn against the afternoon sun. Kristin bit her lip, wondering what to do. Depression suddenly weighed heavily upon her. It was all lost. She would have to leave, and she would have to be grateful that they were alive and accept the fact that nothing else of their life here could be salvaged.

She wasn't sure it mattered. They had already lost so much. Pa. Adam. Her world had been turned upside down. She would have done anything to save it. Anything. But anything just wouldn't be enough.

With a soft sigh, she started up the stairway. At the top of the stairs, she paused, her heart beating hard once again.

There was someone there, on the second floor with her.

There was someone in her parents' bedroom.

She tried to tell herself it was Delilah, or Shannon, but then she heard Delilah calling to Shannon below and heard Shannon's cheerful answer.

"Oh, God," she murmured, her hand traveling to her throat.

Something inside of her went a little berserk. She couldn't bear it if Zeke or one of his cronies had managed to enter that room. Her father's room, a place he had cherished, a place where all his dreams remained alive.

She ran toward the doorway. If Zeke had been in the room, she might have managed to kill him with her bare hands.

But it wasn't Zeke. It was Cole Slater. He had his blanket laid out on the comforter, and he was taking things from it. He looked up at her in surprise as she stared at him from the doorway. He frowned when he noticed the way her breasts heaved and noticed the pulse beating hard at the base of her throat. He strode to her quickly.

"Kristin, what happened?"

She shook her head, unable to speak at first.

"I—I didn't expect you. I mean, I didn't expect you to be here," she said.

He shrugged and walked back into the room, taking a shirt from the blanket and striding toward her father's armoire. "I didn't intend to be here. Delilah insisted there was plenty of room inside the house." He paused and turned back to her. "Is there something wrong with that? Do you want me out of here?"

She shook her head and had to swallow before she could speak again. "No...uh, no. It's fine." He was going to come toward her again. Quickly, before he could come close enough to touch her, Kristin turned and fled to the sanctuary of her own room.

She didn't know what seized her that afternoon. She didn't dare sit and think, and she certainly couldn't allow herself to analyze.

She went out in the early evening to speak with the hands. There was Jacob, who was nearly seventy, and his grandsons, Josh and Trin, who were even younger than she was. Their father had been killed at Manassas at the beginning of the war. And there was Pete, who was older than Jacob, though he wouldn't admit it. That was all she had left—two old men and two young boys. Yet they had survived so far. Somehow they had survived so far.

Cattle were missing again. Kristin just shrugged at the news. Zeke's boys had been through. They had simply taken what they wanted.

Pete wagged a finger at her. "We heard what happened, missy. I think it's time you got out of here."

She ruffled his thin gray hair. "And what about you, Pete?"

"I've gotten along this far. I'll get along the rest of my days."

She smiled at him. "We'll see."

"Hear tell you've got a man named Slater up at the house."

Kristin frowned. "Yes. Why? You know him, Pete?"

Pete looked down at the wood he was whittling, shaking his head. "Can't say that I do."

She thought the old man was lying to her, and she couldn't understand it. He was as loyal as the day was long.

"You just said his name. Slater."

"Yeah, I heard it. From someone. Just like I heard tell that he managed to get rid of the whole lot of the thieving gutter rats." He looked up, wagging his knife at her. "You can't beat the likes of Zeke Moreau, Kristin. He doesn't have a breath of mercy or justice in him." He spat on the floor. "None of them do, not the jayhawkers, not the bushwhackers. It's time to get out."

"Well, maybe," Kristin said distractedly. She stood from the pile of hay she'd been sitting on. "Maybe."

"Your Pa's dead, Kristin. You're smart and you're tough. But not tough enough to take on Zeke on your own."

He looked at her expectantly. She felt like laughing. Everyone thought she could help. Everyone thought that all she had to do was bat her eyelashes at Cole Slater and he'd come straight to their rescue. If they only knew.

"We'll talk about it in the morning," she told him.

When she returned to the house, it was dinnertime.

Delilah had set out the good china and fine crystal again. She'd made a honeyed ham, candied yams, turnip greens and a blueberry pie.

Shannon and Cole Slater talked all through the meal. There might not have been a war on. There might not have been anything wrong with the world at all, the way the two of them talked. Shannon was beautiful and charming, and Cole was the perfect gentleman.

Kristin tried to smile, and she tried to answer direct questions. But all she could remember was that he had rejected her—and that she needed him desperately. She hated him, yet trembled if their hands so much as brushed when they reached for something at the same time.

She drank far too much Madeira with dinner.

When he went out back to smoke a cigar afterward, Kristin decided to take another bath. She hoped Delilah would think she hadn't been able to wash away the miserable stench of the morning.

Shannon was a sweetheart, tender and caring. Kristin realized when Shannon kissed her good-night that her sister was suffering more then she had realized. She was just taking it all stoically, trying to ease Kristin's pain with smiles and laughter.

Shannon went to bed.

Kristin dressed in her best nightgown. It had been part of her mother's trousseau. It was soft, sheer silk that hugged her breasts in a pattern of lace, then fell in gentle swirls around her legs.

She sat at the foot of her bed in the gown, and she waited. She was still, but fires raged inside her.

She had to make him stay, no matter what it took.

This was something that she had to do.

She heard his footsteps on the stairs at last. She heard him walk down the hallway, and then she heard the door to her parents' room open and close.

She waited, waited as long as she could, as long as she dared. Then she stood and drifted barefoot across the hardwood floor. She opened her door and started across the hall. She nearly panicked and fled, but something drew her onward. She wondered if she had gone mad, wondered if the world really had been turned upside down. Nothing could ever be the same again.

She hated him, she told herself. And he had already turned her down once. One day she would best him.

She placed her hand on the doorknob and turned it slowly. Then she pushed open the door.

The room was dark. Only a streak of moonlight relieved the blackness. Kristin stood there for several seconds, blinking, trying to orient herself. It was foolish. She had waited too long. He was probably fast asleep.

He wasn't asleep. He was wide awake. He was sitting up in bed, his chest bare. He was watching her. Despite the darkness, she knew that he was watching her, that he had been waiting for her and that he was amused.

"Come on, Kristin," he said softly. He wasn't whispering like a man afraid of being caught at some dishonorable deed. He was speaking softly out of consideration for the others in the house, not out of fear. He wouldn't give a damn about convention, she thought. And yet he seemed to expect her to respect it.

Men.

"I, uh...just wanted to see if you needed anything."

"Sure." He smiled knowingly. "Well, I don't need anything. Thank you."

The bastard. He really meant to make it hard for her.

"That's a nice outfit to wear to check on your male guests, ma'am." He said the last word with a slow, calculated Southern drawl, and she felt her temper flare. Where the hell was he from?

"Glad you like it," she retorted.

"Oh, I do like it. Very much."

This was getting them nowhere. No, it was getting *her* nowhere.

"Well..."

"Come here, Kristin."

"You come here."

He grinned. "If you insist."

She should have known he would be lying there nude beneath the sheets.

Well, she had come to seduce him, after all.

She just hadn't imagined his body. The length of it. She couldn't remember what she had imagined. Darkness, and tangle of sheets... She had known it involved a naked man, but she hadn't known just how a naked man could be.

She tried to keep her eyes on his, aware that a crimson tide was rushing to her face. She wished she had the nerve to shout, to run, to scream, but she didn't seem to be able to do anything at all.

Her eyes slipped despite her best efforts, slipped and then widened. She knew that he saw it, and she knew that he was amused. But she didn't move and she didn't speak, and when he stood before her at last, his hands on his hips, she managed to toss her head back and meet his gaze with a certain bravado.

He placed his hands against the wall on either side of her head. "Like what you see?" he inquired politely.

"Someone should really slap the living daylights out of you," she told him sweetly.

"You didn't do badly."

"Good." She was beginning to shake. Right now it was a mere tremor, but it was growing. He was so close that...that part of his body was nearly touching the swirling silk of her gown. She felt his breath against her cheek. She felt the heat radiating from him. She bit her lip, trying to keep it from quivering.

He pushed away from the wall. He touched her cheek with his palm, then stroked it softly with his knuckles. She stared at him, unable to move. She knew then that he could see that she was trembling. His eyes remained locked with hers. He moved his hand downward and cupped her breast.

The touch was so intimate, so bold, that she nearly cried out. He grazed her nipple with his thumb, and sensations shot through her with an almost painful intensity. She caught her breath, trying desperately to keep from crying out. And then she realized that he was watching her eyes carefully, gauging her reactions.

She knocked his hand away and tried to push by him, but he caught her shoulders and threw her against the wall.

"I hurt your feelings before. But then, I don't think that you were lacking in self-confidence. You must know that you're beautiful. Your hair is so golden and you have the bearing of a young Venus. Kristin, it isn't you. It's me. I haven't got any emotion left. I haven't got what you need, what you want. Damn it, don't you understand? I want you. I'm made out of flesh and blood and whatever else it is that God puts into men. I want you. Now. Hell, I could have wanted you right after I ripped another man away from you. I'm no better than he is, not really. Don't you understand?"

She drew herself up against the wall. She hated him, and she hated herself. She had lost again.

"I only know that I need you. Emotion! I saw my father murdered, and Adam..."

"Yes, and Adam."

"And Adam is dead, too. So if you're worried about some kind of emotional commitment, you're a fool. I want help against Zeke Moreau."

"You want me to kill him."

"It's worth any price."

"I told you...I don't murder men in cold blood."

"Then I just want protection."

"How badly?"

"Desperately. You know that."

"Show me."

She stepped toward him and placed her hands around his neck. Suddenly she realized that she hadn't the least idea of what to do. Instinct guided her, instinct and nothing more.

She stepped closer, pressing against him so that she could feel the length of his naked body through the thin silk of her gown. She wound her arms around his neck and came up on tiptoe to press her lips against his, summoning up the memory of the kiss he had given her. She felt him, felt the instrument of his desire pulsing against her. She felt the muscles of his chest and belly and thighs. Then she felt his arms, powerful around her.

Then she plunged her tongue into his mouth and the world began to spin. She had come to seduce him, and she was ready to fall against him, longing for him to sweep her away.

To help her...

She felt the passion in him as he held her, and for a moment, victory was hers. She burned, she longed, with an astonishing hunger, and she could not know where it would lead. His lips held hers, his mouth devoured hers, and with each second that passed she entered deeper into a world that was pure sensation. Her pulse soared, and there was a pounding in her ears that was like the rush of the sea. His kiss was her life, his body was her support. She was afraid, and she was ecstatic.

And then he suddenly pushed her away.

His breathing was coming rough and ragged.

He watched her for a long, long moment. She felt his eyes on her, felt them as she would have felt an approaching storm. Then he shook his head.

"Go to bed, Kristin."

She inhaled sharply, furiously. "You let me make a complete fool of myself and then you— Damn you!"

Kristin slammed her fists against his shoulders, catching him off guard. He staggered, and she found the doorknob. Throwing the door open, she tore across the hall. She threw herself onto her own bed, tears hovering behind her lashes, fury rising in her throat.

The door crashed open behind her, and she spun around. He had followed her across the hall without even bothering to dress.

"Get out of here!" she snapped, enraged.

He ignored her and strode calmly toward the bed. Kristin shot up, determined to fight. It was all to no avail. His long stride quickly brought him to her. She came to her knees hastily, but he joined her on the bed, grabbing her hands and pressing her down.

"I should scream!" she told him. "Samson would come and—"

"Then scream."

She held her breath. He pressed her down on the bed and straddled her.

"Why won't you leave me alone?"

"You wanted to make a deal," he said harshly.

"What?"

"You said you wanted to make a deal. All right. Let's talk. I'm willing to negotiate."

PART 2   The Lover

Chapter Four

Kristin was glad the room was steeped in darkness. His features were shadowed, his body was shadowed, and she prayed that her own emotions were hidden by the night. She wanted to hate him. She could not. She wanted to think, to reason, and she could think of nothing but the hard male body so hot and intimate against her own.

He had come here, naked, to accept her proposition, it seemed. And yet he was angry again, angrier even than before. Hard and bitter and angry.

Moonlight cast a sudden soft glow over the room. She saw his features, and they were harsh, taut, almost cruel, as if he were fighting some inner pain.

"Negotiate?" she whispered.

"First, Miss Kristin, if you're going to play a game of chance, make sure you're playing with a full deck."

"I don't know what—"

"Exactly. That's why I'm going to explain things to you. I'll meet any man in a fair fight, but I won't go out and commit murder, not for you, not for myself, not for anyone. Do you understand?"

She nodded. She didn't understand him at all, but she was suddenly too afraid to do anything else. She had lost her mind. The war and the bloodshed had made her insane. She, Kristin McCahy, raised to live up to the highest standards of Southern womanhood, was lying on her bed with a naked stranger.

And she wasn't screaming.

"No involvement, Miss Kristin." The mock drawl was back in his voice, making her wonder again where he hailed from. She was filled with awareness of him. His muscled chest was plastered with crisp dark hair. She thought of how quickly he had drawn his Colts and his rifle, and she shivered. He carried with him an aura of danger that drew her to him despite her best intentions.

His sex pulsed against her belly, and she fought wildly to keep her eyes glued to his. It was all she could do to remember that she had intended to seduce him, to leave him gasping and longing and aching, his tongue hanging out for her.

He would never long for her that way, she realized now. Nor would he be denied. He had mocked her, but now he was determined to have her, and she felt sure he must despise her more with each passing second.

She steeled herself and whispered harshly, "No involvement. You needn't worry. I need a gunslinger. I could never love one."

A slight smile curved his lip. "This deal is made on my terms, lady. No involvement, no questions. And I won't murder Zeke. I'll go after him when I can. I'll do my damnedest to keep you and Shannon safe and your place together. But I've got other commitments, too, Kristin. And I can't forget them."

She didn't say anything. She didn't know what to say or do, didn't know where to go from here. This was so easy for him. He was so casual. He didn't even seem to know he was naked.

He touched her cheek, brushing it with his fingertips. "Why?" he said suddenly.

She shook her head, uncomprehending. "Why what?"

"This is all Zeke wanted."

"I hate Zeke. I hate him more than you could ever imagine. He killed my father. I'd rather bed a bison than that bastard."

"I see. And I'm a step above a bison?"

"A step below."

"I can still leave."

Panic filled her. She wanted to reach out and keep him from disappearing, but her pride wouldn't let her. Then she realized that he was smiling again, that he was amused. He leaned down low and spoke to her softly. His breath caressed her flesh, and the soft hair of his beard teased her chin. "There's one more point to this bargain, Miss McCahy."

Her heart was suddenly pounding mercilessly, her body aching, her nerves screaming.

"What's that, Slater?"

"I like my women hungry. No, ma'am, maybe that's not enough. I like them starving."

Words and whispers could do so much. As much as his slow, lazy, taunting smile. Fever ran through her, rife and rampant. She wanted to strike him because she felt so lost, and in spite of herself, she was afraid. She wasn't afraid he would hurt her. She might have gone insane, but she believed with all her heart that he would never hurt her. And she wondered, too, if this madness hadn't been spawned by the very way he made her feel, alive as she had never been before, haunted and shaken and...hungry, hungry for some sweet sensation that teased her mind and heart when he was near.

And yet she lay stiff and unyielding, numbed by the fear that swept through her, the fear that she would be unable to please him, the fear that she didn't have what it would take to hold him. Women... He had used the plural of the word. He liked his women hungry....

No, starving.

She didn't know him, and she didn't want involvement any more than he did, and yet this very intimacy was involvement. Even as she lay there, unable to move, she felt a painful stirring of jealousy. She had sacrificed so very much pride and dignity and morality for this man, and he was herding her together with every other female he had ever known.

He touched her chin. Then he brushed her lips with his, with the soft sweep of his mustache.

"Hungry, sweetheart." She sensed his smile, hovering above her in the dark. "This is as exciting as bedding a large chunk of ice."

She struck out at him blindly, but he caught her arms and lowered his weight onto her. She clenched her teeth as his laughing eyes drew near.

"Excuse me, Mr. Slater. My experience is limited. You wouldn't let me run out and screw a ranch hand, remember?"

"Kristin, damn you—"

"No, damn you!" she retorted, painfully close to tears. This couldn't be it. This couldn't be the night, the magic night she had wondered about in her dreams. No, it couldn't be, she thought bitterly. In her dreams this night had

come after she had been married. And Adam had been in her dreams. And there
had been nothing ugly or awkward about it. There hadn't even been any nude
bodies, except beneath the sheets, and even then she had been cloaked all in
white and he had whispered about how much he loved her and how beautiful
she was and it had been wondrously pure and innocent....

She hadn't known these feelings then. And she hadn't known she could sell
herself to a man who didn't even really want her.

"Please!" she cried suddenly, trying to escape his touch. Tears were beginning to sting her eyes, and she didn't want him to see them. She couldn't bear
any more humiliation. "Just leave me alone. I—I can't be what you want, I
can't—"

"Kristin!"

She went still when she heard the pained tenderness in his voice. He touched
her cheek gently. Then he lay beside her and swept her into his arms.

She was stunned to realize that he was trembling, too, that his body was
racked by heat and fever. He murmured her name again and again, and his lips
brushed over her brow, as light as air. "Don't you see? I don't want to need
you like this. I don't want to want you!"

There was passion in his voice, dark and disturbing. There was bitterness in
it, too, pained and fervent, and as he continued to touch her, his emotions seemed
to burn and sear her along with his touch. His hands were tender, then demanding, then gentle again.

"I don't want to want you," he murmured, "but God help me, I do."

Then he kissed her, and there was nothing left to worry about, for she was
suddenly riding swiftly across the dark heavens and there was no time to think,
no time for reason. She could only hold tight.

It all seemed to come together, everything she had felt since she had first set
eyes on the man. Hungry...his mouth was hungry, and he was devouring her.
His lips molded and shaped hers, and his tongue seemed to plunge to the very
depths of her being, licking her deep, deep inside, taunting her, arousing her still
more.

His hands roamed her body with abandon, abandon and a kind of recklessness.
He caressed her tenderly, even delicately, then touched her with a force that told
her that he wanted to brand her, wanted to leave his mark on her.

She never knew where the awe and the trembling and fear ceased and something entirely different began. She didn't even know when she lost the elegant
nightgown brought west in her mother's trousseau, for his touch was so sweeping, so swift, so heady. She knew only that her breast was suddenly bare and
his mouth was upon it. He cupped the soft mound of flesh with his hand, his
lips hard around the nipple, drawing, suckling, raking the peak with his teeth as
he demanded more and more.

She nearly screamed. She had never imagined such intimacy, and she never
dreamed that there could be anything like the sensation that gripped her now
with burning fingers, drawing a line of raw excitement down her spine and into
her loins. She clutched his shoulders, barely aware that her nails were digging
into him, that she was clutching him as if he were a lifeline in a storm-swept
sea.

And still the tempest raged. His lips found her throat, and he raked his palm
down the length of her, kneading her thigh and her buttocks. He moved swiftly,
and she tried to follow, but she could not, for she was breathless, gasping in
shock and amazement at each new sensation. He began anew. He touched her,

held her, all over again. His lips trailed a line down the valley between her breasts to her navel, and the soft, bristling hair of his mustache and beard taunted her naked flesh mercilessly. She felt his knee force her thighs apart, and she knew that she was close to the point of no return, to being changed forever, and even then she could not keep pace with the winds that buffeted her.

And then he stopped. His palms on either side of her head, he caressed her with that curious tenderness he possessed and lowered his head to hers, whispering into her mouth.

"Hungry?"

She didn't want to face it. It was too new, too startling. She lowered her head and nodded, but it wasn't enough, not for him.

"Kristin?"

"Please..."

"Tell me."

"Oh, God!" she cried, trying to twist away from him. His palms held her fast, and her eyes were forced to meet his. Her lips were moist and her hair was a mass of gold between them, startlingly pale against the darkness of his chest.

He smiled at her, watching her as he drew his hand down to the pulse at her throat, then over her breast, down, down, to draw a circle on her abdomen and then plunge lower. He kept his eyes on her as he stroked her upper thigh. Then, suddenly, he swept his touch intimately inside her, moving with a sure, languorous rhythm.

She cried out again and tried to burrow against him, but he held her away from him. He watched her eyes, watched the rise and fall of her breasts, watched her gasp for air.

He caught her lips with his own, caught them and kissed them, and then he whispered against them again.

"Yes. You are...hungry."

Was this it? Was this the hunger he demanded, this burning sensation that filled her and engulfed her? She was grateful for the darkness, for the night, for with the moon behind a cloud, she could believe that all her sins were hidden, all that she had bartered, all that she had given so freely. She couldn't believe how she lay there with him, and yet she would not have changed it for the world. A soft cry escaped her, and she threw her arms around his neck, hiding against his chest at last. Something surged within her, and she gasped and murmured against his chest, barely aware that her hips were pulsing to his rhythm, that he hadn't ceased taunting her, that his strokes were growing more enticing.

Cole knew vaguely that he shouldn't be there. He should have told her that morning that nothing could make him stay, nothing could make him help her. She was the last thing in the world he needed. He had commitments of his own, and come heaven or hell or death itself, he meant to see them through.

And this innocence...

This, too, was the last thing he needed. She was hardened, and there were jagged edges to her. War did that. War and death and pain and blood. But the innocence was still there, too. He had thought he could make her run, and he had thought he could be strong enough himself not to touch her. He was used up. He knew that. He was used up, and she deserved more than that. He was still alive, though, still breathing, and she touched every raw cord of desire within him. Maybe he had known what was to come, and maybe he hadn't expected it at all, but now that it was happening, he couldn't even try to deny it. She spun a golden web of arousal and passion as soft and silky and luxuriant as the long strands of hair that tangled around them both, dampened by the glistening sheen of their bodies. She had beautiful features, exquisite features, fine, high cheekbones, a small, slim nose and eyes like an endless blue sky, darkly fringed with rich lashes and glazed now with blossoming passion. And her mouth…it was full and giving, sensual in laughter, sensual when her lips parted beneath his own. She was soft, she was velvet and she was created for desire, with high, firm breasts, a slim waist and flaring hips, and smooth, fascinating buttocks. He hadn't meant to stay. He hadn't meant to come here, and he hadn't meant to stay. He hadn't meant to touch her.…

But he had.

And she moved. She moved with exquisite grace. She made sweet, soft sounds that entered his loins and caused the blood to pound in his head so that he could think no more. Only one thought guided him, and that was that he had to have her, had to have her or go mad. Her nipples pressed against his chest, and she arched against his hand. Despite his best efforts, the agony of the past was erased, the vengeance of the future forgotten. Even the present meant nothing at all. All that mattered was this woman, and she was hot and wet and begging for release.

He pulled her to him almost roughly. Her eyes widened, and he commanded her to hold tight. He caught her lips in a heady kiss and swept his hands beneath her. He fought hard to remember her innocence. He kissed her with sweeping ardor, and then he entered her.

He was slow, achingly slow, and she was sleek and damp, a hot sheath ready to encase him, and still he felt her shudder, heard the sudden agonized cry that she muffled against his chest.

He'd heard it before. On his wedding day.

The irony, the bitter, bitter irony touched him for a moment, and for a moment he hated her and himself. For a moment he was still. Then he felt her shudder again and thought she might be crying, and then he was whispering things without thinking.

Yes…he'd been here before. Making love tenderly to a woman for the very first time. Her very first time.

He held her, caressed her, promised to help her. And then he moved again, slowly at first, carefully, tenderly.

And then she was moving beneath him, subtly at first. She was taking him in, and the tears were gone, and the shock was gone, and the desperate tension was growing again.

Care and consideration left him. A thirst that he was frantic to slake ripped through him and into his loins. He couldn't remember ever being so fevered, and still the sensations grew. He touched her breasts, struck anew by their beauty. He inhaled the clean, sweet scent of her tangled hair and the fever soared higher and higher. He wrapped her legs tightly around him and cupped her buttocks, and rocking hard, filled her with himself again and again. He threw back his head and rough sound tore from him as the relief began to shake and convulse through his body. Again and again he spilled into her. She cried out, her voice ragged. He was aware that she had reached some sweet satisfaction, and he was pleased. She fell still, and the last of the fever raked through him. He thrust deep, deep inside her one last time. It was shattering, and he couldn't remember when he had known such a deeply satisfying climax.

He fell to her side, covered with sweat, breathing heavily.

She was silent. He touched her cheek and found tears there.

Suddenly he was furious with himself and with her. This should never have happened. She should have married some young buck and worn white, and she should have been loved, not just desired.

She twisted away from his touch, and he let her go. She turned her back on him, and he wondered if she was crying again. Maybe she had a right to, but it was damned insulting. He'd taken even greater care with her than he had with—Elizabeth. With Elizabeth.

There. He dared to think her name.

Though he gritted his teeth and wished it away, agony gripped him from head to toe. He wondered if the pain would ever leave him.

"You can...you can go back now," Kristin said suddenly.

"What?" His voice was sharp.

"Our deal." She spoke softly, her voice a mere whisper, as if tears hovered behind her words, tears and just a touch of anxiety. "It's—it's made now, isn't it?"

He hesitated before he answered her. "Yes, your bloody bargain is made, Miss McCahy."

"Then you could...you could go back. Across the hall."

He didn't know what demon seized him. He didn't care if he was heard by the others in the house, didn't care about anything at all. He sat up in a sudden fury and wrenched her around to face him. He spoke bitingly, trying to make every word sting like the stroke of a lash.

"Not on your life, my little prima donna. You invited me in here. Now you've got me. That was the game, Kristin. You knew it was going to go by my rules—"

"My God!" she cried, jerking away from his touch. "Have you no consideration, no—"

"Compassion? Not a whit. This is what you wanted, and now you've got it."

She was beautiful still, he thought. The moonlight was playing over her breasts, and they were damp and shimmering and very, very fine, the nipples still enlarged and hard. He felt a quickening inside him all over again, and with it felt the return of the pain. The pain of betrayal. It was all right with whores, with tavern girls. It was something else with this innocent young beauty.

He scowled fiercely and turned his back on her. "Go to sleep, Kristin."

She didn't move. She didn't answer him. Not for endless seconds.

"Go to sleep?" she repeated incredulously.

"Damn it, yes, go to sleep." He swung around again and pressed her down on the bed. She started to fight him, and he wasn't in the mood to take it. Dark anger was in him, dark, brooding anger, and though he didn't mean to be cruel to her, he didn't seem to be able to help himself. He caught her shoulders and shook them. "Good night, Kristin. Go to sleep."

"Leave," she said stubbornly.

"I'll be damned if I will."

"Then I'll leave."

"And I'll be damned if you'll leave, either. Now go to sleep!"

He turned around, offering her his back once again. He didn't know why he had started this bout, but now that he had begun it, he wasn't about to lose.

He felt it when she started to rise, and he turned with frightening speed, sweeping his arm around her waist and holding her still. He felt her heart beating like that of a doe.

"Go to sleep!"

He heard her teeth grating, but she didn't move, not again. He knew she was planning to wait until he fell asleep, then slip away.

He smiled. She had another think coming. He would feel her slightest movement. He would awaken.

When she did try to move, he kept his eyes closed and held her fast. He heard her swearing softly, and he heard the threat of sobs coming to her whispering voice.

But then it was she who fell into an exhausted sleep. And it was he who awoke first with the morning. He stood and stretched and padded naked to the window and looked out on a beautiful summer's day. It was a fine ranch, he thought. Then he sighed, and he knew that she would think she had sold herself dearly in the night.

He had sold himself dearly, too. He had sold his honor, and he would have to stay, and he would have to protect her.

He walked over to the bed. The evidence of their night together was painfully obvious in the twisted bedding.

Her face was covered by long, soft tendrils of hair that picked up gold from the sun. A hand seemed to tighten around his heart and squeeze. Cole stepped closer to the bed and covered Kristin with the top sheet and the comforter. Then he stepped to the door, glanced out and returned to the room across the hall to wash and dress.

Kristin knew it was late when she awoke. She opened her eyes and saw that the sun had risen high, then closed her eyes again and discovered that she was shaking.

She had almost believed that she had dreamed the entire episode.

But she hadn't. Cole Slater was gone, but he had definitely been there, and just thinking about everything that had happened made her shake again and burn crimson to the roots of her hair.

A knock sounded at her door. "Kristin?"

It was Shannon. Kristin sat bolt upright and looked at the bed. The comforter seemed to hide the sins of the night.

"Shannon, just a minute!" she cried out. Her gown was on the floor beside the bed. She made a dive for it, wincing at the soreness that plagued her thighs. Then she realized that the gown was torn and ragged, and she knew why it had seemed to melt away the night before. Bitterly she wound it into a ball, stuffed it into her dresser and dragged out an old flannel gown. Breathless, she told Shannon to come in.

Shannon came in with a pot of coffee and a cup and breakfast on a silver tray. Kristin stared at it blankly and arched a brow at her younger sister.

"Good morning, sleepyhead," Shannon told her.

"Breakfast? In bed?" The ranch was a place where they barely eked out their existence. Breakfast in bed was a luxury they never afforded themselves. "After I've slept all morning?"

"Delilah was going to wake you. Cole said that maybe things had been hard on you lately and that maybe you needed to sleep."

"Oh, Cole said that, did he?"

Shannon ignored the question. "I rode out to the north pasture with Cole and Pete, and everything's going fine for the day."

Kristin kissed her sister's cheek and plopped on the bed, wincing again. It even hurt a little to sit.

She felt her face flood with color again, and she lowered her head, trying to hide her blush behind her hair. She still didn't know if she hated him, or if her feeling had become something different, something softer.

A little flush of fever seemed to touch her. She was breathing too fast, and her heart was hammering. She couldn't forget the night. She couldn't forget how she had felt, and she didn't know whether to be amazed or grateful or awed— or ashamed. The future loomed before them. They had a deal. He had said he would stay. And he hadn't left her room, and she—

She couldn't help wondering what he intended for their personal future together. Did he mean to do it...again?

"My Lord, Kristin, but you're flushed!" Shannon said with alarm.

"I'm all right," Kristin said hastily. She sipped the coffee too quickly and burned her lip. She set the cup down. "This was really sweet. The breakfast."

"Oh," Shannon said nonchalantly, "this was Cole's idea, too. He seemed to think you might have a little trouble getting up this morning."

"Oh, he did, did he?" She bit so hard into a piece of bacon that her teeth snapped together. He was laughing at her again, it seemed, and he didn't even have the decency to do it to her face. She longed for the chance to give him a good hard slap just once.

She caught herself. He had warned her. They were playing by his rules. And there was only one thing she was gaining from it all. Safety. She had agreed to the rules. She had meant to seduce him, she had meant for it all to happen, she had wanted the deal. It was just that she wasn't at all sure who had seduced whom.

"Where is Cole now?" she asked Shannon. She was surprised to find that she had a ravenous appetite.

Shannon shrugged. "I'm not sure. But do you know what?" she asked excitedly.

"No. What?"

"He says he's going to stay around for a while. Isn't that wonderful, Kristin?"

Kristin swallowed and nodded. "Yes. It's wonderful."

"Samson says it's a miracle. He says God has looked down on us with mercy at long last."

"The Lord certainly does work in mysterious ways," Kristin murmured dryly.

Shannon, who had seated herself at the foot of the bed, leaped up and hugged Kristin. "We're going to make it," she whispered. "We're really going to make it."

She had underestimated Shannon, Kristin realized. She had felt their father's death every bit as keenly as Kristin had.

And because she felt it so strongly, she had learned to hate, just as Kristin had.

"I've got to get back downstairs. Delilah is baking bread and making preserves and I promised to help."

Kristin nodded. "I'll be right down, too."

When her sister had left, Kristin washed hastily. She couldn't help remembering every place he had touched her, everything he had done to her. And then, naturally, she started trembling again, thinking about the feeling that had come over her. In the midst of carnage, a brief, stolen moment of ecstasy.

Shameful ecstasy.

Ecstasy.

She wondered if it had ever really been, if it could ever come again.

She dressed, trying desperately to quit thinking. If she didn't, she would walk around all day as red as a beet.

She dressed for work. There was some fencing down on the north side, and she had told Pete she'd come out and look at it. The stash of gold hidden in the hayloft was dwindling, but they could afford to repair the fencing. And if she could just hang on to her stock a while longer, she could command fair prices from any number of buyers in the spring. She had to remember that she was fighting for the land. Nothing else mattered.

In breeches and boots, Kristin started for the doorway. Then she remembered her bedding, and the telltale sheets.

Delilah usually did the beds. She kept the house with Shannon's help. Samson kept it from falling apart. Pete and Kristin ran the ranch. That was just the way things had worked out.

But she didn't want Delilah doing her bed. Not today.

He liked his women hungry. *Women.* Plural.

Kristin let loose with a furious oath and ripped the sheets from the bed. She jumped up and down on them a few times for good measure, then realized how ridiculous she was being and scooped them up. She carried them down with her to the stables, stuffing them into the huge trash bin. She would burn them later, with some of the empty feed bags.

She headed for the stable, determined to saddle Debutante and ride out. She paused in the doorway, aware that Cole was there, brushing down his black thoroughbred stallion. It was a beautiful animal, Kristin thought.

Very like the man who owned him.

She wasn't ready to see Cole Slater yet. She almost turned around, ready to change her plans for the day to avoid facing him. But he had sensed her there, and he turned, and there seemed to be nothing for her to do but stand there and meet his stare.

It was long, and it was pensive, and it gave no quarter. She would never accuse the man of being overly sensitive or overly polite. His gray eyes were sharp and curious, and she still thought he must be amused by her, because he was smiling slightly. There were times when she thought he hated her, but then he would stare at her in a way that warmed her and offered her a fleeting tenderness.

Very much like the way he made love...

She shouldn't have thought it. The color that had so alarmed her rose to fill her face, and she had to lower her eyes to still the blush. She prayed fervently that she could appear sophisticated for just this one encounter. But it was impossible to stand here now, fully clothed, and not remember what had gone on the night before. Things could never be the same again. She could never see life the same way again. She could never see him the same way again, for she knew the power of the form beneath the shirt and jeans, and he knew all that made up the woman she was.

"Sleep well?" he asked her after a moment.

There was something grating in the question, something mocking, and that helped. She squared her shoulders and tried to walk by him, heading for Debutante's stall. He caught her arm and swung her around. His eyes were serious now.

"Where do you think you're going?"

"Out to the north pasture. I have to see the fencing. I should have gone yesterday, but..." She paused, her voice fading away.

He shook his head impatiently. "I'll meet Pete."

"But it's my ranch!"

"And it's my life, Miss McCahy." He dropped her arm and put his hands, the currycomb in one, on his hips. "You're taking up my time. We made some ridiculous deal—"

"Ridiculous deal!" She was choked with rage. She was going to slap him this time. Right across the face.

She didn't make it. He caught her wrist. "I'm sorry, Kristin. I didn't mean it that way."

"I'm so terribly sorry if I disappointed you."

She'd thought his eyes would drop with shame. They didn't. Hers did. He was still smiling.

"You didn't disappoint me. You surpassed my wildest expectations. I'm sorry. I didn't mean to insult you. I meant that you really should be the hell out of here."

"You're not reneging?" she asked crisply.

He smiled slowly, tilted back his plumed hat and shook his head. "No, Kristin," he said softly. His low, grating voice sent tremors up her spine. "I never renege on a deal. But I'll be damned if I'm going to stick around so you can run off and be swept away beneath my very nose."

"But I—"

"Forget it, Kristin. I warned you. We play by my rules. And you're not riding out anywhere."

"But—"

"You ride out, I ride out."

"But...but you've already been...paid!" Kristin exploded.

His brows shot up, and his lips curled mockingly. "Paid?"

"You know what I mean."

He shook his head. "I sure as hell don't! That was it? One night in your arms and I'm supposed to gladly lay down my life and die?"

"You are no Southern gentleman."

"Did I say I was?"

"You are no gentleman at all!"

"I never claimed to be one, Kristin. In fact, I haven't made any claims to you at all. Remember that."

"I find it difficult to forget."

"Are you trying to renege?" he queried softly.

She drew herself up stiffly, determined to counter-attack. "So you're not from the South?"

"Does it matter where I'm from?"

"Maybe it does!"

He caught her hand and held it. They stared at one another. Behind them, the massive black stallion snorted. Cole stared at her seriously for a long moment and then said, "No, it doesn't, Kristin. Nothing about me matters at all. No questions. No involvement. Remember that."

She jerked her hand away. "I'll remember, Mr. Slater."

She started toward Debutante's stall. Maybe she couldn't go riding, but she had to get away. She would take a moment to stroke the mare's velvet nose, and then she would escape. She didn't know how she would be able to bear it, though. She would be like a caged animal with all the emotions that were playing havoc in her heart.

She patted Debutante's nose and promised the horse in a low whisper that she would come out and give her a good grooming as soon as *he* was out of the stable.

Then she turned around, determined to walk out of the stables with her head held high, determined to hang on to her few remaining shreds of dignity.

"By the way, Kristin..." he began.

She paused, her back to him. She straightened, stiffening her shoulders, and turned in a swift circle. He wasn't watching her. He was combing the stallion's shining flanks.

"Why don't you move your things into the larger bedroom? We'll have more space there."

"What?"

"You heard me."

"But—but everyone will know! And just how many times do you intend to...to..."

"Get paid?" he suggested politely. He didn't even seem to be paying attention to her. He stroked the stallion's ears, then stared directly at her. "You want blood, Kristin. That's an expensive commodity. And as far as everyone knowing is concerned, that's exactly what I want."

"But—"

"I make the rules, remember?"

"I can't! I can't go by this one—"

"Delilah will understand. So will Shannon and Sam and Pete and everyone else. And if Zeke Moreau hears anything about it, he'll get the message, too."

"But—"

"Do it, Kristin."

She spun around in a dead fury again. She didn't look back She stormed into the house, wishing desperately that *she* were a man. She would run away and join the army in two seconds.

She wouldn't even give a damn whose army she joined Just as long as it was someone who hated Quantrill and his animals.

"Kristin, that you?" Delilah came into the hallway, smiling. "Want to give us a hand with the wax? I could surely use some help stirring. I've got Shannon jarring and sealing while I've been kneading the bread."

"Er...of course," Kristin said. She'd much, much rather run away and join the army.

Shannon gave her a bright smile when she came into the kitchen. "Did you find Cole?"

"Yes. I found him."

Shannon nodded. It was obvious that she approved of it all. They were all mad, Kristin decided.

"He wants me to move into Pa's bedroom with him," she blurted out.

Shannon had been holding a jar of jam, sealing it with wax. The jar slipped from her fingers and shattered loudly on the floor.

Delilah sent the bread she was kneading into the air. It fell back on the block table.

Both of them stared at her. Then they glanced at one another. Neither of them said a word.

"Say something!" Kristin demanded. "Help me make some kind of a decision!"

"You can't!" Shannon gasped.

"Seems to me like you've already made your decision," Delilah said softly. "But it ain't right. It just ain't right. Still..."

"He's much, much better than Zeke Moreau," Shannon said. She stooped to pick up the broken glass and the jam that was seeping into the floorboards. "Yes, maybe you have to. And he *is* much better than Zeke."

"So that's why I'm sleeping with a stranger." Kristin sank into a chair before the fire. "I cannot believe I'm doing this," she murmured.

"These are different times," Shannon murmured, staring at the floor. She looked up at her sister. "Kristin, we can't be blind to the facts! We need him. We need him, or else we just have to give up and pull out."

"Shannon!" Kristin exploded. "You're shocked, and you know it. Pa must be turning in his grave. We don't even know where Cole Slater comes from!"

Shannon's beautiful blue eyes widened. "But of course we do, Kristin."

"What?"

Shannon smiled broadly. "He's from Missouri. He was originally from Virginia, but his family bought a big spread out here. I think he comes from tobacco money, a lot of it. He went to West Point. He was in the same class as Jeb Stuart!"

Kristin stared at her sister, who appeared about to swoon. Shannon thought that the Confederate general Jeb Stuart was the handsomest, most gallant gentleman in the whole world. Shannon's reaction to Stuart's name didn't surprise her, but the fact that she seemed to know so much about Cole stunned her.

"What?" she repeated numbly.

Shannon sighed with supreme patience, as if she were the elder, explaining things to a sullen child.

"He's a Virginian, Kristin, moved to Missouri. He went to West Point. Once upon a time he was in the army in Kansas. He and Stuart served together."

"Wonderful," Kristin murmured.

So he *was* a Southerner. And he wasn't in uniform. He was one of them, one of the breed that ran with Quantrill....

She was a Southerner herself, she thought dully. Not all Southerners were like Zeke Moreau.

But Cole...

Cole had talked freely to Shannon. But the questions hadn't all been answered yet.

He had gone to West Point. He had served in the Union Army before the war with the gallant Southern calvary officer, Jeb Stuart.

But he wasn't wearing a uniform now. Not the Union's, and not the Confederacy's. Why not?

Delilah stirred something over the fire. She wiped her hands on her apron. "Well, Kristin? What do we do? If you want, I'll go move your things."

Kristin swallowed. She wanted to protest. She wanted to refuse Cole Slater. She looked at Delilah. Delilah wasn't making any judgments.

Kristin nodded. She could give up the place or she could hold tight to Cole Slater. She really had no choice. But she vowed to herself that she'd find out everything there was to know about the man.

Chapter Five

Kristin spent the day worrying about the night ahead. She prowled around upstairs, trying to keep busy. Though she hated it, she did what Cole had told her to, taking a few of her dresses and nightshirts and putting them in the armoire in her parents' bedroom.

Shannon came upstairs while she was at it. There was something about her knowing glance that made Kristin feel terribly ashamed. "Cole—Mr. Slater— thinks that Zeke ought to think there's something...um, that he and I, that..."

"I understand," Shannon said softly. Even her innocence was dead, Kristin thought. There was an awkward silence, but then Shannon came into the room and hugged her. "I like him," she told Kristin. "I like him a whole lot."

"Only because he knows Jeb Stuart."

Shannon made a face. "That helps." She sat down on the bed. "What happened here?" she queried softly.

"What do you mean?" Kristin asked her.

"So many men are so fine. General Lee is such a gentleman, by all accounts. And Jeb Stuart is so dashing! And then out here..."

"We get the bushwhackers and the jayhawkers," Kristin finished for her. She sat down beside Shannon and hugged her. "And don't forget," she reminded her, "we have a brother fighting in Mr. Lincoln's army."

"I never forget!" Shannon said.

They sat there in silence for a long time. Then suddenly, there was a volley of shots from outside. Kristin leaped to her feet and raced to the window.

Cole was out back with Samson. He'd set a few rows of old liquor and tonic bottles on the back fence to serve as makeshift targets. He'd already shot up the first set.

Kristin watched as he reloaded, then twirled his six-shooter in his hand and shoved it back in its holster. He paused. Then, in the wink of an eye, he cleared away another row. Then he spoke to Samson, and Kristin realized that it was a lesson.

Then it was Samson's turn with the guns. Kristin strained to hear Cole's words.

"Quantrill's boys usually carry four or five Colts, a shotgun or a rifle or maybe both. That's why they keep licking the pants off the Union troops. They're well armed, and the boys in blue are still trying to fire off muzzle-loading carbines. Zeke will always be well armed. So we've always got to be prepared to outshoot him in return. You understand, Sam?"

"Yes, Mr. Slater, that I do."

"Let's try it again. Hold your hand steady, and squeeze the trigger, don't jerk it."

Cole took off his plumed hat, ran his fingers through his hair and set the hat back on his head, low over his eyes. Then he said, "Go!" and Samson drew. He shattered a fair number of the bottles, then laughed. Cole slapped him on the back, congratulating him. Then the men's voices grew low, and Kristin couldn't hear any more.

Suddenly Cole looked up at the window. It was too late. She couldn't draw away.

He smiled and waved. She almost waved back, but then she realized that Shannon had come up beside her and that it was her sister he was waving to, because she was waving down to him.

"We're moving Kristin in!" Shannon called down.

Kristin was mortified. She felt his eyes on her, she saw his slow, lazy smile. She wanted to hit Shannon over the head. She backed away from the window instead.

"You coming up?" Shannon called.

"Shannon!" Kristin hissed.

But Cole shook his head. He looked handsome then, as tall as Samson, and hard and lean in his long coat and his plumed hat. "Tell your sister I'm on my way out to find Pete. Might be gone awhile. If I can take care of some things today, I will."

Shannon turned to Kristin. "Cole said—"

"I heard what Cole said."

"Shannon!" Cole said.

"Yes, Cole?"

"Tell your sister I may be back late. Tell her she doesn't have to wait up."

Shannon turned to Kristin. "Cole said—"

"I heard what Cole said!"

Kristin spun around and stormed out of the room. She returned to her own room and slammed the door. She sat down on her own bed and pressed her hands against her temples. She had a staggering headache, and her nerves were as shattered as the bottles Cole had shot up.

Well, he had shattered her world, too.

She needed to get this over with quickly. She needed him to be around. She wanted him. She hated him.

She wished to God she knew him. She wished to God she could get to know him. But she didn't think he would let anyone get close to him. Anyone at all.

No involvement...

She didn't want any involvement. And he couldn't possibly make her as nervous as Zeke Moreau made her hateful.

Or could he?

If he came back at all that night, Kristin never knew it. She lay on her parents' bed until the wee hours of the morning, and then exhaustion claimed her. When she awoke, it was almost noon. No one came for her. When she dressed and went downstairs, Delilah was busy with a big pot of lye and Shannon was putting their last two-year-old colt through his paces. Kristin longed to do something, to ride somewhere, but Samson found her in the stable and warned her that Cole had said she should stay close to home. She bit her lip but did as she was told, and Samson proudly showed her something of what he had learned.

Kristin was impressed with his newfound skill with a gun, and she told him so, but then she rested her chin on the fence and sighed. "Is it enough, Samson? Is it enough against Zeke?"

"Maybe not me alone, Miss Kristin, but Mr. Slater had all the boys out here this morning, and he can teach a whole lot about gun play, as well as practice it."

"You sound like you like him a lot, Samson."

"Yep. Yes, miss, I do. He complimented me on my language this morning, and when I told him how big your pa was on learning he said that he thought fine men came in both black and white, and that he was mighty proud to know me."

Kristin smiled. "That's nice, Samson. That's mighty nice."

They were both silent for a moment. Then Kristin began to grow uncomfortable, wondering what he really thought of what was going on with Cole Slater.

"The world just ain't the same anymore, Miss Kristin," Samson said at last. "The world just ain't the same." He chewed on a long blade of grass and stared out at the pastureland. "No, the world just ain't the same, and we can only pray that it'll right itself when this awful war is over."

Kristin nodded. Then she turned to him and gave him a big hug. She didn't know what she'd do without him and Delilah.

She didn't see Cole again all that day and night. He was still out with Pete and the boys at dinnertime, and later, much later, she heard laughter and the strains of Pete's fiddle coming from the bunkhouse. That night she slept alone again in the big sleigh bed in her parents' room.

In the morning she didn't know if he had ever come to bed or not. For some reason, she didn't think he had, and she wondered why he was taunting her this way when he seemed to have so little real interest in her. Her temper rose, but then she remembered that she should be grateful to have him here. And then she was afraid he would leave.

And then she hated him. He was supposed to want her. They were supposed to have a deal. She was supposed to loathe him for taking advantage of her weakness. But she was the one left wondering and wanting. No, not wanting. Merely curious, she assured herself. But she couldn't deny that she had been in a fever ever since he had come. She simply couldn't deny her emotions.

Then he was there. He was there all day. He passed her in the hallway and tipped his hat to her, a smile of amusement tugging at his lips.

"Wait!" she cried. "Where are you going?"

"Rounding up strays."

"Let me come."

His smile faded. "No."

"But—"

"My rules, Kristin."

"But—"

"My rules."

She gritted her teeth and stiffened, watching him for a moment in simmering silence. He smiled again. "But I will be back for supper this evening. Steak and sweet potatoes and Delilah's black-eyed peas, and blueberry pie for dessert. And then..." He let his voice trail off. Then he lifted his hat again and turned and left.

And she didn't even know where he had spent the night.

It was another wretched day. She fed the chickens. She groomed her horse. She played with little Daniel, marveling in spite of herself at the way the child grew daily. She wandered around upstairs. Then she found herself sitting at the foot of the big sleigh bed.

His blanket lay on the floor next to the dresser. Kristin hesitated, staring at it for a long while. Then she got up and went over to it.

And then she unrolled it and went through his personal belongings.

There wasn't much. If he had a wallet, he had it with him. There was a shaving mug and a tin plate, a leather sack of tobacco, another sack of coffee and a roll of hard tack.

And there was a small silver Daguerreotype frame.

Kristin stared at it for a moment then found the little silver clasp and flicked it open.

There were two pictures in the double frame. The first was of a woman alone, a very beautiful woman, with enormous eyes and dark hair and a dazzling smile.

In the second picture the woman was with a man. Cole.

He was in a U.S. Cavalry uniform, so the picture must have been made before the war. The woman wore a beautiful, voluminous gown with majestic hoops, and a fine bonnet with a slew of feathers. They weren't looking at the camera. They were looking at one another.

There was such tenderness, such love in their eyes, that Kristin felt she was intruding on something sacred. She closed the frame with a firm snap and put it back inside the blanket, trying to put everything back together as if she hadn't touched it at all. It didn't make any difference, she told herself dully. He should expect people who didn't know a thing about him to check up on him. No, that didn't wash, not at all, not even with her.

The woman was dead, she thought.

She didn't know how she knew, but she knew. Cole Slater had loved her, and Kristin was certain that he wouldn't be here with her now if the woman in the picture were still alive.

There seemed to be an ominous silence all over the house as dinnertime approached. Delilah had been out to feed the hands, and the table was set for the family.

Set for three.

They weren't using the fine service that evening. Shannon had set out the pewter plates, and the atmosphere in the dining room seemed as muted and subdued as the dull color of the dishes.

Cole had stayed out all day. Kristin had done her best to be useful, but the day had been a waste. There was no way out of it. She couldn't forget Cole's promise that he would be there that night, and she couldn't forget the woman in the picture, and she couldn't forget the startling array of emotions that it had all raised within her.

Kristin had dressed for dinner.

She was a rancher, and this ranch on the border between Kansas and Missouri was a far cry from the fine parlors and plantations back east, but she was still a woman and she loved clothes.

It was a weakness with her, Pa had told her once, but he'd had a twinkle in his eyes when he'd said it. He'd always been determined that his daughters should be ladies. Capable women, but ladies for all that. He had always been pleased to indulge her whims, letting her study fabrics, and to pick up her *Lady Godoy's* the minute the fashion magazine reached the local mercantile. Her armoire was still filled with gowns, and her trunks and dressers held an endless assortment of petticoats and hoops, chemises and corsets, stockings and pantalets. They had all lent a certain grace to life once upon a time. Before the carnage had begun. By day they had worked for their dream, and the dust and the tumbleweed of the prairie had settled on them. At night they had washed away the dust and the dirt, and after dinner Pa had settled back in his chair with a cigar and she and Shannon had taken turns at the spinet. Her own voice was passable. Shannon's was like that of a nightingale.

And there had been nights when Adam had been there, too. Sometimes winter had raged beyond the windows, but they had been warm inside, warmed by the fire and by the love and laughter that had surrounded them.

That was what Zeke had hated so much, she thought. He had never understood that laughter and love could not be bought or stolen. He had called her a traitor to the Southern cause, but she had never betrayed the South. She had merely learned to despise him, and so she had lost her father, and then Adam, too.

Today she could remember Adam all too clearly. He had loved books. He had always looked so handsome, leaning against the fireplace, his features animated as he spoke about the works of Hawthorne and Sir Walter Scott.

No one had told her that Adam was riding out after Zeke. She'd never had the chance to try to stop him.

And now she wondered painfully if she had ever really loved him. Oh, she had cared for him dearly. He had been a fine man, good and decent and caring, and he had often made her laugh.

But she had never, never thought of Adam in the way that she had Cole Slater, had never even imagined doing with Adam the things she had actually done with Cole Slater.

And she didn't love Cole Slater. She couldn't love him. No, she couldn't love him, not even now. How could a woman love a man who had treated her the way he had?

But how could she forget him? How could she forget all she had felt since she'd first seen the man? How could she forget all that had passed between them? Kristin realized that it was difficult just to be in the same room with him now. Her breath shortened instantly, and she couldn't keep her gaze steady, and she wanted to run away every time he looked her way. She couldn't look at him without remembering their night together, and when she did she wanted to crawl into a hole in the ground and hide. She was ashamed, not so much because of what she had done but because she had been so fascinated by it. Because she still felt the little trickles of excitement stir within her whenever he entered the room, whenever she felt his presence.

She knew instinctively when he came into the house for dinner.

Fall was coming on, and the evening was cool. She had dressed in a soft white velvet gown with black cord trim. The bodice was low, and the half sleeves were trimmed in black cord, too. The skirt was sweeping, and she had chosen to wear a hoop and three petticoats.

She'd made Delilah tie her corset so tightly that she wasn't sure she'd be able to breathe all evening.

Her appearance had suddenly become very, very important to her. He hadn't been cruel to her, but he had been mocking, and he'd warned her again and again that this terribly intimate thing between them had nothing to do with involvement. Her pride was badly bruised, and all she had to cling to was her dream of leaving him panting in the dust. Someday. When she didn't need him anymore.

She'd braided her hair and curled it high atop her head, except for one long lock that swept around the column of her neck and the curve of her shoulder to rest on the mound of her cleavage.

She never used rouge—Pa hadn't allowed it in the house—but she pinched her cheeks and bit her lips, to bring some color to her features. Still, when she gazed at her reflection in the mirror over the dresser—she had refused to dress in the other room—she was terribly pale, and she looked more like a nervous girl than a sophisticated woman in charge of her life, owner of her property, mistress of her own destiny.

She tried to sweep elegantly down the stairs, but her knees were weak, so she gave up and came down as quickly as she could. Shannon was setting cups on the table. She stared at Kristin with wide blue eyes, but she didn't say anything. Nor did Kristin have to question her about Cole.

"He's in Pa's office," Shannon mouthed. Kristin nodded. Nervously, she started through the house. She passed through the parlor and came around, pausing in the doorway.

He was sitting at her father's desk, reading the newspaper, and his brows were drawn into such a dark and brooding frown that she nearly turned away. Then he looked up. She was certain that he started for a moment, but he hid it quickly and stood politely. His gaze never left her.

"Bad news?" she asked him, looking at the paper.

He shrugged. "Not much of anything today," he said.

"No great Southern victory? No wonderful Union rout?"

"You sound bitter."

"I am."

"You got kin in the army?"

"My brother."

"North or South?"

"North. He's with an Illinois troop." Kristin hesitated. She didn't want him to feel that they were traitors to the Southern cause. "Matthew was here when Pa was killed. He learned a whole lot about hatred."

"I understand."

She nodded. Then curiously she asked him. "And have you got kin in the army, Mr. Slater?"

"Yes."

"North or South?"

He hesitated. "Both."

"You were in the Union Army."

"Yes." Again he paused. Then he spoke softly. "Yes. And every time I see a list of the dead—either side—it hurts like hell. You've seen the worst of it, Kristin. There are men on both sides of this thing who are fine and gallant, the very best we've ever bred, no matter what state they've hailed from."

It was a curious moment. Kristin felt warm, almost felt cherished. She sensed depths to him that went very far beyond her understanding, and she was glad that he was here for her.

However briefly.

But then he turned, and she saw his profile. She saw its strengths, and she saw the marks that time had left upon it, and she remembered the woman in the picture, and that he didn't really love her at all. And she felt awkward, her nerves on edge again.

"Supper's about on the table," she said.

He nodded.

"Can I...can I get you a drink? Or something?"

Or something. She saw the slow smile seep into his lips at her words, and she blushed, feeling like a fool despite herself. He nodded again.

"Madeira?"

"A shot of whiskey would be fine."

Kristin nodded, wondering what had prompted her to say such a thing. He was closer to the whiskey than she was, and he knew it, but he didn't make a move to get it. He kept staring at her, his smile mocking again.

She swept into the room and took the whiskey from the drawer. They were very close to one another. He hadn't changed. He was still wearing tight breeches and a cotton shirt and his riding boots. She knew he had ridden out to meet with Pete, and she knew, too, that he seemed to know something about ranching. Well, he was from somewhere around here, according to Shannon.

She poured him out a double shot of the amber liquid, feeling him watching her every second. She started to hand him the glass, but he didn't seem to notice. His eyes were on hers, grown dark, like the sky before a tornado.

He reached out and touched the golden lock of hair that curled over the rise of her breasts. He curled it around his finger, his thumb grazing her bare flesh. She couldn't move. A soft sound came from her throat, and suddenly it was as if all the fires of hell had risen up to sweep through her, robbing her of all strength. She stared up at him, but his eyes were on her hair, and on her flesh where he touched her. She felt heat radiating from the length and breadth of his body, and yet she shivered, remembering the strength of his shoulders, the hardness of his belly, the power of his thighs.

And she remembered the speed of his draw. He was a gunslinger, she thought, bred to violence.

No. He had been to West Point. He had served as a captain in the U.S. cavalry. That was what he had told Shannon, at least.

Did any of it matter? He was here, and as long as he was here she felt safe from the Zeke Moreaus of the world. And yet, she thought, their's must surely be a bargain made in hell, for when he looked at her, when he touched her even as lightly as he did now, she felt the slow fires of sure damnation seize her.

"Do you always dress so for dinner?" he asked her, and the timbre of his voice sent new shivers skating down her spine.

"Always," she managed to murmur.

His knuckles hovered over her breasts. Then his eyes met hers, and he slowly relinquished the golden curl he held. Expectation swirled around them, and Kristin was afraid that her knees would give, that she would fall against him. The whiskey in the glass she held threatened to spill over. He took the glass from her and set it on the desk. She felt heat where his fingers had brushed hers, and it seemed that the air, the very space between them, hummed with a palpable tension.

"You are a very beautiful woman, Miss McCahy," he told her softly, and she felt his male voice, male and sensual, wash over her.

"Then, you're not...you're not too disappointed in our deal?"

He smiled again, and his silver-gray eyes brightened wickedly. "Did we need a deal?"

"I don't know what you mean," she told him, though she knew exactly what he meant.

The light went out of his eyes. He picked up the whiskey and swallowed it quickly. "I'm still damned if I know what the hell I'm doing here," he muttered.

"I thought—" she began, and her face flamed.

He touched her cheek. "You thought the payoff went well, is that it?"

She shoved his hand away. She didn't want him to touch her, not then. "You do have a talent for making a woman feel just like river slime," she said, as sweetly as she could. He arched a brow, and she saw fleeting amusement light his features. She could hold her own in any fight, she thought, but only for so long. She needed to escape him now.

"I didn't mean to make you feel like...river slime."

"Don't worry. You already did so. Last night." With a sweetly mocking smile, Kristin turned to leave.

Then she paused and turned toward him again, biting her lip. She kept forgetting how much she needed him. Her eyes must have widened with the realization, for he was smiling cynically again and pouring himself another shot of whiskey.

"Don't worry," he told her smoothly. "I'm not walking out on you. Not yet."

Kristin moistened her lips. "Not yet?" she whispered.

"Why, Miss McCahy! I really couldn't leave a lady in such distress, could I?"

"What do you mean by that?"

He raised the glass. "Take it as you will, ma'am."

Kristin swore under her breath and strode over to him again. She snatched the glass from his hand and thought seriously of pouring the contents over his head. His eyes narrowed, and she quickly reconsidered.

She swallowed the whiskey down so quickly that her head spun in an instant and her throat burned with the fury of a brush fire. A double shot, straight. But she steeled herself, and she still managed to smile sweetly. "You don't owe me anything."

"No, darlin'. You owe me." He smiled, took the glass from her and poured another double. "And I'm real anxious for the next installment."

Kristin snatched the glass again and swallowed the liquid down. She didn't know if she was alive with anger or with desire.

She slammed the glass down and tried to spin around. He caught her arm, pulling her back. She tossed her head back, staring into his eyes.

"Isn't it what you want?" he asked her.

"I want revenge, nothing more," she told him.

"Nothing more?"

"I want you to—I want you to stay. I want to hold on to the ranch. I just want to hold on to what is mine."

"The precious ranch," he muttered darkly.

Fear fluttered briefly in her heart. "Cole...Mr. Slater, you really wouldn't...you wouldn't go back on your word, would you?"

"Not so long as you follow the rules."

Her head was really spinning now. He had poured so much whiskey, and she'd swallowed it down so fast. He was so warm, and so damn vibrant, and so shockingly male. And she'd already been in bed with him.

Her mother would be spinning in her grave, Kristin thought.

He was using her. He was using her because he had loved another woman and now he just didn't give a damn.

"Your rules! Just don't forget that the place belongs to me!"

She wrenched free of him, and this time she walked out. She wasn't afraid of him leaving. He was having too fine a time torturing her to leave now.

When she reached the dining room, she was startled to discover that he was behind her. He had followed her, as silent as a wraith. It was disconcerting.

"Stop it!" she demanded.

Shannon came out of the kitchen. Delilah was behind her. Both women stopped, startled.

Cole ignored them both. "Stop what?" he demanded irritably.

"Sneaking up on me!"

"I wasn't sneaking up on you. You told me it was time for supper, so I followed you."

"Whoa!" Shannon murmured, looking at her sister. "Kristin, you've been drinking!"

"Yes!" she snapped, glaring at Cole. "And I'll probably do a whole lot more drinking before...before..."

"Oh, hell, will you just sit the hell down!" Cole growled. He caught her hand, pulled out a chair and directed her into it with little grace. Her wide skirts flew. He pressed them down and shoved her chair in.

Kristin wanted to be dignified. She wanted to be sophisticated and elegant, and most of all she wanted to be in control. "You arrogant scallywag!" she said quietly, her voice husky with emotion.

"Kristin, shut up."

That was it. She started to push herself away from the table, but his hand slammed down on hers, holding her fast. "Kristin, shut up."

"Bas—"

"Now, Kristin." He came closer to her, much closer, and spoke in a whisper. This was between the two of them. "Or else we can get up and settle this outside."

The whiskey seemed to hit her anew right then, hit her hard. She thought she was going to scream. She burst into laughter instead. "Outside? With pistols?"

"Hardly, but you can call it what you want, darlin'."

The buzz of the liquor was nice. If he stayed around too long, Kristin thought, she'd find herself turning into a regular old drunk.

"Shall we eat?" Cole asked politely.

There was silence in the room. Shannon was staring at him.

"Sit!" he told her.

Shannon sat hastily, then lowered her head before looking surreptitiously over at Kristin, who hiccuped loudly.

Cole groaned, then he looked up at Delilah. "Don't you and Samson usually eat?"

"Oh, no, sir!" Delilah protested. "Why, you know it just wouldn't be right for black folks—"

"Delilah, cut the...er—" He broke off, looking from Samson to Kristin. Shannon was about to laugh.

"Manure," Kristin supplied.

Shannon did burst into laughter. Even Delilah grinned. Cole said, "Get your husband, woman, and sit down and eat. I once had the opportunity to discover that a black man could save my hide as good as a white one. Let's just have supper and get it over with, shall we?''

''Yessir, yessir,'' Delilah said, chuckling. ''My, my, my,'' she muttered, moving off toward the kitchen.

Kristin sat primly, her hands folded in her lap. Her dress felt ridiculously heavy, now that she was sitting. She felt as if she was about to fall over. She realized that Cole was looking at her, but it didn't matter very much, and that was a nice feeling.

Delilah walked back in from the kitchen.

Cole gazed at her expectantly. ''You've never washed her mouth out with soap, huh?'' He indicated Kristin.

Kristin decided that she could sit straight. She told Cole that he reminded her of the stuff that people needed to wipe off their boots before they came in from the barn.

Shannon gasped, and then she began to giggle. Delilah stood stock-still. Samson, coming in behind his wife, turned an ashen color.

Cole was dead still. Explosively still. And then explosively in motion.

He was up, and Kristin sobered enough to know a moment's panic as he came around behind her and purposely pulled her chair away from the table. He lifted her, and her petticoats and hoops and shirt went flying. Kristin swore at him and pounded on his back.

''Cole!'' Kristin gasped.

What manner of man had she let loose in her home, she wondered.

He started for the stairs.

''What are you doing?'' she shrieked.

''Putting you to bed.''

''I don't want to go!''

''My rules, Miss McCahy.''

They were all watching her, Shannon and Delilah and Samson, and they weren't doing a thing to save her. They were just staring. She raised her head and saw that Delilah was openly grinning and Samson was hiding a smile.

''You son of a bitch!'' she yelled.

''We are going to have to do something about that mouth of yours,'' Cole vowed grimly.

''This is my house!''

''My rules!''

She told him what he could do with his rules, but it was too late. They were already up the stairs. He booted open the door to the room he had decreed they would share, and before she knew it she had landed on the bed. She wanted to get back up, but she groaned instead and clutched her temples.

His leering face was above her.

''Why, what's the matter, Miss McCahy? Why, I would have thought you could drink any man west of the Mississippi under the table.''

''Madeira,'' she whispered. ''Not whiskey.''

He showed her no mercy. Suddenly his hand was on her leg and he was pulling off her shoe. She managed to pull herself up to a sitting position and pummel his back. ''What are you doing?''

''Taking your shoes off.'' But her shoes were off, and his hands were still on her, slipping along her calf, then her thigh. When his fingers touched her thigh, she gasped and tried to stop him. ''Damn you Cole Slater—''

Her words ended in a gasp, for he turned quickly, pulling hard on her ankle so that she was lying flat on her back again. Her silk stockings came free in his hands, and he tossed them carelessly on the floor. She tried to rise, and he came down beside her on the bed, his weight on her.

"Where the hell are the damn ties to these things?" he muttered, working on her hoop.

Kristin struggled to stop him, but he found the ties. She reached for his hands, but they had already moved, freeing her from her hoop and petticoats, and he pulled her up, working on the hooks of her gown. In seconds he had it free and she was down to her pantalets, chemise and corset.

"Come here!" he demanded roughly. Kristin cried out, trying to elude him, but he pulled her back by the corset ties. He lossened the ties, and she gasped, amazed by the air that rushed into her lungs. But then she was naked except for her sheer chemise and pantalets, and his presence was overwhelming.

She began to protest. He caught her shoulders and slammed her down on the bed.

"Calm down and sleep it off!" he commanded.

He was straddling her, and his eyes were like steel. She wanted to slap his superior face. She tried. She missed by a mile, and he caught her hand.

"My rules."

She told him again what he could do with his rules.

"Stay here alone, or I'll stay here with you."

She went still, trying to grasp the meaning of his words. The room was spinning madly.

Then she understood. He stared at her. Then he lowered his head toward her and kissed her, and somewhere, within her hazy mind and her bruised heart she knew that he did desire her. And she knew, too, that he didn't love her, not at all.

His kiss was hard and demanding and, in its way, punishing. But then it deepened, and it was rich, and it betrayed a growing passion and hunger. She felt her body respond. She felt his hands move over her, felt him grow warm and hard. She began to tremble and suddenly she wanted him, but she wanted him loving her, loving her tenderly, not just wanting her with the raw desire that had finally brought him to her.

His mouth opened and closed hungrily upon her flesh. His teeth grazed her throat, and the tip of his tongue teased the valley between her breasts. He was a flame setting on her, seeping into her, and she was stunned that he could so easily elicit this willingness...

This eagerness...

Within her. She stiffened, fighting the whiskey haze in her heart and in her mind. She had to stop him. He hadn't meant to do this, not now. He had stayed away from her on purpose, she was certain of it. He wanted no involvements.

And she could too easily fall in love with him.

She forced herself to feel nothing, to allow the bitterness of the last years to invade her, so that his searing warmth could not touch her. When he rose above her, she met his steely gaze and spoke to him in a quiet, toneless voice.

"Who was she? Your wife?"

She might have struck him. All the heat left him. It was as if he turned to ice. He stared at her, his jaw constricted, his features as harsh as a desert. He rolled away from her and sat on the side of the bed. His fingers threaded through his hair, and he pressed his hand against his temple as if he were trying to soothe some awful pain.

"Go to sleep," he told her. "And stay off the hard stuff from now on."

Kristin cast her arm over her eyes. "Your rules," she murmured.

"I don't like this kind of a fight, Kristin," he said dully, "but..."

"But?"

"You start it, and I'll end it. Every time."

She felt his weight lift from the bed, and she started to shiver. Suddenly she was warmed. He had laid a blanket over her, and he was close by her again.

"Go to sleep," he said softly, his voice almost tender again.

Almost.

He got up and walked away. She heard the door close quietly, and to her great dismay she closed her eyes and started to cry as she hadn't done since they had come to tell her that Adam was dead.

Chapter Six

It was the liquor, Kristin thought. Lying in the darkness, feeling miserable, she put her arm over her eyes and felt her head spin, and she wondered what had made her drink so much so fast. She was humiliated, but it was her own fault, and she was in no mood to do anything about it, except to suffer in silence.

And, in a way, she wasn't sorry. She could dimly hear the sounds of dinner, and she wondered if Samson and Delilah had sat down to eat. Cole Slater was an unusual man. A very unusual man.

The darkness closed in and whirled around her. She knew she ought to be sorry she had let the liquor ignite her temper, but instead she was glad of it. She didn't feel the awful pain for once. She didn't remember what it had been like to see Pa die, to see Matthew turn his back on his own people and ride away with the Union forces.

She didn't even quite remember what it was like to be with Cole Slater. To be so nervous that she lost all the wisdom her harsh life had taught her. To be afraid in a way, and yet to want something, some intangible thing, so badly.

Curiously—bless the liquor—she felt at peace.

She closed her eyes, and she must have dozed. Then she must have awakened, or else she was dreaming, because when she opened her eyes, the room was bathed in moonlight. Her mind was still spinning, and she still felt at peace.

He was in the room with her.

He had come in quietly, and the door had closed softly behind him. He stood just inside of it, his hands on his hips, and watched her where she lay upon the bed. The moonlight fell on his features, and they were both harsh and curiously beautiful. For the longest time he stood there. The wind seemed to rise, not to a moan, but to a whisper. She imagined that outside tumbleweeds were being caught and tossed in the strange, sweet dance of the West, buffeted as she was being buffeted. Her heart rose and fell like that tumbleweed, tossed around heedlessly.

No...

He was a marvelous creature sleek as a cougar, sharp as an eagle. He was still standing there, his hands on his hips, his head at an angle, as if he were waiting, as if he were listening to the curiously tender whispering of the wind.

Then he moved. He unbuttoned his cuffs. He took off his boots and stripped off his socks. He came to her in silence, barefoot, and he dropped his gun belt beside the bed. Then he looked down at her, and saw that her eyes were open.

"You're still awake."

She nodded gravely, and then she smiled. "I'm sorry. I was out of line this evening. And I...I don't want to fight."

Unbuttoning his shirt, he sat beside her on the bed. His eyes remained on hers. He reached over and touched her cheek. "I don't want to fight, either, Kristin. You've had a hard time of it, and you've done well. Someone else might have shattered a long, long time ago."

The gentle whisper of the wind was in his voice, and there was an evocative tenderness in his fingertips as they brushed her cheek. She didn't reply, but kept her eyes on his, and then the whisper of the wind seemed to sweep into her, to permeate her flesh and fill her veins. She was warm, and achingly aware of herself, and of the man. Surely, she was still asleep. Surely it was all a dream. It was a spell cast by the moonlight. It lived in the clouds of imagination.

But it was real. Very real. He leaned over then and caught her lips in a curious kiss. It was light at first. He tasted her lips, teasing them with the tip of his tongue. Then he plunged his tongue deep into her mouth, and she wrapped her arms around his neck and felt the rugged, steel-muscled frame of his chest against her. She felt his hands on her, rough and tender. Then his hands were in her hair, threading through the tendrils, and he was stroking her arm as he moved his lips over her throat and down to the place where her breasts spilled provocatively from her lace chemise. His mouth fastened over her nipple through the sheer fabric, and she cried out softly. He shifted swiftly, taking her mouth again, taking her cry into him.

He stood, dropping his shirt and stripping away his pants. The moonlight fell on him. He was tall and rugged, lean and sinewed, his skin shining almost copper in that light, his shoulders shimmering with it. She stared at him. If this was a dream, she was grateful for it. She wanted him. She wanted him with her heart and with her mind, she wanted him with every fiber of her being. She wanted him desperately.

She was not to be denied.

He came down beside her and took her in his arms, and she strained to meet his kiss again. He unlaced her chemise, and her breast spilled from it. He lowered his head again, touching her nipple with his tongue, fondling the weight of her breast with a touch so achingly soft.... She was barely aware that she arched to him, that she dug her fingers into his hair and cried incoherently for him to come to her. But it was not to be. His hands brushed her flesh, and where they had been she yearned for them again. His kisses ranged over the length of her, a mere breath, a mere whisper, and then were gone. She writhed. She tried to hold him, to pin him down. And she felt something move in her, like lava rising to the surface of the earth. She felt the earth teeming and bubbling with heat and steam, and still he pressed her. She moved her hands against him, felt the tension in his taut muscles, and touching him inflamed her, bringing her to still greater heights. She no longer knew herself. She had become some strange wanton. She felt his hands on her hips, and on her belly and she moved toward the feel of them, the promise of them. He made her touch him, and the pulsing heat and size of him gave her pause. Then a curious elation filled her, and for a moment she was afraid she might faint.

Her remaining clothes were gone now. Like him, she lay naked in the moonlight, her skin shimmering like copper beneath its glow.

Time had lost all meaning. She lay upon clouds of moonlight, and all that was real was the hardness of this man, the demand in his eyes. The wind had become the ragged cry of his breath, and the storm was the near-savage urgency that drove him. He did not tease. He sucked hard on her breast until she thought she would explode. He did not shyly caress her thighs, but stroked within, to the heart of her, and as he touched her, he caught her cries again with his lips. He knelt before her, caught her eyes again, then watched her, before he caught the supple length of her legs and brought them around him. He stared at her as he lowered his head, and she opened her mouth to stop him, but she could not.

He touched her intimately, with a searing demand, and she tossed her head, savagely biting her own lip so as not to scream. She could not bear it, and despite her efforts she did cry out. She lunged forward, she convulsed and she heard the soft tenor of his laughter. She longed to strike him, to hide from him. But he was above her, and he had her hands, and suddenly he was within her, igniting a fierce burning, and it was all happening again, all beginning again. His hands roughly cupped her buttocks, and again he led her into a shattering rhythm.

The clouds danced around them. She closed her eyes and buried her face against his chest, and she tasted the salt on his body. There was nothing gentle in him then. He moved in a frenzy, violent, urgent, and though she feared she would lose herself in him, she clung to him and fought to meet his every move. Ecstasy burst through again, even stronger than before, and she dug her fingers into his flesh, convulsing against him. He shuddered strongly against her, and she was filled with their mutual heat. Then he fell from her, smoothing the wild tangle of her hair.

They didn't say anything. Not anything at all.

The wind had died down again. It was a mere whisper. It caught the tumbleweeds down below and tossed them around.

Her heart was still beating savagely,. He must have felt it when he put his arm around her and pulled her against him. It was a wonderful way to sleep, her back to his chest, his fingers just below the full curve of her breast. She didn't think about the wind, or the night. The moonlight was still shining down on them. Perhaps it had all been a dream. She didn't want to know. She closed her eyes, and at long last the spinning in her head stopped. She slept.

He slept, too, and it was his turn to dream. The nightmare of the past, the nightmare that haunted him whether he was awake or asleep, came back to him now.

The dream unfolded slowly, so slowly. It always came to him first with sound...a soft, continual thunder, like the beating of drums. It was the sound of hooves driving across the earth, driving hard. Then he heard the shouts. They made no sense at first, they meant nothing, nothing at all. Then he realized that the hooves were churning beneath him. He was the rider. He was riding hard, riding desperately, and all he wanted to do was get home before...

Smoke. He inhaled sharply and it filled his nostrils and mouth with an acrid taste. There was something about that smell... He could feel a trail of ice streak along his spine. He recognized the awful odor of burning flesh.

Then he saw the horror up ahead. The house was burning; the barn was burning.

And he saw Elizabeth.

She was running, trying to reach him. He screamed her name, his voice ragged and harsh, and still he felt the movement beneath him, the endless thunder of the horse's hooves. He rode across the plain, across the scrub brush. And she kept coming. She was calling to him, but the sound of her voice could not reach him. She could not reach him.

She fell and disappeared from sight. He rode harder, and then he leaped from the horse, still shouting her name, over and over. He searched through the grass until he found her. Her hair, long and lustrous and ebony black, was spread over the earth in soft, silken waves.

"Elizabeth..."

He took her into his arms, and he looked down, and all that he saw was red. Red, spilling over him, filling his hands. Red, flowing in rivers, red...the color of blood.

He cast back his head, and he screamed, and the scream echoed and echoed across the plain....

He awoke with a start.

He was covered in sweat, and he was trembling. He shook his head, trying to clear it, and gazed at the woman beside him. He saw her golden hair, and the easy rise and fall of her chest with her breath.

She hadn't awakened.

He rose and went to the window, where he stared out at the moon. He hadn't woken her; it was going to be all right. Maybe he was getting better; at least he wasn't screaming out loud anymore.

He walked over to the bed and stared down at her; and she seemed incredibly young and pure, and very lovely. His fingers itched, and he wanted to shake her, to tell her that she didn't understand how deadly the game she was playing could be.

His fingers eased. Maybe she knew.

He went back to the window and stared at the moon again. Slowly, the tension left him, and he sighed. He went back to bed, but he couldn't bear to touch her, even though he knew that someday soon he would. He needed to touch her, just as he needed air to breathe.

He didn't sleep. In time, dawn came. He rose and dressed, then went outside. He gazed out over the plain, and in his mind he saw Elizabeth again, running toward him. He closed his eyes, and she was gone, but the pain was still with him, filling him, gnawing at his insides. He straightened his shoulders, and the pain slowly began to ebb, but it never fully left him. It clutched his heart with icy fingers, and he wondered what the hell he was doing here, then reminded himself that he had agreed to a "deal," and he might as well get on with it. He turned around and stared at her window. She was sleeping just beyond it. He marched back to the house.

She'd never expected to be awakened so rudely. One second she was so deep in blissful sleep, and the next she felt his hand against her rump. Her *bare* rump. He'd pulled the covers away from her.

Protesting, she grabbed the covers and sat with them pulled up to her chin, her eyes blazing with fury and indignation. He was up and dressed, standing at the foot of the bed and surveying her with cold eyes.

"I want you in the office. Now. If you want my help, you'd better show me the books."

"I'll come down to the office when I'm ready," she snapped. She couldn't understand the man. She couldn't understand his strange, distant behavior after the things they had shared in the night. It hurt.

"Get up."

She narrowed her eyes at this new battle.

"You get out and then I'll get up. When I'm ready."

He grabbed the sheets again. She lunged for them but she was too late, and he stripped them away. He eyed her dispassionately, his steely gaze sweeping over her form. She jumped out of bed, swearing once again, and leaped toward him, her temper soaring. He caught her arms, and his smile was curiously grim and somehow self-satisfied. It was as if he had been trying to pick a fight. She tried to wrench free of his touch. She didn't like the daylight on her naked flesh, and she didn't like the disadvantage of being undressed while he was clad from his scarf to his boots. He pulled her close against him. She felt the bite of his belt buckle and the texture of his shirt, but most of all she felt a hot tempest of emotions within him, no matter how calm, cold and in control he looked.

"I told you," he said sharply, "I call the shots. And you can't laze in bed all morning. You're a rancher. You should know that. Or do you just play at this thing? When you feel like riding with the boys, you do. And when you feel like playing the Southern belle, then you do that, too."

She was furious, but she smiled to hide it. Tense and still against him and staring up into his eyes, she smiled. "I don't play at anything, Mr. Slater. I am a rancher, and probably better at it than you ever were or could be. I just don't have to be as ugly as a mule's rump to do it. You call the shots? Well, that's just fine. When you want me up from now on, you knock. One knock, Mr. Slater, and I promise I'll be right out in less than five minutes. But don't you ever, ever touch me like that again!"

His brow arched slowly, and she saw his smile deepen. He released her and put his hands on his hips. She felt his gaze sweep over her again like fire. For a moment she thought he was going to sweep her up in his arms, right there, right then, in broad daylight. For a moment she was certain he was going to carry her over to the bed and take her there and then, with the morning sun shining on them.

She'd have to protest, she'd have to scream....

For the life of her she didn't know if she was afraid or if she wished he'd take a step forward and sweep her up in his arms....

He tipped his hat to her.

"I call all the shots, Kristin. All of them."

He turned around then and left her. The door closed sharply behind him.

She washed and dressed, wondering again what kind of a monster she had brought into her home. She touched her cheeks, and it was as if they were on fire.

When she came down the stairs, he was just finishing his breakfast. He tossed his checkered napkin on the table and rose at the sight of her. Kristin went to her chair.

"Flapjacks, honey?" Delilah asked her.

Cole was around the table before she had a chance to sit. He took her arm.

"Give her a cup of coffee, Delilah. Nothing else for the moment. We've got work to do."

She could make a scene, as she had at dinner. Delilah was staring at her, and Samson was staring at her, and so was Shannon. Her sister's eyes were very wide. They were all waiting.

Bastard! she thought. He was at fault! But she had been at fault the night before, and she knew she would look like a spoiled fool again if she created a problem.

"That's right. This is a busy, busy day, isn't it?" she said sweetly. "Coffee, Delilah." She accepted a cup and smiled her gratitude, gritting her teeth. She freed her arm from Cole's grasp. "Do come, Mr. Slater. The day is wearing on."

He followed her into the office, then swept past her, taking a seat behind her father's desk. He'd already been in there that morning, she was certain. He had the ledgers out, and before she could even seat herself he was firing out a barrage of questions. Where did she buy her feed, how much, how often? Had she considered moving any of the herd to avoid soldiers, Union and Confederate? Had she thought of leaving more pasture time, had she thought of introducing new strains? And on and on.

She didn't falter once. She was a rancher. She was bright, determined and well schooled, and she wanted him to know it. It occurred to her that he was just some drifter, that he had no rights here at all. But then she remembered that she had asked him to stay, that she had been desperate for him to stay.

That she had been willing to do anything at all to make him stay. And he had stayed, and she wasn't the same person anymore, not in any way. But whoever she was now, he wasn't going to treat her this way.

Suddenly he slammed the ledger he was examining shut and stood up. He stared across the desk at her, and for a moment she thought he must hate her.

He had saved her from Zeke, she reminded herself. He had ridden in, all honor and chivalry, and he had saved her from Zeke. Now he looked as if he wanted to flay her alive himself.

He looked as if he were about to say something. He shook his head impatiently. "I'm going out," he said. He jammed his hat low on his head, and came around the desk.

Kristin rose quickly and, she hoped, with dignity. "If you'd let me come with you—"

"No. I don't want you with me."

"I could show you—"

"God damn you, can't you hear? Or are you just incapable of listening? I'll see things myself. I'll see what I want to see. And you'll stay here by the house. Roam too far and come across Zeke and you'll wind up on your own this time. I swear it."

It might be better! she longed to shout. But she didn't do it, because it wasn't true. Zeke had killed her father. No matter how outrageously bad Cole's manners were turning out to be, he didn't compare with Zeke.

She crossed her arms over her chest and leaned back. "Don't let me keep you," she said sarcastically.

He walked past her.

She didn't know where he went. She was pretty sure he was never far away, but he didn't come by the house.

He had left a newspaper on the table, and she sat down and stared at the articles. War. It was all about war. About the Union troops holding Kansas, about the measures they intended to take against Quantrill and his raiders.

War and more war. The Union held New Orleans, and Grant was swearing he'd have Vicksburg soon. But whether the Union held sway or not, there was something that couldn't be changed. In the East, Lee was leading them all a merry chase. He had fewer men, he had less ammunition, he had less food. But he was brilliant, and not even the fact that the paper had been published in a town filled with Yankees could change the tenor of the articles. The South was strong. They could beat her and beat her, but she had the genius of Lee and Stonewall Jackson, and she had the daring of Jeb Stuart and Morgan Hunt and others like them.

Kristin laid her face against the cool wood of her father's desk. The news didn't make her happy or proud. It filled her heart with dread. It meant the war was going to go on and on. Nobody was going to go out and whomp the pants off anybody else. It was just going to keep going.

And Quantrill's outlaws would keep raiding and raiding....

After a while, Kristin lifted her head. There was a knock at the door. Delilah was there. She stuck her head in hesitantly.

"How about something to eat? Flapjacks and bacon?"

Her stomach was rumbling. She was starving. She hadn't had any supper, and she hadn't had any breakfast. She stood up and slid her hands into her back pockets.

"Flapjacks sound great."

"Fine. Come along."

"Delilah, wait."

Delilah hesitated there in the doorway. She met Kristin's eyes.

"Delilah, am I doing the right thing?"

"Honey, you're doing the only thing."

Kristin shook her head. "He made a fool out of me last night, Delilah."

"You let that happen."

"Yes, I did. But—"

"We need him," Delilah said bluntly. Then she smiled and gazed at Kristin, and Kristin was sure she was blushing beneath the gold and mahogany of her coloring. "We need him, and I like him. I like him just fine. You did well."

Kristin blushed herself. "I didn't marry him, Delilah. I'm...I'm his...mistress, Delilah."

"You did well," Delilah repeated. "I like him. I don't care what he seems to be, he's a right honorable fellow." She was silent for a moment. "You come along now and have something to eat."

Kristin did.

Then she set to the housework with a vengeance, cleaning and sweeping. Later she went out to the barn and spent some time grooming the horses that weren't out with the hands. She came back in and bathed, and while she sat in the tub she decided that although her feelings about him were entirely different from her feelings about Zeke, she still hated Cole Slater. She couldn't even take a bath in peace anymore. She kept thinking about him the entire time. She wanted to be clean, and she wanted to smell sweet, because she could just imagine him...

She promised herself she would be cool and aloof and dignified through dinner and all through the evening.

She promised herself she would be cool and aloof and wouldn't allow him to touch her.

But he didn't come back for dinner. He didn't come back at all. At midnight she gave up and went upstairs. She managed to stay awake for an hour, but then she fell asleep. She had taken care to dress in a high-necked nightgown, one with a multitude of delicate little buttons at the throat.

Cole stayed out for a long time that night, waiting for her to fall asleep. He smoked a cigar and sipped a brandy and wondered where Quantrill's boys might be.

Quantrill was no bargain, Cole thought, but he wasn't the worst of the lot. He rode with some frightening company. Bill Anderson was a blood-thirsty soul. Zeke was a horror. Cole had heard that some of the men liked to fight the way the Indians did, taking scalps from their victims.

Quantrill for the South...

And the likes of Lane and Jennison for the North. Killing anyone and anything that stood in their way. Making a jest out of a war that was being fought desperately on both sides for different sets of ideals.

Smoke rose high above him, and he shivered suddenly. He hadn't been able to get Elizabeth's face out of his mind all day. But now, curiously, when he closed his eyes, he saw Kristin. Saw her fighting for all she was worth. Saw her fallen in the dirt.

He stood up and dusted off his hands on his pants.

Kristin was alive, and Elizabeth wasn't. Elizabeth had died because of Doc Jennison and his jayhawkers; Kristin had been attacked by the bushwhackers.

He was angry with her for being alive, he realized. She was alive and Elizabeth wasn't. And he knew he couldn't explain that to her.

He threw his cigar down in the dirt and snuffed it out with the heel of his boot. Then he turned around. He couldn't back down on any of the demands he had made of her. Not ever. It was just part of his nature, he supposed. And it was important that Quantrill know that he was living with her—intimately.

He looked up at the house and swore, then entered it quietly. For a moment he paused in the darkness of the entry. It was a good house. It had been built sturdy and strong, and it had been made into a home. It had grace.

He paused and inhaled deeply. Then he started for the stairway and climbed the steps silently. He reached his room and opened the door, thinking that she must have returned to her own room.

She hadn't. She was curled up on the bed. Her hair spilled over on his pillow.

He cast aside his clothes impatiently and approached the bed, but before he could pull back the covers, his hand brushed a tendril of hair that lay on his pillow, and its soft scent rose up to greet him. Heat immediately snaked through him. He didn't want it this way. But all he had to do was touch her hair and see her innocent form and he was tied into harsh knots of desire.

He didn't have to give in to it, he reminded himself.

He stretched out and stared at the ceiling, drumming his fingers on his chest. She was sound asleep, and even if she were not she would surely not be particularly fond of him at the moment.

A minute later he was on his side, just watching her. He throbbed, he ached, his desire thundering, clamoring for release.

He touched her hair again and reminded himself that it should be black. He didn't love this girl.

He slipped his hand beneath her gown and slowly, lightly stroked her flesh, following the line of her calf, the length of her thigh, the curve of her hip. He rounded her buttocks with a feathery touch, then gently tugged her around and pressed his lips against hers.

She responded, warmly and sweetly and instinctively, to his touch. Her arms swept around him and her body pressed against his. Her lips parted and he plundered the honey-warm depths of her mouth with his tongue. His body pressed against hers intimately. He pulled her gown up further and wedged his hips between her bare thighs. Her eyes remained closed. She was barely awake.

Then she awoke fully. Her eyes widened, and she pressed furiously against his shoulders. He thought he saw tears sting her eyes as she pronounced him a son of a bitch.

"I know," he told her.

"If you know—"

"I'm sorry."

He tried to kiss her again, but she twisted her head, and his lips fell against her throat.

"You behave like a tyrant."

"I know. I'm sorry."

"You treat people like servants—"

"I know. I'm sorry."

"You behave—"

Her mouth was open, and he caught her lower lip between his teeth and bathed it with his tongue. Then he began to move against her. He caught her cheeks between his palms and stroked her hair, and when she stared up at him again, gasping for breath, he kissed her again quickly, speaking against her lips.

"I am sorry. So damned sorry, for so damned much."

She was silent then, staring at him in the darkness. She was very still, very aware of his sex throbbing against her, so close. If she fought him he would leave.

She didn't fight him. She continued to stare at him, and he met her eyes. Then he moved, thrusting deep inside her. She let out a garbled little sound, and her arms came around him and she buried her face against the hard dampness of his shoulder. Her long limbs came around him, and he sank deeper into her and then deeper still.

She was instinctively sensual, and she offered him greater solace than he could ever have imagined. When it was over he lay with her hair tangling over his naked chest and reminded himself again that it was blond and not ebony black. They were strangers who had stumbled together. They had answered one another's needs, and that was all.

If he closed his eyes he would see her, Elizabeth, racing toward him. Running, running, running...

But it was not Elizabeth's face he saw in his dreams. Sweet blond hair flowed behind the woman who ran to him in his dreams. Kristin raced to him in the night, and he wanted to reach for her, but he was afraid to. He was afraid he might fail.

He was afraid he would take her in his arms and find her blood on his hands. He was afraid he would see Kristin's exquisite blue eyes on his and see her blood running red onto his hands.

Chapter Seven

When Kristin awoke, she could hear gunfire. Looking out the window, she saw that Samson and Delilah were practicing with Cole's six-shooters. She dressed quickly in a cotton shirt and pants and boots and hurried downstairs and out to the pasture. Delilah stumbled from the recoil every time she fired, but she had a set and determined expression on her face. Samson laughed at her, and she gave him a good hard shove. Cole actually grinned. Then he looked at Kristin and saw that she wasn't happy at all. Perched on a fence, he nodded to her and arched a brow, and she flushed. The nights they shared were real, she thought. But the nights were one thing, and the harsh light of day was another. She wasn't going to act like a child again, and she wasn't going to try to pretend that he hadn't touched her in a way she would never forget, that he hadn't awakened her to something incredible. What if it was wrong according to all moral and social standards? Murder was wrong, too. The world wasn't run according to moral standards anymore. She didn't mind getting close to Cole. He knew how to treat a woman, knew when to be tender, knew when to let the wild winds rage. Even now, as his eyes flickered over her, she felt the warmth of their intimacy, and it wasn't an unpleasant feeling, despite her current impatience. Cole just didn't seem to understand what he was doing to her. He didn't speak. He watched her. Waiting.

"Miz Kristin, I am going to get this down pat!" Delilah swore.

Kristin tried to smile. "Delilah, you can master anything you set your mind to. I've see you." She set her thumbs in the pockets of her pants and said to Cole, "May I speak with you a moment?"

"Speak," Cole said flatly. He had said he was sorry about lots of things, but his manner toward her didn't seem to be much better today than it had been before. And he didn't come down from the fence.

"Alone," she said.

He shrugged, and started to climb down.

"Don't you bother, Mr. Slater," Samson said behind her. Kristin whirled around in surprise. Samson looked at her, his expression almost sorrowful, and gave her a rueful grin. "Meaning no disrespect, Miz Kristin, and you know it. But you're gonna tell him that you don't want him teaching us any more about gunfire. 'Cause of us being free blacks. She thinks that if we don't shoot they'll just put us on a block and not think to shoot us or string us up. Delilah and me talked about it a long, long time. We're in this together. If there's more trouble, we got to stick together. Delilah's got to shoot just like everybody else. You see, Miz Kristin, I been a free man now a long time. And it's mighty sweet."

"Samson..." Kristin swallowed and closed her eyes. "Samson, if you're alive, you can get free again. If you're dead—"

"I believe in the good Lord, Miz Kristin. And one day there's going to be a meetin' 'cross that river. And I ain't going to that meetin' being no coward, or a man who didn't live up to what I believe in. We're in this together, Mis Kristin."

She stared furiously at Cole. He shrugged.

"You fool!" she snapped at him. "Samson is a black man."

"Samson is a man," he replied. "A free man. Your daddy made him so. The way I see it, he's made his choice."

They were all staring at her. No one said anything, and no one moved. The sun streamed down on them all. Cole kept watching her. She couldn't begin to read the emotions in his eyes. I don't know this man, I don't know him at all, she thought in sudden panic. But did it matter? she asked herself. It couldn't matter. The die had been cast.

"I've got to get back to the house now," Delilah said. "I've got to get Daniel and let Shannon come on down here."

"Shannon?" Kristin whispered.

Cole hopped down from the fence at last. He took his gun from Delilah, and he slowly and deliberately reloaded it. His hat shaded his eyes from her when he spoke. "You want your little sister to be defenseless?" He looked straight at her.

Kristin smiled sweetly and took the gun from him. He had a row of bottles set up on the back fence. She took her time, aiming as slowly and deliberately as he had loaded. She remembered everything her father and Adam had ever taught her. Remember the recoil, and remember that it can be a hell of a lot for a small woman to handle. Squeeze the trigger gently. Don't jerk back on it...

She didn't miss once. Six shots, six bottles blown to bits, the glass tinkling and reflecting the sunlight as it scattered. With a very pleasant smile, she turned to Cole, daintily handing him the Colt.

He wasn't amazed; he didn't even seem surprised. He studied her. He slipped a second Colt from his gunbelt and handed it to her.

"What happens when the target moves?" he demanded.

"Try me."

Cole nodded to Samson. Samson grinned approvingly. He picked up a bottle and sent it flying high and fast into the air. Kristin caught the missile at its peak, just before it curved back downward to earth. Once again the sun shimmered on the exploding pieces, and they fell in a rainbow of color.

"Not bad," Cole murmured. He nudged back his hat and looked at her sharply. "And Shannon?"

Shannon was already on her way to the yard from the house. Delilah had gone inside. Shannon was dressed like a ranch hand today, too. She seemed all the more feminine for the way her budding curves filled out her shirt and breeches. She glanced slyly at Kristin, and Kristin knew that she was thinking of the fiasco at dinner the night before. She was tempted to give her a sharp slap, but that would be wrong, and she knew it. She decided to ignore her sister's amusement. "Shannon, Cole wants to see you shoot."

"I know." She smiled at Cole. Shannon liked him. A lot. Kristin wanted to spin her around and shake her. He'll be gone in a blink one day! she wanted to tell her sister. Don't care too much!

Then she wondered if Shannon needed the warning, or if Kristin did.

"Show him," Kristin suggested.

Shannon proceeded to do so. She was an even better shot than Kristin, and Cole told her so. He didn't seem to give anyone lavish praise, but he was always gentler with Shannon than with anyone else.

"Good. Damned good," Cole told her.

Shannon flushed, delighted by the compliment.

Kristin turned on her heel and headed for the house. He didn't want her riding away from the house, and he would insist that she stay. If she didn't, he would leave her to the mercy of the bushwhackers. She was going to be mature today, mature and dignified, and she wasn't going to get into any fights over the ranch.

"Kristin!" he called to her.

She turned to look at him.

"What are you doing?" His plumed hat was set at a cocky angle, his hands were on his hips, and his frock coat hung down the length of his back. There was something implacable about him as he stood there, implacable, unfathomable and hard. But that was why she had wanted him. He couldn't be beaten. Not by Quantrill's gang. Not by her.

That last thought made her tremble slightly. She clamped down hard on her jaw and wondered just how long the war could last, and wondered if maybe she shouldn't run after all.

"Paperwork," she told him calmly. "I wouldn't dream of going against your rules, Mr. Slater," she said, and walked away.

He rode out later. She knew when he rode out; she heard the sound of his horse's hooves as she sat in the office, trying hard to concentrate on numbers. She walked out front and watched him, and she was restless. This was hard. She had always been such an important part of things.

But they were playing for high stakes. Damned high stakes. She forced herself to sit down again. She weighed the prices she could receive for her beef against the distances she would have to take the herd to collect the money. Then her pencil stopped moving, and she paused and chewed the eraser, and she wondered what it would be like when he came home for dinner that night.

If he came home for dinner that night.

It didn't matter, she told herself. She was forgetting that this whole thing was business. She was certain Cole never forgot for a moment that it was a deal they had made and nothing more.

She had to learn to be aloof. Polite and courteous and mature, but aloof. She had to keep her distance from him. If she didn't, she would get hurt.

Maybe it was too late already. Maybe she had already come too close to the fire. Maybe no matter what happened she was doomed to be hurt. She wasn't so naive that she didn't know she pleased him, but neither was she so foolish as to imagine that it meant anything to him. There was a coldness about him that was like a deep winter frost. It wasn't that he didn't care at all—he did care. But not enough. And he never could care enough, she was certain.

She gave herself a mental shake and decided that she would have to remember herself that it was business—all business. But still she wondered what he would be like if he returned for dinner, and she swore to herself that her own behavior would be the very best the South had ever had to offer.

Cole did return.

And Kristin was charming. She dressed for dinner again, elegantly, in a soft blue brocade with underpanels and a massive, stylish skirt. She remembered her mother, and she was every bit as gracious as she had been. She was careful to refer to him as "Mr. Slater" all the way through the meal. He watched her and he replied in kind, perfectly courteous, as if he'd been trained for society in the finest drawing rooms back East.

When the meal was over, he disappeared outside. Kristin tried to stay up, but at last everyone else had gone to bed, and she walked up the stairs and to the window. She could see him out on the porch, smoking one of her father's fine cigars and drinking brandy from a snifter. He was leaning against one of the pillars and looking up at the night sky.

She wondered what he was thinking, where his heart really lay.

He turned and stared up at her, there in the window. Her face flamed, but he smiled at her.

"Evening," he said softly.

She couldn't reply to him. He watched her curiously for another moment, and his smile deepened, striking against his well-trimmed beard and mustache.

"I'll be right up."

Her heart hammered and slammed against her chest, and she nearly struck her head trying to bring it back in beneath the window frame. She clutched her heart and reminded herself that she had decided to be mature and dignified and not get as flustered as a schoolgirl.

But she was still trembling when he came up the steps. She heard his footsteps in the hallway, and then he opened the door and came into the room. She was still dressed in her blue brocade. He stared at her for a moment, watching the way her breasts rose and fell above the deep décolletage of her gown. He saw the pulse that vibrated against the long, smooth line of her throat. He smiled, and she sensed the curious tenderness that could come to his eyes. "Come here," he told her softly. He held out a hand to her, and she took it and found herself in this arms. And there was nothing awkward about it at all. He kissed her and touched her face, and then he turned her around, and the touch of his fingers against her bare back as he released her gown set her skin to glowing. Like her heart, her flesh seemed to pulse. It occurred to her that he disrobed her so expertly because he had done the same for many women, but it didn't really matter. All that mattered was that her clothing was strewn on the floor and that he was lifting her in his arms and that the soft glow of the moon was with them again. He carried her to the sleigh bed and set her down, and she saw the passion rise in his eyes and come into his touch. She wrapped her arms around him and sighed, savoring the exquisite feel of him against her, the masculine hardness of muscle and limb, the starkly demanding feel of his shaft against her. Somewhere the tumbleweeds tossed, and somewhere the wind blew harsh and wicked and cruel, but here a tempest rose sweet and exciting, wild and exhilarating.

Somewhere battles raged. Somewhere Northerner fought Southerner, and the nation ran with the blood shed by her youth. Blood washed over Kansas and Missouri as if some shared artery had been slashed, but for tonight, Kristin didn't care.

She was alive in his arms, feline and sensual. She was learning where to touch him, how to move with him and against him and how to leave the world behind when she was with him. No drug and no liquor could be so powerful as this elation, so sweet, so all-encompassing.

That night he slept. She stared at his features, and she longed to reach out and touch them, but she did not. She decided that even his nose was strong, long and straight, like a beak against his features. His cheekbones were high, his forehead was wide and his jaw was fine and square beneath the hair of his beard. She wondered at the fine scars that criss-crossed his shoulders and his chest, and then she remembered that he had been with the Union cavalry before the war, and she wondered what battles had done this to him. She longed to touch him so badly....

She reached out, then withdrew her hand. He was an enigma, and he was fascinating. He drew her like the warmth of a fire, and she was afraid. There was so much she didn't know about him. But her fear went deeper than that, for she sensed that though he cared he would never stay. He liked her well enough. He could even be patient with her temper and her uncertainties. He could be careful, and he could be tender, and he seemed as immersed in this startling passion as she was.

But she sensed that he would not stay, could not stay. Not for long. Worse, she sensed that he could never love her, and that she could fall in love with him all too easily. Already, she thought, other men seemed to pale beside him.

Other men...if any remained when the carnage was over.

She walked to the window and looked out at the night. The moon was high, and the paddocks and the outbuildings looked so peaceful there, rising against the flatland. She sighed. For the rest of the country the war had begun when the first shots had been fired at Ford Sumter back in April of '61, but Kansas seemed to have been bleeding forever, and Missouri along with it. The Army of Northern Virginia had defeated the Army of the Potomac at Manassas twice, while along the Mississippi the Union troops were faring a bit better. The North had won the Battle of Shiloh, and just last April New Orleans had fallen to Union troops under Farragut.

It should matter, she thought. It should matter to her who lost and who won. She should care. At Sharpsburg, Maryland, by Antietam Creek, both sides had suffered horribly. She had been in town when the list of the dead had arrived, and it had been devastating. The papers had all cried that the single bloodiest battle of the war had been fought there, and that men had slipped in the blood, and that bodies had fallen on top of other bodies. All she had seen was the tears of the mothers, the sweethearts, the lovers—the families of boys who had left to join the Union Army and the families who had sons fighting with the Confederacy. She had looked for Matthew's name, and she had not seen it, and she had thanked God. But then she had felt the tears around her, felt the agony of the parents, the sisters, the brothers. And yet sometimes it felt as if the real war were remote here. Here the war had been reduced to sheer terrorism. Men did not battle men; they set out to commit murder.

Here it had become a question of survival. All she wanted to do was survive.

She shivered suddenly and realized that she had come naked from the bed and that the night air was cold. She turned and saw that Cole was awake. His eyes were caught by the moonlight as he watched her. They glimmered curiously, and again she wondered at his secret thoughts. Then his gaze fell slowly over the length of her and she realized again that she was naked, and that his very eyes could touch her like a caress.

"Are you all right?" he asked her.

She felt as if she were going to cry, and she didn't know why.

"I was just thinking about the war," she said quietly.

Something covered his eyes, some careful shield. "It seems far away right now, doesn't it? Then again, I don't think we're even fighting the same war as the rest of the country here." There was a harsh bitterness in his tone, and she suddenly felt cold, as if she had turned him against her, or as if she had even made him forget she was there. But then his eyes focused on her again, and they were rueful and surprisingly tender. "Don't think about it," he told her. "Don't think about the war. You can't change it."

She wanted to say something, but she couldn't find her voice, and so she nodded.

"Come back to bed. It's late," he said. Even when he whispered, his voice was so deep. It entered into her and became the wind again.

She forgot about the war. She forgot about the rest of the world. His voice, his beckoning, had that power over her. Her stomach fluttered and her nipples hardened, and she felt she had to cover herself quickly. She had become so bold, so brash. She was standing here naked as a jaybird, and they were talking, and she should have the decency to reach out for something and cover her nudity.

But she did not. She straightened and tossed back her head, and her hair, golden fire in the moonlight, tumbled down the length of her back. She walked toward him. If nothing else, perhaps they could have honesty between them. She honestly wanted him. She wanted these nights. She wanted the way she felt in his arms, wanted this ecstasy that seemed sweeter than life itself.

She came, he thought, very slowly, very sinuously. She allowed a natural sway to come into her walk, and she moved with a feline grace and purpose that set his blood aflame. He was glad that covers lay over his body, for his response to her was instant and instinctive. He clenched his fists at his sides and waited for her. Waited until she stood above him. Then he reached out, pulled her down to him and held her in his arms. He savaged her lips, groaning with the sweet, aching pleasure of it.

He had never thought it could happen, but he had found an oasis with her. He had known she was beautiful, like a sunrise, like the corn that had grown endlessly in the fields before they had run with blood. He had known that he wanted her.

He had not known how badly, how completely, he would come to need her.

Her eyes were a distant sea that claimed him, and the golden skeins of her hair were webs that entrapped him and brought him softly into a dream of paradise. He could not love her, but he could want her, and he did. He hungered for her, as if he could not be filled. She sated him completely, but then she touched him again, or she moved, or she whispered, and he wanted her again. He had taken her from innocence and he had set the woman within her free, and though she came to him with sensual grace, she held on to something of innocence too, and he wondered at that gift. He had to touch her, had to run his fingers over the fine, delicate beauty of her face, had to press his palms against the lush curve of her breast. He had to breathe in her scent.

It had to end, he knew. But he groaned aloud as her nails stroked against his back, as her hips thrust forward. It had to end, he reminded himself....

But then he ceased to think and gave way to urgent need and fevered desire. He looked into her eyes, blue eyes that were soft, radiant and glazed with passion. He swept her beneath him, and he sank into her as he sank into the dream. She eased the pain. She gave him moments of ecstasy. He could not remember ever having needed a woman so badly. He could not remember so insistent a beat, so desperate, so thunderous a rhythm.

This was like nothing he had ever known. Beautiful, sleek, sensual, she moved beneath him. He became as taut as wire, then shook and shuddered, and spasms continued to rack him.

Later she slept. He cast an elbow behind his head and stared bleakly at the ceiling, shadowed in the moonlight.

It was wrong, he thought. When vengeance lay upon his soul and his heart was barren, it was wrong.

But he could not, would not, make himself cease. She had come to him with the deal. He had not wrung it from her.

That didn't excuse him.

But he needed her....

That didn't excuse him, either. But it mattered. Somehow they had interwoven their lives, and that—as with so many other things—was simply the way it was.

That was simply the way it was.

But still he turned to her. He saw the beautiful curves of her body as she slept, and the tangle of her hair over her shoulders, falling to her flanks, wild and yet somehow virginal. He saw her features, her parted lips and the soft way she breathed. He saw her brow, and he touched it gently, trying to ease the frown line from it. She seemed so very young to have suffered so very much. But she was a fighter. No matter what they had done to her, she had come back up, kicking, fighting. Maybe that was why he couldn't leave her.

He had to leave her, he reminded himself. Soon.

This time it was he who rose. He walked to the window and looked out at the moon. He would have to leave soon, for a time, at least.

He watched the moon, and at last he shrugged. He'd get to the telegraph office tomorrow and hope he could get a message through. He didn't know how long he would have to be gone, but he didn't want her alone. Not now.

Just how long could he guard her?

And would he keep dreaming? He closed his eyes. Dreaming again and again, of one death, of another...

The question washed over his heart, cold as ice. He didn't know. No, he did know. Come hell or high water—or Yankees or Quantrill's raiders—he would find a way to guard her. He wasn't sure why. Maybe it was because this was a matter of honor, and there wasn't much honor left in his world.

And maybe it was because he wanted her so badly. Because she was the only antidote to pain. Because when he was with her he could almost forget...

He didn't want to forget.

Yes, he did. For those few moments.

Whatever the reason, he thought impatiently, he had struck a bargain. He would protect her. He would protect her if she grew hair all over her body and sprouted a full mustache, he swore to himself.

Then he smiled slowly. He was one hell of a liar, he thought, even to himself. She needed him, and he wanted her. That was the bargain.

No. He would protect her, damn it and he would do it so that he never had to hold her bleeding in his arms. He clenched his jaw to keep from crying out. He would protect her because he could not let it happen again.

He breathed slowly and tried to relax.

He would protect her. He had the power. They would help each other, and then he would ride away. The war had to end some day.

Please, God, he thought bleakly. It had to.

The days passed and things were very much the same. After a few days Cole let Kristin ride with him. It was necessary, because the men were busy with the cattle. Kristin showed Cole the length and breadth of her land. She showed him the water holes, and where the land was apt to flood when the rains came too heavily. They went out together searching for a calf that had strayed, and they went into town to buy a length of fencing for the north pasture.

But things felt strange even though they were together. They were polite workmates, cool, courteous acquaintances. Kristin and Shannon always dressed for dinner, because Kristin was determined to cling to what was left of civilization in her life, and the evening meal was her chance to do that. But the conversation there was stilted, too. Cole seldom had much to say to her that wasn't directly concerned with the ranch, with guns, with warnings about the future. She was never to wander around unarmed, and neither was Shannon. He didn't seem to need to warn Delilah or Samson.

He was always polite to Shannon. It seemed to Kristin that her little sister was growing up before her very eyes. Shannon would be eighteen soon, and she was beginning to look every inch the woman. Cole treated her like a child, not condescendingly but with a gentle patience that irritated Kristin. She would have liked some of that patience for herself. Sometimes she asked him very blunt questions, but he invariably ignored her or turned the tables on her. When she demanded to know why he insisted on being such a mystery to her, he merely replied that she had no right to know anything about his past or his future and that she shouldn't be asking.

It didn't matter if she walked away from him, and it didn't matter if she made a sharp reply. He just let her go, or he let her say whatever she wanted and then walked away himself.

But the nights were always the same.

There were times when she couldn't believe she was the same girl who had first met him, innocent, frightened, naive. Even when she felt her temper soar she longed for the night. And even if she turned away from him he stroked her back slowly, moving his fingers down her spine to her buttocks, so lightly that she thought she had imagined it. But his touch was lightning, and it always instilled the same seeds of desire within her. If she really tried to ignore him and he let her be, she sometimes resorted to a soft sigh, feigning sleep, and rolled against him...until he touched her again. Then she sensed his smile, and knew that he knew that she wasn't asleep at all, and that he didn't mind pretending that he needed her more than she needed him.

It went on....

It went on until she woke up one morning, cold and alone. That wasn't so unusual. He was able to get by on much less sleep than she. But somehow she didn't think he had awakened and gone downstairs. She felt a growing sense of dread.

He was gone.

She heard sounds. A rider. Wrenching a sheet from the bed, she raced to the window and stared down at the paddock area. A man had just come riding in on a big bay horse.

She put her hand to her mouth, biting down hard to keep from crying out. He was dressed in gray. She studied the uniform and gold trim.

Cavalry. The man was a Southern cavalry officer.

She turned around and dressed quickly, finding pants and a shirt and her boots. She told herself that she was a Southerner, that she had been born a Southerner and that only Quantrill had made her fear and hate her own people.

She tried to smile, reminding herself that Shannon's great hero was Jeb Stuart, a Southern cavalry officer.

It didn't help. Fear raced through her, and she wondered if the officer had been sent by Zeke or his men.

Cole had told her never to walk around unarmed. She had proven she could use a Colt six-shooter and use it well. She slid her narrow gun belt over her hips and nervously checked to see that her weapons were loaded. Then she started down the stairs.

The house was silent. Where was Shannon? she wondered. She couldn't help it. She had awful visions of her beautiful sister caught in the stables with the men all out on the ranch, caught and thrown down in the hay and viciously raped.

She swallowed and tried to tell herself that she was panicking for nothing. But the house was silent, and she still sensed that Cole was gone. Not just off on the ranch somewhere—gone. She couldn't have explained how she knew. It was an emptiness. It festered inside her, and it held her in an awful anguish.

But this...

This was more urgent. "Delilah?"

No one answered her. Delilah was not in the kitchen, and neither was Samson. She didn't hear the baby crying, and she had no idea where Shannon was.

And the cavalry officer hadn't come to knock at her door.

She crept out the back door, careful to keep it from slamming behind her. Walking as quickly and silently as she could, she came around the corner of the house. The man was gone, and the horse was gone.

Her heart was beating much too quickly. She dropped low and raced over the dry sand to the barn. She followed the line of the buildings, coming closer and closer to the corner.

She paused and inhaled sharply. Her blood raced, and she tried desperately to still her erratic breathing.

She rounded the corner and she came face-to-face with an Enfield rifle.

Behind it stood the man in the Confederate cavalry officer's uniform. It was worn and faded, the gold epaulets frayed.

"Drop it!" he warned her. His eyes were teal, a beautiful color. They were also sharp as razors.

She realized that she was aiming the Colt at him.

"You drop it!" she barked.

He smiled. She realized that he was young and very, very good-looking. And familiar in some way she couldn't quite put her finger on.

"This Enfield can blow a hole right through you."

"It's not a totally dependable weapon."

"At this range? Impossible to miss."

"A Colt will scalp you faster than an Indian would dare dream."

He was tall, masculine and elegant in the worn uniform. He didn't intend to harm her, she was certain. But she didn't lower the barrel of the gun. She had learned not to take any chances.

"Kristin McCahy?"

"Yes."

He laughed and lowered the rifle. "Why in God's name were you sneaking up on me like that?"

She jammed the Colt into her holster, instinct assuring her that she was in no danger. She shook her head ruefully.

"I'm sorry. This is my property. And you are a total stranger, you know. Slinking around on it. My property, that is. I mean...who the hell are you?"

"Slinking?" he inquired indignantly, but there was a twinkle in his eyes. He swept his hat from his head and bowed deeply, an elegant and manly cavalier. "Miss McCahy, I assure you that Slaters do not slink."

"Slater?" she demanded with a quick frown.

"Captain Malachi Slater, ma'am. Cole's brother. On leave—and on new duty, or so it seems. You mean to tell me that Cole didn't say anything?"

She felt as if her knees were going to crumble. Cole was gone. And he hadn't even said goodbye.

"Cole—"

"He had a few things to attend to. I'll be with you for a while. If you don't mind."

She did mind. She minded terribly. Not that Malachi was here, but that Cole was gone. She forced herself to smile and to extend her hand. "Why, Mr. Slater, I'm thrilled and grateful for your appearance. Completely thrilled and entirely grateful."

"Thank you, Miss McCahy." He took her hand and raised it to his lips. Then his blue eyes met hers again and she was certain that he knew everything. And there was something in his gaze that suggested that he understood her feelings.

She withdrew her hand suddenly. "Oh, my God!"

"What?"

"You're a Confederate officer."

He stiffened, and his jaw took on a stubborn set that reminded her of his brother. "Miss, last I heard, Missourians were still considering themselves Southerners—for the most part, that is."

Kristin nodded vaguely. "Well, yes, Mr. Slater. But this is a border country. Half the land around here is occupied by Federal forces."

"Don't worry about me. I'll change into civilian clothing quickly, and I'll avoid the Federals."

She shook her head again. "It's just that, well, I have a brother who is a—"

"A Yankee?"

"Ah...yes, a Yankee."

He looked a lot like Cole. A whole lot. He was very tall and very broad-shouldered in his dress shirt and cape, and at the moment he looked very severe, as if he were about to explode.

But he didn't explode. He suddenly started laughing. "Well, it's one hell of a war, isn't it, Miss McCahy? One hell of a war."

Suddenly the wall behind them exploded. Wood chips went flying from the solid impact of a bullet.

"What the hell?" Malachi shouted. He dragged her to the ground, shielding her with his body. Once again there was the sound of gunfire, and another bullet tore into the walls, sending more wood chips cascading down on them.

"Damn it, what the hell!" Malachi repeated.

What the hell indeed? Kristin had no idea who was firing at them.

Chapter Eight

Kristin lay facedown on the ground, dirt in her mouth, with Malachi on top of her, protecting her. Finally the firing stopped and she heard soft footsteps.

"Get off her, Reb!" Kristin almost laughed out loud with relief. It was Shannon.

"Watch it with that thing, little girl," Malachi said slowly, easing himself away from Kristin. He had angry narrowed eyes leveled on her sister. Kristin sprang to her feet and stepped between them. Shannon's temper was flaring, and her eyes were sparkling dangerously.

"I'm not a little girl, Reb, and I swear I'm damned accurate with this Colt," Shannon replied.

"Why, you little—" Malachi began.

"Stop, stop!" Kristin begged, reaching for the gun. She couldn't imagine trying to explain to Cole Slater why they had murdered his brother. "Shannon—"

"He's a Reb, Kristin. He's probably one of Quantrill's—"

"Don't you know a regular cavalry uniform when you see one, girl?"

Kristin lost patience and swung around. "Mr. Slater, please, just for a minute, shut up. Shannon, this is Cole's brother."

"Brother?"

Her eyes wide, she looked at Malachi, then at Kristin again. "Are you sure? They don't look much alike!"

"We have identical big toes," Malachi snapped sarcastically. Shannon stiffened.

Then, suddenly, there was the sound of another explosion. The three of them stared at one another blankly. Wood chips flew as a second bullet struck the barn wall above their heads.

"Get down—" Malachi began.

"Drop that gun!" The order was spoken in a commanding, masculine tone.

Shannon wasn't about to obey. She spun around, aiming. Malachi swore and slammed his fist down on her wrists. The Colt fell to the ground, and Shannon turned on Malachi, swearing and flailing at him with her fists. Malachi swore in return, and Kristin wondered how the two of them could be going at one another this way when someone else was firing at all three of them. They were warning shots, she realized. She stared blankly across the yard and saw that another man had come out of the shadows of the porch. He was younger than Cole and Malachi and dressed like a rancher in high boots, a long railway frock coat and a slouch hat that sat low on his forehead. Malachi paid no attention to him. As he came forward, the stranger tipped his hat to Kristin.

"They've got a set of rotten tempers between them, huh?"

"Do they?" Kristin crossed her arms over her chest and stared at the young man who had been doing the shooting. Shannon was still shrieking, fighting the hold Malachi had on her. Kristin ignored them both and kept staring at the newcomer. "Why were you shooting at us?"

"I thought she meant to poke a hole right through old Malachi there," he said solemnly. He had cloudlike blue-gray eyes and tawny hair. He smiled again. It was an engaging smile, and Kristin almost smiled, too, in spite of herself.

"I take it you're another Slater? Or are you a friend of the family?"

He stuck out his hand. "Jamie, ma'am."

Malachi let out something that sounded like a growl. "Damned brat bit me!" he thundered.

"Shannon!" Kristin implored.

She might have bitten Malachi, but the bite didn't keep him from maintaining his hold upon her, his arms around her waist. Her toes were barely touching the ground.

"Ah, Malachi." Jamie shook his head sorrowfully and said to Kristin, "He met Grant at Shiloh but he can't handle a little wisp of a girl."

"I'm not—" Shannon began.

"You are a foolish little brat!" Malachi said, releasing her at last and shoving her towards Kristin. She would have swung at him again, but Kristin caught her sister's arms. "Shannon, please!"

But Shannon was still staring at Malachi, seething. "I am not a brat, Reb. You attacked my sister—"

"And you attacked my brother," Jamie said pleasantly. "We're all even. And if Cole were here he'd say the entire lot of us were a pack of fools playing around with firearms. But then, Cole isn't here, and that's why Malachi and I are. Maybe we ought to try and start over."

"Cole sent you, too?" Kristin asked Jamie.

"Yes, ma'am, he did."

"I see," Kristin said stiffly.

Jamie grinned broadly. "No, ma'am, I doubt if you see at all. He had some business to attend to."

"I told her," Malachi said.

"My brother is a cavalry officer," Shannon snapped at Malachi, ignoring everything else. "And if he knew you were on his property he'd skewer you right through!"

He shook his head, looking as if he were about to explode. Then he exhaled in an exaggerated display of patience. "I thought I was supposed to be looking out for Quantrill, not a two-bit piece of baggage!" He shoved his hat down hard over his forehead and started walking toward the house. Kristin, amused, stared after him. Shannon, amazed, placed her hands on her hips.

"Where do you think you're going?" she called.

Malachi stopped and swung around. "In. For coffee and breakfast. And if you don't like it, little girl, that's just too damned bad. You take it up with Cole the next time you see him. He asked me to be here, and I'm here, and I won't be leaving, not until he gets back. Until that time, you do us both a favor. You stay clear of me. Way clear." He paused, then swore softly again. "Hell, I could still be out there with the Yankees. It'd be a hell of a lot less nerve-racking than a morning here!'' Once again he turned. Kristin saw that Delilah was on the steps, watching them. She was grinning broadly.

"You must be Mr. Malachi.''

Delilah's voice floated down to Kristin, and Kristin arched a brow at her. She and Shannon hadn't known that Cole's brothers were coming, but Delilah had. Cole had told Delilah what he was up to, and he hadn't said a word to them.

She gritted her teeth, damning Cole a thousand times over. What was this business he had to attend to? They had made a deal. Zeke was still out there somewhere. She didn't need a pair of baby-sitters. She needed to have Zeke taken care of.

And she needed to have Cole talk to her, to tell her about his life, not just walk away from her when the sun came up.

"You come on in,'' Delilah was saying to Malachi. "Breakfast's on the table, boys. Breakfast's on the table.''

Kristin felt Jamie watching her. She turned to him, and she flushed, surprised by the knowing assessment she saw in his eyes. He had been reading her mind, or else he had been wondering about her relationship with his brother. No, he seemed to know what their relationship was already. She could read that in the look he was giving her.

Then he smiled, as if he had already decided that he liked her, and so she smiled, too. She liked Jamie. And she liked Malachi. She even liked the war he was waging with Shannon. She had felt like laughing as she'd watched them and she hadn't felt like laughing in a long time.

"I'm awful hungry, too,'' Jamie said. He offered her his arm. "Shall we go in for breakfast?''

Kristin hesitated, then took his arm, and they started toward the house. She paused, turning back to her sister. "Shannon?''

"I'll skip breakfast,'' Shannon said heatedly, her bright blue eyes still on Malachi's retreating back. "I don't rightly feel like sitting down with—'' She paused when she saw that Jamie was studying her intently. "I'm not hungry.'' She spun around and stomped off to the barn. Kristin looked at Jamie again.

"Just where is Cole? I don't need looking after like this, you know. Cole and I had a—an agreement.''

She studied his eyes, trying hard not to flush.

"You talk to Cole about his whereabouts later,'' Jamie said flatly. Neither of the Slaters was going to say a thing about Cole's absence, she realized. "And we're here 'cause of your agreement. We know Quantrill and his boys. We're just here to see that you're safe. Do you really mind? Terribly?''

"No, I, uh…of course not. You're both very welcome,'' she said, forcing herself to smile. They were welcome, they really were. It was just that…

It was just that she wondered where the hell Cole had gone. She wondered if it had to do with another woman, and she wondered if she could bear it if it did.

Don't fall in love with him! she warned herself again. But he was gone, and she was aching, and it was too late. He wasn't involved and she was, and it was gnawing away at her. She forced her smile to remain in place. "Jamie, you are very welcome. Come on. Delilah makes an incredible breakfast.''

He rode southeast the first day. The farther east he went in Missouri, the more closemouthed and careful people were about Quantrill and his gang.

It was natural, he supposed. It had all turned into such a hideous, ugly thing.

The ugliness had taken hold way back in the 1850s when John Brown had come into Missouri with his followers and killed slaveholders. Cole didn't really know what to think of John Brown. He had seen the man at his trial, and he had thought then that old John Brown spoke like a fanatic. But he had also thought that he spoke from conviction, too, when he said that only a bloodbath could cleanse the country of the sin of slavery.

John Brown and his followers had gone on to raid the arsenal at Harper's Ferry. Robert E. Lee—then an officer of the United States Army—had been sent in to capture John Brown. Jeb Stuart had been with the forces sent to Harper's Ferry, too.

Cole had been with them himself, riding right alongside Jeb. They had captured John Brown and taken him to Charlestown to stand trial. There hadn't been any Confederacy then. And Cole hadn't known what was to come.

In the North they had quickly begun to sing, "John Brown's body lies a-molderin' in the grave," conveniently forgetting that even if the man had been a God-fearing murderer, he had still been a murderer.

And in Missouri men had learned to retaliate.

Quantrill and his raiders were worshipped by the people here, people who had known nothing but death and destruction from the Kansas jayhawkers. Cole had to be careful. When he stopped at a farmhouse, he quickly made his presence known. He asked for a sip of water from a well, then asked if anyone knew where he might find Quantrill or any of his boys. He was polite, and he smiled, and he used his best country accent, and he kept it filled with respect.

In return he was pointed more and more toward the south. Finally, in a small town almost fifty miles south of Osceola, he heard that Quantrill was at the local saloon.

No one was afraid there. Quantrill's boys were in charge. The South had a good grip on its own here. At a farmhouse outside the town, Cole was invited in for a meal, and the farmer assured him that he could find Quantrill at the saloon at about six that evening.

Cole rode in carefully. If he saw Quantrill first, or Anderson, he'd be all right, but he didn't want to run into Zeke, not now. In case he did, though, he rode in with his six-shooters and two shotguns loaded and ready.

Things were quiet enough as he rode into town. It was almost as if there were no war. Nicely dressed women with stylish hats stood outside the mercantile. As he rode slowly along the dusty main street, they stared at him, and he tipped his hat. They blushed and whispered to one another.

That was when Cole realized that the quiet little town was pulsing with an inner excitement and that things weren't really quiet at all. He could hear the sound of laughter and piano music up ahead and saw a sign that read Red Door Saloon. There were at least eight horses tethered out front.

Quantrill and company do reign here, he thought. He reined in his horse and dismounted, dropping the reins over the post in front of the saloon and dusting off his hands. Then he headed for the red door that had given the saloon its name.

He opened the door and stood there, blinking in the dim light. Then he swiftly cast his gaze over the Red Door's patrons.

Zeke wasn't there.

But William Clarke Quantrill was, playing cards at a round table, leaning back with a thin cigar in his mouth. He was a pale, ashen man with dark hair and a neat brown mustache. He saw Cole just as Cole saw him, and he smiled.

He tossed his cards down and stood. He was of average height, about five foot nine. There was nothing about the man to label him the scourge of the West. Nothing except his eyes. They were pale blue and as cold as death.

"Cole. Cole Slater. Well, I'll be damned. To what do I owe this honor?"

Cole didn't answer him. He'd already looked around the room, and looked hard. Zeke wasn't there, but Cole was certain that Quantrill wasn't alone. He wasn't. Cole recognized the other four around the table as young recruits. The two James boys, Jesse and Frank, were there, along with Bill Anderson and little Archie Clements. Cole was sure, too, that Quantrill had more men in the saloon. It wasn't that he had anything to fear here. He was a hero in these parts. It didn't matter that he made out lists of men to be executed. It didn't matter that his men were rapists, murderers and thieves. All that mattered was that what had been done to the Missourians by the jayhawkers was being returned to the Kansans twice over by the bushwhackers.

Cole hadn't come here to do battle, anyway. He strode into the saloon, toward the poker table. The piano player had stopped playing. Everyone in the room was watching him.

He reached Quantrill. Quantrill had his hand extended. Cole took it. "Quantrill," he acknowledged quietly, nodding to the other men at the table. "Jesse. Frank. Archie. Bill. You all look fit. War seems to agree with you."

"Bushwhacking agrees with me," Archie Clements admitted freely. He was dark and had a mean streak a yard wide. "Hell, Cole, I couldn't make it in no ordinary unit. Besides, I'm fighting Yanks for Missouri, and that's it. 'Course, now, you aren't so much regular army, either, are you, Cole? What do they call you? A spy? A scout? Or are you still just a raider?"

"I'm a major, Archie, and that's what they call me," Cole said flatly.

Quantrill was watching the two of them. He turned to the piano player and said, "Hey, what's the problem there, Judah? Let's have something light and fancy here, shall we? Archie, you and Bill take the James boys over to the bar for a whiskey. Seems to me that Cole must have made this trip 'cause he's got something to say. I want to hear it."

Archie stood, but he looked at Cole suspiciously.

"You alone, Cole?"

"That's right, Archie. I'm alone."

Archie nodded at last. Young Jesse James kept staring at Cole. "It was good to see you again, Major Slater. We miss you when we ride. You were damned good."

Damned good with his guns, that was what the boy meant. What the hell was going to be in store for these men when the war was over? If they survived the war.

"You take care, Jesse. You, too, Frank," Cole said. He drew up a chair next to Quantrill. Quantrill started to deal out the cards. "You still a gambling man, Cole?"

"Always," Cole told him, picking up his cards. A buxom brunette with a headful of rich curls, black fishnet stockings and a blood-red dress came over. She nudged up against Quantrill's back but flashed Cole a deep, welcoming smile.

"Want some whiskey for your friend there, Willy?"

"Sure. Bring over the best. We've got a genuine Confederate scout in our midst. But he used to be one of mine, Jennifer. Yep, for a while there he was one of my best."

"He'd be one of anybody's best, I'm sure," Jennifer drawled, fluttering her dark lashes.

Cole flashed her an easy smile, surprised to discover that he felt nothing when he looked at her. She was a pretty thing, very sexual, but she didn't arouse him in the least. You're too satisfied, he warned himself. He found himself frowning and wondering if he shouldn't be interested. At least then he'd know he could be. He shrugged. He was committed—for the moment. And he'd be taking a long ride away soon enough. There'd be plenty of time to prove things to himself then if he had to. That bothered him, too. He shouldn't have to feel the need to prove things to himself.

He shouldn't feel any of these things. Not when his wife lay dead.

"Get the man a whiskey," Quantrill said sharply. Jennifer pouted, then spun around. "What's this all about?" he demanded of Cole.

"The McCahy girls," Cole said flatly.

Quantrill frowned. He didn't seem to recognize the name, and Cole felt sure he wasn't acting. "I don't know them."

Jennifer returned with a new bottle of good Irish whiskey and a pair of shot glasses. She was going to pour out the amber liquid, but Quantrill shooed her away and poured out the shots himself.

"Your man Zeke has been after them."

Quantrill met his frown. "Zeke? Zeke Moreau? I didn't even know the two of you had met. Zeke came in after you were gone."

"Not quite. We met. But I don't think he remembered me when we met again."

Comprehension dawned in Quantrill's cold eyes. "The farmhouse? Near the border? That was you, Cole?"

"Yeah, that was me." Cole leaned forward. He picked up his glass and swallowed down its contents. It was good. Smooth. The kind of stuff that was becoming rare in the South as the war went on and on. He poured himself another shot. He could feel Quantrill's eyes on him. He sensed that Quantrill wasn't angry. He seemed amused more than anything else.

"So you came back to beat my boys up, huh?"

Quantrill poured himself another glass of whiskey, then sat back, swirling the liquid, studying its amber color. Cole looked at him. "No, I just happened by your boys at work, and I'll admit I was kind of sick to my stomach at the war they were waging. They dragged out an old man and killed him. Then they came back after his daughter. Seems the lady had the bad luck to dislike Zeke."

Quantrill shrugged. His amusement was fading. "You don't like my methods?"

"You've become a cold-blooded killer, Quantrill."

"I didn't know anything about the McCahy place."

"I believe you," Cole said.

Quantrill watched him for a moment, a sly smile creeping onto his lips again. "Hell, Cole, you're starting to sound like some damned Yankee."

"I'm not a Yankee."

"Yankee lover, then."

"I don't want the girl touched, Quantrill."

"My, my..." Quantrill leaned back, idly running a finger around the rim of his glass. "Seems to me that you weren't so finicky back in February of '61, Mr. Slater. Who was heading up the jayhawkers back then? Was it Jim Lane, or was Doc Jennison calling the shots by then? Don't make no real matter, does it? They came riding down into Missouri like a twister." He came forward, resting his elbows on the table. "Yessir, just like a twister. They burned down your place, but that wasn't enough. They had to have their fun with Mrs. Slater. Course, she was a beauty, wasn't she, Cole?"

Cole felt his face constrict. He felt his pulse hammering against his throat. He longed to jump forward and throttle the life out of Quantrill, to close those pale, calculating eyes forever.

"Nope, you weren't so finicky about methods when I met you first, Cole Slater. You had revenge on your mind, and nothing more."

Cole forced his lips to curl into a humorless smile. "You're wrong, Quantrill. Yeah, I wanted vengeance. But I could never see murder done in cold blood. I could never draw up a list of men to be gunned down. I could never see dragging terrified, innocent women out of their beds to be raped and abused. Or shooting down children."

"Hell, Cole. Children fight in this war."

"And that's the hell of it, Quantrill. That's the whole bloody hell of it. The war is hell enough. The savagery is too much."

"We fight like we've been attacked, and that's the plain truth of it. You go see the likes of Lane or Jennison. Tell them about innocents. You can't change the war, Cole. Not you, and not anybody else. Not anybody."

"I didn't come here today to end the war, Quantrill," Cole said calmly.

"You just want me to rein in on Zeke, is that it?"

"Well," Cole told him casually, "you can rein in on him or I can kill him."

Quantrill grinned and shrugged. "You're overestimating my power, Slater. You want me to call Zeke in when this girl isn't anything to you. Not anything at all. She's not your sister and she's not your wife. Hell, from what I understand, Zeke saw her first. So what do you think I can do?"

"You can stop him."

Quantrill sat back again, perplexed. He lifted a hand idly, then let it fall to his lap. "What are you so worried about? You can outdraw Zeke. You can outdraw any ten men I know."

"I don't perform executions, Quantrill."

"Ah...and you're not going to be around for the winter, huh? Well, neither are we. We'll be moving south soon enough—"

"I want a guarantee, Quantrill."

Quantrill was silent. He lifted his glass, tossed back his head and swallowed the whiskey down in a gulp, then wiped his mouth with his sleeve. His eyes remained on Cole. He set the glass down.

"Marry her."

"What?" Cole said sharply.

"You want me to give the girl a guarantee of safety. A girl Zeke saw first. A girl he wants—badly, I'd say. So you give me something. Give me a reason to keep him away from her. Let me be able to tell the men that she's your wife. That's why they have to stay clear. She'll be the wife of a good loyal Confederate. They'll understand that."

Cole shook his head. "I'm not marrying again, Quantrill. Not ever."

"Then what is this McCahy girl to you?"

What indeed, he wondered. "I just don't want her hurt anymore, that's all."

Quantrill shook his head slowly, and there was a flash of something that might have been compassion in his pale eyes. "There's nothing that I can do, Slater. Nothing. Not unless you can give me something to go on."

The damnedest thing about it, Cole thought, was that Quantrill seemed to want to help him. He wasn't trying to be difficult and he wasn't looking for a fight. He was just telling it the way it was.

"We will be gone pretty soon," Quantrill said. "Another month of raids, maybe. Then the winter will come crashing down. I intend to be farther south by then. Kansas winter ain't no time to be foraging and fighting. Maybe she'll be safe. From us, at least. The jayhawkers might come down on the ranch, but Quantrill and company will be seeking some warmth."

"Another month," Cole muttered.

Quantrill shrugged.

The two men sat staring at one another for several moments. Then Quantrill poured more whiskey.

He couldn't marry her. She couldn't be his wife. He'd had a wife. His wife was dead.

He picked up the whiskey and drank it down in one swallow. It burned. It tore a path of fire straight down his throat and into his gut.

"You going east?" Quantrill asked.

Cole nodded. Maybe he shouldn't have, but Quantrill knew he would have to get to Richmond sooner or later, and probably sooner.

Cole let out a snarl and slammed his glass down on the table. The piano player stopped playing again. Silence filled the saloon, like something living and breathing. All eyes turned toward Cole and Quantrill.

Cole stood. "I'm going to marry her," he told Quantrill. Then he looked around at the sea of faces. "I'm going to marry Kristin McCahy, and I don't want her touched. Not her, and not her sister. The McCahy ranch is going to be my ranch, and I'm promising a slow, painful death to any man who thinks about molesting any of my property."

Quantrill stood slowly and looked around at his men. "Hell, Cole, we're all on the same side here, aren't we, boys?"

There was silence, and then a murmur of assent. Quantrill lifted the whiskey bottle. "Let's drink! Let's drink to Cole Slater's bride, Miss McCahy! Why, Slater, not a man jack here would think to molest your property, or your woman. She's under our protection. You've got my word on it."

Quantrill spoke loudly, in a clear voice. He meant what he said. Kristin would be safe.

Quantrill offered Cole his hand, and Cole took it. They held fast for a moment, their eyes locked. Quantrill smiled. Cole stepped back, looked around the room and turned to leave. He had his back to the room, but he had probably never been safer in his life. Quantrill had guaranteed his safety.

He walked through the red door, his shoulders squared. Outside, he felt the sun on his face, but the breeze was cool. Fall was fading, and winter was on its way.

He had just said he would marry her.

Hell.

The sun was bright, the air was cool, and the sky was cloudless and blue. He stared at the sun, and he felt cold. He felt a coldness that seeped right into him, that swept right around his heart. It was a bitter cold, so deep that it hurt.

He found his horse's reins and pushed the huge animal back from the others almost savagely so that he could mount. Then he turned and started at a trot down the street.

It couldn't be helped. He had said he would do it, and he had to carry it through.

He had to marry her.

It wouldn't be real, though. It wouldn't mean anything at all. It would just be the way it had to be, and that would be that.

The cold seeped into him again. It encompassed and encircled his heart, and he felt the numbness there again, and then the pain.

He couldn't do it. He couldn't marry another woman. He couldn't call her his wife.

He would marry her. But he never would call her his wife.

Malachi was the more serious of Cole's two brothers, Kristin quickly discovered. Like Cole, he had gone to West Point. He had studied warfare, from the campaigns of Alexander the Great to the American Revolution to Napoleon's grand attempts to take over Europe and Russia. He understood the South's situation in the present struggle for independence, and perhaps that understanding was the cause of gravity. He was on leave for no more than three weeks, so he would have to be returning soon to his unit. Kristin wondered if that meant Cole would return soon. Malachi was courteous to her. He seemed to be the last of the great Southern gentleman, perhaps the last cavalier. Shannon retained her hostility toward him, though. Since Malachi's arrival, she had become a Unionist. She loved to warn both Malachi and Jamie that her brother would come back and make them into nothing more than dust in the wind. Jamie was amused by Shannon. Malachi considered her a dangerous annoyance. Since Kristin had her own problems with Cole, she decided that Shannon was on her own.

Kristin didn't think Matthew would make it home. The last letter she had received from him had stated that his company had been sent East and that he was fighting with the Army of the Potomac.

Malachi didn't wear his cavalry butternut and gray while he was with them at the ranch. He fit into Matthew's breeches fine, and since Federal patrols had been known to wander over the border, it seemed best for him to dress in civilian clothing. Two weeks after his arrival, Kristin heard hoofbeats outside and hurried to the porch. To her vast astonishment, Jamie sat whittling on the steps while Malachi held Shannon in a deep engrossing embrace, kissing her as hotly as a newlywed. Stunned, Kristin stared at Jamie. Jamie pointed to two men in Union blue who were riding away.

"She started to mention that things might not be all they seemed," Jamie drawled. "Malachi didn't take kindly to the notion of spending the rest of the war in a Yankee prison camp."

There was a sharp crack. Kristin spun around to see that Shannon had just slapped Malachi.

Her sister's language was colorful, to say the least. She compared Malachi Slater to a milk rat, a rattlesnake and a Texas scorpion. Malachi, her fingerprints staining his face, didn't appreciate her words. Kristin gasped when he dragged her onto his lap and prepared to bruise her derriere.

Shannon screamed. Jamie shrugged. Kristin decided she had to step in at last. Kristin pleaded with him, but he ignored her at first. She hadn't the strength to come to physical blows with him, so all she could do was appeal to his valor. "Malachi, I'm sure she didn't mean—"

"She damned well did mean!" Malachi shouted. "And I may fall to a Yankee bullet, but I'll be damned if I'll rot in a hellhole because this little piece of baggage has a vicious heart!''

His palm cracked just once against Shannon's flesh.

"Rodent!" Shannon screeched.

"Please—" Kristin began.

Malachi shifted Shannon into his arms, ready to lecture here.

Then Jamie suddenly stood up, dropped his knife and the wood he'd been whittling and reached for his Colt.

"Horses!" he hissed.

A sudden silence settled over them. Malachi didn't release Shannon, but she froze, too, neither sniffling in indignation nor screaming out her hatred.

Kristin glanced at Jamie. She could tell he was afraid that the Union patrol was on its way back. That Malachi's act just hadn't been good enough. That Shannon had exposed them all to danger.

They all saw the riders. Two of them.

Kristin saw Jamie's tension ease, and then Malachi, too, seemed to relax. Even his desire for vengeance against Shannon seemed to have ebbed. He suddenly set her down on the wooden step, not brutally but absently. Still, Shannon gasped out, startled. Malachi ignored her. Even Kristin ignored her. Kristin still couldn't see the riders clearly, but apparently Malachi and Jamie knew something.

Then she realized it was Cole's horse. It was Cole, returning.

Instantly she felt hot and then cold. Her heart seemed to flutter in her breast. Then butterfly wings seemed to soar within her, and she was hot and then cold all over again.

Cole...

No matter what she wanted to think or believe, she had thought of nothing but him since he had gone away. Waking or sleeping, he had filled her heart and her mind. She had touched the bedding where he had lain and remembered how he had stood, naked, by the window. She had remembered him with the length of her, remembered the feel of his fingers on her flesh, the staggering heat of his body against hers, the tempest of his movement. She had burned with the thoughts and she had railed against herself for them, but they had remained. And in her dreams she had seen him naked and agile and silent and sleek and coming to her again. And he would take her so tenderly into his arms...

And in her dreams it would be more than the fire. He would smile, and he would smile with an encompassing tenderness that meant everything. He would whisper to her, and the whispers would never be clear, but she would know what they meant.

He loved her....

He did not love her.

He rode closer, a plump, middle-aged man at his side. She barely noticed the other man. Her eyes were for Cole, and his rested upon her.

And her heart ran cold then, for he was staring at her with a startling dark hatred.

Her fingers went to her throat, and she backed away slightly, wondering what had happened, why he should look at her so.

"Cole's back," Jamie said unnecessarily.

"Cole!"

It was Shannon who called out his name, Shannon who went running out to him as if he were a long-lost hero. Kristin couldn't move.

Cole's horse came to a prancing halt, and Shannon stood there, staring up at him in adoration, reaching for him. To his credit, Kristin admitted bitterly, he was good to Shannon. His eyes gentled when they fell upon her, and if there was a certain impatience about him, he hid it from her well. He dismounted from his horse in front of the house. Both Jamie and Malachi stood there watching him in silence, waiting for him to speak. He stepped forward and greeted both of his brothers.

"Malachi, Jamie."

He grasped both their hands, and Jamie smiled crookedly while Malachi continued to observe him gravely. Then Cole's eyes came to her again, and she would have backed up again if she hadn't already been flush against the door. His gaze came over her, as cold as the wind of a twister, and perhaps, for just a second, with the same blinding torment. Then the emotion was gone, and all that remained was the staggering chill.

Her mouth was dry, her throat was dry, and she couldn't speak. She was grateful then for Shannon, who told Cole how glad she was to see him, how grateful she was that he was back.

Then she was suddenly still, and Kristin realized that the pudgy middle-aged man was still sitting atop his horse, looking at them all. She was the hostess here. She should be asking him in and offering him something cool to his throat from the dust and dirt of his ride. She should be doing something for Cole, too. If she could only move. Cole should be doing something, too, she thought, not leaving the little man just sitting there.

She forced her eyes away from Cole's to meet those of the man. She even made her lips curl into a semblance of a welcoming smile. "Hello, sir. Won't you come in?"

Jamie smiled. "Welcome, stranger. Cole, you're forgetting your manners. Who is this man?"

Cole turned to the man on the horse. "Sorry, Reverend. Please, come down."

"Much obliged," the man said, dismounting from his horse. Jamie stepped forward to tether the horses. The wind picked up and blew a handful of dirt around.

"This is the Reverend Samuel Cotter," Cole said. "Reverend, my brothers, Malachi and Jamie. And Miss Kristin McCahy in the doorway there, and Miss Shannon McCahy here by my side."

The reverend tipped his hat. "A pleasure, ladies. Gentlemen."

Then they were all just standing there again. The reverend turned his hat awkwardly in his hands. He had a nice face, Kristin thought. Heavy-jowled, with a nice, full smile and bright little eyes. She wished she could be more neighborly, but she was still having difficulty moving.

"Maybe we should all move into the house," Jamie suggested.

"Perhaps the reverend would like a sherry," Shannon murmured.

"The reverend would just love a whiskey!" the little man said, his eyes lighting up.

Malachi laughed. Cole came forward, his hands on his hips. He stood right in front of Kristin, and his eyes were just like the steel of Malachi's cavalry sword. His hands fell on her shoulders, and she almost screamed.

"You're blocking the door, Kristin," he said.

"Oh!" She moved quickly, jumping away from his touch. Her face flushed with color. She looked at the little man. "Forgive me my lack of manners, sir. Please, please, do come in." She paused, looking at Cole's hard, dispassionate features, then back at the reverend. "Um...just what are you doing here, sir?"

The little man's brows shot up. "Why, I've come to marry you, miss."

"Marry me?"

"Why, not myself!" He laughed hard, enjoying his own joke. "I've come to marry you to Mr. Slater here."

"What!" Kristin gasped. She turned to stare at Cole again. She saw the ice, and the hatred in his eyes, and she thought it must be some horrible joke.

"Oh, no! I can't marry Mr. Slater." She said it flatly and with grim determination.

His hands were on her shoulders once again. His eyes bored into hers, ruthless, demanding. His fingers bit into her flesh, brutal and challenging.

"You will marry me, Kristin. Now. While we have the nice reverend here. It took me four days to find him, and I don't intend to have trouble now."

She gritted her teeth against the pain of his touch, against the force of his will. She wanted to cry, but she couldn't do that, and she couldn't explain that she couldn't possibly marry him, not when the mere idea made him look at her with such hatred.

"I will not—"

"You will!"

He turned around and shoved her through the door to the house. His touch stayed upon her, the warmth and strength of his body radiated along her spine, and his whisper touched her ear like the wind.

"Damn it, Kristin, stop it! You will do this!"

Suddenly tears glistened in her eyes. She'd dreamed about just such an occasion, but it hadn't been like this. He hadn't looked at her this way.

"Why?" she managed to whisper.

"We have to."

"But..." She had to salvage some pride. "I don't love you."

"I don't love you."

"Then—"

"Kristin, you've got your choices."

"I see. This is another threat. If I don't go through with this, you'll ride away."

"I have to ride away, Kristin. No matter what. And this is the only safeguard I could find for you."

"I can't do it—"

"Then plan on entertaining Zeke Moreau, Kristin. And if you can't think about yourself, think about Shannon."

"This is a travesty!"

His eyes burned with silver emotion for a moment. He was a stranger again as he stood there, touching her yet somehow distant from her.

"War is a travesty, Kristin. Cheer up. If it ever ends, you can divorce me. I'm sure you'll have plenty of cause. But for the moment, Miss McCahy, get into the parlor, stand sweetly and smile for the nice reverend, please."

PART 3   *The Husband*

Chapter Nine

It was not what she had expected her wedding day to be like, and it was certainly not what she had dreamed it would be like.

Cole and the reverend were still covered with dust from their ride. She wore a simple cotton day dress with a single petticoat, since Cole had sworn impatiently when she had murmured something about changing. Shannon was wearing a shirt and trousers. The only concession to the fact that it was a wedding was the little bouquet she held, hurriedly put together by Delilah from ferns and late-blooming daisies.

They stood stiffly in the parlor. Cole was brusque, and the reverend tried to be kind. Malachi stood up for Cole, and Shannon acted as bridesmaid. Jamie, Delilah and Samson looked on. The reverend kept clearing his throat. He wanted to say more, wanted to speak about the sanctity of marriage and the commitment made thereby between a man and a woman. Cole kept shifting his weight from foot to foot. Then he snapped at the man, "Get on with it!"

Hastily the reverend went on.

Kristin listened to the droning voice and found herself looking around her mother's beautiful parlor and wondering what it had been like for her parents. Not like this: They had loved one another, she knew. She could remember her father's eyes, and the way they had misted over when her mother's name had been spoken. They had built their lives on a dream, and the dream had been a good one.

But they weren't living in a world of dreams, and Cole didn't love her. He didn't even pretend to love her.

"Kristin?"

"What?"

Startled, she looked up at him. She realized that they were standing side by side, she in simple cotton, he in denim and Missouri dust. His hand was around hers, and his flesh felt dry and hot. He squeezed her hand, and she gasped at the pressure, her eyes widening.

"Kristin!" His eyes were sizzling silver and dangerous. "The reverend just asked you a question."

She looked at the reverend. He was flushed and obviously uncomfortable, but he tried to smile again.

"Kristin…do you take this man for your lawful wedded husband, to have and to hold, from this day forward, to love, to cherish and to obey in all the things of this earth?"

She stared at him blankly. It wasn't right. He didn't love her. And she was falling in love with him.

"I, er…"

"Kristin!" The pressure of his fingers around hers was becoming painful.

"Cole..." She turned to him, trying to free her hand from his grasp. "Cole, this is marvelously noble of you, honestly. But I'm sorry, I don't think—"

"Kristin!" Shannon gasped.

"Kristin..." Cole began, and there was a definite threat in his tone, like a low rumble of thunder. What could he do to her, here, with all these people, she wondered recklessly.

He caught her shoulders and jerked her against him. The revered was sucking air in and out out of his cheeks very quickly. "Mr. Slater, if the young lady isn't prepared to take this step, if she isn't completely enamored of you—"

"She's enamored, she's enamored!" Cole snapped. He wound his fingers into Kristin's hair and kissed her hotly. He kissed her with such conviction and passion that she felt herself color from the roots of her hair to her toes. His lips molded around hers, and his tongue plunged deep into her mouth. She couldn't breathe, and she could barely stand, and her knees were beginning to shake.

"Really, now—" the reverend protested.

"They really *are* in love!" Jamie assured him cheerfully.

"Cole—" Malachi tapped his brother on the shoulder, "I—er...think you've made your point."

Cole lifted his lips from Kristin's by just a whisper. His eyes burned into hers. "Say 'I do,' Kristin. Say it."

She inhaled. Her ribs felt as if they had been crushed. She tried to shake her head, but it wouldn't move. "Say 'I do,'" he insisted.

She felt as if the trembling in her heart were an earthquake beneath her feet. She parted her lips, and they felt damp and swollen.

"For God's sake, do it!" Shannon whispered. "We need him. Don't be so naive!"

She nodded, but she couldn't speak. Cole caught her fingers and brought their hands together and squeezed. "'I do,' Kristin! Say it!"

She formed the words at last. I do.

"Go on!" Cole roared at the reverend.

The reverend asked Cole the same question he'd asked Kristin.

He almost spat out the answer. "I do!" His lips twisted bitterly, as if, having forced her to do what he wanted, he had found a new contempt for her. She tried to wrench her hand away from him, but he held her firm and slipped a ring on her finger. It was a wide gold band, and it was too big for her.

She heard Delilah saying that if they twined some string around it it would fit fine.

Then the reverend announced that they were man and wife, and Cole released her. No one said anything, not a single word. The silence went on and on, but Delilah finally broke it.

"This calls for some of that fine white wine in the cellar, I think. Samson, you go fetch it up here, please."

"Yessir, a wedding sure calls for wine," Samson agreed.

The room seemed very still, and Kristin was still unable to move. She was hot and cold by turns. She had never felt more alone in her life. Cole had moved away from her, far away, as if he couldn't bear to touch her now that the words had been spoken. He thanked the reverend and paid him. Then he seemed to notice Kristin again. She had to sign the marriage certificate.

She balked again. He grabbed her hand and guided it to the paper, and she managed to scratch our her name. Nothing seemed real. Delilah said she would set out a cold supper, and Shannon promised to help. Somehow Kristin wound up in one of the big plush wing chairs in the parlor. Jamie stood beside her, resting a hand on her shoulder.

"He's really not as bad as he seems, you know," he whispered.

She clenched her teeth together to keep them from chattering. "No, he's worse." Jamie laughed, but there was an edge to his laughter. He sat down on the sofa across from her and took her hands in his. His eyes were serious. "Kristin, you have to try to understand Cole."

"He doesn't want to be understood," she replied softly.

"You're not afraid of him, are you?" he asked.

She thought for a moment, then shook her head, smiling ruefully. "Afraid of Cole? Never. He saved my life. No, Jamie, I'm not afraid of him. I just wish that—"

"That what?" Jamie murmured.

They could both see Cole. He was rubbing the back of his neck as he talked to Malachi. He looked tired, Kristin thought. She bit her lower lip, and wished for a moment that the marriage was real. She wanted to tiptoe up behind him and touch his shoulders with soothing fingers. She wanted to press her face against the coolness of his back and pretend there was no war, no Zeke, no chaos.

"I wish I understood him," she said at last, staring straight at Jamie. "Want to help?"

He straightened and released her hands. "I'm sorry, Kristin. I can't." He stood and smiled down at her. "Look at that, will you? Delilah is a gem. A cold supper, indeed. She's got biscuits and gravy, turnip greens and a shank of ham over there. Come on!" He took her hands in his again and pulled her to her feet. Suddenly, impulsively, he gave her a kiss on the cheek. "Hey, welcome, sister," he whispered.

Some instinct caused her to look behind him. Cole was watching them. He scowled darkly and turned his attention to Malachi again.

"I'm not very hungry, Jamie," Kristin said. It was true. She wasn't hungry at all. She smiled at him, though and whispered, "Thank you, Jamie!" She felt like crying again, and she shook herself impatiently. It was absurd. She had stood tall in the face of tragedy. Now there was only confusion, but it was tearing her apart.

Cole didn't seem to be very hungry, either. He waited with barely concealed impatience for his brothers to finish their meal. When they had, he started toward the door with long strides, and they followed. He paused in the doorway and said to Kristin, "We're going to ride out and take a look at things. I want to tell the ranch hands."

He was going to announce their wedding the way he might have spread the news of a battle. She nodded, wondering again at the fever that touched his eyes. He couldn't wait to be away from her, she thought. Then why, she thought angrily, had he done it at all? Surely his obligation to her wasn't as great as that.

She didn't say anything. He looked at the reverend, thanking him again for making the trip and urging him to make himself at home. Then he paused again. Malachi and Jamie shifted uncomfortably, exchanging worried glances.

"Write to your brother," Cole told Kristin. "Write to him immediately. There's a good possibility I may stop a Yankee bullet before this is all over, but I don't intend it to be because of a stupid mistake."

Then the three of them were gone. Kristin stood up, watching as the door closed, listening as their booted feet fell against the floorboards of the front porch.

Then, ridiculously, she felt her knees wobbling. She heard a humming in the air, and it was as if wind were rising again, bringing with it a dark mist.

"Kristin!"

She heard Shannon calling her name, and then she heard nothing. She sank to the floor in a dead faint.

Several hours later the Slater brothers rode back from their inspection of the ranch. They'd told all the ranch hands about the marriage. Old Pete had spit on the ground and told Cole he was damned glad. He seemed to understand that with Cole and Kristin married, they were all safer from Zeke Moreau. He didn't seem to care much whether the marriage was real. He seemed to think it was none of his business.

The brothers had gone on to ride around the perimeters of the McCahy ranch. It was a quiet day. By the time they headed back for the house, night was coming and coming fast. Still, when they were within sight of the place, Cole suddenly decided he wanted to stop and set up camp.

Jamie built a fire, and Malachi unsaddled the horses. Cole produced a bottle of whiskey and the dried beef and hard tack. By then the stars had risen, bright against the endless black velvet of the night sky.

Malachi watched Cole, and he noticed the nervous tension that refused to ease from his features. There was a hardness about him today. Malachi understood it. He just didn't know how to ease it.

Let it rest! Malachi thought. Let it go. Kristin McCahy—no, Slater now— was young, beautiful and intelligent, and if he wasn't mistaken, she was in love with Cole. Cole was too caught up in his memories of tragedy to see it. Even if he did see it, it might not change anything. Malachi knew his brother had acted out of a sense of chivalry. He also knew Kristin would have preferred he hadn't. Malachi sighed. Their personal lives were none of his business. He had to leave. He was a regular soldier in a regular army, and his leave was about up.

"This is kind of dumb, ain't it?" Jamie demanded, swallowing some of the whiskey.

"Dumb?" Cole asked.

"Hell, yes. You've got yourself a gorgeous bride, young and shapely—"

"And what the hell do you know about her shape?" Cole demanded heatedly.

"Come on, you can't miss it," Malachi protested dryly. He was determined to have a peaceful evening. He sent Jamie a warning scowl. They both knew what was bothering Cole. "Jamie...stop it."

"Why? Does Cole think he's the only one who's been hurt by this war?"

"Damned brat—" Cole began angrily.

"But the damned brat came running when you asked, Cole, so sit back. Hell, come on, both of you stop it."

"I just think he should appreciate the woman, that's all. And if he didn't mean to, damn it, he shouldn't have tied her up in chains like that."

Cole, exasperated, stared at Malachi. "Will you shut him up, or should I?"

"There's a war on, boys!" Malachi reminded them both.

"He should be decent to her—" Jamie began.

"Damn it, I am decent to her!" Cole roared.

"Leaving her alone on her wedding night—"

"Leaving her alone was the most decent damned thing I could do!" Cole said. He wrenched the whiskey bottle from his brother's hands. "You're too young for this stuff."

"Hell, I'm too old," Jamie said softly. He grinned ruefully at his brother, and all the tension between them seemed to dissipate. "I'm twenty, Cole. By some standards, that's real old. Seventeen-year-old boys are dying all over the place."

"Quantrill is running a bunch of boys," Cole said. He lifted his hand in a vague gesture. "The James boys. The Youngers. And that butcher Bill Anderson. He's just a kid."

He swallowed the liquor, then swallowed again. He felt like being drunk. Really drunk.

Malachi reached for the bottle. The firelight played over his hair, and he arched his golden brows at Cole. "You think that Quantrill can really control his men? That marrying Kristin can keep her safe?"

Cole looked out at the Missouri plain before him, gnawing on a blade of grass. He spit out the grass and looked over at his brothers, who were both looking at him anxiously. If he hadn't been knotted up inside he might have smiled. They were both concerned. There was something about the McCahy place that got to a man. He could understand how even the great struggle between North and South had ceased to matter here, had ceased to matter to Kristin. The brutality here was too much. It left the mind numbed.

"I know Quantrill is about to head south for the winter. He doesn't like the cold. He'll make one more raid, I'm certain. Then he'll head on somewhere south—maybe Arkansas, maybe Texas. I'll stick around until he moves on. Then I'll go on over to Richmond. If I can just find some train tracks that are still holding together, I should make it in time."

"If Jefferson Davis is still in the Cabinet," Jamie said glumly.

Cole looked at him sharply. "Why? What have you heard?"

"Nothing. It's just that the battle of Sharpsburg left a lot of dead men. A whole lot of dead men."

"Watch your step around here," Malachi warned Cole. "There's Federal patrols wandering all around the McCahy place."

"Yeah, I know."

"That little witch just about got me hauled in today."

"Witch?" Cole asked.

"Shannon," Jamie supplied.

Malachi grunted. "I envy you your wife, Cole, but not your in-laws."

"And he doesn't mean the Yankee brother." Jamie laughed. "It's a good thing Malachi has to ride out soon. I don't think she's too fond of him, either."

Malachi looked as if he wanted to kill somebody, Jamie thought, but at least Cole laughed, and Cole needed it the most. "What have I missed?" Cole asked.

"The antics of a child," Malachi replied, waving a dismissing hand in the air. He reached for the liquor bottle. It was going down quickly.

"Some child!" Jamie said. "Why, she's coming along just as nicely as that wife of yours, Cole."

Malachi and Cole looked at one another. "We could end this war if we just sent this boy to Washington to heckle the Union commanders," Malachi said.

Cole grunted his agreement. Jamie grinned and lay back against his saddle, staring up at the stars. "You know, Cole," he said suddenly, "I am sorry about the past. I sure am."

There was a long silence. The fire snapped and crackled. Malachi held his breath and held his peace.

"But if I were you," Jamie went on, "I wouldn't be out here with my brothers. Not when I had a woman like that waiting. A woman with beautiful blond hair and eyes like sapphires. And the way she walks, her hips swinging and all... Why, I can just imagine what it'd be like—"

"Son of a bitch!" Cole roared suddenly. He stood up, slamming the nearly empty whiskey bottle into the fire. The liquor hissed and sizzled. Jamie leaped to his feet, startled by the deadly dark danger in his brother's eyes. Malachi, too, leaped to his feet. He couldn't believe that Cole would really go for Jamie, but then he had never seen Cole in a torment like this. Nor had he ever seen Jamie so determined to irk him.

"Cole—" Malachi reached for his brother's arm, and they stared at one another in the golden firelight.

"No!" Jamie told Malachi, his eyes on Cole. "If he wants to beat me up, let him. If he thinks he can strike out at me and feel better, fine. Let him hurt me instead of that poor girl waiting for him at the house. At least I understand why he strikes out. Hell, she doesn't even know why he's so damned hateful."

"What the hell difference does it make?" Cole thundered. "All she wanted from me was protection!"

"She deserves some damned decency from you!"

"I told you—"

"Yeah, yeah, you came up with some puny excuse. You are a bastard."

"You don't know—"

"I know that it wasn't my wife killed by the jayhawkers, but we loved her, too, Cole. And she loved you, and she wouldn't want you making your whole life nothing but ugly vengeance."

"Why, I ought to—"

"Cole!" Malachi shouted. Between the three of them, they'd consumed almost an entire bottle of liquor. This wasn't a good time for Jamie to be goading Cole, but Jamie didn't seem to care. And now Cole was losing control. He shook off Malachi's arm and lunged at Jamie with a sudden fury. Then the two of them were rolling in the dust.

"Jesus in heaven!" Malachi breathed. "Will the two of you—"

"You don't know! You don't know anything!" Cole raged at Jamie. "You didn't find her, you didn't feel the blood pouring out all over you! You didn't see her eyes close, you didn't see the love as it died. You didn't watch her eyes close and feel her flesh grow cold!"

"Cole!"

His hands were around Jamie's neck, and Jamie wasn't doing anything at all. He was letting Cole throttle him. Malachi tried to pull him off, and Cole suddenly realized what he was doing. Horrified, he released his brother. Then he stood and walked away, his back to his brothers.

"I need to stay away from Kristin," he said softly.

Jamie looked at Malachi and rubbed his throat. Malachi spoke to Cole.

"No. You don't need to stay away from her. You need to go to her."

Cole turned around. He came over to Jamie and planted his hands on his brother's shoulders. "You all right?"

Jamie nodded and grinned. "I'm all right."

Cole walked over to his horse. He untied the reins which were tethered to a tree, and walked the horse into the open. Then he leaped up on the animal's back without bothering to saddle it.

"You going back?" Malachi asked.

"Just for another bottle of whiskey."

Malachi and Jamie nodded. They watched as Cole started back toward the house, the horse's hooves suddenly taking flight in the darkness.

"He's just going back for another whiskey bottle," Jamie said.

Malachi laughed. "We betting on when he's going to make it back?"

Jamie grinned. "You get to bring his saddle in the morning." He lay down again and stretched out, feeling his throat. "Too bad I wasn't blessed with sisters!" He groaned.

Malachi grunted, pulled his hat low over his face and closed his eyes. The fire crackled and burned low, and at last the two of them slept.

Cole heard one of Pete's hounds barking as he approached the house. Then Pete himself, shirtless, the top of his long johns showing above his hastily donned trousers, came out to challenge him.

"Just me, Pete," Cole assured him.

"Evening, boss," Pete said agreeably, and headed back to the bunkhouse.

Cole dismounted from his horse, sliding from the animal's back without his accustomed grace. He gave his head a shake to clear it. The whiskey had gotten to him more than he would have cared to admit, but not enough to really knock him out the way he wanted, not enough to take away the last of his pain. He was determined to be quiet, but it seemed to him that his boots made an ungodly noise on the floorboards of the porch.

The house was dark. He stumbled through the hall and the parlor and into what had been Gabriel McCahy's office. He fumbled around for a match and lit the oil lamp on the desk, then came around and sat in the chair, putting his feet up on the desk and digging in the lower right hand drawer for a bottle of liquor—any kind of liquor.

Then he heard a click, and the hair on the back of his neck stood straight up. His whiskey-dulled reflexes came to life, and he slammed his feet to the floor, reaching for his revolver.

He pointed it at the doorway—and right at Kristin, who stood there with a double-barreled shotgun aimed at his head. He swore irritably, returning his gun to his holster and sinking back into his chair.

"What the hell are you doing?" he growled.

"What am I doing? You son of a bitch—" She lowered the shotgun and moved into the room. She stopped in front of the desk, caught in the soft glow of the lamplight. Her hair was loose, a soft storm of sunshine falling over her shoulders. She was dressed chastely enough, in a nightgown that buttoned to her throat, but the lamplight went through the fabric and caressed her body. He could see all too clearly the sway of her hips, which Jamie had so admired. He could see the curve of her breasts, the flow and shape of her limbs, and suddenly the sight of her hurt him. It was as if some mighty hand reached down and took hold of him, squeezing the life from him. He felt his heart pounding, felt his shuddering pulse enter his groin and take root there. His fingers itched to reach out to her, to touch her. She was staring at him, her blue eyes a raging sea of fury, and not even that deterred him. It only made the pulse within him beat all the harder.

He didn't love her. To love her would be disloyal. But he had married her. What the hell else could she want?

"What are you doing in here?" she snapped.

"Kristin, put the gun down. Go to bed."

"You scared me to death! And *you* taught *me* not to go wandering around unarmed!"

"Kristin, put the gun down." He hesitated. Then he smiled suddenly. "Come on. We'll go to bed. Together."

Her eyes widened. "You're out of your mind, Cole Slater."

"Am I?" He came around the desk, slowly, lazily, yet purposefully. Kristin raised the shotgun again.

"Yes! You are out of your mind."

"You're my wife."

"And you walked out of here this afternoon and didn't come back until three in the morning—after treating me with the manners of a rabid squirrel. I promise you, Mr. Slater, if you think you're going to touch me, you're out of your mind."

He *was* out of his mind, and he knew it. He swallowed raggedly. He had forgotten so much. He had tried to forget. He had forgotten that she could hold her head with such incredible pride. He had forgotten her eyes could snap this way, and he had forgotten that her mouth was wide and generous and beautifully shaped. He had forgotten that she was beautiful and sensuous, and that her touch was more potent than whiskey or wine or the finest brandy. He had forgotten so much....

But now he remembered. The revealing lamplight glowed on the lush curves of her body, and the thunder inside him became almost unbearable. He took a step forward, and she cocked the shotgun. His smile deepened.

"Fire it, Kristin."

"I will, damn you!"

He laughed triumphantly, stepped toward her again and took the shotgun from her hands. He pulled her hard against him, and he lowered his head and seized her lips in a kiss. It was not at all brutal, but it was filled with a shocking need and a shocking thirst. For an instant she thought to twist from him, but his kiss filled her with a searing, liquid heat, and she felt as if she were bursting with the desire to touch him, to be touched by him.

He broke away from her, and his eyes sought hers. "No!" she told him angrily, but he smiled and swept her up into his arms. Her eyes were still angry but she locked her arms around his neck. He carried her effortlessly through the darkened parlor, up the stairs and into the bedroom. He closed the door with his foot and set her down by the window. The moonlight found her there, dancing over her fine, delicate features and her rich, feminine curves.

"You're horrid," she told him.

He smiled tenderly. "You're beautiful."

"You're filthy."

He kissed her forehead, and he kissed her cheeks, and he rimmed her lips with the tip of his tongue, teasing them, dampening them. His fingers went to the tiny buttons of her gown, and he tried to undo them but they wouldn't give, and he finally ripped the gown open impatiently. The moonlight fell on her naked flesh. He groaned and kissed her shoulder and her throat, feeling the urgent quickening of her heart.

"Does it matter so terribly much?" he whispered.

She didn't answer. He stroked her breast. Then he lowered his head and touched his lips to the nipple. He teased it with his teeth, then sucked it hard into his mouth and finally gentled it with his tongue. Rivers of pleasure streaked through her, and she threaded her fingers roughly into his hair, and he savored the little tug of pain. He lowered himself slowly to his knees, holding her hips, then her buttocks.

"Does it matter so terribly much?" he repeated, looking up into her dazed eyes. He teased her navel with the tip of his tongue.

"Yes!" she whispered. He started to move away from her, but she wouldn't let him. He bathed her belly with kisses, cupping her buttocks hard and pressing close to her, sliding his tongue along the apex of her thighs and into the golden triangle there. She shuddered and cried out, but he held her firmly, and when it seemed she was about to fall he lowered her carefully to the floor. He touched her gently and tenderly, and then he brought his mouth over hers again. "Does it really matter so terribly much?" he demanded.

She closed her eyes and wrapped her arms around his neck. "No," she whispered, and she released him to tug at his buttons and then at his belt buckle. She groaned in frustration, and he helped her, stripping quickly. She was so very beautiful, there in the full flood of the moonlight. All of him quickened, and desire spread through him like a raging wind, and he cried out in a ragged voice. She was there, there to take him, there to close around him, a sweet and secret haven. Nothing on earth was like this.

He sank into her, swept into her, again and again. She rose to meet his every thrust, and the pulse raged between them. She was liquid fire when she moved. She was made to have him, made to love him, made to take him. The culmination burst upon them swiftly. She gasped and shuddered, and he thrust heatedly, again and felt his climax spew from him. He held her tight. He felt the sweat, slick between them. He felt the rise and fall of her breath and the clamor of her heart, slowing at last.

He stroked her hair, and he marveled at the ecstasy of it.

Then he remembered that he had made her his wife, and suddenly he hated himself again.

He should have said something. He should have whispered something to her. Anything. Anything that was tender, anything that was kind.

He couldn't bring himself to do it.

Instead, he rose, his skin glistening in the moonlight. Then he bent down and took her naked form in his arms. She was silent, her eyes lowered, her hair a tangle around them.

He laid her down upon the bed. Her eyes met his at last, and he saw in them a torment that seemed to match that within his heart. She was so very beautiful. Naked, she was a goddess, her breasts firm and full and perfect, her limbs shapely and slim, her belly a fascinating plane between her hips. He pulled the covers over her. Her sapphire eyes still studied him.

"I'm...I'm sorry," he muttered at last.

She let out a strangled oath and turned away from him.

He hesitated, then slipped in beside her. He crossed his arms behind his head and stared up at the ceiling, wishing he were drunker, wishing fervently he could go to sleep.

But he lay awake a long, long time. And he knew she didn't sleep, either.

At dawn he rose and left.

And at dawn Kristin finally slept. She had the right to stay in bed all day, she told herself bitterly. She was a bride, and this was the morning after her wedding day.

Cole wasn't in the house when she finally did get up. Shannon told her he had gone out with Malachi.

Jamie was there, though. He told her that they were low on salt and that they needed a couple of blocks for the cattle to lick through the winter. Cole had said that she and Pete were to go into town and buy them.

The Union had control of most of the border area—despite Quantrill's sporadic raids—and the town had managed to remain quieter than the McCahy ranch. Kristin was glad to take the buckboard and ride into town with Pete. She was glad to be away from the house.

It was a three-hour ride. The town of Little Ford was small, but it did have two saloons, one reputable hotel, two doctors old enough to be exempted from military service and three mercantile stores. In Jaffe's Mercantile she saw Tommy Norley, a newspaperman and and old friend of Adam's from over the Kansas border.

"Kristin!"

He was limping when he came over to her. He tipped his hat quickly, then took both her hands in his. "Kristin, how are you doing out there? Is everything all right? You and Shannon should have moved on, I think. Or maybe into town. Or maybe out to California!"

She smiled. He was a slim man, pale-faced, with a pencil-thin mustache and dark, soulful eyes.

"I'm doing well, Tommy, thank you." She searched his eyes. She had last seen him when they had buried her father. He had written a scathing article about guerrilla attacks.

"You should move, Kristin."

She chose to ignore his words. "Tommy, you're limping."

He smiled grimly. "I just got caught by Quantrill."

Her heart skipped a beat. "What do you mean? What happened?"

"The bastard attacked Shawneetown last week. I was with the Federal supply train he and his maniacs caught up with on their way in." He paused and looked at her, wondering how much he should say to a lady.

"Tommy, tell me! What happened?"

He took a deep breath. "Kristin, it was awful. Quantrill and his men came after us like a pack of Indians, howling, shouting. They gunned down fifteen men, drivers and escorts. I rolled off the side of the road, into the foliage. I took a bullet in the calf, but I lived to tell the tale. Kristin, they went on into town and murdered ten more men there. Then they burned the village to the ground."

"Oh, God! How horrible!" Kristin gasped.

"Kristin, come to Kansas. I'm opening an office in Lawrence, and I'm sure you'll be safe."

She smiled. "Tommy, my home is in Missouri."

"But you're in danger."

"I can't leave the ranch, Tommy." She wondered if she should tell him that she had married to save her ranch and that she would probably be in real danger from her new husband if she deserted him and ran off to Kansas.

"You should have seen them," Tommy murmured. "Kristin, they were savages. You should have seen them."

She held on to the counter in the mercantile, suddenly feeling ill. He kept talking, and she answered him as politely as she could. She cared about Tommy. He had been a good friend to Adam. It was just that Adam had begun to fade from her life. It was not that she hadn't loved him. She had. But Cole was a stronger force in her life.

Kristin hesitated, then asked him if he thought he could get a message to Matthew for her. He promised to try, and she bought some stationery from Mr. Jaffe and quickly wrote a letter to Matthew. It wasn't easy to explain her marriage. She did it as carefully and as cheerfully as she could, then turned the letter over to Tommy, hoping she had done well.

She kissed Tommy and left him. Pete had gotten the salt licks, and he had stacked the remaining space in the buckboard with alfalfa to help get them through the coming winter.

She told him about Shawneetown, then fell silent. The news bothered her all the way home.

When they arrived at the ranch, she still felt ill. She went out back and stood over her parents' graves. Cold and chilled, she tried to pray, but no thoughts came to her mind.

A while later she felt a presence behind her, and she knew that it was Cole. She was angry, and she didn't know why, unless it was because she knew he didn't love her, and because she knew she was falling in love with him. He was attracted to her, certainly. Maybe he even needed her. But he didn't love her.

She spun around, ready to do battle.

"Quantrill and his animals attacked Shawneetown last week. They killed the men escorting a supply train, and then they went into the village and killed some more, and then they burned the whole place down."

His eyes narrowed, and he stared at her warily, but he didn't say anything. She walked up to him and slammed her fists against his chest. "He's a captain! The Confederates made him a captain!"

He grabbed her wrists hard. "I don't condone Quantrill, and you know it. The Missouri governor considers him and his raiders like an elephant won at a raffle."

"Let go of me!" she hissed furiously.

"No. You listen to me for a minute, lady. Quantrill has no monopoly on brutality! Quantrill came *after* the likes of Lane and Jennison. Unionists, Kristin! Jayhawkers! You want to know some of the things they've done? They've ridden up to farmhouses and dragged men out and killed them—men *and* women! They've murdered and they've raped and they've tortured, exactly the same way Quantrill has! You remember that, Kristin! You bear that in mind real well!"

He pushed her away from him and turned, his long, angry strides taking him toward the house. The rear door opened and then slammed shut, and he disappeared inside.

She waited a moment, and then she followed him. She didn't know if she wanted to continue the fight or try to make up with him somehow.

It didn't matter. He wasn't in the house anymore.

And that night he didn't come back at all.

Chapter Ten

Cole might have slept somewhere else during the night, but he appeared at the breakfast table in the morning. Kristin was angry and wondered what everyone must think. He came and went like the breeze, with no regard for her feelings. Kristin was sharp when he spoke to her. When he asked her to pass him the milk, she seriously considered splashing it in his face or pouring it in his lap. He caught her hand and the pitcher before she could do either. He stared at her hard, and she looked away.

She didn't like Cole's ability to stay away from her. She wanted to fight with him. She wanted to do anything just to bring him close to her again. It was an effort to turn away from him, to find some trivial thing to discuss with Jamie and Shannon.

Cole remained in a foul temper all day. With winter coming on, there was a lot to do. Cole was anxious to have it all done before he left for the East and before Malachi and Jamie had to leave to rejoin their units. They spent the day gathering up as much of the herd as they could for Pete to drive to market. Kristin had been surprised that Cole was willing to let her sell the beef on the Union side of the line, but he had reminded her that the ranch belonged to her brother, Matthew, and that Matthew was fighting for the Union. Cole couldn't go north himself, but Pete could handle the cattle drive, and Malachi and Jamie would be around until he got back at the end of the week.

By dinnertime, Cole seemed to be in a somewhat better mood, and Kristin maintained a polite distance from him. Cole, Jamie and Malachi all sat down to dinner with Kristin and Shannon that night. Delilah refused to sit and made a big fuss over everyone. Jamie made the meal a pleasant affair. He told the two girls about a pair of hammers his mother had bought for Cole and Malachi when they were boys and about how the two of them had used their hammers on one another. Even Shannon laughed and refrained from engaging in verbal warfare with Malachi. Cole listened to the story with a smile on his face, and at one point his eyes met Kristin's and he gave her an entrancing grin and a sheepish shrug.

After dinner, Kristin played the spinet and Shannon sang. She sang a few light tunes, then gave a haunting rendition of "Lorena", a ballad about a soldier who returns from the wars to find that his love is gone. When it was over, they were all silent. Then Cole stood up and told Shannon in a strangled voice that her singing was very beautiful. He excused himself and left them.

Kristin bit her lip as she watched him leave the room. Jamie gave her an encouraging pat on the knee, and Malachi practically shoved Shannon out of the way and began a rousing chorus of "Dixie."

When he had finished, Shannon regained her place and sang "John Brown's Body."

"Shannon McCahy, you are a brat," Malachi told her.

"And you're a rodent," Shannon replied sweetly.

"Children, children!" Jamie protested with a sigh.

But Shannon said something, and though Kristin could see that Malachi was striving for patience, he replied sharply, and the battle was on once again.

Kristin rose and left them bickering. She went upstairs and was surprised to find that Cole was already in bed. She thought he was asleep, but when she crawled in beside him, trying not to disturb him, he turned over and took her in his arms. She tried to study his eyes in the darkness, but she could see only their silver glow. She tried to speak, but he silenced her with a kiss. Tenderly at first, and then with a growing passion, he made love to her. When it was over, he held her close, his bearded chin resting against the top of her head. He didn't speak, and neither did she. She knew he lay there awake for a long time, and she wished she could reach out to him, wished she knew what to say to him. She could not apologize, for she had done nothing wrong. She kept silent.

Eventually Kristin fell asleep.

Sometime later, something woke her. She didn't know what it was at first. She heard something, some hoarse, whispered words that she didn't understand. Struggling to free herself from the web of sleep, she opened her eyes, just as Cole's arm came flying out and slammed against her shoulder.

She sat up in bed, calling out his name. He didn't answer her, and she fumbled for a match to light the oil lamp on the bedside table. The glow filled the room and fell on Cole.

The bare flesh of his shoulders and chest was gleaming with sweat. The muscles there were tense and rigid and knotted. His fingers plucked at the sheet that lay over him.

His features contorted, his head tossing from side to side, he screamed, "No!" His entire body was stiff and hard.

"Cole!" Kristin pleaded, shaking him. "Cole—"

"No!" he screamed again.

She straddled him, took him by the shoulders and shook him hard, determined to wake him.

His eyes flew open, but he didn't see her. He called out again, and then he struck out at her, and the force sent her flying to the floor. He jerked upright as she fell. Stunned, Kristin sat on the hard floor, rubbing her bruised behind.

"Kristin?"

He whispered her name slowly, fearfully. There was something in his voice that she had never heard before, a frightened tone, and it touched her deeply.

"I'm here," she whispered ruefully.

He looked over the side of the bed and swore. He leaped swiftly from the bed, and took her in his arms. She felt the pounding of his heart, felt the tremors that still racked him as he laid her down on the bed again.

"I hurt you. I'm so sorry."

His voice was deep, husky. She felt her own throat constrict, and she shook her head, burrowing more deeply against his naked chest. "No. You didn't hurt me. I'm all right, really."

He didn't say anything. He didn't even move. He just held her.

She wanted to stay there, where she was, forever. She had never felt so cherished before. Desired, admired, even needed. But never so cherished.

"You had a nightmare," she told him tentatively.

"Yes," he said.

"I wish you would tell me—"

"No."

It wasn't that he spoke so harshly, but that he spoke with absolute finality. Kristin stiffened, and she knew he felt it. He set her from him and rose. She watched as he walked over to the window, and as he stood there in the moonlight a dark web of pain seemed to encircle her heart. He walked with a pride that was uniquely his. He stood there for a long time, naked and sinewed and gleaming in the moonlight, and stared out at the night. Kristin watched as his muscles slowly, slowly eased, losing some of their awful rigor.

"Cole—" she whispered.

He turned back to her at last. He walked across the room, and she was glad when he lifted the covers and lay beside her again, drawing his arm around her and bringing her head to his chest. He stroked her hair.

"Cole, please—"

"Kristin, please. Don't."

She fell silent. His touch remained gentle.

"I have to leave tomorrow," he said at last.

"Where are you going?"

"East."

"Why?"

He hesitated for a long time. "Kristin, there are things that you probably don't want to hear, and there's no good reason for me to tell you."

"No questions, no involvement," she murmured. He didn't answer her, but she felt him tighten beneath her.

"It's late," he said at last. "You should—"

She rose up and touched his lips with her own, cutting off his words. She wondered if she should be angry, or at least cool and distant. Nothing had changed. He had married her, but he still didn't want any involvement.

That didn't matter to her. Not at that moment. She only knew that he was leaving, and that in these times any man's future was uncertain at best. She ceased the flow of his words with the soft play of her tongue and leaned the length of her body over his, undulating her hips against his groin and the hardened peaks of her breasts against his chest. She savored the sharp intake of his breath and the quick, heady pressure of his hands upon her back and her buttocks.

Now it was her turn to inflame him. She nuzzled her face against his beard, and she teased his throat and the hard contours of his shoulders and chest. She tempted him with her tongue and with her fingertips and with the entire length of her body. She moved against him, crying out again and again at the sweet feel of their flesh touching. She teased him with her teeth, moving lower and lower against him. He tore his fingers into her hair and hoarsely gasped out her name. She barely knew herself. She was at once serene and excited, and she was certain of her power. She took all of him without hesitation. She loved him until he dragged her back to him and kissed her feverishly on the lips, then drew her beneath him. There was a new tension etched into his features, and a new blaze in his eyes. Taut as wire, he hovered above her. Then he came to her, fierce and savage and yet uniquely tender.

She thought she died just a little when it was over. The world was radiant, painted with shocking strips of sunlight and starlight, and then it was black and she was drifting again.

He held her still. He didn't speak, but his fingers stroked her hair, and for the moment it was enough. His hand lay over her abdomen. Tentatively she placed her fingers over his. He laced them through his own, and they slept.

But in the morning when she awoke, he was gone.

Three days later, Kristin was pumping water into the trough when she looked up to see a lone rider on the horizon, coming toward the house. For a moment her heart fluttered and she wondered if it might be Cole returning. Then she realized it couldn't be him. It wasn't his horse, and the rider wasn't sitting the horse the way he did.

"Malachi!" she called. He and Jamie would be with her for another few days. She frowned and bit her lip as she watched the approaching rider. It wasn't Zeke, she knew. Zeke never rode alone. Besides, there was no reason for her to be afraid of Quantrill's boys. Cole had gone through with the wedding to protect her, and anyway, Quantrill was supposed to be moving south for the winter. There was no reason to be afraid.

She was afraid anyway.

"Malachi—" she began again.

"Kristin?" He appeared at the door to the barn, his thumbs hooked in his belt, his golden brows knit into a furrow. He hurried over to her and watched the rider come. His eyes narrowed.

"Anderson," he murmured.

"Who?"

"It's a boy named Bill Anderson. He's...he's one of Quantrill's. One of his young recruits."

"What does he want? He is alone, isn't he?" Kristin asked anxiously.

"Yes, he's alone," Malachi assured her.

Jamie appeared then, coming out of the barn, his sleeves rolled up, his jacket off. He looked at Malachi. "I thought Quantrill was already on his way south That's Bill Anderson."

Malachi nodded. "He seems to be alone."

The rider came closer and closer. He was young, very young, with a broad smile. He had dark, curly hair and a dark mustache and beard, but he still had an absurdly innocent face. Kristin shivered, thinking that he was far too young to be going around committing murder.

He drew his horse up in front of them. He was well armed, Kristin saw, with Colts at his waist and a rifle on either side of his saddle.

"Howdy, Malachi, Jamie."

"Bill," Malachi said amiably enough. Jamie nodded an acknowledgment.

"Cole's headed east, huh?" Anderson asked. He smiled at Kristin, waiting for an introduction. "You his new wife, ma'am? It's a pleasure to meet you."

He stuck out his hand. Kristin thought about all the blood that was probably on that hand, but she took it anyway and forced herself to smile.

"I'm his new wife," Kristin said. She couldn't bring herself to say that it was a pleasure to meet him, too. She could barely stand there.

"Kristin Slater, this is Bill Anderson. Bill, what the hell are you doing here? There's a lot of Union soldiers around these parts, you know," Malachi said.

"Yep," Jamie agreed cheerfully. "Lots and lots of Federals in these parts.

And you know what they've been saying about you boys? No mercy. If they get their hands on you they intend to hang you high and dry."

"Yeah. I've heard what the Union has to say. But you've been safe enough here, huh, Malachi? And you, too, Jamie."

"Hell, we're regular army," Jamie said.

Anderson shrugged. "They have to catch us before they can hang us. And I'm not staying. I just had...well, I had some business hereabouts. I've got to join Quantrill in Arkansas. I just thought maybe I could come by here for a nice home-cooked meal."

Malachi answered before Kristin could. "Sure, Bill. Jamie, why don't you go on in and ask Delilah to cook up something special. Tell her we've got one of Quantrill's boys here."

Jamie turned around and hurried to the house. Delilah was already standing in the doorway. As Kristin watched, Shannon's blond head appeared. There was a squeal of outrage, and then the door slammed. Jamie came hurrying back to them.

"Malachi, Delilah says she needs you. There's a bit of a problem to be dealt with."

Malachi lifted an eyebrow, then hurried to the house. Kristin stood there staring foolishly at Bill Anderson with a grin plastered to her face. She wanted to shriek, and rip his baby face to shreds. Didn't he understand? Didn't he know she didn't want him here?

Men using Quantrill's name had come here and murdered her father. Men just like this one. She wanted to spit in his face.

But he had evidently come for a reason, and Malachi seemed to think it was necessary that he be convinced that Kristin was Cole's wife and that this was Cole's place now.

Kristin heard an outraged scream from the house. She bit her lip. Shannon obviously realized that one of Quantrill's men was here, and she didn't intend to keep quiet. She certainly didn't intend to sit down to a meal with him.

Anderson looked toward the house, hiking a brow.

"My sister," Kristin said sweetly.

"Her baby sister," Jamie said. He smiled at Kristin, but there was a warning in his eyes. They had to make Bill Anderson think Shannon was just a little girl.

And they had to keep her away from him.

Apparently that was what Malachi was doing, because the screams became muffled, and then they were silenced.

Malachi—the marks of Shannon's fingernails on his cheek—reappeared on the front porch. "Come on in, Bill. We'll have a brandy, and then Delilah will have lunch all set."

Bill looked from Malachi to Kristin and grinned. "That came from your, uh...baby sister, Mrs. Slater?"

"She can be wild when she wants," Kristin said sweetly. She stared hard at Malachi. He touched his cheek and shrugged. Kristin walked by him. "Too bad they can't send her up to take on the Army of the Potomac. We'd win this war in a matter of hours. Old Abe Lincoln himself would think that secession was a fine thing just as long as Shannon McCahy went with the Confederacy."

"Malachi!" Kristin whispered harshly. "You're talking about my sister!"

"I ought to turn her over to Bill Anderson!" he muttered.

"Malachi!"

Anderson turned around, looking at them curiously. "Where is your sister?" he asked.

"The baby is tucked in for her nap," Malachi said with a grin. "We don't let her dine with adults when we have company in the house. She spits her peas out sometimes. You know how young 'uns are."

Kristin gazed at him, and he looked innocently back at her. She swept by him. "Mr. Anderson, can we get you a drink? A shot of whiskey?"

"Yes, ma'am, you can."

Kristin took him into her father's study and poured him a drink. As he looked around the room, admiring the furnishings, Malachi came in and whispered in her ear.

"Shannon's in the cellar."

"And she's just staying there?" Kristin asked, her eyes wide.

"Sure she's just staying there," Malachi said.

Soon they sat down to eat. Sizzling steaks from the ranch's own fresh beef, fried potatoes, fall squash and apple pie. Bill Anderson did have one big appetite. Kristin reminded herself dryly that he was a growing boy.

He was polite, every inch the Southern cavalier, all through the meal. Only when coffee was served with the pie did he sit back and give them an indication of why he had come.

"Saw your husband the other day, ma'am."

Kristin paused just a second in scooping him out a second slice of pie. "Did you?" she said sweetly.

"Sure, when he came to see Quantrill. He was mighty worried about you. It was a touching scene."

She set the pie down. "Was it?" She glanced at Malachi. His eyes were narrowed, and he was very still.

"He used to be one of us, you know."

"What?"

Despite herself, Kristin sat. She sank right into her chair. "What?" she repeated.

Jamie cleared his throat. Malachi still hadn't moved.

Bill Anderson wiped his face with his napkin and smiled pleasantly. "Cole is one of the finest marksmen I ever did see. Hell, he's a one-man army, he's so damned good. It was nice when he was riding with us."

Kristin didn't say anything. She knew all the blood had fled from her face.

Bill Anderson forked up a piece of pie. "Yep, Cole Slater was just the same as Zeke Moreau. Just the same."

Malachi was on his feet in a second, his knife at Anderson's throat. "My brother was never anything like Zeke Moreau!"

Jamie jumped up behind him. He was so tense that Jamie couldn't pull him away. Kristin rushed around and tugged at his arm. "Malachi!"

He backed away. Bill Anderson stood and straightened his jacket. He gazed at Malachi, murder in his eyes. "You'll die for that, Slater."

"Maybe I'll die, but not for that, Anderson!" Malachi said.

"Gentlemen, gentlemen!" Kristin breathed, using her softest voice. "Please, aren't we forgetting ourselves here?"

It worked. Like most young men in the South, they had both been taught to be courteous to females, that a lack of manners was a horrible fault. They stepped away from each other, but their tempers were still hot.

"You came here just to do that, didn't you?" Malachi said quietly. "Just to upset my sister-in-law. I'm willing to bet Zeke Moreau asked you to do it."

"Maybe, and maybe not," Anderson said. He reached over to the sideboard for his hat. "Maybe she's just got the right to know that Cole Slater was a bushwhacker. You want to deny that, Malachi?"

Kristin looked at Malachi. His face was white, but he said nothing.

Anderson slammed his hat on his head. He turned to Kristin. "Mighty obliged for the meal, ma'am. Mighty obliged. Cap'n Quantrill wants you to know that you should feel safe, and he's sorry about any harm that's been done to you or yours. If he had understood that your loyalties lay with the Confederacy, none of it would have come about."

It was a lie, a bald-faced lie, but Kristin didn't say anything. Anderson turned around, and she heard the door slam shut as he left the house.

Delilah came in from the kitchen. The old grandfather clock in the parlor struck the hour. They all stood there, just stood there, dead still, until they heard Bill Anderson mount his horse, until they heard the hoofbeats disappear across the Missouri dust.

Then Kristin spun around, gripping the back of a chair and staring hard at Malachi. "Is it true?"

"Kristin—" he began unhappily.

"Is it true?" she screeched. "Is Cole one of them?"

"No!" Jamie protested, stepping forward. "He isn't one of them, not now."

She whirled around again, looking at Jamie. "But he was! That's the truth, isn't it?"

"Yes, damn it, all right, he was. But there was a damned good reason for it."

"Jamie!" Malachi snapped.

"Oh, God!" Kristin breathed. She came around and fell into the chair. Malachi tried to take her hand. She wrenched it away and jumped to her feet. "Don't, please don't! Can't you understand? They are murderers! They dragged my father out and they killed him!"

"There are a lot of murderers in this war, Kristin," Malachi said. "Quantrill isn't the only one."

"It was Quantrill's men who killed my father," she said dully. "It was Quantrill's men who came after me."

Malachi didn't come near her again. He stood at the end of the table, his face pinched. "Kristin, Cole's business is Cole's business, and when he chooses, maybe he'll explain things to you. He's asked us to mind our own concerns. Maybe he knew you'd react just like this if you heard something. I don't know. But you remember this while you're busy hating him. He stumbled into this situation. He didn't come here to hurt you." He turned and walked to the door.

"He rode with Quantrill!" she whispered desperately.

"He's done the best he knows how for you," Malachi said quietly. He paused and looked back at her. "You might want to let your sister go when you get the chance. I tied her up downstairs so she wouldn't take a trip up here to meet Bill Anderson. He might not have liked what she had to say very much...and he might have liked the way that she looked too much."

He went out. The clock suddenly seemed to be ticking very loudly. Kristin looked miserably at Jamie.

He tried to smile, but the attempt fell flat. "I guess I can't tell you too much of anything, Kristin. But I love my brother, and I think he's a fine man. There are things that maybe you can't understand just yet, and they are his business to discuss." He paused, watching her awkwardly. Then he shrugged and he, too, left her.

It wasn't a good day. She sat there for a long time. She even forgot about Shannon, and it was almost an hour before she went downstairs to release her. When she did, it was as if she had let loose a wounded tigress. Shannon cursed and ranted and raved and swore that someday, somehow if the war didn't kill Malachi, she would see to it that he was laid out herself.

She would probably have gone out and torn Malachi to shreds right then and there, but fortunately he had ridden out to take a look at some fencing.

Shannon was even furious with Kristin. "How could you? How could you? You let that man into our house, into Pa's house! After everything that has been done—"

"I did it so that Quantrill would leave us alone from now on! Maybe you've forgotten Zeke. I haven't!"

"Wait until Matthew comes back!" Shannon cried. "He'll take care of the Quantrill murderers and Malachi and—"

"Shannon," Kristin said wearily, "I thought you were going to take care of Malachi yourself?" She was hurt, and she was tired, and she couldn't keep the anger from her voice. "If you want to kill one of the Slater brothers, why don't you go after the right one?"

"What do you mean?" Shannon demanded.

"Cole," Kristin said softly. She stared ruefully at her sister. "Cole Slater. The man I married. He rode with Quantrill, Shannon. He was one of them."

"Cole?" Shannon's beautiful eyes were fierce. "I don't believe you!"

"It's the truth. That's why Bill Anderson came here. He wanted me to know that I had married a man every bit as bad as Zeke Moreau."

"He's lying."

"He wasn't lying. Malachi admitted it."

"Then Malachi was lying."

"No, Shannon. You two have your differences, but Malachi wouldn't lie to me."

Shannon was silent for several seconds. Then she turned on Kristin. "They are Missourians, Kristin. They can't help being Confederates. We were Confederates, I guess, until...until they came for Pa. Until Matthew joined up with the Union. And if Cole did ride with Quantrill, well, I'm sure he had his reasons. Cole is nothing like Zeke. You know that, and I know that."

Kristin smiled. Shannon was right, and so was Malachi. Cole was nothing like Zeke, and she knew it. But she was still hurt, and she was still angry. She was angry because she was frightened.

And because she loved him.

"Maybe you're right, Shannon," she said softly.

"Cole would never do anything dishonorable! He wouldn't!" Shannon said savagely. "And—"

"And what?"

"He's your husband, Kristin. You have to remember that. You married him. He's your husband now."

"I'll give him a chance to explain," was all that Kristin said. She would give him a chance. But when? He was gone, and winter was coming, and she didn't know when she would see him again.

* * *

Two days later Pete and the hands returned from the cattle drive, and Jamie and Malachi prepared to ride back to the war. Kristin was sorry she had argued with Malachi, and she hugged him tightly, promising to pray for him. She kissed Jamie, and he assured her that since his unit was stationed not far away he would be back now and then to see how she and Shannon were doing.

Shannon kissed Jamie—and then Malachi, too. He held her for a moment, smiling ruefully.

Then the two of them rode away.

Kristin stood with Shannon at her side, and they watched until they could no longer see the horses. A cool breeze came up, lifting Kristin's hair from her shoulders and swirling around her skirts. Winter was on its way. She was very cold, she realized. She was very cold, and she was very much alone.

Chapter Eleven

Winter was long, hard and bitterly cold. In December Shannon turned eighteen and in January Kristin quietly celebrated her nineteenth birthday. They awaited news from the front, but there was none. The winter was not only cold, it was also quiet, ominously quiet.

Late in February, a Union company came by and took Kristin's plow mules. The young captain leading the company compensated her in Yankee dollars which, she reflected, would help her little when she went out to buy seed for the spring planting. The captain did, however, bring her a letter from Matthew, a letter that had passed from soldier to soldier until it had come to her.

Matthew had apparently not received the letter she had written him. He made no mention of her marriage in his letter to her. Nor did he seem to know anything about Zeke Moreau's attack on the ranch after their father's murder.

It was a sad letter to read. Matthew first wrote that he prayed she and Shannon were well. Then he went into a long missive on the rigors of war—up at five in the morning, sleeping in tents, drilling endlessly, in the rain and even in the snow. Then there was an account of the first major battle in which he had been involved—the dread of waiting, the roar of the cannons, the blast of the guns, the screams of the dying. Nightfall was often the worst of all, when the picket's were close enough to call out to one another. He wrote:

We warn them, Kristin. "Reb! You're in the moonlight!" we call out, lest our sharpshooters take an unwary lad. We were camped on the river last month; fought by day, traded by night. We were low on tobacco, well supplied with coffee, and the Mississippi boys were heavy on tobacco, low on coffee, so we remedied that situation. By the end of it all we skirmished. I came face-to-face with Henry, with whom I had been trading. I could not pull the trigger of my rifle, nor lift my cavalry sword. Henry was shot from behind, and he toppled over my horse, and he looked up at me before he died and said please, would I get rid of his tobacco, his ma didn't know that he was smoking. But what if you fall? he asks me next, and I try to laugh, and I tell him that my Ma is dead, and my Pa is dead, and that my sisters are very understanding, so it is all right if I die with tobacco and cards and all. He tried to smile. He closed his eyes then, and he died, and my dear sisters, I tell you that I was shaken. Sometimes they egg me on both sides—what is a Missouri boy doing in blue? I can only tell them that they do not understand. The worst of it is this—war is pure horror, but it is better than being at home. It is better than Quantrill and Jim lane and

Doc Jennison. We kill people here, but we do not murder in cold blood. We do not rob, and we do not steal, nor engage in any raping or slaughter. Sometimes it is hard to remember that I was once a border rancher and that I did not want war at all, nor did I have sympathy for either side. Only Jake Armstrong from Kansas understands. If the jayhawkers robbed and stole and murdered against you, then you find yourself a Confederate. If the bushwhackers burnt down your place, then you ride for the Union, and the place of your birth doesn't mean a whit.

Well, sisters, I do not mean to depress you. Again, I pray that my letter finds you well. Kristin, again I urge you to take Shannon and leave if you should feel the slightest threat of danger again. They have murdered Pa, and that is what they wanted, but I still worry for you both, and I pray that I will get leave to come and see you soon. I assure you that I am well, as of this writing, which nears Christmas, 1862. I send you all my love. Your brother, Matthew.

He had also sent her his Union pay. Kristin fingered the money, then went out to the barn and dug up the strongbox where she kept the gold from the cattle sales and the Yankee dollars from the captain. She added the money from Matthew. She had been feeling dark and depressed and worried, but now, despite the contents of Matthew's letter, she felt her strength renewed. She had to keep fighting. One day Matthew would come home. One day the war would be over and her brother would return. Until then she would maintain his ranch.

By April she still hadn't been able to buy any mules, so she and Samson and Shannon went out to till the fields. It was hard, backbreaking labor, but she knew that food was growing scarcer and scarcer, and that it was imperative that they grow their own vegetables. Shannon and she took turns behind the plow while Samson used his great bulk to pull it forward. The herd was small, though there would be new calves soon enough. By morning Kristin planned the day with Pete, by day she worked near the house, and supper did not come until the last of the daylight was gone. Kristin went to bed each night so exhausted that she thought very little about the war.

She didn't let herself think about Cole, though sometimes he stole into her dreams uninvited. Sometimes, no matter how exhausted she was when she went to bed, she imagined that he was with her. She forgot then that he had been one of Quantrill's raiders. She remembered only that he was the man who had touched her, the man who had awakened her. She lay in the moonlight and remembered him, remembered his sleek-muscled form walking silent and naked to her by night, remembered the way the moonlight had played over them both...

Sometimes she would awaken and she would be shaking, and she would remind herself that he had ridden with Quantrill, just like Zeke Moreau. She might be married to him now, but she could never, never lie with him again as she had before. He was another of Quantrill's killers, just like Zeke. Riding, burning, pillaging, murdering—raping, perhaps. She didn't know. He had come to her like a savior, but Quantrill's men had never obeyed laws of morality or decency. She wanted him to come back to her because she could not imagine him dead. She wanted him to come back to her and deny it all.

But he could not deny it, because it was the truth. Malachi had said so. Malachi had known how the truth would hurt, but hadn't been able to lie. There was no way for Cole to come and deny it. There was just no way at all.

Spring wore on. In May, while she was out in the south field with Samson, Pete suddenly came riding in from the north pasture. He ignored the newly sown field, riding over it to stop in front of Kristin.

"He's back, Miz Slater, he's back. They say that Quantrill is back, and that Quantrill and company do reign here again!"

The house was still a long way off when Cole reined in his horse and looked across the plain at it. Things looked peaceful, mighty peaceful. Daisies were growing by the porch, and someone—Kristin? Shannon?—had hung little flowerpots from the handsome gingerbread on the front of the house.

It looked peaceful, mighty peaceful.

His heart hammered uncomfortably, and Cole realized that it had taken him a long time to come back. He didn't know quite why, but it had taken him longer than necessary. He hadn't been worried at all, at least not until he had heard that Quantrill was back. He didn't understand it. All through the winter, all through the early spring, he'd had dreams about her. He had wanted her. Wanted her with a longing that burned and ached and kept him staring at the ceiling or the night sky. Sometimes it had been as if he could reach out and touch her. And then everything had come back to him. The silky feel of her flesh and the velvety feel of her hair falling over his shoulders. The startling blue of her eyes, the sun gold of her hair, the fullness of her breasts in his hands...

Then, if he was sound asleep, he would remember the smell of smoke, and he would hear the sound of the shot, and he would see his wife, his first wife, his real wife.... Running, running... And the smoke would be acrid on the air, and the hair that spilled over him would be a sable brown, and it would be blood that filled his hands.

It hurt to stay away. He needed her. He wanted her, wanted her with a raw, blinding, burning hunger. But the nightmares would never stay away. Never. Not while his wife's killer lived. Not while the war raged on.

He picked up the reins again and nudged his mount and started the slow trek toward the house. His breath had quickened. His blood had quickened. It coursed through him, raced through him, and it made him hot, and it made him nervous. Suddenly it seemed a long, long time since he had seen her last. It had been a long time. Almost half a year.

But she was his wife.

He swallowed harshly and wondered what his homecoming would be like. He remembered the night before he had left, and his groin went tight as wire and the excitement seemed to sweep like fire into his limbs, into his fingertips, into his heart and into his lungs.

They hadn't done so badly, he thought. Folks had surely done worse under the best of circumstances.

When the war ended...

Cole paused again, wondering if the war would ever end. Those in Kansas and Missouri had been living with the skirmishing since 1855, and hell, the first shots at Fort Sumter had only been fired in April of '61. Back then, Cole thought grimly, the rebels had thought they could whomp the Yankees in two weeks, and the Yankees had thought, before the first battle at Manassas, it would be easy to whip the Confederacy. But the North had been more determined than the South had ever imagined, and the South had been more resolute than the

North had ever believed possible. And the war had dragged on and on. It had been more than two years now, and there was no end in sight.

So many battles. An Eastern front, a Western front. A Union navy, a Confederate navy, a battle of ironclads. New Orleans fallen, and now Vicksburg under seige. And men were still talking about the battle at Antietam Creek, where the bodies had piled high and the corn had been mown down by bullets and the stream had run red with blood.

He lifted his hands and looked at his threadbare gloves. He was wearing his full dress uniform, but his gold gloves were threadbare. His gray wool tunic and coat carried the gold epaulets of the cavalry, for though he was officially classified a scout he'd been assigned to the cavalry and was therefore no longer considered a spy. It was a fine distinction, Cole thought. And it was damned peculiar that as a scout he should spend so much of his time spying on both sides of the Missouri-Kansas border. He wondered bleakly what it was all worth. In January he'd appeared before the Confederate Cabinet, and he'd reported honestly, as honestly as he could, on the jayhawkers' activities. Jim Lane and Doc Jennison, who had led the jayhawkers—the red-legs as they were sometimes known because of their uniforms—were animals. Jim Lane might be a U.S. senator, but he was still a fanatic and a murderer, every bit as bad as Quantrill. But the Union had gotten control of most of the jayhawkers. Most of them had been conscripted into the Union army and sent far away from the border. As the Seventh Kansas, a number of jayhawkers had still been able to carry out raids on the Missouri side of the border, plundering and burning town after town, but then Major General Henry Halleck had ordered the company so far into the center of Kansas that it had been virtually impossible for the boys to jayhawk.

As long as he lived, Cole would hate the jayhawkers. As long as he lived, he would seek revenge. But his hatred had cooled enough that he could see that there was a real war being fought, a war in which men in blue and men in gray fought with a certain decency, a certain humanity. There were powerful Union politicians and military men who knew their own jayhawkers for the savages they were, and there were men like Halleck who were learning to control them. No one had control of Quantrill.

By that spring, General Robert E. Lee had been given command of the entire Confederate Army. When he had met with that tall, dignified, soft-spoken man, Cole had felt as if the place he had left behind could not be real. War was ugly, blood and death were ugly, and screaming soldiers maimed and dying on torn-up earth were ugly, too. But nothing was so ugly as the total disregard for humanity that reigned on the border between Kansas and Missouri. Lee had listened to Cole, and Jefferson Davis, the Confederate president, had listened long and carefully to him, too. Judah P. Benjamin, secretary of war, had taken his advice and when Quantrill had demanded a promotion and recognition, his request had been denied.

Cole wondered briefly if the violence would ever stop. He wondered if he would ever be able to cleanse his own heart of hatred.

Suddenly he forgot the war, forgot everything.

He could see the well to the left of the house, near the trough, and he could see Kristin standing there. She had just pulled up a pail of water.

Her hair was in braids, but a few golden strands had escaped from her hairpins and curled over her shoulders. She was dressed in simple gingham—no petticoats today—and she had opened the top buttons of her blouse. She dipped a handkerchief into the bucket and doused herself with the cool water, her face, her throat, her collarbone, then flesh bared by the open flaps of her blouse. Hot and dusty, she lifted the dipper from the pail and drank from it. Then she leaned back slightly and allowed the cool water to spill over her face and throat.

Cole's stomach tightened, and he felt his heartbeat in his throat, and he wondered what it was about the way she was standing, savoring the water, that was so provocative, so beguiling, so sensual. He nudged his horse again, eager to greet her.

He came in at a gallop. She spun around, startled. The water spilled over her blouse, and the wet fabric outlined her young breasts. Her eyes widened at the sight of him, first with panic, he thought, then with startled recognition. He drew up in front of her and dismounted in a leap. Her blouse was soaked, and her face was damp. Her lips were parted, and her face was streaked with dust. She was beautiful.

"Cole..." she murmured.

He pulled her hard against him. He found her lips, and he kissed her deeply, and she tasted even sweeter than he remembered. She was vibrant and feminine. He choked out something and touched her breast, feeling her nipple hard as a pebble beneath his palm. She melted against him. She gasped, and she trembled beneath his touch. Her lips parted more fully, and his tongue swept into the hot dampness of her mouth.

Then, suddenly, she twisted away from him with another choking sound. Startled, he released her. She shoved hard against his chest, backing away from him, wiping her mouth with her hands as if she had taken poison. Her eyes remained very wide and very blue. "Bastard!" she hissed at him. She looked him up and down. "Stupid bastard! In a Confederate uniform, no less! Don't you know this whole area is crawling with Yankees?"

"I'll take my clothes right off," he offered dryly.

She shook her head stubbornly. She was still trembling, he saw. Her fingers worked into the fabric of her skirt, released it, then clenched the material again. Her breasts were still outlined by her wet blouse, the nipples clearly delineated. He took a step toward her. "For God's sake, Kristin, what the hell is the matter with you? You're my wife, remember—"

"Don't touch me!"

"Why the hell not?"

"You're a bushwhacker!" she spat out. "You're his—you belong to Quantrill, just like Zeke."

That stopped him dead in his tracks. He wondered how she had found out. A haze fell over his eyes, a cool haze of distance. It didn't really matter. He'd had his reasons. And though he wasn't with Quantrill anymore, if he'd found the right man when he had been with him, he would have been as savage as any of them.

"A friend of yours stopped by here right after you left in the fall," Kristin informed him. "Bill Anderson. You remember him? He remembered you!"

"Kristin, I'm not with Quantrill any longer."

"Oh, I can see that. You got yourself a real Reb uniform. It's a nice one, Cole. You wear it well. But it doesn't cover what you really are! Who did you steal it from? Some poor dead boy?"

His hand slashed out and he almost struck her. He stopped himself just in time.

"The uniform is mine, Kristin," he said through clenched teeth. "Just as you're my wife."

He didn't touch her. Her face was white, and she was as stiff as a board. He started to walk past her, heading straight for the house. Then he spun around. She cringed, but he reached for her shoulders anyway.

"Kristin—" he began. But he was interrupted by a man's voice.

"You leave her alone, Johnny Reb!"

Cole spun around, reaching for his Colt. He was fast, but not fast enough.

"No!" he heard Kristin scream. "Matthew, no, you can't! Cole, no—" She threw herself against his hand, and he lost his chance to fire. She tore her eyes from his and looked over at the tall man in the Union blue coming toward them with a sharpshooter's rifle raised. Kristin screamed again and threw herself against Cole. He staggered and fell, and he was falling when the bullet hit him. It grazed the side of his head. He felt the impact, felt the spurt of blood. He felt a sheet of blackness descend over him, and wondered if he was dying. As he railed against himself in black silence for being so involved with Kristin that he never heard or saw the danger, Cole heard the next words spoken as the man who had called to him, the man who had shot him, came forward.

"Oh, no! Oh, my God—"

"Kristin! What's the matter with you? I'm trying to save you from this jackal—"

"Matthew, this jackal is my husband!"

As he slowly regained consciousness, Cole realized he wasn't dead. He wasn't dead, but he'd probably lost a lot of blood, and it seemed as if he had been out for hours, for it was no longer daylight. Night had fallen. An oil lamp glowed softly at his side.

He was in the bedroom they had shared, the bedroom with the sleigh bed. Everything was blurred. He blinked, and the room began to come into focus. He could see the windows and a trickle of moonlight. He touched his head and discovered that it had been bandaged. He drew his fingers away. At least he couldn't feel any blood. Someone had stripped off his uniform and bathed the dust of the road from him and tucked him between cool, clean sheets.

Someone. His wife. No, not his wife. Kristin. Yes, his wife. He had married her. She was his wife now.

She had stopped him from killing the man.

But she had stopped the man from killing him, too.

A sudden pain streaked through him. He was going to have one terrible headache, he realized. But he was alive, and he was certain that the bullet wasn't embedded in his skull. It had just grazed him.

He heard footsteps on the stairs, and then on the floor outside his door. He closed his eyes quickly as someone came into the room. It was Delilah. She spoke in a whisper. "Dat boy is still out cold." She touched his throat, then his chest. "But he's living, all right. He's still living, and he don't seem to have no fever."

"Thank God!" came in a whisper. Kristin. Cole could smell the faint scent of her subtle perfume. He felt her fingers, cool and gentle, against his face. Then he heard the man's voice again. Matthew. She had called him Matthew. Of course. The brother. The one he had told her to write to just so that this wouldn't happen.

"A Reb, Kristin? After everything that happened—"

"Yes, damn you! After everything that happened!" Kristin whispered harshly. "Matthew, don't you dare preach to me! You left, you got to go off and join up with the army! Shannon and I didn't have that luxury. And Zeke came back—"

"Moreau came back?" Matthew roared.

"Shut up, will you, Matthew?" Kristin said wearily. She sounded so tired. So worn, so weary. Cole wanted to open his eyes, wanted to take her into his arms, wanted to soothe away all the terrible things that the war had done to her. He could not, and he knew it.

She probably didn't want him to, anyway. She would probably never forgive him for his time with Quantrill. Well, he didn't owe anyone any apologies for it, and he'd be damned if he'd explain himself to her. And yet...

"Kristin," Matthew was saying huskily, "what happened?"

"Nothing happened, Matthew. Oh, it almost did. Zeke was going to rape me, and let every man with him rape me, and then he was probably going to shoot me. He was going to sell Samson and Delilah. But nothing happened because of this man. He's a better shot than Shannon or me. He's even a better shot than you. He happened by and it was all over for Zeke."

"Zeke is dead?"

"No. Zeke rode away." A curious note came into her voice. "You see, Matthew, he won't murder a man in cold blood. I wanted him to, but he wouldn't. And after that, well, it's a long story. But since he's married me, none of them will harm me, or this place. They're—they're afraid of him."

"Damn, Kristin—" He broke off. Cole heard a strangled sound, and then he knew that brother and sister were in one another's arms. Kristin was crying softly, and Matthew was comforting her. Cole gritted his teeth, for the sound of her weeping was more painful to him than his wound. I will never be able to touch her like that, he thought. He opened his eyes a fraction and took a good look at Matthew McCahy. He was a tall man with tawny hair and blue eyes like his sisters. He was lean, too, and probably very strong, Cole thought. He was probably a young man to be reckoned with.

He shifted and opened his eyes wider. Sister and brother broke apart. Kristin bent down by him and touched his forehead. Her hair was loose, and it teased the bare flesh of his chest. "Cole?"

He didn't speak. He nodded, and he saw that her brow was furrowed with worry, and he was glad of that. She hated him for his past, but at least she didn't want him dead.

"Cole, this is Matthew. My brother. I wrote him, but the letter never reached him. He didn't know that—he didn't know that we were married."

Cole nodded again and looked over at Matthew. He was still in full-dress uniform—navy-blue full-dress uniform. As his gaze swept over Matthew, Cole couldn't help noticing that Matthew McCahy's uniform was in far better shape than his own, and in much better condition than that of the majority of the uniforms worn by the men of the South. The blockade was tightening. The South was running short of everything—medicine, clothing, ammunition, food. Everything. He smiled bitterly. The South had brilliance. Lee was brilliant, Jackson was brilliant, Stuart was brilliant. But when a Southerner fell in battle, he could not be replaced. Men were the most precious commodity in war, and the Confederacy did not have nearly enough.

The Union, however, seemed to have an inexhaustible supply of soldiers, volunteers and mercenaries.

Cole knew a sudden, bleak flash of insight. The South could not win the war.

"Reb—Sorry, your name is Cole, right? Cole Slater." Matthew came around and sat at the foot of the bed. He swallowed uncomfortably. "You saved my sisters' lives, and I'm grateful to you. I wouldn't have shot you if I'd known. It was the uniform. I'm with the North." He said it defensively. It was not easy for a Missourian to fight for the North.

"You had just cause," Cole said. His voice was raspy, his throat dry. His mouth tasted of blood.

Matthew nodded. "Yes. I had just cause." He hesitated. "Well, I'm home on leave, and I guess that you are, too."

"Something like that," Cole said. Kristin made a little sound of distress, but she quickly swallowed it down. Cole didn't glance her way. He smiled at Matthew and reached for her hand. She was playing the loving wife for her brother, he knew, and he wondered how far she would go. She let him take her hand, let him pull her down beside him.

"We'll have to manage while we're both here," Matthew said. He stretched out a hand to Cole, and Cole released Kristin's long enough to take it. "Does that sound fair to you, Reb?"

"It sounds fine to me, Yankee."

Matthew flushed suddenly. "Well, maybe I'd best leave the two of you alone." He rose quickly.

Kristin was on her feet instantly. "No! I'm coming with you!"

Matthew's brow furrowed suspiciously. "Kristin—"

"Sweetheart..." Cole murmured plaintively.

"Darling!" Kristin replied sweetly, syrup dripping from her tone, "I wouldn't dream of disturbing you now. You must rest!"

She gave him a peck on the forehead, and then she was gone, practically running out of the room.

Matthew smiled at Cole. "Too bad there's a war on, ain't it?"

"Yeah. It's too damn bad," Cole agreed.

"She's stubborn," Matthew said.

"Yeah. I've noticed."

"Just like a mule."

"Well, I guess I agree with you there, Yankee."

Matthew laughed, then left and closed the door behind him.

Three days later, Cole was feeling damned good, and damned frustrated. Kristin had managed to elude him ever since his return, sweetly pleading his weakened condition. She had spent her nights in her own room, leaving him to lie there alone. But as night fell on his third day back, Cole jerked awake from a doze to realize that Kristin had come into the room.

He heard her breathing in the darkness, each breath coming in a little pant. Her back was against the door, and she seemed to be listening. She thought he was sleeping, he realized.

Cole rose silently and moved toward her in the dark. He clamped a hand over her mouth and pulled her against the length of his naked body. She gave a muffled gasp and stiffened then began to struggle to free herself.

"Shush!" he warned her.

She bit his hand, and he swore softly.

"Let me go!" she whispered.

"Not on your life, Mrs. Slater."

"Bushwhacker!"

His mouth tightened grimly. "You're still my wife, Kristin."

"Try to rape me and I'll scream. Matthew will kill you. You don't even have a gun up here!"

"If I touch you, Kristin, it wouldn't be rape," Cole assured her.

"Let go—"

He did not let go. He kissed her, plunging his tongue deep into her mouth, holding her so firmly that she could not deny him. He caught her wrists and held them fast behind her back, pressing his naked body still closer to hers. She wore a thin white cotton nightgown buttoned to the throat. It was so thin that he could feel all the sweet secrets her body had to offer.

He raised his lips from hers at last, and she gasped for breath. He pressed his lips to her breast and took the nipple into his mouth through the fabric, savoring it with his tongue.

"I'll scream!" she whispered.

"Scream, then," he told her. He lifted her into his arms and carried her to the bed, searching feverishly for the hem of the gown. He found it and pulled it up, and then they were together, bare flesh touching bare flesh. He seared the length of her with his lips, and she raged against him with husky words and whispers. But then she rose against him. She wrapped her arms around him and pulled his head down to hers and kissed him again. And then she told him he was a bastard, but she gasped when he caressed her thighs, and she buried her face against him when his touch grew intimate and demanding.

"Scream," he whispered to her. "Scream, if you feel you must..."

He thrust deep into her. She cried out, but his mouth muffled the cry, and then his tongue filled her mouth.

It had been so very long, and she had dreamed of him so many times.

He stroked and caressed her insides until she was in a frenzy. Then he drove into her with all the force he possessed, and she felt the familiar sweetness invade her once, and then again and again. Then, suddenly, he was gone from her. She was cold, and she was lost, but then he was kissing her again, her forehead, her cheeks, her breasts, her thighs.... He turned her over gently, and his lips trailed a path of fire down her spine. Then she was on her back again, and his silver-gray eyes were upon her and she swallowed back a shriek of pleasure as he came to her again....

The night was swept away.

Later, as she lay awake in the ravaged bed, Kristin berated herself furiously for her lack of principles. She reminded herself again that he had been with Quantrill, and she fought back tears of fury.

She slept with her back to him, and he did not try to touch her again. In the morning, she avoided him. At dinner she was polite, though she wanted to scream. She was disturbed to see that her brother and Cole talked about the cattle and the ranch easily, like two old friends. Shannon had talked to Matthew, and Shannon thought Cole was a hero, no matter what.

He's a bushwhacker! she wanted to shriek to her brother, but of course she could not. Matthew would want to kill Cole, if he knew. And Kristin had never seen anyone as talented with a gun as Cole. No one. If Matthew tried to kill him, Matthew would be the one who died.

Later that evening, when it was time for bed, Matthew walked upstairs with them, and Kristin had no choice but to follow Cole into her parents' bedroom.

When the door closed behind them, Kristin stared at it. Cole was behind her, so close that she could feel his warm breath on the back of her neck.

"I hate you," she told him.

He was silent for a long time. She longed to turn around, but she did not.

"I don't think you do, Kristin," he said at last. "But have it however you want it."

He stripped off his clothes and let them lay where they fell, and he crawled into bed. She stayed where she was for a long time. She heard him move to blow out the lamp, and still she stood by the door. Then, finally, she stripped down to her chemise and climbed gingerly into the bed. She knew he was still awake, but he did not try to touch her. She lay awake for hours, and then she drifted off to sleep. While she slept, she rolled against him, and cast her leg over his. Their arms became entwined, and her hair fell over him like a soft blanket.

They awoke that way. Her chemise was up to her waist, her shoulders were bare, and her breast was peeking out. She gazed over at Cole and saw that he was awake and that he was watching her. Then she felt him, felt him like a pulsing rod against her flesh. He moved toward her, very, very slowly, giving her every chance to escape. She couldn't move. Her flesh was alive, her every nerve awake to shimmering sensation, and when he came inside her she shuddered at the pleasure of it, of having him with her, of touching him again, of savoring the subtle movement of his muscles, of feeling the hardness of him as he moved inside her.

And yet, when it was over, she could still find nothing to say to him. She rose quickly and dressed, aware all the while of his brooding eyes upon her.

"Where have you been?" she demanded at last.

"In Richmond."

"Not with—"

"You know I wasn't with Quantrill. You saw my uniform."

Kristin shrugged. "Some of them wear Confederate uniforms."

"I wasn't with Quantrill."

Kristin hesitated, struggling with her buttons. Cole rose and came up behind her, and she swallowed down a protest as he took over the task. "How long are you staying?"

"I've got another week."

"The same as Matthew," she murmured.

"The same as Matthew."

"And where are you going now?"

"Malachi's unit."

She hesitated. Liar! she longed to shout. Tears stung her eyes. She didn't know if he was lying or not.

He swung her around to face him. "I'm a special attaché to General Lee, Kristin. Officially, I'm cavalry. A major, but the only man I have to answer to is the grand old man himself. I do my best to tell him what's going on back here."

Kristin lifted her chin. "And what do you tell him?"

"The truth."

"The truth?"

"The truth as I see it, Kristin."

They stared at one another for a moment, enemies again. Hostility glistened in her eyes and narrowed his sharply.

"I'm sorry, Cole," Kristin said at last. "I can't forgive you."

"Damn you, Kristin, when did I ever ask you to forgive me?" he replied. He turned around. He had dismissed her, she realized. Biting her lip, she fled the room.

She avoided him all that day. She was tense at dinner as she listened to the conversation that flowed around her. Matthew, puzzled by her silence, asked if she was unwell, and she told him she was just tired. She went up to bed early.

She went to bed naked, and she lay awake, and she waited.

When Cole came to bed, she rolled into his arms, and he thought she made love more sweetly than ever before, more sweetly and with a greater desperation.

It went on that way, day after day, night after night, until the time came for Matthew to ride away again.

And for Cole to ride away again.

And then they were standing in front of the house, ready to mount up, one man she loved dressed in blue, one man she loved dressed in gray. Both handsome, both young, both carrying her heart with them, though she could not admit that to the man in gray.

Kristin was silent. Shannon cried and hugged them both again and again.

Kristin kissed and hugged her brother, and then, because there was an audience, she had to kiss Cole.

Then, suddenly, the audience didn't matter. May was over. They had heard that Vicksburg had fallen, and Kristin thought of all the men who would die in the days to come, and she didn't want to let either of them go.

She didn't want to let Cole go. She couldn't explain anything to him, couldn't tell him that she didn't hate him, that she loved him, but she didn't want to let him go.

She hugged him fiercely, and she kissed him passionately, until they were both breathless and they both had to step away. His eyes searched hers, and then he mounted up.

Shannon and Kristin stood together and watched as the two men clasped hands.

Then one rode west, the other east. Cole to Kansas, Matthew deeper into Missouri.

Shannon let out a long, gasping sob.

"They're gone again!" she said, and pulled her sister closer to her. "Come on. We'll weed out the garden. It's hot, and it'll be a miserable task, and we won't think about the men at all."

"We'll think about them," Shannon said. She was close to tears again, Kristin thought. Shannon, who was always so fierce, so feisty. And Kristin knew that if Shannon cried again, she would sob all day, too.

"Let's get to work."

They had barely set to work when they heard the sounds of hooves again. Kristin spun around hopefully, thinking that either her brother or her husband had returned.

Shannon called out a warning.

It was Zeke, Kristin thought instantly.

But it was not. It was a company of Union soldiers. At its head was a captain. His uniform was just like Matthew's. They stopped in front of the house, but they did not dismount.

"Kristin Slater!" the captain called out.

He was about Matthew's age, too, Kristin thought.

"Yes?" she said, stepping forward.

He swallowed uncomfortably. "You're under arrest."

"What?" she said, astonished.

His Adam's apple bobbed. "Yes, ma'am. I'm sorry. You and your sister are under arrest, by order of General Halleck. I'm right sorry, but we're rounding up all the womenfolk giving aid and succor to Quantrill and his boys."

"Aid and succor!" Kristin shrieked.

She might have been all right if she hadn't begun to laugh. But she did begin to laugh, and before she knew it, she was hysterical.

"Take her, boys."

"Now, you just wait!" Delilah cried from the porch.

The captain shook his head. "Take Mrs. Slater, and the young one, too."

One of the soldiers got down from his horse and tugged at Kristin's arm. She tore it fiercely from his grasp.

The young man ruefully addressed his captain. "Sir..."

"My brother is in the Union army!" Kristin raged. "My father was killed by bushwhackers, and now you're arresting me...for helping Quantrill? No!"

The soldier reached for her again, and she hit him in the stomach. Shannon started to scream, and Delilah came running down the steps with her rolling pin.

"God help us, if the Rebs ain't enough, Halleck has to pit us against the womenfolk!" the young captain complained. He dismounted and walked over to Kristin. "Hold her, men."

Two of them caught her arms. She stared at him.

"Sorry, ma'am," he said sincerely.

Then he struck her hard across the chin, and she fell meekly into his arms.

Chapter Twelve

❦❦❦❦❦❦

"**Y**'all have just the blondest hair! And I do mean the blondest!" Josephine Anderson said as she pulled Shannon's locks into a set of high curls on top of her head. She was a pretty young woman herself, with plump cheeks and a flashing smile and a tendency to blush easily. She never smiled when their Yankee captors were around, though. Josephine was a hard-core Confederate. She and her sister Mary had been brought in a week after Kristin and Shannon, and they all shared a corner of a big room on the second floor of a building in Kansas City. Josephine and Mary were both very sweet, and Kristin liked them well enough, despite their fanaticism. They had both wanted her and Shannon to meet their brother Billy—who turned out to be none other than Bill Anderson, the Bill Anderson who had stopped by the house to make sure that Kristin knew about Cole's position with Quantrill's raiders.

That was all right. At the very beginning, Kristin had sweetly told the girls that she did know their Billy. She also told them what had happened to her father—and that she wished that she were anything other than what she was: a citizen of a country whose people tore one another to shreds.

Josephine and Mary had turned away from her in amazement, but then the next day they had been friendly. They respected her right to have a passionate stand—even if it was a strange one.

And when Cole's name was mentioned, Mary acted just the way Shannon did. "Ooh! You're really married to him?" she gushed.

It seemed that Cole had been to dinner once at their house with Bill when he had first started out with Quantrill. But they didn't know very much about him, only that there was some deep secret in his past.

"He can be real quiet like, you know!" Mary said.

"But, oh, those eyes!" Josephine rolled her own.

"It's such a pity he left Quantrill!" Mary told her fiercely. "Why, he'd have cleaned out half of Kansas by now; I just know it."

Kristin assured them that Cole was still with the Confederate Army—in the cavalry, like his brothers. Then Shannon went on to tell them about their brother Matthew and how he had gone off to join up with the Union Army after their father's death.

Mary and Josephine thought that was a terrible tragedy, but they understood that, too. "I'm surprised he didn't become a jayhawker, because that's how it goes, you know! They say that old John Brown was attacked way back in '55, that one of his sons was killed. So he killed some Missourians, and some Missourians went up and killed some more Kansans. But you two—why, I feel right sorry for you! Missourians, with a brother in blue and your husband in gray. It's a shame, a damned shame, that's all.''

It was a good thing they were able to come to an understanding. All summer long, General Ewing, the local Union commander, had women picked up so that their men couldn't come to them for food or supplies. There were a great many of them living at very close quarters. The authorities holding them weren't cruel, and the women weren't hurt in any way. A number of the young officers were remarkably patient, in fact, for the women could be extraordinarily abusive when they spoke to their captors. But though the men behaved decently toward their prisoners, the living conditions were horrid. The building itself was in terrible shape, with weak and rotting timbers, the food was barely adequate, and the bedding was full of insects.

Kristin wanted desperately to go home. At first she had been angry. She had fought and argued endlessly with various commanders, and they had all apologized and looked uncomfortable and shuffled their feet, but none of them had been willing to let her go. And finally she had become resigned.

She grew more and more wretched. She had often been sick in the first weeks of her captivity and she had thought it must be the food. She was still queasy much of the time, but, though she hadn't told anyone, she knew why now. She was pregnant. Sometime in February of the following year she was going to have Cole's baby. She had been stunned at first, but then she had taunted herself endlessly. Why should she be surprised, after all. Children were the result of a man being with a woman.

She wasn't sure how she felt. Sometimes she lay there and railed against a God that could let her have a baby in a world where its blood relations were destined to be its mortal enemies, in a world where murder and bloodshed were the order of the day.

Then there were nights when she touched her still-flat belly and dreamed, and wondered what the baby would look like. And then, even if she was furious with Cole, even if she had convinced herself that he was as evil as Zeke, she knew she loved him. And she did want his child. A little boy with his shimmering silver eyes. Or a girl. Or maybe the child would be light, with her hair and eyes. Whoever the child took after, it was destined to be beautiful, she was certain. Cole's baby. She longed to hold it in her arms. She dreamed about seeing him again, about telling him.

And then there were times when she sank into depression. Cole probably wouldn't be the least bit pleased. He probably intended to divorce her as soon as the war was over, she thought bitterly. She was imprisoned for being the wife of a man who intended to divorce her.

Then not even that mattered. She wanted the baby. She wanted the baby to hold and to love, and she wanted it to be born to peace. The war could not go on forever. She didn't care who won. She just wanted it to be over. She wanted her baby to be able to run laughing through the cornfields, to look up at the sun and feel its warmth. She wanted peace for her child.

And most of all, she wanted it to be born at home. She did not want to bear her baby here, in this awful, crowded place of degradation.

Kristin looked up from the letter she was writing to her brother asking if there was anything he could do to get the authorities to free Shannon and herself. The three other women in the room looked as if they were preparing for a ball.

Josephine stepped back. "Oh, Shannon, that just looks lovely, really lovely."

"Why, thank you, ma'am," Shannon said sweetly. Then she sighed. "I wish I could see it better."

Mary dug under her pillow and found her little hand mirror. "Here, Shannon."

Suddenly the room fell silent. One of the young Federal officers, a Captain Ellsworth, had come in. The women looked at him suspiciously.

His dark brown eyes fell on Kristin. "Mrs. Slater, would you come with me, please?"

She quickly set aside her paper and pen and rose, nervously folding her fingers in front of her and winding them tightly together.

A middle-aged woman called out to the captain, "Don't walk too hard on this here floor, sonny! Those Yankee boots will make you come right through it!"

He nodded sadly to the woman. "Sorry, Mrs. Todd. The place is awful, I know. I'm working on it."

"Don't work on it!" Mary Anderson called out gaily. "You tell them to let us go home. You tell them that my brother will come after them, and that he'll kill them all."

"Yes, miss," Captain Ellsworth said, staring straight at her. "That's the problem, Miss Anderson. Your brother already does come to murder us all." He bowed to her politely. Then he took Kristin's elbow and led her out of the room. He preceded her down the groaning staircase to the doorway of the office below. Kristin looked at him nervously.

"It's all right, Mrs. Slater. Major Emery is in there. He wants to talk to you."

He opened the door for her, and Kristin walked in. She had never seen Major Emery before. He was a tall, heavyset man, with thick, wavy, iron-gray hair and great drooping mustache to match. His eyebrows were wild and of the same gray, and beneath them his eyes were a soft flower blue. He seemed a kind man, Kristin thought instantly, a gentleman.

"Mrs. Slater, sit, please." Kristin silently did so. The major dismissed Captain Ellsworth, then smiled at Kristin. "Can I get you some tea, Mrs. Slater?"

"No, thank you." She sat very straight, reminding herself that, no matter how kindly he looked, he was still her captor. He smiled again and leaned back in his chair.

"Mrs. Slater, I'm trying very hard to get an order to have you and your sister released."

A gasp of surprise escaped Kristin. Major Emery's smile deepened, and he leaned forward again. "It will take a few days, I'm afraid."

Kristin and Shannon had been here almost three months. A few more days meant nothing.

"Because of my brother?" Kristin said. "Did Matthew find out that we were here? I didn't want to tell him at first because I didn't want him going into battle worrying, but I was just writing to him—"

"No, no, Mrs. Slater. I haven't heard anything from your brother at all."

"Oh, I see," Kristin murmured bitterly. "You've finally decided that a woman who had her father killed by some of Quantrill's men is not likely to give aid and comfort to the enemy, is that it?"

Major Emery shook his head. "No. Because of your husband," he said quietly.

"What?" Kristin demanded suspiciously. "Major, I'm in here because I'm married to Cole Slater. No one seems to believe me when I say that he isn't with Quantrill anymore.''

Major Emery stood and looked out the window. Then he turned back to Kristin. ''Do you believe it yourself, young lady?''

''What?'' She was certain she was blushing, certain her face had turned a flaming red.

''Do you believe in him yourself, Mrs. Slater?''

''Why...of course!'' she said, though she was not at all sure she did.

Emery took his seat again and smiled. ''I'm not sure, Mrs. Slater, I'm not sure. But that doesn't really matter. You see, I do have faith in your husband. Complete faith.''

Kristin stared at him blankly. She lifted a hand in the air. ''Do go on, major. Please, do go on.''

''I'm wiling to bet I know your husband better than you do, Mrs. Slater. In certain ways, at least.''

She tightened her jaw against his mischievous grin. He was a nice man, she decided, a gentle, fatherly type, but he seemed to be having a good time at her expense at the moment.

''Major...''

His smile faded. He looked a little sad. ''He was a military man, you know. He went to West Point. He was in the same class as Jeb Stuart. Did you know that?''

Yes, he had said something to Shannon about it. To Shannon. Not to her.

''I know that he was in the military, yes.''

Major Emery nodded. ''Cole Slater was one of the most promising young cavalrymen I ever knew. He fought in Mexico, and he was with me in the West. He's good with the Indians—fighting them and, more importantly, talking with them, making truces. Keeping truces. Then the war came.''

''And he resigned,'' Kristin murmured.

''No, not right away. He didn't resign until they burned down his house and killed his wife.''

''Killed? His wife?'' She didn't realize that she had gotten to her feet until Major Emery came around the desk and gently pushed her back into her chair. Then he leaned against the desk and crossed his arms over his chest, smiling down at her kindly. ''I reckoned you might not know everything. Cole is a closemouthed man. Tight-lipped, yes sirree. He was an officer in the Union Army when South Carolina seceded from the Union. That didn't matter none to the jayhawkers. He was a Missourian. And Jim Lane had sent out an order that anybody who was disloyal to the Union was to be killed. The boys got pretty carried away. They rode to his place and they set it on fire. Cole was out riding the range. I imagine he was giving his position some pretty grave thought. Anyway, Jim Lane's jayhawkers rode in and set fire to his place. His wife was a pretty thing, real pretty. Sweet, gentle girl from New Orleans. She came running out, and the boys grabbed hold of her. Seems she learned something about gunfire from Cole, though. She shot up a few of them when they tried to get their hands on her. Cole came riding in, and by then she was running to him. Only some fool had already put a bullet in her back, and when Cole reached her, she was dying. She was expecting their first child right then, too. She was about five months along, so they tell me. Of course, after killing his pregnant wife, none of the men was willing to let him live, either. Someone shot Cole, too, and left him for dead. But he's a tough customer. He lived.''

"And he joined up with Quantrill," Kristin whispered. She swallowed. She could almost see the fire, could almost smell the smoke, could almost hear the screams. She suddenly felt ill. As if she were going to throw up.

"Oh, my God!" she whispered, jumping to her feet. Major Emery, too was on his feet in an instant, yelling for a pail and some water.

To her horror, she *was* sick. Major Emery was a perfect gentleman, cooling her forehead with a damp cloth and then insisting that she have tea with lots of milk to settle her stomach. When it was over and they were alone again, he said to her, "You are expecting a child, Mrs. Slater?"

She nodded bleakly.

"Well, my point exactly. I just don't think you should be here anymore. And I don't think Cole is still with Quantrill, because it just isn't his style. Ma'am, I want you to know that I find our jayhawkers every bit as loathsome as the bushwhackers. They're all murderers, pure and simple. Cole isn't a murderer. I think he went with Quantrill to try to get the man who led the attack on his ranch, and only for that reason. Only he wasn't easy to find, because he retired along with Lane. Hell, Lane is a U.S. senator! But the man who attacked Cole's place is back in the center of Kansas, and like Lane, he owns a lot of things, and a lot of people. Cole knew he couldn't get to him, not with Quantrill. And he knew that what Quantrill was up to was murder. He's regular army now, all right."

Kristin swallowed some of her tea and nodded painfully. She hurt all over, inside and out. She had despised Cole, despite everything that he had done for her, just because Bill Anderson had told her that Cole had ridden with Quantrill. She desperately wanted to see him again. She wanted to hold him. She wanted to make him forget, if only for a moment, what had been done to him.

It made men hard, this war did. It had made her hard, she knew, and it had made him harder. She realized anew that he did not love her, and now, she thought, he never would. He had loved his first wife.

"Mrs. Slater?"

Kristin looked at the major. "Yes...yes I think that he's in the regular army. That's—that's what he said."

The major frowned suddenly, his hands flat on his desk. He looked up at the ceiling.

Then Kristin felt it. There was a trembling in the floor beneath her, in the very air around her.

"Hellfire and damnation!" Major Emery shouted. He leaped to his feet, hopped over his desk and pulled her out of her chair. He dragged her over to the door and kicked it open, then huddled with her beneath the frame, shielding her with his bulk.

Suddenly floorboards and nails were flying everywhere and great clouds of dust filled the room. Dirt flew into Kristin's mouth and into her eyes, and she heard screams, terrible screams, agonized screams.

The whole building was caving in. The awful place had been faulty structurally and decaying and now it was actually caving in.

"Shannon!" Kristin screamed. "Shannon!" She tried to pull away from the major, but she couldn't. He was holding her too tightly. The rumbling continued, and inside was chaos. Boards were falling and breaking and clattering on the floor. A woman's body fell right next to Kristin, who was able to pull away from the major at last to kneel down by the girl.

It was Josephine Anderson, and Kristin knew instantly that she was dead. Her eyes were wide open, glazed as only death could glaze them. "Jo!" she cried out, falling to her knees. She touched the still-warm body and closed the pathetic, staring eyes. Then she looked up from the body to the gaping hole above her. "Shannon!" she screamed. She twisted around to look at what had been the hallway and the stairs. Only the bannister was left. Everywhere, the floor had crumbled. Tears and screams filled the air. "Shannon!"

"Mrs. Slater! You must remember your child!" the major urged her, grabbing her arm.

"Please!" She shook herself free and stumbled through the wreckage that littered the floor. She found Mary, her body grotesquely twisted beneath a pile of boards. "Mary!" After clawing away the debris, Kristin knelt and felt for the other woman's pulse. Mary was alive. She opened her eyes. "Jo?"

"It's Kristin, Mary. Everything...everything is going to be all right." She squeezed the girl's hand and turned around, searching for someone, anyone. "Get help here!" Kristin shouted, suddenly choking back tears. Where was Shannon? The girls had all been together.

Several young medics rushed in. Kristin moved away as they knelt over Mary. There were clanging bells sounding from outside, and the sound of horses' hooves was loud as a fire hose was brought around.

"Mrs. Slater!"

The major was still trying to get her out.

"Shannon!"

An arm was protruding from a pile of lumber. Kristin began to tear away the planks. This was the worst of it. The woman beneath was dead. Kristin inhaled on a sob and turned away.

"Kristin!"

She looked up. Shannon, deathly pale, was clinging to a board that looked as if it were just about to give way.

"Shannon! Hold on! Just hold on a little longer—"

There was a cracking sound. The board began to break. Shannon's toes dangled ten feet over Kristin's head. "Hold on!"

"No, Miss McCahy, let go now! I'm here. I'll catch you!"

It was Captain Ellsworth. He stepped in front of Kristin and reached out his arms to Shannon. Shannon still clung to the board. "Come down, now! Please, before it breaks!"

Kristin saw the problem. If the board broke, Shannon could fall on a splinter in one of the beams that had been exposed, and she would be skewered alive.

"Shannon! Where the hell is your courage? Jump!" Kristin called out. She watched as Shannon's eyes fell on the splintered beams below her. But then Shannon looked down at her and she grinned. "What the hell! We can't all live forever, now, can we? Thumbs up, Kristin. Say a prayer."

Shannon released her hold on the board. She fell, her skirts billowing out around her, and suddenly, Captain Ellsworth was falling, too. He had caught her and the impact had brought him down with her.

"Get them both out of here!" Major Emery shouted. He picked Kristin up bodily and carried her outside. Captain Ellsworth swept Shannon up and followed. When they were finally out in the street, Kristin and Shannon hugged each other, sobbing.

"Jo—"

"Jo is dead," Kristin said softly. Then they stared at one another as they realized how lucky they were to be alive. And they just hugged one another again and sobbed, and listened to the chaos as more women were carried from the building, some alive, some injured...and some dead.

A week later, Kristin and Shannon were in the home of Captain Ellsworth's sister, Betty.

Four women besides Josephine Anderson had been killed. Rumor had it that Bill Anderson had gone berserk, foaming at the mouth, when he had heard that one of his sisters had been killed and the other had been seriously injured. Many Confederates were saying that General Ewing had purposely ordered that the women be incarcerated in the ramshackle building so that just such a tragedy might occur. There would be repercussions. To make matters worse, General Ewing had issued his General Order Number Ten, ordering all wives and children of known bushwhackers to move out of the state of Missouri.

That night, Major Emery rode out to the small house on the outskirts of the city with Captain Ellsworth beside him. It was quite apparent that an attachment was forming between Shannon and the captain, and Kristin didn't mind at all. After all, the young captain had come valiantly to her rescue. Kristin liked him herself. He was quiet and well read and unfailingly polite. And Shannon was eighteen, a young woman who already knew her own mind.

But though both the captain and the major were charming in Betty's parlor, Kristin knew that something was very wrong. The major called her onto the porch.

He looked at the moon, twirling his hat in his hand. "Quantrill attacked Lawrence, Kansas, yesterday."

"Oh, God!" Kristin murmured.

"It was a massacre," Major Ellsworth said grimly. "Almost the entire town was razed to the ground. At least one hundred men were killed...one twelve-year-old boy was shot down for being dressed up in an old Union uniform. And Quantrill only lost one of his boys. A former Baptist preacher named Larkin Skaggs. He was too drunk to ride away with Quantrill. An Indian found him and shot him dead, and then the survivors ripped him to shreds." Major Emery was silent for a moment. "What is it coming to? None of us, not one of us, it seems, is any better than a bloody savage."

Kristin wanted to say something to comfort him. A lot of good men were experiencing the same despair, she knew. But she could think of nothing to say.

He turned around and tipped his hat to her. "You're free, young lady. I'm going to see to it that an escort takes you and your sister home."

"But how—"

A grin tugged at his lower lip. "Someone got through to your brother, and he raised all kinds of hell with the higher-ups. And then..."

"And then?"

He shrugged. His eyes twinkled. "Well, you see, Kristin, I know Cole. And a lot of other cavalry boys know Cole, so we know damned well that he isn't any outlaw. But people who don't know him, well, they're still convinced that he's a bad 'un. At the moment, that's all right, because there's a rumor out that he's heard about you and Shannon being held up here and that he's steaming. After everything that's happened, well...we can't have troops everywhere. Some folks are afraid he might ride in here and destroy the town just to get to you. I decided not to dispute that with any of them. I thought you deserved the right to go home if that was what you wanted."

Kristin stared at him a long time. Then she kissed him on the cheek. "Thank you."

"You see Cole, you tell him I sent my regards. You tell him I miss him. I never did meet another man who could ride or shoot like him."

She nodded. "Thank you. Thank you so much. For everything."

"Be there for him. He probably needs you."

Kristin smiled ruefully. "He doesn't love me, you know. You see, he only married me because he felt he had to. To protect me."

"Love comes in a lot of ways, young lady. You give him a little time. Maybe this war will end one day."

He tipped his hat to her again, and then he was gone.

In retaliation for the attack on Lawrence, General Ewing issued General Order Number Eleven, which forced almost everyone in Missouri to leave. People were given fifteen days to leave their property. The exodus was a terrible thing to watch, one of the worst things Kristin had seen in all the years since the fighting had begun. Poor farmers were forced to leave behind what little they possessed, and others were shot down where they stood because they refused to leave. Because the McCahy ranch belonged to Matthew, a soldier serving in the Union army, Major Emery was able to keep his promise and send Kristin and Shannon home, however.

The young lieutenant who escorted them was appalled by what he saw of the evacuation. Once he even told her that it was one of the cruellest measures he had ever seen taken. "This war will never end," he said glumly. "We will not let it end, it seems. The people who do not fight are ordered to leave, and the bushwhackers will come through here when they're gone, stealing whatever they leave behind!"

It was true, Kristin discovered. Even when they were home, when it seemed that they had returned to something like a normal life, Peter often came to her at night to tell her that he had seen another house burning somewhere, or that he had found cattle slaughtered, a sure sign that guerrillas had been in the area, living off the land.

In the middle of September they had a letter from Matthew. He was trying to get leave to come and see them, but so far he hadn't been able to manage it. He explained:

But the Rebels are in worse shape than we are. I think that perhaps by Christmas I will be able to come home. There was a battle fought in a little town in Pennsylvania called Gettysburg. Kristin, they say it was the most awful yet, but General Lee was stopped, and he was forced to retreat back to the South. Since then, there has been new hope that the war may end. Some of these fellows say that they will force the South to her knees. They do not know Southerners. I cannot imagine your husband on his knees, nor do I ever quite forget that I am a Missourian myself. But I pray for it to end. I watched another friend die yesterday of the dysentery, and it seems that we do not even have to catch bullets to drop off like flies. John Maple, who was injured in our last skirmish, had to have his leg amputated. Kristin, if I am caught at all by shot, I hope that the ball passes straight to my heart, for those operations are fearful things to witness. There was no morphine, but we did have some whiskey, and still, John screamed so horribly. Now we must all pray that the rot does not set in, else he will die anyway.

Kristin, forgive me, I wander again into subjects that do not fit a lady's ears, but you are my sister. I am still so grateful that you and Shannon are home. Every man who heard of the incident in Kansas City was appalled, and none was proud. That you might have been killed there chilled me to the bone, and I waited very anxiously for the news that you were safe.

As I said before, the Rebs are hurting badly. They have good generals, and good men, but those that die cannot be replaced. I am telling you this, aware that you must be worried for your husband. If you do not see him, you must not instantly fear the worst. They have probably refused to give him leave. They are desperate now to hold on to Virginia, and perhaps they are keeping him in the East.

Kristin set her brother's letter down and stared out the window. She wondered if Cole would come if she thought hard enough about him. Then she wondered, not for the first time, if he had been at the battle of Gettysburg. They talked of it constantly in Kansas City. It seemed that the death toll had been terrible there, but she had read the lists endlessly, looking for his name, and she had not found it. She had thought, too, that he might have been with John Hunt Morgan, along with Malachi, but she had read that Morgan had been captured in July, though what had become of his men was unknown. She had checked the lists of the dead again and again. Once her heart had nearly ceased to beat when she had read that a Slater had been killed, but it had been Samuel Slater from South Carolina, no relation, she hoped, to Cole.

Looking out the window would not bring Cole back to her. Wishing for him to appear would not help, either.

Every night she left a light burning in the window, hoping he would return. Even if he were to try, it would be hard for him to do so, she knew. The Union was getting a firm grip on the area. There were almost always patrols somewhere in the vicinity.

Every night she stood on the steps before going up to bed, and she lifted her chin, and she felt the breeze, and she waited. But it was all to no avail.

All to no avail...

Until one night in late September.

There had been no breeze all day, but there was the slightest whisper of one now. The night had been still, but now a tumbleweed lifted from the ground. Fall was coming, and in the pale glow of the moon the world was dark brown and pale gold and rich orange.

She thought she had imagined the sound at first. The sound of hoofbeats. But she had learned how to listen, and she closed her eyes, and she felt the wood beneath her feet shiver.

She stumbled out onto the porch and down onto the bare earth. She felt the hoofbeats more clearly. A rider was approaching, a single rider.

She needed to run into the house. She needed to grab one of the Colt six-shooters, or her rifle. The breeze was cool, and she was standing there barefoot on the cold ground, dressed only in a white cotton nightgown. The wind swept the gown around her and molded it to her breasts and hips and thighs. The breeze picked up the tendrils of her hair and sent them cascading behind her.

Then she saw the horse, and saw the rider, and she was exhilarated and incredulous and jubilant.

"Cole!"

"Kristin!" He reined in his horse, cast his leg over the animal's haunches and slid quickly to the ground. He frowned at the sight of her there, but she ran to him, laughing, and threw herself into his arms.

They closed around her.

Cole felt her, felt her soft and fresh and fragrant and clean, the way he had dreamed her, the way he had imagined her, the way he had feared he would never feel her again. The road home was always long and hard and dangerous. He had been riding for days, trying to avoid the Union patrols that were all over the place.

But now she was in his arms. There were no questions, no answers. She was in his arms, whispering his name. He began to shake. Her hair spilled over his hands like raw silk. She pressed against him, and she was so feminine and sweet that he nearly lost his breath. He breathed deeply, and her scent filled him, and it made his heart pound and his loins quicken.

"Kristin—"

She caught his face in her hands and kissed him. She kissed him as if she had starved for him, she kissed him deeply, passionately, like a woman. She kissed him with the fullness of her mouth and with the fullness of her body. Her tongue was wickedly sensual, touching all of him, plunging deep into his mouth. When his tongue invaded her mouth in turn, she moaned and fell against him, suddenly weak. After a long time he lifted his head to stare down into her eyes, eyes as blue as sapphires beneath the moon.

"What are you doing out here?"

"Waiting."

"You couldn't have known I was coming."

"I'm always waiting," she told him, and she smiled. It was just the slightest curve of her mouth, a rueful admission that left him feeling as if the earth trembled beneath his feet. He swept her hard against him again, heedless of whether she felt the emotion that racked him.

"I heard about Kansas City. I tried to come for you. Malachi and Jamie knocked me flat. Then I heard about the building, and I heard they let you go at the same time—"

"Hush!" She pressed a finger to his lips. She smiled again, and it was a dazzling smile. She was so soft, all of her. Her arms wound around him. Her thighs molded to his, naked beneath the gown. Her breasts pressed against his chest, against the gray wool of his uniform. "It's all right. We're home. Shannon and I are home, and you've come home now, too."

It wasn't his home. He could have told her that. But he didn't want to. Not tonight. She might not understand.

He wove his fingers into her hair, savoring the feel of her. Then he swept her up into his arms and stumbled up the steps, somehow keeping eyes locked with hers.

It seemed to take forever to reach their room, and it was not until much later that he wondered if his poor horse had managed to wander to the trough and into the barn. If not, the animal had known much worse nights upon the road.

For the moment, all that he knew was the woman in his arms and the sweetness of his homecoming.

When they were alone in their room he set her down. With trembling fingers, he undid the buttons of her nightgown and let it float to the floor. He stared at her. He wanted this moment to be etched in his memory forever, and he wanted the memory to be as incredible as the reality. Her eyes luminous. Her smile welcoming. Her breasts full and round and firm, more entrancing even than he had remembered. Her legs long and beautifully shaped.

Then he touched her.

And he wanted, too, to remember the feel of her skin against his fingertips, and so he touched her again and again, marvelling at the softness of her. And he kissed her, for he had to remember the taste of her. He kissed her lips, and he kissed her forehead, and he found the pulse at the base of her throat. He kissed her breasts, and the desire inside him grew. He savored the taste of her shoulders, of the little hollows there. He turned her around and kissed her back, trailing his fingers down the beautiful line of her spine and over the curve of her buttocks. He had to touch and taste and feel all of her. He went on and on, drinking deeply of her, until the whole of his body shook and trembled, until she cried out his name with such anguish and passion that he came to his feet, crushed her in his arms and lifted her again, bearing her to the bed.

Whispering to him, telling him how much she wanted him, how she needed him, how she desired him, she feverishly helped him out of his clothes, desperate to touch him as he had touched her. Soft as a feather, gentle as a breeze, sensual as the earth, she touched and petted and loved him. Then, at last, they came together, a man and a woman meeting in a breathless fusion.

All that night she felt she was riding the wind, an endless, sweet, wild wind that swept away the horrors of the world and left her drifting on the clouds of heaven. Anticipation had sown its seeds, and their first time together was erratic and wild and thunderous for them both. Barely had they climaxed before he touched her again, and again the clamor of need rose quickly in them. They were slower this time, easier, for the first desperate hunger had been appeased.

And still the night lay ahead of them.

She never knew just how many times they loved that night, never knew when she slept and dreamed, never knew when she awakened to find that he was holding her again. She only knew that it was heaven, and that however long she lived, however old she grew, she would never, never forget it, or the crystalline beauty of the desire that surged between them.

It was morning before they spoke.

Dazed and still delighted, Kristin lay in his arms, wondering lazily how to tell him about the child. She wondered if he could tell by the subtle changes in her body. He hadn't said anything. She smiled. His need for her had been too great for him to have noticed anything. She thought to speak then, but he was speaking already. He was talking about the war, and his tone was cold.

"Stonewall Jackson was the greatest loss. Lee might have taken Gettysburg if he hadn't lost Stonewall. It was the first battle he had to go into without Jackson. God, how I shall miss that man!"

"Sh..." she murmured. She drew a finger across the planes of his face, and she felt the tightness there, and the pain. It was a strong face, she thought, a striking face. And it was so hard now.

"And Morgan...God help Morgan. He has to escape." He shook his head. Then he turned to her and took her in his arms, whispering, "How can I say these things to you? You've been through so much already, you've witnessed so much. That horror in Kansas City..."

"The deaths were terrible," Kristin admitted. She drew away, smiling at him. "But Major Emery was very kind."

Suddenly Cole was stiff as steel, and every bit as cold. "Emery?"

She didn't understand the abrupt change in him. "Yes. He said that you had been with him, before the war. He—"

He sat up and ran his fingers through his hair. "He what?" She didn't answer, and he turned, setting his hands firmly on her shoulders. "He what?"

"Stop it! You're hurting me!" Kristin pulled away from him. "He told me about—he told me about your wife."

Cole smiled suddenly. It was a bitter smile. "I see," he said softly.

"What do you see?" she demanded.

"Nothing, Kristin, nothing at all." He tossed the covers aside and stood and wandered around the room, picking up his clothes.

"Cole!"

He stepped into his gray trousers and pulled on his shirt. Still ignoring her, he sat and pulled on his boots. She frowned when she realized that he was putting his uniform back on—something he wouldn't be doing if he was staying.

"Cole, you can't be leaving already?"

He stood up, buckling on his scabbard. He nodded gravely. Then he walked to her and stroked her chin. "I only had five days. It took me three to find my way through the Federal troops. I have to pray I can make it back more quickly." He bent down and touched her lips lightly with his own. "You are so very beautiful, Kristin," he murmured to her. But he was still distant from her. Very distant.

"Cole—" She choked on his name. Her heart was aching. There were so many things that needed to be said, and none of them mattered. She had said or done something to offend him and she didn't even know what it was. "Cole, I don't understand—"

"Kristin, I don't want your pity."

"What?"

"Pity, Kristin. I don't want it. It's worthless stuff, and it isn't good for anyone. I wondered what last night was all about. You were barely civil to me when I left in May. Hate me, Kristin. Hate me all you want. But for God's sake, Kristin, don't pity me!"

Incredulous, she stiffened, staring at him, fighting the tears that stung her eyes.

"I've thought about having you and Shannon move to London until this thing is over with. I had a little power with Quantrill, but I'm afraid my influence with the Yankees is at a low ebb. This is a dangerous place—"

"Go!" Kristin said.

"Kristin—"

"Go back to your bleeding Confederacy!" Kristin said heatedly. "I've already met with the Yankees, thanks, and they were damned civil."

"Kristin—"

"I'm all right here! I swear it. We are fine."

He hesitated, then swept his frock coat over his shoulders and picked up his plumed hat.

"Kristin—"

"Cole, damn you, get out of here! You don't want my pity, you want my hatred! Well, then, you've got it! Go!"

"Damn you, Kristin!"

He came back to the bed and took her in his arms. The covers fell away, and she pressed against the wool of his uniform, felt the hot, determined yearning of his kiss. She wanted to fight him. She wanted to tell him that she really did hate him. But he was going away again, going away to the war. And she was afraid of the war. The war killed people.

And so she kissed him back. She wound her arms around him and kissed him back every bit as passionately as he did her. And she felt his fingers move over her breast, and she savored every sensation.

Then he lifted his lips from hers, and their eyes met, and he very slowly and carefully let her fall back to the bed.

They didn't speak again. He kissed her forehead lightly, and then he left her.

Chapter Thirteen

June, 1864

He never should have come to Kansas.

Cole knew he should never have come to Kansas. A scouting mission in Kentucky was one thing. He could slip into Virginia or even Maryland easily enough. Even in Ohio he might be all right. In the East they were slower to hang a man as a spy. In the East they didn't shoot a man down where he stood, not often, not that Cole had heard about anyway.

He should never have come to Kansas.

But the war effort was going badly, very badly. First General Lee had lost Stonewall Jackson. Then Jeb Stuart had been shot, and they had carried him back to Richmond, and he had died there. Countless men had died, some of them brilliant men, some of them men who were perhaps not so brilliant but who were blessed with an endless supply of courage and a fine bravado, even in the face of death.

Jeb was the greatest loss, though. Cole could remember their days at West Point, and he could remember the pranks they had pulled when they had been assigned out west together. The only comfort in Jeb's death was the fact that his little daughter had died just weeks before. They said that when he lay dying he had talked of holding her again in heaven. They had buried him in Hollywood Cemetery. Cole had been with Kristin when they had buried him, but he had visited the grave when he'd come to Richmond, and he still found it impossible to believe that James Ewell Brown Stuart, his friend, the dashing cavalier, could be dead. He had visited Flora, Jeb's wife, and they'd laughed about some of their days back in Kansas, but then Flora had begun to cry, and he had thought it best to leave. Flora had just lost her husband, a Confederate general. Her father, a Union general, was still fighting.

The war had never been fair.

Cole had to head out again, this time to the Indian Nation, to confer with the Cherokees and Choctaws who had been persuaded to fight for the Confederacy. The Union armies were closing in on Richmond, and Lee was hard pressed to protect the capital without Jackson to harass the Federals as they made their way through the Shenandoah Valley.

When he had left Virginia Cole had gone to Tennessee, and from Tennessee he had been ordered to rejoin his brother's unit. The noose was closing tighter and tighter around the neck of the Confederacy. John Hunt Morgan had managed to escape his captors, and he needed information about the Union troops being sent into Kentucky and Tennessee from Kansas City. Cole had taken the assignment in the little town outside the big city for only one reason—he would be close to Kristin. He had to see her. It had been so long, and they had parted so bitterly. He'd received a few letters from her, terse, quick notes telling him that they were all fine, telling him that the Union was in firm control of the part of Missouri where the ranch sat, that he was better off away and that he should take care.

Jamie and Malachi had received warmer letters. Much warmer letters. But still, even to his brothers, Kristin had said very little. Every letter was the same. She related some silly little anecdote that was sure to make them laugh, and then she closed, telling them she was praying for them all. She thought there might be a wedding as soon as the war was over or maybe even before. Shannon was corresponding regularly with a Captain Ellsworth, and Kristin said she, too, thought he was a charming gentleman. He was a Yankee, but she was sure the family would forget that once the war was over. They would all have to, she added forcefully, if there was to be a future.

Cole wasn't sure there could be. There was that one part of his past that he couldn't forget, and he never would be able to forget it, not unless he could finish it off, bury it completely. Not until the redlegs who had razed his place and killed his wife were dead could he ever really rest. No matter how sweet the temptation.

Sitting at a corner table in the saloon, his feet propped and his hat pulled low, he sipped a whiskey and listened to the conversation at the bar. He learned quickly that Lieutenant Billingsley would be transferring eight hundred troops from Kansas to Tupelo and then on to Kentucky by the following week. The saloon was crowded with Union soldiers, green recruits by the looks of them— he didn't think many of the boys even had to shave as yet—but they had one or two older soldiers with them. No one had paid Cole much heed. He was dressed in denim and cotton, with a cattleman's chaps and silver spurs in place and a cowhide vest. He didn't look much like a man who gave a damn about the war one way or the other. One man had asked him what he was doing out of uniform, and he'd quickly invented a story about being sent home, full of shrapnel, after the battle of Shiloh. After that, someone had sent over a bottle of whiskey and he'd set his hat low over his forehead and he'd listened. Now that he had his information, it was time to go. He wanted to reach his wife.

His wife.

He could even say it out loud now. And only once in a while did the bitterness assail him. His wife... His wife had been slain, but he had married a little spitfire of a blonde, and she was his woman now. His wife.

He tensed, remembering that she knew, knew everything about him, about his past. Damn Emery! He'd had no right to spill out the past like that for her. Now he would never know...

Know what? he asked himself.

What her feelings were, what her feelings really were. Hell, it was a damnable time for a marriage. He could still count on his fingers the times he had seen her....Kristin. He'd been impatient with her, and he'd been furious with her, but he'd always admired her courage, no matter what, and from the beginning he'd been determined to protect her.

Then he'd discovered that he needed her.

Like air. Like water. Like the very earth. He needed her. When he'd been away from her he'd still had the nightmares, but time had slowly taken them away. When visions of a woman came to haunt him while he slept, it was Kristin's delicate features he saw, her soft, slow smile, her wide, luminous eyes.

He'd never denied that he cared for her.

He just hadn't wanted to admit how much.

He didn't want a wife feeling sorry for him. He didn't want her holding on, afraid to hurt a traumatized soldier. The whole thing made him seethe inside. He'd swear that he'd be quit of her as soon as the war was over, and then he'd panic, and he'd pray that everything was all right, and he would wish with all his heart that he could just get back to that little patch of Missouri on the border where he could reach out and just touch her face, her hand....

And if he did, he wondered glumly, what good could it do him? He could never stop. Not until one of them lay dead. Him or Fitz. Maybe Fitz hadn't fired the shot that had killed his wife, but he had ordered the raid on Cole's place, and he had led it. In the few months that he had ridden with Quantrill, Cole had managed to meet up with a number of the men who had been in on the raid.

But he'd never found Henry Fitz.

His thoughts suddenly shifted. He didn't know what it was that told him he was in danger, but suddenly he knew that he was. Maybe it was in the thud of a new pair of shiny Union boots on the floor, maybe it was something in the air. And maybe he had lived with the danger for so damned long that he could smell it.

He should never have come to Kansas.

It wasn't that he wasn't armed. He was. And the poor green boys in the saloon were carrying muzzle-loading rifles. He could probably kill the dozen or so of them in the room before they could even load their weapons.

He didn't want to kill them. He'd always hated that kind of warfare. Hell, that was why Quantrill had been able to run circles around the Federals for years. Quantrill's men were so well armed that they could gun down an entire company before they could get off a single shot.

He prepared to leave, praying that the newcomer wasn't someone he knew. But when he saw the man's face beneath the brim of his hat, his heart sank.

The man was his own age, and he wore a lieutenant's insignia. He had dark hair and a long, dark beard, and the lines that furrowed his face said that he should have been older than thirty-two.

It's been a long hard war for all of us, Cole thought bleakly.

The Union officer's name was Kurt Taylor, and he had ridden escort and trails out in the Indian country with Cole when he had been with Stuart. Another West Pointer. They'd fought the Sioux side by side many times.

But now they were on opposite sides.

When Cole stood, Taylor saw him. The men stared straight at one another.

Cole hesitated. He wasn't going to fire, not unless he had to. He didn't cotton to killing children, and that was about what it would be. He looked at the boys standing at the bar. Hell, most of them wouldn't even have started school when the trouble had started in Kansas.

Do something, Taylor, Cole thought. Say something. But the man didn't move. The two of them just stood there staring at one another, and it was as if the world stood still.

Then, miraculously, Taylor lifted his hat.

"Howdy," he said, and walked on by.

Taylor had recognized him. Cole knew it. He had seen the flash of recognition in his eyes. But Taylor wasn't going to turn him in.

Taylor walked up to the bar. The soldiers saluted him, and he told them to be at ease. They returned to their conversations, but they were no longer as relaxed as they had been. They were in the presence of a commissioned officer now.

But Kurt Taylor ignored the men, just as he was ignoring Cole. He ordered himself a brandy, swallowed it down quickly and ordered himself another. Then he turned around, leaned his elbows on the bar and looked out over the room.

"You know, boys," he said, "war itself, soldiering, never did bother me. Joining the army seemed to be a right noble position in life. We had to defend American settlers from the Indians. We had to keep an eye on Mexico, and then suddenly we had our folks moving into Texas. Next thing you know, our great nation is divided, and we're at war with our Southern cousins. And even that's all right, 'cause we all know a man's gotta do what a man's gotta do." He paused and drained his second brandy. He didn't look at Cole, but Cole knew damned well that Taylor was talking straight to him.

"Bushwhackers!" Kurt Taylor spit on the floor. Then he added, "And bloody murdering jayhawkers. I tell you, one is just as bad as the next, and if he claims to wear my colors, well, he's a liar. Those jayhawkers we've got up here, hell, they turned half of Kansas and Missouri against the Union. Folks that didn't own no slaves, that didn't care one way or another about the war, we lost them to the Confederacy because they so abhorred the murder that was being done. Quantrill's boys started up after Lane and Jennison began their goddamn raiding."

"Pardon me—" one young man began.

"No, sir! I do not pardon you!" Kurt Taylor snapped. "Murder is murder. And I hear tell that one of the worst of our Kansas murderers is right here, right here in this town. His name is Henry Fitz. He thought he could make himself a political career out of killing Missourians. He forgot there were decent folk in Kansas who would never condone the killing of women and children, whether it was done by bushwhackers or jayhawkers." He stared straight at Cole, and then he turned his back on him.

He knew Cole wouldn't shoot him.

He knew Cole wouldn't shoot a man in the back.

Cole was trembling, and his fingers were itching. He didn't even want to draw his gun. He wanted to find Fitz and wrap his fingers around the bastard's throat and choke the life out of him.

"Give me another brandy there, barkeep. Boys, you watch your step while Fitz is around. He's down Main Street at the McKinley barn with his troops. I'd say there's about a dozen of those marauders. Yep, I think you ought to steer clear of the area."

He tossed back another brandy, and then he turned and looked at Cole again. And then he walked out of the saloon.

Cole left a few minutes after Taylor did. He wondered if his old comrade in arms had put on the performance he had so that Cole would get out of town or so that he would stay in it.

He came out on the steps and looked up at the noonday sun, and he smiled. He came out to the hitching post and mounted his horse, a bay he had borrowed from Malachi because he had been afraid his own stallion was too well known here.

Taylor had even told him where to find Fitz. Straight down Main Street.

Cole started the bay at a walk. Within seconds he had urged the horse to a trot, and then to a canter, and then to a gallop. The barbershop whizzed by him, then the savings bank, the newspaper office and Ed Foley's Mercantile. He passed rows of neat houses with white picket fences and summer gardens, and then he was on the stretch of road leading to the farms beyond the town limits.

He must have headed out in the right direction, because suddenly there was a line of troops coming toward him. Redlegs, so called for the color of their leggings. Raiders. Murderers. Jim Lane had led them once. Now Senator Jim Lane was in Washington, and even Doc Jennison, who had taken command of them after Lane, had gone on to new pursuits. But Henry Fitz was still leading his band, and still striking terror into the hearts of innocent men, women and children.

Cole slowed the bay to a walk as the men approached. Henry Fitz sat atop a piebald, dead center. He had narrowed his dark little eyes, and he was staring down the road at Cole.

Cole kept moving. He had to do this. He had to kill Fitz. And if he died, too...

Would Kristin care? he found himself wondering. He had never doubted her gratitude, but he wondered now what she would feel if she heard that he had been gunned down on a Kansas road. Would she shed any tears for him? Would she miss him? Would she revile him for dying a senseless death, for leaving her alone?

He closed his eyes for a moment. He had to do this. If they were to have any kind of a future together, he had to do this. Now.

For a moment he remembered the flames, remembered them clearly. He remembered the crackling of the fire and he remembered the acrid smell of the smoke. And he remembered her, running, running to him. He remembered reaching out and touching her, and he remembered the way she had looked into his eyes and smiled and died. And he remembered the blood that had stained his hands...

I loved you! his heart cried out. I loved you, Elizabeth! With all my heart and with all my soul.

And in that moment he knew at last that he loved Kristin, too. He had to bury the past, because he longed for a future with her. He had been afraid to love again. He had not wanted to destroy Elizabeth's memory by loving again. Yet he knew now that if Elizabeth could speak to him she would tell him to love Kristin, to love her deeply and well, in memory of all they had once shared.

He brought the bay to a halt and watched the road. The redlegs were trotting along easily, none of them expecting trouble from a lone man atop a single bay horse. But in the center of the group, the frown upon Henry Fitz's face was deepening. Another five feet—ten—and he would recognize Cole.

"Howdy, there," Fitz began, drawing in on his reins. The rest of the party stopped along with him. His hat was tilted low over his thickly bearded face, and his eyes seemed to disappear into folds of flesh. "I'll be damned!" he said suddenly. Then he laughed. "Come all the way to Kansas to die, boy?"

And he reached for his revolver.

Cole had been fast before the war. He had been fast in the West. He was faster now.

Fitz had been the inspiration that had taught him how to draw faster than sound, faster than light. He had always known that someday, somehow, he would meet up with this man.

And he did now, guns blazing. Holding the reins in his teeth, he tightened his thighs around the bay and rode into the group.

He watched Fitz fall. He saw the blood stain his shirt crimson, and he watched him fall. The rest of it was a blur. He heard men and horses screaming as he galloped through their midst. A bullet struck his saddle, and then the bay went down beneath him. Cole tasted the dust roused by the multitude of horses. He jumped away from the fallen bay, grabbed his rifles and fired again. The gunfire seemed to go on forever.

Then there was silence. He spun around, a cocked rifle in either hand.

Three men remained alive. They stared at him and raised their hands. Their faces meant nothing to him.

He hurried away from his fallen horse and leaped into the saddle of a large, powerful-looking buckskin. Warily eyeing the three men, he nudged the horse forward. The buckskin had been a good choice. It surged forward, and Cole could feel the animal's strength and sense its speed. He raced forward, his heart pounding, adrenaline pumping furiously through his system.

He was alive.

But as he raced toward the town he saw the soldiers. Rows of blue uniforms. Navy blue. On both sides of the road. He slowed his horse to a walk. There was nowhere to go. It was over. They would build a gallows in the middle of town, and they would hang him as a bushwhacker.

Suddenly Kurt Taylor was riding toward Cole. "Hear there's been some shooting up at the end of town, stranger. You might want to hurry along and let the army do the picking up."

Cole couldn't breathe. Taylor lifted a brow and grinned at him. Cole looked down at his hands where they rested on the pommel. They were shaking.

He saluted Taylor.

Taylor saluted back. "Someone ought to tell Cole Slater that the man who killed his wife is dead. And someone also ought to warn him that he's an outlaw in these parts. Someone ought to warn him that he'd best spend his time way, way deep in Dixie. I know that the man isn't any criminal, but there aren't many who served with him like I did. The rest think he ought to wear a rope around his neck."

"Thank you kindly, sir," Cole said at last. "If I meet up with him, I'll tell him."

He rode on, straight through the ranks of blue uniforms. He kept riding. He didn't look back, not even when he heard a cheer and realized that the Union soldiers were saluting him, that Kurt Taylor had won him a few friends.

His thigh was bleeding, he realized. He had been shot after all, and he hadn't even known it. It didn't matter much. He had to keep riding. He wanted to get home. Night was falling. It was a good time to ride.

A little farther down the road he became aware that he was being followed. He quickly left the road and dismounted, whispering to the buckskin, encouraging it to follow him into the brush.

He was being followed by a single horseman. He hid behind an oak tree and listened to the hoofbeats. He waited until the rider was right by his side. Then he sprang up and knocked the man to the ground.

"Damn you, Cole Slater! Get off me."

"Taylor!"

Cole stood and dragged Taylor to his feet.

"You son of a bitch!" Taylor laughed, and then he clapped Cole hard on the shoulders. "You damned son of a bitch! Hasn't anybody told you that the South is going to lose the war?"

"It wouldn't matter what they told me," Cole said. "I can't much help what I am." He paused a moment, and then he grinned, because Kurt really had been one damned good friend. "Thank you. Thank you for what you did back there. I've seen so many men tearing one another to shreds. The truth meant more to you than the color of a uniform. I won't forget that, Kurt. Ever."

"I didn't do anything that God wouldn't call right," Kurt said. "You got him, Cole. You got that mangy bastard. 'Course, you do know they'll shoot you on sight now and ask questions later."

"Yes, I know that."

"You're heading south, I hope?"

"East, and then south."

"Don't stay around the border too long," Taylor warned him. "Even to see your boy. Major Emery said that if I ever came across you I was to warn you—"

"What?" Cole snapped, his hands on Taylor's shoulders.

"I'm trying to tell you. Major Emery said—"

"The hell with Emery! What boy?"

Taylor cocked his head, frowning. "Why, yours, of course. Born last February. A fine boy, I understand. Captain Ellsworth gets out there now and again, and he reported to the major that both mother and child were doing fine. Don't rightly recall what they named him, but Ellsworth says he's big and healthy and has a head of hair to put many a fine lass to shame. Cole, let go, you're about to snap my damned shoulder blade. Oh, hell! You mean you didn't know? Listen to me now. Don't you go running off half-cocked after everything that happened here today. You move slow, and you move careful, you hear me, Slater? Most of the Union boys would shoot me if they knew I let you slip through my fingers. Cole?"

"I'll move careful," Cole said.

Yes, he'd move careful. He'd move damned careful. Just to make sure he lived long enough to tan Kristin's sweet hide.

Why in God's name hadn't she told him?

It was hot and humid on the Fourth of July, 1864. Scarcely a breeze had stirred all day.

It had been a difficult day for Kristin. She had learned long ago to keep her mind off her worries, to try not to think too much, to concentrate on her tasks. Anything was better than worrying. If she worried all the time she would drive herself mad.

But the fourth was a particularly difficult day.

There were celebrations going on everywhere. Union soldiers letting off volleys of rifle fire, ranchers setting off fireworks. Every gunshot reminded Kristin that her husband could meet her brother on the field of battle at any time, that they were still at war, that the nation celebrating its birthday was still bitterly divided.

There was smoke in the air, and the noise was making the baby restless. She'd had him with her down in the parlor, and Delilah's Daniel, almost three years old now, had been laughing and entertaining the baby with silly faces. But then Cole Gabriel Slater had decided enough was enough, and he had jammed one of his pudgy little fists into his mouth and started to cry.

"Oh, I've had it with the entire day anyway!" Kristin declared to everyone in the room and to no one in particular. She picked up the baby and started up the stairs. Delilah, sewing, stared after her. Shannon, running her fingers idly over the spinet, paused. Samson rolled his eyes. "Hot days, yes, Lordy, hot days," he mumbled. He stood up. "The hands will be back in soon enough. I'll carry that stew on out to the bunkhouse."

Upstairs, Kristin lay down with her fretful baby and opened her blouse so that he could nurse. She started, then smiled, as he latched on to her nipple with a surprising power. Then, as always, an incredibly sweet feeling swept through her, and she pulled his little body still closer to her. His eyes met hers. In the last month they had turned a silver gray, just like Cole's. His hair was hers, though, a thatch of it, blond, almost white. He was a beautiful baby, incredibly beautiful. He had been born on the tenth of February. Stroking his soft cheek, she felt her smile deepen as she remembered the day. It had been snowing, and it had been bitterly cold, and she had been dragging hay down for the horses when she had felt the first pain and panicked. It would have been impossible for Dr. Cavanaugh to come out from town, and it would have been impossible for her to reach town. Pete had been terribly upset, and that had calmed her somehow, and Delilah had assured her that it would be hours before the baby actually came.

Hours!

It had been awful, and it had been agony, and she had decided that it was extremely unfair that men should be the ones to go off to war to get shot at when women were the ones stuck with having babies. She had ranted and raved, and she had assured both Delilah and Shannon in no uncertain terms that she despised Cole Slater—and every other living soul who wore britches, as a matter of fact—and that if she lived she would never do this again.

Delilah smirked and assured her that she was going to live and that she would probably have half a dozen more children. Shannon waltzed around in a daydream, saying that she wouldn't be complaining one whit if she were the one about to have the baby—if the baby belonged to Captain Ellsworth.

The pain subsided for a moment, and Kristin had smiled up at her sister, who was pushing back her soaked hair. It was "colder than a witch's teat," as Pete had said, but she was drenched with sweat.

"You really love him, don't you, your Captain Ellsworth?"

Shannon nodded, her eyes on fire. "Oh, Kristin! He saved my life. He caught me when I fell. He was such a wonderful hero. Oh, Kristin! Don't you feel that about Cole?"

She hesitated, and she remembered how happy she had been to see him. And she remembered how they had made love, how tender he had been with her, how passionate. With a certain awe she remembered the way his eyes had fallen upon her, how cherished that look had made her feel. And she remembered the ecstasy...

But then she remembered his anger and his impatience, and how he had grown cold and distant when she had mentioned his past. He was in love with another woman, and though that woman lay dead, she was a rival Kristin could not best.

"Cole was a hero!" Shannon whispered. "Kristin, how can you forget that? He rode in here and he saved our lives! And if you think you're having a difficult labor, well, then...that is God's way of telling you you had no right to keep the information about this baby from your husband!"

I meant to tell him.... Kristin almost said it. But if she did she would have to explain how he had acted when she had mentioned his past, and she would have to think about the fact that he didn't love her, right in the middle of having his child. She shrugged instead. "What can he do? There is a war on."

A vicious pain seized her again, and she assured Shannon that Cole was a rodent, and Shannon laughed. And then, miraculously—for it had been hours and hours, and it was nearly dawn—Delilah told Kristin that the baby's head was showing and that it was time for her to push.

When he lay in her arms, red and squalling, Kristin knew that she had never imagined such a love as swelled within her.

And she prayed with all her heart that her son's father was alive, that he would come home to them all. She vowed that she would ask no questions he could not answer, that she would not ask for anything he could not give.

Lying with the baby, nursing him as she did now, was the greatest pleasure of her life. Kristin forgot the world outside, and she forgot the war, and she even forgot that his father probably did not know he existed. She loved his grave little eyes, and she loved the way his mouth tugged on her breast. She counted his fingers endlessly, and his toes, and she thought that he was gaining weight wonderfully and that he was very long—even Delilah said he would grow to be very tall—and that his face was adorable. He had a little dimple in his chin, and Kristin wondered if Cole had a dimple like it. She had seen all of his body, but she had never seen his naked chin. He had always had a beard.

Delilah had warned her to let Gabe, as they called him, nurse only so long at one breast. If she did he would ignore the other, and she would experience grave discomfort. Consequently she gently loosened his grasp on her left breast, laughing at his howl of outrage.

"Heavens! You're more demanding than that father of yours!" she told her baby, cradling him against her shoulder and patting his back. Then, suddenly, she realized that she was not alone. She had been so engrossed with her son that the door had opened and closed without her noticing it.

A peculiar sensation made its way up her spine, and suddenly she was breathless. She dared to look at the door, and found him standing there.

Her hero.

He was in full dress uniform, tattered gray and gold, his sword hanging dangerously from its scabbard. He was leaner than she remembered him, and his face was ashen, and his eyes...his eyes burned through her, seared into her.

"Cole!" she whispered. She wondered how long he had been standing there, and suddenly she was blushing, and it didn't matter that he was the child's father, she felt awkward and vulnerable and exposed.

He pushed away from the door and strode toward her, and despite herself she shrank away from him. He reached for the baby, and she clung to her child. Then she heard him speak, his voice low and hoarse.

"My God, Kristin, give him to me."

"Cole—"

She had to release the baby for Cole meant to take him. She nervously pulled her dress together but he had no eyes for her. He was looking at the baby. She wanted to shriek his name, wanted to run to him. It had been so long since she had seen him last, and even that had seemed like a dream. But she couldn't run to him, couldn't throw her arms around him. He was cold and forbidding. He was a stranger to her now.

He ignored her completely, setting the squalling child down on his back at the foot of the bed, freeing him from all his swaddling so that he could look at the whole of him. Kristin could have told him that Gabe was perfect in every way, but she kept silent. She knew he had to discover it for himself. Suddenly she was more than a little afraid of her husband. Should she have written to him? What good would it have done? Cole shouldn't be here even now. There were far too many Union troops around. Was that the real reason? she wondered. She had hesitated once because he had made her angry, because she had realized that he did not love her. But she hadn't written, she knew, because she had been afraid that he would be determined to come home, and that that determination would make him careless.

For a moment Gabe quieted and stared up at his father. He studied Cole's face as gravely and as purposefully as Cole studied him. His little body was perfectly still.

Then he had had enough of his father. His mother was the one he wanted. He lifted up his chubby little legs and screwed up his face and kicked out and howled in outrage all at once. The cry brought a surge to Kristin's breasts that soaked the bodice of the gown she held so tightly against her. Cole covered his son again, then picked him up and set him against his chest. Kristin reached out her arms.

"Please, Cole, give him back to me. He's...he's hungry."

Cole hesitated, staring at her hard. Then he handed the baby to her. Kristin lowered her head and wished he would go away, but then she remembered that he had just come, and that if he went away again he might be killed this time. Color spilled over her cheeks, and she remembered just how they had gotten the baby, and she touched the baby's cheek with her finger and let her bodice fall open and led his little mouth to her breast. He latched on with an awful, pigletlike sound, and she found that she couldn't look up at all, even though she knew that Cole was still in the room and that his eyes were still on her.

The room was silent except for the baby's slurping. Then even that stopped, and Kristin realized he had fallen asleep. She lifted him to her shoulder and tried to get him to burp, but he was sleeping too soundly. Biting her lip, she rose and set him in the cradle that Samson had brought down from the attic. All the while she felt Cole's eyes on her.

Still, he didn't touch her, and he didn't speak to her. He stood by the cradle and stared down at the child. He was going to touch him again. Kristin bit her lips to keep from protesting. She watched in silence as Cole's long fingers tenderly touched the tiny cheek. She tried to button her bodice, then realized that she was drenched and that it was a foolish gesture. Flushing, she hurried to change her gown, but it didn't matter. Cole didn't seem to have noticed. She wondered if she should tiptoe away and leave him alone, but the moment she started for the door he was on his feet, and she realized that he had noted her every movement.

"Where do you think you're going?"

His voice was low, but there was real anger in it, and real menace.

"I thought you might be hungry."

He was silent. His gaze fell over her. Then he took a step toward her, and she almost screamed when his fingers gripped her arms and he shook her.

"Damn you, Kristin! Damn you a thousand times over! You knew! You knew—and you didn't tell me! What right did you have to keep him from me?"

She tried to free herself, but she could not. She looked in his eyes, and she hated what she saw there, the uncompromising hardness.

"What rights have you got!" she choked out. "You ride in whenever you choose.... You may feel you have obligations, but that is all you have! I—"

"I ride in when I can get here!" he snapped, shaking her again. Her head fell back, and her eyes, glazed suddenly with tears, stared into his. "Lady, there is a war being fought out there! You know that. Of all women, you know that. I have done everything that is humanly possible, I have given you everything—"

"No! No, you have not given me everything! You have never given me the least little part of your—"

"I could have been killed. I don't know how many times I could have been killed on some stinking battlefield, and I wouldn't even have known I had a son!"

"Let me go!"

"No!"

"Please!" He was so close to her, and he felt so good. He was so warm, and she could feel the hardness of his body, and the touch of his hands. She wanted to touch his face and soothe away the lines around his eyes, and she wanted to fill the emptiness in his heart. She wanted to see his eyes alight with passion again. As she thought of the passion they had known together, her breasts seemed to fill again, but it was not for her child this time, it was for him. She needed to be held, to be touched.

To be loved.

"Please!" she repeated softly. She was so glad to see him, and their time together should be a precious respite against the war that raged on around them.

"Cole, I wanted to tell you when you were here, but all of a sudden we were fighting, because Major Emery had committed the horrible sin of telling me that you had been hurt. Mr. Cole Slater had been hurt, cut open and left bleeding, and he just couldn't bear that! Well, you are human, Cole, and you're supposed to bleed! And I should hurt for you, too, because damn it, what happened was awful!"

"Kristin, stop—"

"No! No, I will not stop! What have you got now? One week, one day? One lousy hour? Not long, I'll warrant. There are too many Federals around. So you stop, and you listen to me! I am grateful to you, Cole, eternally grateful. And I've been glad of this bargain of ours, heartily glad. You have fulfilled every promise you ever made me. But don't you dare yell at me now! I didn't write because I didn't want you getting killed, because I was afraid of your temper."

"My temper! I would never—"

"Yes, you would! You would have taken foolish chances to get here. You would have been afraid because of what happened to you with—"

She broke off, remembering that Emery had said that his wife had been pregnant when she had been killed.

"Oh, God, Cole, I'm sorry. I just realized that you would probably rather that she...that I..."

"What the hell are you saying?" he asked hoarsely.

Kristin shook her head miserably. "Your wife, your first wife... You were expecting a child. I'm sorry, you must be thinking of her, that you would prefer—"

"That she had lived? That you had died? My God, Kristin, don't you ever say such a thing, don't you even think it, do you hear me?" He caught her against him. He threaded his fingers roughly through her hair, and suddenly he lowered his head and buried his face in the fragrant strands. "Don't you ever, ever think that!" he repeated. Then he looked at her again, and he smiled. It was a weary smile, and she saw how much the past few years had aged him, and her heart ached.

"He is a beautiful boy. He is the most wonderful child I've ever seen. And he is mine. Thank you. Thank you so very much."

"Oh, Cole!" she whispered. She was dangerously close to tears. He saw it and his tone changed.

"I'd still like to tan your hide for keeping the truth from me!"

"Cole, I really didn't mean to. I was afraid. I'm always afraid, it seems."

"I know, I know." He held her against him.

"Cole, you must be starved. Let me go down and have Delilah—"

"No, not now."

"Cole, you must need—"

He stepped away from her.

"I need my wife," he said. "I very, very badly need my wife."

He bent his head and kissed her, and then he lifted her into his arms and they fell upon the bed together.

"We have a son, Kristin," he said, and she laughed. "We have a son, and he's beautiful, and...and so are you."

It was a long, long time before either of them thought of any other kind of sustenance.

Chapter Fourteen

The days that followed were glorious for Kristin. It wasn't that anything had been settled between them. It was just that for a time they seemed to have achieved a private peace, and it was wonderful.

They did not stray far from the house. Cole explained how hard it had been to elude the patrols to reach her. But Kristin knew her own land, and she knew where they could safely travel. They picnicked on the banks of the river with the baby, and while he slept they splashed in the deliciously cool water. Kristin was first shocked and then ridiculously excited to dare to strip away her clothes in the broad daylight and make love in the water.

In the evening they sat beneath the moon and felt the cool breezes play over them. Kristin listened while Cole and Samson talked about what was left of the herd, and it seemed that everything that was said began with the words "When the war is over..."

At night, lying curled against her husband's body, Kristin asked him if he thought the war would ever end. He hesitated a long time, stroking her hair.

"It's ending now, Kristin. We're being broken down bit by bit, like a beautiful animal chewed to bits by fleas. We never had the power. We never had the industry. We never had the men. It's going to end. If the Confederacy holds out another year I'll be surprised. Well, we went a long way on courage and tactics. But that Lincoln is a stubborn cuss. Tenacious. He's held on to his Union, so it seems."

He sounded tired, but not bitter. Kristin stroked his chest. "Can't you just stay here now? If you know you're losing..."

"I can't stay, Kristin. You know that."

"I don't know anything of the kind! You've done your best for the Confederacy! You can't—"

"Kristin, Kristin!" He caught her hands. "I'm an outlaw as long as the war is on. If I stay here, I'll be in terrible danger. If some glory-seeking commander hears about it, he might just waltz in and string me up. If I'm going to die, I'd rather it be fighting than dangling from the end of a rope!"

"Cole, stop it—"

"And it isn't over, Kristin. I'm in the game and I have to stay with it. If I don't go back, Malachi will come here and shoot me for a traitor."

"He would not!"

"Well, someone would," he said.

"Cole—"

"Kristin, I have to go back."

"Cole—"

He rolled over and swept her into his arms and kissed her and then looked into her eyes. "When I ride now, I will think of my son. Thank you for Gabe, Kristin. Thank you." He nuzzled her lips and kissed her forehead and her throat and the valley between her breasts. She tried to keep talking, to keep arguing, but he nuzzled his way down the length of her torso, and she grew breathless and couldn't speak. When he had finished she couldn't remember what she had wanted to say, only that it was terribly important that she hold him as long as she could.

The next day Kristin was overjoyed when Matthew arrived unexpectedly. He quickly warned her that both he and Cole could be shot if they were caught together. Still, for a few hours, it was a wonderful homecoming. Matthew admired his nephew, and Shannon clung to her brother, and Delilah managed a fine feast. Then Cole and Matthew shut themselves up in the library together. Kristin finally had to force her way in.

"You're discussing me, I know it, and I will know what is going on!" she insisted.

"Cole has to leave," Matthew told her. "Right away. Tonight."

"Why?"

Matthew looked unhappily at Cole. Cole shrugged and gave her the explanation. "Matthew is putting the ranch under the protection of a Federal troop."

"But—"

"I can't be here, Kristin. And Quantrill's group has split up."

"What?"

"During the spring," Matthew explained, "Quantrill and his men got into some heavy feuding in Texas. Bill Anderson has some men under him, and George Todd has a group, too. Quantrill still has his followers. Bill attacked some Federals during the summer, and Archie Clements scalped the men he murdered. The situation is frightening, and no one knows where Zeke Moreau is, or who he's with. So you see, Kristin, Cole has to get out of here. And you have to be protected."

Tears stung her eyes, and she gritted her teeth to keep from spilling them. She turned away from the men.

"I fixed the tear in your frock coat, Cole. And Delilah has been washing everything. The two of you, sometimes your clothes smell as if you'd been sleeping with skunks for a year. I'll see that you're packed up and have Shannon wrap up a supply of jerky."

She stumbled into the hallway. Cole found her there and swept her into his arms and took her upstairs to their room. She cried the whole time they made love, her tears spilling over his shoulders and his chest and dampening his cheeks.

Then he kissed her and held the baby tightly. She insisted on coming down with him, and when he was mounted he leaned down to kiss her again. Holding their child close to her breast, Kristin waved as he left.

That night some Union soldiers moved into the bunkhouse. Kristin supposed it was necessary. But it was still hard.

The bushwhacker situation grew much worse. On the thirtieth of September Kristin was surprised when she came out on the porch to see that Major Emery was riding toward her. She stood and smiled, ready to greet him, but her smile died when she saw his face. She went pale herself, and the world spun, and she was afraid that she was going to faint.

"Oh, my God, it's Cole—"

"No, no, Mrs. Slater," he assured her hastily, taking Gabe from her. "He's a fine boy, ma'am. A fine boy." He looked around uncomfortably. "I don't think your sister should know the whole of this, ma'am, but...Captain Ellsworth is dead."

"Oh, no!"

"That damned Bill Anderson! Since his sister died they say he froths at the mouth every time he fights. Fights—bah!" He spat into the dirt. "He tore up Centralia. He made twenty-five unarmed soldiers strip, and then he shot twenty-three of them dead. The troops that went out after him fared worse. It was a massacre. At least a hundred killed. Stripped, scalped, dismembered, their bodies mutilated as they died—"

"Oh, God! Oh, God!"

They both heard the scream. Kristin turned around to see that Shannon was standing in the doorway. She had heard every word. She knew.

"Oh, God! No!" she shrieked. Major Emery took a step toward her, barely managing to catch her as she pitched forward in a dead faint.

"Could you take her to her room for me, please?" Kristin whispered.

Major Emery nodded and carried Shannon upstairs. "We've a company surgeon out in your bunkhouse. I'll send him over and see that he gives her something."

The doctor didn't come soon enough. Shannon awoke, and she started to cry. She cried so hard that Kristin was afraid she would hurt herself. Then she was silent, and the silence was even worse. Kristin stayed with her, holding her hand, but she knew that she hadn't reached her sister, and she wondered if anyone ever would again.

Fall came, and with it more tragedy for the South. General Sherman was marching to the sea through Georgia and the Carolinas, and the reports of his scorched earth policy were chilling. In the west, the Union bottleneck was almost complete.

On the twenty-first of October George Todd died when a sniper caught him in the neck. Five days later Bill Anderson was killed in the northwestern corner of Missouri.

Kristin was alarmed to see how eagerly Shannon received the news of their deaths.

Thanksgiving came and went. It was a very quiet affair. Kristin was Matthew McCahy's sister, but she was also Cole Slater's wife, and so it didn't seem right to invite any of the Union men in for a fancy supper.

Matthew made it back for Christmas Day, and Kristin was delighted to see him. She asked if he had heard anything, and he told her that the last he had heard, Cole Slater was still at large. John Hunt Morgan, the dashing cavalry commander, had been killed late in the year, and Matthew hadn't heard anything about where Cole or Malachi or Jamie had been assigned.

She cried that night, cried because no news was good news. It seemed so long since she had lost her father, and she could hardly remember Adam's face. She didn't want to lose anyone else. She could hardly stand to see Shannon's pale face anymore. She hadn't seen her sister smile since Captain Ellsworth had been killed. Not once.

After Christmas dinner, Kristin sat before the fire in the parlor with her brother and her sister. She began to play a Christmas carol on the spinet, but Shannon broke down and ran upstairs to her room. Kristin sat staring silently at her hands for a long time.

Finally Matthew spoke.

"Kristin, nothing's going to get better, not for a long, long time, you know."

"They say it's almost over. They say the war is almost over."

"The war, but not the hatred. I doubt they'll fix that for a hundred years, Kristin. It isn't going to be easy. The healing will be slow and hard."

"I know," Kristin whispered.

"You just make sure, Kristin, that if Cole comes around you get him out of here fast. He isn't going to be safe anywhere near this place, not until some kind of a peace is made, and then only if amnesty is given."

Kristin's fingers trembled. She nodded. "He won't come back. Not until...not until it's over."

Matthew kissed her and went upstairs. Kristin stared at the fire until it had burned very low in the grate.

In February Gabriel had his first birthday. The news that month was good for the Union, grim for the Confederacy. Sherman had devastated the South. Robert E. Lee was struggling in Virginia, and Jefferson Davis and the Confederate cabinet had abandoned Richmond half a dozen times.

By March, everyone was talking about the campaign for Petersburg. Grant had been pounding away at the Virginia city since the previous summer, and the fighting had been fierce. The Union had tried to dig a tunnel under the Confederate lines. Mines had exploded, and many Confederates had been killed, but then they had rallied and shot down the Union soldiers who had filled in the crater. The soldiers shuddered when they spoke of it.

Kristin had become accustomed to the men who had made their headquarters on her land. They were mostly farmers and ranchers, and more and more she heard them speak wistfully of the time when the war would be over, when they could go home. The Confederate general Kirby-Smith was still raising hell in the West, and the Southern forces were still fighting valiantly in the East, but the death throes had already set in for a nation that had never had a chance to truly breathe the air of independence. Major Emery came one day and sat with them on the porch while the first warmth of spring touched them. Morosely he told Kristin that the death estimates for the country were nearing the half-million mark. "Bullet, sword and disease!" He shook his head. "So many mothers' sons!"

When he left her that afternoon, Kristin had no idea that she would never see him again alive.

April came. General Lee's forces were gathering around Richmond for a desperate defense of the capital. Gabe was learning to walk, and Kristin had agreed with Samson and Pete that he might be allowed to try sitting on top of a horse.

Kristin came outside one April afternoon, and she knew instantly that something was wrong. There was a peculiar stillness in the air.

There should have been noise. There should have been laughter. The dozen or so Union troops billeted on the ranch should have been out and about, grooming their horses, hurrying here and there in their smart blue uniforms with their correspondence and their missives.

Pete was nowhere in sight, and neither was Samson.

"Samson?" Kristin called out.

Then she heard the barn door creak as if the breeze had moved it, but there wasn't any breeze. She looked toward it, and she saw a hand. Its fingers were curled and crumpled, and it was attached to a bloodstained blue-clad arm. Kristin felt a scream rising in her throat, but she didn't dare release it. She wrenched Gabe into her arms and ran for the house as fast as she could.

"Shannon!" she screamed. In the hall she found a gun belt with the two Colt six-shooters Cole had insisted she keep loaded and ready. With trembling fingers she wound the belt around her waist and reached for the Spencer repeating rifle Matthew had brought at Christmas.

"Shannon!" she called again.

Her sister came running down the steps, her eyes wide, her face pale.

"Something is wrong. Take Gabe—"

"No! Give me the rifle!"

"Shannon, please—"

"I'm a better shot than you are, damn it!"

"Maybe, yes! But I'm not as desperate and reckless as you are!" Kristin snapped. "Shannon, for God's sake, you are the best shot! So for the love of God take Gabriel and get upstairs and try to pick them off if they come for me."

"Who?"

She didn't know how she could be certain, but she was.

"Zeke is back. He's out there somewhere. Shannon, please, don't let them get my baby!"

With that she pushed Gabriel into her sister's arms and started out the door again. Shannon watched her. Gabriel began to cry, and she pulled him close and hurried up the stairs.

"Holy Mary!" Private Watson muttered. "Will you look at that? Fool Yankee, he's all alone and coming right at us!"

Cole looked up from where he sat polishing the butt of his rifle. His eyes narrowed as he watched the trotting horse. Judging by the way the man riding it sat, he was injured, and injured pretty badly.

"Should we shoot him?" someone murmured uncertainly.

"Somebody already done shot him," came the wry answer.

"Leave him be, boys," Cole said, rising curiously. Cole had been promoted to Colonel, which made him the highest-ranking officer in the group. Malachi was now a major and Jamie a captain. The three of them were with a small company of men simply because small companies were all that was left in their sector of the West. They had decided to find Kirby-Smith, wherever he was, and join forces with him, but for the last month they had kept a field headquarters in this abandoned farmhouse deep inside an overgrown orchard.

"I know that man," Cole muttered suddenly. He hurried forward, his brothers and his ragged troops at his heels.

He reached the horse, and the Yankee fell right into his arms. Cole eased him down to the ground, wresting his own scarf from around his neck to soak up the blood pouring from the wound beneath the man's shoulder blade.

"Matthew McCahy, what the hell happened to you, boy?" he said gruffly. He looked at Captain Roger Turnbill, the company surgeon, and then he looked down at Matthew and wondered how the hell his brother-in-law had found him. Then he decided it didn't matter, not until Matthew was looked after.

"Let's get inside the house," Captain Turnbill said.

The men started to lift him. Matthew opened his eyes, huge blue eyes that reminded Cole painfully of his wife, so very close by, so endlessly far away. Matthew reached up and clutched the lapel of Cole's frock coat.

"Cole, listen to me—"

"You know this blue belly well, colonel?" Captain Turnbill asked.

"He's my wife's brother. I know him well enough."

"Then let's get him inside. He's bleeding like a stuck pig."

"Matthew—" Cole gripped the hand that clutched him so tightly. "Matthew, the captain is going to help you. I swear it." Cole wondered if Matthew was delirious, or if he was merely wary of the Confederate surgeon. Doctors on both sides had been known to boast that they had killed more of the enemy than all the artillery shells in the service.

"Cole! For God's sake, listen to me!" Matthew rasped out. His fingers held Cole's like a vise. "It's Zeke—"

"What?"

Matthew swallowed painfully. "We met up with him southeast of here, in a little two-bit place called James Fork. We were a small detachment, thirty of us, heading over to Tennessee. I went down, I was knocked out and they took me for dead. I heard him talking over me. Said he couldn't wait to get to the McCahy place and tell Kristin McCahy that he'd managed to murder her brother now, too. They spent the night at James Fork. I waited till they were drunk and I found a horse, and here I am—"

Cole was ashen and tense. He didn't realize how hard he was gripping Matthew's shoulders until Captain Turnbill said softly, "Ease off, colonel."

"How did you find us?" Jamie asked carefully. He was the only one who seemed to be capable of rational thought at the moment.

Matthew smiled. "Your location isn't exactly a secret, gentlemen. Kurt Taylor was out here with a scouting party a few weeks ago. Some of the higher-ups know where you are.... They're just hoping the war will be over before they have to come in and clean you out." His smile faded, and he choked and coughed and then groaned in pain.

"Get him up and in the house!" Turnbill ordered. A half-dozen men quickly obeyed him, Jamie Slater tensely and carefully taking Matthew's head and his wounded shoulder.

"Slater! You've got to get there. You and your men, you've got a chance. Riding straight west—"

Cole followed after him. "There's a dozen Yankees on the ranch," he said tensely. "I know it."

"So does Zeke Moreau," Matthew gasped out.

Then he was suddenly silent.

"Is he dead?" Malachi asked tonelessly.

Turnbill shook his head. "Passed out from loss of blood. It's amazing that he made it here."

Cole didn't follow any farther. He paused in the yard in front of the farmhouse and looked around at the men who remained with him. Besides his brothers and the doctor, he had one sergeant, two corporals and twenty-two privates. They had survived a hell of a lot. How could he ask them to die at this point?

"I've got to leave you, boys," he said. The soldiers who hadn't helped carry

Matthew into the house ranged silently around him. "This is a private battle, and some of you might say it's being waged against one of your own—"

"Hell, Quantrill and his kind were never one of my own," Bo Jenkins, a shopkeeper in peacetime, said. "My kind of Southerner ain't never shot down a man in cold blood."

"Glad to hear it, private," Cole said quietly. "But still, I can't rightly ask you to come along and get killed—"

"Hell, colonel, how's this any different from all the other times?" Jenkins said.

His brother John stepped up beside him. "Seems like we've been following you a long time, sir. We'll keep on doing that. I mean, what the hell, colonel? You think we all want to live forever?"

Cole felt a smile tug at his lips. "Then let's get ready. We've got to ride fast. We've got to ride like the wind."

Armed and ready, Kristin came out of the house and moved quickly toward the barn, toward the bloody hand lying in the spring sunshine.

She paused at the gaping doorway and flattened herself against the wall. Then she kicked open the door and stepped inside, both her Colts cocked and ready to fire.

She heard nothing, saw nothing. She blinked in the dim light, then she saw that at least five men in Yankee blue lay on the ground and in the hay. Their killer or killers had interrupted them in the middle of a poker game. The cards were still sitting on a bale of hay in the center of the barn.

Someone had been holding a full house.

Kristin swallowed painfully.

"Drop 'em," came a sneering voice from behind her. It was one of Zeke's men. She didn't know his name, but she recognized the voice from its jeering tone. She had heard the man's raucous laughter when her father had died.

She froze, aware that she hadn't a chance in hell of turning quickly enough to kill the man. She wondered whether she shouldn't turn anyway and die quickly. Zeke surely no longer desired her. All he wanted was revenge.

Suddenly there was an explosion right over her shoulder. She screamed, stunned, wondering if she'd been hit. She hadn't. She stared toward the center of the barn, and there lay one of the Yankee soldiers she had thought were all dead. Blood was pouring from his temple, but he was smiling at her, and his pistol was smoking. She whirled around. The man behind her lay dead, very dead. There was a black hole burned right into his chest.

She slammed the Colts back into the gun belt and ran over to the Yankee who had saved her life, falling down on her knees beside him. "Bless you! What can I—"

"Lady, you can save yourself!" the man whispered, and he winced. "If all goes well, then you come back for me. Damn it to hell, but I can't help you no more now. My leg is all busted up. You go careful. He's in the house."

Chills swept up her spine. "He's...where?"

"Moreau, their leader. He's up in the house."

He was in the house, with her sister and her child. Kristin raced for the doorway. She found Samson and Pete slumped against the far wall of the barn. Pete was dead, his eyes wide open and staring. Samson was still breathing, a thin stream of blood trickled from his forehead.

She paused for a split second to tear apart her skirt and dab at the wound.

She lowered him to the ground and pressed the hastily made bandage against his forehead. Then she raced into the yard, across the paddock and toward the house, easing the Colts from the belt once again.

Suddenly there was a shot. She stopped where she stood, feeling the dust rise around her feet where a bullet had bitten into the earth. She looked up, way up, to her bedroom window.

Zeke was standing there, a handful of Shannon's hair caught in his filthy fingers.

"Drop the guns, Mrs. Slater," Zeke drawled. "Drop 'em right now, else I'll let this pretty gold stuff in my fingers run red with McCahy blood."

Kristin stared up at him in despair. She heard a shuffling around her, and she knew that his men were emerging from the bunkhouse, from the far side of the house, from behind the watering trough. She looked around, and the faces spun before her. How many of them were there? Twenty? Thirty? It was hard to tell.

"Drop 'em in the dust, Kristin, slow and careful!" Zeke laughed then, fingering Shannon's hair. "She sure did come along nicely, Kristin. Why, I think she's even prettier than you are. Hard to tell, though. You're both nasty as rattlers."

Shannon cursed and bit Zeke's hand savagely. Zeke swore in turn and cuffed her hard. Suddenly Gabe began to cry. Kristin cried out involuntarily and bit her lip.

Shannon screamed as Zeke tore at her hair. Zeke, shouting insanely, addressed Kristin again.

"Drop the guns or else I'll kill the kid first. Slow. I'll blow off his legs one by one, and then his arms and then, if he's still alive, I'll cut off his ears!"

Kristin set the Colts on the ground. She heard Zeke's wild laughter, and then he and Shannon disappeared from the window. The shuffling around her began again. She closed her eyes and tried to ignore the soft jeers and the horrible smell as the men moved closer and closer.

The door to the house burst open, and Zeke appeared, shoving Shannon before him. Shannon was white, but Kristin was, perhaps ridiculously, glad to see that her sister's hatred seemed to outweigh her fear. There would be plenty of time for fear.

Zeke, keeping his punishing grip on Shannon's hair, forced her into the center of the circle. He came close to Kristin, and he smiled. "I'm going to tell you about the afternoon, Kristin. Just so you can anticipate it all. Every sweet moment. See Harry over there? The guy with the peg leg and the rotten teeth? He's had a real hankering for you, so he gets to go first. I'm going for little sister here. Fresh meat. Then, well...hell, we've learned to share and share alike. We are going to make sure you stay alive, though. At least until we've had a chance to fire the house and the barn. You should get to hear the horses scream. That's a real fine sound. Then—maybe—Harry will scalp you. He learned the art real well from little Archie Clements himself. But we'll see how the afternoon goes. We may not have time for everything. There's lots of Yankees in these parts. Did you know that, Mrs. Slater? Sure you did. Your brother's a turncoat Yankee, ain't he? But don't worry about him none. I killed him last night."

Kristin's knees sagged, and she fell into the dirt. Matthew! It couldn't be. No!

Zeke started to laugh.

Something inside her snapped. She catapulted from the ground, flying at him in a fury. Shannon screamed but quickly rallied, and together they fell on him, biting him, tearing at him with their nails. Zeke screamed but none of his men moved to help him at first. And they couldn't shoot. They might kill him.

Then they heard it. The unmistakable sound of hoofbeats pounding the Missouri earth, pounding like thunder, coming closer and closer.

"Take cover!" one of the bushwhackers shouted.

Zeke let out a terrible growl and threw Shannon down hard in the dirt. He slammed the back of his hand against Kristin's cheek, and when she reeled, stunned by the blow, he caught her by the hair and dragged her up the steps to the porch and behind the oak rocker.

The hoofbeats came closer, thundering like a thousand drums. "Bastard!" Zeke muttered. "How could they know…"

It was only then, as Zeke aimed his gun through the slits in the back of the rocker, that Kristin got her first glimpse of the riders.

They were dressed in gray, and they might have been a sorry sight had they not ridden with such grace and style. A rebel yell suddenly rose up in the air, and the horses tore around the front of the house. Dust flew everywhere. Gunfire erupted, and Kristin bit back a scream.

Cole was leading them, whirling his horse around, his head held high. Malachi was there, too, and Jamie.

The Union army had failed endlessly against the bushwhackers because the bushwhackers were so well armed and so fast. But now they were fighting a man who knew their ways. A man who was faster. A man with a company of soldiers who were every bit as well armed as they were, a company of soldiers who were determined to salvage something of honor and chivalry from a war they were destined to lose. They fought their own kind, for their own kind had defied the very code of the South that so many had fought to preserve.

Kristin couldn't see for the clouds of dust the horses and the gunfire had churned up. All she knew was that Zeke was dragging her viciously along the porch.

She fought him. He swore he would turn around and shoot her, but she didn't really care. He had murdered Matthew, and he had murdered her father, and he was probably going to murder her. All she dared hope for was that Delilah had hidden somewhere, and that she had found Gabe. She wanted her son to live. She wanted something good to rise from the dust and ashes of this war. She wanted her child, Cole's child, to live, to remember, to start over.

"Damn you!" Zeke screamed. He twisted her arm cruelly behind her back, and she cried out in pain. He pushed her to the front door and then into the house. He pushed her toward the stairs, and the pain in her arm was so piercing that she had to stumble up the steps.

"Maybe we do have a little time. Maybe they'll all stay real busy out there for a long, long time. I wouldn't mind having you on Cole Slater's bed while he chokes on his own blood down below."

Suddenly the front door flew open and Cole was standing in the doorway. Zeke whirled, and Kristin stumbled and almost fell, but Zeke caught her and held her in front of him.

Framed by the doorway, the sunlight behind him, Cole was frightening and yet strangely beautiful. In his left hand he held his cavalry saber, and with his right he aimed his Colt.

"Put it down nice and easy, Slater, nice and easy," Zeke said. He pulled Kristin close against him, so close that she could breathe in the reek of his breath and feel the sweat of his body.

"You get your filthy hands off my wife, Zeke."

"You know, Slater, I started in with Quantrill late. That's why I didn't remember you the first time we met here. But now I remember you real well. And I've thought about this moment. I've dreamed about it. So you put the gun down. See how I've got this beautiful silver barrel aimed right at her throat? Think about how her blood will pour out where the artery's cut...."

Suddenly they heard a cry. It was Gabriel, crying in fear and rage. Delilah must have him in a closet close by, Kristin thought.

Her stomach twisted, and she saw that Cole had gone white. She sensed that Zeke was smiling. Now Cole was forced to think not only about her but about his son.

"That's a real fine boy you got there, Slater," Zeke drawled. He moved the barrel of the gun against Kristin's cheek. "A real fine wife, a real fine boy. You want to see them live, you'll set that gun down, slow and easy. No fast moves."

"No fast moves," Cole echoed tonelessly.

Gabe was still crying. Kristin bit into her lip. As soon as Cole set the gun down, Zeke would shoot him, and there was so much she had to tell him. Gabe was walking now, could say so many words. She had taught him to say papa. He had the most wonderful laugh in the whole world, and his eyes were so very much like his father's....

"Cole, no!" she cried out.

He smiled at her. "I have to do this, Kristin."

Zeke laughed. "Yeah, he has to."

Cole was looking at her. A curious smile touched his lips. "I never got a chance to tell you that I loved you, Kristin. I do, you know. With all my heart."

"Oh, God, Cole!"

"I love you. I love you. Duck, Kristin."

"What?" she gasped,

He didn't drop his Colt. He aimed it right over her head. She screamed, and the world exploded.

Chapter Fifteen

Kristin fell, and it was as if the earth had opened up beneath her feet. All she knew was that Cole had fired.

And that Zeke had not.

Zeke's body was tumbling down the stairs after hers. Kristin came to a halt at the landing, and something fell hard on top of her. She stared up at Zeke, at his wide, staring eyes, at his forehead, where flesh and bone had been ripped away. She pushed away from him, desperate to get him away from her.

"Kristin, Kristin!"

Strong arms were around her, pulling her up from beneath him. She couldn't tear her eyes away from him. His face was still frozen in a sneer, even in death.

"Kristin!"

Cole turned her into his arms. "Kristin!" She looked up and saw his face, his eyes. Concern furrowed his brow as he eased his knuckles over her cheek. "Are you hurt?" he asked anxiously.

She shook her head. She couldn't speak. She stared at him blankly, and then she shrieked out his name and threw herself against him and started to cry. He stroked her hair and murmured comfortingly to her. Then he held her away from him and studied her anxiously. She struggled desperately for control.

"Oh, Cole! How did you know to come? They slaughtered all the Yankees.... Oh, no, a few of them might still be alive. You have to help them. Him. One of them saved me." Tears flooded her eyes. No matter how hard she tried, she couldn't keep from crying. "Cole! He killed Matthew! He found my brother and he killed him."

"Hush, Kristin, hush," Cole murmured. He pulled her against his body again and smoothed back her hair. Then he tilted her chin and sought her eyes. He had to make sure she understood. "Kristin, Matthew is fine. Well, I'm sorry, I suppose he's not fine. He's injured, but he's alive, Kristin. I would never have known—" He was suddenly unable to speak. It was all over, and now he was suddenly paralyzed by the fear. His hands trembled as he held her. "Kristin, Matthew's company was attacked. Zeke left him for dead, but he wasn't dead, and he got away in the night. Thank God, the Yanks knew where I had my men all along, and Matthew knew the area so well that he came straight to me."

Her eyes were wide with hope, with a joy she dared not feel. "Oh, Cole! Please, don't tell me that unless—"

"It's the truth, Kristin, I swear it."

"But they didn't come after you? The Yankees, they let you be?"

"I have a few friends in the right places," Cole said with a wry smile. "It gives me hope. Maybe, when this thing is over, some of the hatreds will be patched up. Some of them won't be. But, oh, God, I want it to end. I want it to be over!''

He pulled her against him again and she felt the beating of his heart. The rough wool of his frock coat tickled her cheek, and she had never been so glad of anything in her life. She wanted to look at him again. She wanted to study his features, and she wanted to see him smile, because he was young again when he smiled. She wanted to see the silver light in his eyes when he held her, and most of all she wanted to hear him speak again. She wanted to hear him say he loved her.

Of course, this wasn't really the right time. There was a dead man at her feet, and though the guns had gone silent outside the house, dead men littered the earth there, too, and—please God—a few living men, too. She had to go back to the barn for the young Yankee who had saved her life, and she had to find her son.

"Kristin—" Cole began, but he was interrupted by an outraged cry.

"Miz Kristin! Mister Cole! Why, thank the Lord,'' Delilah called. She was at the top of the stairs with Gabe, who was struggling fiercely to free himself from her grasp. Cole stared at his son with the awe of a parent who has not seen his child in a long, long time. Gabe might have been a grown man the way Cole was staring at him.

Kristin's eyes twinkled. "He walks now. And he talks. I taught him how to say papa.''

Delilah hurried down the stairs. She saw Zeke's body, but she didn't pause. She spat on it and stepped over it, and then she set Gabriel down. He tottered for a moment. Kristin watched Cole as he went down on his knees and reached out for the boy. Gabe waddled carefully over to inspect the stranger.

"Say papa!'' Kristin urged him.

Gabriel wasn't interested in saying anything. He turned away from the stranger who was his father and buried his face in his mother's skirts. He reached out his arms, and Kristin laughed and picked him up. Then, suddenly, she crushed him against her, so hard that he cried out in protest. "Oh, Gabriel!'' she murmured, holding him tight.

Cole came to his feet and rescued his screaming son. He lifted Gabriel very high and silver eyes gazed into silver eyes. "I'm your papa, little man!'' He laughed. "And you'd best get used to the idea.''

Gabriel couldn't possibly have understood what Cole had said to him, of course, but he smiled anyway, as if he had decided to accept the stranger in gold and gray. Cole lowered him at last and set him on his hip, smiling at Kristin.

Suddenly there was an awful commotion at the door.

"Put me down, you piece of trash!'' Shannon shrieked.

Malachi—Shannon thrown over his shoulder—came through the doorway, his face dark and thunderous. "I don't mind bushwhackers, and I don't mind the damn Yankees, but Cole, I will be damned if I'll be responsible for this brat!''

"Put me down!'' Shannon screamed.

He did. He dumped her in front of Cole, and she was thrashing and flailing, trying to get her balance. She rolled over and came face-to-face with Zeke Moreau's body.

"Oh!'' she gasped, and fell silent at last.

Kristin looked at Malachi and arched a brow.

He sighed with great patience. "Kristin, I didn't know what the hell was happening in here. I didn't want her barging in to get shot, or to cause you or Cole to get shot. Mainly. It would be her own damn fault if she did get shot, but since she is your sister, I thought I'd try to save her sweet, darling, precious little life!"

For once Shannon didn't reply. She was still staring at Zeke's face. She began to tremble uncontrollably, and then she burst into tears.

Kristin started toward her sister, but Cole pulled her back. Malachi was kneeling beside Shannon, and he pulled her up and away from the body.

"It's over! It's all over!" he told her roughly. "Don't go falling apart now."

Shannon stiffened momentarily, and then she hiccuped. Malachi gave her his handkerchief, and she dried her face, nodding an acknowledgement. Then she jammed it back into his hand.

"I never fell apart, you backwoods bastard!"

"Well, good. Get your derriere out there and start helping!"

"Helping?"

"There are injured men out there. Unless you're too damned prissy to help the men who were willing to die to save your miserable life."

"Miserable?"

"Go!"

"I am going, Malachi Slater! I'm going because those are fine men out there—even the rebels! I'm going for them, and I'm going because I choose to go, and I'll never, never do anything because you tell me to, do you understand?"

With an elegant toss of her golden curls, she swept past him. It was a splendid exit except for one thing. Malachi smacked her rump soundly as she went past. She yelped in outrage and slapped him hard across the face. He caught her by the elbow and turned her toward him, his face dark with rage.

"Malachi! Please! She is my sister," Kristin reminded him sweetly.

Slowly, his eyes narrowed, he released Shannon. "Why, thank you, kind sir!" she said. Then she kicked him hard in the shin and raced out the door.

Kristin began to smirk, and then Cole laughed, and the baby giggled. Delilah laughed along with them, but then her laughter faded, and she gasped, "Samson! My man! Oh, Mister Slater—"

"The barn," Kristin said quickly, her eyes on Cole. "He was breathing—"

Cole ran out the door, Delilah hard on his heels. Kristin followed but when she stepped out on the porch she stood there stunned, her son in her arms, staring at the scene of destruction.

There were bodies everywhere. Men in gray were collecting them, dragging them away. A weary-looking young man nodded to her in grim acknowledgment as he passed her. She swallowed and caught his arm. "Thank you. Thank you for coming here."

He smiled and tipped his hat. "I'd go anywhere Colonel Slater invited me, ma'am. I'm right glad we got here in time."

He had work to do, and he went back to it. Dazed, Kristin stepped down into the yard.

Then someone called out, asking for water. She hurried over to the trough and found one of Cole's boys behind it, clutching his shoulder and trying to stand.

"Here, here!" she whispered, ladling up some water. Gabe gurgled. He seemed to think they were playing.

"Thank you, ma'am," the soldier said. Then he winced, and she saw that he had a ball lodged in his flesh.

"Help me over here!" she called. Another soldier lifted the wounded man, and within minutes she had him in the house and on the couch and she had Cole's men scurrying around, boiling water, ripping up sheets for bandages, setting up the parlor as a temporary infirmary.

Gabriel refused to sleep, so she set up a little playpen in the parlor and busied herself with the injured. Shannon was at her side and Delilah, too, now that she knew that Samson was all right. He had been knocked cold, and he had a blinding headache, but otherwise he was none the worse for wear.

Samson was out on burial detail now. Zeke Moreau's body had been removed from the house.

There had been a scene when that had happened. Shannon had followed them out. She had stood on the porch and begged the men, "Please...please! Don't bury that man's body anywhere on this property!"

"Miss McCahy—"

"Please! Let the vultures eat him, let the wolves finish him, but I beg you, don't bury him near here!"

And so some of the men had set out with a wagon, and they were taking Zeke and the bodies of the other bushwhackers far, far away. Pete was dead, and he was family, and three of Cole's men had fallen, and there were the Yankees that the bushwhackers had killed. They were being laid to rest with infinite tenderness in the family plot, beside Kristin's mother and father.

By nightfall, most of the traces of the gun battle had been cleared away. Delilah managed to produce a hearty stew in abundance to feed everyone.

At ten they heard the sound of a wagon creaking along. Cole had just finished eating, and he was sipping a brandy on the porch. Gabriel was in bed, and Kristin was sitting at Cole's feet, listening to a sad tune being played on a harmonica somewhere nearby.

She felt Cole stiffen. Then she realized that he had sentries posted, for there was something like a Rebel yell in the darkness, and then the wagon came through.

"Cole?" Kristin murmured.

"It's a surprise," he said, squeezing her shoulder. She followed him down the steps and out to the yard. There was something lumpy in the back of the wagon, something cried out plaintively, "Kristin, Shannon?"

"Matthew!" She screamed her brother's name and flew to the wagon. She kissed him, and she held him so tightly that he muttered, "Kristin, I survived being shot, you're going to kill me here in my home at last with kindness!"

"Oh, Matthew!"

Then Shannon was flying down the steps. The three McCahy's greeted one another, and the men looked on, and then the harmonica player started up again, with "Lorena" this time bringing tears to eyes that had nearly run dry in all the years of bloodshed.

Matthew was brought in and put to bed in his own room. Once he was tucked in, he caught his sister's hand, and Kristin smiled and kissed him on the forehead again and told him to rest.

"Kristin!" He pulled her back. "Kristin, there'll be a bunch of Yankees here soon. They'll find out that Major Emery and his men were slaughtered, and they'll know that Cole and his men came in for the cleanup, and they'll be damned glad. But there's still a war on. They'll have to take them prisoner, or else they'll have to fight, and a lot of men will die needlessly. They're true heroes—to both sides, probably—but that won't make any difference. Kristin, are you understanding me?''

No, she wasn't. Or perhaps she was and she wanted to deny it. She couldn't have her husband taken away from her so soon.

"Kristin, Cole is considered an outlaw. Worse than ever before."

"Why? What do you mean?"

"He'll have to explain that to you himself. But be prepared. They need to sneak away now, tonight."

She felt weak, as if she had been drowning and she had reached and reached for a rope and it had been viciously wrenched away.

"Thank you, Matthew," she told her brother.

She blew out the lamp and left him. She hesitated, leaning against the door.

When she came back downstairs, she quickly discovered that everything that Matthew had said was true. The Confederate surgeon who had so carefully tended to her brother was checking the men she had sutured and bandaged—and preparing them for travel. He smiled at her when he saw her.

"Your brother is going to be just fine. Keep the wound clean. Never use the same sponge twice when you're cleaning out a wound. I'm becoming more and more convinced that rot travels that way. Seems we have been doing better with sanitation than the blue bellies." He paused, and she thought that he, too, looked weary. "He's a fine young man, your brother. You take care of him."

"Thank you, Captain Turnbill," said Kristin. He was about to turn away, but she stopped him with a hand set lightly upon his arm. "Captain, are you sure these men are fit to travel?"

"The worst wounded are the Yankees we found in the bunkhouse and the barn, and they don't have to travel anywhere. My men have one broken arm, a broken leg, some shot in the shoulder and two concussions. They'll be all right." He paused, looking at her unhappily. "Mrs. Slater, they'll be a lot better off traveling now than they would be in a Yankee prison camp. I'm not a man to say that all Yanks are butchers, but there's not much good to be said about prison camps, whether they're Yankee camps or Confederate camps."

The able-bodied men were walking past her, making ready to leave. Kristin couldn't see her husband anywhere.

Malachi came around behind her and squeezed her shoulders. He turned her around. "Hope Cole won't mind," he said, and he hugged her and gave her a kiss on the cheek. "Hell, I don't care if Cole does mind!" he said, and he kissed her again. She didn't know there was a tear on her cheek until he wiped it away

"Oh, Malachi…"

"It's all right. We won't be far away."

"Not far away at all."

It was Jamie who spoke. He was right behind Malachi, and he took her from his brother and kissed her cheek, too. "You take care of yourself, little sister you hear? Take good care of that nephew of mine, too."

She nodded, unable to speak for a few seconds.

"Cole—'

"Cole is right here, ' her husband said. Tears blurred her vision. He took her in his arms "Hey!" he whispered, his lips nuzzling her throat. "Stop that! You can't send my brothers away with tears in your eyes."

"Your brothers…"

She whirled around in his arms. Cole looked over her head. Malachi tipped his hat and grinned, and Cole grinned back. The two of them went out, and the house slowly fell silent. "I'm not leaving tonight, Kristin."

"What?" she whispered.

There was a bit of a commotion outside. Shannon was saying goodbye nicely to Jamie, and not so nicely to Malachi. Cole grinned, and Kristin grinned back, her eyes searching his. Then the door slammed, and Shannon whispered. "Oh, excuse me!"

Neither of them turned around. They heard Shannon tiptoe into the parlor to stay with the Union injured.

He was beautiful, Kristin thought. He was the most beautiful man she had ever seen. He was leaner than he had been that first day she had seen him. Strands of gray were creeping into his hair and into his beard, but somehow they were beautiful, too. They went well with the silver light in his eyes, with the handsome, dignified planes of his face.

"Oh!" she whispered heatedly. "You have to leave! Matthew says they consider you an outlaw—"

"They won't know I'm here, Kristin. My men are gone. They've taken my horse. They've learned how to disappear with the night. And for now I'm staying with my wife."

"Oh!"

"If she'll have me."

"Oh!" She touched his cheek, tenderly moving her fingertips over the coarse beard there. "Oh, she will have you!" she breathed.

He caught her hand and kissed her fingertips. Silently he led her up the stairs and through the doorway to their bedroom. Then he leaned against the door, and she smiled as she watched him.

"I never thought I would be here with you now!" he whispered.

"But you are," she said.

"Yes, I am."

Kristin walked over to him. She lifted off his hat and tossed it on the floor, and she unbuckled his scabbard and his gun belt and cast his weapons aside. Studiously, she unbuttoned his frock coat and his uniform shirt, and when his shoulders and chest were bare she felt the sweet thrill of anticipation invade her. Her fingers grew awkward, and she found that she was trembling. She whispered his name, and she pressed her lips to his chest and to the pulse at the base of his throat. He caught her lips and kissed her hungrily, tasting and tasting her mouth, trembling with ever-greater ardor. She was breathless when he released her and turned her around to work at the tiny buttons of her dress. He was shaking as badly as she, but was more practiced, and more determined, and she was startled when the dress fell quickly away from her, and then her chemise, and then her petticoats. He lifted her up with her stockings and shoes still on and carried her quickly to the bed, pausing with a rueful laugh to check on Gabriel, who was sleeping sweetly in the little bed in the corner.

Then he tossed her on the bed and fell upon her, and she threaded her fingers joyously through his hair. He groaned and kissed her again, and then he kissed her breasts, staring at them, savoring them, easing his tongue over each nipple, then his teeth, then the fullness of his mouth.

"Oh, Cole!" Her head tossed from side to side, and lightning swept through her, embedding a sweet, swirling heat at the apex of her thighs, a dizzying need for him. He filled it, touching her with a light and tender stroke and then with a demanding one, watching her eyes, watching her body, feeling the thunder of the desire that grew and grew within him.

He kissed her belly, and he stroked her thighs, and he played his touch over the golden triangle at their juncture, and then he delved within it. He made an incredibly sensual act of taking off her shoes, peeling away her garters and hose. Then he rose boldly above her. He drew a steady pattern with the searing tip of his tongue from her throat down the valley between her breasts to her navel and into the very heart of her fire. And she cried out for him, and he came to her.

Then he hovered, just above her, and she opened her eyes wide, waiting, pleading, wondering why he denied her. A great sound of agony escaped him, and he buried his head against her breasts.

"I do love you, Kristin. I do love you."

"Oh, Cole!" she said, clinging to him. "Please..."

He pushed away from her, and stared at her. "Well?"

And then it dawned on her what he wanted, and she pressed hard against him, arching to meet his need. "Cole, I have loved you for ages! I love you so very much. I could never admit it, I was so afraid, I knew you didn't love me."

"I just didn't dare admit it," he said softly.

"Say it again!" she demanded.

"I love you. I love you, Kristin McCahy Slater, and I swear that I will do so until the end of time."

"Oh, Cole!" She buried her face against his chest. It was hot and sleek and damp with perspiration. And he chose that moment to plunge deep, deep within her, and even as he did he was whispering again, the sweet words over and over again.

He loved her.

Later that night—much later, for making love took on a sweet new dimension when the words were spoken, and they were tempted to explore that dimension again and again—Cole held her in his arms and told her everything. First he told her about the day the jayhawkers had come, and how they had burned down his home and killed his wife. She heard the agony in his voice, but she didn't stop him, because it was important that he say everything, that he lay his soul bare for her, as she had hers. He needed to trust her in that way, and, Kristin thought, he needed the healing power of words. His heart needed the cleansing.

She listened, and she was not afraid of the past, merely saddened. Then she listened as he told her what had happened in Kansas, how his old friend Kurt Taylor had been there and how he had purposely alerted Cole to the fact that Henry Fitz was in town with his jayhawkers.

"I killed him, Kristin. I knew what I was doing. I knew exactly what danger I was riding into, but I had to face him." His arms tightened around her. "If we were to have a future, I just had to do it. Can you understand that?"

She didn't really have to answer him. She planted little kisses over his chest, and he groaned, and his hands rode roughly over her hair, and then they were in one another's arms once again. They were still so desperate, so hungry, so determined to have all that they could of one another, to cherish, to hold, to keep always for their dreams.

It was near dawn before they dozed off. Kristin was startled when she awoke almost before she had slept. Day was breaking, bright and fresh as a rainbow. Pink light fell upon her.

She heard the sounds of hoofbeats below.

With a soft gasp, she rose and raced to the window.

Down by the well she saw a single Union officer. She glanced at Cole, and he seemed to be asleep. He seemed at peace, the lines of strain erased from his features at last.

Kristin struggled into her gown and left the room without stockings or shoes, closing the door behind her. She padded silently down the stairs and hurried out to the well.

She couldn't imagine how she looked to the man, her face pale, her blue eyes wide, her hair in complete and lovely disarray around her fine-boned, very worried face.

He smiled at her and looked her up and down. He suddenly envied Cole Slater very much.

"Good morning, ma'am. This the McCahy ranch?"

"It is. My brother, a Union officer, is inside, recovering from wounds."

And your husband, a Southern officer, is inside, too, I'd wager, he thought, but he was silent.

"This is sweet, clear water. Thank you."

"You're very welcome to it."

"Zeke Moreau came here and gunned down most of the men?"

Kristin swallowed and nodded.

"There's a detachment of medics coming for the injured later today."

"That's fine. We're doing our best."

"I'm sure you are."

"Would you like to come in?"

He shook his head. "No thanks. I'm not here officially." He spoke softly. "I came here to tell you that the war is over. Well, all but the shouting. I'm sure it will take a while for all the troops to surrender. Kirby-Smith is a tenacious soul. Proud man, fine fighter, but—"

"The…the war is over?" Kristin breathed.

"Yes, ma'am, like I said, all but the shouting. Two mornings ago, on April twelfth, General Robert E. Lee surrendered the Army of Northern Virginia to General Ulysses S. Grant at a little place called Appomattox Courthouse. Word has it that President Lincoln is determined that this great nation must unite in peace and brotherhood as quickly as possible, and he seems determined that there be brotherhood between North and South again."

She was shaking. She had to sit down. He saw her lips and her limbs tremble, and he came around to her and helped her over to the porch. He gave her a sip of water, and she nodded her thanks.

"The war…is really over?"

"Really over." He smiled. "I hear tell that Colonel Slater and his men came in here yesterday. Yep, I hear tell they cut down Zeke Moreau and his bloody bushwhackers. That must have been a fine piece of work, yes, ma'am. I'd have liked to have been here. No doubt the Union commanders—and the law—will hear about it." He smiled at her again. "'Course, Slater's men are gone, I take it?"

Kristin nodded. "Yes…they're gone."

"You his wife?"

"I'm his wife."

"Someone ought to tell him that the war is over. 'Course, they should warn him that he needs to take care. Some people still don't take kindly to a few of his exploits. Once with Quantrill, you know, and then there was Kansas…" He shrugged. "If you should happen to see him, Mrs. Slater, you might warn him to lie low for a while. Ride on to Texas, maybe. Fitz had a brother, and he's sure to make an outcry. But tell him that he has to remember—the war is over. It will all come right. You hear? Tell him Kurt Taylor said so.''

Kristin nodded.

"Thanks for the water. That's mighty good water.''

"You're welcome, sir. Mighty welcome.''

Kristin stood and waited. She waited until the Union officer in his blue uniform had disappeared on the dusty Missouri horizon.

Then she turned and screamed, ''Cole! Cole!''

She tore up the stairs. He was up. He had been watching her and the officer from the window. Kristin threw herself at him, sending him flying across the room.

"It's over, it's over! The war is over! Lee has surrendered! Oh, there are still troops that haven't surrendered yet, but they're saying it's over! Oh, Cole!'' She caught his face between her hands, and she kissed him. She kissed his throat and his shoulders, and she was so alive and vibrant that even though he had been worried and wary he had to laugh.

"Kristin, Kristin, it can't be that easy—''

"No, it isn't that easy," she said solemnly, and she told him what the man had said. "His name was Kurt Taylor, and he said you should head for Texas.''

"I will," Cole said.

Kristin corrected him. "We will.''

"We will?" he asked her, arching a brow. "I do seem to recall that there was once a woman who would not leave this ranch. She sold her honor to a disreputable rebel in order to stay right here on this property.''

Kristin smiled at him. She had never felt so deliciously alive and sensual and vibrant and aware of all the world around her. It was spring—and the war was over. Over.

"It isn't my ranch. I was just holding on to it for Matthew, and Matthew is here now. You see, it's time to move on, anyway. And I consider that my honor was sold for a fair price. It was rather useless, you see, while my son—he's just magnificent. And—''

"And?''

"Well, there is this other minor thing. I fell desperately in love with that disreputable rebel. Even when I wanted to hang him myself, I was very much in love.''

"Very much?''

"Incredibly, inestimably, most desperately in love.''

"Really?" He laced his fingers through hers and bent his head and kissed her. She felt a shudder rake through him, and she sought his eyes.

"Cole?''

"We really have a future.''

"Yes!''

"We can watch Gabriel grow, and we can have more children. And I can hold them when they are little tiny infants—''

"And you can change their little bottoms, too," Kristin informed him sweetly.

He smiled, and he kissed her again, and she let out a sweet, shuddering sigh. "Cole?''

"My love?''

She smiled, slowly, lazily, sensuously. "If you go to Texas, I will follow you wherever you may lead. But for the moment...''

"Yes?"

"We've never made love in peacetime before. Never," she told him with very wide eyes. "We've never made love in peacetime, whispering that we love one another!"

He threw back his head and laughed, and his eyes sizzled, silver and mercury, into hers, and she thought that he would always be her cavalier, the tall, dark stranger with the plumed hat who had stepped into her life like a hero, taking her from darkness into light. They weren't clear of the darkness yet. There would be pain. There would be time to mourn Pete, who had always been her friend, always at her side. There would be time to mourn Major Emery, who had been their friend, too, noble and caring, until the very end.

For now, though, they had one another.

Cole grinned wickedly. "Then," he said, "we must make love at peace, and whisper that we love one another. Kristin!"

"Yes?"

. He came close against her lips, his mouth a breath away from hers.

"I love you!" he whispered fervently. "I love you, I love you, I love you!"

And though they were at peace they soared. into the sweetest tempest, and through it all they never ceased to whisper the words.

The sun entered their room, and a new day had truly dawned.

Cole stroked his wife's beautiful hair, luxuriating in the sweet satisfaction she brought him. He stared at the ceiling, at the new light of day.

It would take the country a long time to heal, he knew. A long, long time. A long time to unite.

But she had brought healing to him, and his heart was united with hers now. "A new age," he murmured.

"What?"

"I said I love you!" Cole lied, and he turned to her again.

The war wouldn't end as easily as Kristin thought. Life was never as easy as that. But they did have a future.

And Texas could wait just a little while longer.

* * * * *

Author's Note

The war did not end easily, and especially not in the West, on the Kansas-Missouri border where it had really begun, long before shots rang out at Fort Sumter.

General Kirby-Smith was determined, and he held out with his troops until the twenty-sixth of May, holding the last Southern command to stand in the field.

William C. Quantrill died on June 6, 1865, fatally wounded by Union troops while conducting a raid on Louisville, Kentucky. On his deathbed he swore that if he had captured Jim Lane, leader of the jayhawkers before Doc Jennison, he would have burned him at the stake.

Jim Lane himself fired his last shot on July 1, 1865—with his revolver in his own mouth.

Frank and Jesse James and the Younger brothers—Quantrill's men—went on to find a separate infamy.

For Cole and Kristin, all those things were in the future. Cole was to have his own problems.

But those are really part of Malachi and Shannon's story, and must be told by them.

#1 *New York Times* bestselling author

NORA ROBERTS

Presents a brand-new book in the beloved MacGregor series:

THE WINNING HAND
(SSE#1202)

October 1998 in

Silhouette®SPECIAL EDITION®

Innocent Darcy Wallace needs Mac Blade's protection in the high-stakes world she's entered. But who will protect Mac from the irresistible allure of this vulnerable beauty?

**Coming in March, the much-anticipated novel,
THE MACGREGOR GROOMS
Also, watch for the MacGregor stories
where it all began!**

**December 1998:
THE MACGREGORS: Serena—Caine**

**February 1999:
THE MACGREGORS: Alan—Grant**

**April 1999:
THE MACGREGORS: Daniel—Ian**

Available at your favorite retail outlet, only from

▼ *Silhouette*®
TM

Look us up on-line at: http://www.romance.net   SSEMACS1-T

Harlequin®
Historical

From rugged lawmen and
valiant knights to defiant heiresses
and spirited frontierswomen,
Harlequin Historicals will
capture your imagination with their
dramatic scope, passion
and adventure.

Harlequin Historicals...
they're too good to miss!

HHGENR-T